NEW YORK REVIEW BOOKS
CLASSICS

KOLYMA STORIES

VARLAM SHALAMOV (1907–1982) was born in Vologda in western Russia to a Russian Orthodox priest and his wife. After being expelled from law school for his political beliefs, Shalamov worked as a journalist in Moscow. In 1929, he was arrested at an underground printshop and sentenced to three years' hard labor in the Ural Mountains, where he met his first wife, Galina Gudz. The two returned to Moscow after Shalamov's release in 1931; they were married in 1934 and had a daughter, Elena, in 1935. Shalamov resumed work as a journalist and writer, publishing his first short story, "The Three Deaths of Doctor Austino," in 1936. The following year, he was arrested again for counterrevolutionary activities and shipped to the Far Northeast of the Kolyma basin. Over the next fifteen years, he was moved from labor camp to labor camp; imprisoned many times for anti-Soviet propaganda; forced to mine gold and coal; quarantined for typhus; and, finally, assigned to work as a paramedic. Upon his release in 1951, he made his way back to Moscow where he divorced his wife and began writing what would become the *Kolyma Stories* and *Sketches of the Criminal World*. He also wrote many volumes of poetry, including *Ognivo* (Flint, 1961) and *Moskovskiye oblaka* (Moscow Clouds, 1972). Severely weakened by his years in the camps, in 1979 Shalamov was committed to a decrepit nursing home north of Moscow. In 1981, he was awarded the French PEN Club's Liberty Prize; he died of pneumonia in 1982.

DONALD RAYFIELD is Emeritus Professor of Russian and Georgian at Queen Mary University of London. As well as books and articles on Russian literature (notably *A Life of Anton Chekhov*), he is the author of many articles on Georgian writers and of a history of Georgian literature. In 2012 he published *Edge of Empires: A History of Georgia*, which has recently come out in an expanded Russian edition, as have his *Life of Chekhov* and *Stalin and His Hangmen*. He was the chief editor of *A Comprehensive Georgian-English Dictionary*. He has translated several novels, including Hamid Ismailov's *Devils' Dance*, Nikolai Gogol's *Dead Souls* (an NYRB Classic), and Shalamov's second volume of Kolyma stories, *Sketches of the Criminal World* (also an NYRB Classic).

Апостол Павел.

Когда я вплотную ступил, поравнялся ...

A manuscript page from Shalamov's story "The Apostle Paul"

KOLYMA STORIES
Volume One

VARLAM SHALAMOV

*Translated from the Russian and with
an introduction by*

DONALD RAYFIELD

NEW YORK REVIEW BOOKS

New York

THIS IS A NEW YORK REVIEW BOOK
PUBLISHED BY THE NEW YORK REVIEW OF BOOKS
435 Hudson Street, New York, NY 10014
www.nyrb.com

English publishing rights acquired via FTM Agency, Ltd., Russia in 2015.
Originally published in Russian in *Sobranie sochinenii v 6 + 1 tomakh* (Collected
Works, vols. 1–7) by TERRA-Knizhnyï klub in 2013.

The publication was effected under the auspices of the
Mikhail Prokhorov Foundation TRANSCRIPT Pro-
gramme to Support Translations of Russian Literature.

Library of Congress Cataloging-in-Publication Data
Names: Shalamov, Varlam, author. | Rayfield, Donald, 1942– translator, writer of
   introduction.
Title: Kolyma stories / by Varlam Shalamov ; translated and with an introduction
   by Donald Rayfield.
Other titles: Kolymskie rasskazy. English
Description: New York : New York Review Books, 2018. | Series: New York
   Review Books classics
Identifiers: LCCN 2017046693 (print) | LCCN 2017049306 (ebook) | ISBN
   9781681372150 (epub) | ISBN 9781681372143 (alk. paper)
Subjects: LCSH: Political prisoners—Soviet Union—Fiction. | Kolyma
   (Concentration camp)—Fiction.
Classification: LCC PG3487.A592 (ebook) | LCC PG3487.A592 K6413 2018
   (print) | DDC 891.73/44—dc23
LC record available at https://lccn.loc.gov/2017046693

ISBN 978-1-68137-214-3
Available as an electronic book; ISBN 978-1-68137-215-0

Printed in the United States of America on acid-free paper.
10 9 8 7 6 5 4 3

CONTENTS

BOOK TWO: THE LEFT BANK

BOOK THREE: THE SPADE ARTIST

INTRODUCTION

VARLAM SHALAMOV (1907–1982) was one of the rare survivors of fifteen years in the worst of Stalin's Gulag, spending six years as a slave in the gold mines of Kolyma, one of the coldest and most inhospitable places on earth, before finding a less intolerable life as a paramedic in the prison camps. He had written a few prose pieces and some verse before these years of imprisonment, but his seven volumes of prose, verse, and drama stem almost entirely from the years after Stalin's death in 1953 to Shalamov's own physical and mental decline in the late 1970s.

What we have collected and translated are the six books of short stories, to be published in two volumes of three books each, mostly about his period in Kolyma but including a few about an early spell from 1929 to 1931 of "corrective labor" in camps in the northern Urals, and one or two that recall his youth in Vologda. The line between autobiography and fiction is very fuzzy: virtually everything in these stories was experienced or witnessed by Shalamov. His work is full of many real names of prisoners and their oppressors. He himself appears simply as "I" or "Shalamov," sometimes under pseudonyms, such as Andreyev or Krist. A reading of the stories thus provides us with a biography of the first fifty years of his life.

Born in Vologda, a northern town that since medieval times has been a place for political exiles, Shalamov as a small boy might well have crossed paths with his nemesis Joseph Stalin, who in 1911 and 1912 regularly walked from his lodgings in Vologda to its excellent public library. The son of a priest, Shalamov (like Anton Chekhov) was saturated in religious imagery and language, but rejected all faith from an early age. He inherited from his father (an extraordinary man who had been a missionary in the Aleutian Islands, who sympathized with political liberalism, who preached tolerance of other religions, but who tyrannized his family) an intractable stubbornness and resistance to authority. Shalamov's father went blind after refusing a simple operation; he also would not let Shalamov have a much-needed nasal operation, which deprived his son of a sense of smell and may have contributed to the Ménière's disease that incapacitated him in old age.

Vologda was the scene of appalling atrocities during the Russian Civil War, particularly in 1918, when the psychopath Mikhail Kedrov shot civilian hostages, including Shalamov's chemistry teacher. Nevertheless, Shalamov sympathized with the revolution, particularly the Trotskyist factions, even though, as the son of a priest, he was excluded by the Communists from higher education. His parents, now expelled from church premises, lived in extreme poverty (see the story "The Cross"), which Shalamov's casual earnings were too small to alleviate. By working in a leather factory and achieving high marks in mathematics and physics, he was eventually allowed to enroll at Moscow University (to study Soviet law), but a fellow student denounced him for "concealing his social origins," and he was expelled. He then earned a precarious living by journalism, and was arrested for the first time for participating in a student movement that demanded (as did many Trotskyists) the publication of Lenin's Testament, a document that named Stalin as too rude and power-hungry to be appointed as secretary-general of the party.

Shalamov spent three years at a chemical construction site in conditions that were made to seem tolerable only by comparison to Kolyma. In 1931 he was released against the wishes of OGPU, as the secret police was then called, but was able to live and work in Moscow without harassment. In 1934 he married Galina Gudz; a daughter, Elena, was born in 1935. Galina's brother, Boris Gudz, an OGPU agent, was horrified by this connection. He pressed Shalamov to write to the secret police, by now the NKVD (People's Commissariat of Internal Affairs). The result was disastrous: Shalamov was arrested and given an initial five-year sentence in Kolyma for counterrevolutionary Trotskyist activity, just when the Great Terror was ensuring that most "Trotskyists" were to be shot. (The Gudz family did not escape repression: Shalamov's wife and daughter were exiled to Turkmenistan; Boris Gudz was dismissed from the secret police and became a bus driver, while his oldest sister, Aleksandra, was also repressed.)

In his prose, Shalamov avoided all mention of his marital troubles. His Kolyma experiences and the miracle of his survival are graphically documented in the stories. His biography on his release and after his "rehabilitation" (an admission by the authorities of his innocence and two months' salary) has, however, to be reconstructed from records of conversations and a few surviving letters. His marriage soon collapsed. His daughter, as a conventionally brought up Stalinist, preferred to think of him as dead or as a criminal. Two years later, Shalamov married Olga Nekliudova. The marriage lasted until 1966 but was never a happy one. Shalamov, like many former Gulag prisoners, stuck to the principle of speaking as little as possible, and never when a third person (who might be an informant) was present; in any case, like his father, he took a patriarchal view of women.

Shalamov initially had high hopes of a literary career. Boris Pasternak greatly praised his poetic talents, and Aleksandr Solzhenitsyn had shown in *One Day in the Life of Ivan Denisovich* that it was possible to write about the camps. But Pasternak, hounded by the Soviet authorities for publishing *Doctor Zhivago* abroad, died in 1960, and it became clear that Solzhenitsyn could publish—and then just for a few years—only because he had won the favor of Nikita Khrushchev, now the party's leader, and of Aleksandr Tvardovsky, the editor of the influential journal *New World*. Shalamov's initial idolization of Solzhenitsyn was met with a friendly response, even an invitation to collaborate on the compilation of *The Gulag Archipelago*. But, like nearly all of Shalamov's contacts, relations rapidly soured: Shalamov clearly disapproved of Solzhenitsyn's adherence to some of the Christian values of the nineteenth century and to some of the ethics of Soviet society, particularly the faith in the redemptive power of manual work. Whereas Solzhenitsyn moved from writing short stories to colossal novels, Shalamov disapproved of novels as elaborate structures that falsified their material. (His memoir of corrective labor in the Urals is entitled *Vishera: An Antinovel.*) Shalamov distanced himself from other survivors of the Gulag, such as Yevgeniya Ginzburg, accusing them of being too soft on the villains who had caused their suffering.

Shalamov was initially close to Nadezhda, the widow of Osip Mandelstam—he dedicated two of his best stories to both her and the poet—but was alienated by her role as queen bee, surrounded by admirers and dissidents.

Despite this isolation, and the hostile attentions of the KGB, Shalamov managed to publish four books of poetry. While his poetry, strongly reminiscent in its techniques and subjects of the symbolist school of prerevolutionary Russia, aroused no official antagonism, publishing his stories in the USSR proved impossible, except for one in 1965, the least controversial, "The Dwarf Pine," and even that caused the editorial board of *Country Youth* to be dismissed. In 1968—whether with Shalamov's complicity or against his will is not certain—individual stories, and then the whole of the first book, *Kolyma Stories*, were leaked in the West and were published, first in émigré Russian journals, and then in German and French translation under the name Shalanov. Shalamov protested privately (though asking for copies and payment), and then, evidently acting under compulsion, publicly in the official *Literary Newspaper*. For his condemnation of "anti-Soviet" émigré and Western publishers, he was rewarded with belated admission to the Union of Writers, without whose membership no Soviet writer could hope to make a living.

At the end of the 1960s Shalamov was befriended by Irina Sirotinskaya, who deposited his manuscripts with the Russian State Archive of Literature and Art. Sirotinskaya has given a detailed account of a relationship based on mutual affection and respect. Certainly, Shalamov's work might have met the same fate of destruction as that of other dissident writers had it not been for Sirotinskaya's intervention. More skeptical friends of Shalamov, particularly those who were dissidents or ex-prisoners, or both, had their doubts about this friendship: all state archivists in the USSR were subordinate to the KGB, and the transfer of a writer's work to the archives during his lifetime could be seen as sequestration as well as preservation. But in my own work in the Soviet archives, I found that there were archivists who despite their "security clearance" were genuinely devoted to the literature to which they controlled access. There is no doubt that Sirotinskaya played a major part in helping Shalamov at least to publish his poetry.

In the late 1970s, Shalamov, homeless and increasingly ill, disappeared from view into a home for the elderly. Conditions there were truly appalling—ironically, as bad as the worst institutions in the Gulag. When friends, including the granddaughter of one of the imprisoned professors who had trained Shalamov as a paramedic in Kolyma, discovered him, they were allowed to alleviate his conditions slightly but were hindered by the attentions of the KGB and the indifference of the "medical" staff. By now Sirotinskaya, a married woman who felt her relationship with Shalamov had to be subordinated to her family's interests, seems to have distanced herself from the writer. In January 1982, a psychiatric commission diagnosed Shalamov's condition—extreme deafness, loss of muscular control, and acute suspicion of strangers—as dementia, and he was moved, almost naked in the freezing cold, to a "psychiatric hospital" to which visitors had almost no access. In a few days he died of pneumonia. In her memoir, Sirotinskaya states that she visited him just before his death and that he dictated to her the text of a collection of poems. Shalamov also wrote a will naming her as his heir, and dedicated two of his unpublished collections of stories to her. The authenticity of these last dispositions has been disputed by Shalamov's dissident associates, notably Sergei Grigoriants. Again, because Shalamov disliked speaking in the presence of a third party (an old camp habit), none of his reported conversations can be corroborated.

On the grounds that Shalamov, as the son of a priest, had been baptized, friends and people from the world of Soviet literature organized a church funeral and burial.

Once perestroika was firmly established, in 1988–89, Sirotinskaya prepared Shalamov's manuscripts—he had a calligraphic hand and there were no problems of decipherment—and organized their publication. No editing, however, was carried out, and readers will notice that in the later books themes, incidents, and characters sometimes recur, and there are even contradictions and similarities in name between disparate characters. Nevertheless, the relentless power of these works, in which the author refuses to soften or mitigate anything, including his own misjudgments, and which show an extraordinary memory, visual and oral, make them unique in the record of twentieth-century horrors, whether Nazi or Soviet. There is no consolation, no faith in Providence or humanity, despite the isolated incidences of kindness he encountered in the Gulag. Only animals behave chivalrously—the male bear and the bullfinch who draw the hunter's fire so that their mates can escape, the husky that trusted prisoners and growled at guards, or the cat that helps a prisoner catch fish.

Apart from their artistic power, Shalamov's stories are a shocking testimony. One of the many examples is the way which, from 1942 to 1945, American lend-lease sent bulldozers to Kolyma to dig the mass graves, trucks to carry the gold ore, spades and pickaxes for the slaves to use, and food and clothes for the guards. As one of Shalamov's fellow prisoners put it, Kolyma was "Auschwitz without the ovens."

In some ways, Shalamov could be accused of complicity: he himself shows admiration for the Red heroes of the Civil War who perpetrated acts of cruelty as ruthless as their Stalinist successors. "The Gold Medal,"[1] one of his longest stories, almost deifies the Socialist Revolutionary terrorist Nadia Klimova. For all that Shalamov suffered, he never renounced revolutionary killers when they were prompted by idealism and prepared to pay with their own death. And although he declared that he would never accept a post in which he collaborated with the system of forced labor, once he was a paramedic, he was, as he recounts in "Permafrost,"[2] responsible for the suicide of a young man whom he refused to allow to go on washing floors in the hospital and dispatched to hard labor back in the mines.

Shalamov claimed not to have learned anything from Kolyma, except how to wheel a loaded barrow. But one of his fragmentary writings, dated 1961, tells us rather more:

WHAT I SAW AND UNDERSTOOD IN THE CAMPS

1. The extreme fragility of human culture, civilization. A man becomes a beast in three weeks, given heavy labor, cold, hunger, and beatings.

2. The main means for depraving the soul is the cold. Presumably in Central Asian camps people held out longer, for it was warmer there.

3. I realized that friendship, comradeship, would never arise in really difficult, life-threatening conditions. Friendship arises in difficult but bearable conditions (in the hospital, but not at the pit face).

4. I realized that the feeling a man preserves longest is anger. There is only enough flesh on a hungry man for anger: everything else leaves him indifferent.

5. I realized that Stalin's "victories" were due to his killing the innocent—an organization a tenth the size would have swept Stalin away in two days.

6. I realized that humans were human because they were physically stronger and clung to life more than any other animal: no horse can survive work in the Far North.

7. I saw that the only group of people able to preserve a minimum of humanity in conditions of starvation and abuse were the religious believers, the sectarians (almost all of them), and most priests.

8. Party workers and the military are the first to fall apart and do so most easily.

9. I saw what a weighty argument for the intellectual is the most ordinary slap in the face.

10. Ordinary people distinguish their bosses by how hard their bosses hit them, how enthusiastically their bosses beat them.

11. Beatings are almost totally effective as an argument (method number three).[3]

12. I discovered from experts the truth about how mysterious show trials are set up.

13. I understood why prisoners hear political news (arrests, etc.) before the outside world does.

14. I found out that the prison (and camp) "grapevine" is never just a "grapevine."

15. I realized that one can live on anger.

16. I realized that one can live on indifference.

17. I understood why people do not live on hope—there isn't any hope. Nor can they survive by means of free will—what free will is there? They live by instinct, a feeling of self-preservation, on the same basis as a tree, a stone, an animal.

18. I am proud to have decided right at the beginning, in 1937, that I would never be a foreman if my freedom could lead to another man's death, if my freedom had to serve the bosses by oppressing other people, prisoners like myself.

19. Both my physical and my spiritual strength turned out to be stronger than I thought in this great test, and I am proud that I never sold anyone, never sent anyone to their death or to another sentence, and never denounced anyone.

20. I am proud that I never wrote an official request until 1955.[4]

21. I saw the so-called Beria amnesty where it took place, and it was a sight worth seeing.

22. I saw that women are more decent and self-sacrificing than men: in Kolyma there were no cases of a husband following his wife. But wives would come, many of them (Faina Rabinovich, Krivoshei's wife).[5]

23. I saw amazing northern families (free-contract workers and former prisoners) with letters "to legitimate husbands and wives," etc.

24. I saw "the first Rockefellers," the underworld millionaires. I heard their confessions.

25. I saw men doing penal servitude, as well as numerous people of "contingents" D, B, etc., "Berlag."[6]

26. I realized that you can achieve a great deal—time in the hospital, a transfer—but only by risking your life, taking beatings, enduring solitary confinement in ice.

27. I saw solitary confinement in ice, hacked out of a rock, and spent a night in it myself.

28. The passion for power, to be able to kill at will, is great—from top bosses to the rank-and-file guards (Seroshapka[7] and similar men).

29. Russians' uncontrollable urge to denounce and complain.

30. I discovered that the world should be divided not into good

and bad people but into cowards and non-cowards. Ninety-five percent of cowards are capable of the vilest things, lethal things, at the mildest threat.

31. I am convinced that the camps—all of them—are a negative school; you can't even spend an hour in one without being depraved. The camps never gave, and never could give, anyone anything positive. The camps act by depraving everyone, prisoners and free-contract workers alike.

32. Every province had its own camps, at every construction site. Millions, tens of millions of prisoners.

33. Repressions affected not just the top layer but every layer of society—in any village, at any factory, in any family there were either relatives or friends who were repressed.

34. I consider the best period of my life the months I spent in a cell in Butyrki prison, where I managed to strengthen the spirit of the weak, and where everyone spoke freely.

35. I learned to "plan" my life one day ahead, no more.

36. I realized that the thieves were not human.

37. I realized that there were no criminals in the camps, that the people next to you (and who would be next to you tomorrow) were within the boundaries of the law and had not trespassed them.

38. I realized what a terrible thing is the self-esteem of a boy or a youth: it's better to steal than to ask. That self-esteem and boastfulness are what make boys sink to the bottom.

39. In my life women have not played a major part: the camp is the reason.

40. Knowing people is useless, for I am unable to change my attitude toward any scoundrel.

41. The people whom everyone—guards, fellow prisoners—hates are the last in the ranks, those who lag behind, those who are sick, weak, those who can't run when the temperature is below zero.

42. I understood what power is and what a man with a rifle is.

43. I understood that the scales had been displaced and that this displacement was what was most typical of the camps.

44. I understood that moving from the condition of a prisoner to the condition of a free man is very difficult, almost impossible without a long period of amortization.

45. I understood that a writer has to be a foreigner in the questions he is dealing with, and if he knows his material well, he will write in such a way that nobody will understand him.

It was only in 2013 that a reasonably complete collection of Shalamov's work appeared (in seven volumes) in Russia. Abroad, he became most widely known in Germany, where four of the six books translated here, and in the forthcoming volume, have been published. The first reliable English translation of a selection of the Kolyma stories appeared in 1980 as *Kolyma Tales*, translated by John Glad; in 1994 a handful of other stories from the later books was added to *Kolyma Tales*. The present volume and its companion will more than double the amount of Shalamov's work available in English. Unfortunately, there is as yet no biography of Shalamov or study of his work in English. Those who read German will enjoy Wilfried F. Schoeller's *Leben oder Schreiben: Der Erzähler Warlam Schalamow.*[8]

On the one hand, translating Shalamov is straightforward. He avoids any stylistic effects; most stories are deliberately written "roughly," without fear of repeating the same adjective, with a minimum of metaphor. One aspect, however, must defeat the translator, and that is the language, *fenia* or *blatnoi yazyk*, of the gangsters, the hereditary and professional thieves and murderers who made the life of political prisoners even more hellish. *Fenia* is a dialect that draws on Odessa Yiddish, on various Slavic and even Turkic sources, and has been stable for perhaps two hundred years. Criminal jargons in English, however, vary with each decade and every city. Only in eighteenth-century London was there a stable criminal language, and just a few specialists today would understand it. For that reason, in this English version Shalamov's gangsters talk like anyone else, with just a few well-known slang terms. Interestingly, Shalamov wrote only one prose work while in Kolyma: a 600-word dictionary of gangster language for Podosionov, an imprisoned engineer who was in charge of a chemical laboratory (see the story "Galina Pavlovna Zybalova" in the forthcoming volume). Podosionov was killed by a passing truck, and the manuscript of this dictionary was lost—which has not made the interpretation of gangster language any easier, despite the proliferation in Russia of dictionaries of criminal slang.

I am immensely grateful to my wife, Anna Pilkington, for reading the first version of these translations and saving me from a number of blunders, infelicities, and omissions. The task was especially difficult for her, given that her father, Dmitri Vitkovsky, like Shalamov, spent half his life in the Gulag. I also want to thank Susan Barba for her tactful but meticulous editing, and Natalia Efimova of the Russian State Archive of Literature and Art for checking Shalamov's manuscripts when I (wrongly) suspected a misprint in the published text.

Despite his own assertion in the last point of "What I Saw and Understood in the Camps," Shalamov knew his material perfectly, and he wrote in a way that everyone can understand.

—DONALD RAYFIELD

BOOK ONE
Kolyma Stories

TRAMPLING THE SNOW

How do you trample a road through virgin snow? One man walks ahead, sweating and cursing, barely able to put one foot in front of the other, getting stuck every minute in the deep, porous snow. This man goes a long way ahead, leaving a trail of uneven black holes. He gets tired, lies down in the snow, lights a cigarette, and the tobacco smoke forms a blue cloud over the brilliant white snow. Even when he has moved on, the smoke cloud still hovers over his resting place. The air is almost motionless. Roads are always made on calm days, so that human labor is not swept away by wind. A man makes his own landmarks in this unbounded snowy waste: a rock, a tall tree. He steers his body through the snow like a helmsman steering a boat along a river, from one bend to the next.

The narrow, uncertain footprints he leaves are followed by five or six men walking shoulder to shoulder. They step around the footprints, not in them. When they reach a point agreed on in advance, they turn around and walk back so as to trample down this virgin snow where no human foot has trodden. And so a trail is blazed. People, convoys of sleds, tractors can use it. If they had walked in single file, there would have been a barely passable narrow trail, a path, not a road: a series of holes that would be harder to walk over than virgin snow. The first man has the hardest job, and when he is completely exhausted, another man from this pioneer group of five steps forward. Of all the men following the trailblazer, even the smallest, the weakest must not just follow someone else's footprints but must walk a stretch of virgin snow himself. As for riding tractors or horses, that is the privilege of the bosses, not the underlings.

1956

ON THE SLATE

THE HORSE herder Naumov was hosting a card game. The duty guards never even poked their heads into the horse herders' barracks, since they quite rightly considered their main job to be watching prisoners convicted under article 58. In any case, counterrevolutionaries were not generally allowed to look after horses. The more pragmatic bosses did, admittedly, quietly grumble that this rule deprived them of the best and most conscientious workmen, but their instructions on this question were unambiguously strict. So the horse herders' barracks was the safest place to be, and every night the gangsters gathered there to fight it out over a game of cards.

The bottom bunks in the right-hand corner of the barracks were covered with quilts of various colors. A twist of wire held an improvised Kolyma lamp, fueled by kerosene fumes, to the corner pillar. Three or four lengths of copper pipe were soldered onto a jam-jar lid—that was all you needed to make the lamp—and to light it a burning coal was put on the lid; it heated the gas, so that the fumes rose up the pipes and could be lit by a match.

A filthy down pillow was placed on the quilts. The pair of cardplayers sat on either side of the pillow, their legs beneath them Mongol-style. This was the classic setup for a prison card duel. A fresh pack of cards was put on the pillow. They were no ordinary cards; the pack was cobbled together with amazing speed in the prison by highly skilled men. To do this they needed paper (any book), a piece of bread (chewed and then filtered through a rag to make starch to stick the paper together), the stub of an indelible pencil (a substitute for printer's ink), and a knife (to cut out the cards and to make stencils for the diamonds, spades, etc.).

The cards this time had just been made from a volume of Victor Hugo that someone had forgotten to take home from the office. The paper was nice and thick, so there was no need to stick sheets together, as one had to when the paper was too thin. Whenever a search was carried out in the camp, all the indelible pencils were confiscated without fail. They were even removed when prisoners' parcels were delivered. The reason for this was not only to prevent documents and official stamps from being forged (and there were a lot of talented prisoners who did that sort of thing) but to eliminate anything that might infringe the state's monopoly on playing cards. Indelible pencils were used to make ink and, by using stencils, the ink was used to make patterns on the cards: queens, jacks, tens in all suits. Prison cards were all the same color; no player needed to have both red and black. The jack of spades, for instance, could be recognized by the spades on two opposite corners of the card. The layout and shape of the patterns had not changed for centuries, and knowing how to make cards yourself was part of the "courtly" training of any young gangster.

The new pack of cards lay there on the pillow. One of the players would clap his filthy hand on it—but his fine, white fingers showed he had never done any dirty work. The nail of his little finger was unnaturally long, another sign of gangster chic, just like his fixes—gold, or actually bronze, veneers stuck onto perfectly healthy teeth. There were even craftsmen, self-taught dental technicians, who earned a good living making these crowns, for which there was a constant demand. As for fingernails, there would certainly have been a fashion for varnishing them, if only prison conditions had allowed the import of lacquer. The carefully burnished yellow fingernail shone like a jewel. The owner of the fingernail ran his left hand through his sticky, dirty fair hair. He had a very professional army-style crew cut. His brow was low, free of wrinkles, with bushy yellow eyebrows, and his mouth was sharply defined, like a woman's, and this gave his face a quality sought after by thieves: he was unremarkable. His was a face you could never remember. You would forget him a moment after you looked at him; all his features vanished and when you next met him, you wouldn't recognize him. This man was Sevochka, famous for his skill at terzo (a prison version of bezique), shtoss, and various kinds of bura (thirty-one), and he was a genius at expounding the thousands of rules of these games, rules that had to be strictly observed in the battle to come. People said of Sevochka that he was really good at "laying it down," in other words he had the knowledge and deftness of a cardsharp. He was, of course, a cardsharp, for an honest game among thieves is a game of deception; you have the right to watch and catch out your partner, and you have to be just as good as he is at cheating and at holding on to your dubious winnings.

The game was always a duel between two players. None of the professionals would lower himself by taking part in games for more players, such as Russian blackjack. They never hesitated to play against someone who could "lay it down," just as a real chess player always looks for the strongest opponent he can find.

Sevochka's partner was Naumov, the foreman of the horse herders. He was older (not that anyone knew Sevochka's age—twenty, thirty, forty?), a dark-haired fellow whose sunken black eyes had such a long-suffering expression that, had I not known Naumov to be a railway thief from the Kuban, I might have taken him to be a wandering monk or a member of the "trust in God alone" sect, such as you could come across over the last few decades in the camps. This impression was heightened by the pewter cross hanging from a chain around his neck, his shirt open to reveal it. The cross was not a blasphemous joke nor a passing whim. In those days all the gangsters wore aluminum crosses, as much an indication of their profession as a tattoo.

In the 1920s gangsters liked to wear workmen's caps; before that they wore naval officers' caps. In the 1940s they wore flat round cossack caps, turned down the tops of their felt boots, and hung crosses around their necks. The cross was usually plain, but any available artist could be made to use a needle to scratch the criminals' favorite patterns: a heart, a card, a naked woman.... Naumov's cross was plain. It hung on his dark, bare chest, and it was hard to read his blue tattoo, a quotation from Yesenin, the only poet recognized and canonized by the criminal world:

How few the roads I have trodden,
How many the mistakes I have made.

"What are you staking?" Sevochka asked, his clenched lips expressing infinite contempt—this was considered the height of good manners at the start of a game.

"These rags of mine: this suit," replied Naumov, clapping his hands to his shoulders.

"I'll call that five hundred, then," was Sevochka's evaluation of Naumov's clothes. The response was a loud and lengthy series of obscenities, meant to persuade the opponent that the stake was worth far more. The spectators crowding around the players patiently waited for this traditional opening move to end. Sevochka gave as good as he got, cursing even more viciously in order to knock the price down. In the end Naumov's clothes were valued at a thousand. In response, Sevochka staked a few well-worn sweaters. After the sweaters had been valued and thrown down on the quilt, Sevochka shuffled the cards.

Garkunov, a former textile engineer, and I were sawing firewood for Naumov's barracks. This was moonlighting. After our day's work at the pit face, we had to saw and chop enough firewood to last twenty-four hours. As soon as supper was over, we went to see the horse herders; it was warmer there than in our barracks. After we'd done the job, the man on duty in Naumov's barracks would fill our pans with cold "broth," the leftovers from the sole and invariable dish, which in the refectory was called "Ukrainian dumplings," along with a piece of bread each. We would find somewhere on the floor to sit and quickly eat what we had earned. We ate in complete darkness since the kerosene lamps only lit up the card game, but as the old prison hands observed so rightly, the spoon never missed the mouth. Now we watched Sevochka and Naumov playing each other.

Naumov lost his "rubbish." His trousers and jacket were lying on the quilt next to Sevochka. The pillow was now the stake. Sevochka's fingernail traced elaborate patterns in the air. Cards would disappear in his hand and then reappear. Naumov was wearing just his vest; his satin side-buttoned shirt had gone the same way as his trousers. Helping hands tried to put a quilted jacket over his shoulders, but he brusquely threw it off onto the floor. Suddenly there was a silence. Sevochka slowly brushed the pillow with his fingernail.

"I'll stake the quilt," said Naumov. His voice was hoarse.

"Two hundred," Sevochka replied indifferently.

"A thousand, you bitch!" Naumov yelled.

"For that? That's not worth having. It's crap, it's rubbish," Sevochka decreed. "Just for you, I'll put it at three hundred."

The battle continued. The rules state that no battle is over as long as the opponent can come up with a response.

"I'll stake my felt boots."

"I don't play for felt boots," said Sevochka firmly. "I don't accept government rags."

A Ukrainian rug decorated with roosters, a cigarette case with Gogol's face embossed on it, both valued at a few rubles, were lost, like everything else, to Sevochka. Naumov's dark-skinned cheeks began to blush deep red.

"Put it on the slate," Naumov pleaded.

"Like hell I will," retorted Sevochka as he stretched his hand out behind him. Someone immediately put a lit cigarette into it. Sevochka took a deep puff and started coughing. "What use is your slate to me? There isn't going to be another batch of prisoners, so where will you get the money? From the guards, I suppose?"

Agreeing to gamble "on the slate," that is, on credit, was an optional favor according to the rules, but Sevochka didn't want to rub Naumov's nose in it or deprive him of any chance of recuperating his losses.

"I stake a hundred," he said slowly. "I give you an hour's credit."

"Give me a card," said Naumov, adjusting his cross as he sat down. He won back the quilt, the pillow, and his trousers, and then lost everything again.

"Let's brew up some chifir," said Sevochka as he put away his winnings in a big fiber suitcase. "I'll wait."

"Brew it up, boys," said Naumov.

They meant that amazing northern drink chifir, very strong tea made by brewing more than two ounces of tea in a small mug. This makes an extremely bitter drink, gulped down with the help of salted fish. It keeps you awake, so it is highly valued by gangsters and by long-distance truck drivers in the north. Chifir must have a very bad effect on the heart, but I have known people addicted to it for many years who suffered almost no side effects. When the mug was handed to him, Sevochka took a sip.

Naumov looked around at everyone, his gaze grim and dark. He was disheveled. When he caught sight of me, he fixed me with a stare. A thought flashed in Naumov's brain.

"You there, come up here."

I came into the light.

"Take off your padded jacket."

There was no mistaking his intentions, and everyone was interested to see what would come of Naumov's idea.

All I had under my padded jacket was prison-issue linen. The tunic had been issued about two years ago, and it was falling apart. I put my jacket back on.

"Then you come here," said Naumov, pointing at Garkunov.

Garkunov took off his padded jacket. His face turned white. He was wearing a woolen sweater under his filthy shirt. The sweater was the last thing his wife had passed to him before he was sent off to the Far North, and I knew how carefully Garkunov looked after it. He washed it when in the bathhouse, dried it on his body, and never let go of it for a minute: a woolen sweater would have immediately been stolen by his fellow prisoners.

"Go on, take it off," said Naumov.

Sevochka made an approving gesture with his finger. Woolen garments were highly valued. If he had the wool sweater laundered and then had the lice steamed out of it, he could wear it himself. It had a nice pattern.

"I'm not taking it off," gasped Garkunov. "You'll have to flay me first."

Men hurled themselves at him and threw him to the floor.

"He's biting," someone shouted.

Garkunov slowly got up and used his sleeve to wipe the blood off his face. Right then Sashka, the same Sashka, Naumov's duty orderly, who had an hour ago given us soup for sawing the wood, squatted down and snatched something from the top of his felt boot. Then he moved his arm toward Garkunov; Garkunov gave a sobbing gasp and then slumped down onto his side.

"Did you have to do that?" Sevochka yelled. In the flickering light of the kerosene lamp you could see Garkunov's face draining of color.

Sashka stretched out the dead man's arms, tore the shirt open, and pulled the sweater off over his head. The sweater was red, so you could hardly see the bloodstains. Sevochka, carefully avoiding getting his fingers dirty, put the sweater away in his suitcase. The game was over, and I could go home. Now I had to find someone else to saw firewood with me.

1956

AT NIGHT

Supper was over. Glebov took his time licking his bowl clean, then carefully raked the bread crumbs off the table into his left hand, which he lifted to his mouth so as to lick every crumb off his palm. Without swallowing them, he could feel the saliva in his mouth greedily covering the tiny lump of bread in a thick layer. Glebov could not have said whether it tasted good. Taste was something different, too weak compared with the passionate, oblivious feeling that food gave him. Glebov took his time before swallowing; the bread melted in his mouth and it melted quickly.

Bagretsov could not take his sunken, shining eyes off Glebov's mouth. Nobody had the strength of will to avert their eyes from food disappearing into somebody else's mouth. Glebov swallowed his saliva, and Bagretsov immediately shifted his gaze to the horizon, where a big orange moon was creeping out into the sky.

"It's time," said Bagretsov.

Without speaking, they followed the path to the rock and climbed to a small ledge that went around the bare hill. The sun had only just set, but the stones, which had burned the soles of their feet through the rubber shoes (worn without socks), were already cold. Glebov buttoned up his padded jacket. Walking didn't make him any warmer.

"Is it much farther?" he whispered.

"It's quite far," Bagretsov answered quietly.

They sat down for a rest. There was nothing to talk about, and nothing to think about, either: everything was clear and simple. On a square at the end of the terrace were heaps of stones that had been turned over, and lumps of moss that had been torn off and left to dry.

"I could have done this on my own," Bagretsov said with a laugh, "but it's more fun if there are two of us. Anyway, for an old friend. . . ."

They had been brought here last year on the same ship. Bagretsov stopped.

"We've got to lie down, or we'll be seen."

They lay down and started throwing the stones aside. None of the stones here were too big for two men to lift or move, because the men who had dumped them here in the morning had been no stronger than Glebov.

Bagretsov cursed quietly: he had grazed a finger, and it was bleeding. He put some sand on the wound, tore a lump of cotton wool from his jacket lining and pressed it on the wound, but the finger still bled.

"Bad clotting," said Glebov in a bored tone.

"Are you a doctor, then?" asked Bagretsov, as he sucked at the blood.

Glebov remained silent. It seemed a very long time ago that he had been a doctor. And had he ever been one? Far too often, the world beyond these mountains and seas seemed to him like a dream or a fiction. What was real was the minute, the hour, the day from reveille to the order to stop work. He never let his mind wander any further and he could not have found the strength to do so. Like everyone else.

He knew nothing of the past life of the people around him, and he was not interested. Yet, if the next day Bagretsov were to announce he was a doctor of philosophy or a major general in the air force, Glebov would have believed him without hesitating. Had he himself ever been a doctor? He had lost his reflexive judgments, even his reflexive observational powers. Glebov could see Bagretsov was sucking the blood from his dirty finger, but he said nothing. It just flashed through his mind, but he couldn't find the will to reply, and he wasn't trying. Whatever mind he still had left, and it might well no longer be a human mind, had too few facets. At the moment it was focused on one thing only: to move the stones as fast as possible.

"I expect it's deep down, is it?" Glebov asked, once they had lain down to rest.

"How could it be deep?" replied Bagretsov.

Glebov realized that his question was idiotic and that the pit couldn't possibly be deep.

"Here we are," said Bagretsov.

He had touched a human digit. A big toe was poking out of the stones, and it was perfectly visible in the moonlight. The toe was not like Glebov's or Bagretsov's, not just because it was lifeless and stiff—theirs were, too. The dead man's toenails had been cut, and the toe was fatter and softer than Glebov's. They quickly flung aside the stones dumped over the body.

"Quite young," said Bagretsov.

It was an effort for the two of them to drag the corpse out by its legs.

"A pretty big lad," said Glebov, who was out of breath.

"If he hadn't been such a big lad," said Bagretsov, "he'd have been buried like the rest of us, and we wouldn't have had to come all this way today."

They straightened out the corpse's arms and pulled off his shirt.

"His underpants are quite new," said Bagretsov with satisfaction.

So they pulled the underpants off too. Glebov stuffed the bundle of linen under his padded jacket.

"It'd be better if you put them on," said Bagretsov.

"No, I'd rather not," mumbled Glebov.

They placed the corpse back in the grave and covered it with stones.

The blue light of the moon, which had now risen, shone on the stones, on the thin polar forest, picking out every ledge, every tree in a special light that was not like daylight. Everything seemed real in its own way, but not its daytime self. This was a sort of second, nocturnal aspect of the world.

The corpse's linen grew warm from being close to Glebov's body. It no longer seemed to belong to someone else.

"I could do with a smoke," said Glebov dreamily.

"You can have a smoke tomorrow," said Bagretsov, smiling. Tomorrow they would sell the clothes and get some bread, perhaps even a bit of tobacco in exchange....

1954

CARPENTERS

THERE had been a white mist for days on end. It was so thick that a man became invisible two yards away. Not that there was any reason to go far on one's own. The few routes—to the refectory, the hospital, or the guardhouse—could be divined by some mysterious instinct, like the capacity for orientation that animals have and that, given the right circumstances, can be activated in human beings.

The workmen were not allowed to see a thermometer, and they didn't need one. No matter what the temperature was, they had to go to work. In any case, the old hands could tell almost exactly how many degrees below zero it was. If there was a frosty mist, then it was minus forty centigrade outside; if there was a noise when you breathed out but you could still breathe normally, then it was minus forty-five; if your breath was noisy and you were out of breath, then it was minus fifty. Below fifty-five degrees a gob of spit freezes solid in midair. Spit had been freezing in midair for two weeks.

Potashnikov woke up each morning hoping that the freezing temperatures had abated. After last winter, experience told him that, however cold it was, what you needed to feel warm was a sharp change in temperature, a contrast. Even if the weather got no warmer than minus forty or minus forty-five, you'd feel warm for a couple of days, and there was no point making any plans for longer than two days.

But there was no letup in the cold, and Potashnikov realized that he could not stand it anymore. Breakfast gave him the ability to endure an hour's work at most, and then he was overcome by tiredness and the cold got to his very bones: an idiomatic expression that was literally true. All you could do, so as not to freeze to death by lunchtime, was to wave your pickax or spade about and hop from one leg to the other.

The hot lunch, the notorious dumpling soup and two spoonfuls of porridge, did little to restore your strength, but it did warm you up. Once again, you had the strength to work for an hour, after which Potashnikov was overcome by a desire, if not to get warm, then just to lie down on the sharp edges of the frozen stones and die. But the day still came to an end and after supper, with a drink of water and a mouthful of bread, which all the workmen took back to the barracks, never eating it with the refectory soup, Potashnikov would immediately lie down to sleep.

Naturally, he slept on the top bunk; the lower bunks were like an ice cellar, and those who slept there spent half the night standing by the stove, taking turns to put their arms around it and get the remnants of its warmth. There was never enough firewood. You had to go four kilometers after work to fetch wood, and everyone used any excuse they could to get out of this task. It was warmer up on top, although people slept in their work clothes, wearing hats, padded jackets, pea jackets, quilted trousers. It was warmer up on top, but even there your hair froze to the pillow in the night.

Potashnikov could feel his strength waning every day. He was a man of thirty, but he now found it hard to climb to the top bunk and hard to get down. His neighbor had died the day before, just died. He'd failed to wake up, and nobody was curious as to why he had died, as if there was only one reason for dying and everyone knew what it was. The duty orderly was pleased that the death had happened in the morning instead of the evening; he would get the dead man's rations for that day. Everyone understood that, and Potashnikov was bold enough to approach the orderly and say, "Leave a crust for me." But the orderly responded with the violent cursing that can only come from a man who was once weak and is now strong and who knows that he can curse with impunity. A weak man curses a strong man only in extraordinary circumstances, when moved by the boldness of despair. Potashnikov said nothing and retreated.

He had to decide to do something, to make his enfeebled brain think up something. Or die. Potashnikov wasn't afraid of death. But he did have a secret passionate desire, a last stubborn resolve, a desire to die somewhere like a hospital, in a bunk or a bed, being attended to, even if only by prison authorities, but not to die outside in the freezing cold or kicked to death by the guards, not in the barracks to the sound of loud quarreling, in filth and surrounded by everyone's indifference. He didn't blame people for being indifferent. He had realized a long time ago what caused this dulling of the spirit, this cold lack of sympathy. The same cold that turned saliva to ice in midair had gotten to the human soul. If your bones could freeze, then your brain could freeze into insensitivity and so could your soul. You couldn't think about anything in the freezing cold. Everything was simple. A cold hungry brain couldn't take in nutrition, the brain cells withered; this was clearly a physical process, and God knew if the pathosis could ever be reversed, as a medical man would put it, like frostbite, or if the destruction was permanent. That was what happened to the soul: it froze, it shrank, and, maybe, it would stay cold forever. All this had occurred to Potashnikov before, and now all that was left was a desire to endure, to outlive the spell of freezing cold.

Of course, the first thing was to find some means of salvation. There were few such means. You could become a foreman or a guard, just hang around the bosses. Or around the kitchen. But there were hundreds competing for the kitchen, and Potashnikov had refused a year ago to be a foreman, because he had promised himself that he would not allow himself to enslave another human being here. Even if his own life was at stake, he refused to have his dying comrades hurl their last curses in his face. Potashnikov was expecting death any day now, and the day appeared to have come.

He gulped down a bowl of warm soup and chewed the last lump of bread, then, barely able to drag his feet, went to his workplace. The brigade was lined up for the start of work; a fat, red-faced man in a reindeer-skin hat, Yakut reindeer-skin boots, and a white fur jacket walked up and down the line. He surveyed the workmen's emaciated, filthy, expressionless faces. The men were shuffling their feet, waiting for this unexpected delay to be over. The foreman was there too, respectfully reporting something to the man in the reindeer-skin hat.

"I promise you, sir, I don't have anyone like that. You should go and see Soboliov and the nonpolitical convicts. These people are the educated ones, sir, and they're nothing but trouble."

The man in the reindeer-skin hat, Aleksandr Evgeniyevich, stopped examining the workmen and turned to the foreman.

"You foremen don't know your men, you don't want to know them and don't want to help us," he said hoarsely.

"Whatever you say, sir."

"I'll show you what's what. What's your name?"

"Ivanov, sir."

"Now watch me. Hey, men, pay attention." The man in the reindeer-skin hat addressed the brigade. "The administration needs carpenters to make boxes for carrying earth."

There was no response.

"You see, sir," whispered the foreman.

Potashnikov suddenly heard his own voice: "Yes, sir, I'm a carpenter." He took a step forward.

Another man silently took a step from the right flank. Potashnikov knew him: Grigoriev.

"Well," said the man in the reindeer-skin hat, turning to the foreman, "you're a useless piece of shit. You two, follow me."

Potashnikov and Grigoriev staggered after the man in the reindeer-skin hat, who halted.

"If that's how we're walking," he rasped, "we won't arrive until dinnertime. I'll tell you what: I'll go ahead, and you go straight to the carpentry shop and see the construction man, Sergeyev. Do you know where the carpentry shop is?"

"We do, we do!" Grigoriev shouted. "Could you let us have a cigarette, please?"

"I was expecting that," murmured the man in the reindeer-skin hat, gritting his teeth. Without taking the pack from his pocket, he pulled out two cigarettes.

Potashnikov walked in front, thinking hard. Today he would spend in the warm carpentry shop and sharpen an ax and make an ax handle. And sharpen a saw, too. There would be no hurry. They would get their tools by dinner, order things, and find the store man. And by evening, when it was discovered that he didn't know how to make an ax handle or to set a saw, he'd be thrown out and be back in his brigade the next day. But today he'd be warm. It was even possible that he could pass as a carpenter tomorrow and the day after, as long as Grigoriev was a carpenter. He would be Grigoriev's apprentice. Winter was coming to an end. Summer was short, so he might somehow get through it.

Potashnikov stopped, to allow Grigoriev to catch up.

"Can you do this . . . carpentry stuff?" he managed to say, panting with sudden hope.

"You know," said Grigoriev cheerfully, "I have a postgraduate degree from the Moscow Institute of Philology. I think that anyone with higher education, especially in the humanities, ought to be able to carve an ax handle and set a saw, especially if this is to be done next to a hot stove."

"So, you aren't either—"

"That doesn't matter. We can fool them for a couple of days, and then, who cares what happens then?"

"We can fool them for one day. Tomorrow we'll be sent back to the brigade."

"No, it will take them longer than a day to get us transferred to the carpentry shop. They have to hand over all the details, make lists. Then they'll have to do the same when they transfer us back again."

The two of them barely had the strength to open the door, which had frozen shut. A red-hot iron stove was burning in the middle of the carpentry shop, and five carpenters, without jackets or hats, were bent over their workbenches. The two new arrivals kneeled in front of the stove's open door, worshiping the god of fire, one of humanity's first gods. They took off their gloves and held out their hands to the heat, almost shoving them into the fire. Their fingers, so often frostbitten, had lost their sensitivity and took time to feel the heat. After a minute, Grigoriev and Potashnikov took off their hats and undid their pea jackets but remained kneeling.

"What are you here for?" the carpenter asked them in an unwelcoming tone.

"We're carpenters. We're going to be working here," said Grigoriev.

"It's on Aleksandr Evgeniyevich's orders," Potashnikov hastily explained.

"So the construction engineer meant you when he said we were to hand out axes," said Arnshtrem, an elderly toolman, who was in the corner, planing spade handles.

"It was us, us."

"Here you are," Arnshtrem told them, after giving them a mistrustful look. "Two axes, a saw, and a saw-setting tool. Give me back the setting tool when you've finished. Here's my ax—make me a new handle for it." Arnshtrem smiled. "My norm for ax handles is thirty per day," he said.

Grigoriev took a block of wood from Arnshtrem and started carving. The dinner siren sounded. Still in his indoor clothes, Arnshtrem watched Grigoriev at work and said not a word.

"Now you," he told Potashnikov.

Potashnikov placed a log on the chopping block, picked up the ax, and started hacking.

"That's enough," said Arnshtrem.

The carpenters had gone to dinner, and the three of them were alone in the shop.

"Take these two ax handles I've made," said Arnshtrem, handing two finished handles to Grigoriev, "and fit the ax heads to them. Sharpen the saw. You can warm yourselves by the stove today and tomorrow. The day after tomorrow go back where you came from. Here's a piece of bread for your dinner."

That day and the next they warmed themselves by the stove; the following day the freezing cold suddenly let up. It was now only minus thirty, and winter was coming to an end.

1954

A PERSONAL QUOTA

ONE EVENING the guard said, as he rolled up his tape measure, that Dugayev would be getting a personal quota for the next day. The foreman, who was standing next to them and had been asking the guard to credit them with "a dozen cubic meters until the day after tomorrow," suddenly fell silent and moved his gaze to the evening star, which was glimmering over the crest of the bare hill. Baranov, who was Dugayev's work partner and had been helping the guard to measure the work they had done, picked up his spade and set to clearing the pit face, which had been cleaned out long ago anyway.

Dugayev was twenty-three years old and was more amazed than frightened by everything he had seen and heard here.

The brigade gathered for roll call, handed in their tools, and, in the prisoners' typical straggling line, went back to their barracks. A hard day's labor was over. Dugayev didn't sit down in the refectory; he drank the thin cold barley soup straight out of the bowl. His day's ration of bread, issued in the morning, had since been eaten. He longed to smoke. He looked around, working out whom he could beg a cigarette end from. Baranov was by the windowsill, scraping into a piece of paper tobacco dust left after someone had emptied their tobacco pouch. After carefully gathering the tobacco, Baranov rolled a thin cigarette and passed it to Dugayev.

"Have a smoke and leave some for me," he offered. Dugayev was amazed, for he and Baranov weren't friends. Not that any friendship could arise between hungry, cold, and sleepless men. Dugayev, despite his youth, understood how false were all the proverbs about friendship tested by misfortune and misery. Real friendship needed to have firm foundations laid before the conditions of everyday life had reached the extreme point beyond which human beings have nothing human about them except mistrust, anger, and lies. Dugayev never forgot the saying in the north, that there are three commandments for prisoners: don't trust, don't be afraid, don't ask.

Dugayev greedily sucked in the sweet tobacco smoke; his head began to spin.

"I'm getting weak," he said.

Baranov did not reply.

Dugayev went back to the barracks, lay down, and shut his eyes. Recently he had not been sleeping well; hunger stopped him from sleeping properly. He had particularly upsetting dreams: loaves of bread, rich steaming soups. . . . It took a long time for oblivion to come, and still Dugayev's eyes were open half an hour before reveille.

The brigade reached its workplace; everyone went to their pit face.

"You wait here," the foreman told Dugayev. "The guard will tell you where to go."

Dugayev sat down on the ground. He was already so worn out that he was completely indifferent to any change in his fate.

The first wheelbarrows came thundering down the ramp; spades rasped noisily as they struck stone.

"Come here," the guard ordered Dugayev. "This is your place." He marked out a cubic measure of the pit face and designated a piece of quartz as the boundary. "Up to here," he said. "The ramp man will give you a board to join the main ramp. You have to barrow it to the same place as everybody else. Here's your spade, pickax, crowbar, barrow: get a move on."

Dugayev meekly set to work.

"This is even better," he thought. None of his fellow workers would be grumbling that he wasn't doing his job. People who had once worked the land had no need to understand or know that Dugayev was new to the work, that he had gone straight from school to university, and then from the lecture room straight to this pit face. Everyone was on their own. They didn't want or need to know that he had long been exhausted and starved, that he didn't know how to steal. Knowing how to steal is the main virtue in the north and takes many forms, beginning with stealing your workmate's bread and ending by defrauding the bosses of thousand of rubles in bonuses for nonexistent and impossible production achievements. Nobody cared if Dugayev couldn't stand a sixteen-hour working day.

Dugayev barrowed, pickaxed, filled his barrow, barrowed again, and pickaxed and filled again.

After the lunch interval the guard came to look at what Dugayev had done and then left without saying a word. Dugayev pickaxed and filled his barrow again. The quartz marker was still a long way away.

In the evening the guard reappeared and unwound his tape measure. He measured what Dugayev had done.

"Twenty-five percent," he said, and then gave Dugayev a look. "Twenty-five percent. Are you listening?"

"I am," said Dugayev. He was astonished by this figure. The work was so hard, the spade budged so little stone, and it was so difficult to use the pickax. Even the figure of twenty-five percent of the norm seemed to Dugayev to be very high. His calves ached, his arms, shoulders, and head hurt unbearably from constantly pushing the barrow. He had long ago stopped feeling hungry. Dugayev ate because he saw other people eating and something told him that he had to eat. But he didn't want to.

"Right then," said the guard as he left. "Good luck to you."

That evening Dugayev was summoned to see the interrogator. He replied to the four questions: first name, surname, Criminal Code article, sentence—the four questions a prisoner can be asked thirty times a day. Then Dugayev went off to sleep. The next day he was again working with the rest of the brigade, but the following night he was taken by soldiers behind the stables and then led along a forest path to a place where a tall fence, topped with barbed wire, cordoned off most of a small ravine. At nights you could hear from this point the rumbling of tractors. Dugayev realized what was about to happen: he wished he hadn't wasted his time working and suffering all this day, his last.

1955

THE PARCEL

Parcels were issued in the guardhouse. The foremen checked the identity of the recipient. The fiberboard broke and cracked in a special fiberboard way. Here, trees broke differently and made a different noise when they broke. Behind a barrier made of benches, men with clean hands and in exceedingly neat military uniforms were opening, checking, shaking out, and issuing things. The boxes the parcels came in had barely survived a journey of many months; they were thrown with practiced skill into the air so as to split open when they hit the floor. Pieces of sugar, dried fruit, rotting onions, crumpled packets of tobacco flew all over the floor. Nobody picked up the spillage. The addressees of the parcels made no protests; just to get a parcel was a real miracle.

The escort guards stood by the guardhouse, rifles at the ready; unidentifiable figures moved around in the white frosty mist.

I was standing by the wall, waiting for my turn. Those light blue fragments weren't ice: they were sugar! Sugar! Sugar! In an hour I would be holding them in my hands, and they wouldn't melt away. They would only melt in my mouth. A lump that big would give me two, even three mouthfuls.

What about the tobacco? Real homegrown tobacco! Tobacco from mainland Russia. Yaroslavl Squirrel or Kremenchug No. 2. I'd smoke it, I'd treat absolutely everybody, everybody, above all the people who'd let me smoke their cigarette stubs all this year. Mainland tobacco! We did get tobacco as part of our rations, but it was so old that it had been written off from army supplies—that was a gigantic fraud, because any produce whose shelf life had expired was written off and sold to the camps. Now, however, I'd be smoking proper tobacco. And if my wife didn't know that what was needed was the strongest possible tobacco, someone would have let her know.

"Surname?"

The parcel split open, and the box spilled out leathery fruit: prunes. Where was the sugar, then? And there were only a couple or so handfuls of prunes, anyway.

"Soft boots for you? Pilot's soft boots! Ha, ha, ha! With rubber soles! Ha, ha, ha! Just like the chief mining engineer's! Here, take them!"

I stood there dumbfounded. What did I want soft boots for? Here you could only wear them on days off, and there were no days off. If only they were reindeer-fur snow boots, Yakut boots, or ordinary felt boots. Soft boots were far too fashionable. That wouldn't go down well. What's more—

"Listen, you..." A hand touched my shoulder.

I turned around so that I could see the soft boots, the box with a few prunes at the bottom, as well as the people in charge, and the face of the man holding my shoulder. It was Andrei Boiko, our warden at the mine.

Boiko was whispering quickly: "Sell me the boots. I'll give you money. A hundred rubles. You won't get as far as the barracks carrying them. Someone out there will take them off you, snatch them." Boiko pointed a finger into the white mist. "In any case they'd be stolen in the barracks. Before the night is over."

"You'd be the one who sent the thief," I thought, then said, "All right, give me the money."

"You can see I'm good," said Boiko as he counted out the money. "I'm not cheating you like others would. I said a hundred and I'm giving you a hundred." Boiko was afraid he'd paid too much.

I folded the dirty money double, four times, eight times and hid it away in my trouser pocket. I took the prunes out of the box and put them into my jacket lining; the pockets had long ago been torn out to make tobacco pouches.

"I'll buy some butter! A kilogram! And I'll have butter with my bread, soup, and porridge. And I'll buy sugar! And I'll get a bag off somebody, a fabric bag with a rope handle: that's what every self-respecting political prisoner has to have. Ordinary criminals won't be seen dead with them."

I went back to the barracks. Everyone was on their bunks, except for Yefremov, who was sitting with his hands on the stove, which had gone out. Yefremov, reluctant to get to his feet and tear himself away from the stove, had his face against the last remnants of warmth.

"Why don't you stoke it?"

The orderly came up.

"Yefremov is on duty. The foreman said he can take the wood wherever he can find it, but there's got to be firewood. Anyway, I won't let you go to sleep. Go before it's too late."

Yefremov slipped through the barracks door.

"Where's your parcel, then?" he asked.

"It was all a mistake."

I ran to the shop. Shaparenko, the shop manager, was still doing business. There was nobody else.

"Shaparenko, give me some bread and butter."

"You'll be the death of me."

"Take whatever it costs."

"Can't you see how much money I've got?" said Shaparenko. "What use is a drip like you to me? Take your bread and butter and clear off."

I had forgotten to ask him for sugar. I had a kilo of butter and a kilo of bread. I would go and see Semion Sheinin. Sheinin used to be an adviser to Kirov, and he hadn't been executed yet. We used to work together in the same brigade, but by a quirk of fate we'd been separated.

Sheinin was in the barracks.

"Let's eat. Butter, bread."

Sheinin's hungry eyes lit up. "I'll go and get some hot water—"

"There's no need for hot water!"

"No, I'll be right back." He disappeared.

At that moment someone hit me on the head with a heavy object; when I got up and came to my senses, my bag was gone. Everyone was where they had been, looking at me with spiteful pleasure. This was the best sort of entertainment. Incidents like this gave double the pleasure: first, someone is having a bad time; second, it isn't them. It certainly isn't envy.

I didn't cry. I was lucky to be alive. This was all thirty years ago, but I can remember in detail the barracks in semidarkness, the spiteful, happy faces of my comrades, the unseasoned log on the floor, Sheinin's pale cheeks.

I went back to the shop. I didn't ask for more butter, I didn't ask for sugar, either. I managed to get some bread, went back to the barracks, thawed some snow, and set about boiling my prunes.

The barracks was fast asleep: groaning, snoring, rasping, and coughing. Three of us stood by the stove, each doing our own cooking: Sintsov was boiling a crust of bread he'd saved from dinner so as to have it hot and sticky and then greedily drink the hot water made from melted snow, which smelled of rain and bread. The lucky, cunning Gubariov had taken a pot and pounded leaves of frozen cabbage. The cabbage smelled like the best Ukrainian borscht. And I was stewing the prunes from my parcel. None of us could help looking in the others' pots.

Somebody kicked the barracks doors open. Two soldiers emerged from a cloud of frozen mist. The younger one was the camp chief Kovalenko; the older one was the mine chief Riabov. Riabov was wearing pilot's boots—could they have been mine? It took me some time to realize that this was a mistake and that the boots belonged to Riabov.

Kovalenko rushed to the stove, waving a pickax he had brought with him.

"Cooking pots again? I'll show you what happens to cooking pots. I'll teach you to foul the place up!"

Kovalenko tipped over the pots of soup, bread crusts, cabbage leaves, and prunes and smashed a hole in each pot with his pickax.

Riabov warmed his hands on the stovepipe.

"If you've got pots, that means you've got food to cook," the mine chief expounded with an air of profundity. "That, you know, is a sign of plenty."

"Well you ought to see what they've been cooking," said Kovalenko as he trampled the pots flat.

The chiefs left, and we started sorting out the crushed pots and picking out our own food: I got my prunes, Sintsov his shapeless soaked bread, Gubariov his crumbled cabbage leaves. We ate it all straightaway: that was the safest option.

I swallowed a few prunes and went to sleep. Long ago I had learned to go to sleep before my feet got warm; at first I couldn't do that, but experience is experience. Sleep was just like oblivion.

Life recurred as a dream: the doors were flung open again—white puffs of steam kept to the floor as they ran to the far wall of the barracks, while there were people in white fur jackets that stank from being new and unworn, and something that didn't move but was alive, grunted after it fell to the floor.

The orderly struck a pose that suggested bewilderment as well as respect as he bowed down to the white sheepskin jackets of the supervisors.

"Is that your man?" asked the guard, pointing to a bundle of dirty rags lying on the floor.

"That's Yefremov," said the orderly.

"This will teach him to steal other people's firewood."

Yefremov spent many weeks lying on his bunk next to me before he was carted off to die in the buildings set aside for invalids. His "innards" had been smashed up; there were quite a few experts in the mines who knew how to do that. He never complained; he just lay there, quietly groaning.

1960

RAIN

THIS WAS the third day that we had been drilling at the new site. Each man had his own prospecting shaft and by now none of us had gotten any deeper than half a meter. Nobody had yet reached permafrost, even though the crowbars and pickaxes were being repaired quickly. This was unusual, but the blacksmiths had no reason to hold things up, because ours was the only brigade at work. The basic problem was the rain, which had been pouring without a break for seventy-two hours. When the ground was stony you couldn't tell if it had rained for an hour or a month. The rain was cold and fine. The brigades working next to us had been taken off the job and sent home some time ago, but these were brigades of gangsters, and we didn't even have the strength to envy them.

Our guard rarely appeared. He wore a soaking-wet enormous hooded canvas cloak that was as angular as a pyramid. The bosses were relying on the rain, the cold streams of water lashing our backs. We had long been wet through—not to our underwear, though, because we didn't have any underwear. The bosses' crude secret calculation was that rain and wind would make us work. But our hatred of the work was even stronger, and every evening the guard cursed as he lowered his wooden ruler with its markers into the shaft. The escort guards kept watch over us from under their "mushroom," a well-known piece of camp equipment.

We couldn't climb out of the shafts, or we would have been shot. Only our foreman was allowed to move from shaft to shaft. We were not allowed to shout to one another, or we would have been shot. So we stood silently, up to our waists in the ground, in stone pits, a long chain of shafts that stretched along the banks of a dried-out stream.

The nights were too short to dry out our pea jackets; at night we nearly managed to get the tunics and trousers dry on our bodies. I was hungry and angry, but I knew that nothing in the world would make me commit suicide. This was when I began to understand the essence of life's great instinct, the quality that human beings possess in the highest degree. I could see our horses getting worn out and dying—that's the only way I can put it, there are no other verbs to apply to the horses' existence. The horses were no different from the human beings. The north, the unbearable workload, the bad food, the beatings were killing them, and although they suffered only a thousandth of what the human beings suffered, they died first. I also understood the main thing: man was human not because he was God's creation, or because he had an amazing thumb on both hands, but because he was physically stronger, more enduring than any other animal and, eventually, because he succeeded in making his spiritual side the effective servant of his physical side.

That's what I was thinking about for the hundredth time in this shaft. I knew I wouldn't kill myself because I had tested my will to live. In a similar shaft, only a deeper one, I had recently taken out an enormous stone with my pickax. I spent many days carefully freeing its terrible weight. From this unkind weight, as the Russian poet[1] put it, I thought I could make something fine. I thought I could save my life by breaking my leg. This really was a fine intention, a purely aesthetic prospect. The stone was meant to tumble out and shatter my leg. And I would be a permanent invalid! This passionate dream depended on careful planning, so I took care to find the right spot to place my leg, and I imagined how I would make a slight twist of the pickax, and the stone would tumble down. I'd decided on the day, the hour, and the minute, and they came. I placed my right leg under the hanging stone, praised my own calmness, raised a hand, and, as if it were a lever, turned the pickax wedged behind the stone. The stone started moving down the shaft wall to the place I had carefully calculated. But I don't know how it happened: I jerked my leg back. The shaft was tight, so my leg was squashed, and I had two bruises and an abrasion—a meager result for such a well-planned job.

So I realized that I was no more suited to self-harm than to suicide.

All I could do now was wait for small disasters to alternate with small successes, until the big disaster ran its course. The next success was the end of the working day and three mouthfuls of hot soup; even if the soup was cold it could be warmed up on the iron stove in a pan that I had made of a three-liter tin can. I could light a cigarette, or rather a stub I could beg off our orderly Stepan.

That's how I waited, mingling "astral" questions with trivia, soaked to the skin but calm. Were these reflections a form of brain training? Certainly not. This was all quite normal, it was life. I understood that my body, and thus my brain cells, were short of nourishment. My brain had been on starvation rations for such a long time, and this would inevitably result in madness, early sclerosis, or something worse.... I found it a cheering thought that I wouldn't live that long, that I would never live long enough to get sclerosis. The rain poured down.

I remembered a woman who had passed along the path near where we were working and who paid no attention to the guards' shouts. We greeted her and thought she was beautiful. She was the first woman we had seen in three years. She waved to us, pointed to the sky, at some angle to the firmament, and shouted, "Not long, boys, not long!" We answered with a joyful roar. I never saw her again, but I have remembered ever since how she found a way of understanding and consoling us. When she pointed to the sky, she certainly didn't mean the next world. No, she was just showing an invisible sun setting in the west, which meant that the working day would soon be over. In her own way she was repeating Goethe's words about the mountain peaks. What I was thinking about was the wisdom and magnanimity of this simple woman, who was or had been a prostitute—for there were then no other sorts of women in these regions. The sound of falling rain was a good accompaniment to these thoughts. The gray stony riverbank, the gray mountains, the gray sky, men in torn gray clothes—all that was very easy on the eye, very much in harmony. Everything had a mono-chrome harmony, a satanic harmony.

This was when we heard a faint cry from the next shaft. My neighbor was a certain Rozovsky, an elderly agronomist whose fairly specialized knowledge, like those of the doctors, engineers, and economists, was wasted here. He was calling my name, so I responded, paying no attention to the threatening gesture coming from a guard, sheltering far off under his "mushroom."

"Listen," Rozovsky was calling, "listen! I've been thinking for a long time. And I've realized that there is no sense in life ... none—"

Then I leapt out of my shaft and ran to intercept him before he rushed at the guards. Both guards were coming toward us.

"He's sick," I said.

Just then we caught the distant sound of the siren, muted by the rain, and we started forming ranks.

Rozovsky and I went on working together for a while, until he threw himself under a loaded wagon that was rolling downhill. He stuck his leg under the wheel, but the wagon just leapt over him, without even bruising him. All the same, he was charged with attempted suicide and tried for it. We then parted, for there was a rule that anyone convicted after a trial would be sent to some other camp. The authorities were afraid that the victim might take revenge on his interrogator or the witnesses. That was a wise rule. But there was no need to apply it to Rozovsky.

1958

PUSHOVER

THE BARE hills were white with a bluish tinge, like loaves of sugar. Round and treeless, they were covered with a thick layer of packed snow, which the winds had consolidated. In the gullies the snow was deep and strong enough to hold a man, but on the hill slopes it was puffed up as if in enormous bubbles. These were bushes of dwarf pine that crept over the ground and flattened themselves for hibernation before the first snow fell. This pine was what we were after.

Of all the trees in the north, the dwarf pine or cedar was my favorite.

I had long ago understood and treasured the enviable haste with which impoverished northern nature, destitute as it was, strove to share its simple riches with human beings by producing all of its flowers as quickly as it could. It took only a week to bring everything into blossom, and in little more than a month after the beginning of summer, when the sun never set, the mountains would shine red with lingonberries and black with blueberries. The bushes of large, watery yellow rowan were so low you didn't have to lift your hand. The honey-flavored mountain briar had rose petals, the only local flower that smelled of flowers. All the other flowers smelled only of damp, of marsh, and that fit with the silence of the birds in spring, the silence of the larch forest, whose branches were slow to grow green needles. The briar held on to its hips until the first frosts and would offer us its chewy wrinkled berries, with a hard violet skin concealing their sweet, dark yellow flesh. I knew the cheerful vines that in spring changed color many times from dark pink to orange to pale green, as if bound in colored leather. The larches stretched out their fine fingers and green fingernails, while ubiquitous thick willow herb covered the ground wherever the forest had been burned down. All this was beautiful, trusting, noisy, and hasty, but it happened only in summer when the old olive-green grass mingled with the new grass on the mossy rocks that shone in the sun and suddenly turned out to be green instead of gray and brown.

In winter all this vanished: it was covered with porous, hard snow, driven by the wind into the gullies and packed down so hard that you had to cut steps with an ax if you wanted to climb a hill. You could see a man in the forest half a mile away, so bare was the landscape. There was only one evergreen tree, the dwarf pine or dwarf evergreen cedar. It forecast the weather. Two or three days before the first snow fell, when there was still an autumnal warmth in the air and the sky was cloudless and nobody wanted to think about the approach of winter, the dwarf pine would suddenly lower its enormous, twelve-foot paws and bend its straight black trunk, as thick as two fists, so as to lie facedown on the ground. One or two days would pass and a small cloud would appear; by the next evening a blizzard would gather and snow would fall. If in late autumn, low snow clouds gathered and a cold wind blew, but the dwarf pine did not lie down, then you could be absolutely sure that there would be no snow.

At the end of March and in April, before there was even a hint of spring, and when the air had its wintry thinness and dryness, the dwarf pine would suddenly rise up, shaking the snow off its green, slightly reddish clothing. A day or two later the wind would change and warm streams of air would bring spring with them.

The dwarf pine was a very precise instrument, so sensitive that at times it could make mistakes: it would rise up during a thaw, if the thaw was prolonged. It never rose up before a thaw. But before the thaw ended it would quickly lie down in the snow again. Occasionally something else would happen. If you got a hot campfire going in the morning so as to have somewhere to warm your hands and legs at dinnertime, you would put on as many logs as you could and then go to work. Two or three hours later the dwarf pine would poke its branches out of the snow and carefully straighten up, thinking spring had come. Before the fire had gone out, however, the dwarf pine would bed itself down in the snow again. In these regions winter has two colors: the pale blue of the high sky, and the white of the earth. In spring last year's dirty yellow rags are revealed; for a very long time the earth is dressed in these pauper's clothes, until the new greenery gets enough strength to start to bloom, hastily and violently. It is in the middle of this mournful spring and pitiless winter that the dwarf pine turns a bright, dazzling green and shines forth. What's more, it produces nuts, tiny pine nuts. This is a delicacy that people share with nutcracker birds, bears, squirrels, and chipmunks.

We chose an area on the windward side of the hill; we dragged a load of small and slightly larger branches; we tore up dry grass on the bare patches where the wind had driven the snow off the hill. Before we left the barracks, we had taken some smoldering coals from the stove, since there were no matches to be had.

We carried the coals in a big tin can with a piece of wire for a handle; we took care to keep the coals alight on our journey. When I took them out of the can, I blew on them, gathered the smoldering lumps in a pile, raised a flame, and put them on the branches with some dry grass and twigs to make a bonfire. I then covered it all with bigger branches, and soon the wind drew forth a precarious bluish smoke.

This was the first time I had worked in a brigade collecting dwarf pine needles. The work had to be done by hand, the dry green needles had to be plucked like game-bird feathers; you had to take as big a handful as you could, then stuff them into sacks, and in the evening you handed over your harvest to the guard. The pine needles were then carted off to a mysterious vitamin processing plant, where they produced a thick, sticky, dark yellow extract that tasted unspeakably foul. Every time before we had lunch, we were made to drink or eat this extract (you got it down the best way you could). The taste not only spoiled lunch and dinner but many people regarded this medication as just an extra way for the camp to get at you. You weren't given your lunch until you'd downed a small glass of this medication; they were strict about that. Scurvy affected everyone, and dwarf pine needles were the only treatment approved by medicine. Faith conquers all things, and although this concoction was later proven to be utterly useless as a means of preventing scurvy[2] and then renounced, and the processing plant was closed down, in our time people still had to take this stinking rubbish, spitting afterward to get rid of the taste, as they recovered from scurvy, or, rather, failed to recover, or recovered from scurvy despite not taking it. There were rose hips to be had everywhere, but nobody processed them or used them to combat scurvy, since rose hips were not mentioned in the instructions issued in Moscow. (A few years later they started importing rose hips from the mainland, but as far as I know, nobody ever thought of processing the local ones.)

The instructions considered pine needles to be the sole source of vitamin C, and I was now a producer of this valuable raw material. I had lost my strength, so I was transferred from the gold-mine pit face to pick pine needles.

"You'll go and gather dwarf pine needles," the supervisor told me one morning. "I'll give you a pushover of a job for a few days."

"Pushover," or *kant*, was a widespread term in the camps, meaning something like a temporary break, not a complete break (for that the term was "a swell"—someone would be "swelling" for a day); pushover meant work that didn't exhaust you, temporary light work.

Dwarf pine work was considered not merely easy but in fact very easy. It was prized because you had no guards on your back.

After many months of work in icy open pits where every stone, shining with frost, burned your hands, after the clicking of rifle bolts, the barking of dogs, and the foul cursing of the guards behind you, working with dwarf pines was an enormous pleasure that was relished by every single tired muscle. Normally, people were sent to work while it was still dark; for pine needles you were sent off later.

It was good to warm your hands on a can full of smoldering coals, to amble slowly to the hills, which were so impossibly far away, I used to think, as I climbed higher and higher, all the time relishing my isolation and the deep silence of the mountains in winter as an unexpected joy, as if everything bad in the world had vanished and there was only yourself and your comrade and the endless narrow dark path in the snow, leading high up to somewhere in the mountains.

My comrade didn't approve of my slowness. He had been gathering pine needles for a long time and quite rightly suspected that I would be a weak and incompetent partner. The work was done in pairs, and the results were shared equally between us.

"I'll cut the branches, and you sit down and pick the needles," he told me. "And be lively about it, or we won't meet the norm. I don't want to be sent back to the mines again."

He chopped down a pile of dwarf pine branches and dragged the gigantic heap toward the bonfire. I broke off the smallest branches and stripped the needles and the bark, starting at the end of the branch. The needles and bark were like green tassels.

"You have to work faster," my partner said when he came back with another armful. "That's no good, man."

I didn't need telling that it was no good, but I couldn't work any faster. I had a ringing in my ears, and my fingers, which had been frostbitten that winter, were aching again with a familiar dull throb. I stripped the needles, broke up whole branches into smaller pieces, trying not to strip the bark, and stuffed the result into the sack. But there was no way I could fill the sack. There was now a whole mountain of stripped branches, looking like washed bones, surrounding the bonfire, but the sack still had plenty of room and could take in more armfuls of needles.

My partner began helping me. Things moved faster.

"Time we went home," he suddenly said. "Or we'll miss supper. This isn't enough for the norm." Then he picked a big stone from the bonfire ash and shoved it into the sack.

"They won't untie the sack there," he said with a frown. "Now we've met the norm."

I got up, scattered the burning branches, and raked snow over the still-red coals. The bonfire hissed and went out; it instantly became cold, and it was clear that evening was falling. My partner helped me shoulder the sack: I swayed under the weight.

"Then drag it on the ground," he said. "It's downhill all the way."

We were only just in time to get our soup and tea. Men doing such light work were not meant to have a second course.

1956

FIELD RATIONS

When the four of us had reached the Duskania spring we were so pleased that we almost stopped talking to one another. We were afraid that our journey had been a mistake or a joke on somebody's part, that we would be sent back to the stone pit faces of the mines, so ominous, flooded with water from melting ice. Our prison-issue rubber boots were no protection for our feet, which suffered frostbite again and again.

We had been following the tracks left by tractors, like the footprints of some prehistoric animal; then the tractor path ended, and we walked on a footpath that was hard to make out, until we reached a small log cabin with two windows and a door that hung from a hinge made from a car tire and fixed with nails. The little door had an enormous wooden handle, like the handles on restaurant doors in big cities. Inside the cabin were bare bunks made of whole floorboards, and a big, soot-covered tin can lay on the earth floor. Many cans of the same sort, yellow with rust, were scattered around the moss-covered cabin. This was the mining prospectors' hut where nobody had lived for many a year. We had to stay here and cut a clearing, for which we had brought axes and saws.

This was the first time we had been handed out field rations. I had the standard bag of grain, sugar, dried fish, and edible fats. The bag was tied at various places with odd ends of rope, just like sausages. There was sugar and two sorts of grain—barley and millet. Saveliev had exactly the same bag, while Ivan Ivanovich had two whole bags, which had been made with crude masculine stitches. The fourth man in our group, Fedia Shchapov, had foolishly filled the pockets of his pea jacket with pearl barley and tied granulated sugar in his foot bindings. Fedia used the pocket he had torn out of his jacket as a tobacco pouch, in which he carefully put away any cigarette ends he found.

Rations meant to last ten days looked intimidating. We were reluctant to think that all this had to be divided into thirty parts if we were to have breakfast, lunch, and dinner, or twenty parts if we were to eat twice a day. We had taken two days' supply of bread, because a guard would be bringing more. It was unthinkable to let even the smallest group of workmen go without a guard. We weren't interested in who he might be. We were told that we had to reach somewhere for him to stay before he came.

We were all sick of the barracks food. We could have wept every time we saw the big zinc cauldrons of soup being carried on long poles into the barracks. We were ready to weep from fear that the soup was thin gruel. And when by some miracle the soup was thick, we couldn't believe it and were so joyful that we ate it as slowly as we could. But even thick soup in a warmed-up stomach left us with a nagging pain, so long had we been starving. Any human feelings—love, friendship, envy, charity, mercy, ambition, decency—had vanished along with the flesh we had lost during our prolonged starvation. The minuscule layer of muscle that was still left on our bones, and which allowed us to eat, move, breathe, even saw beams, fill barrows with spadefuls of stone and sand, even push a barrow up an endless wooden ramp in the gold mine, had only enough room for resentful anger, the most lasting of human feelings.

Saveliev and I decided to eat our food separately. Cooking is a special sort of pleasure for prisoners. It gives you a satisfaction beyond compare to cook your own food with your own hands and eat it, even if you cook worse than a professional. Our culinary knowledge was minimal, and we didn't know enough even to make a basic soup or porridge. Nevertheless, Saveliev and I collected and cleaned tin cans, heated them over a campfire, soaked and boiled various things, learning from each other.

Ivan Ivanovich and Fedia mixed up their food. Fedia carefully turned out his pockets, checked every seam, and used his dirty broken fingernail to scrape out the grains.

All four of us were well prepared for a journey into the future, to heaven, if not on earth. We knew what science dictated as the minimum nutritional requirements, and we knew our tables for comparing the value of different foodstuffs, which showed that ten liters of water had the same caloric value as a hundred grams of meat. We had learned to be meek; we had forgotten how to be astonished. We had no pride, no self-esteem or self-respect, while jealousy or passion seemed to us to be something only Martians might feel and, in any case, was nonsense. It was far more important to learn the skills needed to button up your trousers in sub-zero winter temperatures. Grown men would weep when they found they could not do that. We realized that death was no worse than life and we were afraid of neither. We were in thrall to total indifference. We knew we could put a stop to this life tomorrow, if we wanted, and sometimes we decided to do so, but every time we were stopped by some trivial thing that was part of life. Either we were going to get a "box," a bonus kilogram of bread, today and it would be simply stupid to end such a day by committing suicide. Or the orderly in the next barracks would have promised to repay an old debt by giving us a cigarette that evening.

We understood that even the worst sort of life is made up of alternating joy and grief, good luck and bad, and there was no point fearing that the bad luck would outweigh the good.

We were disciplined and obedient to authority. We realized that truth and lies were twin sisters, and that truth on earth came in thousands of different forms.

We considered ourselves to be almost saintly, thinking that we must have expiated all our sins by the years spent in the camps.

We had learned to understand people, to foresee their actions and guess what they were up to.

Above all, we understood that our knowledge of people was of no use to us in everyday life. What was the point of my understanding, feeling, guessing, foreseeing another person's actions? All the same I couldn't alter my behavior toward someone, I wouldn't inform on another prisoner like myself, whatever he might be up to. I wasn't going to try and get the foreman's job, even though it gave you a chance of staying alive, for the worst thing in the camps was forcing another person, a prisoner like yourself, to bow to your will (or anyone else's).

What did it matter that I knew that Ivanov was a swine, that Petrov was a spy and Zaslavsky a false witness?

The impossibility of exploiting the usual types of weapon made us weak compared with some of our neighbors in the camp bunks. We had learned to be satisfied with little and to get pleasure from little things.

We also understood an amazing thing: in the eyes of the state and its representatives, a physically strong man is better—and I mean better, more moral, more valuable—than a weak man, a man who is incapable of throwing twenty-five cubic meters of earth out of a trench in one shift. The strong man is more moral than the weak; he is fulfilling the "percentage," that is, he is carrying out his duty to the state and to society and is therefore respected. That is why he is consulted and taken into consideration, invited to discussions and meetings that may have as their topic something quite unconnected with questions of throwing heavy slippery earth out of wet sticky ditches.

Thanks to his physical advantages, such a man becomes a moral force in decisions affecting the numerous everyday questions of camp life. But he is a moral force only as long as he has physical strength.

Tsar Paul I's aphorism runs: "In Russia the man I am talking to is noble, as long as I am talking to him." And it obtained a surprising new validity in the mines of the Far North.

In the first months of his life in the mines, Ivan Ivanovich was a model hard worker. Now he's lost his strength and fails to understand why everyone he meets hits him; it doesn't hurt, but he still gets beaten by the orderly, the barber, the supervisor, the barracks chief, the foreman, the guard. Ivan Ivanovich was happy to leave all that behind for the job in the forest.

Fedia Shchapov, an adolescent from the Altai, became a goner before anyone else because his body was half child, half adolescent, and it couldn't cope. So Fedia weakened more quickly and lasted about two weeks less than the others. He was a widow's only son, and he was convicted of illegally slaughtering sheep: He had slaughtered his only ewe, something forbidden by law. Fedia was given ten years, and the pace of labor in the mines, quite unlike agricultural work, was too hard for him. Fedia was bewitched by the easygoing life of the gangsters at the mines, but there was something about him that prevented him from mingling with thieves. This healthy peasant element, a natural love of labor, rather than a revulsion toward it, helped him a little. He was the youngest among us and he attached himself straightaway to the oldest and most positive, Ivan Ivanovich.

Saveliev had been a student at the Moscow Communications Institute, and I had shared a cell with him in Butyrki prison in Moscow. Shaken by all he had seen, he wrote a letter from his cell, like the true Komsomol member he was, to the leader of the party, since he was sure that the leader was unaware of all this information. His own case was trivial (correspondence with his fiancée), the evidence for agitation (paragraph 10 of article 58) was merely the letters of two people about to be married, so that his "organization" (paragraph 11 of the same article) consisted of just two persons. This was in all seriousness recorded on the interrogation forms. Everyone thought that Saveliev would be let off with exile, even given the scales of punishment at the time.

Shortly after he dispatched the letter on one of the days set aside for prisoners' "petitions," Saveliev was called out into the corridor and told to sign a receipt of a warrant. The chief prosecutor was informing him that he personally would be examining Saveliev's case. After that Saveliev was called out just once, to be handed the special assize's sentence: ten years in the camps.

Once in the camp, Saveliev very quickly was in a world of his own. He still couldn't understand the ominous punishment he had been dealt. We weren't exactly friends; we just liked recalling Moscow, its streets, its monuments, the Moskva River covered with a mother-of-pearl-like oil slick. Leningrad, Kiev, and Odessa don't have such admirers, connoisseurs, and lovers. We were capable of talking endlessly about Moscow.

We brought the iron stove we had carried with us into the hut and, although it was summer, stoked it. The dry warm air had an extraordinary, wonderful smell. We all had gotten used to breathing the sour smell of worn clothes and sweat; it was just as well that tears don't smell.

On Ivan Ivanovich's advice we took off our underwear and buried it overnight in the ground, keeping each shirt and pair of underpants separate and leaving just a corner unburied. This was a folk way of getting rid of lice; in the mines we had no means of fighting them. In fact, by morning the lice had gathered on the shirt corners that were left unburied. The earth, covered by permafrost, nevertheless thawed enough here to let us bury our underwear. Of course, it was the local earth, more stones than soil. But even this frozen stony soil produced thick forests of enormous larches, whose trunks took three men to embrace them, so powerful was the life force of the trees, a great and instructive example given to us by nature.

We burned the lice by placing our shirts next to a burning coal from a bonfire. Unfortunately, this clever device did not exterminate the vermin, so that same day we spent a lot of time furiously boiling our linen in big tin cans, and this time the disinfection proved effective.

Later we discovered the miraculous qualities of the land when we caught mice, crows, seagulls, and squirrels. Any animal meat loses its particular smell if you bury it in the ground before cooking it.

We took special care to keep our fire going nonstop, since we had between us only a few matches that Ivan Ivanovich had hung on to. He had wrapped the valuable matches with extreme care in a piece of canvas and then in rags.

Every evening we placed two burning coals together so that they would smolder until morning without going out or flaring up. Three coals would have burned up. Saveliev and I had known this principle since we were at school, while Ivan Ivanovich and Fedia had learned it as children at home. In the morning we would blow the coals into life, a yellow flame would flare up, and we would put a nice thick lump of wood on the burning fire.

I divided my barley into ten portions, but found that too frightening. The operation of feeding the five thousand with five loaves of bread was probably easier and simpler than a prisoner's division of his ten days' ration into thirty portions. Rations and ration cards were always for ten days. In the mainland they'd long given up on five-day periods, ten-day periods, and nonstop working weeks, but here the decimal system was kept going far more thoroughly. Nobody here considered Sunday to be a day off. Prisoners who got their days off long after our spell as lumberjacks were eventually given three days a month at the whim of the local prison bosses, who had the right to designate rainy days in summer or excessively cold days in winter as prisoners' rest days, official days off.

I poured all the barley back, being unable to stand this new torment. I asked Ivan Ivanovich and Fedia to let me go in with them, and handed my rations over to the common kitty. Saveliev followed my example.

All four of us in concert took the wise decision to cook twice a day. There certainly wasn't enough food for three meals a day.

"We'll gather berries and mushrooms," said Ivan Ivanovich. "We'll catch mice and birds. And for one or two days out of ten we'll just eat bread."

"But if we're going to go without food for a couple of days before we get supplies," said Saveliev, "how can we stop ourselves eating too much when they do bring something to cook?"

We decided to eat twice a day, whatever the consequences, and, if we had to, to make the soup as thin as we could. After all, nobody here was going to steal anything and we were getting the full norm. We had no drunken cooks or thieving store men, no greedy overseers or thieves who grabbed the best food for themselves; we had none of the countless bosses who deprived the prisoners of food and clothing, and who were deterred by nothing, for they had no fear and no conscience.

We had our full ration of fats in the form of a lump of hydrogenated fat; our sugar was less than the gold dust I washed out with my pan; the bread was sticky and astringent, since it was produced by the great, inimitable experts at makeweight, who also fed the bosses of the bakeries; the grain in twenty different sorts—millet, kibbled wheat. All that was extremely mysterious, and frightening, too.

Fish, which according to some secret scale of values was substituted for meat, came in the form of rust-colored herring and was meant to make up for our increased loss of proteins.

Unfortunately, even the full norm was not enough to nourish or satisfy us. We needed three or four times as much; our bodies had been starving for a long time. We didn't then understand this simple truth. We trusted the norms, but we didn't know of the familiar cook's observation that it is easier to cook for twenty than for four. There was only one thing we were perfectly clear about: we didn't have enough to last us. This amazed us more than it scared us. We had to start working, we had to smash a clearing through fallen trees.

In the north trees die lying down, like people. Their enormous bared roots look like the claws of a giant predatory bird caught in a rock. From these gigantic talons thousands of tiny tentacles, whitish offshoots covered with warm brown bark, stretched down into the permafrost. Each summer the permafrost retreated a little and a tentacle-like root would then immediately use its fine hairs to pierce and anchor itself in each inch of thawed ground. Larches reach maturity at three hundred years, slowly raising their mighty, heavy bodies on weak roots that are spread all over the stony ground. A powerful storm easily fells these weak-kneed trees. Larches would fall on their backs, with their heads in the same direction, and they died lying on a thick soft layer of bright green and bright pink moss.

Only the twisted, crooked, low-growing trees, exhausted by constantly turning toward the sun for warmth, stayed obstinately on their own, keeping their distance from one another. They had kept up this intensive struggle for life for so long that their tortured, crushed heartwood was of no use. A short, many branched trunk, covered all around with terrible growths, like the scarred bark when a branch has been broken off, was unusable for construction, even in the north, where nobody was fussy about the quality of house-building materials. These twisted trees could not even be used for firewood, since their resistance to the ax could exhaust any workman. This is how they avenged themselves on the whole world for the damage the north had done to their life.

Our task was to make a clearing, and we boldly set to work. We sawed from sunrise to sunset, we felled timber, we cut it into blocks and piled it in stacks. We forgot everything else, we wanted to stay here as long as we could, we feared going back to the gold mines. But the stacks rose too slowly and by the end of our second day of intensive work it was clear that we had not done enough and that we didn't have the strength to do more. Ivan Ivanovich made a meter-long ruler by measuring out five of his hand spans on a young ten-year-old larch he had felled.

That evening the guard came, measured our work using a staff with notches, and shook his head. We had done only ten percent of the norm.

Ivan Ivanovich tried to argue with him and took measurements, but the guard was implacable. He mumbled about "face meters" and "solid bodies," which was way above our heads. One thing was clear: we were going to be put back in the camp precinct. Once again we would go through the gates with their inevitable official, government inscription: "Labor is a matter of honor, a matter of glory, a matter of valor and heroism." It's said that a quotation from Nietzsche was used over the gates of German concentration camps: "To each man his due." By imitating Hitler, Beria outdid him in cynicism.

The camp was a place where you were taught to hate physical labor, or labor of any sort. The most privileged group among the camp's population were the professional criminals. Was it for them, perhaps, that labor was heroism and valor?

But we weren't afraid. On the contrary, by recognizing how hopeless our work was, how pathetic our physical capabilities were, the guard had brought us unprecedented relief, without upsetting us or frightening us.

We went with the stream, and we were "drifting to the end," to use the camp terminology. Nothing bothered us anymore; we found living according to somebody else's will easy. We weren't even concerned about staying alive, and if we slept, it was also to obey orders, the camp's daily agenda. The peace of mind achieved by dulling all our feelings was rather like that "higher freedom of the barracks" that T. E. Lawrence dreamed of, like Tolstoy's nonresistance to evil. Someone else's will was constantly watching over our peace of mind.

We had long been fatalists and never gave a thought to our life more than a day ahead. It would have been logical to eat all our food at once and then go back and serve the prescribed sentence in a solitary cell or go out to work at the pit face, but we didn't do that. Any interference with fate or the will of the gods was improper, for it broke the code of camp behavior.

The guard left and we stayed on to cut a clearing and make more stacks of wood. Now we did so more calmly, caring less. We no longer quarreled about who had to get under the butt of a beam and who would take the top end when it had to be carried to the stacks, or "skidded," to use the forester's term.

We took more rests, we paid more attention to the sun, to the forest, to the high pale blue sky. We loafed.

One morning Saveliev and I managed to fell an enormous black larch that had by some miracle survived storms and fires. We threw the saw down on the grass, it rang as it hit a stone, and we sat on the trunk of the tree we had felled.

"Right," said Saveliev, "let's dream a bit. We'll get through this, we'll go back to the mainland, we'll soon get old and we'll be sick old men. We'll get stabbing pains in the heart, or rheumatism will give us no peace, or we'll have chest pains. Everything we are doing now, the way we're spending our youth—sleepless nights, hunger, hard work for long hours, gold mining in icy water, cold in winter, beatings from the guards—all of that will leave its mark on us, even if we stay alive. We'll be sick without knowing why, we'll be groaning and going to outpatient clinics. Work that is beyond our strength will have given us incurable injuries, and in our old age our whole life will be one of pain, various unending physical and mental pains. But these terrible future days will be interspersed with days when we breathe more easily, when we are almost well, and when our sufferings stop bothering us. There won't be many days like that. They will equal in number the number of days we will have managed to loaf while in the camp."

"How about honest labor?" I asked.

"The only people who call on you to do honest labor are the swine and the people who beat us, cripple us, eat our food, and work living skeletons to death. They believe in that fiction even less than we do."

That evening we were sitting around our much loved stove, while Fedia Shchapov listened attentively to Saveliev's hoarse voice.

"Well, I refused to work. They drew up a statement, saying I was dressed 'right for the season.'"

"What does dressed 'right for the season' mean?" asked Fedia.

"Well, so they don't have to list all the winter things and summer things you're wearing. They can't draw up a statement in winter that you were sent to work with no jacket or no gloves. How many times have you stayed behind when there were no gloves?"

"We weren't allowed to stay behind," Fedia said shyly. "The boss made us tramp down the road. Otherwise that would be called 'stayed behind because improperly dressed.'"

"Just what I meant."

"Go on, tell us about the metro."

And Saveliev told Fedia about the Moscow metro. Ivan Ivanovich and I also found it interesting to listen to Saveliev. He knew things that I, though a Muscovite, had never even guessed at.

"Muslims, Fedia," said Saveliev, glad to find his brain was still versatile, "are called to prayer by a muezzin. Muhammad decided that the voice was the best signal to call people to prayer. Muhammad had tried everything—a trumpet, a drum roll, a bonfire—and rejected them all. Fifteen hundred years later, when they tried different signals on the metro, it turned out that whistles, horns, sirens can't catch the train driver's ear as reliably and precisely as the human voice of a platform controller shouting, 'Ready!'"

Fedia gasped with delight. Of all of us, he was the best suited to forest life. Despite his youth, he had more experience than any of us. Fedia could do carpentry, he could make a simple log cabin in the taiga, he knew how to fell a tree and how to use branches to make a strong night shelter. Fedia was a hunter, too. In his home country people learned to use guns when they were children. But cold and hunger made all of Fedia's qualities useless; the earth scorned his knowledge and his skills. Fedia didn't merely envy the townsmen, he bowed down before them, and he could listen endlessly, despite his hunger, to stories about the achievements of technology and urban wonders.

Friendship never arises in a state of deprivation or misery. The "difficult" conditions of life, which writers of fairy tales tell us are a precondition for friendship, are simply not difficult enough. If deprivation or misery ever gave people solidarity and friendship, then the deprivation was not extreme and the misery was not very great. Grief is not acute or deep enough if you can share it with friends. In the deprivation we underwent, all you are aware of is your own mental and physical strength, and you find out the limits of your capacities, your physical endurance, and your moral strength.

We all understood that survival was a matter of pure luck. Oddly enough, in my younger days I used to have a saying that I repeated whenever I had bad luck or a failure: "Well, we're not going to starve to death." Every fiber of my body believed that phrase. And at the age of thirty I found myself in the situation of a man really starving to death, literally fighting over a piece of bread. And all that was before the war.

When the four of us gathered at the Duskania spring, we all knew we weren't there to be friends; we knew that if we survived, we wouldn't care to meet one another. We would find it unpleasant to recall bad things: hunger that drove you mad, steaming out the lice in the pots you cooked dinner in, a constant stream of nonsensical talk around the fire, pointless daydreaming, gastronomical fairy tales, quarrels with each other, lonely dreams—for we all dreamed the same dreams: loaves of rye bread flying over us like fireballs or angels.

What makes a man happy is his ability to forget. One's memory is always ready to discard bad things and retain just good things. There was nothing good at the Duskania spring, nor on the paths any of us had trodden or would tread. We were permanently poisoned by the north, and we realized that. Three of us had stopped resisting fate; only Ivan Ivanovich went on working with the same tragic devotion as he had before.

During one of our cigarette breaks, Saveliev tried to make Ivan Ivanovich see sense. A cigarette break is the most banal form of rest, even for people who don't smoke, since we hadn't had any tobacco for a year, and yet we still had cigarette breaks. Smokers in the taiga would gather and dry black-currant leaves, and there were lengthy discussions, with all the passion that prisoners can muster, about whether bilberry or black currant had the nicer leaves. Connoisseurs considered that neither of them were any good, since your body demands poisonous nicotine, not just smoke, but one couldn't help deceiving one's brain cells with such an easy ploy. For cigarette breaks black-currant leaves were fine, since the concept of a "rest" from work was in the camps far too hateful; it clashed with the basic rules of production morality, rules that were inculcated in the Far North. "Resting" every other hour was a challenge to authority, a crime, but a cigarette break every hour was in order. Here, as in the rest of the north, what actually happened didn't correspond to the rules. Dried black-currant leaves were natural camouflage.

"Listen, Ivan," said Saveliev, "I'll tell you something that happened to me. In the Baikal-Amur camp we used to barrow sand along the second rail track. It was a long way to deliver the sand and our norm was twenty-five cubic meters. If you didn't make fifty percent of the norm, you got punishment rations: three hundred grams and gruel once a day. If you made the norm, you got a kilo of bread as well as something to cook up, and you had the right to buy another kilo of bread in the shop for cash. People worked in pairs, but the norms were impossible. So we found a way to get around it. One day the two of us would both barrow from his pit face and get enough for the norm. We then get two kilos of bread and my three hundred grams of punishment rations, so each of us gets a kilo and a hundred and fifty grams. The next day we work together for my norm. What's so bad about that? The main thing was the guard was a softie. He knew, of course. It was even good for him, since people didn't lose their strength so fast and the total production didn't go down. But one of the bosses exposed this trick and that was the end of our good times."

"Well, do you want to try that here?" asked Ivan Ivanovich.

"No, I don't. We'll just help you."

"How about yourself?"

"We don't care, old pal."

"In that case, I don't care either. The sergeant can come as far as I'm concerned."

The sergeant, that is the guard, came a few days later. Our worst fears came true.

"Well, you've had your rest, it's time you stopped. You've got to let others have your job. Your work is more like a sanatorium or a relief team," said the guard, joking grimly.

"Yes," responded Saveliev.

"First convalescent centers, then the teams,
A tag on your ankle, and now sweet dreams!"

We laughed out of politeness.

"When do we have to go back?"

"We're off tomorrow."

Ivan Ivanovich was calm again. That night he hanged himself from the fork in a tree trunk, ten yards from the hut; he didn't use any rope—this was the first suicide of that kind I had seen. Saveliev found him—he saw him from the path and shouted out. The guard ran over but forbad us to remove the body until the "investigating team" turned up. He hurried us off.

Fedia Shchapov and I got ready to go. We were very perturbed, for Ivan Ivanovich had good foot bindings that were still intact; he had bags, a towel, a spare calico vest, from which he had now steamed out the lice; quilted soft boots that had been repaired; and his pea jacket was lying on his bunk. We had a brief discussion and then took all these things for ourselves. Saveliev did not take part in sharing the dead man's things. He kept walking around Ivan Ivanovich's body. Outside prison, a dead body always and anywhere arouses a repressed interest—it has a magnetic attraction. That is not true in war or in the camps, where death is so banal and feelings are so dulled that a dead body holds no interest. But Saveliev was affected by Ivan Ivanovich's death: it lit up and disturbed some dark corners of his soul and propelled him to make certain decisions.

He went into the cabin, took an ax from the corner, and crossed the threshold. The guard, who was sitting on the mound of earth outside, leapt up and roared something we could not make out. Fedia and I rushed into the yard.

Saveliev went up to the thick short larch beam that we used to saw firewood on; the beam was slashed by saw marks, and its bark had been chopped off. Saveliev put his left hand on the beam, spread out his fingers and swung the ax.

The guard shrieked in a squeaky penetrating voice. Fedia threw himself at Saveliev: four fingers flew off into the sawdust, and it took time to see them among the branches and wood chips. Scarlet blood gushed from his fingers. Fedia and I ripped up Ivan Ivanovich's shirt, made a tourniquet that we wrapped around Saveliev's hand and bandaged the wound.

The guard took us all back to the camp. Saveliev was taken to the clinic to be bandaged and then to the criminal investigation section for the start of a case of malicious self-harm. Fedia and I went back to the same tent we had left two weeks before with such hopes and expectations of happiness.

Our places on the top bunks had been taken by other men, but that did not bother us. It was summer now, and in fact the lower bunks were actually better than the top ones; by the time winter came there would be many, many changes.

I went to sleep quickly but woke up in the middle of the night and went to the duty orderly's table. Fedia had made himself comfortable there; he was holding a piece of paper. I read over his shoulder what he had written: "Mom, I'm living well. Mom, I'm dressed right for the season. . . ."

1959

THE INJECTOR

From the head of the Golden Spring sector, L. V. Kudinov, to the director of mines, Comrade A. S. Koroliov.

A REPORT

IN ACCORDANCE with your instructions to provide explanations for the six-hour stand-down of the fourth brigade of prisoners, which took place on November 12 of this year in the Golden Spring sector of the gold mines under your management, I report:

The air temperature in the morning was below minus fifty degrees. Our thermometer had been broken by the supervisor on duty, a fact that I have reported to you. However, it was possible to measure the temperature because a gob of spit froze in midair.

The brigade was brought out to work in good time but was unable to start work because the injector on the boiler that serves our sector and warms up the frozen subsoil refused to work. I have on many occasions informed the chief engineer that the injector has been working badly, but no measures have been taken, and the injector has now completely fallen apart. The chief engineer refuses to replace it at the present time.

Because the injector has been working badly, the earth has not been made ready, and we were forced to keep the brigade idle for several hours. We have nowhere to keep warm, and we are forbidden to start fires, while the escort guards will not allow us to send the brigade back to barracks.

I have written to every authority I can that I am no longer able to work with an injector like this. For five years now its performance has been terrible, yet fulfilling the plan for our sector depends on it. We cannot cope with it, but the chief engineer refuses to pay attention and goes on demanding his cubic meters.

Signed by the head of the Golden Spring sector,
mining engineer L. V. Kudinov

Across this report is written diagonally in clear handwriting the following:

1) For refusing to work more than five days and causing a breakdown in production on the sector, prisoner Injector is to be arrested for seventy-two hours and not allowed to go out to work. He will be put in a squad working under intensive conditions. The case is to be handed to the investigative organs so that prisoner Injector can be held legally answerable.

2) I notify chief engineer Gorev that there is an absence of discipline in production. I recommend replacing prisoner Injector with free hired labor.

Director of Mines, Aleksandr Koroliov

1956

THE APOSTLE PAUL

WHEN I dislocated my foot, by falling down a slippery pole ladder in the open pit, the authorities realized that I would be lame for a long time. As sitting idly was out of the question, they transferred me to work as an assistant to our carpenter Adam Frizorger, which both of us, Frizorger and I, were very happy about.

In his first life Frizorger had been a pastor in a German village near Marxstadt on the Volga. We met at one of the big transit camps while we were being quarantined for typhus, and we came here together to prospect for coal. Like me, Frizorger had been in the taiga before, and he had been listed as a goner; he had been taken from the mines to the transit camp in a semi-insane state. As invalids, we were sent to prospect for coal. We were meant to provide backup since the workforce in prospecting was made up exclusively from free hired labor. True, these free laborers had in the recent past been prisoners, but they had just completed their "terms" or sentences, and they were known in the camps a little contemptuously as "freebies." When we were transferred, the forty free hired men could barely scrape together two rubles when they needed to buy tobacco; all the same they were now a class above us. It was generally understood that in two or three months they would get decent clothes, be able to get a drink, receive ID papers, and, after a year, perhaps even return home. These hopes were brighter still when Paramonov, the man in charge of prospecting, promised them fantastic salaries and Polar Circle rations. "You'll be wearing top hats when you go home," the boss kept telling them. No such talk of top hats or Polar Circle rations was ever directed at us prisoners, though.

At least Paramonov was polite to us. He wasn't allotted any prisoners for prospecting, and getting five men to provide backup services was the most that Paramonov could get out of the authorities.

We didn't know each other when our names were called from a list and we left the barracks to be inspected by his sharp shining eyes. He was very pleased by the answers to his questions. One of us, Izgibin, a wit with a gray mustache, was a baker; he hadn't lost his natural vitality in the camps. His skills were of some help to him, so that he wasn't as emaciated as the rest. The second man was a one-eyed giant from Kamenets-Podolsk, a "stoker on a steam locomotive," he told Paramonov.

"So you can do a bit of metalwork," said Paramonov.

"I can, I can," the stoker confirmed willingly. He had long ago figured out that working with free prospectors would be very much to his advantage.

The agronomist Riazanov was the third man. Agronomy was a profession that delighted Paramonov. No attention, naturally, was paid to the torn rags the agronomist was wearing. In the camps people are not judged by their clothes, and Paramonov knew enough about the camps.

I was the fourth man. I was neither a baker, nor a metalworker, nor an agronomist. But I was tall, and that seemed to reassure Paramonov; in any case, it wasn't worth going to the trouble of altering the list for the sake of one man. He nodded at me.

But our fifth man behaved very oddly. He mumbled the words of a prayer and covered his face with his hands, so that he couldn't hear Paramonov's voice. That, however, didn't surprise the chief. Paramonov turned to the supervisor who was standing next to him with a pile of yellow folders—our so-called personal files—in his hand.

"He's a carpenter," said the supervisor, guessing what Paramonov meant to ask. The induction was over, and we were taken to the prospectors' camp.

Later, Frizorger told me that when he was called on, he thought he was being singled out to be shot, so badly had he been threatened by the interrogator when he was still in the mines. We spent a year together in the same barracks and we never ever had an argument. That was rare among prisoners, whether in the camps or the prisons. Quarrels started over the most trivial things, and in no time cursing could reach such a degree that the next step, it seemed, could only be a knife or, at best, a red-hot poker. I had soon learned not to pay much attention to the florid cursing. The heat soon died down, and if both sides continued for some time to curse each other idly, that was only done for show, to "save face."

So I never had a quarrel with Frizorger. I think that this was thanks to him, because he was the most peaceful person on earth. He never disparaged anyone, he spoke very little. He had an old man's voice, quivery, but the quivering seemed somehow put on, overdone. It was how young actors speak in the theater when they are playing old men. In the camps many men try (and often successfully) to seem older and physically weaker than they really are. They don't always do so for any conscious purpose; it's instinctive. The ironic trick played by life is that at least half of the people who exaggerated their age and underplayed their strength ended up in an even worse state than the state they were imitating.

But in fact there was no pretense about Frizorger's voice.

Every morning and evening he would pray, too quietly to be heard; he turned away from everyone and looked at the floor. If he took part in the general conversation, it was only when the subject was religion, so he took part very seldom, since prisoners dislike talking about religion. Our beloved Izgibin, who always loved obscenity, would try to tease Frizorger, but the only response to his jokes was a smile so peaceful that his sallies were wasted. Frizorger was liked by all the prospectors, even by Paramonov, for whom Frizorger made a remarkable desk, which took him, apparently, six months to complete.

We had neighboring bunks, so we often chatted; sometimes Frizorger waved his little hands like a child when he was amazed by my knowledge of popular Gospel stories, material that he was simpleminded enough to think was the preserve of a narrow circle of religious people. He giggled and showed great pleasure when I revealed such knowledge. It stimulated him into starting to tell me things from the Gospels I could recall only shakily or not at all.

Once, however, Frizorger made a mistake when he listed the names of the twelve apostles. He included the apostle Paul. With the self-assurance of an ignoramus, I had always considered the apostle Paul as the real creator and theoretical leader of the Christian religion; I knew a little of Paul's biography and didn't miss my chance of correcting Frizorger.

"No, no," said Frizorger, laughing. "You don't know: listen...." He started bending his fingers. "Peter, Paul, Mark...."

I told him everything I knew about the apostle Paul. He listened to me carefully and said nothing. It was now late, time to go to sleep. I woke up in the night, and in the flickering smoky light of the kerosene lamp I saw Frizorger's eyes were open and I heard him whisper, "Lord, help me. Peter, Paul, Mark...." He stayed awake until morning. Then he went to work early and returned late in the evening, when I was already asleep. I was woken by an old man's quiet weeping. Frizorger was on his knees, praying.

"What's wrong?" I asked, after he finished praying.

Frizorger searched for my hand and squeezed it. "You're right," he said. "Paul was not one of the twelve apostles. I forgot about Bartholomew."

I said nothing.

"Are you surprised at my tears?" he asked. "They're tears of shame. I could not, should not have forgotten such things. That's a sin, a great sin. A stranger has to point out an unforgivable mistake by me, Adam Frizorger. No, no, it's not your fault at all. It's me, it's my sin. But it's good that you corrected me. Everything will be well."

I had trouble reassuring him and after that (shortly before I dislocated my foot) we became even greater friends.

Once, when there was nobody in the carpentry workshop, Frizorger took a greasy cloth wallet out of his pocket and with a gesture got me to come to the window.

"Here," he said, showing me a tiny cracked photograph, "look at this snapshot." It was a photograph of a young woman with the casual expression you get on all snapshots. The yellowed, cracked picture had been carefully framed with colored paper.

"That's my daughter," said Frizorger solemnly. "My only daughter. My wife died a long time ago. True, my daughter doesn't write, she probably doesn't know the address. I've written a lot to her and I still do. Only to her. I never show anyone this photo. I brought it from home. Six years ago I took it off the chest of drawers."

Paramonov came through the workshop door. He had not made a sound.

"Your daughter, is it?" he said, after a quick look at the photo.

"My daughter, sir," said Frizorger with a smile.

"Does she write to you?"

"No."

"How can she forget her old man? Write me a request to search for her, and I'll send it off. What's wrong with your leg?"

"I'm lame, sir."

"Well, if you're lame, you're lame." Paramonov then went out.

After that Frizorger was no longer secretive with me. When he finished his evening prayers and lay down on his bunk, he would get out the photograph of his daughter and stroke its colored frame.

We lived like this, without incident, for about six months, and then they brought the mail. At the time, Paramonov was away prospecting, and his secretary, a prisoner called Riazanov, took delivery of the mail. (Riazanov turned out to be an Esperanto speaker, not an agronomist, not that this was a hindrance to him. He was very deft at flaying dead horses, at bending thick iron pipes by filling them with sand and heating them red-hot on a bonfire, and at doing all of his boss's office work.)

"Take a look at this," he said to me. "Look at this declaration we've received about Frizorger."

The packet was an official statement with a request to inform prisoner Frizorger (article of criminal code, sentence) of his daughter's declaration, a copy of which was attached. Her declaration was a brief and clear statement that, being convinced that her father was an enemy of the people, she renounced him and asked that her relationship to him be annulled.

Riazanov held on to the piece of paper and turned it over and over.

"What a nasty piece of work!" he said. "What did she have to do that for? She isn't joining the party, is she?"

I was thinking of something else: why send declarations like that to your father when he's in prison? Was it a peculiar sort of sadism, like the authorities' habit of notifying relatives of a prisoner's fictional death, or was it just a desire to do everything according to the rules? Or something else?

"Listen, Vania," I told Riazanov, "have you made a record of the incoming mail?"

"How could I? It's only just come in."

"Then let me have that packet," and I told Riazanov what it was all about.

"How about the letter?" he said hesitantly. "She's probably going to write to him, too."

"You can intercept the letter, too."

"All right, take it."

I crumpled up the package and threw it through the open door of the stove, which was alight.

A month later the letter arrived. It was just as brief as the declaration, and we burned it in the same stove.

Not long after, I was moved somewhere else, and Frizorger was left behind. I don't know what happened to him afterward. I often recalled him, while I still had the strength to recall anything. I could hear his quivery, anxious whisper: "Peter, Paul, Mark...."

1954

BERRIES

FADEYEV said, "Wait a bit, I'll have a talk with him myself." And he came up to me and put the butt of his rifle by my head.

I was lying in the snow, my arms around a beam which had been on my shoulder and which I had dropped. I couldn't lift it or go back to my place in the file of men who were going down the mountain; each man had a beam on his shoulder, "a stick of firewood," some bigger, some smaller. Everyone was in a hurry to get home, guards and prisoners, everyone wanted to eat and sleep. They were all utterly fed up with the endless winter day. And there I was, lying in the snow.

Fadeyev always used the polite form of the verb to prisoners.

"Listen, old man," he said, "I can't believe that a bruiser like you can't carry a log as small as that, a stick you could call it. You're obviously a malingerer. You're a fascist. When the motherland is fighting the enemy, you go and put a wrench in the works."

"I'm not a fascist," I said. "I'm a sick, hungry man. You're the fascist. You read in the papers about fascists killing old men. Think about telling the girl you're going to marry about what you did in Kolyma."

I didn't care. I couldn't stand these rosy-cheeked, healthy, well-fed, well-clothed people, and I wasn't afraid. I curled up to protect my belly, but that was an instinctive movement inherited from my Stone Age ancestors: I had no fear at all of being hit in the belly. Fadeyev's boot kicked me in the back. I suddenly felt warm. It didn't hurt at all. If I died, so much the better.

"Listen," said Fadeyev when he turned me on my back with the toe caps of his boots, "I've been working with people like you for some time, I know your sort."

Another guard, Seroshapka, came up.

"Right then, show me your face, so I remember you. What a nasty ugly brute you are. Tomorrow I'll shoot you personally. Got it?"

"Got it," I said, as I stood up and spat out salty blood and saliva.

I dragged the beam along the ground while my fellow prisoners mocked me with whooping noises, yelling and cursing. They had been freezing all the time I was being beaten.

The next morning Seroshapka led us out to work in a forest that had been hacked down the previous winter. We had to collect anything that could be burned in the iron stoves this winter. As the forest had been felled in winter, the stumps were high. We tore them out of the ground using levers and cables, and then we sawed them up and stacked them.

Seroshapka hung up some marker bundles from the very few trees still standing where we were working. The bundles of yellow and gray hay marked out the zone we were forbidden to cross.

Our foreman made a bonfire on a hillock for Seroshapka's benefit— only the guard was allowed to have a bonfire during working hours— and brought him a supply of firewood.

The snow had long been driven away by the wind. The dead, frost-covered grass was slippery to the touch and changed color on contact with a human hand. Low mountain briars froze on the hills; their frozen dark-violet berries had an extraordinary smell. The bilberries, a bluish gray, touched by the frost and overripe, were even better to eat than the briar hips. Blueberries hung from short straight twigs; they were bright blue, wrinkled like empty leather purses, but they contained a dark, bluish-black juice of an indescribable taste.

At this time of the year, the frosted berries were quite unlike ripe berries when they are full of juice. They had a much more subtle taste.

My comrade Rybakov collected berries in a jar whenever we broke off for a cigarette and whenever Seroshapka wasn't looking in our direction. If Rybakov collected a whole jarful, then the guards' cook would give him bread in exchange. Rybakov's enterprise immediately became crucial to him.

I didn't have a customer like his, so I ate the berries myself, my tongue carefully and eagerly pressing each one to my palate. The sweet aromatic juice of each squashed berry intoxicated me for a second.

I never thought of helping Rybakov to pick berries, and he would have refused any help, for he would then have to share the bread.

Rybakov's jar was filling up too slowly, it was getting harder and harder to find a berry, and, without having noticed, we were getting close to the limits of our zone. The markers were hanging over our heads.

"Watch out," I told Rybakov. "Let's go back."

Ahead of us were tussocks covered with briar hips, blueberries, and lingonberries. We'd spotted these tussocks before. It would have been all right if the tree from which a marker bundle was hanging had been two meters farther off.

Rybakov pointed to his jar, which was still not full, to the sun, which was now setting, and began slowly to approach the enchanted berries.

There was the dry crack of a rifle shot, and Rybakov fell facedown between the tussocks. Seroshapka waved his rifle about, shouting, "Leave him where he is, don't come near!"

With a click of his bolt Seroshapka reloaded and fired another shot. We knew what that second shot meant. So did Seroshapka. There were supposed to be two shots: the first a warning shot.

Rybakov lay between the tussocks. He looked surprisingly small. The sky, mountains, and river were enormous: God knows how many people you could have laid down on the footpaths between the tussocks in these mountains.

Rybakov's jar rolled some distance away, but I managed to pick it up and put it in my pocket. Perhaps I might get some bread for the berries: I knew whom Rybakov was picking them for.

Seroshapka calmly assembled our small squad, counted us, gave the order, and took us home.

He touched my shoulder with the tip of his rifle. I turned around.

"I meant to get you," said Seroshapka, "but you wouldn't stick your head out, you bastard!"

1959

TAMARA THE BITCH

TAMARA the bitch was brought from the taiga by our blacksmith, Moisei Moiseyevich Kuznetsov. Judging by his surname,[3] the profession was inherited from his forefathers. Moisei came from Minsk. Kuznetsov was an orphan, as you could tell by his first name and patronymic, for Jews have their father's name only if, and always if, the father died before the son was born. Moisei learned his trade as a boy from his uncle, who was a blacksmith, as his father had been.

Kuznetsov's wife was a waitress in one of the Minsk restaurants; she was much younger than her forty-year-old husband, and in 1937, on the advice of her close friend, an assistant in the restaurant, she wrote a denunciation of her husband. At the time this was a much more reliable way out than any plot or slander, even more reliable than sulfuric acid. The husband, Moisei, immediately disappeared. Moisei was no ordinary blacksmith. He worked in a factory; he was a master craftsman, even a bit of a poet. He was the sort of blacksmith who could make a wrought-iron rose. The tools he used, he made himself. These tools—tongs, chisels, hammers, sledgehammers—were especially elegant, which showed his love of his craft and his craftsman's understanding of its soul. We aren't talking of symmetry or asymmetry but of something deeper, more inward. Every horseshoe or nail forged by Moisei was elegant, and the mark of the craftsman could be found on every item that came from his hands. He was reluctant to end work on anything he was making; he always felt that it needed one more blow of the hammer to make it even better, even easier to use.

The authorities valued him highly, although there was not much blacksmithery to be done on a geological site. Moisei sometimes played jokes on the bosses, but he was forgiven because of his good work. For

63

instance, he assured the bosses that it was better to temper drills in oil than in water, and the boss ordered butter, naturally a very small quantity, for the forge. Kuznetsov threw a bit of this butter into the water and the tips of the steel drills took on a gentle shine that was never seen after the usual tempering. Kuznetsov and his hammerman ate the rest of the butter. The boss was very soon informed of the blacksmith's trick, but no reprisals followed. Later, Kuznetsov, insisting on the high quality of tempering with butter, asked the boss to let him have the offcuts of rolls of butter that had gone moldy in the stores. He then melted down these offcuts into clarified butter that was just a little bit bitter. He was a good, quiet man who wished everyone well.

Our boss knew all the fine points about life here. Like Lycurgus, he made sure that his taiga state had two paramedics, two blacksmiths, two foremen, two cooks, and two bookkeepers. One paramedic would treat the patients, while the other would do physical labor but keep an eye on his colleague. If the first paramedic abused drugs by taking a bit of codeine or a bit of caffeine, then he would be exposed, punished, and sent back to do hard labor with the other prisoners, while his colleague, after drawing up and signing the inventory, would be installed in the medical ward. The boss was of the opinion that a reserve supply of specialists not only ensured that a replacement was available when needed but encouraged discipline, which would, of course, have lapsed if any single specialist were to feel he was indispensable.

But the bookkeepers, paramedics, and foremen were replaced at a rate that was quite mad, and none of them would ever refuse a glass of alcohol, even if the man offering it was operating a sting.

The blacksmith who had been selected by the boss as a counterweight to Moisei never even picked up a hammer, because Moisei was irreproachable and invulnerable; in any case, Moisei's qualifications were too good.

It was Moisei who on a path in the taiga came across a stray Yakut dog that looked like a wolf. It was a bitch with a patch of abraded fur on its white chest—evidently it had been a sled dog.

There were no Yakut settlements or nomadic camps anywhere near us. The dog suddenly appeared in front of Kuznetsov on the taiga path, frightening him badly. Moisei thought it was a wolf and ran back, stamping his boots loudly on the path, to warn the other men following him.

But the "wolf" lay on its belly and crawled toward the people, wagging its tail as it did so. They stroked it, patted its emaciated flanks, and fed it.

The dog stayed with us. Soon it was obvious why it didn't risk looking for its real owners in the taiga: it was about to have puppies. The very first evening it began digging a pit under a tent. It was in a hurry and barely acknowledged people's greetings. Every one of fifty men wanted to stroke it, show it affection, and tell the animal of their own longing for affection.

Even Kasayev, the chief of works, a geologist of about thirty who had just completed ten years' work in the Far North, came out, still strumming the guitar he could not be parted from, to look at our latest inhabitant.

"We can call it 'Fighter,'" he said.

"It's a bitch, Valentin Ivanovich," said Slavka Ganushkin, the cook.

"A bitch? So it is. Then let's call it Tamara." And the chief of works went off.

Smiling, the dog watched the chief leave; it wagged its tail. It very soon established good relations with all the right people. Tamara understood the importance of Kasayev and of the foreman Vasilenko in our settlement, and she realized how crucial it was to make friends with the cook. At night she settled in with the night watchman.

We soon realized that Tamara would only accept food she was given, that she never touched anything in the kitchen or the tent, whether there were people there or not.

These firm moral principles were what won over the inhabitants of the settlement, men who had seen everything and had had a tough life.

They placed tinned meat and bread and butter on the floor under Tamara's nose. The dog sniffed the food and always chose to take away the same thing: a piece of salted salmon, the most familiar, tasty, and, probably, safest food for her.

Very soon she gave birth: six tiny puppies in a dark pit. We made a kennel for them and moved them into it. Tamara was anxious for some time, fawning, wagging her tail, but it must have been all right, for the puppies were unharmed.

This was when the prospecting group had to move another three or so kilometers farther into the mountains, away from the base where the stores, the kitchen, the head office were, so they were about seven kilometers from their living quarters. We took the kennel and the puppies to the new place, and two or three times a day Tamara would run to see the cook and carry back in her mouth a bone that he had given her. We would have fed the puppies in any case, but Tamara was never sure of that.

It then happened that a special operations squad came on skis to our settlement. They were prowling the taiga looking for escaped prisoners. People very rarely tried to escape in winter, but the squad had information that five prisoners had run away from a nearby mine, and they were combing the taiga.

Instead of a tent like ours, the skiers were given the only log building in the settlement, the bathhouse. The ski squad's mission was too important for anyone to protest, as our chief of works, Kasayev, explained to us.

Everyone treated these uninvited visitors with the usual indifference and resignation. Only one creature expressed severe displeasure about their visit.

Tamara the bitch hurled herself at the nearest special operations guard and bit through his felt boot. Tamara's hackles were up, and her eyes were full of fearless hatred. It was hard to chase the dog off and restrain it.

The special operations chief, Nazarov, whom we'd heard something about previously, was about to grab his automatic and shoot the dog, but Kasayev held his arm and dragged him off to the bathhouse.

On the advice of our carpenter Semion Parmenov, we put Tamara on a rope strap and tied her to a tree. The special operations squad wasn't going to be here permanently.

Like all the Yakut dogs, Tamara couldn't bark. She growled, and her old canines tried to gnaw through the rope. She was no longer the easygoing Yakut bitch who'd spent the winter with us. Her hatred was extraordinary, and it revealed what her past life had been. Everyone could see that this was not the first time the dog had encountered guards.

What forest tragedy had fixed itself in the dog's memory? Was this terrible past event the reason why the Yakut bitch had turned up in the taiga near our settlement?

Nazarov could probably have told us a few things, if he remembered animals as well as he did people.

About five days later three of the skiers left, while Nazarov and one of his friends were preparing to depart with the chief of works the next morning. They spent the night drinking, had a hair of the dog in the morning, and then left.

Tamara growled. Nazarov turned back, took his automatic off his shoulder, and let off a round point-blank at the dog. Tamara twitched and fell silent. At the sound of the shots people were already running out of their tents, grabbing axes and crowbars as they came. The chief of works rushed to intercept the workmen, and Nazarov disappeared in the forest.

Sometimes one's desires are fulfilled; perhaps the hatred that fifty men felt for this squad leader was so passionate and powerful that it became an actual force and caught up with Nazarov.

Nazarov and his assistant both skied off. They didn't follow the completely frozen river, which was the best winter road to get to the highway twenty kilometers from our settlement. Instead, they went across the mountain pass. Nazarov was afraid of being pursued; the mountain route was shorter and he was an excellent skier.

It was dark by the time they reached the pass. There was still daylight on the mountain peaks, but the deep ravines were in darkness. Nazarov started descending the mountain at an angle, where the forest became thicker. He understood that he had to stop, but his skis were sweeping him downhill, and he flew into the snow-covered stump of a fallen larch, which had been sharpened by the passage of time. The stump ripped open Nazarov's belly and back, tearing through his greatcoat. The second special operations man was skiing much farther down the hill. He sped to the highway, but only managed to raise the alarm the next day. Two days later they found Nazarov hanging from the stump, frozen stiff in the pose of a running man, rather like one of those figures in a battle diorama.

Tamara was flayed and her skin was stretched by nailing it to the stable wall. But it was stretched badly and the skin, when it dried out, was tiny, and you wouldn't have thought that it came from a big Yakut sled husky.

Very soon the forester came to draw up backdated certificates for the cutting of timber that had been done more than a year before. When the trees were being felled, nobody gave a thought about the height of the stumps, and they turned out to be higher than the norm, so that the work had to be done again. That was an easy job. The forester was allowed to buy a few things in the shop, and was given money and alcohol. When he was leaving, he asked if he could have the dog skin hanging on the stable wall. He would tan it and make sledder's gloves: gauntlets made from northern dog skin with the fur on the outside. According to him, the bullet holes in the skin didn't matter.

1959

CHERRY BRANDY[4]

THE POET was dying. His big hands, swollen by starvation, with their bloodless white fingers and dirty, overgrown, curling nails, lay exposed on his chest, despite the cold. Before then he had held them against his naked body, but that body now had too little warmth. His gloves had been stolen a long time ago. Stealing was just a matter of shamelessness, and thieves operated in broad daylight. The dim electric lightbulb, covered in fly droppings and caged in by a round grid, was fixed high up near the ceiling. The light fell on the poet's feet. He was lying as if in a box in the dark depths of the lower row of a continuous row of two-story bunks. From time to time his fingers moved and clicked like castanets, as they felt for a button, a loop, a hole in his jacket, or brushed away a bit of dirt, before stopping again. The poet was taking so long to die that he had stopped understanding that he was dying. Occasionally some simple, powerful thought would force its morbid and almost palpable way through his brain: that the bread he'd put under his head had been stolen. And this terrible thought burned him so much that he wanted to quarrel, curse, fight, search, argue. But he didn't have the strength for any of that, and the thought of his bread died away.... At the moment he was thinking of something else: that everyone was going to be taken over the sea, that the ship was delayed and it was lucky he was here. And he had the same light fleeting thought about the big birthmark on the face of the barracks orderly. For most of the past twenty-four hours he had been thinking of the events of his life here. The visions he was seeing were not those of childhood, youth, or his prime. All his life he had been in a hurry to get somewhere. What was wonderful was that now he didn't have to hurry, that he could think slowly. And he thought at leisure of the great monotony of

69

deathbed movements, something that doctors had understood and described long before artists and poets. The features of Hippocrates, a man's death mask, are familiar to every medical student. This mysterious monotony of deathbed movements provoked Freud's most daring hypotheses. Monotony and repetition are the essential basis of science. What is unique about death was sought by poets, not by doctors. It was pleasant to be aware that he could still think. He had long been used to the nausea of hunger. And everything was of equal status: Hippocrates, the orderly with the birthmark, and his own dirty fingernails.

Life was ebbing and flowing in him: he was dying. But life kept reappearing, his eyes would open, thoughts would emerge. Only desires failed to appear. He had long been living in a world where people often have to be brought back to life—by artificial respiration, glucose, camphor, caffeine. The dead became the living again. And why not? He believed in immortality, in real human immortality. He had often thought there were simply no biological reasons why man shouldn't live forever. Old age is merely a curable disease, and if it weren't for this still-unsolved tragic misunderstanding, he could live forever. Or at least until he was tired of life. And he hadn't tired of life at all. Even now in this transit barracks, the *tranzitka*, as its inhabitants lovingly called it. This transit camp was the antechamber to horror, but it wasn't horror itself. On the contrary, there was a living spirit of freedom here, and everyone could sense that. The camps were yet to come, the prisons were in the past. This was "peace on the way there," and the poet understood that.

There was another path to immortality, as set out by Tyutchev:

Blessed is he who visits this world
In its most fateful moments.

But if he was apparently not fated to be immortal in his human form, as a physical entity, at least he had earned creative immortality. He had been named the greatest Russian poet of the twentieth century, and he often thought that this was true. He believed in the immortality of his poetry. He had no pupils, but do poets put up with pupils?

He had written prose, too—bad prose—and he had written articles. But only in verse had he found things that were new to poetry and important, as he always thought. His entire past life was literature, books, fairy tales, dreams, and only this present day was real life.

All these thoughts took place not as a dispute but secretly, deep down in his inner self. He didn't have enough passion for such reflections. Indifference had long taken possession of him. How trivial it all was, like mice scrabbling about, compared with the unkind weight of life. He was amazed at himself. How could he be thinking like this about verses when everything had been decided, and he knew it very well, better than anyone? Who needed him here, and who cared? But why did this all have to be understood, and he waited . . . then he understood.

At the moments when life flowed back to his body and his half-open glazed eyes suddenly began to see, his eyelids quivered and his fingers fidgeted, then he was revisited by thoughts he didn't think were his last ones.

Life entered unasked, like a self-confident lady of the house. He hadn't invited it, but it still came into his body, his brain, coming like verses, like inspiration. And the meaning of that word was for the first time revealed to him in its full sense. Verses were the life-giving force keeping him alive. That was it. He didn't live for poetry, he lived by it.

It was now so obvious, so palpably clear that inspiration was the same as life. On the verge of death he was allowed to learn that life was inspiration, inspiration alone.

And he was glad that he had been allowed to learn this final truth.

Everything, the whole world was comparable to verse: work, the sound of horse hooves, a house, a bird, a rock, love—all of life easily found its way into verse and settled there comfortably. And that was how it should be, for verses were the word.

Even now stanzas arose easily, one after the other, and although he hadn't written down any for a long time, and couldn't write down his verse, the words still came without effort in a rhythm that was predetermined and, on every occasion, unusual. Rhyme was a search tool, an instrument for the magnetic search of words and concepts. Each word was part of the world, it responded to rhyme, and the whole world rushed past with the speed of some electronic machine. Everything cried out, "Take me! No, me!" You never had to look for anything. You had only to reject. There seemed to be two people here: the one who composes, who has got the wheel spinning at top speed, and the other one who makes his choice and from time to time stops the machine the first one has set in motion. Having seen that he was two people, the poet realized that he was now composing real poetry. What did it matter that it wasn't written down? Writing down and printing was just vanity of vanities. The best was the unrecorded, what vanished after it was composed, what melted away without a trace; only the creative joy that he felt, and which could not be mistaken for anything else, proved that the poem had been created, that something fine had been created. Could he be mistaken? Was his creative joy infallible?

He remembered how bad, how poetically feeble were Aleksandr Blok's last poems, and that Blok apparently was not aware of the fact....

The poet forced himself to pause. Pausing was easier to do here than anywhere in Leningrad or Moscow.

At this point he suddenly realized he hadn't thought about anything for some time. Life was again ebbing away.

For long hours he lay motionless, then he suddenly saw before him something like a rifle target or a geological map. Whatever it was, it was mute, and his efforts to understand what it represented were fruitless. Quite a lot of time passed before he worked out that he was looking at his own fingers. The tips of his fingers still had brown traces of cheap cigarettes that had been smoked, then sucked to the very end; the pads had a marked dactyloscopic pattern like a relief map of a mountain. All ten digits had the same pattern of concentric circles, like tree rings on a log. He recalled once upon a time in childhood being stopped on the boulevard by a Chinese laundryman, who worked in a laundry in the basement of the house where he grew up. The Chinese man casually took one hand, then the other hand, turned his palms up and excitedly shouted something in Chinese. It turned out that he was announcing that the boy was fortunate and had the marks to prove it. The poet very often recalled this mark of good fortune, especially when he had printed his first book. Now he remembered the Chinese man without any bad feelings or irony. He didn't care one way or the other.

The main thing was that he wasn't dead yet. Actually, what did it mean to say "died as a poet"? There had to be something childlike and naïve about such a death. Or was there something preplanned, theatrical about it, like Yesenin's or Mayakovsky's death.

"Died as an actor": that made sense. But "died as a poet"?

Yes, he had some inkling of what lay ahead for him. The transit camp had given him time to understand and guess a lot of things. And he was glad, quietly glad of his feeble state, and he hoped he would die. He remembered a prison argument from some way back: what's worse, more frightful—camp or prison? Nobody knew anything for real, the arguments were speculative, and how cruel was the smile of a man who had been brought to that prison from a camp. The poet never forgot that man's smile, so much so that he was afraid to recall it.

Think how neatly he'd trick the people who'd brought him here if he died now. He'd cheat them of a whole ten years. A few years ago he had been in exile, and he then knew he had been permanently put on a special list. Permanently?! The scales had changed, and words had acquired new meanings.

He felt another flow of strength starting, like an incoming sea tide. High tide for several hours, and then low tide. But the sea does not retreat from us forever. He could still recover.

Suddenly he felt hungry, but he didn't have the strength to move. Slowly and with difficulty he recalled that today he had given his soup to his neighbor, that a mug of boiled water was all the nourishment he had taken over the last twenty-four hours. Apart from bread, of course. But the bread had been issued a very, very long time ago. And yesterday's bread had been stolen. Someone still had the strength to steal.

So he lay, at ease and without thoughts, until morning came. The electric light became just a little more yellow; they brought bread on big plywood trays, as they did every day.

But he was no longer anxious; he didn't bother trying to spot a crusty piece, he didn't weep if someone else got that crust, his quivering fingers didn't stuff the makeweight piece of bread into his mouth, and it instantly melted away in his mouth and his whole being could sense the taste and the smell of fresh rye bread. That makeweight piece was no longer in his mouth, even though he hadn't had time to swallow anything or even move his jaw. A piece of bread had melted away, vanished, and that was a miracle, one of many miracles here. No, he wasn't anxious for now. But when they put his day's ration into his hands, he clutched it with his bloodless fingers and pressed the bread to his mouth. He bit the bread with his scurvy-ridden teeth, his gums began to bleed and his teeth rocked. But he felt no pain. He pressed the bread to his mouth with all his strength, sucking, tearing, and gnawing it....

His neighbors tried to stop him.

"Don't eat it all, it's better to eat it later, later...."

And the poet understood. He opened his eyes wide, his fingers not letting go of the bloodstained bread.

"What do you mean, later?" he pronounced precisely and clearly. Then he closed his eyes.

By evening he was dead.

But they wrote him off two days later. His enterprising neighbors managed to get a dead man's bread for two days; when it was distributed, the dead man's hand rose up like a puppet's. Therefore he died earlier than the date of his death, quite an important detail for his future biographers.

1958

CHILDREN'S PICTURES

WE WERE forced to go to work without any lists being drawn up. They counted us in fives at the gates. They always lined us up in fives, since very few of the escort guards knew their multiplication tables well. Any mathematical operation carried out in below-zero temperatures on living beings is no joke. The cup of prisoners' patience can suddenly run over, and the authorities took heed of this.

This time we had easy work, the sort given to the gangsters: cutting up firewood with a circular saw. The saw revolved on its bench, banging gently. We heaved an enormous trunk onto the bench and slowly pushed it toward the saw blade.

The saw would shriek and growl furiously. It liked work in the Far North no more than we did, but we kept moving the trunk on and on until it fell apart and gave us unexpectedly lightweight offcuts.

Our third workmate chopped the firewood with a heavy, bluish chopping ax with a long yellow handle. He chopped the edges off the thick logs and split the thinner ones with one blow. He didn't hit them very hard, our workmate was just as starved as we were, but frozen larch wood was easy to split. Nature in the north is not indifferent or unbiased; it is in league with the people who sent us here.

We finished the job, stacked the firewood, and began to wait for our escort guard. We had a guard; he was warming himself in the institution for which we had been sawing firewood, but we were supposed to return home in proper formation, after splitting into small groups in the town.

After work we didn't go to warm ourselves. We had noticed earlier a big pile of rubbish by a fence, something that could not be ignored. Both of my workmates examined the heap with practiced skill, removing one frozen layer after the other. Their loot was pieces of frozen bread, a frozen clump of burgers, and torn men's socks. The socks were the most precious item, and I was sorry they didn't fall to me. Socks, scarves, gloves, shirts, civilian trousers—"civvies"—were highly valued by people who had worn only government-issue for decades. Socks could be darned or patched, and you could get tobacco or bread for them.

My workmates' success made me restless. I too used my hands and feet to break off the many-hued pieces of the rubbish heap. After removing a rag that looked like human guts, I saw, for the first time in many years, a schoolchild's gray exercise book.

It was an ordinary school exercise book, a child's book for drawing in. Every page was covered in colored paintings, done carefully and lovingly. I turned the paper, made fragile by the sub-zero temperatures, and the frost-covered cold, bright, naïve sheets. I used to paint, but that was a long time ago, when I settled down at the dining table on which was a kerosene lamp with a half-inch wick. Just a touch of the magic brushes brought to life a dead fairy-tale hero, as if he'd been sprinkled with magic, life-giving water. My watercolors, which looked like women's buttons, were kept in a white tin box. Prince Ivan would gallop on his gray wolf through the fir forest. The firs were smaller than the gray wolf. Prince Ivan rode the wolf the way the Evenki ride their reindeer, their heels almost touching the mossy ground. Smoke would spiral up to the sky, and birds, like upside-down ticks, could be seen in the blue star-studded sky.

The more strongly I reimagined my childhood, the more clearly I understood that my childhood would not be repeated, that I wouldn't find even a shadow of it in someone else's childhood exercise book.

It was a terrible exercise book.

The northern town was built of wood; the house walls and fences were painted bright ocher, and the young artist's brush had faithfully reproduced the yellow color wherever the boy had wanted to speak of street buildings and things made by human hands.

There were many, very many fences in the book. People and houses in almost every painting were fenced in with even yellow fences, topped by black lines of barbed wire. Steel was strung out in the official pattern over all the fences in the child's exercise book.

People stood by the fence. In this book people were not peasants, nor workmen, nor hunters; they were soldiers, escort guards, and sentries with rifles. The "mushroom" rain shelters around which the young artist had grouped his guards and sentries stood at the foot of enormous guard towers. On the towers there were soldiers, walking about with shiny rifle barrels.

The exercise book was quite small, but the boy had managed to paint every season of the year in his hometown.

Brightly colored earth, a monotonous green, as in an early Matisse painting, and a perfectly bright blue sky, fresh, pure, and clear. The sunsets and sunrises were solid red, and that was not due to a child's inability to find a halftone or intermediate colors or to discover the secrets of chiaroscuro.

The color combinations in this schoolbook were true representations of the Far North sky, whose colors are extraordinarily pure and clear and have no halftones.

I recalled the old northern legend about a god who created the taiga when he was still a child. He didn't have many colors, and they were childlike in their purity, and the paintings were simple and clear, and their subjects were elementary.

Afterward, when the god grew up and reached adulthood, he learned to carve the strange patterns of leaves, he invented a lot of many-colored birds. This god was bored with the childish world and covered his taiga creation with snow, leaving it forever to go south. So went the legend.

Even in his winter paintings, the child had kept to the truth. Green vanished. Trees were black and bare. They were Dahurian larches, not the pines and firs of my childhood.

A northern hunt was in full swing. A German shepherd, its big teeth bared, was tugging at a leash held by Prince Ivan, who was wearing a military-style hat with earflaps, a white sheepskin jacket, felt boots, and long gauntlets, *kragi* as they are called in the Far North. He had an automatic gun over his shoulder. Bare triangular trees poked here and there out of the snow.

The child had seen and remembered nothing but yellow houses, barbed wire, towers, sheepdogs, guards with automatics, and the dark, dark blue sky.

My workmate took a look at the exercise book and felt the pages.

"It'd be better to find some newspaper to make cigarettes," he said, snatching the exercise book from my hands, crumpling it, and throwing it back on the rubbish heap. The book started to frost over.

1959

CONDENSED MILK

HUNGER made our envy as dull and feeble as all our other feelings. We had no strength left for feelings, to search for easier work, to walk, to ask, to beg. We envied only those we knew, with whom we had come into this world, if they had managed to get work in the office, the hospital, or the stables, where there were no long hours of heavy physical work, which was glorified on the arches over all the gates as a matter for valor and heroism. In a word, we envied only Shestakov.

Only something external was capable of taking us out of our indifference, of distracting us from the death that was slowly getting nearer. An external, not an internal force. Internally, everything was burned out, devastated; we didn't care, and we made plans only as far as the next day.

Now, for instance, I wanted to get away to the barracks, lie down on the bunks, but I was still standing by the doors of the food shop. The only people allowed to buy things in the shop were those convicted of nonpolitical crimes, including recidivist thieves who were classified as "friends of the people." There was no point in our being there, but we couldn't take our eyes off the chocolate-colored loaves of bread; the heavy, sweet smell of fresh bread teased our nostrils and even made our heads spin. So I stood there looking at the bread, not knowing when I would find the strength to go back to the barracks. That was when Shestakov called me over.

I had gotten to know Shestakov on the mainland, in Moscow's Butyrki prison. We were in the same cell. We were acquaintances then, not friends. When we were in the camps, Shestakov did not work at the mine pit face. He was a geological engineer, so he was taken on to work as a prospecting geologist, presumably in the office. The lucky man barely acknowledged his Moscow acquaintances. We didn't take offense—God knows what orders he might have had on that account. Charity begins at home, etc.

"Have a smoke," Shestakov said as he offered me a piece of newspaper, tipped some tobacco into it, and lit a match, a real match.

I lit up.

"I need to have a word with you," said Shestakov.

"With me?"

"Yes."

We moved behind the barracks and sat on the edge of an old pit face. My legs immediately felt heavy, while Shestakov cheerfully swung his nice new government boots—they had a faint whiff of cod-liver oil. His trousers were rolled up, showing chessboard-patterned socks. I surveyed Shestakov's legs with genuine delight and even a certain amount of pride. At least one man from our cell was not wearing foot bindings instead of socks. The ground beneath us was shaking from muffled explosions as the earth was being prepared for the night shift. Small pebbles were falling with a rustling sound by our feet; they were as gray and inconspicuous as birds.

"Let's move a bit farther," said Shestakov.

"It won't kill you, no need to be afraid. Your socks won't be damaged."

"I'm not thinking about my socks," said Shestakov, pointing his index finger along the line of the horizon. "What's your view about all this?"

"We'll probably die," I said. That was the last thing I wanted to think about.

"No, I'm not willing to die."

"Well?"

"I have a map," Shestakov said in a wan voice. "I'm going to take some workmen—I'll take you—and we'll go to Black Springs, fifteen kilometers from here. I'll have a pass. And we can get to the sea. Are you willing?" He explained this plan in a hurry, showing no emotion.

"And when we reach the sea? Are we sailing somewhere?"

"That doesn't matter. The important thing is to make a start. I can't go on living like this. 'Better to die on one's feet than live on one's knees,'" Shestakov pronounced solemnly. "Who said that?"

Very true. The phrase was familiar. But I couldn't find the strength to recall who said it and when. I'd forgotten everything in books. I didn't believe in bookish things. I rolled up my trousers and showed him my red sores from scurvy.

"Well, being in the forest will cure that," said Shestakov, "what with the berries and the vitamins. I'll get you out, I know the way. I have a map."

I shut my eyes and thought. There were three ways of getting from here to the sea, and they all involved a journey of five hundred kilometers, at least. I wouldn't make it, nor would Shestakov. He wasn't taking me as food for the journey, was he? Of course not. But why was he lying? He knew that just as well as I did. Suddenly I was frightened of Shestakov, the only one of us who'd managed to get a job that matched his qualifications. Who fixed him up here, and what had it cost? Anything like that had to be paid for. With someone else's blood, someone else's life.

"I'm willing," I said, opening my eyes. "Only I've got to feed myself up first."

"That's fine, fine. I'll see you get more food. I'll bring you some . . . tinned food. We've got lots. . . ."

There are lots of different tinned foods—meat, fish, fruit, vegetables—but the best of all is milk, condensed milk. Condensed milk doesn't have to be mixed with boiling water. You eat it with a spoon, or spread it on bread, or swallow it drop by drop from the tin, eating it slowly, watching the bright liquid mass turn yellow with starry little drops of sugar forming on the can. . . .

"Tomorrow," I said, gasping with joy, "tinned milk."

"Fine, fine. Milk." And Shestakov went off.

I returned to the barracks, lay down, and shut my eyes. It was hard to think. Thinking was a physical process. For the first time I saw the full extent of the material nature of our psyche, and I felt its palpability. Thinking hurt. But thinking had to be done. He was going to get us to make a run for it and then hand us in: that much was completely obvious. He would pay for his office job with our blood, my blood. We'd either be killed at Black Springs, or we'd be brought back alive and given a new sentence: another fifteen years or so. He must be aware that getting out of here was impossible. But milk, condensed milk. . . .

I fell asleep and in my spasmodic hungry sleep I dreamed of Shestakov's can of condensed milk: a monstrous tin can with a sky-blue label. Enormous, blue as the night sky, the can had thousands of holes in it and milk was oozing out and flowing in a broad stream like the Milky Way. And I had no trouble reaching up to the sky to eat the thick, sweet, starry milk.

I don't remember what I did that day or how I worked. I was waiting and waiting for the sun to sink in the west, for the horses to start neighing, for they were better than people at sensing that the working day was ending.

The siren rang out hoarsely; I went to the barracks where Shestakov lived. He was waiting for me on the porch. The pockets of his quilted jacket were bulging.

We sat at a big, scrubbed table in the barracks, and Shestakov pulled two cans of condensed milk out of a pocket.

I used the corner of an ax to pierce a hole in one can. A thick white stream flowed onto the lid and onto my hand.

"You should have made two holes. To let the air in," said Shestakov.

"Doesn't matter," I said, licking my sweet dirty fingers.

"Give us a spoon," Shestakov asked, turning to the workmen who were standing around us. Ten shiny, well-licked spoons were stretched over the table. They were all standing to watch me eat. That wasn't for lack of tact or out of any hidden desire to help themselves. None of them even hoped that I would share this milk with them. That would have been unprecedented; any interest in what someone else was eating was selfless. I also knew that it was impossible not to look at food disappearing into someone else's mouth. I made myself as comfortable as I could and consumed the milk without bread, just washing it down occasionally with cold water. I finished the two cans. The spectators moved away; the show was over. Shestakov looked at me with sympathy.

"You know what," I said, carefully licking the spoon. "I've changed my mind. You can leave without me."

Shestakov understood me and walked out without saying a thing.

This was, of course, a petty revenge, as weak as my feelings. But what else could I have done? I couldn't warn the others: I didn't know them. But I should have warned them: Shestakov had managed to persuade five others. A week later they ran off; two were killed not far from Black Springs, three were tried a month later. Shestakov's own case was set aside in the process, and he was soon moved away somewhere. I met him at another mine six months later. He didn't get an additional sentence for escaping. The authorities had used him but had kept to the rules. Things might have been different.

He was working as a geological prospector, he was clean-shaven and well-fed, and his chess-pattern socks were still intact. He didn't greet me when he saw me, which was a pity. Two tins of condensed milk was not really worth making a fuss about, after all.

1956

BREAD

THE ENORMOUS double door opened, and the delivery man entered the transit prisoners' barracks. He stood out in the broad band of morning light reflected by the blue snow. Two thousand eyes looked from all directions at him: from below, under the bunks; at his level; from the side and from above; from the height of the four-story bunks where those who still had the strength had clambered up a ladder. Today was herring day, and an enormous plywood tray, bending under the weight of a mountain of herrings split in two, was brought in behind the delivery man. The tray was followed by the duty supervisor, wearing a white tanned sheepskin jacket that shone like the sun. Herrings were issued in the mornings, half a herring per person every other day. Whatever calculations were made about the protein and calories in them, nobody knew, and nobody cared about such academic concerns. Hundreds of people were whispering the same thing: "Tails." A wise camp chief had taken into account the prisoners' psychology when he ordered either herring heads or herring tails to be issued at any one time. There were frequent discussions about the merits of one or the other: the tail apparently contained more fish oil, but the head was more satisfying. The process of swallowing the food was prolonged by having to suck the gills and extract the brain. The herrings that were issued had not been gutted, which everyone preferred; they ate it with all the bones and the skin. Any nostalgia for the fish heads was a short-lived thing; the tails were a fact to be contended with. In any case, the tray was coming nearer and the most anxious minute was approaching. How big a piece would you get, since you couldn't swap, let alone protest, and everything depended on your luck, your card in this game with hunger. The man who was careless about cutting up the herrings into portions didn't always understand (or had simply forgotten) that ten grams more or ten grams less—ten grams that looked like ten grams—could lead to a dramatic conflict, possibly to bloodshed. We needn't mention tears, for tears were frequent; they were understood by everyone, and nobody laughed at those who wept.

While the deliveryman came nearer, each prisoner calculated which piece this uncaring hand would offer him. Each man had time for disappointment or joy, to prepare himself for a miracle or to plumb the depths of despair if he had gotten his hurried calculations wrong. Some would screw up their eyes because they couldn't cope with the anxiety, and would open them only when the deliveryman jolted them to offer their ration of herring. Grabbing the herring with dirty fingers, stroking it, squeezing it quickly but gently to see whether it was a dry or a juicy portion (Sea of Okhotsk herrings are not always juicy, and this gesture with the fingers was another sort of preparation for a miracle), a man could not help casting a quick glance at the hands of people all around him who were also stroking and squeezing their pieces of herring, afraid to be too quick to swallow this tiny tail. A man didn't eat the herring; he licked and licked, as the tail gradually vanished from his fingers. All that was left were the bones, and he carefully chewed them, chewed them thriftily, so that the bones also melted away and vanished. Then he would start on the bread—the daily ration of five hundred grams was issued in the morning—pinching off a tiny piece and putting it in his mouth. Everyone ate the bread immediately so that it wouldn't be stolen or taken away; in any case, they didn't have the strength to hold on to it. The main thing was not to hurry, not to wash it down with water, not to chew it. It had to be sucked, like sugar, like a boiled sweet. After that you could take your mug of tea, or rather warm water, turned black by adding burned bark.

The herring is eaten, so is the bread, and the tea is drunk. You immediately feel hot and you don't want to go anywhere; you want to lie down, but now you've got to get dressed, to put on your torn quilted jacket that has been your blanket, to take some string and tie soles to your torn soft boots, quilted with cotton wool, boots that have been your pillow. You have to hurry, because the doors are wide open again and the escort guards and their dogs are waiting on the other side of the barbed-wire enclosure....

We were in quarantine, in typhus quarantine, but we weren't allowed to lie there idly. We were herded out to work. There were no lists, they just counted us by fives at the gates. There was a fairly reliable way of ending up each day with a relatively advantageous job. All you needed was patience and endurance. Advantageous jobs are always those where only a few people are taken on—two, three, or four men. Jobs needing twenty, thirty, or a hundred meant heavy labor, usually involving digging. Although a prisoner is never told in advance where he's going to work, he finds out on his way there, and it is the people with patience who are lucky in this terrible lottery. You have to loiter at the back, joining other people's ranks, move aside but rush forward when a small group is being assembled. If the group is going to be large, then the best job is in the stores sorting vegetables, or in the bakery, in other words, anywhere where the work is connected with food, future or present. It is there that you will always find leftovers, ends, offcuts of something edible.

We were lined up and led down a dirty April road. The guards' boots cheerfully splashed as they passed through the puddles. We were not allowed to break ranks while within town boundaries, so nobody avoided the puddles. Our feet got wet, but nobody paid any attention, for they weren't afraid of catching a chill. They'd caught chills thousands of times, and the most dreadful thing that could happen was pneumonia, and that would get you into the longed-for hospital.

"To the bakery, do you hear? We're headed for the bakery!"

There are people who always know everything and guess everything right. There are also people who try to make the best of everything, and their sanguine temperament will find some sort of accord with life in the worst of situations. But for others, events get worse as they unfold, and these people distrust any alleviation as a mere oversight by fate. This difference in attitudes has little to do with personal experience; it seems to be determined in childhood for the rest of their lives.

The wildest hopes came true: we were at the bakery gates. Twenty men, their hands tucked into their sleeves, were shuffling their feet, turning their backs to the piercing wind. The guards stood aside to have a smoke. From a door built into the gates emerged a bareheaded man wearing blue overalls. He spoke to the guards and then came up to us. He slowly inspected us all. Everyone becomes a psychologist in Kolyma, and he had a lot to consider in just a minute. He had to choose two men out of twenty ruffians to work indoors in the bakery workshop. These people had to be among the strongest; they had to be able to drag trays of smashed bricks that were all that was left after the ovens had been reconstructed. But they mustn't be thieves or gangsters, or else the working day would be wasted on all sorts of encounters and smuggled notes instead of work. They mustn't have reached the point at which any man may be driven by hunger to steal, for there were no guards in the bakery teams. They mustn't be inclined to attempt to escape. They must....

All that had to be read from twenty prisoners' faces in a minute; a selection and decision had to be made.

"Step forward," the bareheaded man told me. "You, too." He stuck a finger at my freckled know-it-all of a neighbor. "I'll take these two," he told the guard.

"Okay," said the guard, as if he didn't care.

Envious eyes saw us off.

All five human senses never work at full intensity at the same time. I can't hear the radio when I'm concentrating on reading. The lines begin to jump before my eyes if I concentrate on listening to a broadcast; although the automatic process of reading carries on and I let my eyes follow the lines, I will suddenly discover that I can't remember anything of what I have just read. The same thing happens if you start thinking about something different when you're in the middle of reading something: some inner switches come into operation. There's a well-known folk saying: "When I'm eating, I'm deaf and dumb." You could add "and blind," since your visual functions when you're eating eagerly are focused on helping your taste perceptions. When I grope for something deep in a cupboard and my perceptions are localized in my fingertips, I don't see or hear anything, for everything is suppressed by the tension of palpation. This was what was happening now: once I crossed the threshold of the bakery, I stood, unable to see the workmen's sympathetic and benevolent faces (former prisoners were working alongside current prisoners here), and unable to hear what the master baker, the familiar bareheaded man, was saying when he explained that we had to drag the smashed bricks outside, that we were not to visit the other workshops, that we mustn't steal, because he was going to give us bread in any case. I heard none of that. I didn't even feel the warmth of the overheated workshop, warmth that my body had longed for so desperately all that endless winter.

I was breathing in the smell of bread, the dense aroma of the loaves, in which the smell of hot oil mingled with the smell of roasted flour. I had greedily tried to catch a minute part of this overwhelming aroma in the mornings, when I pressed my nose against a crust of my ration that I had not yet eaten. Here the aroma came in all its density and power. It seemed to tear my poor nostrils apart.

The master baker put an end to my enchantment.

"You've had a good enough look," he said. "Let's go to the boiler room." We went down to the basement. My workmate was already sitting by the stoker's table in the boiler room, which had been swept clean. The stoker, wearing the same blue overalls as the master baker, was smoking by the stove, and you could see through an opening in the door of the cast-iron stove the flame inside flaring and blazing—it turned from red to yellow, and spasms of fire made the boiler walls shake and hum.

The baker put a kettle, a mug full of jam, and a loaf of white bread on the table.

"See they have something to drink," he told the stoker. "I'll come back in about twenty minutes. But don't drag it out, eat quickly. We'll give you more bread in the evening, and then you'd better break it into pieces, or it will be taken off you in the camp."

The baker left.

"What a swine," said the stoker, turning the loaf over in his hands. "Too mean to give you the seventy percent wheat, the sod. Hang on a moment."

He followed the baker out and a minute later came back, tossing a different loaf in his hands.

"Nice and hot," he said, throwing the loaf to the freckled lad. "Thirty percent rye. You see, he was trying to get away with a half-and-half! Give it here." Taking hold of the loaf the master baker had left us, the stoker flung open the stove door and tossed it into the roaring, howling fire. He slammed the door shut and laughed. "So there," he said happily, turning to face us.

"Why do that?" I asked. "We could have taken it with us."

"We'll give you something else to take home," said the stoker. Neither I nor the freckled lad were able to break the new loaf in two.

"Would you have a knife?" I asked the stoker.

"No. What do you need a knife for?"

The stoker picked up the loaf in both hands and easily broke it apart. Hot aromatic steam flowed out of the broken round loaf. The stoker stuck a finger into the soft bread.

"Fedka's a great baker, good man," he said in praise.

But we didn't have time to find out who Fedka was. We'd started eating, burning our mouths on the bread and the hot water that we added the jam to. Hot sweat was streaming off us. We were in a hurry; the master baker had come to fetch us.

He had brought us the carrying tray and dragged it to a pile of smashed bricks; he'd brought spades, and he personally filled the first box. We set to work. Suddenly it was obvious that the carrying tray was far too heavy for us, that it was stretching our sinews, so that our arms suddenly weakened and lost their strength. Our heads spun, we began to stagger. On the next tray I put half the load we had put on the first.

"That'll do, that'll do," said the freckled lad. He was even paler than me, or his freckles made his pallor look worse.

"Take a break, lads," said a baker who was passing by. He wasn't being at all sarcastic, so we obeyed and sat down to rest. The master baker passed by but said nothing.

After our break we got back to work, but after every two tray loads or so, we would sit down again—the pile of rubble was not getting any smaller.

"Have a cigarette, lads," said the same baker when he reappeared.

"We haven't got any tobacco."

"I'll give you enough for a roll-up each. But you've got to go outside. There's no smoking here."

We divided the tobacco and each of us smoked a cigarette: a long-forgotten luxury. I drew on it slowly a few times, carefully put it out, wrapped it in paper, and hid it under my shirt.

"Quite right," said the freckled lad. "I didn't think of that."

By the lunch break we had gotten so accustomed to it all that we even took a look into the neighboring rooms that had the same baker's ovens. Everywhere, iron bread tins and trays shrieked as they came out of ovens; on all the shelves there was nothing but bread, bread, bread. Every now and again a trolley would roll up and the baked bread was loaded and taken away, but not to where we had to return that evening —this was white bread.

You could see through the broad, unbarred window that the sun was now heading for the west. There was a cold draft coming from the doors. The master baker came.

"Right, stop now. Leave the carrying trays on the rubble. You haven't done very much. It'll take you slackers more than a week to move this heap."

We were given a loaf of bread each, which we broke into pieces and then stuffed into our pockets. But how much could we get into our pockets?

"Put it straight down your trousers," the freckled lad ordered me.

We walked out into the evening cold of the yard. The work party was now forming ranks, and we were led back. Nobody searched us when we reached the camp guardhouse, nobody had any bread in their hands. I went back to my place, shared the bread I'd brought with my neighbors, and fell asleep as soon as my wet, frozen feet had warmed up.

All night I dreamed of loaves of bread and the mischievous face of the stoker as he tossed bread into the stove's fiery maw.

1956

THE SNAKE CHARMER

WE WERE sitting on an enormous larch tree that had been knocked over by a storm. In the permafrost region trees have a very weak hold on the inhospitable ground and are easily pulled down, roots and all, by a storm. Platonov was telling me the story of his life here, our second life in this world. I frowned when he mentioned the Jankhara mine. I had been in bad and difficult places, but the terrible reputation of Jankhara resounded everywhere.

"Were you at Jankhara for long?"

"A year," Platonov answered quietly. His eyes narrowed, his wrinkles deepened: I was looking at a different Platonov, ten years older than the first one.

"Though it was hard just at the beginning, for two or three months. Only thieves worked there. I was the sole . . . literate man there. I'd tell them stories, 'churn out novels' as the gangster slang puts it. In the evenings I'd retell them Dumas, Conan Doyle, Wallace. In exchange they'd feed me, give me clothes, and I didn't have to work too much. I expect you've benefited too in your time here from the unique advantage of being literate."

"No," I said, "I haven't. I always thought that was the ultimate humiliation, the end. I never retold novels in exchange for soup. But I know what you're talking about. I've heard the 'novelists.'"

"So you disapprove of it, do you?" asked Platonov.

"Not at all," I replied. "A hungry man can be forgiven many things, many things."

"If I survive," Platonov pronounced the sacred phrase that opens all reflections about any time further than the next day, "I'll write a story about this. I've already thought of a title: 'The Snake Charmer.' Do you like it?"

"I do. You just have to survive. That's the main thing."

Andrei Fiodorovich Platonov, a film scriptwriter in his former life, died about three weeks after this conversation. He died the same death as many others did: he swung his pickax, lost his footing, and fell facedown onto the stones. Intravenous glucose or a strong heart drug might have revived him, for he went on rasping for an hour or ninety minutes, but he'd stopped making any noise by the time the stretcher-bearers came from the hospital, and his little corpse, a light load of skin and bones, was carried off to the morgue.

I was fond of Platonov because he hadn't lost interest in life beyond the blue sea, beyond the high mountains, from which we were separated by so many kilometers and years, and in whose existence we had almost stopped believing, or rather, we believed in the same way as schoolchildren believe in the existence of America, for example. God knows how, but Platonov had books and, when it wasn't too cold, for instance in July, he would shun conversations on the topics that animated everyone else—what soup there would be or had been for supper, whether we would get bread three times a day or just once in the morning, whether tomorrow's weather would be rainy or clear.

I was fond of Platonov, and I'll try now to write his story "The Snake Charmer."

The end of work is by no means the end of work. After the siren you have to gather all your tools, take them to the store, line up, go through two of the ten daily roll calls, listening to guards' foul curses and the pitiless shouts and insults from your own comrades, as long as they are stronger than you are, comrades who are also tired, anxious to get home, and angry at any delay. You have to endure another roll call, line up, and set off five kilometers into the forest to fetch firewood. The nearby forest was cleared and burned a long time ago. A brigade of lumberjacks gets the firewood ready, and the mine workers each carry home a big log. Nobody knows how to bring home the logs that are too big even for two men to carry. Trucks are never sent out for fire-wood, and all the horses are too sick to leave the stables. A horse loses its strength far more quickly than a human being, even though the difference between their former and present living conditions is min-imal, compared to what people undergo. It often seems, and perhaps it really is so, that the reason human beings rose to the top of the ani-mal kingdom and became human, that is, became a creature that could think up such things as our islands, however improbable life there might be, is that humans are physically tougher than any other animal. The ape wasn't humanized by having a hand, or an embryonic brain, or a soul; there are dogs and bears that behave more intelligently and morally than human beings. And the reason was not the taming of fire. All of that happened after the main requirement for the transfor-mation was met. Given that other conditions were equal at the time, man turned out to be considerably stronger and tougher physically, and only physically. He was as hard to kill as a cat, but that saying isn't quite accurate. It would be better to say that the cat is as hard to kill as a man. A horse cannot stand a month of life here in the winter, in cold stables with hours and hours of heavy labor in sub-zero tempera-tures. Unless it's a Yakut horse. But Yakut horses aren't used for hard labor. True, they're not fed, either. Like reindeer, in winter they paw at the snow and pull out last year's dried grass. Human beings survive. Perhaps they survive on hope? But they don't have any hope. Unless a man is a fool, he cannot live on hope. That is why there are so many suicides.

But the feeling of self-preservation, clinging onto life, a literally physical clinging that subordinates his mind, is what saves a man. He lives by the same principle as a stone, a tree, a bird, a dog. But he clings more tightly to life than they do. And he can endure more than any animal.

All that was what Platonov was thinking about as he stood by the entrance gates, a log on his shoulders, waiting for the next roll call. The wood had been brought and stacked; people crowded as, hurrying and cursing, they entered the dark log barracks.

When his eyes got used to the darkness, Platonov saw that by no means had all the workmen been to work. In the far right-hand corner seven or eight men were sitting on the upper bunks; they had taken over the only lamp, a smoking kerosene lamp with no glass, and were surrounding two other men, who sat with their legs tucked under them, like Tatars, with a greasy pillow between them, playing cards. The light of the fuming lamp shuddered, the fire swayed the shadows and made them seem longer.

Platonov sat down on the edge of the bunk. His shoulders and knees ached, his muscles were quivering. Platonov had been brought to Jankhara that same morning and this was his first day at work. There were no free places on the bunks.

"As soon as they all move away," Platonov thought, "I'll lie down." And he dozed off.

The game above him ended. A dark-haired man with a little mustache and a long fingernail on the little finger of his left hand rolled over to the edge of the bunk.

"Hey, call that Ivan Ivanovich over," he said.

Platonov was woken by someone jerking his back.

"You...you're wanted."

"Well, where is this Ivan Ivanovich?" came a call from the upper bunk.

"I'm not Ivan Ivanovich," said Platonov, screwing up his eyes.

"He won't come, Fedia."

"What do you mean he won't?"

Platonov was pushed into the light.

"Do you want to stay alive?" Fedia asked him quietly, revolving his little finger with its dirty overgrown nail near Platonov's eyes.

"I do," Platonov replied.

He was knocked to the ground by a powerful punch in the face. Platonov got up and wiped the blood with his sleeve.

"That's no way to answer," Fedia explained gently. "Ivan Ivanovich, was that how you were brought up in your boarding school?"

Platonov stayed silent.

"Clear off, you piece of shit," said Fedia. "Go and lie down next to the piss pot. That's your place. And if you make a noise, we'll choke you."

That was no empty threat. Platonov had twice witnessed men being choked to death with a towel to settle some thief's sense of justice. Platonov lay down on the stinking wet boards.

"I'm bored, mates," said Fedia with a yawn. "Why doesn't someone tickle my heels, then?"

"Mashka, hey Mashka, come and tickle Fedia's heels."

Mashka, a pale, good-looking boy-thief of eighteen, suddenly dived into the lamp's light, carefully removed Fedia's dirty, torn socks, and, smiling, started tickling his feet. The tickling made Fedia giggle and shake.

"Get out of here," Fedia suddenly said. "You can't tickle me. You don't know how."

"Fedia, I was only—"

"Get out, I told you. Scraping and scratching: you've got no tenderness."

The men around Fedia nodded their heads in sympathy.

"You remember that Jew I had at Kosoye? He could tickle. Mates, he really tickled. He was an engineer."

And Fedia plunged into his memories of the Jew who had tickled his heels.

"Fedia, Fedia, how about this new man.... Do you want to try him?"

"To hell with him," said Fedia. "People like him can't tickle. Anyway, get him up."

Platonov was brought out into the light.

"Hey, you, Ivan Ivanovich, adjust the lamp," Fedia ordered. "And you're going to put more wood in the stove at night. In the morning you take the piss pot out. The orderly will show you where to empty it...."

Platonov submissively said nothing.

"And for that," Fedia explained, "you'll get a bowl of soup. I don't eat dumpling soup anyway. Go and sleep."

Platonov went back to his old place. Almost all the workmen were asleep, curling up in pairs or in threes for the warmth.

"God, I'm bored. The nights are long," said Fedia. "Why doesn't someone 'churn out a novel'? When I was at Kosoye, I had—"

"Fedia, Fedia, how about this new man. Why not try him?"

"Right." Fedia came to life. "Get him up."

They roused Platonov.

"Listen," said Fedia, smiling almost ingratiatingly. "Sorry I got a bit overexcited."

"That's all right," said Platonov, gritting his teeth.

"Listen, can you 'churn out novels'?"

Platonov's dull eyes briefly blazed. Of course he could. The whole cell in the pretrial prison was captivated by his retelling of *Dracula*. But those prisoners had been human. Whereas here? Was he to be the clown at the court of the Duke of Milan, to be fed for a good joke and beaten for a bad one? There was after all another side to this business: he would be exposing them to real literature. He would be an educator, he would awaken their interest in literature; here, in the lower depths of life, he would be doing his job, his duty. Old habits blinded Platonov to the fact that he would only be fed, would get an extra soup for a job that was different, more dignified than carrying out the piss pot. But was it dignified at all? It was more like tickling the thief's dirty heels than giving him an education. But the hunger, the cold, the beatings....

Fedia was smiling intently as he waited for an answer.

"I c-c-can," Platonov managed to say, and he smiled for the first time that difficult day. "I can 'churn them out.'"

"Oh my darling man!" Fedia suddenly became joyful. "Come and climb in here. Here's a piece of bread for you. You'll get something to eat tomorrow. Sit here on the blanket. Have a cigarette."

Platonov hadn't smoked for a week and sucked at the cigarette stub with morbid enjoyment.

"What's your name, then?"

"Andrei," said Platonov.

"Well, Andrei, I need something really long, really spicy. Like *The Count of Monte Cristo*. I don't want stories about tractors."

"*Les Misérables*, perhaps?" Platonov suggested.

"Is that the one about Jean Valjean? I had that 'churned out' for me at Kosoye."

"Then how about *The Jack of Hearts Club*[5] or *The Vampire*?"

"That's the thing. Give us the *Jack*. Shut up, you bastards."

Platonov cleared his throat. "In the city of Saint Petersburg in 1893 a mysterious crime was committed...."

Day was breaking by the time Platonov completely lost his strength.

"Here ends the first part," he said.

"Well that was good," said Fedia. "He did a good job. Lie down here with us. You won't get much sleep, it's dawn. You can get some sleep at work. Save your strength for the evening."

Platonov was already asleep.

They were taken out to work. A tall peasant lad who had slept through the previous night's *Jack of Hearts* gave Platonov a vicious shove in the doorway.

"You swine, look where you're going."

Someone immediately whispered something into the lad's ear.

They lined up in rows, and the tall lad came up to Platonov.

"Don't tell Fedia that I hit you, pal. I didn't know that you were a novelist."

"I won't tell him," Platonov replied.

1954

THE TATAR MULLAH AND CLEAN AIR

THE HEAT in the prison cell was so great that you didn't see a single fly. The enormous iron-barred windows were open wide, but this brought no relief, for the yard's almost molten asphalt sent up waves of hot air, and it was actually cooler in the cell than outside. Everyone had stripped, and a hundred naked bodies exuding a heavy, damp heat tossed and turned on the floor, pouring with sweat. It was too hot to lie on the bunks. When the superintendent carried out his roll call, the prisoners lined up in just their underpants, and when they went to relieve themselves, they hung about for an hour in the washrooms, pouring cold water from the sink all over themselves. But this was no help in the long run. Those who slept under the bunks suddenly found that they were in possession of the best places. They had to prepare themselves for the region of "distant camps," and the typically grim prison joke was that after torture by steaming they could expect torture by freezing.

A Tatar mullah, who was still being interrogated as part of the notorious Greater Tatary case, which we knew about long before the newspapers gave any hint of it, a strong, sanguine man of sixty, with a powerful chest covered in gray hair and animated dark round eyes, used to say as he endlessly rubbed his shiny bald skull with a damp rag: "As long as they don't shoot me. That's a frightening sentence only for someone who expects to die at forty. If they give me ten years, that's nothing. I intend to live to eighty."

The mullah was never out of breath, even when he ran up to the fifth story after coming back from his exercise walk.

"If they give me more than ten years," he continued calculating, "I'll live about another twenty in prison. But if it's in a camp," the mullah was silent for a while, "in clean air, it will be just ten."

Today, when I was reading Dostoyevsky's *Notes from the House of the Dead*, I recalled that cheerful, intelligent mullah. The mullah knew what "clean air" was.

Morozov and Figner each survived twenty years of the harshest regime in the Shlisselburg fortress and were perfectly fit for work when they came out. Figner found enough strength to take an active role in the revolution and then wrote ten volumes of memoirs about the horrors she had endured; Morozov wrote a series of well-known scholarly works and married a schoolgirl for love.

In the camps, however, to turn a healthy young man, who had begun his career in the clean winter air of the gold mines, into a goner, all that was needed, at a conservative estimate, was a term of twenty to thirty days of sixteen hours of work per day, with no rest days, with systematic starvation, torn clothes, and nights spent in temperatures of minus sixty degrees in a canvas tent with holes in it, and being beaten by the foremen, the criminal gang masters, and the guards. The length of time required has been proven many times. Brigades that start the gold-mining season (the brigades are named after their foremen) have, by the end of the season, not a single man left alive from the start of the season, except for the foreman and one or two of the foreman's personal friends. The rest of the brigade is replaced several times over the summer. A gold mine constantly discards its production refuse into the hospitals, the so-called convalescent teams, invalid settlements, and mass graves.

The gold-mining season begins on the fifteenth of May and ends on the fifteenth of September: four months. There's no need to talk about winter work. By the next summer the basic mining brigades are formed from new people who haven't yet spent a winter here.

Prisoners, once they were given their sentence, couldn't get to the camps from the prisons fast enough. In the camps they would have work, healthy country air, early release, correspondence, parcels from relatives, the chance to earn money. People always believe in the best. Day and night passengers en route for the camps would crowd around the cracks in the doors of the cattle cars in which we were taken to the

Far East, ecstatically breathing in the quiet cool evening air that was saturated with the scent of wildflowers activated by the passing of the train. This air was unlike the stale prison-cell air, which smelled of carbolic and human sweat; the cells had become such hateful places after many months of interrogation. Memories of reviled and trampled honor were left behind in those cells, memories that people wanted to lose.

People are simpleminded enough to imagine that a pretrial prison is the cruelest experience to turn their lives upside down. Their actual arrest was for them the worst moral shock. Now, in their haste to leave the prison, they subconsciously want to believe in freedom, albeit relative freedom but a life free of the accursed bars and grids, of the humiliating, demeaning interrogations. A new life was beginning with none of the efforts of will constantly required to endure interrogation while the investigation is still going on. They felt a deep relief, knowing that everything was irrevocably settled, they had received their sentence, they needn't think about how to answer the interrogator, they needn't worry about their relatives, or make any future plans, or fight for a piece of bread. They were now subject to someone else's will, nothing could be changed, there was no turning off this shiny railway journey that was slowly but relentlessly taking them to the north.

The train was moving toward winter. Each night was colder than the previous one, and the thick green poplar leaves here already had a bright yellow tinge. The sun was no longer so hot or bright, as if the maple, poplar, birch, and aspen leaves had ingested and absorbed the heat. The sunlight now shone from the leaves themselves, while the pale, anemic sun, as it mostly hid behind warm gray clouds, which had yet to hint at snow, could not even warm the cattle car. But snow would soon come.

Transit camp is yet another route to the north. The bay of the sea met them with a small blizzard. The snow hadn't yet settled; the wind swept it off the frozen yellow cliffs into a pit full of dirty, turbid water. You could see through the blizzard. The snowfall was thin, like a fisherman's net of white threads cast over the town. You couldn't even see the snow over the sea; the dark green crested waves slowly lapped onto the slippery, weed-covered stones. A ship was anchored offshore;

from above it looked like a toy, and even when they were taken by launch to board it and they climbed one by one onto the deck, only to separate and vanish immediately into the maw of the holds, the ship was surprisingly small, surrounded as it was by so much water.

Five days later they disembarked on the harsh and gloomy shores of the taiga, and trucks distributed them to the places where they would be living and surviving.

They had left their healthy country air on the other side of the sea. Here they were surrounded by thin air that was saturated with the exudations of the bogs. The bare hills were covered with marshy ground, and only the bald, unforested hills shone, thanks to the limestone, polished by storms and winds. Their legs sank in the marshy moss, and their feet were rarely dry on a summer's day. In winter everything turned to ice. The mountains, the rivers, and the bogs seemed in winter to be one and the same being, ominous and hostile.

For anyone with a weak heart the air was too heavy in summer and in winter just unbearable. When the temperature was really low, people breathed in short gasps. Nobody here moved at a run, except perhaps the very youngest, and they skipped along rather than ran.

Your face was covered with clouds of mosquitoes, and you couldn't take a step without a face net. The face net stifled you and kept you from breathing when you were working, yet you couldn't lift it because of the mosquitoes.

People then worked for sixteen hours a day, and the norms were set accordingly. If you took into consideration that reveille, breakfast, the assembly, and walk to work took a minimum of an hour and a half, while lunch was an hour and dinner, followed by getting ready for bed, took an hour and a half, then all you had left for sleep after heavy physical labor in the open air was four hours. As soon as he stopped moving, a man fell asleep; he learned to sleep walking or standing. Sleep deprivation took away more strength than did hunger. Failure to fulfill the norm was liable to get you punishment rations, three hundred grams of bread a day and no gruel.

The first illusion was soon shed. This was the illusion about work, the labor about which an inscription, prescribed by the camp constitution, is placed over the gates of all sections of the camps: "Labor is a matter of honor, a matter of glory, a matter of valor and heroism." The actual camp could only inspire a hatred and loathing of labor.

Once a month the camp postman would take away the accumulated mail to be censored. Letters to and from the mainland took six months, if they arrived at all. Parcels were issued only to those who had fulfilled the norm; others had their parcels confiscated. None of this was arbitrary, not at all. Orders to these effects were read out, and in especially serious cases every single person was made to acknowledge them with a signature. This wasn't the wild imaginings of a depraved camp boss; it was an order coming from the very top.

But even if someone received a parcel—you could promise some protector half and still not get your half—then there was nowhere to take that parcel. The gangsters would already be waiting for you in the barracks, so as to snatch it from you in front of everyone and share it with their Vanias and Senias. You immediately had to either eat or sell what you'd been sent. There were all the buyers you could want: guards, bosses, doctors.

There was in fact a third way out, the most widespread. Many people handed their parcels for safekeeping to people whom they knew in the camp or prison and who had some position or job where they could lock away and hide things. Or they handed them to the free hired workers. There was always a risk in both cases: nobody believed in the good faith of those above him. But this was the only way to save what you had received.

Money was never paid. Not a penny. Only the best brigades were paid, and they received trivial amounts that couldn't give them any significant relief. In many brigades the foreman acted by ascribing the production to two or three men, so they had more than a hundred percent production and were entitled to a cash bonus. Then the other twenty or thirty men in the brigade were liable to get punishment rations. This was a cunning solution. If the earnings had been divided equally among everyone, then nobody would have received a penny. But now two or three men, chosen quite arbitrarily to figure in the certificate, often without the foreman's say-so, would get something.

Everyone knew that the norms could not possibly be achieved, that nothing was or could be earned. Yet people still followed the foreman, asking about the proceeds, or ran to meet the cashier or visited the office for information.

What was going on? Was this a desire to insist that you were a hard worker, to improve your reputation in the bosses' eyes, or was it a mental illness due to malnourishment? The latter is more likely.

Now that they were here in the camp, the bright, clean, warm pretrial prison, which they had so recently and so infinitely long ago left, seemed to absolutely everyone the best place on earth. All the wrongs done to them in prison were forgotten, and everyone excitedly recalled listening to lectures by real scholars and to stories told by people who had seen a lot of the world. They recalled reading books, sleeping, and eating their fill, going to a wonderful bathhouse, getting parcels from relatives, feeling that their family was close by them, just beyond the double iron gates; they remembered speaking freely about whatever they liked (for doing that in the camp you could get an extra sentence), not fearing informers or wardens. The pretrial prison seemed to them freer and cozier than their family home. Quite a few, dreaming in their hospital bunks, would say, even though they did not have long to live, "Of course, I'd like to see my family, to leave here. But I'd like even more to get back to my cell in the pretrial prison. It was more comfortable and interesting even than home. And I'd tell all the newcomers what 'clean air' really was."

If you added to everything else the almost universal scurvy, which had turned, as in Behring's times, into a terrible and dangerous epidemic taking the lives of thousands; as well as the dysentery, since people ate whatever they could find in their urge to just fill an aching stomach, gathering kitchen refuse from the rubbish heaps, which were thickly covered with flies; not to speak of the pellagra, an emaciating disease of the poor, which peels the skin like a glove off a man's palms and soles, and makes the whole body a mangy mass of large round petals, like fingerprints; and lastly, the famous alimentary dystrophy, the disease of the starving, which was called by its real name only after the blockade of Leningrad. Before then dystrophy had various names—in medical diagnosis it was APE, which stood for acute physical emaciation; more often, it was polyavitaminosis, a wonderful Latin term describing the lack of several vitamins in a person's body, but which reassured the doctors in that they had a convenient and legitimate Latin formula to denote what was just starvation.

If you remember the unheated damp barracks, with a thick layer of ice filling all the crevices inside, as if a tallow candle had melted in a corner of the barracks; if you account for the bad clothing and starvation rations, the frostbitten digits (frostbite meant everlasting agony, even if amputation was not resorted to); if you imagine how frequent were the inevitable appearances of flu, pneumonia, all sorts of chills and of tuberculosis in these marshy mountains, so fatal for anyone with heart trouble; if you recall the epidemics of self-harming by chopping off a limb or a digit; if you also consider the appalling moral dejection and the hopelessness, then you can easily see how much more dangerous clean air was to human health than prison.

That is why there is no point arguing with Dostoyevsky about the advantages of "work," when you are sentenced to hard labor, over the idleness of prison life, or about the merits of "clean air." Dostoyevsky's times were different, and hard labor had then not reached the heights described here. It is difficult to form a true idea of this in advance, for everything there is too unusual, too improbable, and a poor human brain is simply incapable of conceiving concrete images of life there, a life of which our prison acquaintance, the Tatar mullah, had a vague, uncertain idea.

1955

MY FIRST DEATH

I WITNESSED a lot of human deaths in the north—in fact, too many for one man to see—but the first death I saw made the deepest impression on my memory.

That winter we found ourselves working the night shift. I saw a tiny light gray moon in a black sky; the moon was surrounded by a rainbow-colored halo that appeared when the temperature was very low. We never saw the sun at all; we got back to the barracks (not home, nobody called the barracks home) and we left them while it was dark. In any case, the sun appeared for such a short period that it didn't have time even to take a good look at the earth through the thick white gauze of frosty mist. We had to guess where the sun might be; it gave no light or warmth.

It was a long walk, two or three kilometers, to the pit face, and we had to pass between two enormous, six-meter-high walls of snow. That winter saw heavy snowdrifts and after each blizzard the pit face had to be dug clear. Thousands of people with spades came out to clear the road so that the trucks could pass. Everyone who worked on road clearance was surrounded by a shift of guards with their dogs, and they were kept at work for days on end, not allowed to warm themselves nor go anywhere warm to eat. Packhorses brought rations of half-frozen bread and sometimes, if the job dragged out, tinned food: one can for two men. The same horses took the sick and the exhausted back to the camp. Only when the job was done were people allowed to go back to sleep and then out into the sub-zero cold again to do their "proper" work. It was then that I noticed something remarkable: when you work for many hours on end, it is only hard and agonizingly difficult for the first six or seven hours. After that you lose your sense of time, you subconsciously watch out only for the danger of freezing to death; you stamp your feet, you wave your spade about, but you don't think about anything at all and don't hope for anything.

The end of such a job is always unexpected, a sudden stroke of good luck that you seem never to have even dared to count on. Everyone is cheerful and noisy, and for a short time there seems to be no hunger, no deadly fatigue. Hastily lining up in rows, everyone happily runs "home." On either side of us the enormous trench walls of snow rise up, cutting us off from the rest of the world.

The blizzard had stopped long ago, and the fluffy snow had settled, compacted, and now was even more formidable and hard. You could walk on the top of the snow wall and not fall through it. Both walls were intersected at several places by roads that crossed them.

At about two in the morning we got back for dinner and filled the barracks with the noise that people who have been freezing make, with the clanging of spades, the low conversation of those who've come in from outside, talk that only gradually quiets down and then is muffled as it reverts to ordinary human speech. Dinner at night was always in the barracks, not in the freezing refectory where the windows had no glass, a refectory that everyone hated. After dinner those who had tobacco smoked, and those who didn't have any tobacco were given cigarette ends by their workmates. On the whole things worked out so that everyone managed to "have a drag."

Our foreman, Kolia Andreyev, once the manager of a collective's truck and tractor garage but now a plain prisoner condemned to ten years under the fashionable political article 58 of the Criminal Code, always walked at the head of his brigade and walked quickly. Our brigade was not guarded. The explanation for the authorities' trust was that at the time there was a shortage of guards. But knowing we were special, that we had no guards, was, however naïve it seems, of some importance. Everyone valued going to work unguarded; it was the subject of pride and boasting. The brigade did in fact work better than it did later, when there were enough guards and the Andreyev brigade's rights were reduced to the same level as all the others.

On this particular night Andreyev was leading us along a new route, not down below but right on the crest of the snow wall. We could see the mine's golden eyes flickering, the dark mass of the forest on our left, and the distant crowns of the bare hills merging into the sky. For the first time at night we could see from afar where we lived.

When he reached the crossroads, Andreyev suddenly turned sharply to the right and ran downhill through the snow. Meekly repeating his inexplicable movement, a flock of people poured after him, their crowbars, pickaxes, spades all clanging (tools were never left at the workplace, where they would be stolen, and losing your tools incurred punishment).

Two yards from the intersection a man in military uniform stood. He was bareheaded, his short dark hair was disheveled and sprinkled with snow, his greatcoat was unbuttoned. Farther off, its legs buried in deep snow, was a horse, harnessed to a light sleigh.

A woman lay supine at this man's feet. Her fur coat was open, her brightly colored dress was creased. A black crumpled shawl was lying by her head. The shawl had been trodden into the snow, as had her blond hair, which seemed almost white in the moonlight. Her thin throat was open, and dark oval stains showed on the right and left of her neck. Her face was white, bloodless, and when I had taken a good look, I recognized Anna Pavlovna, the secretary to the chief of our mine.

Her face was familiar to us all; there were very few women at the mine. One evening about six months previously she had passed our brigade, and the prisoners' delighted looks followed her thin figure as she passed. She had smiled at us and pointed to the sun, which was already heavy as it sank to the horizon.

"It won't be long, boys, not long!" she'd shouted.

Like the camp horses, we spent the whole working day thinking only about the minute it would end. We were touched by the fact that our simple thoughts had been so well understood, and what's more by a woman who was so beautiful (according to our ideas at the time). Our brigade loved Anna.

Now she was lying there dead, strangled by the fingers of the man in military uniform who was looking around him with a wild, bewildered gaze. He was much more familiar to me: this was Shtemenko, the interrogator at our mine, the man who set in motion criminal cases against so many of the prisoners. He would interrogate relentlessly, and would bribe false witnesses and slanderers, recruited from the hungry prisoners, with a pinch of tobacco or a bowl of soup. He assured some victims that the state required them to lie, threatened others, and bribed the rest. He never bothered, before arresting a new suspect, to get to know him or to summon him, even though we all lived at the same mine. In the interrogator's office any arrested man could expect ready-made statements and beatings.

Shtemenko was the boss who had visited our barracks about three months previously and destroyed all the prisoners' cooking pots, which they had made from old cans and in which they cooked anything that could be cooked and eaten. The cans were used to carry dinner from the refectory so as to heat it up over the barracks stove and eat it sitting down. A champion of cleanliness and discipline, Shtemenko ordered someone to give him a pickax and then personally smashed in the bottoms of the tin cans.

Now he noticed Andreyev just two yards away. He grabbed his pistol holster but, seeing the crowd of men armed with crowbars and pickaxes, decided not to draw his weapon. But people were already tying his hands behind his back. They did so with such passion and tied the knot so tightly that it later had to be undone with a knife.

Anna's corpse was put onto the sleigh and taken to the settlement, to the mine chief's house. Not everyone accompanied Andreyev; many made a beeline for the barracks and their soup.

When he saw the crowd of prisoners gathered around the doors of his house, the chief took his time before opening up. In the end Andreyev managed to explain what the matter was, and along with Shtemenko, who was still tied up, and two other prisoners, Andreyev went into the house.

Dinner took a long time that night. Andreyev was taken off somewhere to give evidence. But he came back later, gave us our orders, and we went off to work.

Shtemenko was quickly sentenced to ten years for murder due to jealousy. The punishment was minimal. His trial was at our mine, and after the sentence he was taken away. In such cases, former camp bosses are kept in a special place. Nobody ever came across them in the ordinary camps.

1956

AUNTIE POLIA

AUNTIE Polia died in the hospital of stomach cancer. She was fifty-two years old. The autopsy confirmed the diagnosis made by the doctor treating her. Not that the pathologist's report often differed from the clinician's in either the best or the worst hospitals.

Only the office knew Auntie Polia's surname. Even the wife of the boss whom Polia had served for seven years as an "orderly"—that is, a servant—couldn't remember her actual surname.

Everyone knows what an orderly, male or female, is, but not everyone knows what they can be: a trusted confidant of an inaccessible master of the fates of thousands of human beings; a witness to his failings and dark sides; a person who knows the shadowy aspects of the home; a slave, but a constant participant in the submarine, subterranean war for accommodation; a participant, or at the very least an observer, in domestic battles; a secret arbiter in quarrels between husband and wife; the master's chief housekeeper, increasing his wealth, and not only by being economical and honest. There was one orderly who traded in cigarettes to make a profit for his master; he sold them to prisoners for ten rubles each. The camp chamber of weights and measures had decreed that a matchbox held enough tobacco to make eight roll-ups, and eight matchboxes of tobacco contained a total of two ounces of tobacco. These dry-matter measures applied to one-eighth of the territory of the Soviet Union—that is, all of eastern Siberia.

Our orderly would earn six hundred and forty rubles from each two-ounce packet of tobacco. But even this figure was not what you would call the limit. You didn't have to pack the matchboxes fully. To the untrained eye there was no discernible difference, and nobody wanted to quarrel with the boss's orderly. You could just roll your cigarettes more tightly. The roll-up's contents were a matter for the orderly's hands and conscience. Our orderly bought his tobacco from the boss for five hundred rubles a packet. The one hundred and forty ruble profit went into the orderly's pocket.

Auntie Polia's boss didn't trade in tobacco, and he didn't make her do any underhanded trading. Auntie Polia was a magnificent cook, and orderlies who were culinary experts were valued especially highly. Auntie Polia could undertake—and she actually did so—to get any of her fellow Ukrainians an easy job or to get them onto a list for release. The help Auntie Polia gave her fellow countrymen was very substantial. She didn't help anyone else, except perhaps with a word of advice.

Auntie Polia had been working for her boss for more than six years, and she believed she'd serve her entire ten-year sentence with no problems.

Auntie Polia was calculating but not avaricious; she rightly thought that her indifference to gifts and money was bound to be highly appreciated by any boss. Her calculations proved to be right. She was one of the boss's family, and a plan for her release had already been drawn up—she was going to be registered as a truck loader at the mine where her boss's brother worked, and the mine had put in a request for her release.

But Auntie Polia fell ill; she got worse and worse and was sent to the hospital. The doctor in charge saw to it that she had a separate ward. Ten moribund patients were dragged out into a cold corridor to make room for the boss's orderly.

The hospital stirred to life. Every afternoon jeeps would arrive, as would trucks; ladies in sheepskin jackets and men in military uniform would get out of the cabs, all rushing to see Auntie Polia. And she promised each one that, if she recovered, she would put in a word for them to her boss.

Every Sunday a ZIS-101 limousine would pass through the hospital gates, bringing a parcel and a note from the boss's wife.

Auntie Polia gave all the treats to the nurses after sampling just a spoonful. She knew what was wrong with her.

But Auntie Polia couldn't recover. Eventually an extraordinary visitor, Father Piotr, as he introduced himself to the hospital manager, came to the hospital, carrying a note from the boss. It turned out that Auntie Polia wanted to take confession.

This extraordinary visitor was Piotr Abramov. Everyone knew him. He'd even been a patient in the hospital some months previously. But now he was Father Piotr.

The most reverend priest's visit bewildered the whole hospital: apparently there were priests in our region! There was nothing but talk of Auntie Polia's confession in the hospital's biggest ward, ward two, where the time between lunch and dinner was taken up by one of the patients telling a story about food—not to stimulate the patients' appetites but to meet a starving man's need to have his dietary emotions stimulated.

Father Piotr was wearing a peaked cap and a pea jacket. His quilted trousers were tucked into old boots made from kersey.[6] His hair was cut very short for a cleric, far shorter than the Elvis-style haircuts of the 1950s. Father Piotr unbuttoned his pea jacket and quilted waistcoat so that the blue peasant shirt and the big cross around his neck could be seen. This was no ordinary cross; it was a homemade one, the work of a skilled hand lacking the necessary tools.

Father Piotr heard Auntie Polia's confession and left. He spent some time standing on the highway, raising his arm whenever trucks appeared. Two trucks passed but did not stop. Then Father Piotr took a ready-rolled cigarette from under his jacket and raised it over his head. The very first truck braked and the driver hospitably opened the cab door.

Auntie Polia died and was buried in the hospital cemetery. This was a big cemetery at the bottom of a hill (the patients used to say "to end up down the hill" instead of "to die"), with mass graves A, B, C, and D, and a few lines, looking like spinal columns, of single graves. Auntie Polia's burial was not attended by her boss, the boss's wife, or Father Piotr. The ceremony was the usual one; the hospital manager tied a wooden tag to Auntie Polia's left calf. The tag bore a number, the number of her personal file. The rules stated that the number had to be written with an ordinary, not an indelible, black pencil, just like the topographical reference points foresters mark trees with.

The usual gravedigger janitors covered Auntie Polia's withered body with stones. The manager fixed a stick into the stones, bearing the same personal file number as the tag.

A few days later, Father Piotr appeared at the hospital. He had been to the cemetery and was now causing an uproar in the hospital office.

"You have to put up a cross. A cross."

"Like hell I will," replied the manager.

They swore at each other for a long time. Finally Father Piotr announced: "I'm giving you a week. If no cross is erected in that time, I shall complain about you to the chief of the administration. If he won't help, I'll write to the chief of Far East Development. If he won't help, I shall complain about him to the Council of People's Commissars. If they refuse to intervene, I'll write to the synod." Father Piotr was roaring.

The manager had been a prisoner himself and was well aware of the "Wonderland" he lived in—he knew that the most unexpected things could happen. After pondering a little, he decided to put this whole business to the doctor in charge.

The doctor in charge, who had once been a minister or a deputy minister, advised the manager not to argue but to erect a cross over Auntie Polia's grave.

"If that priest is so sure of what he's saying, then there may be something in it. He knows something. Anything's possible, anything's possible," mumbled the former minister.

A cross, the first cross in that cemetery, was erected. It could be seen a long way away. Although it was the only one, the whole area now began to look like a real cemetery. All the ambulatory patients would come to look at this cross. It even had a board with a black frame nailed to it. An old artist who had been a patient in the hospital for more than a year was entrusted with inscribing the board. He wasn't actually bedridden, he just had a bed assigned to him. He spent all his time mass-producing copies of three paintings: *Golden Autumn*, *Three Knights*, and *The Death of Ivan the Terrible*. The artist swore that he could do these copies with his eyes closed. His clients included all the bosses and chiefs in the settlement and the hospital.

But the artist did agree to do a board for Auntie Polia's cross. He asked what it should say. The manager dug about in his lists.

"I can only find her initials," he said. "Timoshenko, P. I. So write Polina Ivanovna. Died on such-and-such a date."

The artist never argued with his clients, so that is what he wrote. A week later to the day, Piotr Abramov, that is Father Piotr, reappeared. He said that Auntie Polia's name was Praskovia, not Polina, and her patronymic was Ilyinichna, not Ivanovna. He gave her date of birth and demanded that it be included in the inscription over her grave. The inscription was corrected in Father Piotr's presence.

1958

THE NECKTIE

HOW CAN I write the story of that damned necktie?

This is something true but peculiar: it is true reality. But this is a story, not a sketch. How am I to make it a piece of the prose of the future, something like the stories of Saint-Exupéry, who revealed the air to us?

In the past and at present a writer needs to be someone like a foreigner in the country he is writing about if he wants to be a success. He has to write from the viewpoint—interests, vision—of the people he grew up among and from whom he got his habits, tastes, and views. A writer writes in the language of those in whose name he speaks. And that is all. If a writer knows his material too well, the people for whom he is writing won't understand him. The writer will have betrayed them and gone over to the side of his material.

You mustn't know your material too well. Every writer in the past and the present had that defect, but the prose of the future demands something different. It will be professionals with a gift for writing who will speak out, not writers. And they will tell us only about what they know and have seen. Plausible accuracy is the force behind the literature of the future.

But speculation may be irrelevant in this case, and the main thing is to try and remember, to remember in every detail Marusia Kriukova, a lame girl who took an overdose of veronal by saving up some tiny, shiny, yellow oval tablets and swallowing them. She got the veronal by swapping it for bread, porridge, or a portion of herring from other patients in her ward who had been prescribed the drug. The paramedics knew that veronal was being traded, and so they forced patients to swallow the tablet while they were watching, but the tablets had a hard coating, and patients could usually manage to tuck the veronal behind their cheeks or under their tongues and, once the paramedic had gone, spit it out onto their palms.

Marusia Kriukova hadn't worked out the right dose. She didn't die, she just vomited, and, after she had received aid in the form of a stomach pump, she was discharged and sent to the transit camp. But all this happened long after the incident with the necktie.

Marusia Kriukova arrived from Japan at the end of the 1930s. The daughter of an émigré who was living on the outskirts of Kyoto, Marusia, along with her brother, joined a union called Return to Russia, contacted the Soviet consulate, and in 1939 received a Russian entry visa. Marusia, her brother, and their fellow returnees were arrested in Vladivostok; Marusia was taken to Moscow and never saw any of her friends again.

Marusia's leg was broken under interrogation, and when the bone mended she was sent to Kolyma to serve a twenty-five-year term of imprisonment. Marusia was a superb craftswoman, a specialist in embroidery, and it was this skill that allowed her to support her family in Kyoto.

The bosses in Kolyma immediately discovered Marusia's skills. She was never paid for her embroidery; she would be brought a piece of bread, two bits of sugar, or cigarettes—but Marusia never learned to smoke. Her wonderful hand embroidery, worth several hundred rubles, stayed in the possession of the bosses.

The woman in charge of the camp health service heard of Marusia's abilities and admitted her to the hospital, so that from then on Marusia did embroidery for the chief female doctor.

Then a telegram arrived at the state collective where Marusia was employed, instructing that all women with seamstress skills should be sent by the next vehicle going that way to X ... for redeployment. The camp chief had been concealing Marusia's existence, for his wife had a big commission for the craftswoman. But someone immediately wrote a denunciation to the higher authorities and Marusia had to be sent off. Where to?

The central Kolyma highway stretches its winding path over two thousand kilometers, passing through bare hills, ravines, milestones, rails, and bridges....There aren't any rails on the Kolyma highway. Nevertheless people have never stopped reciting Nekrasov's poem "The Railway."[7] Why compose a poem when there is a perfectly apt text already in existence? The road was entirely built by pickax and spade, wheelbarrow and drill....

Every four or five hundred kilometers along the highway is a "director's house," a super-luxury hotel at the personal disposal of the director of Far East Development, who is equivalent to the governor-general of Kolyma. He alone may spend the night there during his travels over the district entrusted to him. Expensive carpets, bronze sculptures, and mirrors. Original paintings by quite a few first-rate artists, such as Shukhayev. In 1957 there was an exhibition at Kuznetsky Most[8] in Moscow of Shukhayev's works, the story of his life. The exhibition began with bright landscapes from Belgium and France, and a self-portrait of the artist wearing a harlequin's camisole. Then came the Magadan period: two small portraits in oil, one of his wife and one self-portrait in gloomy brown tones, all he had done over ten years. The portraits were of people who had seen something terrible. Apart from these portraits there were only sketches for theater decorations.

After the war Shukhayev was released. He went to Tbilisi, south, south, taking with him his loathing of the north. He was a broken man. He painted a sycophantic picture called *Stalin Taking the Oath in Gori*. He was a broken man. There were portraits of shock workers, of leading production workers. *A Lady in a Golden Hat*. The radiance in this portrait shows a lack of balance; the artist seems to be forcing himself to forget the limitations of the northern palette. And everything else. He might as well have died.

For the "director's house" artists also painted copies: *Ivan the Terrible Killing His Son*, Shishkin's *Morning in a Pine Forest*. These two paintings are classics of hack work.

But the most amazing feature of the "house" was the embroidery. Silk curtains, blinds, portieres were all embroidered by hand. Rugs, pillowcases, towels—any piece of cloth was transformed into a thing of value by the hands of the imprisoned craftswomen.

The director of Far East Development spent a night in one of his "houses," of which there were several along the highway, two or three times a year. The rest of the time there were guards, a housekeeper, a cook, and a house manager, four hired free workers, who waited for him to arrive, and who got bonuses on their salary because they were working in the Far East. They waited, they prepared, they stoked the stoves in winter and aired the "house."

Marusia Kriukova had been brought here to embroider the curtains, pillowcases, and anything else they could think of. There were two other fine seamstresses whose skills and inventiveness were as good as Marusia's. Russia is a country of checks, a country of monitoring. The dream of every good Russian, prisoner or free worker, was to be employed someplace where he or she could check up on someone else. First of all, "I am in charge of somebody." Second, "I am trusted." Third, "I'm less answerable for this work than I would be for my own labor." And fourth, remember the attack on *In the Trenches of Stalingrad* by Viktor Nekrasov.[9]

Marusia and her new friends were under the supervision of a female party member who issued their material and threads daily. At the end of the working day this woman took their work and checked what they had done. She herself did no work but was attached to the staff of the central hospital as a senior nurse in the operating room. She was a thorough overseer, convinced that she only had to turn her back and a piece of heavy blue silk would vanish.

The seamstresses were long used to this sort of guard. And although it probably would not have been hard to pull the wool over this woman's eyes, they didn't steal. All three craftswomen had been sentenced under article 58 of the Criminal Code.

The seamstresses had their quarters in the camp, in the zone over whose gates, as over all camp zones in the Soviet Union, were inscribed the unforgettable words: "Labor is a matter of honor, a matter of glory, a matter of valor and heroism." The quotation sounded ironic, since it was an astonishing take on the sense and content of the word "labor" in the camp. Labor was anything you like, but not a matter of glory. As for the surname of the author of this quotation, in 1906, a publishing house that was run in part by Socialist Revolutionaries printed a booklet called *The Complete Collected Speeches of Nicolas II*. These were pieces reprinted from the *Government Herald* at the time of the tsar's coronation and consisted of toasts he had offered: "I drink to the health of the Kekstolm regiment!" "I drink to the health of the fine young men of Chernigov."

These toasts were preceded by a foreword, written in chauvinist-patriotic tones: "These words, like a drop of water, reflect all the wisdom of our great monarch," etc.

The compilers of this collection were exiled to Siberia. What happened to the people who took the quotation about labor and raised it on the gates of the camp zones of all the Soviet Union?

As a reward for their excellent conduct and success in fulfilling the plan, the seamstresses were allowed to attend the cinema when there were showings for prisoners.

The showings for free workers had a slightly different arrangement than the prisoners' showings.

The projector was the same; there were intervals between the reels.

Once the film shown was *Enough Stupidity in Every Wise Man*. The first reel finished, the lights, as always, came on, and then, as always, went out, and you could hear the projector crackling and see a yellow beam hit the screen.

Everyone started stamping their feet and shouting. The projectionist had clearly blundered and was showing the first reel again. Three hundred people—including bemedaled soldiers from the front, distinguished doctors who had come for a conference—everyone who had bought a ticket for this free workers' showing, was shouting and stomping their feet.

The projectionist was in no great hurry. He let the first reel roll and then put the auditorium lights on. Everyone understood what was going on. The deputy chief of the hospital management, Dolmatov, had come in. He had missed the first reel, so the film was shown from the start again.

The second reel began, and everything went normally. Everyone understood the Kolyma ways of doing things—the doctors very well, the soldiers from the front not so well.

If tickets weren't selling briskly, then there was a general showing for everybody, and the best seats, at the back, went to the free workers, while the front rows were for the prisoners—women to the left and men to the right of the aisle. The aisle thus divided the auditorium like a cross into four sections, which was very convenient for working out the camp rules.

A lame girl, noticeably lame even at film showings, had ended up in the women's section of the hospital. No small wards had yet been built; the whole women's section filled a single military dormitory of at least fifty beds. Marusia was sent to the surgeon for treatment.

"What's wrong with her?"

"Osteomyelitis," said Valentin Nikolayevich, the surgeon.

"Is she going to lose a foot?"

"No, why should she?"

I used to come and bandage Kriukova, and I'd already told him about her life. A week later her temperature had gone down and the following week she was discharged.

"I'll give you a necktie, you and Valentin Nikolayevich. They'll be good ties."

"Fine, fine, Marusia."

It was just a strip of silk taken from tens, hundreds of meters of fabric, which she had embroidered and decorated over several shifts in the "director's house."

"How about the inspections?"

"I'll ask Anna Andreyevna." That, apparently, was her supervisor's name.

"Anna Andreyevna said I could. I kept embroidering, embroidering. I don't know how to explain it, but Dolmatov came in and took it away."

"What do you mean 'took it away'?"

"He took what I was sewing. Valentin Nikolayevich's was already finished, and yours was almost done. It was gray. The door opened. 'Are you embroidering a tie?' He searched my sewing box. He put the tie in his pocket and left."

"Now you'll be sent away."

"Not me. I've got too much work still to do. But I did want so much to give you a tie...."

"It doesn't matter, Marusia, I wouldn't have worn it anyway. I suppose I could have sold it."

Dolmatov was as late for the camp amateur concert as he had been for the cinema. Overweight and potbellied, as if he were much older, he made for the first empty bench.

Kriukova got up and waved her arms. I realized she was signaling to me.

"The tie, the tie!"

I managed to get a look at the boss's necktie. Dolmatov's tie was gray, patterned, high-quality.

"It's your tie," Marusia was shouting. "Yours, or Valentin Nikolayevich's!"

Dolmatov sat down on his bench, the curtains were drawn back as in an old-fashioned theater, and the amateur concert began.

1960

THE GOLDEN TAIGA

"THE LESSER ZONE" means the transit camps. "The Greater Zone" means the camps run by the mining administration—endless squat barracks, streets for the prisoners, a triple barrier of barbed wire, winter-proof guard towers that look like starling nesting boxes. The Lesser Zone has even more barbed wire, more towers, locks, and bolts; after all, it houses passing prisoners, prisoners in transit who could cause all sorts of trouble.

The Lesser Zone architecture is perfect: one enormous square barracks with four-story rows of bunks and a "statutory" room for no less than five hundred men. So, if need be, you can house thousands in it. But it is winter now, there aren't many new trainloads of prisoners, and the interior of the zone seems almost empty. The barracks interior still hasn't dried out; there's a white mist and ice on the walls. At the entrance is an enormous thousand-watt electric light, which dims to yellow or flares up dazzling white—the supply voltage varies.

By day the zone is asleep. At night the doors open and people appear in the lamplight. They are holding lists and they call our surnames in voices that are hoarse from the freezing cold. Those whose names are called do up all the buttons on their pea jackets, step over the threshold, and disappear, never to be seen again. Outside the escort guards are waiting for them, the truck engines are sputtering somewhere nearby, and the prisoners are taken to mines, to state farms, or to sections of road that need building....

I am also lying there, on the lower bunk not far from the door. It's cold down below, but I'm reluctant to climb higher up, where it's warmer, in case I'm thrown down by someone. The higher places are reserved for the strong, above all for the thieves. Anyway, I couldn't climb on the rungs that are nailed to a pillar. I'm better off down below. If there's any fight over a place on the lower bunks, I'll crawl under them.

I can't bite or fight, even though I've learned all the tricks of fighting in prison. The limitations of space—prison cell, railway cattle car, tight-packed barracks—have dictated the ways you can grab or bite someone, or break their bones. But I no longer have the strength even for that. All I can do is growl and swear. I have to fight for every day, for every hour of rest. Every fragment of my body tells me how I have to behave.

I was called out on my very first night, but I didn't do up my trousers, even though I had a piece of string, and I didn't button my jacket.

The door shut behind me and I was standing in the lobby.

A brigade consisting of twenty men, the usual load for one truck, was standing by the next door, through which a thick frozen fog was oozing.

The supervisor and the guard sergeant were counting and examining the men. On the right there was another man, wearing a padded jacket, quilted trousers, a hat with earflaps, and waving about his fur gauntlets. He was the man I needed to speak to. I'd been taken off to work so often that I knew the rules to perfection.

The man in the gauntlets was the mine representative who took on people and had the right to refuse to take someone on.

The supervisor shouted out my name at the top of his voice, just as loudly as he had shouted in the enormous barracks. But I was looking only at the man in the gauntlets.

"Don't take me, chief. I'm sick and I'm not going to work at the mine. I need to go to the hospital."

The representative hesitated. Back at the mine he'd been told to select only those fit for work, and that the mine didn't want anyone else. That was why he had come in person.

The representative took a good look at me. My ragged pea jacket, my grease-stained tunic that had lost its buttons, my dirty bare chest covered in sores where I had been scratching at the lice, the bits of rag I had bandaged my fingers with, the rope footwear (despite a temperature of minus sixty), my inflamed hungry eyes, my extreme emaciation: he knew very well what all that meant.

The representative took a red pencil and promptly crossed off my surname.

"Clear off, you swine," the zone works manager told me.

The door opened again and I was back in the Lesser Zone. My place had now been taken, but I dragged off to one side the man who had taken it. He growled with annoyance but soon calmed down.

And I fell into a sleep that was very much like oblivion, but I woke up at the first slight noise. Like a wild animal, a savage, I'd learned to wake up without any intermediate state.

I opened my eyes. A foot in a slipper, which was worn to an extreme but was at least not a prison-issue boot, was hanging down from the top bunk. A filthy adolescent thief suddenly appeared in front of me and spoke to someone up above in the languid tones of a pederast.

"Tell Valia," he said to this invisible person on the upper bunk, "that the artists have arrived."

A pause. Then a hoarse voice from above: "Valia wants to know who they are."

"The artists from the Culture Brigade. A magician and two singers. One of the singers is from Harbin."

The slipper started moving and then vanished. The voice above said, "Bring them in."

I moved over to the edge of the bunk. Three men were standing in the lamplight: two wearing pea jackets, one in a civilian "city" sheepskin jacket. Their faces all expressed veneration.

"Who's the man from Harbin?" a voice asked.

"That's me," replied a man in an old-fashioned fur-trimmed coat.

"Valia says you've got to sing something."

"In Russian? French? Italian? English?" the singer asked, stretching his neck upward.

"Valia said in Russian."

"How about the guards? Can I do it quietly?"

"Don't worry about them. Give it all you've got, like in Harbin."

The singer moved back and sang "The Toreador Song." Cold fog burst from his mouth with every breath.

There was a deep grumbling, and a voice from above: "Valia said, a song."

The singer turned pale and sang:

"Rustle, my golden, rustle, my golden
My golden taiga.
Oh, wind, my roads, one or the other
Into our unbounded land."

The voice from above said, "Valia said, good."

The singer sighed with relief. His forehead, damp with anxiety, was steaming, forming something like a halo around his head. The singer wiped the sweat with his palm and the halo disappeared.

"And now," said the voice, "take off that city jacket of yours. I'll swap it for this."

A torn quilted jacket was flung down from above.

The singer said nothing as he took off his city jacket and put on the quilted jacket.

"Clear off now," said the voice above. "Valia wants to sleep."

The Harbin singer and his friends melted away in the barracks mist.

I moved back deeper in, curled in a ball, stuck my hands up my jacket sleeves, and went to sleep.

It seemed as if I was immediately woken by a loud, expressive whisper.

"In 1937 we were in Ulaanbaatar and a friend and I were going down the street. It was lunchtime. There was a Chinese restaurant on the corner, so we went in. I looked at the menu: Chinese pelmeni.[10] I'm from Siberia, I know what Siberian or Urals pelmeni are. And now, suddenly, there are Chinese ones. We decided to have a hundred each. The Chinese cook laughed and said, 'Will be too much,' and his mouth stretched from ear to ear. 'All right, ten each, then?' Loud laughter: 'Will be too much.' 'All right, a couple each!' He shrugged, went to the kitchen, and brought out pelmeni, each one as big as your hand, all covered in hot fat. Well, the two of us managed half a pelmeni each and we left."

"And I...."

It took all my willpower not to listen but to go back to sleep again. I was woken by the smell of smoke. Somewhere up above, in the thieves' kingdom, people were smoking. Someone climbed down, a cigarette in his mouth, and woke everyone with the sweet, sharp smell of the smoke.

Then there was more whispering: "In our district committee in Severnoye, my God, my God, there were so many cigarette stubs. Auntie Polia, the cleaner, never stopped cursing. She was always sweeping them up. At the time I had no idea what a cigarette end, a fag end, a butt meant."

I fell asleep again.

Someone was shaking me by the leg. It was the supervisor. His inflamed eyes had a vicious expression. He made me stand by the door under the lamp's yellow light.

"Well," he said, "you refuse to go to the mine."

I said nothing.

"How about the state collective? A nice warm state collective, to hell with you, I wouldn't mind that myself."

"No."

"How about roadworks? You can make brooms. Making brooms, think about it."

"I know," I said. "One day you make brooms, the next you're pushing a wheelbarrow."

"Then what do you want?"

"To go to the hospital! I'm sick."

The supervisor wrote something in his book and left. Three days later a paramedic came to the Lesser Zone and summoned me. He took my temperature, examined the scars on my back left by carbuncles, and rubbed in some ointment or other.

1961

VASKA DENISOV, PIG RUSTLER

For traveling after dark he needed to borrow a pea jacket from a fellow prisoner. Vaska's jacket was too dirty and torn; he wouldn't have made it two meters down the settlement without any free worker grabbing hold of him.

People like Vaska are only allowed to move around the settlement under guard, lined up with other prisoners. The free inhabitants, military or civilian, don't like people of Vaska's sort walking the settlement streets on their own. The only time Vaska's sort doesn't attract suspicion is when they're carrying firewood on their shoulders: a small log, or as they say here "a stoveful of firewood."

One such stoveful of firewood was buried in the snow not far from the truck station, the sixth telegraph pole from the turning, in a drainage ditch. That had been done the previous evening, after work.

This time a driver he knew stopped his truck, and later, Vaska Denisov bent over the side and clambered down to the ground. He immediately found where he had buried the log; you could see even in the twilight that the bluish snow was a slightly darker color and a little bit compacted. Vaska leapt into the ditch and scraped away the snow with his feet. The log came into sight: gray, sharp-edged, like a big frozen fish. Vaska dragged it out onto the road, lifted it upright so as to knock the snow off; then he bent down, put his shoulder against it, and helped it up with his hands. The log swung sideways and settled on his shoulder. Vaska strode off to the settlement, changing shoulders every now and again. Because he was weak and emaciated, he warmed up quickly, but the warmth didn't last long. However much he felt the weight of the log, Vaska couldn't stay warm. The twilight was thickened by a white haze, and all the electric lights in the settlement came on.

Vaska gave a laugh, pleased he had worked things out correctly. The white mist would make it easy for him to reach his goal without being noticed. He passed an enormous broken larch, a silver stump covered in hoarfrost: so it was the next building.

Vaska threw the log down by the porch, brushed the snow off his felt boots with his gloves, and knocked at the door to the apartment. The door half opened, and Vaska was admitted. An elderly woman, her hair hanging loose, gave Vaska a frightened, questioning look. She was wearing a short fur jacket, unbuttoned, over her body.

"I've brought you a bit of firewood," said Vaska, who now found it hard to shape his frozen facial skin into a smile. "Can I see Ivan Petrovich?"

Ivan Petrovich, lifting up the door curtain, had already emerged.

"That's good," he said. "Where is it?"

"In the yard," said Vaska.

"Just wait there, we'll saw it up. I'll get my clothes on."

It took Ivan a long time to find his gloves. They went out onto the porch and, not having a saw bench, they held the log between their legs to raise it, and then sawed it up. The saw was blunt and needed resetting.

"Come back later," said Ivan, "and you can set the saw. Now here's the splitting ax. After that you can stack it, but bring it into the apartment, don't leave it in the corridor."

Vaska was dizzy with hunger, but he chopped up all the firewood and carried it into the apartment.

"Right, that's it," said the woman, coming out from behind the curtain. "Finished."

But Vaska stayed where he was, shuffling his feet by the door. Ivan reappeared.

"Listen," he said, "I don't have any bread at the moment, the soup has been taken to feed the piglets, so I haven't got anything to give you at the moment. Drop in next week. . . ."

Vaska said nothing, but still wouldn't leave.

Ivan poked about in his wallet. "Here's three rubles for you. Just for you, for that firewood, but as for tobacco—you know how it is! Tobacco's expensive these days."

Vaska stuffed the crumpled banknote under his shirt and left. Three rubles wouldn't buy him even a pinch of tobacco.

He was still standing on the porch, nauseous with hunger. The piglets had eaten Vaska's bread and soup. Vaska took out the green banknote and tore it into shreds. The scraps of paper were snatched by the wind and whirled over the shiny polished covering of snow for a long time. When the last shreds had vanished in the white mist, Vaska got off the porch. Staggering with exhaustion, he walked on, not homeward but toward the center of the settlement; he kept walking and walking toward single-story houses, then two-story and three-story palaces....

He went to the very first porch he saw and tugged at the door handle. The door squeaked and slowly opened. Vaska entered a dark corridor, dimly lit by a small lightbulb. He went past the doors leading to the apartments. At the end of the corridor was a pantry; Vaska put his weight to the door, opened it, and crossed the threshold. In the pantry were sacks of onions and perhaps salt. Vaska ripped open one of the sacks. It was pearl barley. Frustration spurred him on. He put his shoulder to the sack and moved it aside. Under the sacks there were frozen pig carcasses. Vaska yelled with fury. He didn't have the strength to tear even a piece of meat off a carcass. But farther down under the sacks there were frozen piglets, and Vaska had eyes only for them. He tore a frozen piglet off the mass, held it in his hands like a doll, and left for the exit. But people were now coming out of their rooms, and white mist was filling the corridor. Someone shouted "Stop!" and threw himself at Vaska's legs. Vaska leapt into the air, still hanging on to the piglet, and ran out of the building. The inhabitants rushed in pursuit. Someone was firing a gun at him, someone was roaring like a wild beast, but Vaska was blindly racing away. A few minutes later he realized that his legs were carrying him off to the only official building in the settlement that he knew of, the center for the vitamin expeditions: Vaska had worked for one of them collecting dwarf pine needles.

His pursuers were getting nearer. Vaska ran up the porch, pushed the janitor aside, and rushed down a corridor. A crowd of pursuers came crashing up behind him. Vaska dived into the office of the head of cultural work and then leapt through the next door, the Lenin room.

He was trapped. Only now did Vaska see that he had lost his hat. He was still holding the frozen piglet. Vaska put it on the floor, turned the massive bench on its end, and used it to block the door. He dragged the speaker's platform up to reinforce the bench. Someone shook the door, and then there was silence.

Vaska then sat down on the floor, took the piglet—raw and frozen —in both hands, and gnawed and gnawed at it....

By the time a squad of armed men had been called in and the doors had been opened and the barricade dismantled, Vaska had managed to eat half the piglet....

1958

SERAFIM

THE LETTER was lying on the black, soot-stained table, like a shard of ice. The doors of the iron barrel stove were wide open and the coals were as red as the bilberry jam that came in cans, so the ice shard should have melted, turned into a sliver, and vanished. But the ice wasn't melting, and Serafim was frightened when he realized that the shard of ice was in fact a letter, and a letter addressed to him, to Serafim. Serafim was afraid of letters, especially ones that had not been paid for and bore government stamps. He had grown up in the countryside where any telegram, received or sent (the term was "tapped off"), would be about some tragic event: funeral, death, serious illness. . . .

The letter was lying facedown on Serafim's table, not showing the address. Taking off his scarf, unbuttoning his sheepskin coat, which was stiff from the freezing cold, Serafim stared fixedly at the envelope.

He had come all these twelve thousand kilometers, over high mountains, over blue seas, wanting to forget and forgive everything, but the past would not leave him in peace. A letter had come from the other side of the mountains, a letter from the other world, which he had not yet forgotten. The letter had been brought by train, by airplane, by steamship, truck, and reindeer sled to the settlement where Serafim had hidden himself away.

And here was the letter, in the small chemical laboratory where Serafim worked as an assistant.

The laboratory's log walls, ceiling, and cupboards had turned black not from time but from the nonstop burning stoves, and the interior of the little building seemed like some ancient peasant cottage. The laboratory's square windows were like the mica windows in the times of Peter the Great. The mines were sparing of glass, and the window frames were more like little grids, so that the smallest piece of glass, even a broken bottle, could be used for glazing. A yellow lightbulb in a metal shade hung from the ceiling beam, like a suicide. Its light would go dim or flare up, since the power was provided by tractor engines, instead of proper generators.

Serafim took off his outdoor clothes and sat close to the stove; he still would not touch the envelope. He was alone in the laboratory.

A year ago, when what is called a "family breakdown" happened, he had refused to compromise. The reason he had left for the Far East was not because he was a romantic or a man of duty. The extra rubles didn't tempt him, either. But Serafim considered, in accordance with the views of thousands of philosophers and a dozen local people that he knew, that separation would extinguish love and that kilometers and years would deal with the unhappiness love had brought.

A year had passed, but Serafim's heart had not changed. He was secretly amazed by the firmness of his feelings. That may have been because he no longer spoke to women; there just weren't any around. There were the wives of the big bosses, a social class above a laboratory assistant like Serafim. Every one of these well-fed ladies considered herself to be a beauty. Such ladies lived in settlements where there were more entertainments, and the men who appreciated their charms were somewhat wealthier. In any case, there were a lot of military men in the settlements, so that no lady felt she was in danger of a sudden gang rape by chauffeurs or convicted gangsters, something that constantly happened on the road or in small remote places.

For this reason the geological prospectors and the camp chiefs kept their wives in the larger settlements, places where a manicurist could earn herself a fortune.

But there was another side to all this: "Physical frustration" turned out to be a far less terrible thing than Serafim had thought when he was younger. You just had to think less about it.

The mines were worked by prisoners, and in summer Serafim had frequently watched the gray ranks of prisoners crawling into the main gallery and, when the shift was over, crawling out again.

Two prisoners who were engineers worked in the laboratory; a guard would bring them and take them away. Serafim was afraid to talk to them. They asked only questions to do with work: the results of an analysis or a test sample. When Serafim answered, he averted his eyes. Serafim had been warned off any contact when he was still in Moscow, being hired for the Far North. He was told that there were dangerous state criminals there. So he was afraid to bring his fellow workers even a piece of sugar or white bread. In any case, he was being watched by the laboratory chief Persikov, a member of the Komsomol, who was disoriented by the extraordinarily high salary and senior position he got immediately after graduating. He considered his main duty to be the political supervision (possibly, all that was demanded of him) of his colleagues, whether prisoners or free hired workers.

Serafim was rather older than his manager, but he obediently did everything he was ordered to do, as far as the all-important vigilance and circumspection were concerned.

For a whole year, apart from what work demanded, he hadn't even spoken a dozen words to the engineer prisoners. And he had never said anything at all to the orderly or the night watchman.

Every six months his salary as a contractor for the Far North was raised by ten percent. After his second raise, Serafim asked to be allowed a trip to the nearest settlement, a mere hundred kilometers away, so as to buy something, go to the movies, have dinner in a proper refectory, "see a bit of skirt," and have a shave at the barber.

Serafim climbed into a truck cab, raised his collar, wrapped himself up as tight as he could, and the truck sped off.

About ninety minutes later, the truck stopped outside a small building. Serafim got out, screwing up his eyes as the spring sunlight was so dazzling.

Two men with rifles were standing in front of him.

"Papers!"

Serafim put his hand in his jacket pocket and suddenly felt a chill: he'd left his ID at home. Worse, he didn't have a single document to confirm his identity. All he had was an analysis of the air in the mine shaft. Serafim was ordered into the hut.

The truck drove off.

Serafim hadn't shaved, and his hair was cut very short. He did not inspire the officer with any confidence.

"Where have you escaped from?"

"I'm not an escapee—"

A sudden box on the ears knocked Serafim to the ground.

"Give me a proper answer!"

"I'm going to make a complaint!" Serafim yelled.

"Oh, you're going to complain, are you? Hey, Semion!"

Semion took careful aim and with a gymnast's practiced accuracy deftly kicked Serafim in the solar plexus.

Serafim groaned briefly and lost consciousness.

He vaguely recalled being dragged straight down the road somewhere and losing his hat. Then a lock clanged, a door screeched, and soldiers threw Serafim into a stinking shed. At least it was warm.

A few hours later Serafim got his breath back and realized he was in special confinement, like all captured escapees and repeat offenders who were the prisoners in the settlement.

"Got any tobacco?" someone asked in the darkness.

"No, I don't smoke," Serafim said apologetically.

"Damned fool. Has he got anything?"

"No, nothing. Do you think those gulls would leave anything over?"

It took Serafim a great effort to work out that he was the subject of this exchange, and that the gulls were what the guards were called because of their all-encompassing greed.

"I had money," said Serafim.

"'Had' is the word."

Serafim felt happier and fell silent. He'd taken two thousand rubles for the journey and, thank God, this money had been removed and was in the guards' safekeeping. Everything would soon be sorted out, and Serafim would be released and given back his money. He became quite cheerful.

"I'll have to give the guards a hundred," he thought, "for safekeeping." Though why should he? For beating him up?

In this confined, completely windowless hut, where the only source of fresh air was through the door and the cracks in the wall, which were packed with ice, about twenty men were lying on the bare earth.

Serafim felt hungry. He asked the man next to him when supper would be.

"What, are you really not a convict? You won't get food until tomorrow. We get what the authorities allow: a mug of water and three hundred grams of bread is our daily ration. And seven kilos of firewood."

Serafim wasn't summoned; he spent all of five days there. The first day he yelled and banged on the door, but he stopped complaining after the warden on duty managed to smash his rifle butt into Serafim's forehead. To replace the hat he had lost, Serafim was given a piece of crumpled material that he had trouble fixing onto his head.

On the sixth day he was summoned to the office, where the same officer who had taken him in was sitting; the laboratory manager was standing by the wall, extremely displeased both by Serafim's absence without leave and by the time he himself had wasted traveling here to confirm his assistant's identity.

Presniakov gasped quietly when he saw Serafim, who had a blue bruise under his right eye and a torn hat made of dirty, rough cloth, with no straps. Serafim was wearing a ripped quilted jacket with no buttons (he had been forced to leave his fur coat in the cell); he had grown a beard and he was filthy. His eyes were red and inflamed. He made a powerful impression.

"Well," said Presniakov, "it's him. Can we go?" And the laboratory manager dragged Serafim to the exit.

"How about my m-m-money?" bellowed Serafim, digging his heels in and pushing Presniakov away.

"What money?" the officer's voice rang out like a piece of metal.

"Two thousand rubles. I had them on me."

"You see," the officer roared with laughter, "what did I say? Drunk, with no hat...."

Serafim strode out and said nothing until they got back home.

After this incident Serafim began thinking about suicide. He even asked an imprisoned engineer why he, a prisoner, hadn't committed suicide.

The engineer was struck dumb. For a year Serafim hadn't said more than a couple of words. He stayed silent as he tried to understand Serafim.

"But how do you manage? How can you live?" Serafim whispered passionately.

"Yes, a prisoner's life is nothing but a series of humiliations, from the moment he opens his eyes to the beginning of a merciful sleep. Yes, all that's true, but you get used to anything. Even here some days are better than others, days of despair alternate with days of hope. A man doesn't live because he believes in something or hopes for something. He's kept going by the instinct for life, just like any other animal. And any tree or any stone could say the same. Watch out when you find yourself struggling for life within yourself, when your nerves are stretched to the maximum, inflamed; watch out you don't bare your heart or reveal your mind in any unusual way. When you focus what's left of your strength to fight something, beware of a blow struck from behind. You may not have the strength for a new struggle, a struggle you're not prepared for. Any suicide is the inevitable result of a double effect, of at least two causes. Do you understand me?"

Serafim did.

Now he was sitting in the soot-stained laboratory, remembering his trip with, for some reason, shame and a burdensome feeling of responsibility, which he was not going to get rid of. He didn't want to live.

The letter was still there on the black laboratory table, and he was too afraid to pick it up.

Serafim could imagine the lines and his wife's left-sloping handwriting. It was this handwriting that gave away her age, for in the 1920s schools stopped teaching children to slope their letters to the right and everyone wrote as they liked.

Serafim imagined the lines of the letter, as if he were reading it without opening the envelope. The letter could start "My dear" or "Dear Sima" or "Serafim." The last of these was what he feared.

Supposing he just tore the envelope into shreds and threw it into the glowing red stove fire, without reading it? Then the spell it was casting would vanish, and he would find it easier to breathe—at least until the next letter came. But he wasn't that much of a coward, after all! He wasn't a coward in any case: the engineer was the coward, and he'd show him. He'd show everybody.

Serafim picked up the letter and turned it over to read the address. He had guessed right: it was from his wife in Moscow. In his rage he tore the envelope open and, going up to the lamp, read the letter without sitting down. His wife was writing about a divorce.

Serafim threw the letter in the stove, where it flared up with a white flame edged with blue and then disappeared.

Serafim went into action, decisively and without haste. He took the keys from his pocket and opened the cupboard in Presniakov's room. He took a pinch of gray powder from a glass jar and tipped it into a measuring glass. Then he dipped a jug into the water bucket and poured the water into the measuring glass, mixed it with the powder, and drank it.

His throat burned, he felt slightly nauseous, but that was all.

He sat there, watching the pendulum clock, not recalling anything, for all of thirty minutes. There was no effect, apart from the burning in his throat. Then Serafim made haste. He opened the desk drawer and took out his penknife. He opened a vein on his left arm, and the dark blood poured onto the floor. Serafim felt a joyful weakness. But the blood was flowing more and more weakly.

Serafim realized that he wouldn't bleed to death, that he would survive, that his body's defenses were stronger than his desire to die. He now remembered what he had to do. Somehow, using one hand, he got his fur jacket on—otherwise it would be too cold outside—and bareheaded, his collar turned up, he ran to the stream that flowed a hundred yards from the laboratory. It was a mountain stream, with deep, narrow flood hollows that steamed like boiling water in the dark, frosty air.

Serafim remembered the first snowfall late last autumn, when the river was covered with a thin layer of ice. And a duck, lagging behind in its migration, weakened by struggling with the snow, fell onto the new ice. Serafim remembered a man, a prisoner, running out, spreading his arms in a ridiculous way as he tried to catch the duck. The duck ran over the ice to the flooded hollow, dived under the ice, and reemerged in the next hole in the ice. The man kept running, cursing the duck. He was as exhausted as the duck but kept running after it from one flood hollow to the next. Twice he fell over on the ice and, cursing foully, took some time to clamber up onto an ice floe.

There were a lot of people around, but nobody came to the aid of the duck or the hunter. The duck was his quarry, his booty, and help would have to be paid for with a share. Worn out, the man crawled over the ice, cursing the whole world. It ended with the duck diving and not reappearing. Presumably, it was so tired that it drowned.

Serafim remembered that he then tried to imagine the duck's death, as it flailed about in the water, beating its head against the ice and seeing the blue sky through the ice. Serafim was now running to the same spot on the river.

He leapt straight into the steaming, icy water, breaking the crust of blue ice with its dusting of snow. He was up to his waist in water, but the current was strong and Serafim was knocked off his feet. He threw off his jacket and put his arms together, forcing himself to dive under the ice.

People were now shouting and running up, however. They dragged boards and laid them over the flooded hollow. Someone managed to grab Serafim by the hair.

He was carried straight to the hospital, undressed, and warmed up. They tried to pour warm sweet tea down his throat. Serafim silently waved his head from side to side.

The hospital doctor came up to him with a syringe full of glucose solution but saw the torn vein and raised his eyes to meet Serafim's.

Serafim smiled. They injected the glucose into his right arm. The old doctor, who had been through it all, parted Serafim's teeth with a spatula, looked at his throat, and called for a surgeon.

An operation was carried out immediately, but even that was too late. Serafim's stomach walls and esophagus were eaten away by acid. His initial calculation had been perfectly correct.

1959

A DAY OFF

Two DARK blue squirrels with black faces and black tails were completely absorbed in what was happening behind the silver larches. I went up to the tree where they were in the branches and was close enough to touch the tree before they noticed me. Squirrel claws rustled over the bark, the blue bodies hurled themselves upward and fell silent only when they were somewhere very high. Then I saw what the squirrels had been examining.

A man was praying in the forest clearing. His fabric hat, with earflaps, lay in a heap by his feet, and hoarfrost had already turned his short-cropped hair white. His face had an extraordinary expression, the expression of someone remembering childhood or something equally precious. The man was crossing himself with wide, rapid sweeps of his arm; the three fingers of his right hand seemed to be pulling his head down. I didn't recognize him at first, his facial features seemed so very unfamiliar. It was the prisoner Zamiatin, a priest from the same barracks as me.

Still unaware of my presence, his lips, growing mute with cold, were quietly and solemnly uttering the words that I remembered from my childhood. It was the Slavonic form of the liturgy: Zamiatin was saying Mass in the silvery forest.

He slowly crossed himself, straightened up, and saw me. His face lost its solemnity and inner joy, and the usual folds on the bridge of his nose united his eyebrows in a frown. Zamiatin hated jokes. He picked up his hat, shook it, and put it on.

"You were saying Mass," I began.

"No, no," said Zamiatin, smiling at my ignorance. "How can I say

Mass? I don't have the wine and bread, I don't have my priest's stole. This is a prison towel."

And he adjusted the dirty cellulose rag hanging around his neck. It did in fact look like a priest's stole. The frost had covered the towel with crystal-like snow, and the crystals shone in the sun with all the colors of the rainbow, just like embroidered ecclesiastic cloth.

"In any case, I feel ashamed: I don't know where east is. Nowadays the sun rises for two hours and sets behind the same mountain as it rises from. So where is the east?"

"Is it so important to face east?"

"Of course it isn't. Don't go. But I'm telling you I'm not saying Mass, and I can't. I'm simply reciting, remembering the Sunday service. And I don't even know if today is Sunday."

"It's Thursday," I said. "The supervisor said so this morning."

"You see, then: Thursday. No, no, I'm not saying Mass. I just feel better doing this. And I don't feel so hungry," said Zamiatin with a smile.

I knew that everyone here had his own "final thing," the most important thing that helped him to stay alive, to hang on to life, which we were so insistently and stubbornly being deprived of here. If Zamiatin's "final thing" was the liturgy of John Chrysostom, then my final salvation was poetry: favorite verses by other poets, which by some miracle I could remember here, a place where everything else was forgotten, discarded, expelled from the memory. This was the only thing that had not yet been crushed by fatigue, sub-zero temperatures, starvation, and endless humiliations.

The sun set. The hasty mist of an early evening in winter filled the space between the trees. I wended my way back to our barracks, a low, long, narrow hut with small windows—more like a miniature stable. Grabbing the heavy, ice-covered door with both hands, I heard a rustle in the next hut: that was the toolshed, a store where the mine-workers' saws, spades, axes, crowbars, and pickaxes were kept.

On our days off the toolshed was kept locked, but there was no lock now. I went into the shed and the heavy door nearly slammed in my face. There were so many cracks in the storehouse that your eyes quickly got used to the semidarkness.

Two gangsters were tickling a big four-month-old German shepherd puppy; the puppy was lying on its back, squealing and waving all four paws. The older gangster was holding the puppy by the collar. They weren't bothered by my entry; we worked in the same brigade.

"Hey you, who's outside?"

"There's nobody there," I replied.

"All right, come on, then," said the older one.

"Hang on, let me play with him a bit longer," answered the younger one. "Look at him rolling about." He felt the puppy's warm flank near its heart and tickled it.

The trusting puppy squealed and licked the human hand.

"So you're licking...you won't be licking any more. Senia—"

Holding the puppy down with his left hand on its collar, Senia pulled out an ax from behind him and in one fast, short stroke brought it down on the dog's head. The puppy jerked, and blood splashed all over the icy floor of the toolshed.

"Hold him tighter!" Senia yelled, as he raised the ax again.

"No need to hold him, it's not a rooster," said the younger one.

"Take the skin off while it's still warm," Senia instructed him, "and bury it in the snow."

That evening nobody could sleep because of the smell of a meat soup, until the criminals had eaten it all. But there weren't enough criminals in our barracks to eat the whole puppy. There was still some meat left in the pot.

With a wave of his finger Senia invited me: "Take some."

"I don't want any," I said.

"All right, then." Senia surveyed the bunks. "We'll let the priest have it. Hey, Father, have a piece of our mutton. But wash the pot after you."

Zamiatin emerged from the darkness into the yellow light of the smoky kerosene lamp. He took the pot and vanished. Five minutes later he returned with the pot washed.

"That fast?" Senia asked, intrigued. "You get it down quick...like a seagull. Father, that wasn't mutton. It was dog meat. The dog that used to go and see you, the one called North."

Zamiatin looked at Senia but said nothing. Then he turned and left.

I left too. Zamiatin was standing in the snow outside the door. He was vomiting. In the moonlight his face looked leaden. Sticky, clammy saliva hung from his blue lips. He wiped his lips on his sleeve and looked angrily at me.

"What bastards," I said.

"Of course they are," said Zamiatin. "But the meat tasted good. As good as mutton."

1959

DOMINOES

THE MALE nurses lifted me off the platform of the metrical scales. Their powerful, cold hands wouldn't let me touch the floor.

"How much," shouted the doctor, dipping his pen with a bang into his non-spill inkwell.

"Forty-eight."

I was put on a stretcher. I was a hundred and eighty centimeters tall (almost six feet), my normal weight was eighty kilos. My bones, 42 percent of my gross weight, weighed thirty-two kilos. On that icy evening all I had left—skin, flesh, guts, brains—was sixteen kilos, the same as a bushel of wheat. At the time I couldn't work all that out, but I vaguely understood that it was being calculated by the doctor who was frowning at me.

The doctor unlocked his desk drawer, took out a box, from which he removed a thermometer, and then bent over me and cautiously put the thermometer under my left armpit. Then one of the male nurses pressed my left arm to my chest, while the other one grabbed my right wrist with both hands. It was later that I understood the reasons for these practiced, well-rehearsed movements: there was only one thermometer for a hospital of about a hundred beds. The glass tube had wholly new value and importance; it was looked after like a precious heirloom. Only the seriously ill or wholly new patients were allowed to have their temperature taken with this thermometer. Those who were recuperating had their temperatures recorded according to their pulse; only in doubtful cases was the desk drawer unlocked.

The pendulum clock ticked off ten minutes; the doctor carefully removed the thermometer, and the hospital workers relaxed their grip.

"Thirty-four point three," said the doctor. "Can you answer questions?"

I signaled with my eyes that I could. I was saving my strength. My words came out slowly and with difficulty, as if I were translating from a foreign language. I'd forgotten everything. I had gotten out of the habit of remembering. They finished recording the history of the disease; the nurses had no trouble lifting the stretcher on which I lay supine.

"Ward six," said the doctor. "As close as you can to the stove."

I was put on a trestle bed by the stove. The mattresses were stuffed with dwarf pine branches, and the pine needles had dried up and fallen off, so that the curling bare twigs under the dirty striped fabric had something menacing about them. Hay dust puffed out of the tightly stuffed dirty pillow. The thin, worn-out cloth blanket, with the word "feet" stitched in gray at one end, hid me from the rest of the world. My arm and leg muscles, which looked like pieces of rope, ached, and my frostbitten fingers and toes throbbed. But the fatigue was greater than the pain. I rolled up in a ball, grabbed my feet with my hands, and pressed my filthy knees, whose skin was as coarsely grained as crocodile hide, against my chin—then I fell asleep.

Many hours later I woke up. My breakfasts, lunches, and dinners were on the floor next to my bed. I stretched out a hand, grabbed the nearest tin bowl, and started eating nonstop, taking a bite from time to time of my bread ration, which was also lying there. The patients on the other trestle beds looked at me as I swallowed my food. They didn't ask who I was or where I was from; my crocodile hide told them all they needed to know. They would not have even looked at me had it not been for the fact—which I knew from my own experience—that you can't take your eyes off someone else who is eating.

I devoured all the food that had been left. The warmth, the delightful heaviness in my stomach, and more sleep—but not much, because a male nurse had come to fetch me. I threw the ward's only "walking" gown—it was filthy, covered in cigarette burns, heavy with the sweat it had absorbed from many hundreds of patients—over my shoulders, shoved my feet into enormous slippers, and, moving my legs slowly to keep the slippers from falling off, staggered after the nurse into the treatment room.

The same young doctor was standing by the window, looking at the street through the glass, which a buildup of ice had made lacy and shaggy. A rag hung from the corner of the windowsill; water was dripping off it, each drip falling into a tin dinner bowl that had been placed beneath it. The iron stove was humming. I stopped, holding on to the nurse with both hands.

"Let's get on with it," said the doctor.

"I'm cold," I replied quietly. The food I had just eaten was no longer warming me.

"Sit down by the stove. Where did you work before you were in prison?"

I parted my lips and moved my jaw. It was supposed to be a smile. The doctor understood and responded with a smile.

"My name's Andrei Mikhailovich," he said. "You don't need any treatment."

I had a sinking feeling in the pit of my stomach.

"Really," the doctor repeated loudly, "you don't need any treatment. You need to be fed and washed. You need to stay in bed, stay in bed and eat. True, we don't have any feather mattresses. Well, you can still manage. Keep turning over and you won't get any bedsores. Stay in bed for two months or so. And then it will be spring."

The doctor laughed. I felt joyful, of course. What more could I want! Two whole months! But I didn't have the strength to express my joy. I held on to the stool and said nothing. The doctor wrote down something in my notes.

"Off you go."

I went back to the ward. I slept and ate. After a week I could walk unsteadily around the ward, down the corridor, and to other wards. I sought out people who were chewing and swallowing: I looked them in the mouth, for the more I rested, the more acutely hungry I became.

Like in the camp, no one in the hospital was allowed to have spoons. From the start, in the pretrial prison, we had gotten used to doing without knives and forks. We had long ago learned the trick of eating "over the edge," without a spoon—the soup and the porridge were never so thick that you needed a spoon. A finger, a crust of bread would clean the bottom of the pot or bowl, however deep it was.

So I went around searching for people who were chewing. This was an urge that could not be resisted, and Andrei the doctor knew all about it.

At night a male nurse would wake me up. The ward echoed with the usual hospital night noises: rasping, snoring, groans, delirium, coughing —all merged into a peculiar symphony of sounds, if such sounds can be composed into a symphony. But you can take me blindfolded into anywhere that sounds like that, and I'll recognize the camp hospital.

There was a lamp on the windowsill: a tin saucerful of some oil, but not cod-liver oil, with a smoky wick made from a twist of cotton wool. It probably wasn't very late. Our nights began with the end of the work siren, at nine in the evening, and we managed to get to sleep straight-away, once our feet began to warm up.

"Andrei Mikhailovich wants to see you," said the male nurse. "Kozlik here will take you."

The patient called Kozlik was standing in front of me.

I went to the tin sink, washed, returned to the ward, and dried my hands and face on the pillowcase. There was one enormous towel made of a mattress cover, which served a ward of thirty men and was issued only in the morning. Andrei Mikhailovich lived on the premises of the very small wards, the sort that patients were put in after operations. I knocked on the door and entered.

On the desk there were books moved to one side, books that I hadn't held in my hands for so many years. Books were alien, hostile, superfluous. Next to the books was a teapot, two tin mugs, and a bowl full of some sort of porridge.

"Would you like a game of dominoes?" asked Andrei Mikhailovich, giving me a friendly look. "If you have the time...."

I hate dominoes. This is the stupidest, most nonsensical, and boring game there is. Even bingo is more interesting, not to mention cards, any card game. The best would be a game of chess, or at least checkers: I cast a sidelong glance at the cupboard to see if there might be a chess-board, but there wasn't. But I couldn't offend Andrei Mikhailovich by refusing. I had to entertain him, to repay one good deed with another. Never in my life had I played dominoes, but I was sure that it didn't require much intelligence to master the game.

In any case, there were two mugs of tea and a bowl of porridge on the table. And it was warm.

"Let's drink the tea," said Andrei Mikhailovich. "Here's the sugar. Make yourself at home. Eat this porridge and talk about whatever you want to talk about. Not that you can do both things at the same time."

I ate the porridge and the bread, and drank three mugfuls of tea with sugar. I hadn't seen sugar for several years. I warmed myself up, and Andrei Mikhailovich shuffled the domino tiles.

I knew that whoever had a double six began the game: Andrei Mikhailovich threw a double six. After that the players take turns placing tiles according to the number of spots. That was all there was to it, and I boldly got into the spirit of the game, sweating all the time, and burping from all that I had eaten and drunk.

We were playing on Andrei Mikhailovich's bed. It was a pleasure to look at the feather pillow in its dazzling white pillowcase, to see someone else squeezing it with his hand.

"Our game," I said, "is missing its most enchanting side. Dominoes players should bang their tiles on to the table with a wave of the arm." I really wasn't joking. That was what seemed to me to be the key element in a game of dominoes.

"Let's move to the desk," said Andrei Mikhailovich obligingly.

"No, there's no need, I was just recalling all the nuances of this game."

The game took some time. We were telling each other our life stories. Andrei Mikhailovich was a doctor and did not work with the gangs at the mine pit face. He only saw the consequences of that work, in the human refuse, remains, rejects, which the mine dumped in the hospital and the morgue. I too was human slag from the mines.

"Well, so you've won," said Andrei Mikhailovich. "Congratulations, and here is your prize." He took a plastic cigarette case from a bedside table. "When did you last have a cigarette?"

I tore off a piece of newspaper and rolled myself a cigarette. There's nothing better for homegrown tobacco than newsprint. The traces of printer's ink don't spoil the aromas of the tobacco, in fact they enhance it superbly. I lit up the strip of paper from the smoldering embers in the stove, greedily inhaling the nauseously sweet fumes as I smoked the cigarette.

Tobacco was in very short supply for us, and I should have given up smoking long ago, since the conditions were ideal, but I have never given up. It was a frightening thought that I might of my own free will deprive myself of this, the prisoner's sole major pleasure.

"Good night," said Andrei Mikhailovich with a smile. "I was getting ready for bed, but I wanted a game so badly. Thank you."

I left his room for the dark corridor. Someone was by the wall, blocking my path. I recognized Kozlik by his silhouette.

"What's up? Why are you here?"

"For a smoke. I'd like a smoke. Did he give you any?"

I felt ashamed of my greed, ashamed that I hadn't thought of Kozlik or anyone else in the ward, and hadn't brought them a cigarette stub, a crust of bread, or a handful of porridge.

And Kozlik had been waiting for several hours in the dark corridor.

A few more years passed, the war ended, General Vlasov's men[11] replaced us in the gold mines, and I got sent to the Lesser Zone in the transit barracks of the Western Administration. Enormous barracks with multistory bunks housed five to six hundred men each. People were sent from here to the western mines.

There was no sleep at night in this zone. New trainloads arrived, and in the "Lenin corner" of the zone, which was carpeted with the gangsters' dirty quilted blankets, there were concerts every night. What concerts! There were famous singers and storytellers, not just from the camp propaganda brigades but from higher up. There was a baritone from Harbin, who imitated Leshchenko and Vertinsky; there was Vadim Kozin, who imitated himself; and a great number of others who sang nonstop for the gangsters, performing the best of their repertoire. Next to me slept a tank regiment lieutenant, Svechnikov, a tender, rosy-cheeked youth who had been condemned by a military tribunal for offenses committed as a serving officer. Here he was also being investigated: while working in the mine, he was caught eating human flesh from the morgue, after hacking it off ("not the fatty bits, of course," as he explained perfectly calmly).

In a transit barracks you can't choose your neighbors, and no doubt there are worse crimes than dining on a human corpse.

Very, very rarely did a paramedic enter the Lesser Zone to examine those who were running a temperature. The paramedic refused even to look at the carbuncles that were all over my body. My neighbor Svechnikov knew the paramedic from the hospital morgue and talked to him as if they were good friends. Suddenly the paramedic mentioned Andrei Mikhailovich.

I begged the paramedic to take a note to Andrei Mikhailovich; the hospital where he was working was about a kilometer from the Lesser Zone.

My plans changed. Now I had to stay in the zone until I had an answer from Andrei Mikhailovich.

The works manager had already made a note of me and listed me for each party of prisoners leaving the transit barracks. But the mine representatives who took on these parties were just as insistent on crossing my name off the lists. They suspected something amiss, and my appearance was enough for that.

"Why don't you want to go?"

"I'm sick. I need to go to the hospital."

"The hospital's no place for you. We'll send you to do roadworks tomorrow. Are you willing to make brooms?"

"I won't go to roadworks. I won't make brooms."

Day after day passed, and one party after another left. There wasn't sight or sound of the paramedic or of Andrei Mikhailovich.

Toward the end of the week I managed to get a medical examination at the outpatients' clinic about a hundred yards from the Lesser Zone. My fist was clutching a second note for Andrei Mikhailovich. The clerk in the clinic took it from me and promised to give it to Andrei Mikhailovich the next morning.

While I was being examined, I asked the chief of the clinic about Andrei Mikhailovich.

"Yes, there is a doctor of that name among the prisoners. There's no reason why you should see him."

"I know him personally."

"Lots of people do."

The paramedic who'd taken the note from me in the Lesser Zone was standing there. I quietly asked him, "Where's the note?"

"I've never even set eyes on any note."

If I didn't find out anything about Andrei Mikhailovich by the day after tomorrow, I was going to leave ... to do roadworks, or to a village collective, to a mine, to hell and beyond....

The evening of the following day, after the roll call, I was summoned to see the dentist. I went, thinking there had been some mistake, but in the corridor I saw Andrei Mikhailovich's familiar black fur jacket. We hugged each other.

Twenty-four hours later I was summoned again. Four patients were taken from the camp and driven to the hospital. Two were lying in an embrace on a low sled, two followed the sled on foot. Andrei Mikhailovich had not had time to tell me what my diagnosis was: I didn't know what was the matter with me. My illness—dystrophy, pellagra, scurvy—hadn't developed enough to make it necessary to admit me to the camp hospital. I knew I was going to a surgical ward. That was where Andrei Mikhailovich worked, but what illness could I present that required surgery? I didn't have a hernia. Osteomyelitis of four fingers following frostbite was agonizing, but it wasn't enough to be hospitalized. I was sure that Andrei Mikhailovich would find a way of telling me in advance, that we would meet somewhere.

The horses were approaching the hospital, and the male nurses pulled out the stretcher patients, while I and my new partner sat on a bench, took our clothes off, and began washing. Each of us was given a large bowl of warm water.

An elderly doctor in white overalls came into the washroom and looked over the top of his glasses at us.

"What are you here for?" he asked my partner, putting a finger on his shoulder.

The man turned around and, with a grimace, pointed to an enormous inguinal hernia.

I waited to be asked the same and decided to complain of stomach pains.

But the elderly doctor gave me an indifferent look and left.

"Who was that?" I asked.

"Nikolai Ivanovich, the main surgeon here. He's in charge of the department."

A male nurse issued our linen.

"Where do I put you?" That was addressed to me.

"How the hell do I know!" I said, letting my feelings rip: I was no longer afraid.

"Well, what is actually wrong with you, tell me!"

"My belly aches."

"Appendicitis, I expect," said the nurse, who was an old hand.

I saw Andrei Mikhailovich only the next day. He had warned the chief surgeon that I was being hospitalized with semi-acute appendicitis. That evening Andrei Mikhailovich told me his sorry story.

He had gone down with tuberculosis. The X-rays and the laboratory analyses were grim. The district hospital put in a request for the prisoner Andrei Mikhailovich to be transferred to the mainland for treatment. He was on the ship home when someone informed Cherpakov, the head of the medical department, that Andrei Mikhailovich's illness was false, imaginary, "fake" to use the camp terminology.

It may well be that nobody informed on him: Major Cherpakov was just a worthy son of his age of suspicions, mistrust, and vigilance.

The major was furious and arranged to have Andrei Mikhailovich removed from the ship and sent to the remotest place possible, far from the area where we had met. Andrei Mikhailovich had already traveled a thousand kilometers in sub-zero temperatures. In the remote region, however, it turned out that there wasn't a single doctor capable of performing an artificial pneumothorax. Andrei Mikhailovich had already had several insufflations, but the vicious major had declared pneumothorax to be a deceitful trick.

Andrei Mikhailovich was getting worse and worse, and he was at death's door when he managed to persuade Cherpakov to have him sent to the Western Region, the nearest place where there were doctors capable of performing a pneumothorax.

Now Andrei Mikhailovich was somewhat better. He'd had several successful insufflations and had begun to work as a registrar in the surgical department.

After I got some of my strength back, I worked as a nurse for Andrei Mikhailovich. On his insistent recommendation, I left to take a paramedical course, graduated, and worked as a paramedic before returning to the mainland. It is to Andrei Mikhailovich that I owe my life. He died long ago: tuberculosis and Major Cherpakov did their job.

In the hospital where we worked together, we lived in harmony. Our sentences ended in the same year, and that somehow linked our fates and brought us closer to each other.

Once, when we'd finished the evening chores, the male nurses sat in a corner to play dominoes and the tiles were slammed down.

"A stupid game," said Andrei Mikhailovich, his eyes directed at the nurses, and he frowned every time the tiles were banged down.

"I've only ever played dominoes once," I said. "With you, at your invitation. I even won."

"Any fool can win," said Andrei Mikhailovich. "That was the first time for me, too. I wanted to give you some pleasure."

1959

HERCULES

THE LAST guest to arrive for the silver wedding anniversary of Sudarin, the head of the hospital, was late. It was the doctor, Andrei Ivanovich Dudar. He had in his hand a willow basket wrapped in muslin and decorated with paper flowers. Glasses clinked and festive drunken voices roared out as Andrei Ivanovich offered the basket to his host, the hero of the celebration: Sudarin took the basket and weighed it up.

"What is it?"

"Look and you'll see."

The muslin was removed. Inside the basket was a large red-feathered cockerel. It calmly turned its head as it inspected the flushed faces of the noisy, drunken guests.

"Oh, Andrei, what a good idea!" twittered Sudarin's wife, as she stroked the cockerel.

"A wonderful present," babbled the women doctors. "And how handsome he is. That's your favorite pet, Andrei Ivanovich, isn't it?"

Sudarin was moved; he squeezed Dudar's arm.

"Show me, show me," a thin hoarse voice suddenly said.

At the place of honor, at the head of the table, on his host's right, sat a distinguished guest from far away. This guest was Cherpakov, the head of the medical administration, an old friend of Sudarin's; he had driven that morning in his personal Pobeda from the provincial capital, some six hundred kilometers away, just to come to his friend's silver anniversary.

The guest from far away was shown the cockerel in its basket. He looked at it with his lackluster eyes.

"Yes, a nice little cockerel. Yours, is he?" the honored guest's finger pointed at Andrei Ivanovich.

"It's mine now," announced Sudarin with a smile.

The guest of honor was noticeably younger than the bald, gray-haired neurologists, surgeons, general practitioners, and tuberculosis doctors around him. He was about forty. He had an unhealthy, yellow, swollen face and tiny gray eyes, and he wore an immaculate tunic with the silver epaulettes of a colonel in the medical services. The tunic was clearly too small for the colonel and had obviously been made when his belly had not yet become prominent and his neck did not hang over his stiff collar. The guest of honor's face had a bored expression, but each glass of pure spirit (being a Russian and, what's more, a northerner, the guest of honor touched no other inebriating liquid) made his face livelier, and he looked more and more frequently at the medical ladies around him and intervened more and more often in the conversations, which invariably died down whenever his cracked tenor voice made itself heard.

When the party had reached the appropriate level, the guest of honor arose from the table, jolting as he did so a lady doctor who hadn't moved back in time; then he rolled up his sleeves and started lifting the heavy larch-wood chairs, grabbing a front leg with one hand, alternating left and right, showing off his harmonious physical development.

None of the delighted guests could lift chairs as many times as the guest of honor did. After the chairs, he moved to the armchairs and was equally successful. While other guests were lifting chairs, the guest of honor's mighty hand was taking hold of the young lady doctors. They were pink-cheeked with happiness as he made them feel his flexing biceps, a task the lady doctors carried out with obvious delight.

After these exercises the guest of honor, inexhaustibly inventive, decided to show off a national Russian specialty: arm wrestling. He bent his arm at the elbow, put it on the table, and made his opponent do the same. The gray-haired, bald neurologists and general practitioners were unable to put up any serious resistance; only the chief surgeon managed to hold out a little longer than the others.

The guest of honor kept looking for new tests of his Russian might. Apologizing to the ladies, he took off his tunic, which his hostess immediately picked up and hung over the back of a chair. The sudden animation on the guest of honor's face made it obvious that he'd had an idea.

"I can take a sheep, a sheep, you realize, and pull its head back. Crack, and it's dead," said the guest of honor, literally buttonholing Andrei Ivanovich. "As for that . . . present of yours, I can tear the creature's head off," he said, relishing the impression he had made. "Where's the cockerel?"

The cockerel was extracted from the household chicken run where the prudent mistress of the house had already released it. In the north all the bosses kept (in winter, of course) a few dozen chickens at home; whether the boss was a bachelor or married, chickens were always an extremely profitable item.

The guest of honor stepped into the middle of the room with the cockerel in his hands. Andrei Ivanovich's pet lay there just as calmly, both legs folded, and its head hanging to one side. In his lonely apartment Andrei Ivanovich had carried it around like this for two years or so.

Mighty fingers grabbed the cockerel by the neck. The dirty thick skin of the guest of honor's face flushed red. Using the movement that blacksmiths use to straighten a horseshoe, the guest of honor ripped the head off the cockerel. The cockerel's blood splashed his neatly ironed trousers and his silk shirt.

The ladies took out their perfumed handkerchiefs and competed in a rush to wipe the guest of honor's trousers.

"Some eau de cologne."

"Spirits of ammonia."

"Rinse it in cold water."

"What strength, what strength! That really is Russian. Crack, and it's dead," said Sudarin, the host.

The guest of honor was hauled off to the bathroom to clean himself up.

"We'll have dancing in the hall," said the host, as he fussed about. "Well, a real Hercules."

They wound the phonograph. The needle started hissing.

When Andrei Ivanovich got up from the table to take part in the dancing (the guest of honor liked to see everyone dance), his foot hit something soft. He bent down and saw the dead cockerel's body, the headless corpse of his pet.

Andrei Ivanovich straightened up, looked around, and kicked the dead bird farther under the table. Then he hurriedly left the room. The guest of honor didn't like people being late for dancing.

1956

SHOCK THERAPY

EVEN IN that distant blissful period when Merzliakov worked as a stableman and was able, by using a homemade grinder cobbled together from an old tin can with holes in the bottom to make a sieve, to make flaked grain fit for human consumption from the oats that were provided for the horses, and thus cook porridge, a bitter hot gruel that suppressed and reduced his hunger, he was pondering one simple question. The big draft horses brought in from the mainland were given a government oats ration every day which was twice what the squat, shaggy Yakut ponies got, although the draft horses pulled no more than the ponies. Thunder, the monstrous Percheron, had as much oats poured into his trough as five Yakut ponies could eat. This was justifiable, it was done everywhere, and that was not what tormented Merzliakov. He couldn't understand why the human rations in the camp, the mysterious prescription of proteins, fats, vitamins, and calories destined to be swallowed by prisoners and called the "pot sheet," were drawn up with absolutely no consideration of people's live weight. If they were to be treated as beasts of burden, then questions of rations should be dealt with more logically, instead of observing some terrible mathematical average or bureaucratic whim. At best this terrible average would benefit only the lightweights, and in fact those who weighed less took longer than the others to become goners. Merzliakov had a constitution like that of Thunder, the Percheron, and that pathetic breakfast of three spoonfuls of porridge only increased the nagging pain in his stomach. Yet a workman in a brigade could get almost nothing in addition to his ration. The most precious items—butter, sugar, and meat—were never added to the pot in the quantity prescribed by the pot sheet. There were other things that Merzliakov had seen: tall people were the first to die. Being inured to heavy labor made absolutely no difference. An intellectual weakling still held out longer than a giant from Kaluga, where tilling the earth was in the blood, if they received the same food, in accordance with camp rations. There was not much advantage in increasing your ration by exceeding the production norm by a percentage either, because the basic prescription was unchanged and still did not match the needs of tall men. If you wanted to eat better, you had to work better; but if you wanted to work better, you had to eat better. Everywhere, Estonians, Latvians, Lithuanians were the first to die. They were the first to become goners, which always led the doctors to remark that the Baltic peoples were weaker than the Russians. True, the living standards of the Latvians and Estonians were far higher than those of the camps, or even of the Russian peasant, so they found things harder. But the main cause lay elsewhere: they weren't less tough, they were just taller.

About eighteen months earlier, after an attack of scurvy, which quickly knocked out anyone new to the camps, Merzliakov was given a job as a temporary nurse in the tiny local hospital. He saw there that medicines were dispensed in doses according to the patient's weight. New medicines were tested on rabbits, mice, or guinea pigs, and human doses were determined by calculating body weight. Children's doses were less than adult doses.

But the camp rations were not calculated according to the weight of the human body. This was, then, the wrong answer to the question that astonished and worried Merzliakov. But before he became hopelessly weak, he managed by some miracle to get a stableman's job, where he could steal the horses' oats and stuff his own stomach with them. Merzliakov was already thinking he could get through the winter and then face whatever was coming. But things worked out differently. The stable manager was dismissed for drunkenness, and a senior stableman was promoted. He was one of the men who had shown Merzliakov how to use a tin can to make porridge oats. The senior stableman had himself been something of an oats thief and knew perfectly well how it was done. He now felt the need to ingratiate himself with his bosses, and he no longer needed any oat flakes. He therefore personally sought out and destroyed all the homemade grinders. People started roasting, boiling, and eating oats, husk and all, treating their stomachs as if they were horses. The new manager wrote a report to the authorities. Several stablemen, including Merzliakov, were put in solitary confinement for stealing oats and then sent from the stables back to where they had come from: ordinary manual labor.

Doing manual labor, Merzliakov soon realized that death was imminent. He staggered under the weight of the beams he had to drag around. The foreman took a dislike to the idle bruiser ("bruiser" is what they called anyone tall in the camp) and always put Merzliakov "under the butt," that is, made him carry the heavy butt end of the beam. Once Merzliakov fell down and could not at first get up from the snow-covered ground; he suddenly decided to refuse to carry this damned beam. It was late, dark, and the guards were in a hurry to get to their indoctrination class, while the workmen wanted to reach the barracks and food as fast as they could; that evening the foreman was late for a card-game duel. Merzliakov was blamed for all the delay. So he was punished. First, he was beaten up by his workmates, then by the foreman and the guards. The beam lay abandoned in the snow and, instead of the beam, it was Merzliakov that was carried to the camp. He was let off work and lay on the bunk. The small of his back hurt. The paramedic rubbed him down with tallow—the medical center hadn't had any proper ointments for ages. Merzliakov lay there, bent half double, all the time complaining of pain in the small of his back. The pain had gone long ago, his broken rib had quickly mended, but Merzliakov was determined, using any lie he could, to put off being declared fit for work. They didn't declare him fit. One day they put his outdoor clothes on, laid him on a stretcher, and loaded him into the cab of a truck to take him, with other patients, to the district hospital. There was no X-ray machine there. Some serious thinking had to be done about everything, and Merzliakov thought. He stayed there for some months, still bent half double; he was then transferred to the central hospital where, of course, there was an X-ray machine, and where Merzliakov was put in the surgical section, in the ward for traumatic illnesses (the patients, unaware of the irony in the pun, called these illnesses "dramatic").

"And this man, too," said the surgeon, pointing to Merzliakov's notes, "we'll hand over to you, Piotr Ivanovich. He doesn't need treatment in the surgical section."

"But you've written a diagnosis of ankylosis due to spinal trauma. Why should I have him?"

"Well, of course there is ankylosis. What else can I put down? Worse than that can happen after a beating. I had a case at the Gray mine, where the foreman beat up a good worker—"

"Seriozha, I haven't got time to listen to your cases. I'm asking why you're transferring him."

"But I've written 'To be examined with a view to documentation.' Poke him with needles, let's document him and get him on a ship. Then he can be a free man."

"But you've taken X-rays, haven't you? We shouldn't need needles to detect any abnormalities."

"I have. Have a look, if you'd care to," and the surgeon placed a dark film negative on the muslin screen. "This picture makes no sense at all. Until we get proper lighting, proper voltage, our X-ray photographers will go on giving us this fuzz."

"It really is fuzzy," said Piotr Ivanovich. "All right, so be it." And he signed his name on the notes, agreeing to accept Merzliakov's transfer.

The surgical section was noisy, chaotic, overcrowded with cases of frostbite, dislocated limbs, fractures, burns—the northern mines were no joke—and some of the patients lay on the ward and corridor floors; just one young, infinitely tired surgeon and four paramedics worked there, none of them sleeping for more than three or four hours a night. Nobody had the time to give Merzliakov proper attention. In the neurology section, however, where Merzliakov had been so suddenly transferred, he realized that a really close examination would begin.

All his desperate prisoner's willpower had long been focused on one thing: to not unbend. And he didn't. His body so very much wanted to straighten out, if only for a second. But he recalled the mine, the piercing breath of the cold air, the slippery frozen stones of the gold-mine pit face, which shone from the sub-zero temperatures; the little bowl of soup, his dinner, which he devoured in one gulp, not needing any spoon; the rifle butts of the guards and the boots of the foremen— then he found the strength to stay doubled up. In any case, it was now easier than it had been in the first weeks. He didn't sleep much, since he was afraid of unbending while he slept. He knew that the duty nurses had long ago been ordered to watch him and catch him faking. And if he was caught—Merzliakov knew this, too—he would imme-diately be send to the punishment mines, and what would a punishment mine be like, if the ordinary one left Merzliakov with such terrible memories?

The day after he was transferred, Merzliakov was taken to see the doctor. The chief of the section asked him briefly about the early stages of the illness and nodded in sympathy. The doctor told him, as if by the way, that even healthy muscles could get used to being in an unnatural position after many months, and that a man can turn himself into an invalid. Then Piotr Ivanovich started examining his patient. As the doctor inserted needles, tapped away with a rubber mallet, and pressed certain points, Merzliakov gave random answers to his questions.

Piotr Ivanovich devoted more than half of his working hours to exposing malingerers. Of course, he understood the reasons that induced prisoners to fake their symptoms. Piotr Ivanovich had been a prisoner not so long ago, and he wasn't surprised by the childish stubbornness of malingerers, nor by the primitive and frivolous nature of their faked symptoms. Piotr Ivanovich, formerly a lecturer at a Siberian medical institute, had made his professional career in the same snowy world as the one where his patients tried to save their lives by trying to deceive him. One cannot deny that he felt sorry for people. But he was more a doctor than a human being and he was, above all, a specialist. He was proud of the fact that a year of manual labor in the camps had not destroyed the specialist doctor in him. He looked at the problem of exposing malingerers not from a lofty, statesmanlike point of view, and not morally. He saw this problem as a proper use of his knowledge, of his psychological skill in setting traps for hungry, half-insane, wretched people to fall into, to the greater glory of science. In this battle between doctor and malingerer, everything favored the doctor: thousands of subtle medicines, hundreds of textbooks, a wide array of equipment, the help of the guards, and the enormous experience of a specialist, while all the patient had on his side was his horror of the world that he had left for the hospital and was afraid of being returned to. It was this horror that gave the prisoner the strength to battle on. Exposing yet another malingerer gave Piotr Ivanovich deep satisfaction. Once more he had proof from real life that he was a good doctor, that instead of losing his skills, he had enhanced them, perfected them—in other words, that he still could....

"What fools those surgeons are," he thought, as he lit a cigarette after Merzliakov had left. "They don't know topographical anatomy, or they've forgotten it, and they never have known what reflexes are. X-rays are their only answer. If they haven't got an X-ray, they can't be sure even about a simple fracture. Yet they're so conceited." Piotr Ivanovich, naturally, had no doubt that Merzliakov was a malingerer. "All right, he can stay in bed for a week. That week will give us time to do all the analyses, so we jump through all the hoops. We'll stick all the right bits of paper in his notes." Piotr Ivanovich smiled as he anticipated the theatrical effect of this, his next unmasking.

A week later the hospital would be getting a party of patients ready to be shipped home to the mainland. The papers were being drawn up in the ward and the chairman of the medical commission had come from the administration building to examine personally the patients whom the hospital had prepared for dispatch. The chairman's job was limited to examining the documentation, checking that the proper formulas had been used—actual examination of a patient took only thirty seconds.

"I have in my lists a certain Merzliakov. The guards broke his back a year ago. I'd like to send him off. He's recently been transferred to the neurology section. Here are his documents, all ready for dispatch." The chairman of the commission turned to face the neurologist.

"Bring Merzliakov," said Piotr Ivanovich. They brought in the patient, bent nearly double. The chairman gave him a cursory glance.

"What a gorilla," he said. "Yes, of course, there's no point keeping men like that." Picking up his pen, he reached for the lists.

"Personally, I'm not signing for him," said Piotr Ivanovich in a clear, loud voice. "He's a malingerer, and tomorrow I shall have the privilege of showing him up to you and to the surgeon."

"Right, then we'll leave him out," said the chairman indifferently, and put his pen down. "Anyway, it's time we stopped, it's getting late."

"He's a malingerer, Seriozha," Piotr Ivanovich said as he took the surgeon by the arm, when they were leaving the ward.

The surgeon freed his arm.

"He may be," he said, frowning with distaste. "Good luck with exposing him. You'll get an enormous amount of pleasure."

The next day, at a meeting with the head of the hospital, Piotr Ivanovich reported in detail on Merzliakov's case.

"I think," he concluded, "that we can expose Merzliakov in two stages. First comes Rausch anesthesia, which you, Seriozha, have forgotten about," he said triumphantly, turning to face the surgeon. "That should have been done straightaway. Then if Rausch anesthesia doesn't work," Piotr Ivanovich spread his arms, "it's shock therapy. That's a very intriguing procedure, I assure you."

"Not too intriguing?" asked Aleksandra Sergeyevna, the manager of the biggest section in the hospital, the tuberculosis section. She was a stout, heavily built woman who had only recently arrived from European Russia.

"Well," said the hospital chief, "for a bastard like that. . . ." The presence of ladies didn't inhibit him much.

"Let's see what the Rausch anesthesia does," said Piotr Ivanovich in a conciliatory tone.

Rausch is short-term anesthesia administered by an overwhelming dose of ether. The patient goes to sleep for fifteen or twenty minutes, enough time for a surgeon to manipulate a dislocation, amputate a finger, or lance an infected boil.

The hospital chiefs, dressed in white gowns, surrounded an operating table on which a submissive, half-bent Merzliakov had been put. Male nurses picked up the linen straps that usually tie patients down on the operating table.

"No need, no need," shouted Piotr Ivanovich, as he ran forward. "Straps are the last thing we need."

Merzliakov's face was turned upward. The surgeon placed an anesthesia mask over it and picked up a bottle of ether.

"Start, Seriozha!"

The ether began dripping.

"Breathe in deeper, deeper, Merzliakov! Count aloud!"

"Twenty-six, twenty-seven," Merzliakov counted in a lazy voice; then, suddenly stopping counting, he started saying broken phrases, making no sense at first, some of them obscene curses.

Piotr Ivanovich was holding Merzliakov's left hand. After a few minutes, that hand relaxed and Piotr Ivanovich let go of it. The hand fell gently, like a dead object, onto the edge of the table. Piotr Ivanovich slowly and solemnly unbent Merzliakov's body. Everyone gasped with amazement.

"Now tie him down," Piotr Ivanovich told the nurses.

Merzliakov opened his eyes and saw the hospital chief's hairy fist.

"How about that, you reptile?" the chief was rasping at him. "You'll be charged and tried."

"Congratulations, Piotr Ivanovich, congratulations!" repeated the chairman of the commission, clapping the neurologist on the shoulder. "To think that only yesterday I was about to give that gorilla his freedom!"

"Untie him!" ordered Piotr Ivanovich. "Get off the table."

Merzliakov hadn't fully regained consciousness. His temples throbbed, and he could still taste the sickeningly sweet ether in his mouth. Even now he didn't understand whether he was awake or dreaming, and it may be that he'd had dreams like this before.

"To hell with the lot of you!" he suddenly yelled out, and bent himself double, as he had been.

Broad-shouldered, bony, his thick long fingers almost touching the floor, his eyes clouded, and his hair disheveled, Merzliakov really did look like a gorilla. He left the bandaging room and Piotr Ivanovich was told that the patient Merzliakov was lying on his bed in his usual posture. The doctor ordered him to be brought to his office.

"You've been exposed, Merzliakov," said the neurologist. "But I've asked the chief, and you won't be charged, you won't be sent to a punishment mine. You'll simply be discharged from hospital and go back to your mine to do what you were doing. You're a hero, man. You've pulled the wool over our eyes for a whole year."

"I don't know anything about that," said the gorilla, not lifting his eyes.

"What do you mean, you don't know? We've only just straightened you out!"

"Nobody straightened me out."

"Look, dear man," said the neurologist. "There's no need for all this. I wanted to do it the nice way. Otherwise, watch out, because in a week's time you yourself will be asking to be discharged."

"What do I care what's going to happen in a week's time?" Merzliakov said quietly. How could he explain that just one extra week, an extra day, an extra hour spent somewhere that was not the mine was his idea of happiness. If the doctor couldn't understand that, how could he explain it? Merzliakov said nothing and stared at the floor.

Merzliakov was taken away; Piotr Ivanovich went to see the hospital chief.

"Well, you could do it tomorrow, instead of in a week," said his boss after he'd listened to Piotr Ivanovich's proposal.

"I promised him a week," said Piotr Ivanovich. "It won't bankrupt the hospital."

"All right," said the chief. "In a week, then. But bring me along. Are you going to tie him down?"

"You can't tie him down," said the neurologist. "He'd dislocate an arm or a leg. He'll be held down." Taking Merzliakov's notes with him, Piotr Ivanovich wrote in the treatment column "shock therapy" and named a date.

Shock therapy consists of intravenously injecting the patient with a quantity of camphor oil several times higher than the dose used subcutaneously for maintaining a seriously ill patient's cardiac activity. The camphor oil acts by causing a sudden attack, like an attack of violent madness of epilepsy. A rush of camphor causes a sharp increase in all of the patient's muscular activity and motor forces. Muscles are tensed as never before and the patient's strength, although he has lost consciousness, is increased tenfold. The attack lasts several minutes.

Several days passed without Merzliakov thinking of unbending of his own free will. The morning named in his notes came and he was taken to see Piotr Ivanovich. Any entertainment is highly appreciated in the north, so the doctor's office was crowded. Eight burly male nurses were lined up against the wall. A divan was placed in the middle of the office.

"We'll do it here," said Piotr Ivanovich, getting up from his desk. "We shan't bother the surgeons. Where's Sergei Fiodorovich, by the way?"

"He's not coming," said Anna Ivanovna, the sister on duty. "He said he was busy."

"Busy, busy," repeated Piotr Ivanovich. "It would do him good to watch me doing his job for him."

Merzliakov's sleeve was rolled up and the paramedic rubbed some iodine on his arm. Taking a syringe in his right hand, the paramedic pierced a vein near the patient's elbow joint. Dark blood flowed through the needle into the syringe. With a gentle movement of his thumb the paramedic pressed the plunger and a yellow solution began entering the vein.

"Get it in as fast as you can!" said Piotr Ivanovich. "And then stand aside quickly. As for you," he told the male nurses, "hold him."

Merzliakov's enormous body leapt up and writhed in the nurses' hands. Eight men were holding him down. He rasped, he struggled, he kicked, but the nurses were holding tight and he started quieting down.

"You can restrain a tiger like that, a tiger," shouted Piotr Ivanovich in his delight. "On the other side of Lake Baikal that's how they catch tigers by hand. Now watch closely," he told the hospital chief, "see how Gogol exaggerated. Do you remember the end of *Taras Bulba*? 'Almost thirty men were hanging on to his arms and legs.' Well, this gorilla is rather bigger than Taras Bulba. And he only needs eight men."

"Yes, yes," said the chief. He didn't remember Gogol, but he did like the shock therapy enormously.

The next morning Piotr Ivanovich did his rounds and stopped at Merzliakov's bed.

"Well, then," he asked, "what's your decision?"

"You can discharge me," said Merzliakov.

1956

THE DWARF PINE

In the far north, where the taiga meets the treeless tundra, among the dwarf birches, the low-growing rowan bushes with their surprisingly large, bright yellow, juicy berries, and the six-hundred-year-old larches (they reach maturity at three hundred years), there is a special tree, the dwarf pine. It is a distant relative of the Siberian cedar or pine, an evergreen bush with a trunk that is thicker than a human arm and two or three meters long. It doesn't mind where it grows; its roots will cling to cracks in the rocks on mountain slopes. It is manly and stubborn, like all northern trees. Its sensitivity is extraordinary.

It's late autumn and snow and winter are long overdue. For many days there have been low, bluish clouds moving along the edge of the white horizon: storm clouds that look as if they are covered in bruises. This morning the piercing autumn wind has turned ominously quiet. Is there a hint of snow? No. There won't be any snow. The dwarf pine hasn't lain down yet. Days pass, and still there's no snow and the heavy clouds wander about somewhere behind the bare hills, while a small pale sun has risen in the high sky, and everything is as it should be in autumn.

Then the dwarf pine bends. It bends lower and lower, as if under an immense, ever-increasing weight. Its crown scratches the rock and huddles against the ground as it stretches out its emerald paws. It is making its bed. It's like an octopus dressed in green feathers. Once it has lain down, it waits a day or two, and now the white sky delivers a shower of snow, like powder, and the dwarf pine sinks into hibernation, like a bear. Enormous snowy blisters swell up on the white mountain: the dwarf pine bushes in their winter sleep.

When winter ends, but a three-meter layer of snow still covers the ground and in the gullies the blizzards have compacted the snow so firmly that only an iron tool can shift it, people search nature in vain for any signs of spring. The calendar says that it's high time spring came. But the days are the same as in winter. The air is rarefied and dry, just as it was in January. Fortunately, human senses are too crude and their perceptions too primitive. In any case humans have only their five senses, which are not enough to foretell or intuit anything.

Nature's feelings are more subtle. We already know that to some extent. Do you remember the salmon family of fish that come and spawn only in the river where the eggs they hatched from were spawned? Do you remember the mysterious routes taken by migratory birds? There are quite a few plants and flowers known to act as barometers.

And so the dwarf pine rises amid the boundless white snowy wastes, amid this complete hopelessness. It shakes off the snow, straightens up to its full height, raises its green, ice-covered, slightly reddish needles toward the sky. It can sense what we can not: the call of spring. Trusting in spring, it rises before anyone else in the north. Winter is over.

It might rise for other reasons: a bonfire. The dwarf pine is too trusting. It dislikes winter so much that it will trust the heat of a fire. If you light a fire in winter next to a bent, twisted, hibernating dwarf pine bush, it will rise up. When the fire goes out, the disillusioned pine, weeping with disappointment, bends again and lies down where it had been. And snow covers it again.

No, it is not just a predictor of the weather. The dwarf pine is a tree of hope, the only evergreen tree in the Far North. Against the radiant white snow, its matt-green coniferous paws speak of the south, of warmth, of life. In summer it is modest and goes unnoticed. Everything around it is hurriedly blooming, trying to blossom during the short northern summer. Spring, summer, and autumn flowers race one another in a single furious stormy flowering season. But autumn is close, and the larch is stripped bare as it scatters its fine, yellow needles; the light-brown grass curls up and withers, the forest is emptied, and then you can see in the distance the enormous green torches of the dwarf pine burning in that forest amid the pale yellow grass and the gray moss.

I always used to think of the dwarf pine as the most poetic Russian tree, rather better than the much vaunted weeping willow, the plane tree, or the cypress. And dwarf pine firewood burns hotter.

1960

THE RED CROSS

CAMP LIFE is organized in such a way that only a medical worker can offer a prisoner any real, effective help. Protecting labor means protecting health, and that means protecting life. The camp authorities are numerous: the camp chief and the supervisors subordinate to him; the chief guard with his detachment of fighting men serving as escort guards; the chief of the district section of the Ministry of Internal Affairs with his organization for investigation and interrogation; the camp enlightenment organizer, who is the head of the culture and education section and has his own inspectorate. The maintenance of the regime is entrusted to the benevolence or malevolence of these people. As far as the prisoners are concerned, all of these people stand for oppression and compulsion. These people force prisoners to work, they guard them night and day in case prisoners try to escape, watch them in case they eat or drink more than they should. All these people repeat, every day and every hour, just one order: "Work! Move!"

Only one person in the camp doesn't address the prisoners with these words that the camp finds so terrible, loathsome, and hateful. This person is the doctor. The doctor uses different words: "Rest, you're tired, don't work tomorrow, you're sick." Only the doctor refrains from sending a prisoner into the white winter darkness, to the ice-covered rock pit face for many hours every day. The doctor is by profession the prisoner's protector, shielding him from the bosses' arbitrary orders, from the excessive enthusiasm of the old hands in the service of the camps.

There were years when big printed announcements were hung up in camp barracks: "The Prisoner's Rights and Obligations." There were a lot of obligations and not many rights: the "right" to make a complaint to the boss was for individuals only; the "right" to write a letter to relatives was only through the camp censors; the "right" to medical assistance....

This last right was extremely important, even though the assistance was perfunctory. In many mine clinics dysentery was treated by potassium permanganate, which was the same solution that was used in a rather thicker form to anoint festering sores or frostbitten digits.

A doctor could officially exempt a prisoner from manual labor by a note in a book; he could send him to a hospital bed, or find him a place in a sanatorium, or increase his ration. The main thing in a labor camp was that a doctor determined the "labor category," the degree to which a man was capable of manual labor, which then determined the norm he had to fulfill. A doctor could even recommend release from prison on the grounds of an invalid state, according to the notorious 450th article of the Criminal Code. Nobody could force a man to do manual labor if he had been exempted from work for reasons of illness. The doctor had total discretion. Only senior medical officers could overrule him. As far as medicine was concerned, the doctor did not answer to anyone.

It must also be remembered that control over what products went into the cooking pots was the job of the doctor, as was supervision of the quality of the food that was cooked.

The prisoner's only defender, his real defender, was the camp doctor. His power was very great, for none of the camp bosses was able to interfere with the actions of a specialist professional. If a doctor gave a wrong or misleading diagnosis, only a medical worker of superior or equal status—another professional—could be the judge. Almost all the camp chiefs were at war with their medics; the demands of their work pulled them in opposite directions. A boss would want group B (sick persons temporarily exempted from work) to be as few as possible, so that the camp could send the maximum number of people out on manual labor. But the doctor could see that the boundaries of good and evil were being transgressed, that people going out to work were sick, tired, emaciated and therefore had a right to be released from labor in far greater numbers than the authorities considered necessary.

If the doctor had a strong enough character, he could insist on people being exempted from work. Not a single camp chief would send people out to work without the doctor's say-so.

A doctor could save a prisoner from heavy manual labor. All the prisoners were classified, like horses, into work categories. These categories—there were three, four, even five—were known as labor categories, although that sounds more like an expression from a dictionary of philosophy. That was one of life's little jokes, or rather grimaces.

Putting someone in the category of light labor often meant saving a man from death. The saddest fact was that people who desperately wanted to be in the light labor category and tried to deceive the doctor were in fact far more seriously ill than they themselves knew.

A doctor could give a prisoner a rest, could send him to the hospital, could even "document" him, that is, draw up a document certifying an invalid state, which meant that the prisoner might be sent back to the mainland. True, a hospital bed and documentation by the medical commission did not depend on the doctor who issued the permit, but the important thing was to begin this process.

All this, and many other things, subsidiary, everyday things, were perfectly well understood and assessed by the gangsters. Special consideration for the doctor was an integral part of the thieves' moral code. Along with the prison bread allowance and the gentleman thief, the prison world believed firmly in the legend of the Red Cross.

"The Red Cross" was criminal slang, and every time I hear the term, I go on the alert.

The criminals made their respect for medical workers very clear by promising them every support and by not including doctors in their unlimited category of *freiers*, meaning "pushovers" and "suckers."

A legend was created, and it is still current in the camps, that some petty thieves ("muggers") once robbed a doctor and the big thieves investigated and returned the stolen goods with an apology. Just like the story of Édouard Herriot's gold watch.[12]

In fact, doctors were never robbed; the thieves made an effort. Doctors were given presents—in goods and money—if they were free workers. They received begging requests and threats of murder if they were prisoners themselves. Doctors who treated the gangsters were rewarded with praise.

The dream of every gang of thieves was to have "hooked" a doctor. A criminal could be coarse and rude to any boss (this was a style, a sign of spirit that a gangster was under certain circumstances obliged to demonstrate to the full), but the same gangster would fawn on the doctor and would not think of referring to the doctor in coarse language, unless he saw that the doctor didn't trust him or had no intention of giving in to his brazen demands.

It was said that no medical worker ever had to worry about his fate in the camp, that the criminals would help him, materially and morally. Material help would be stolen—a suit ("glad rags") or just trousers ("squares"); moral help meant that the criminal would be willing to chat with the doctor, visit him, and treat him like a friend.

It didn't take much for a sick "sucker," reduced to skin and bones by exhausting labor, lack of sleep, and beatings, to be turned out of his hospital bed and replaced by a burly pederast, murderer, and extortionist, who would be kept there until he deigned to discharge himself.

It didn't take much for criminals to be regularly released from work so that they could play a profitable game of cards, "hold the king by the beard." Or to send criminals to distant hospitals on medical grounds, if they needed this for their higher criminal purposes. Or to cover up for criminal malingerers. All the criminals were malingerers or at least exaggerated their symptoms, constantly presenting self-inflicted sores and ulcers on their calves and thighs, or slashing their bellies lightly but impressively, etc. Or to treat criminals to a few "powders," a nice dose of codeine or caffeine, diverting your entire stock of narcotics to make flavored alcohol for your benefactors to enjoy.

For a period of many years I was in charge of admissions for new arrivals in a big camp hospital; 100 percent of the malingerers who came carrying medical certificates were thieves. Thieves either bribed or intimidated their local doctor into creating a false medical document.

It often happened that the local doctor or local camp chief wanted to get rid of a troublesome or dangerous element in his organization and would therefore send gangsters to the hospital in the hope that their organization would get some relief, even if the gangsters didn't disappear forever.

If the doctor had been bribed, that was bad, very bad. But if he had been intimidated, that could be excused, since the criminals' threats were by no means empty. At the Spokoiny medical center, where there were a lot of criminal convicts, Surovy, a young doctor and recent graduate of the Moscow Medical Institute, who was, and this is the point, also a prisoner, was sent by the hospital to work at a remote camp. His friends tried to persuade him not to go. He could have refused and done ordinary manual labor, but it was not wise to go somewhere where his work would clearly be dangerous. Surovy had come to the hospital from manual labor and was afraid of going back to it, so he agreed to go to the mine to work as a doctor. The authorities gave Surovy instructions but no advice on how to behave. He was categorically forbidden to send healthy thieves from the mine to the hospital. A month later he was murdered in his surgery; they counted fifty-two knife wounds on his body.

In the women's zone of another mine, Shitsel, an elderly woman doctor, was hacked to death with an ax by her own nurse, the criminal convict Kroshka, who was carrying out a sentence dictated by the criminals.

That was what the "Red Cross" looked like in reality, when the doctors were not sufficiently obliging and refused bribes.

The more naïve doctors tried to find explanations for these contradictions from the ideologues of the gangsters' world. One of these philosopher-gangsters happened to be a patient in the hospital's surgical department. Two months previously, wanting to get out of solitary confinement, he had tried the usual, infallible, but quite dangerous means: he ground an indelible pencil to powder and, to be sure, put the powder in both eyes. Medical assistance happened to arrive too late, and the criminal went blind. In the hospital he was an invalid, preparing to travel back to the mainland. But like the infamous Sir Williams from *Rocambole*,[13] even when blind he took part in planning crimes and was considered an unquestionable authority in courts of honor. When a doctor asked about the "Red Cross" and doctors being murdered by thieves at the mines, this Sir Williams replied, with the criminal's typical soft vowels after his *sh* and *ch* sounds: "There are various situations in life when the law must not be applied." This Sir Williams knew his dialectics.

In his *Notes from the House of the Dead*, Dostoyevsky was moved to wonderment when he noted the actions of wretches: behaving like overgrown children, carried away by the theater, quarreling like a child, when they weren't really angry. Dostoyevsky never met or knew people from the real criminal world. Dostoyevsky would never have let himself utter a word of sympathy with that world.

The evil acts committed by the thieves in the camps are beyond counting. The wretches were the people doing hard labor, from whom the thieves took their last rags, their last bit of money, while the worker was too afraid to complain, for he saw that the thief was stronger than the authorities. The worker was beaten by the thief and forced to work; tens of thousands were beaten to death by the thieves. Hundreds of thousands of people, once they were imprisoned, were corrupted by the thieves' ideology and ceased to be human beings. Something gangsterish got into their souls and stayed there. Thieves and their morality could leave an indelible trace in anyone's soul.

The bosses were coarse and cruel, the propagandist was a liar, the doctor had no conscience, but all that was trivial compared to the power of the criminal world to deprave others. The bosses, propagandist, and doctor were still human and there were very occasionally glimpses of something human in them. But the criminals were not human.

Their influence on camp life knew no bounds and was ubiquitous. The camps are a negative school of life in every possible way. Nobody can get anything useful or necessary out of the camps, neither prisoner nor chief, neither the guards nor the casual witnesses, such as engineers, geologists, and doctors, neither the bosses nor their subordinates.

Every minute of camp life is poisoned.

There is a lot in the camps that a man must not know or see, and if he does see it, he is better off dead.

Prisoners in the camps learn to hate labor. That is all they can learn there.

They are taught flattery, lying, vileness, petty and serious, and they become egotists.

When they are released, they see that not only have they failed to grow while in the camps but that their interests have narrowed and become wretched and coarse.

Moral barriers have been pushed aside.

You find out that you can do something vile and still live.

You can lie and still live.

You can make promises and fail to keep them and still live.

You can spend a friend's money on drink.

You can beg for charity and still live! You can live as a beggar.

It turns out that a man who has done something vile doesn't then die.

He learns to live a life of idleness, deceit, and resentment against everyone and everything.

He overvalues his own sufferings and forgets that everyone has their own grief. He has forgotten how to sympathize with someone else's grief; he just can't understand it and doesn't want to.

Skepticism is all very well, and that is the best you can take away from the camp.

The prisoner learns to hate people.

He is afraid that he is a coward. He is afraid that he will suffer the same fate again. He is afraid of denunciations, of his neighbors, of everything a human being should not be afraid of.

He is morally crushed. His ideas of morality have changed and he hasn't noticed.

In the camp, a boss gets used to almost infinite power over convicts, gets used to seeing himself as a god, as the only plenipotentiary representative of power, as a member of a superior race.

As for the escort guard who has many times held human lives in his hands and has often killed prisoners who stepped outside the closed zone, what is he going to tell the girl he marries about his work in the Far North? Will he tell her about using his rifle butt to hit starving old men who could no longer walk?

A young peasant who finds himself a prisoner sees that only the professional criminals have a relatively good life in this hell, and that they are respected, and that the almighty authorities are frightened of them. The criminals are well-dressed, well-fed, and support one another.

The young peasant takes all this in. He begins to suspect that in camp life the gangsters are on the right side, that just by imitating their behavior he will find the right way to save his own life. It now appears that there are people who can live even in the lowest depths. So the peasant begins to imitate the gangsters and to act like them. He goes along with everything they say, is ready to carry out anything they ask him to do, and speaks about them with fear and veneration. He cannot wait to color his speech with their jargon. Nobody, male or female, prisoner or free, who spent any time in Kolyma, ever came back without criminal slang in their vocabulary.

These slang words are a poison, a venom that gets into a man's soul. The moment you master the criminal dialect is the moment a "sucker" begins to join the criminal world.

An intellectual, once imprisoned, is crushed by the camp. Everything that used to be dear to him is trampled into the dust, and he sheds his civilization and culture in the shortest imaginable time, a matter of weeks.

In any discussion the main argument is a fist or a stick. The means of compulsion is a rifle butt or a punch in the mouth.

An intellectual turns into a coward, and his own brain suggests a justification for his actions. He can persuade himself of anything, he can take any side in an argument. The criminal world calls intellectuals "life teachers," fighters "for the people's rights."

A "slapping," a punch, is enough to turn an intellectual into the obedient servant of some thieving Senia or Kostia.

Physical influence becomes moral influence.

The intellectual becomes a permanently scared creature. His spirit is broken. Even when he gets back to life in freedom, he will still have this intimidated and broken spirit.

Engineers, geologists, and doctors who come to Kolyma on Far East Development contracts are very quickly debauched. The extra rubles, the law of the taiga, slave labor that is so easy and profitable to use, a reduction of cultural interests—all this corrupts and depraves. A man who has spent some time working in the camps doesn't go back to the mainland, he is worthless trash there, but he has gotten used to a rich life with all the facilities. It's this depravity that is referred to in literature as "the call of the north."

The blame for this debauchery of the human soul falls to a significant extent on the world of the gangsters, the recidivists whose tastes and habits are interlinked with all of Kolyma's life.

1959

THE LAWYERS' CONSPIRACY

SHMELIOV'S brigade was a dumping ground for human slag, the waste people from the gold-mine pit face. There were three ways out of the seam from where sand was extracted and peat was removed: "down the hill"—which meant into mass graves—to the hospital, or to Shmeliov's brigade. These were the three paths open to goners. This brigade worked at the same pit face, but it was given less important tasks. The slogans "Fulfilling the plan is the law" and "Let's take the plan to the pit-face workers" weren't idle words. They were interpreted as "If you don't fulfill the norm, you've broken the law, deceived the state, and must pay for it with a prison sentence, if not your life."

The Shmeliov men were fed worse and less. But I remembered well the local saying: "What kills you in the camps is the big ration, not the small one." I wasn't making any effort to get the big ration that the core pit-face brigades got.

I had only recently, three weeks previously, been transferred to Shmeliov's brigade, and I didn't know the foreman Shmeliov by face. It was the depths of winter and the foreman's head was ingeniously wrapped in a torn scarf, while in the evenings it was dark in the barracks, where the improvised kerosene lamp barely lit up the door. And so I don't remember his face, only his voice, which was hoarse from the freezing cold.

We were working a December night shift and every night seemed like torture—minus fifty is no joke. Even so, the night shift was better, calmer, with fewer bosses at the pit face and less cursing and beating.

The brigade was lining up to leave. In winter we lined up inside the barracks, and even now it is agonizing to recall those last minutes before you left for an icy twelve-hour night shift. Here, wanly jostling by the half-open doors, from which came an icy mist, human beings showed their real nature. One man would overcome his shivering and stride straight out into the darkness; another man would hastily finish sucking a cigarette end he had gotten from God knows where, since there wasn't a whiff or even a trace of tobacco here; a third man would shield his face from the cold wind; a fourth would stand over the stove, holding out his gloves to gather the warmth.

The last men were pushed out of the barracks by the orderly. That was what happened to the weakest everywhere, in every brigade.

I was not yet being dragged out in that brigade. There were people weaker than me there, which gave me a certain comfort, an unexpected joy. Here I was still human. I had left the orderly's shoves and punches behind in the "golden" brigade from which I had been moved to Shmeliov's.

The brigade was standing by the barracks door, ready to go outside. Shmeliov came up to me.

"You're staying behind," he rasped.

"Have I been moved to the morning shift, then?" I asked mistrustfully.

Any transfer from one shift to another always happened just before the beginning of the first hour, so that no working day was lost and so that the prisoner would not have any extra rest hours. I knew how it worked.

"No, Romanov is summoning you."

"Romanov? Who's Romanov?"

"What a jerk! Doesn't know who Romanov is," the orderly intervened.

"He's the NKVD officer, got it? His office is just before the main office. You're to be there at eight."

"At eight!"

I was overwhelmed by a feeling of relief. If the NKVD man kept me until midnight, to night-shift dinner, or even longer, I would have the right to take all night off work. My body immediately felt its fatigue. But this was a joyful fatigue, it was my muscles complaining.

I undid my trouser belt, unbuttoned my pea jacket, and sat down by the stove. I immediately felt warm, and the lice under my tunic started moving about. I scratched my neck and chest with my sorely bitten fingernails. And I dozed off.

"It's time, it's time." The orderly was shaking me by the shoulder. "Off you go, and bring back something to smoke, don't forget."

I knocked at the door of the building where the NKVD officer lived. Bolts were noisily drawn back, locks undone, a great number of bolts and locks, and someone invisible yelled from the other side of the door, "Who are you?"

"Prisoner Andreyev, told to come."

The clanging of bolts and clinking of locks sounded out, then there was silence.

The cold was getting under my jacket, my legs were getting numb. I started banging one soft boot against the other; we weren't wearing felt boots, we had quilted ones made from old trousers and jackets.

There was more noisy clanging of bolts, and the double doors opened, letting out a wave of light, warmth, and music.

I entered. The door from the hall to the dining room was open, and I could hear a radio playing.

NKVD officer Romanov was standing in front of me. Or rather I was in front of him, and he, a squat, stout, restless man who smelled of perfume, was revolving around me, his quick black eyes examining my person.

The prisoner's smell hit his nostrils, and he took out a snow-white handkerchief and shook it. Waves of music, warmth, and eau de cologne washed all over me. The main thing was the warmth. The Dutch stove was red-hot.

"So we meet," Romanov kept saying with delight as he moved around me, waving his scented handkerchief. "So we meet. Well, come through . . . ." And he opened the door to the next room, a little study with a desk and two chairs.

"Sit down. You'll never guess why I've called you in. Have a cigarette." He poked about in the papers on the table. "What's your name? Patronymic?"

I told him.

"Year of birth?"

"It's 1907."

"You're a lawyer?"

"I'm not actually a lawyer, but I was a student of Moscow University law faculty in the second half of the 1920s."

"So you're a lawyer. That's excellent. Just sit there for now and I'll make a few phone calls, and then you and I will take a trip."

Romanov slipped out of the room; shortly afterward the music in the dining room was turned off and a telephone conversation started.

Sitting on a chair, I fell asleep. I even began to dream. Romanov kept vanishing and then reappearing.

"Listen. Do you have any possessions in the barracks?"

"Everything I have is on me."

"That's excellent, really excellent. There'll be a car any moment and you and I will take a trip. Do you know where we're going? You'll never guess. All the way to Khattinakh, to headquarters! Have you ever been there? Well, I'm joking, joking...."

"I don't mind one way or the other."

"That's just fine."

I took off my boots, massaged my toes, and rewrapped my foot bindings.

The pendulum clock on the wall showed half past eleven. Even if all that talk of Khattinakh was a joke, I still wouldn't be going to work this night.

A car sounded its horn just outside, and the headlights shone over the shutters and then the study ceiling.

"Let's go, let's go."

Romanov was wearing a white fur jacket, a Yakut fur hat with earflaps, and embroidered reindeer-skin boots.

I buttoned up my pea jacket, tightened my belt, and held my gloves over the stove.

We went out to the truck. It was a one-and-a-half-ton truck with a covered back.

"What's the temperature today, Misha?" Romanov asked the driver.

"Minus sixty, sir. The night brigades have been stood down."

So our brigade, the Shmeliov brigade, was in the barracks. I hadn't been that lucky after all.

"Right, Andreyev," said the NKVD man, leaping about around me. "You get in the back. We don't have far to go, and Misha will drive as fast as he can. Won't you, Misha?"

Misha said nothing. I got into the back, curled up in a ball, clutching my legs with my hands. Romanov squeezed himself into the cab, and we moved off.

The road was bad and I was thrown about so much that I didn't get cold.

I didn't want to think about anything, not that you can think in the cold.

About two hours later lights were glimmering and the truck stopped by a two-story log cabin. It was dark everywhere. Only one window on the second story had a light burning. Two sentries in sheepskin coats were standing by the large porch.

"Right, we've arrived, that's excellent. He can stay here for a bit." And Romanov disappeared up the big staircase.

It was two in the morning. All the lights were turned off. Only the duty officer's table lamp was on.

I didn't have to wait long. Romanov, who had already changed into an NKVD uniform, ran down the stairs and started waving his arms. "Over here, over here."

Together with the assistant duty officer, we went upstairs and stopped in the upper-story corridor outside a door that had a board on it: "Senior NKVD Officer Smertin." Such a menacing pseudonym (which means "death" and couldn't possibly be a real surname) made an impression even on me, despite my extreme fatigue.

"That's going too far for a pseudonym," I thought, but I now had to enter and walk across an enormous room with a portrait of Stalin covering a whole wall; then I stopped at a desk of gigantic proportions and examined the pale, reddish face of a man who had spent his whole life in rooms like this one.

Romanov was bowing respectfully by the desk.

Senior NKVD officer Smertin fixed his lusterless blue eyes on me. He soon averted them; he was going through some papers, looking for something on the desk. Romanov's fingers obligingly found what needed finding.

"Surname?" asked Smertin, looking into the documents. "Name, patronymic? Article of Criminal Code? Sentence?"

I replied.

"Lawyer?"

"Lawyer."

His pale face rose up from the desk top.

"Have you been writing appeals?"

"I have."

Smertin asked with a sniffling sound, "In exchange for bread?"

"For bread, and just for the sake of it."

"Fine. Take him away."

I made not the slightest effort to sort out or ask anything. Why? At least I was out of the cold, not on the gold-mine night shift. They could sort out whatever they wanted.

The deputy duty officer brought some note or other, and I was taken through the dark settlement to the very edge where four guard towers behind a triple barbed-wire fence protected the special confinement building, the camp prison.

This prison had big cells and one-man cells. I was shoved into one of the one-man cells. I told the men already there who I was, not that I expected them to respond, and I didn't ask them about anything. That was the usual thing to do, to stop people thinking you were a stool pigeon.

Morning, the usual Kolyma winter morning, came, bringing no light and no sun; at first it was indistinguishable from night. An iron rail was banged and a bucket of steaming hot water was brought in. A guard came to fetch me, and I said goodbye to my fellow inmates. I knew nothing about them.

I was brought back to the same building. It now seemed smaller than it had at night. This time I didn't have the privilege of beholding Smertin.

The duty officer told me to sit and wait, so I sat and waited until I heard a familiar voice: "That's wonderful! That's excellent! You'll be off any moment." When not on his own territory, Romanov addressed me as politely as he would a civilian.

Thoughts were slowly, almost palpably revolving in my brain. I now had to think about something new, to which I was unaccustomed, something I didn't know. This was nothing to do with the mine. If we were about to go back to my old Partisan gold mine, Romanov would have said, "We'll be off any moment." This meant that I was being taken somewhere else. To hell with it all, anyway!

Romanov came almost leaping down the staircase. I thought at any moment he might climb onto the banister and slide down like a little boy. He was holding an almost entire loaf of bread.

"Here, this is for the journey. And something else, too." He vanished upstairs and came back with two herrings. "We're doing things properly, aren't we? I think that's it. Ah, I forgot the most important thing, that's because I don't smoke myself."

Romanov went upstairs and reappeared with a newspaper. He'd put some tobacco in it. "Three matchboxes full, I reckon," my experienced eye told me. A two-ounce pack of tobacco fills eight matchboxes —that was how tobacco was weighed out in the camps.

"That's for the journey. Daily rations, you could say."

I nodded.

"Have they got an escort ready?"

"They have," said the duty officer.

Romanov then went to the stairs and vanished.

Two escort guards appeared: one older and pockmarked, wearing a tall sheepskin Caucasian hat; the other young, about twenty, rosy-cheeked, wearing a Red Army helmet.

"This one," said the duty officer, pointing at me.

Both, the young one and the pockmarked one, very carefully examined me from head to toe.

"Where's the chief?" asked the pockmarked one.

"Upstairs. And your package is there."

The pockmarked guard went upstairs and soon came back with Romanov.

They had a quiet conversation, and the pockmarked man kept pointing at me.

"All right," Romanov finally said, "we'll give you a note."

We went outside. By the porch, at the same place the little truck from the Partisan mine had stopped the night before, was a comfortable

Black Maria, a prison bus with barred windows. I got in. The barred doors were closed, the guards took their places by the back doors, and the bus moved off. For some time the Black Maria followed the main highway that transverses the whole Kolyma peninsula, but then it turned off somewhere, and the road wound between bare hills. Every time it climbed a hill, the engine groaned. There were vertical rocks with a thin covering of larch forest and frost-covered branches of shrubby willow. In the end, after several turns among the hills, the bus followed a riverbed and emerged into a small clearing. Here the forest had been felled, there were guard towers, and in the middle, about three hundred yards from the edge, there were slanting towers and a dark mass of barracks, surrounded by barbed wire.

The door of a tiny guard hut on the roadside was opened and the duty guard, a revolver on his belt, emerged.

The bus stopped, but the engine was kept running.

The driver leapt out of the cab and passed by my window.

"You should see all those bends. No wonder it's called Serpantinnaya, the Serpentine."

I had heard that name before, and it said more to me than Smertin's ominous surname. The Serpantinnaya was the famous prison for trials and sentences, where so many people had perished the year before. Their corpses still hadn't decomposed. Actually, their corpses would be intact forever—they were the dead men of the permafrost.

The older guard went down the path toward the prison, while I sat by the window thinking my last hour had finally come, that it was my turn now. Thinking about death was just as hard as thinking about anything else. I didn't try and picture my own execution by shooting: I just sat and waited.

The winter twilight had already fallen. The door of the Black Maria was opened, and the older guard threw me some felt boots.

"Get these on! Take off your cloth boots!"

I took my cloth boots off and tried to get the felt boots on; they were too small.

"You won't make the journey in cloth boots," said the pockmarked guard.

"I will."

The pockmarked guard flung the felt boots into a corner of the bus. "Let's go!"

The bus turned around and sped away from Serpantinnaya.

Soon I could tell by the number of trucks speeding past us that we were back on the main highway.

The bus slowed down; the lights of a large settlement were burning all around us. The bus drove up to the porch of a brightly lit building and I went into a bright corridor, very much like the one in officer Smertin's building. A duty officer with a pistol by his side was sitting behind a wooden barrier next to a wall telephone. This was the Yagodny settlement. Our first day's journey had covered a mere seventeen kilometers. Where were we off to next?

The duty officer showed me into a distant room that turned out to be an isolation cell with a trestle bed, a bucket of water, and a piss pot. A "spy hole" had been cut into the door.

I spent two days there. I even managed to get the bandages on my legs more or less dry and to rewrap them. My legs were covered in festering scurvy sores.

There was a backwoods sleepiness about the NKVD district section building. Sitting in my cubbyhole, I pricked up my ears to hear what I could. Even during the day hardly anyone's boots were heard in the corridor. Keys were rarely turned in the lock, so the cell door was seldom open. The duty officer, always the same unshaven man in a quilted jacket with a Nagant revolver in his shoulder holster, also looked like a backwoodsman. It was not like Khattinakh, where Comrade Smertin made the major decisions. The telephone almost never rang.

"Yes. He's refueling. Yes. I don't know, sir."

"Fine, I'll tell them."

Whom were they talking about? My escort guards? Once a day, just before evening, my cell door was opened and the duty guard brought a pot of soup and a piece of bread.

"Eat!"

That was my dinner. Standard issue. And he brought a spoon, too. The second course was mixed with the first, poured into the soup.

Each time I took the pot, ate the food, and, following the mine worker's habit, licked the bottom of the pot until it shone.

On the third day the door opened and the pockmarked soldier, wearing a sheepskin over his fur jacket, strode into the cell.

"Well, had a good rest? Let's go."

I stood on the porch. I thought we were setting off again in the prison bus, but the Black Maria was nowhere to be seen. An ordinary three-ton truck was standing by the porch.

"Get in."

I obediently climbed in over the side.

The younger soldier got into the cab next to the driver. The pockmarked one sat next to me. The truck moved off and a few minutes later we were on the main highway.

Where was I being taken? North or south? West or east?

There was no point asking, and the guard was not allowed to talk.

Was I being taken to another zone, and if so, which?

The truck shook about for many hours and then suddenly stopped.

"We'll have dinner here. Get out."

I got out.

We went into one of the highway refectories.

The highway is Kolyma's artery and main nerve. Loads of equipment are constantly being moved in both directions. They are not guarded, but trucks with food are always escorted, in case escaped prisoners attack and rob them. An escort guard may not be much protection against the driver's or contractor's thefts, but he can stop general thieving.

The refectories are places where you see geologists and prospectors for mining parties going on leave with their ruble bonuses, black-market tobacco and tea sellers, northern heroes and northern swine. Pure alcohol is always on sale in the refectories. People meet, argue, fight, exchange news, and are always in a hurry. They leave their trucks with the engines running and catch a few hours' sleep in the cab, so that they can get a rest before moving on. This is where you see nice tidy groups of prisoners being taken up-country to the taiga, and filthy heaps of human slag being brought down from up-country, back from the taiga. Here you see the special-operations search parties, hunting for escaped prisoners. And you see the escaped prisoners, too, often wearing military uniform. Here the chiefs, the lords of everyone's life and death, ride in ZIS limousines. A playwright ought to see this—it is in a roadside refectory that you get the best scenes of the north.

I stood there, trying to squeeze my way close to the stove, an enormous barrel stove burning red-hot. The guards were not very worried about my trying to escape: I was obviously too weak. Anyone could see that a goner was not going to get anywhere when the temperature was minus fifty.

"Sit over there, eat."

The guard bought me a plate of hot soup and gave me some bread.

"We'll be off again in a minute," said the young one. "When my chief gets back, we'll go."

But the pockmarked guard came back with somebody else, a middle-aged soldier (they were still called "fighters" then) carrying a rifle and wearing a fur jacket. He looked first at me, then at the pockmarked guard.

"Well, why not? That's all right," he said.

"Let's go," the pockmarked guard told me.

We moved to the opposite corner of the enormous refectory. A man wearing a pea jacket and a black flannel hat with earflaps, as worn by prisoners in the Baikal-Amur camps, was sitting curled up by the wall.

"Sit down here," the pockmarked guard told me.

I obeyed and sank to the floor next to the man, who didn't even turn his head.

The pockmarked guard and the new soldier left. My young guard stayed with us.

"They're giving themselves a break, got it?" the man in the prisoner's hat suddenly whispered to me. "They have no right to do that."

"Who cares what the bastards do?" I said. "They can do as they like. Does it bother you or something?"

The man raised his head. "I'm telling you they don't have the right."

"Where are they taking us?" I asked.

"I don't know where they're taking you, but I'm going to Magadan. To be shot."

"To be shot?"

"Yes. I've got a death sentence. I'm from the Western Administration, from Susuman."

I didn't like that at all. But then I didn't know the procedures that were followed for carrying out the death penalty. I felt embarrassed and said nothing.

The pockmarked soldier and our new traveling companion came up.

They started talking to each other. Whenever the number of guards increased, they became nastier and rougher. I was no longer bought soup in the refectory.

A few more hours passed, and then three more men were brought to join us in the refectory. This made quite a significant batch.

They were like all the goners in Kolyma. You could not tell how old these three men were; their puffy white skin and swollen faces were testimonies to starvation and scurvy. Their faces were covered with frostbite marks.

"Where are you being taken?"

"To Magadan. To be shot. We've got death sentences."

We lay on the back of the three-tonner, huddled, our faces between our knees, our backs against each other's. The three-tonner had good springs, the highway was in an excellent state, so we were hardly thrown about at all, and we began to freeze to death.

We yelled, we groaned, but the guards showed no mercy. We had to reach Sporny before it got dark.

One of those sentenced to death begged to be allowed to "warm up," if only for five minutes.

The truck sped to Sporny, where the lights were already on. The pockmarked guard approached.

"You'll be put in the camp's special prison for the night; we'll move on in the morning."

I was frozen to the marrow of my bones. I could not speak for the freezing cold. I used my last strength to stamp the soles of my cloth boots in the snow. I couldn't get warm. The soldiers were still looking for the camp bosses. Finally, an hour later, we were taken to the frozen, unheated camp prison. Hoarfrost covered all the walls, and the earth floor was covered in ice. Someone brought in a bucket of water. The lock clanged. How about firewood or a stove?

It was that night in Sporny that all my fingers and toes were frost-bitten again, as I tried in vain to get to sleep, if only for a minute.

In the morning we were brought out and put in the truck. The bare hills flashed past; trucks coming the opposite way screeched as they passed. The truck was coming down from the pass and we felt such warmth that we no longer wanted to go anywhere, we wanted to wait, to walk just for a while along this wonderful earth.

The temperature rose by at least ten degrees, and the wind was somehow warm, almost springlike.

"Guard! We need to relieve ourselves."

How else could we tell the soldiers that we were glad of the warmth, the southern wind, of being rescued from the taiga that had covered our souls in ice.

"All right, get out."

The guards also enjoyed relaxing, having a smoke. My seeker of justice was now going up to a guard.

"Can we smoke, citizen soldier?"

"We'll have a smoke. Go back to your place."

One of the new men refused to get out of the truck. But when he saw the relief stop was being extended, he moved to the edge of the truck and gestured to me.

"Help me get down."

I stretched out my arms and, although I was a weak goner, I suddenly felt the extraordinary lightness of his body, a deadly lightness. I moved back. Holding the side of the truck, the man took a few steps.

"How warm it is!" But his eyes were dim and utterly without expression.

"All right, let's go, let's go. It's minus thirty."

Every hour was warmer.

At the refectory in the Palata settlement our guards took their final dinner. The pockmarked one bought me a kilo of bread.

"Here's some white bread for you. We'll be there by evening."

Fine snow was falling when we saw far below us the lights of Magadan. It was about ten degrees below zero. There was no wind. The snow was falling almost perpendicularly, in tiny flakes.

The truck stopped by the district headquarters of the NKVD. The guards entered the building.

A bareheaded man in civilian clothes came out. He was holding an envelope that had been opened.

He called out somebody's surname in the usual ringing tones. The man with the lightweight body did as he gestured and crawled to one side.

"To the prison."

The man in civilian clothes vanished inside the building and reappeared a moment later.

He had a different package in his hand.

"Ivanov!"

"Konstantin Ivanovich," came the reply.

"To the prison."

"Ugritsky!"

"Sergei Fiodorovich."

"To the prison."

"Simonov!"

"Evgeni Petrovich."

"To the prison."

I didn't say goodbye to the guards nor to the men who had come with me to Magadan. Farewells were not customary here.

I and my guards were the only ones left standing by the district headquarters porch.

The man in civilian clothes reappeared on the porch; he had a package in his hand.

"Andreyev. Into the headquarters. I'll give you a receipt in a minute," he told my guards.

I entered the building. My first thought was to locate the stove. There it was: a central-heating radiator. A duty officer behind a wooden barrier. A telephone. Not so luxurious as Comrade Smertin's place at Khattinakh. Perhaps it seemed that way because Smertin's was the first study of that kind that I had seen during my time at Kolyma.

A steep staircase led from the corridor to the second story.

I didn't have to wait long. The same man in civilian clothes who'd met us outside came downstairs.

"Come up here," he said politely.

We went up the narrow stairs to the second floor and reached a door with an inscription: "Y. Atlas, Senior Officer."

"Sit down."

I sat down. Most of the tiny office was taken up by the desk. Papers, files, lists of some kind.

Atlas was between thirty-eight and forty. He was a fairly stout, sporty-looking man with black hair and the beginnings of a bald patch.

"Surname?"

"Andreyev."

"Name, patronymic, article of Criminal Code, sentence?"

I replied.

"Lawyer?"

"Lawyer."

Atlas leapt to his feet and came to my side of the desk.

"Excellent. Captain Rebrov is going to have a talk with you."

"And who is Captain Rebrov?"

"The chief of the Combined Law-Enforcement Organs. Go downstairs."

I went back to my place by the radiator. I pondered all this new information and decided, before it was too late, to eat the kilo of white bread that the guards had given me. There was a cistern of water and a mug attached to it with a chain. The pendulum clock on the wall regularly ticked away the time. Half asleep, I could hear someone stepping quickly as he passed and went upstairs; then the duty officer woke me up.

"You're to see Captain Rebrov."

I was taken to the second floor. The door was opened to a small office, and I heard a brusque voice: "Over here!"

"Surname?"

"Andreyev."

"Name, patronymic? Article of Criminal Code? Sentence? Lawyer?"

"Lawyer."

Captain Rebrov bent over his desk, bringing his glazed eyes close to mine and asked, "Do you know Parfentiev?"

"Yes, I do."

Parfentiev had been my foreman in the brigade working at the mine pit face before I ended up in Shmeliov's brigade. I was transferred from Parfentiev's to Poturayev's, and only then to Shmeliov's. I spent several months working under Parfentiev.

"Yes. I know him. He was my foreman, Dmitri Timofeyevich Parfentiev."

"Right. Good. So you know Parfentiev?"

"Yes, I do."

"Do you know Vinogradov?"

"I don't know Vinogradov."

"Vinogradov, the chairman of the Far East Court?"

"I don't know him."

Captain Rebrov lit a cigarette, took a deep draft, and went on looking at me while thinking about something else.

"So you know Vinogradov, but don't know Parfentiev?"

"No, I don't know Vinogradov...."

"Ah, yes. You know Parfentiev, and you don't know Vinogradov. Never mind!"

Captain Rebrov pressed a button and a bell rang. The door behind me opened.

"To the prison."

A saucer with a cigarette stub and an uneaten crust of cheese were left in the office of the head of the Combined Law-Enforcement Organs, next to a decanter of water.

The guard led me through Magadan, which was asleep in the dead of night.

"Get a move on!"

"I'm in no hurry."

"Another word from you," and the soldier took out his pistol, "and I'll shoot you like a dog. I can easily write you off."

"You can't write me off," I said. "You'll have Captain Rebrov to answer to."

"Move, you bastard."

Magadan is not a big town. We soon reached the Vaskov Building, as the local prison is called. Vaskov had been the deputy of Berzin[14] when Magadan was being built. The wooden prison was one of the first buildings in Magadan, and the prison kept the name of the man who had built it. Since then, some time ago, a stone prison was built in Magadan, but even this new "modern" building, constructed to the latest penitentiary specifications, is called the Vaskov Building.

After a short exchange of words at the guardhouse I was let into the courtyard of the Vaskov Building. The long, low-built, squat block of the prison was made of heavy planed larch beams. At the other end of the courtyard were two stalls, both wooden buildings.

"The second one," a voice behind me ordered.

I grabbed the door handle, opened the door, and went in.

There were double bunks, packed with people. But they weren't packed tight, and there was room. The floor was just earth. A half-barrel stove stood on long iron legs. There was a smell of sweat, Lysol, and dirty bodies.

I had trouble climbing up to a top bunk, where it was warmer, and crawling into a space.

My neighbor woke up. "From the taiga?"

"Yes."

"Have you got lice?"

"Yes."

"Then lie down in the corner. We haven't got lice here. Here there's disinfection."

"Disinfection, that's good," I thought. "But the main thing is that it's warm."

They fed us in the morning: bread, hot water. I wasn't yet on the list for bread. I took my cloth boots off and put them under my head, lowered my quilted trousers so as to warm my feet, and fell asleep. I woke up twenty-four hours later, when bread was being issued, and I was on the list for all the facilities in the Vaskov Building.

We had broth in which dumplings had been boiled and three spoonfuls of wheat porridge. I slept until the morning of the next day, right until the minute when the orderly's savage voice woke me.

"Andreyev! Andreyev! Which one is Andreyev?"

I got off the bunks. "Here I am."

"Go outside, to that porch over there."

The doors of the original Vaskov Building opened before me and I entered a low, dimly lit corridor. The warden undid the lock, pushed aside a massive iron bolt, and opened a tiny cell with double bunks. Two men were sitting curled up in the corner of the lower bunks.

I went to the window and sat down.

Someone was shaking me from behind. It was my mining foreman, Dmitri Timofeyevich Parfentiev.

"Have you any idea what's going on?"

"I can't make head or tail of it. When were you brought here?"

"Three days ago. Atlas brought me in a car."

"Atlas? He's the one who interrogated me in the NKVD headquarters. About forty, going bald. Wears civilian clothes."

"When he brought me here he was wearing a military uniform. What did Captain Rebrov ask you?"

"Whether I knew Vinogradov."

"Well?"

"Why should I know him?"

"Vinogradov is the Far East Court chairman."

"You may know that, but I don't know who he is."

"I was at college with him."

I began to understand a few things. Before he was arrested, Parfentiev was the provincial prosecutor in Cheliabinsk, and then the prosecutor in Karelia. When Vinogradov was passing through Partisan he found out that his old university friend was at the pit face, gave him some money, and asked Anisimov, the chief of Partisan, to help Parfentiev. Parfentiev was transferred to work as a blacksmith at the forge. Anisimov informed Smertin in the NKVD of Vinogradov's request, and Smertin informed Captain Rebrov in Magadan, so the head of the Combined Law-Enforcement Organs started an investigation of Vinogradov's case. All the lawyers who were imprisoned in the mines of the north were arrested. The rest was up to the interrogator's technique.

"Why are we here? I was in a wooden stall—"

"We're being released, you idiot," said Parfentiev.

"Released? Set free? No, I mean, sent to the transit camp."

"Yes," said another man, crawling out into the light and giving me a look of obvious scorn.

He had a well-stuffed fat mug. He was wearing a neat little double-sided fur coat and his fine-cotton shirt was unbuttoned.

"So you know each other? Captain Rebrov didn't manage to wipe you out. He's an enemy of the people."

"And you're a friend of the people, are you?"

"Not a political one, at least. He didn't wear the NKVD diamond shoulder badges. He didn't torment working people. It's because of you, people like you, that we get put in prison."

"You're a gangster, are you?" I asked.

"A gangster to some, a stooge to others."

"Come on, stop it, stop it," Parfentiev intervened, trying to protect me.

"Bastard! I won't stand for it."

The doors clanged.

"Come out!"

There were about seven men jostling around the guardhouse. Parfentiev and I went up to them.

"You wouldn't be lawyers, would you?" asked Parfentiev.

"Yes, yes."

"What's happened, then? Why are we being let out?"

"Captain Rebrov's been arrested. There's been an order to release everyone on his warrants," some know-all said quietly.

1962

THE TYPHUS QUARANTINE

A MAN IN white overalls stretched out a hand, and Andreyev placed his fragile, salt-saturated tunic into the man's wide-stretched, pink, scrubbed fingers with their manicured nails. The man waved it away with a shake of his hand.

"I don't have any underwear," Andreyev said in an indifferent voice.

Then the paramedic picked up Andreyev's tunic in both hands, deftly turned the sleeves inside out, and took a close look.

"He's got them, Lidiya," he said, then roared at Andreyev: "How did you get so lousy, then?"

Lidiya Ivanovna, the doctor, stopped him in his tracks.

"It isn't their fault, is it?" she said quietly and reproachfully, emphasizing the word "their"; then she picked up her stethoscope from the table.

Andreyev remembered that red-haired woman for the rest of his life; he blessed her a thousand times and always recalled her with tenderness and warmth. Why? Because in that phrase, the only phrase Andreyev heard her speak, she had emphasized the word "their." Because of a kind word, said at the right time. Was she ever aware of those blessings he uttered?

It didn't take long to examine him. And the examination didn't need a stethoscope.

Lidiya breathed on her purple stamp and forcefully, using both hands, pressed it on a printed form; she added a few words in writing, and Andreyev was taken away.

The guard was waiting in the clinic lobby; instead of taking Andreyev back to the prison, he led him deep into the settlement, to one of the big warehouses. The door next to the warehouse was protected by ten standard layers of barbed wire with a gate patrolled by a sentry wearing a sheepskin coat and carrying a rifle. They entered the yard and approached the warehouse. Bright electric light beamed through the gap in the doorframe. The guard found it hard to open the door, which was enormous, being designed for trucks, not people; he then disappeared inside the warehouse. Andreyev was struck by the smell of dirty bodies, clothes that had been lain in, and sour human sweat. A dull hum of human voices filled this enormous boxlike space. The four-story bunks, made from hewn larch trunks, were an everlasting structure, made to last for all eternity, like Caesar's bridges. The enormous warehouse's shelving had a thousand men lying on it. This was one of a couple of score of old stores packed to the rafters with new, live goods. There was a typhus quarantine in the port and for a whole month there had been no dispatch or, to use the prison term, "party." The camp's blood circulation, in which living human beings were the red blood cells, had been stopped. The trucks that transported people stood idle. The mines increased the working day for prisoners. In the town itself the bakeries couldn't cope with the amount of bread needed; after all, each man had to have half a kilo per day, so they tried baking bread in private apartments. The authorities' bad temper was made worse by the small groups of prisoner slag, discarded by the mines, which ended up in the town.

In the "section," which was the fashionable name for the warehouse where Andreyev had been taken, there were more than a thousand men. But it wasn't immediately obvious that there were so many. People on the top bunks lay naked because it was so hot; on the lower bunks and beneath them they wore pea jackets, quilted waistcoats, and hats. Most were lying on their backs or facedown (nobody could explain why prisoners almost never sleep on their sides). On the massive bunks, their bodies seemed like tumors, or lumps of wood, or bent planks.

People converged in tightly packed groups next to or around a "novelist"—that is, a storyteller—or around some incident, and inevitably there was a fresh incident every minute, given such a crowd of inmates. Some people had been here for more than a month, not going to work, visiting only the bathhouse to have their things disinfected. Twenty thousand working days lost each day, one hundred and sixty thousand working hours, or perhaps three hundred and twenty thousand working hours, since working days varied. Or you could say twenty thousand days of saved lives.

Twenty thousand days of life. There are various ways to interpret the figures; statistics is a devious science.

When food was being distributed, everyone was in their place (food was issued to ten men at a time). There were so many people that those who delivered the food barely had time to distribute breakfast before the time came to distribute lunch. And they had hardly finished distributing lunch before they began to distribute dinner. From morning to evening food was being distributed in the "section." Yet in the morning all that was given was a day's ration of bread and tea, which was warm boiled water, with half a herring every other day, while lunch was just soup and dinner just porridge.

Even so there wasn't enough time to hand out this modest amount.

The supervisor led Andreyev to the bunks and pointed to the second story: "That's your place."

There were protests from people already up there, but the supervisor swore at them. Andreyev grabbed the edge of the bunks with both hands and tried without success to swing his right leg onto the bunk. The supervisor's powerful arm flung him up and he flopped down heavily amid the naked bodies. Nobody paid any attention to him. This was the end of "registration" and "induction."

Andreyev slept. He awoke only when food was being handed out; after food he carefully, neatly licked his hands clean, and slept again, but not too deeply, for the lice wouldn't let him sleep properly.

Nobody asked him any questions, even though there were a lot of people from the taiga in this transit prison, and everybody else was destined to end up in there. And they understood that. Because they understood, they did not want to know anything about the inevitable taiga. Quite rightly, Andreyev considered: they wouldn't want to know any of what he had seen. Nothing could be avoided, and nothing could be foreseen. What was the point of unnecessary fear? While they were here they were still human, and Andreyev was a representative of the dead. His knowledge, that of a dead man, would be of no use to them while they were still alive.

After two days or so it was bathhouse day. They were all fed up with disinfection and the baths, so they assembled reluctantly, but Andreyev was anxious to get rid of his lice. He now had all the time in the world. Several times a day he examined all the seams in his whitened tunic. But only the disinfection chamber could result in complete success, so he was happy to go and, although he wasn't given any fresh linen and had to put his wet tunic back on his naked body, he no longer felt the usual louse bites.

In the bathhouse they were given their ration of water—one bowl of hot and one bowl of cold—but Andreyev tricked the bathhouse man and got an extra bowlful.

They were issued a tiny piece of soap, but you could collect the scraps of soap off the floor, so Andreyev tried to wash properly. This was his best bath for the whole of that year. He didn't mind the blood and pus flowing from the scurvy sores on his calves, or people staggering to get away from him in the bathhouse. They could, for all he cared, back away in disgust from his louse-ridden clothes.

Clothes were given back after they had been in the disinfection chamber. Ognev, Andreyev's neighbor, got doll's stockings back instead of his sheepskin stockings—the leather had shrunk. Ognev burst into tears. Fur stockings had been his salvation in the north. Andreyev gave him a malevolent look. He'd seen so many men weeping for the most varied reasons. Some were cunning pretenders, some neurotics, some had lost their clothing, some were just embittered, some wept because of the cold. Andreyev hadn't seen anyone weep out of hunger.

They returned through the silent, dark town. The aluminum-colored puddles were frozen, but the air was fresh and springlike. After this bath Andreyev slept especially well, "slept his fill," as his neighbor Ognev put it now that he had forgotten what had happened to him in the bathhouse.

Nobody was being allowed out. But there still was one job in the "section" that allowed you to go beyond the barbed wire. True, this didn't amount to passing the outer barbed wire around the settlement, which consisted of three fences each with ten strands of wire, and a forbidden zone, marked by a wire stretched just above the ground. Nobody even dreamed of getting that far. It was a matter of passing beyond the wire around the courtyard: the refectory, the kitchens, the stores, and the hospital were all there—another life forbidden to Andreyev. The only man who passed beyond the wire was the sanitation man. And when he died suddenly (life is full of merciful chances), Ognev, Andreyev's neighbor, demonstrated prodigious energy and initiative. He stopped eating his bread for two days, then he swapped his bread for a big fiber suitcase.

"We'll see Baron Mandel, Andreyev!"

Baron Mandel! A descendant of Pushkin! Over there, that was Mandel. The baron was a lanky, narrow-shouldered man with a tiny bald skull, and you could see him from afar. But Andreyev was not to make his acquaintance.

Ognev had hung on to the tweed jacket he had worn before he was arrested; he had only been a few months in quarantine.

Ognev offered his jacket and the fiber suitcase to the supervisor and got the job of the deceased sanitation man. About two weeks later, criminal convicts tried to strangle Ognev in the dark—fortunately, they didn't kill him—and took about three thousand rubles off him.

Andreyev seldom met Ognev when the latter's commercial career was at its height. After being badly beaten and tormented, Ognev, returning to his former place, made his confession one night to Andreyev.

Andreyev could have told him about a few things he had seen at the mines, but Ognev had no regrets and no complaints.

"They got me today, I'll get them tomorrow. I'll beat them ... at cards ... I'll fleece them in a game of shtoss, bezique, thirty-one. I'll get it all back!"

Ognev never helped Andreyev out with bread or money, but such help in these circumstances would have contradicted camp ethics, so that was quite normal.

There was one day when Andreyev was amazed to still be alive. It was so difficult to raise himself up on his bunk, but he somehow managed. Above all, he was lying down, not working, and as little as half a kilo of rye bread, three spoonfuls of porridge, and a bowl of thin gruel were enough to resurrect a man: as long as he didn't have to work.

It was at this point that he realized that he felt no fear and that life had no value for him. He also realized that he had undergone a great ordeal and had come out of it alive, that he had been fated to apply the terrible experience of the mines to his own benefit. He realized that, however wretched were the prisoner's possible choices of free will, they still existed. These possibilities were real and could, when necessary, save your life. And Andreyev was ready for the great battle, when he would have to oppose the beast with his own bestial cunning. He had been deceived, and he would deceive them. He wouldn't die, and he didn't intend to.

He would carry out his body's desires, what his body had told him in the gold mine. He had lost a battle in the mines, but that battle was not the last one. He was slag, mine refuse. And he would be that slag. He had seen that the purple stamp made by Lidiya Ivanovna on a piece of paper consisted of three letters: LPL—light physical labor. Andreyev knew that the mine took no heed of these annotations, but here in the center he intended to milk them for all they were worth.

But the possibilities were limited. He could have told the supervisor: "Here's me, Andreyev, lying down, refusing to go anywhere. If I'm sent to the mine, then at the first pass the truck reaches, I'll jump down, and the guard can shoot me if he wants, in any case I'm not going gold mining."

The possibilities were limited. But he was going to be cleverer here and trust his body more. And his body would not let him down. He had been let down by his family and by his country. Love, energy, abilities had all been trampled underfoot and smashed. All the justifications his brain tried to find were false, they were lies, and Andreyev realized this. Only the animal instinct aroused by the mines could and did suggest a way out.

It was here on these cyclopean bunks that Andreyev understood that he had some worth, that he could respect himself. Here he was, still alive, without betraying or selling anybody either under interrogation or in the camp. He had often managed to speak the truth, had managed to suppress his own fear. He had, of course, been afraid, but the moral barriers had become clearer, better defined than previously, everything had become simpler and clearer. For instance, it was clear that Andreyev couldn't survive. His former good health was lost forever, it had been irreparably broken. Irreparably? When Andreyev was brought to this town he thought that he had two or three weeks left to live. If he was to regain his former strength then he needed complete rest for many months in clean air, in spa conditions with milk and chocolate. And as it was perfectly obvious that Andreyev would never see such a spa, he was doomed to die. And yet that didn't frighten him. Many of his comrades had died. But something stronger than death was preventing him from dying. Love? Resentment? No. Man lives by the strength of the same primary causes that keep a tree, a stone, or a dog alive. This is what he had understood, and not just understood but felt deeply, here, in a town transit camp during a typhus quarantine.

The louse bites on his skin healed far more quickly than Andreyev's other wounds. The tortoise armor, which human skin turns into in the mines, was gradually vanishing; the bright pink frostbite scars on the tips of his fingers and toes had turned dark; the thin layer of skin covering them after the frostbite blister burst had become just a little bit tougher. And, above all, his left hand had unbent. Eighteen months of mine work had made both hands bend in a curve that was the same radius as the thickness of a spade or pickax handle; the hands had stuck in this position, Andreyev thought, forever. When he ate, he held the spoon handle, as did all his fellow inmates, like a pinch of salt, with his fingertips; he had forgotten that there was any other way of holding a spoon. His living hand was like an amputee's hook, and it only carried out the movements of an amputee's hook. The one other thing his hand could do was to make the sign of the cross, assuming that Andreyev prayed to God. But there was nothing except anger in his soul. The wounds to his soul were not so easy to heal, and they never would heal.

Yet Andreyev's hand did unbend. Once, in the bathhouse, the fingers of his left hand also unbent. He was astounded. The same would happen to the right hand, too, which was still as bent as ever. At night Andreyev gently touched his right hand, trying to bend back the fingers, and it seemed to him that any time now the hand would uncurl. He bit his fingernails as carefully as he could, and now he was gnawing, bit by bit, at the dirty, thick skin that had become just a little softer. This hygienic operation was one of Andreyev's very few amusements when he wasn't eating or sleeping.

The bleeding cracks in the soles of his feet were no longer as painful as they had been. The scurvy ulcers on his legs had not yet healed and still needed bandaging, but there were fewer and fewer wounds, and they were giving way to bluish-black marks that looked like brands on cattle or those on Negro slaves made by slave owners or slave traders. His big toes were the only parts that would not heal; the frostbite had gotten to the marrow of the bone and made them ooze pus. Admittedly, there was now far less pus than before, when he was in the mines, where so much pus and blood poured into his rubber galoshes (the prisoner's summer footwear) that his feet made a splashing noise with every step, as if he were walking through puddles.

Many years would pass before Andreyev's big toes would heal, and for many years after they healed, whenever the weather turned cold, the throbbing pain they caused would remind him of the northern mines. But Andreyev wasn't thinking about the future. Having learned at the mines not to make plans for his life further than the next day, he tried hard to fight for what was close, as does any man who is only a few feet away from death. At the moment he had only one wish: for the typhus quarantine to go on indefinitely. But that was impossible, and the day came when the quarantine was over.

On that particular morning all the inhabitants of the "section" were herded into the yard. The prisoners spent several hours crowded outside the barbed-wire fence, freezing. The supervisor stood on a barrel and called surnames in his hoarse, despairing voice. Those whose names were called came out through the gate, never to return. On the highway trucks were roaring, roaring so loudly in the frosty morning air that the supervisor couldn't make himself heard.

"Don't let them call me out, don't let them call me out," Andreyev begged fate, like a child repeating a magic formula. No, his luck wouldn't hold. Even if he wasn't called out today, he would be tomorrow. Again he'd go to the gold-mine pit face, to starvation, beatings, and death.

His frostbitten fingers and toes started aching, so did his ears and cheeks. Andreyev kept shifting his feet, more and more frequently, hunching himself and forming his fingers into a tube and breathing into them, but his numb feet and sick hands were not so easy to get warm. Nothing was of any use. He was helpless in this struggle with a gigantic machine whose teeth were grinding up his entire body.

"Voronov! Voronov!" shouted the supervisor, straining his voice to the utmost. "Voronov! I know you're here, you bastard!" And the supervisor angrily chucked the thin yellow file of the prisoner's "case" on the barrel and crushed it with his foot.

It was then that Andreyev understood everything in one second. This was like a flash of lightning in a thunderstorm, showing you the way to salvation. Instantly, worked up to the maximum, he summoned his courage and stepped toward the supervisor, who was calling out surname after surname, while people were leaving the yard one after the other. But the crowd was still too thick. But now, now....

"Andreyev," yelled the supervisor.

Andreyev stayed silent, examining the supervisor's shaven cheeks. After contemplating those cheeks, he switched his gaze to the files with prisoners' "cases." There were only a few left.

"The last truck," Andreyev thought.

The supervisor held Andreyev's file in his hand for a while, then, not repeating his summons, set it aside on the barrel.

"Sychiov! Answer with your name and patronymic!"

"Vladimir Ivanovich," an elderly prisoner answered, as the rules dictated, before pushing the crowd aside.

"Article of Criminal Code? Sentence? Out you go!"

Several more people responded to the summons and left. They were followed by the supervisor. The remaining prisoners were sent back to the "section."

The coughing, foot-stamping, and yells became indistinguishable and merged into the polyphonic conversational voices of hundreds of people.

Andreyev wanted to live. He had set himself two simple aims and decided to attain them. It was extraordinarily clear that he had to hang on here as long as possible, to the last day. He had to be careful not to make mistakes, to control himself....Gold meant death. Nobody in this transit camp knew that better than Andreyev. At all costs he had to avoid the taiga and the gold-mine pit face. How could the disenfranchised slave Andreyev manage that? This was how: during the quarantine the taiga had become depopulated—the cold, starvation, long hours of heavy work, and lack of sleep had deprived the taiga of human resources, which meant that as a matter of priority, trucks would be dispatching people to the "gold" administrations, and only when the mines' human requirements ("Send two hundred trees," they wrote in official telegrams) were met, would they start sending people anywhere other than the taiga or the gold mines. Where that might be didn't matter to Andreyev, as long as it wasn't gold mining.

Andreyev said not a word of this to anyone. He didn't consult anyone, not Ognev, not Parfentiev, his fellow worker at the mine, not a single person of the thousand who shared the bunks with him. He didn't, because he knew that anyone he told about his plan would betray him to the bosses—in exchange for praise, a cigarette stub, or for no reason in particular....

He knew what a burden a secret was, and he could keep a secret, too. This was the one thing that did not frighten him. If you were on your own, it was two, three, four times as easy to pass through the teeth of the machine unharmed. His game was his alone, and that, too, was something the mines had taught him well.

For many days Andreyev refused to respond to the summons. As soon as the quarantine was over, the prisoners began to be forced to go out to work, and as you left, you had to use your ingenuity to avoid being put into large groups, which were usually taken to do earthworks with crowbars, pickaxes, and spades. The smaller groups of two or three men, however, always had a chance of earning an extra piece of bread or even sugar, and Andreyev hadn't seen sugar for more than eighteen months. This was an easy calculation to make, and it was quite right. None of these lesser jobs was legal, of course; these prisoners were listed as being in the big groups, and there were a lot of people who wanted to exploit unpaid labor. Those who ended up doing earthworks went to work with the hope of begging for some tobacco or bread. You could sometimes beg successfully, even from casual passersby. Andreyev went to work at the vegetable stores where he ate all the beetroot and carrots he could and from where he brought "home" a few raw potatoes that he roasted in the stove ashes, pulling them out and eating them when they were still half raw—life here forced you to consume any food as fast as you could, for there were too many starving people around you.

The start of the day now almost made sense, for it was full of activity. Every day began with standing around for two hours or so in the freezing cold, with the supervisor shouting out, "Hey, you, give me your name and patronymic." But when this daily sacrifice to Moloch was over, everyone ran, stamping their feet, back to barracks, from where they were taken off to work. Andreyev also spent time at the bakery, took the rubbish out of the women's transit camp, washed the floors in the guards' barracks, where he collected the sticky, tasty leftover pieces of meat from the plates left behind in the ill-lit refectory. After work there, big bowls were carried to the kitchen. The bowls were full of the milky jelly known as *kisel* and piles of bread, and everyone sat around them, eating and stuffing their pockets.

Only once did Andreyev find he had miscalculated. His motto was, the smaller the group, the better, and being on your own was best of all. But a man on his own was rarely required. Once, the supervisor, who now knew Andreyev's face (but thought his name was Muraviov), said, "I've found you a job you'll never forget: sawing firewood for the top bosses. You can take somebody with you."

They cheerfully ran ahead of their escort, who was wearing a cavalry officer's greatcoat, his boots slipping on the ice, losing his footing, leaping over puddles and then racing to catch up with them, all the time lifting the hem of his greatcoat. Soon they were approaching a small house. Its gate was shut and its fence was topped with barbed wire. Their escort knocked. A dog barked in the yard. The boss's orderly unlocked the gate and without a word showed them into a shed, where he shut them in, releasing an enormous guard dog into the yard. He brought them a bucket of water. Until the prisoners had sawn and split all the firewood in the shed, the dog kept them locked up. Late in the evening they were taken back to the camp. The next day they were to be taken to the same place, but Andreyev hid under the bunks and that day he did not go out to work.

The next morning, before the bread was handed out, a simple idea occurred to him. He acted on it immediately.

He took off his cloth boots and put them on the edge of the bunks, soles facing out, one on top of the other, to look as if he himself were lying in his boots on the bunk. He lay facedown alongside them and rested his head on his elbow.

The bread distributor quickly counted out the next ten rations and gave Andreyev ten portions of bread. Andreyev had two for himself. But this trick was a one-off and unreliable; Andreyev again began looking for work outside.

Was he then thinking about his family? No. About freedom? No. Was he reciting poetry by heart? No. Was he remembering the past? No. He was kept alive by indifference and resentment. This was when he met Captain Schneider.

The gangsters were occupying the area around the stove. Their bunks were covered with dirty quilted blankets and a large number of down pillows of various sizes. A quilted blanket was a successful thief's inalienable possession; he took it with him from one prison or camp to another, and if he didn't have one, he would steal it or take it off somebody else. A pillow, however, was not just something to lay your head on, it was also a card table for the endless dueling card games. That card table could take on any shape. And yet it remained a pillow. Gamblers would rather lose their trousers at cards than their pillow.

The gang leaders, or rather those who were something like gang leaders at any one time, settled on the blankets and pillows. Higher up, on the third row of bunks, where it was dark, there were more blankets and pillows. This was where the thieves dragged up effeminate boy thieves—any boy would do, for almost every thief was a pederast.

The thieves were surrounded by a crowd of serfs and lackeys—court storytellers, for the criminals considered it civilized to take an interest in "novels"; hairdressers with a little bottle of perfume existed even in these conditions; and there was a whole crowd of other eager servants prepared to do anything for a crust of bread or a spoonful of soup.

"Quiet! Senia is talking. Quiet, Senia is going to bed."

A familiar scene at the mines.

Suddenly Andreyev caught sight of a familiar face, familiar features in the crowd of mendicants, the criminals' invariable court; he heard a familiar voice. There was no doubt: it was Captain Schneider, who had been Andreyev's cellmate in Butyrki prison.

Captain Schneider was a German communist, active in the Comintern, a connoisseur of Goethe, an educated Marxist theoretician. Andreyev still remembered conversations with him, "high pressure" conversations in the long prison nights. A cheerful extrovert by nature, the captain had been an oceangoing seaman and kept the prison cell's fighting spirits up.

Andreyev couldn't believe his eyes. "Schneider!"

"Yes? What do you want?" The captain turned around. Gazing with his lusterless blue eyes, he failed to recognize Andreyev.

"Schneider!"

"Well, what do you want? Quiet, or you'll wake Senia."

But the edge of a blanket had been lifted and a pale, sick-looking face was poked out into the light.

"Hey, Captain," said Senia in a weary tenor voice. "I can't get to sleep: I miss you."

"Coming, coming," said the captain, flustered.

He climbed up to the bunk, folded the blanket back, sat down, shoved his hand under the blanket, and started tickling Senia's heels.

Andreyev slowly returned to his place. He wished he were dead. And although this was a minor, harmless event—compared with what he had seen and what he was going to see—Captain Schneider was fixed in his memory forever.

There were fewer and fewer people. The transit camp was emptying. Andreyev came face-to-face with the supervisor.

"What's your surname?"

Andreyev had long been ready for this question.

"Gurov," he meekly responded.

"Wait."

The supervisor flicked through several sheets of the list, on paper as thin as cigarette paper.

"No, no such name."

"Can I go?"

"Clear off, pig," the supervisor roared.

Once he got the job of cleaning and dishwashing in the transit camp refectory for prisoners who had been freed after finishing their sentence and were now leaving. His partner was a walking skeleton, a goner of indeterminate age, who had just been released from the local prison. This was the first time the goner had been out to work. He kept asking what they would be doing, whether they would be fed, and if it would be convenient to ask for something to eat just before they began work. The goner said that he had been a professor of neurology, and Andreyev remembered his name.

Experience had taught Andreyev that camp cooks, and not just the cooks, disliked the "Ivan Ivanoviches," as they called intellectuals. He advised the professor not to ask for anything in advance; he was depressed by the thought that most of the dishwashing and cleaning would fall to him, for the professor was too weak. That was as it should be, and there was no reason to take offense. How many times in the mines had Andreyev himself been a bad, weak workmate for his comrades, and nobody had ever said a word. Where were they all now? Where were Sheinin, Riutin, Khvostov? They'd all died, but he, Andreyev, had come back to life. Actually, he hadn't yet come back to life and probably wouldn't. But he was going to fight for life.

Andreyev's guesses were right after all. The professor did turn out to be a weak, if overeager, helper.

When work was finished, the cook gave them a seat in the kitchen and placed an enormous cauldron of thick fish soup and a big metal plate of porridge before them. The professor clapped his hands with joy, but Andreyev, who at the mine had seen a man eat twenty portions of a three-course dinner, with bread, looked askance and disapprovingly at this offering.

"What, no bread?" he asked, frowning.

"Of course, there's bread: I'll give you a bit each." And the cook took two lumps of bread out of the cupboard.

The free meal didn't take long to eat. When he was a "guest," as in this case, Andreyev had the foresight not to eat the bread. He now put it in his pocket. But the professor broke off chunks of bread, chewing it as he swallowed the soup, and big drops of dirty sweat appeared on his close-shaven gray head.

"Here's a ruble each for you as well," said the cook. "I haven't got any more bread at the moment."

That was excellent pay for the job.

The transit camp had a shop, a stall where you could buy free workers' bread. Andreyev told the professor about it.

"Yes, yes, you're right," said the professor. "But I saw they sell sweet kvass there, too. Or is it lemonade? I'd love to have some lemonade, or anything sweet."

"It's up to you, Professor. But if I were in your shoes, I'd rather buy bread."

"Yes, yes, you're right," repeated the professor. "But I'm desperate for something sweet. You have something to drink, too."

But Andreyev refused outright to have any kvass.

In the end, he got what he wanted: a job on his own. He began washing floors in the transit-camp administration office. Every evening the orderly who was responsible for keeping the office clean would come to fetch him. The office consisted of two tiny rooms filled with desks, each about four meters square. The floors were painted. The job took a mere ten minutes to do, and Andreyev could not at first understand why the orderly took on a workman to do something like this. After all, the orderly even crossed the entire camp to bring the water in person, and clean rags were always waiting and ready. Yet it was generously paid: tobacco, soup and porridge, bread, and sugar. The orderly promised to give Andreyev a summer jacket, but there wasn't time.

Clearly, the orderly thought it beneath him to wash floors, even if it would only take five minutes a day, when he had the power to hire someone to do the dirty work. This attitude was something typical of Russians, which Andreyev had observed in the mines as well. If the boss gave the orderly a handful of tobacco to clean the barracks, the orderly would put half in his own pouch and hire another orderly from the barracks where the political prisoners were housed. This second orderly would then divide his share in half and hire a workman from his barracks to do the job for two cigarettes. So a laborer who'd already done a shift of twelve to fourteen hours would wash the floors at night for those two cigarettes, and what's more, consider it a piece of luck, for he could swap the tobacco for bread.

Questions of exchange rates are the most complex theoretical area of economics. In the camps, too, these questions were complex, and the benchmark currencies were strange: tea, tobacco, and bread were the currencies subject to an exchange rate.

The administration orderly sometimes paid Andreyev with kitchen vouchers. These were stamped pieces of cardboard, something like tokens, giving you ten dinners, five second courses, etc. The orderly gave Andreyev a token for twenty portions of porridge, but these twenty portions weren't enough to cover the bottom of his tin bowl.

Andreyev saw the gangsters pushing bright orange thirty-ruble notes instead of tokens through the window. These banknotes worked without fail. The bowl would be filled with porridge that gushed through the window in response to such a "token."

There were now fewer and fewer people in the transit camp. Finally the day came when the last truck left the camp and there were only about thirty men left in the yard.

This time they were not allowed to go back to the barracks; instead, they were lined up and led across the entire camp.

"All the same, they're not taking us off to be shot," said an enormous, big-handed, one-eyed man, striding along next to Andreyev.

"That's for certain, we're not going to be shot," Andreyev also thought. They were all brought to see the supervisor in the accounting section.

"We're going to take your fingerprints," said the supervisor, coming out onto the porch.

"Well, if it's a matter of fingers, you don't need fingers for that," the one-eyed man said cheerfully.

"My surname is Filippovsky. Georgi Adamovich."

"And yours?"

"Andreyev, Pavel Ivanovich."

The supervisor picked out their personal files.

"We've been looking for you for some time," he said, without resentment. "Go back to the barracks, and I'll tell you later where we're sending you."

Andreyev knew that he had won the battle for his life. It simply was not possible that the taiga still had an appetite for human beings. If there were any departures, they would be for work that was nearby, local. Or even in the town—that was better still. They couldn't send him far, and not only because Andreyev was now assigned "light physical labor." He knew the way that sudden reassignments worked. They couldn't send him far because the taiga recruitment was now completed. Only nearby work trips—where life would be easier, simpler, where he would be better fed, where there were no gold-mine pit faces, and where there was consequently a chance of salvation—were still waiting for their final turn. This was something Andreyev had learned by blood and sweat during his two years of labor in the mines, and by his wild animal's tension during these months of quarantine. Too much had been done. Hopes had to be realized, come what may.

He had only to wait for one more night.

After breakfast the supervisor came rushing into the barracks with a list, a short list, as Andreyev immediately noticed with relief. Lists from the mines had twenty-five names of men to be loaded into a truck, and that always meant a lot of paperwork.

Andreyev's and Filippovsky's names were called out from that list; the list had more people on it, not many, but more than two or three surnames.

Those called out were taken to the familiar door of the accounts section. Three more people were already there: a grave, gray-haired, relaxed old man wearing a good sheepskin jacket and felt boots; a dirty, fidgety man wearing a quilted waistcoat and trousers and rubber boots with foot bindings; the third a dignified old man, looking down at his feet. A man in a military Asiatic coat and a flat fur cossack hat was standing some distance away.

"This is the lot," said the supervisor. "Are they what you want?"

The man in the Asiatic coat gestured to the gray-haired old man with his finger. "Who are you?"

"Izgibin, Yuri Ivanovich, article fifty-eight. Sentence, twenty-five years," the old man reported in a spirited voice.

"No, no." The man in the Asiatic coat frowned. "I meant what is your profession? I can find your standard details on my own."

"Stove builder, sir."

"Anything else?"

"I can do metalwork."

"Very good. You?" The officer turned his gaze to Filippovsky.

The one-eyed giant said that he was a locomotive stoker from Kamenets-Podolsk.

"And you?"

The dignified old man surprised everyone by mumbling a few words in German.

"What's that?" asked the man in the Asiatic coat. He was intrigued.

"Don't worry," said the supervisor. "He's a carpenter, a good carpenter, Frizorger. He's not quite himself. But he'll come around."

"Why is he speaking German?"

"He's from near Saratov, from the autonomous German republic—"

"Ah. And you?" This was directed at Andreyev.

"He needs skilled people and skilled workers," thought Andreyev. "I'll be a leatherworker."

"A tanner, sir."

"Very good. How old are you?"

"Thirty-one."

The officer shook his head. As he was a man of experience and had seen resurrections from the dead before, he did not comment but switched his gaze to the fifth man.

The fifth, the fidget, turned out to be no more or less than an activist in the Esperanto society.

"You see, I'm supposed to be an agronomist, and that's what I've studied, even lectured in, but my case is to do with the Esperanto speakers."

"Spying, is it?" the man in the Asiatic coat asked with no particular interest.

"Yes, yes, something like that," the fidget confirmed.

"Well, what then?" asked the supervisor.

"I'll take them," said the officer. "In any case, that's the best I'll get. There's not much choice now."

All five of them were put in a separate cell, a room attached to the barracks. But there were two or three more surnames on the list, a fact that Andreyev had taken careful note of. The supervisor came.

"Where are we going?"

"You'll be working somewhere local, what else?" said the supervisor. "And that officer will be your boss. We'll send you off in an hour. You've been fattening yourselves up here for three months, my friends, it can't go on forever."

An hour later they were called out, but to a storehouse, not a truck. "Presumably to get new work clothes," Andreyev thought. "Any day now it will be spring. It's April." He'd be given summer clothes, and he'd hand in, throw away, and forget his hateful mining winter clothes. But instead of a summer outfit they were issued more winter clothes. Was it a mistake? No, there was a red-pencil note on the list: "winter things."

Utterly puzzled, on that spring day they dressed in refurbished quilted waistcoats and pea jackets and old felt boots that had been repaired. Jumping as best they could over the puddles, they managed, full of anxiety, to get back to the barracks room that they had left for the storehouse.

Everyone was extremely worried, and nobody spoke. Only Frizorger kept mumbling and mumbling in German.

"He's saying his prayers, the fucker," Filippovsky whispered to Andreyev.

"Well, does anyone here know anything?" asked Andreyev.

The gray-haired stove builder, who looked like a professor, listed all the nearby workplaces: the port, the fourth kilometer, the seventeenth kilometer, the twenty-third, the forty-seventh. . . .

After that there were a series of districts for roadworks, places only a little better than gold mines.

"Out you come! Move to the gates!" They all came out and went to the camp gates. Outside the gates was a big truck, its platform covered with a green tarpaulin.

"Guards, take over."

A guard did a roll call. Andreyev felt his legs and back going cold. . . .

"Get in the truck!"

The guard flung back the edge of the big tarpaulin covering the truck. The truck was full of people, sitting all around the edges.

"Get in!"

All five newcomers sat down together. Nobody spoke. The guard got into the truck, the engine rattled to life, and the truck moved off along the road, turning onto the main highway.

"We're being taken to the fourth kilometer," said the stove maker. The milestones flashed past. All five moved their heads to look through a crack in the tarpaulin. They couldn't believe their eyes....

"Seventeenth kilometer...."

"Twenty-third...." Filippovsky was counting.

"Take us to a local job, you bastards!" the stove maker rasped angrily. For some time now the truck had wended its way along a road that wound between the bare hills. The highway was like a cable pulling the sea toward the sky. The mountains were bending their backs to do the towing.

"Forty-seventh," squeaked the fidgety Esperanto man in despair.

The truck flew past.

"Where are we going?" asked Andreyev, grabbing someone's shoulder.

"We'll spend the night at Atka, at kilometer two hundred and eight."

"And after that?"

"I don't know.... Got anything to smoke?"

The truck puffed heavily as it climbed the pass over the Yablonovy Mountains.

1959

BOOK TWO

The Left Bank

To Ira, my endless recollection, brought to a halt in *The Left Bank*

THE PROCURATOR OF JUDEA

ON DECEMBER 5, 1947, the steamship *KIM* entered Nagayevo Bay with a cargo of human beings. This was the last voyage, the end of the shipping season. Magadan met its visitors with temperatures of forty below zero. Not that these were visitors; they were prisoners, the real masters of this region.

All the town's bosses, military and civilian, were at the port. All available trucks came to meet the *KIM* when it arrived at Nagayevo port. Soldiers and special troops surrounded the pier; unloading began.

As far as five hundred kilometers from the bay every vehicle the mines could spare, summoned by the labor selector, set off empty to Magadan.

The dead were thrown onto the shore and then taken to the cemetery to be laid in mass graves; no tags were attached to the bodies, but a document was drawn up stating that exhumation would be needed at some time in the future.

Those who were most seriously ill, but still alive, were distributed among the prison hospitals of Magadan, Ola, Arman, and Dukcha.

Moderately ill prisoners were taken to the central prison hospital on the left bank of the Kolyma River. This hospital had only recently been moved from the center of Magadan to the twenty-third kilometer out of town. If the *KIM* had arrived a year earlier, there would have been no need to travel another five hundred kilometers.

The head of the surgical department was Kubantsev, who had only just come from the army, from the front, and was shattered by the sight of the prisoners and their terrible injuries, such as he had never witnessed or dreamed of in his life. Every truck that arrived from Magadan had bodies of those who had died on the journey. The surgeon realized that these were the less-seriously sick, who were transportable, and that the worst cases had been left in Magadan.

The surgeon recited the words of General Ridgway, which he had happened to read just after the war: "A soldier's experience at the front cannot prepare him for the spectacle of death in the camps."

Kubantsev had lost his sangfroid. He didn't know what orders to give, where to begin. Kolyma had overwhelmed the surgeon with too great a burden. But something had to be done. The male nurses took the sick from the trucks, carrying them on stretchers into the surgical department, every corridor of which was tightly stacked with stretchers. Smells are as memorable as lines of poetry or human faces. The smell of that first wave of camp pus left a permanent mark on Kubantsev's olfactory memory. He remembered that smell for the rest of his life. You might think that pus smells the same anywhere, and that death too is the same. But that isn't true. All his life Kubantsev felt that he could smell the wounds of his first Kolyma patients.

Kubantsev smoked and, as he smoked, he felt he was losing his self-control, that he didn't know what orders to give the nurses, the paramedics, or the doctors.

"Aleksei Alekseyevich," Kubantsev heard someone next to him say. It was Braude, an ex-prisoner and a surgeon, who used to be in charge of the department and had only just been dismissed on the orders of the authorities, simply because Braude was a former prisoner and, what's more, had a German surname. "Let me give the orders. I know how things are done. I've been here for ten years."

Worried and perturbed, Kubantsev deferred his authority and everything sprang into action. Three surgeons began operating simultaneously. Paramedics acted as their assistants and scrubbed the surgeon's hands. Other paramedics did injections and administered heart medicines by drip.

"Amputations, nothing but amputations," mumbled Braude. He loved surgery and, as he himself said, suffered if he had to endure a day without an operation or an incision. "We're not going to be bored now," said Braude joyfully. "Kubantsev may be a good man, but he's out of his depth. Front-line surgeon! All they know is instructions, plans, orders, but here we've got real life, Kolyma!"

Not that Braude was a spiteful man. Removed quite unjustifiably from his post, he felt no dislike for his successor and didn't put wrenches in the works. Quite the opposite: Braude saw that Kubantsev was at a loss and responded to his gratitude. All the same, Kubantsev had a family, a wife, a school-age son, an officer's Polar Circle rations, a high salary, the ruble bonus. And what did Braude have? A ten-year sentence behind him and a very uncertain future. Braude came from Saratov, he was a student of the famous Krause and had been very promising. But 1937 had smashed his career to smithereens. So he was hardly going to take revenge on Kubantsev for his own misfortunes.

Thus Braude gave the orders, did the cutting and the cursing. Braude lived by forgetting about himself and, although at moments of reflection he often cursed himself for this despicable forgetfulness, he couldn't change.

Today he had decided, "I'll leave the hospital. I'll go to the mainland."

On December 5, 1947, the steamship *KIM* entered Nagayevo Bay with a cargo of human beings—three thousand prisoners. During the voyage the prisoners mutinied and those in charge decided to flood all the holds with water. This was done when the temperature was minus forty. Third- or fourth-degree frostbite (Kubantsev called it "cold-weather injuries") was something Kubantsev was fated to become familiar with, as a reward for his years of service, on his first day of work in Kolyma.

All this had to be forgotten, and Kubantsev, a disciplined man of willpower, forgot it. He made himself forget.

Seventeen years later Kubantsev could remember the name and patronymic of every paramedic-prisoner, of every female nurse; he could remember the camp "love affairs"—which prisoner "lived with" which prisoner. He recalled the exact rank of every one of the more despicable bosses. The only thing that Kubantsev couldn't remember was the steamship *KIM* and its three thousand frostbitten prisoners.

Anatole France wrote the story "The Procurator of Judea," in which Pontius Pilate fails after seventeen years to remember Jesus Christ.

1965

LEPERS

JUST AFTER the war I witnessed another drama, or rather the fifth act of a drama, being played out in the hospital.

The war brought from the lower depths of life into the light layers and pieces of life that had always, everywhere been concealed from bright sunlight. I don't mean criminal or underworld circles: this was something quite different.

In areas where the war was going on the leprosy hospices were demolished and the lepers mingled with the ordinary population. Was this a secret or an open aspect of war? Was it chemical or bacteriological warfare?

People suffering from leprosy had no trouble pretending to be war wounded or war cripples. Lepers mingled with those fleeing eastward, thus returning to real life, however terrifying, where they would be assumed to be victims of war, even heroes.

Lepers lived and worked. Not until the war ended would the doctors remember about the lepers, and the terrible card-index lists of the leprosariums began to fill up again.

Lepers were living among people, sharing retreats, attacks, the joys and miseries of victory. Lepers were working in factories and on the land. They were becoming bosses and subordinates. The one thing they could never be was soldiers, even though the stumps of their fingers and toes were almost indistinguishable from war wounds. In fact, lepers claimed to be war wounded, a small number among the millions of real ones.

Sergei Fedorenko was a stores manager. As a war invalid, he was very clever at managing with his awkward finger stumps and did his job well. He could expect a career, a party ticket, but once there was money he could lay hands on, he began drinking and taking time off work, so that he was arrested, convicted, and arrived at Magadan on one of the Kolyma ship voyages as a prisoner sentenced to ten years for nonpolitical crimes.

Once in Kolyma, Fedorenko changed his diagnosis. There were plenty of cripples here, self-mutilated ones for example. But it was better, more fashionable, and less noticeable to merge with the mass of frostbite victims.

That's how I came across him in the hospital: symptoms of third- or fourth-degree frostbite, sores that would not heal, a stump of a foot, stumps of fingers on both hands.

Fedorenko had treatment: it didn't work. But every patient fought his treatment in any way he could. After many months of trophic ulcers, Fedorenko discharged himself and, wanting to stay in the hospital, became a male nurse, ending up as a senior nurse in a surgical department of some three hundred beds. This was the central hospital, with a thousand beds just for prisoners. On one of the floors there was an annex, a hospital for free contracted workers.

One day the doctor who had Fedorenko's file fell ill and a Dr. Krasinsky, an old military doctor, a lover of Jules Verne (why?), took over his case: Krasinsky, despite living in Kolyma, had not lost his desire to gossip, chatter, and discuss.

Examining Fedorenko, Krasinsky was struck by something he himself couldn't put a finger on. He had known this uncertain feeling ever since he was a student. No, this was not a trophic ulcer, not a stump resulting from an explosion or an ax blow. This was tissue slowly disintegrating. Krasinsky's heart began to pound. He called in Fedorenko again and pulled him over to the window, to the light, where, looking hard at his face, he could not believe what he was seeing. This was leprosy! This was the lion's mask: a human face more like a lion's. Feverishly Krasinsky leafed through his textbooks. He picked up a big needle and pricked repeatedly one of the many white spots on Fedorenko's skin. No pain at all! Pouring sweat, Krasinsky wrote a report to the authorities. The patient Fedorenko was isolated in a separate ward, flakes of skin were sent to the center, first to Magadan, then to Moscow, for a biopsy. A reply came in two weeks. Leprosy! Krasinsky walked about like the hero of the day. One group of authorities corresponded with another about establishing a special squad for a leprosarium in Kolyma. The leprosarium was set up on an island, and at the ferry-crossing points on either bank machine guns were set up. It needed a special squad.

Fedorenko did not deny that he had been in a leprosarium and that the lepers, once abandoned, had fled to freedom. Some had tried to catch up with the retreat, others had gone to welcome Hitler's troops. Just as in life elsewhere. Fedorenko calmly waited to be sent away, but the hospital was seething like an anthill. The whole hospital. Those who'd been badly beaten under interrogation and whose souls had been reduced to dust by a thousand interrogations, while their bodies were wrecked and exhausted by unbearably heavy work, prisoners with sentences of twenty-five years plus five years' deprivation of rights, sentences that were unsurvivable, which you could not hope to come out of alive.... All these people were trembling, yelling, and cursing Fedorenko, because they were afraid of catching leprosy.

This was the same psychological phenomenon that makes an escapee decide to put off a well-prepared escape attempt, just because on that particular day tobacco or parcels are being issued in camp. There are as many peculiar examples that contradict all logic as there are camps.

Human shame, for example. What are its limits and range? People whose lives have been destroyed, whose future and past have been trampled into the ground, suddenly turn out to be in thrall to some trivial prejudice, something banal that for some reason can't be surmounted or set aside. A sudden onset of shame, likewise, comes like the most refined of human feelings and is remembered for a lifetime as something authentic, infinitely precious. There was an incident in the hospital when a paramedic, who was not yet qualified but was just assisting, was given the job of shaving women, a whole newly arrived group of women prisoners. The bosses wanted a bit of amusement, so they ordered women to shave the men and men to shave the women. Everyone amuses themselves as best they can. But the male barber begged a woman he knew to perform this sanitary ceremony herself, and he refused even to think that their lives were in any case ruined, that all these amusements of the camp bosses were just some filthy foam in this terrible cauldron where personal lives were being boiled to death.

The laughable, the tender, the human in human beings is revealed out of the blue.

There was panic in the hospital. Fedorenko had been working for several months there. Unfortunately, in leprosy the dormant period of the infection, before any outward symptoms appear, lasts for several years. Those who were prone to worry were doomed to stay afraid forever, whether they were free or prisoners.

There was panic in the hospital. The doctors feverishly looked for those white insensitive spots on the skin of the patients and the staff. Along with the stethoscope and the rubber mallet, a needle became part of the essential equipment for a doctor's preliminary examination.

The patient Fedorenko was brought and undressed in front of paramedics and doctors. A warder armed with a pistol stood some distance from the patient. Dr. Krasinsky, armed with an enormous pointer, lectured on leprosy, pointing with his stick at the former nurse's lion face, or his missing digits, or the shiny white patches on his back.

Literally every single person in the hospital, free or imprisoned, was reexamined. Suddenly a small white patch, an insensitive white patch, was found on Shura Leshchinskaya's back: she had been a nurse at the front and was now the duty nurse in the women's section. She had only recently, a few months ago, come to the hospital. She did not have a lion face. Her manner was no more severe and no more obliging, her tone no louder and no gentler than any other hospital nurse who was also a prisoner.

Leshchinskaya was locked up in one of the women's wards, and a piece of her skin was sent to Magadan and then to Moscow for analysis. And the reply came: it was leprosy!

Disinfection after leprosy is a difficult business. Any house inhabited by a leper is supposed to be burned, so say the textbooks. But burning down, reducing to cinders a ward in an enormous two-story building, a gigantic building, was something nobody would undertake. Similarly, people will take risks when it comes to disinfecting expensive furs, preferring to leave the microbes alone rather than lose their expensive possessions (for a high-temperature "baking" kills not just the microbes but the fabric they inhabit). The authorities would have kept just as silent if it had been a case even of plague or cholera.

Somebody took the responsibility for not burning the building down. Even the ward in which Fedorenko was locked, while awaiting dispatch to a leprosarium, was not burned. They merely drowned everything by repeatedly spraying phenol and carbolic acid.

Immediately a new and serious cause for alarm appeared. Both Fedorenko and Leshchinskaya were occupying wards big enough to take several beds. A response to this problem, like the special squad of two men to escort them, still had not materialized, despite all the reminders from the bosses in their daily, or rather nightly telegrams to Magadan.

In the basement they set aside an area and built two cells for prisoners with leprosy. This was where they moved Fedorenko and Leshchinskaya. Behind heavy locks, with armed guards, the lepers were left to wait for orders and for the squad to escort them to the leprosarium.

Fedorenko and Leshchinskaya spent twenty-four hours in their cells; the next shift of sentinels found the cells empty.

Panic broke out in the hospital. Everything in those cells was as it should be—windows and doors.

Krasinsky was the first to realize what had happened: they had escaped through the floor.

Fedorenko, a very strong man, had taken the joists apart and gotten into the corridor, raided the bread-cutting room and the operation theater of the surgical department. After collecting all the alcohol and alcoholic extracts from the cupboard, as well as all the codeines, he hauled off his loot to his underground den.

The lepers marked off a place to sleep on which they threw blankets, mattresses; they made a barricade of joists to keep the world, the guards, the hospital, the leprosarium at bay. There they lived as man and wife for several days, three, I believe.

On the third day the searchers and the guard's search dogs found the lepers. I was one of the search party, having to bend only a little under the hospital's tall cellar ceiling. The foundations were very deep. The joists had been taken apart. Down at the bottom, not bothering to get up, lay both lepers, naked. Fedorenko's mutilated dark arms were embracing Leshchinskaya's shining white body. They were both drunk.

They were covered with blankets and taken up to one of the cells: they weren't separated again.

Who covered them with a blanket, who touched those terrible bodies? It was a special male nurse, whom they found in the hospital as one of the employed staff, and to whom they gave seven days off his sentence for every day worked (at the instigation of the top bosses). So he got better terms than he would in the tungsten, lead, or uranium mines. Seven days off for one day worked. His article of the Criminal Code was irrelevant in this case. They had found a front-line soldier who had been given twenty-five plus five years for betraying the motherland: he naïvely supposed that his heroism would reduce his sentence and that the day of his release would be brought nearer.

Prisoner Korolkov, a lieutenant in the war, guarded the cell day and night. He even slept by the cell doors. But when an escort arrived from the island, prisoner Korolkov was taken along with the lepers, to look after them. That was the last I heard of Korolkov, of Fedorenko, or of Leshchinskaya.

1963

IN THE ADMISSIONS ROOM

"A PARTY of prisoners from Zolotistoye!"

"Which mine?"

"Suchi (the Bitches') mine."

"Call for soldiers to search them. They'll be too much for you."

"They'll miss things. They're just regulars."

"No, they won't. I'll be there in the doorway."

"All right, if you think so."

The prisoners, covered in dirt and dust, were unloaded. This was a group of "special cases": there were too many broad-shouldered men, too many bandages, and the percentage of surgical patients was far too high for a party from the mines.

Klavdia Ivanovna, the duty doctor, a free worker, came in.

"Shall we begin?"

"Let's wait until the soldiers come and search them."

"Are those the new rules?"

"Yes. New rules. You'll see what it's all about in a moment, Klavdia."

"Hey you, with the crutches, move to the middle of the room. Your papers!"

The man, a foreman, handed over the papers: a referral to the hospital. The foreman held back his personal files.

"Take off your bandage. Grisha, hand me some bandages. Our own ones. Klavdia, please examine his fracture."

Like a white snake, the old bandage slithered onto the floor. The paramedic kicked it aside. The splint turned out to have something bandaged to it: not a knife but a dagger, made from a big nail, the most portable war weapon for the Bitches. As it fell to the floor, the dagger clanged, and Klavdia turned pale.

The soldiers picked up the dagger.

"Take off all the bandages."

"How about the plaster casts?"

"Break all the plaster casts. New ones can be put on tomorrow."

The paramedic didn't even look as he listened to the usual sounds of bits of metal falling to the stone floor. There was a weapon under every single plaster cast. They had been tucked away before being plastered over.

"You realize what this means, Klavdia."

"I do."

"So do I. We won't be writing a report to the authorities, we'll just tell the head of the mine's health service by word of mouth. Is that all right, Klavdia?"

"Twenty knives. Warden, tell the doctor, that's from a party of fifteen prisoners."

"You call those knives? They're more like daggers."

"Now, Klavdia, send back all those who aren't sick. And then go and see the end of the film. You realize, Klavdia, that this mine has an incompetent doctor: when a patient fell off a truck and broke his bones, he wrote a trauma diagnosis of *prolapsus ex machina* as if it were *prolapsus recti*, a rectal prolapse. But he has learned how to plaster up a weapon."

A despairing and angry pair of eyes was staring at the paramedic.

"Right, anyone sick will be given a hospital bed," said Klavdia. "Come and see me, one by one."

The surgical patients, who expected to be sent back, swore foully: they had nothing to lose. Lost hope had loosened their tongues. The gangsters showered the duty doctor, the paramedic, the guards, the male nurses with obscene curses.

"And I'll cut your eyes out," one patient even ventured to say.

"There's nothing you can do to me, you piece of shit. All you could do is cut a sleeping man's throat. You and your sticks in the mines beat quite a lot of the 1937 politicals to death. Have you forgotten all those old men and four-eyed intellectuals?"

But it wasn't just the "surgical" criminals who had to be closely watched. It was a far more painful business to expose men trying to get to the TB section: a patient would bring a bacteria-infected gob of spit wrapped in a rag, and it was obvious that a TB patient was being manufactured for the doctor to examine. The doctor would say, "Cough it up into this jar." This was an on-the-spot test for the presence of Koch bacillus. Before he was examined by the doctor the patient would put the infected gob of spit in his mouth and would, of course, infect himself with TB. But this would mean getting to the hospital, saving himself from what was most terrible of all—pit-face work in a gold mine. It might only be for an hour, a day, or a month.

It was even more painful to expose those who brought some blood in a vial or scratched a finger to add blood to their urine and enter the hospital on those grounds, if only to get a day or even a week in bed. Afterward, come what may.

There were quite a few of that kind: they were the more sophisticated ones, and wouldn't have put a TB-infected gob of spit in their mouths just to be kept in the hospital. Such men had heard what protein was and why urine was tested, and what the patient could get out of it. Months spent in hospital beds had taught them a lot. There were patients suffering from muscle contracture, which was simulated, so their knees and elbows could be bent straight under anesthetic, Rausch anesthesia. On a couple of occasions, however, the contracture and fusion turned out to be genuine, so that the doctor who was trying to expose them, a man of considerable strength, tore apart living tissue when he tried to straighten a knee: he'd been too eager and had underestimated his own strength.

Most of the newcomers had homemade sores: trophic ulcers made with a needle lubricated with kerosene to cause subcutaneous inflammation. Such patients might or might not be accepted. There were no reliable criteria.

Women sore-makers were particularly common in Elgen state farm; later, when the special Debna women's mine was opened, giving women their own wheelbarrows, spades, and pickaxes, the number of sore-makers at that mine increased sharply. This mine was where the female nurses hacked a female doctor to death with an ax. She was a fine doctor, Shitsel by name, a gray-haired woman from the Crimea. Previously, she had worked at the hospital, but because of her record she was transferred to the mine and doomed to die.

Klavdia Ivanovna went off to see the end of the showing put on by the camp Culture Brigade; the paramedic went to bed. But an hour later he was awoken: "A party of women prisoners from Elgen."

This was a group that would have a lot of possessions: a job for the guards. It was a small party, and Klavdia volunteered to admit them on her own. The paramedic thanked her, but no sooner had he fallen asleep than he was awoken by Klavdia jostling him and weeping, weeping bitter tears. What could have happened there?

"I can't stay here any longer. I can't stand it. I refuse to be a duty doctor."

The paramedic threw a handful of cold tap water over his face, dried himself on his sleeve, and went out to the reception room.

Everyone was howling with laughter: the patients, the guards that brought them, the camp guards. A pretty, very pretty girl was tossing and turning on the couch: this wasn't her first visit to the hospital.

"How are you, Valia Gromova."

"Well, at last, at last I can see a human being."

"What's all the noise about?"

"They won't admit me to the hospital."

"Why aren't we admitting her? She's got a bad case of TB."

"Because she's a dyke," the foreman retorted crudely. "There's been an order about her. She's not to be admitted. After all, she's been having sex without me. Or without any man—"

"They're all lying," Valia Gromova yelled, quite unabashed. "You can see what my fingers are like, the state of the pads...."

The paramedic spat on the floor and went to the next room. Klavdia Ivanovna had an attack of hysterics.

1965

THE GEOLOGISTS

KRIST was woken up one night; the warden on duty took him down endless dark corridors to the office of the chief of the hospital. The chief, a lieutenant colonel in the medical service, was still up. Lvov, a Ministry of the Interior secret police officer, was sitting at the chief's desk, doodling pictures of bored-looking birds on a sheet of paper.

"Reception-room paramedic Krist has come as you asked, sir."

The lieutenant colonel waved a hand and the duty warden who'd brought Krist vanished.

"Listen, Krist," said the boss, "you're going to have visitors."

"A prison party is coming," said the secret policeman.

Krist said nothing, but waited to see what would happen next.

"You'll clean them up. Disinfection and so on."

"Yes, sir."

"Nobody is to know about these people. No communication."

"We are relying on you," explained the secret policeman, who then burst out coughing.

"I can't operate the disinfection chamber on my own, sir," said Krist. "The controls are a long way from the mixer tap. The steam and the water come in different pipes."

"So...."

"I need another hospital worker, sir."

The two officers exchanged looks.

"All right, you can have a male nurse," said the secret policeman.

"You've got it, haven't you? Not a word to anyone."

"I've got it, sir."

Krist and the secret policeman left the room. The chief medical officer got up, turned off the ceiling light, and started to put on his greatcoat.

"Where is this group from?" Krist quietly asked the secret policeman as they passed through the big lobby—civilian or military, it didn't matter which, all the bosses' offices adhered to the Moscow design.

"Where from?" The secret policeman burst out in loud laughter. "Krist, Krist, I never thought you would ask me a question like that. . . ." Then he enounced in cold tones, "From Moscow, by air."

"So they don't know what the camps are like. Prison, interrogation, and all the rest. Anyone who doesn't know the camps thinks this is the crack that gives them their first breath of free air. From Moscow by air. . . ."

The next night the noisy, spacious vestibule was full of newcomers: officers, officers, and more officers. Majors, lieutenant colonels, full colonels. There was even a general, a young, short, black-eyed man. There wasn't a single private in the group.

The chief of the hospital, a tall, skinny old man, had trouble bending down to report to the little general: "Everything's ready for the reception."

"Excellent, excellent."

"Bathhouse!"

The chief waved to Krist, and the doors of the reception room opened.

The crowd of officers in greatcoats parted. The starry gold of their epaulets faded into the background, as all the attention of the newcomers and the reception committee was focused on a little group of filthy people wearing torn and crumpled rags. The rags weren't government issue, they were their civilian clothes, worn during interrogation and ravaged by whatever covered the floors of the cells the prisoners had been lying on.

Twelve men and one woman.

"After you, Anna," said one prisoner, letting the woman go first.

"Certainly not, you go and have a good wash. I'll sit here and rest for now."

The door of the reception room was closed.

Everyone was standing around me, eagerly staring into my eyes, trying to work something out but not yet daring to ask.

"Have you been in Kolyma long?" the boldest man asked, once he saw I was one of those "intellectuals."

"Since '37."

"In '37 we were all still—"

"Shut up," another man, who was older, interrupted.

Our guard came in. It was Khabibulin, the secretary of the party organization, the special confidant of the hospital chief. Khabibulin was keeping an eye on the newcomers and on me.

"How about shaving them?"

"The barber's been called," said Khabibulin. "He's a Persian gangster, Yurka."

The Persian gangster Yurka and his razor soon appeared. He had been given his instructions at the guardhouse, and all he did was grunt.

The newcomers again switched their attention to Krist.

"We won't get you into trouble, will we?"

"How can you get me into trouble? You must be engineers, aren't you?"

"Geologists."

"Geologists, then."

"Where are we, actually?"

"At Kolyma: five hundred kilometers from Magadan."

"Ah well, goodbye. A bathhouse, that's good."

Every one of the geologists had come back from working abroad; they'd gotten sentences from fifteen to twenty-five years. And their fate was in the hands of a special authority that had all those officers and generals and so few common soldiers.

The "business" run by these generals did not come under the Kolyma or the Far East Construction administration. All that Kolyma gave them was mountain air through the barred windows, bigger rations, three visits to the bathhouse per month, bedding and linen with no lice, and a roof. There was no mention so far of being allowed to go out or to the cinema. Moscow had chosen a polar dacha for the geologists.

The geologists had offered to carry out a major job requiring their professional skills, yet another variation on the theme of Ramzin's straight-flow boiler.[1]

What became generally known after the "reforging" of prisoners and many a White Sea canal project is that a spark of creative fire can be struck by using an ordinary stick. A moving scale of encouragement and punishment by increased or diminished food rations, crediting working days against a sentence, and hope are enough to turn slave labor into blessed labor.

The little general came a month later. The geologists had said they wanted to go to the cinema, which was available to prisoners and free workers. The balcony, or upper circle, where the bosses used to sit was screened off and reinforced with prison bars. The geologists were given seats next to the bosses at film showings.

The geologists were not allowed to have books from the libraries, except for technical literature.

The party organization secretary, Khabibulin, a sick old Far East Construction man, acting for the first time in his life as a guard, personally carried bundles of the geologists' washing to the laundry. This was for Khabibulin the most degrading of all his jobs.

The little general came back a month later; the geologists asked if they could have curtains over the windows.

"Curtains," said Khabibulin miserably, "they have to have curtains."

The little general was pleased. The geologists' work was going well. Every ten days the doors of the reception room were opened at night and the geologists could have a bath in the bathhouse.

Krist rarely talked to them. In any case, what could prospecting geologists tell Krist that he hadn't already learned in the camps?

Then the geologists turned their attention to the Persian barber.

"Don't talk to them much, Yurka," Krist said in passing.

"I don't need some *freier* to tell me what to do." The Persian then swore obscenely.

Another bath day passed; the Persian turned up, clearly drunk, or perhaps he had overdone the chifir or was on codeine. Whatever it was, he was too full of energy and in a hurry to get home. He jumped straight out of the guardhouse into the street without waiting for his escort to the camp. Through the open window Krist heard the dry crack of a revolver. The Persian was killed by a guard, a guard he had just shaved, and his curled-up body lay by the porch. The doctor on duty took his pulse and wrote out a certificate. Ashot, another barber, came: Ashot was an Armenian terrorist, from the Armenian Socialist Revolutionary fighters who in 1926 killed three Turkish ministers, the chief victim being Talaat Pasha, who was responsible for the massacre in 1915, when a million Armenians were exterminated. The interrogation service checked Ashot's personal file, and he was banned from shaving geologists. Instead, they found a barber among the gangsters, and a new principle was introduced: on each occasion it was a new barber who did the shaving. That practice was considered safer, because no friendly relations would be started up. This was the system applied to sentries in Butyrki prison: a sliding posting system.

The geologists never found out anything about the Persian or about Ashot. Their work was going well, and the little general, when he next came, allowed the geologists to have half an hour of exercise. This too was sheer humiliation for the old warden Khabibulin. A guard in a camp of submissive, cowed men with no rights is a big boss. But in this case, serving purely as a guard was something Khabibulin disliked.

His eyes became more and more melancholy, his nose ever redder: Khabibulin had definitely taken to drink. On one occasion he fell headfirst off a bridge into the Kolyma River, but he was saved and could continue his important work as a guard. He meekly carried the parcels of linen to the laundry, meekly swept the room and changed the window curtains.

"Well, how's life?" Krist would ask Khabibulin. After all, they had been on duty together for more than a year.

"Bad." Khabibulin sighed.

The little general arrived. The geologists were doing excellent work. Smiling joyfully, the general walked around the geologists' prison. He was getting a bonus for their work.

Khabibulin stood on the threshold at attention, ramrod straight, as he saw the general off.

"Well, good, good. I can see I was right to rely on them," the little general said cheerfully. "As for you," the general turned to look at the guards standing at the threshold, "you should be more polite to them. Or else I'll have you sons of bitches nailed into your coffins."

Then the general left.

Khabibulin staggered as far as the reception room, got a double dose of valerian from Krist and drank it, then wrote a request for an immediate transfer to any other job. He showed his request to Krist, hoping for sympathy. Krist tried to explain to him that the general considered those geologists more important than a hundred Khabibulins, but the senior guard's feelings were so badly hurt that he refused to accept this simple truth.

One night the geologists disappeared.

1965

BEARS

THE KITTEN came out from under the trestle bed and only just managed to jump back when the geologist Filatov flung a boot at it.

"What's gotten into you?" I asked, putting aside a grease-stained volume of *The Count of Monte Cristo*.

"I don't like cats. Now, dogs," said Filatov, grabbing hold of a shaggy gray puppy and patting its neck, "are quite a different matter. A pedigree sheepdog. Go on, bite it, Kazbek, bite it," said the geologist, setting the puppy on the kitten. But the puppy's nose already had two fresh scratches inflicted by a cat's claws, and Kazbek stayed where he was, merely growling.

The kitten had a hard time living with us. Five men took it out on the kitten. They were bored with having nothing to do: the river had flooded, so we couldn't leave; for more than a week Yuzhnikov and Kochubei, the carpenters, had been gambling their future pay in a card game of sixty-six. Sometimes one won, sometimes the other. The cook opened the door and shouted, "Bears!" Everyone rushed headlong to the door.

There were, as I said, five of us, and we had one rifle, the geologist's. We didn't have an ax for everybody, so the cook grabbed his razor-sharp kitchen knife.

The bears, a male and a female, were walking along the mountain slope the other side of the stream. They were shaking the young larches, breaking them, pulling them out by the roots, throwing them into the stream. On that May day in the taiga they were the only moving objects, and we humans got very close to them, about two hundred paces, from the leeward side. The male bear was dark brown with a reddish tinge, twice the size of the female. He was old, for you could see his big yellow canines.

Filatov was the best shot among us. He sat down, laying his rifle on the trunk of a fallen larch so as to be sure of hitting the target. He moved the barrel about as he sought a path for the bullet through the bushes. The leaves were beginning to turn yellow.

"Fire," growled the cook, whose face was white with excitement. "Fire!"

The bears heard the rustling. Their reaction was instantaneous, like that of players in a football match. The female bear rushed uphill and crossed the pass. The old male bear didn't run: he turned his face toward the source of danger, bared his canines, and slowly went along the slope toward a copse of low dwarf-pine bushes. Clearly, he was taking the risk on himself; as a male, he was sacrificing his own life so as to save the life of his mate; he was drawing death away from her and covering her escape.

Filatov fired. As I said, he was a good shot. The bear collapsed and rolled down the slope into the ravine, until a larch tree it had playfully broken stopped the heavy body in its tracks. The female bear had long vanished.

Everything—sky, rocks—was so enormous that the bear seemed to be a toy. It had been killed outright. We tied its feet together, pushed a pole under them and, staggering under the weight of the gigantic carcass, we descended to the bottom of the ravine, onto the slippery two-meter-deep ice that hadn't yet thawed. We then dragged the bear along the ground to the threshold of our hut.

The two-month-old puppy had never seen a bear in its short life; crazed with fear, it hid under a bed. The kitten behaved quite differently. It threw itself as if enraged on the bear's carcass when the five of us were skinning it. The kitten tore off pieces of warm meat, snatched clots of blood, and danced on the animal's magnificent knotted muscles....

The skin measured four square meters.

"That will be about two hundred kilos of meat," the cook told each one of us separately.

This was a lot of booty, but as it was impossible to take it anywhere and sell it, we split it equally there and then. The geologist Filatov's pots and pans were sizzling and simmering day and night, until he had a bellyache. Yuzhnikov and Kochubei found that bear meat was an unsuitable currency for calculating winnings and losses at cards, so they each salted their share in pits they made from stones: every day they checked to see that the meat was still intact. Nobody knew where the cook hid his meat: he had a secret method of salting it but wouldn't tell anyone what it was. I just fed the kitten and the puppy, so we three had more success dealing with our bear meat than the others. The memories of this successful game hunt lasted for two days. We didn't start quarreling until the evening of the third day.

1956

PRINCESS GAGARINA'S NECKLACE

TIME SPENT under interrogation in pretrial prison slips from your memory, leaving no noticeable sharp traces. For anyone who is detained there, the prison and its encounters and people are not the main thing. The main thing is what all your mental, spiritual, and nervous energy is spent on in prison—that is, the battle with your interrogator. What happens in the offices of the interrogation block stays in your memory better than prison life itself. No book you read in such a prison is memorable; the prisons where sentences are served are universities that produce astronomers, novelists, and memoirists. Books read in a pretrial prison are not remembered. For Krist it wasn't the duel with his interrogator that was uppermost in his mind. Krist knew he was doomed, that arrest meant condemnation and slaughter. So Krist was calm. He kept his ability to observe, his capacity to act, despite the lulling effect of the rhythm of prison routine. Krist had several times encountered the fatal human habit of telling someone the most important thing about oneself, of letting your neighbor, your cellmate, the man in the next hospital bed or in the same train compartment know everything about you. Such secrets, kept at the bottom of a human heart, could sometimes be dumbfounding, improbable.

Krist's neighbor on the right, an engineer from a factory in Volokolamsk, when asked to recall the most memorable event, the best event in his life, confided, utterly radiant from the memory he was reexperiencing, that in 1933 he used his ration cards to get twenty cans of tinned vegetables that, when he got home and opened them, turned out to be tinned meat. The engineer took an ax and cut each can into two, after locking himself away from his neighbors. Every can had meat in it, not one had vegetables. In prison nobody laughs at such memories.

The neighbor on the left, the general secretary of the society of pre-revolutionary political prisoners, Aleksandr Georgievich Andreyev, frowned, so that his silvery eyebrows met over his nose and his black eyes shone.

"Yes, there was a day like that in my life: March 12, 1917. I got a life sentence of hard labor under the tsar. Fate would have it that I should mark the twentieth anniversary of that sentence here in prison with you."

A well-built and chubby man climbed off the bunk opposite us.

"Allow me to join in your game. I'm Dr. Miroliubov, Valeri Andreyevich," said the doctor, smiling plaintively.

"Take a seat," said Krist, making room for him, which was very easy, since he had only to bend his legs back, there being no other way to make room. Miroliubov immediately got onto the bunk. The doctor was wearing house slippers. Krist's eyebrows rose in amazement.

"No, I didn't come here straight from home, I came from Taganka prison, where I spent two months. The rules are more relaxed there."

"But Taganka's a prison for common criminals, isn't it?"

"Yes, of course it is," Dr. Miroliubov agreed offhandedly. "Since you came to this cell," Miroliubov said, lifting his eyes to face Krist, "life has changed. The games we play make more sense. Instead of that horrible game, beetle, everyone was so crazy about. People even waited for latrine breaks so that they'd be free for a game of beetle in the wash-rooms. I expect, you've experienced that...."

"I have," said Krist in a firm but melancholic voice.

Miroliubov's kind, prominent, myopic eyes looked into Krist's. "The gangsters took away my glasses. In Taganka."

As usual, questions, presumptions, guesses flashed quickly through Krist's brain.... The doctor was after some advice. He didn't know why he'd been arrested. In any case....

"Why were you moved here from Taganka?"

"I don't know. I haven't been interrogated once in the last two months. But in Taganka I was summoned as a witness in a burglary case. A neighbor in our apartment had a coat stolen. I was interrogated and issued an arrest warrant. Abracadabra. Not a word, and it's been three months. And now they've moved me to Butyrki."

"Well then," said Krist, "be as patient as you can. Get ready for some surprises. There's no abracadabra about it. It's organized chaos, as the critic Iuda Grossman-Roshchin[2] put it. You remember Grossman? A comrade-in-arms of Makhno."[3]

"No, I don't," said the doctor. His hopes that Krist knew everything had faded, and his eyes became lackluster again.

The artistic patterns in the script of the interrogation process were extremely varied. Krist was only too aware of this fact. Someone being called in for a burglary, if only as a witness, reminded him of the famous "amalgams"[4] cases. There was no doubt that Dr. Miroliubov's adventures in Taganka were a camouflage arranged by the interrogators and required for God knows what reasons by the poets of the NKVD.

"Valeri, let's talk about something else: about the best day in our lives. About the event you remember best in your life."

"Yes, I've heard what you've been saying to each other. There was an event that completely transformed my whole life. Only what happened to me isn't at all like what we've heard from Aleksandr Georgievich"—Miroliubov bent to the left where the general secretary of the society of prerevolutionary political prisoners was sitting—"or from this comrade." Miroliubov bent to the right, where the Volokolamsk engineer was sitting. "In 1901, I was a first-year medical student at Moscow University. I was young. Lots of high-minded ideas. I was stupid."

"'A sucker,' as the gangsters would put it," suggested Krist.

"No, not a sucker. After Taganka I know what some of these gangster terms mean. How do you know them?"

"I had a teach-yourself book," said Krist.

"No, what we called ourselves was *gaudeamus*.[5] Get it? That's what it was."

"Get to the point, Valeri," said the Volokolamsk engineer.

"I'm getting to it. We get so little spare time here.... I was reading the papers. There was a big advertisement. Princess Gagarina had lost her diamond necklace. A family heirloom. Five thousand rubles for anyone who found it. I read the paper, crumpled it up, threw it into the trash. Then I went and thought, now I ought to find that necklace. I'd send half the reward to my mother. I'd spend the other half traveling

abroad. I'd buy a good overcoat. And a season ticket to the Maly Theater. There was no Art Theater then.[6] Anyway, I was walking down the
boards of the wooden sidewalk instead of the boulevard: there was
still a nail poking out there you might tread on. So I stepped down
onto the earth to avoid the nail and when I look, there it was in the
ditch.... Anyway, I found the necklace. I sat on the boulevard dreaming away, thinking of how happy I was going to be. I didn't go to the
university but to the trash to get my newspaper; I opened it and found
the address.

"I rang the bell, I kept ringing. A servant. 'I've come about the
necklace.' The prince appears in person. His wife comes running out.
I was twenty then. Just twenty. It was a big test of character. A test of
everything I'd been brought up to believe or that I'd learned to do.... I
had to make up my mind on the spot whether I was a decent man or
not. 'I'll bring the money right away,' the prince said. 'Or would you
prefer a check? Please sit down.' The princess was right there, just two
steps from me. I stayed standing, and said I was a student, that I'd
hadn't brought the necklace just to get a reward. 'Ah, so that's how it
is,' the prince said. 'Please forgive us. Won't you come and have breakfast with us?' And his wife, Irina Sergeyevna, kissed me."

"Five thousand," the Volokolamsk engineer enounced. He was
spellbound.

"A real test of character," said the general secretary of the society of
prerevolutionary political prisoners. "Just like when I threw my first
bomb in the Crimea."

"Then I started visiting the prince almost every day. I fell in love
with his wife. I went abroad with them every year for three years—by
then I was a doctor. So I never got married. Thanks to that necklace
I've been a bachelor all my life.... Then came the revolution. And the
civil war. During the civil war I got to know Putna well, Vitovt Putna.[7]
I was his personal doctor. Putna was a good man, but of course he was
no Prince Gagarin. There was something missing. And he didn't have
a wife like Gagarin's."

"The fact is you were twenty years older, twenty years older than a
gaudeamus."

"Maybe…"

"Where's Putna now?"

"He's the military attaché in England."

Aleksandr Georgievich, the doctor's neighbor on his left, smiled. "I think you should be looking for the explanation for your troubles, as Musset liked to put it, in Putna and all that group. Eh?"

"How can that be?"

"That's something your interrogators know. Take an old man's advice: prepare for battle under Putna's flag."

"Old man? You're younger than I am."

"That doesn't matter, it's just I've got less *gaudeamus* in me, and more bombs," said Andreyev smiling. "Let's not quarrel."

"And what's your opinion?"

"I agree with Aleksandr," said Krist.

Miroliubov's face went red, but he restrained himself. In prison, quarrels break out like fires in a dry forest. Krist and Andreyev both knew this. Miroliubov had yet to learn about it.

A day came when Miroliubov underwent such an interrogation that he lay facedown for forty-eight hours and didn't go out for his walk.

On the third day Valeri Andreyevich stood and went up to Krist, his fingers touching the reddened eyelids of his blue eyes, and said, "You were right."

It was Andreyev, not Krist who'd been right, but this was a subtle way of admitting mistakes, a subtlety that both Krist and Andreyev recognized.

"Putna?"

"Putna. It's all too horrible, too horrible." Valeri Andreyevich burst into tears. He'd held out for forty-eight hours but couldn't take any more. Neither Andreyev nor Krist liked to see a man cry.

"Calm down."

At night Krist was woken up by Miroliubov's feverish whispering. "I'll tell you everything. I'm as good as dead. I don't know what to do. I'm Putna's personal doctor. Now they're not interrogating me about a burglary but about something too terrible to contemplate: about planning an assassination of the government."

"Valeri," said Krist, yawning as he tried to shake off his sleepiness, "you're not the only one in this cell being accused of that. Over there is Lionka from Tuma district in Moscow Province: he can't read or write. Lionka was unscrewing the bolts on the railway track to use as fishing weights, just like in Chekhov's story 'The Malefactor.' You know your literature, you know all those *gaudeamuses*. Lionka is accused of sabotage and terrorism. And he's not hysterical. Next to Lionka you can see a potbellied man, Voronkov: he's the head chef in the Moscow Café, it used to be called the Pushkin, on Strastnaya Square. Have you been there? The café was decorated in brown. Voronkov was persuaded to move to the Prague Restaurant on Arbat Square, where the manager was Filippov. Well, in Voronkov's file it's all recorded by the interrogator, and every page is signed by Voronkov, that Filippov offered Voronkov a three-room apartment, trips abroad to get higher qualifications. There's a dearth of chef's skills at the moment, after all. . . . 'The manager of the Prague Restaurant offered me all this if I agreed to a transfer, and when I refused he suggested that I should poison the government. And I agreed.' Your case, Valeri, also belongs to the category of 'techniques bordering on fantasy.'"

"Is that your way of reassuring me? What do you know? I've been with Putna practically ever since the revolution. Ever since the civil war. I was with him on the Pacific coast and in the south. Only I wasn't allowed to go to England. They refused me a visa."

"And is Putna in England?"

"I told you, he was in England. He was. But now he's not in England, he's in here with us."

"So that's how it is."

"A couple of days ago," Miroliubov whispered, "I had two interrogations. At the first one I was asked to write down everything I knew about Putna's terrorist activities and his statements in that respect. And who visited him. What they talked about. I wrote it all down. In detail. I never heard any terrorist talk, none of the visitors. . . . Then there was a break. Dinner. I was given dinner, too. Two courses. Peas for the second course. Here in Butyrki we're always given beans for pulses, but there you get peas. After dinner, they gave me a cigarette—I don't usually smoke, but I've gotten into the habit in prison—and we got down to writing statements again. The interrogator said, 'Now you, Dr. Miroliubov, are so devoted to defending and protecting Putna, your friend and employer for so many years. That's to your credit, Dr. Miroliubov. Putna takes quite a different attitude to you, however. . . .' 'What do you mean?' 'Well, look. This is what Putna's written. Read it.' The interrogator gave me pages and pages of statements written in Putna's hand."

"So that's it. . . ."

"Yes. I could feel my hair turning gray. Putna's declaration said, 'Yes, a terrorist assassination was planned in my apartment, a conspiracy was being drawn up against members of the government, against Stalin, Molotov. The closest, the most active role in all these conversations was that of Kliment Yefremovich Voroshilov.'[8] And there is a final phrase, which is burned into my memory: 'All this can be confirmed by my personal doctor, Dr. Miroliubov.'"

Krist whistled. Death had moved too close to Miroliubov.

"What am I to do? What? What can I say? It's Putna's genuine handwriting. I know his handwriting only too well. And his hands didn't tremble, any more than Tsarevich Alexei after torture with the knout—you remember those historic criminal investigations, the interrogation statements from the times of Peter the Great."

"I really do envy you," said Krist, "because your love of literature overcomes everything else. Or rather, love of history. But if you've got the moral strength to make these analogies, then you have enough to take a rational view of your case. One thing is clear: Putna's been arrested."

"Yes, he's here."

"Or at Lubyanka. Or in Lefortovo. But not in England. Tell me, Valeri, honestly, were any disparaging remarks made at all?" Krist twirled imaginary mustaches, as if he were Stalin. "Even if they were very vague?"

"Never."

"Or say: 'Never in my presence.' You must know about these subtleties under interrogation."

"No, never. Putna is an utterly loyal comrade. A military man. A bit of a rough diamond."

"Just one last question. Psychologically, it's the most important. But be honest."

"I give the same answer no matter where I am."

"Well, keep your temper, Marquis de Posa."

"I have the feeling you're laughing at me."

"No, I'm not. Tell me frankly, what did Putna think of Voroshilov?"

"Putna loathed him," Miroliubov said in one feverish breath.

"Well, there's our solution, Valeri. This isn't hypnosis, it's not Ornaldo⁹ at work, it's not injections or drugs. It's not even threats, it's not even being interrogated nonstop without sleep. It's a doomed man's cold-blooded calculation. Putna's last battle. You're a pawn in this game, Valeri. Do you remember Pushkin's *Poltava*? 'To lose your life and your honor, too, / To take your enemies with you to the scaffold.'"

"'To take your friends with you to the scaffold.'" Miroliubov corrected the quotation.

"No. 'Friends' is a reading that suits you and people like you. Valeri, my dear *gaudeamus*, you have to rely more on your enemies than on your friends. Take as many enemies with you as you can; your friends will be taken anyway."

"But what am I myself to do?"

"Do you want some good advice, Valeri?"

"Good or bad, I don't care. I don't want to die."

"It's only good advice. Tell only the truth in your statements. If Putna decided to lie before he dies, that's his business. Your only salvation is the truth, just the truth, nothing but the truth."

"I have always said nothing but the truth."

"And were your statements the truth? There are a lot of nuances. Lying to save someone, for instance. Or there's the interests of society and the state. An individual's class interests and personal morality. Formal logic and informal logic."

"Just the truth!"

"All the better. So you have experience in making true statements. Keep it up."

"Your advice doesn't amount to much," said Miroliubov, who was disappointed.

"Yours is a difficult case," said Krist. "Let's believe that where it matters they know perfectly well what's what. If they need your death, you'll die. If they don't, you'll be saved."

"Wretched advice."

"That's all there is."

Krist encountered Miroliubov on the steamship *Kulu* during its fifth voyage of the shipping season of 1937. The voyage was from Vladivostok to Magadan.

Prince Gagarin's and Vitovt Putna's personal doctor greeted Krist coldly: Krist had been a witness to his moral weakness at a dangerous hour of his life and, Miroliubov felt, had utterly failed to help him at a difficult, lethal moment.

Krist and Miroliubov exchanged handshakes.

"Glad to see you're alive," said Krist. "How many?"

"Five years. You're making fun of me. I haven't done anything wrong, after all. And then I get five years in the camps. Kolyma."

"You were in a very dangerous position. It was a deadly position. Your luck held out," said Krist.

"To hell with you, and to hell with my luck."

It occurred to Krist that Miroliubov was right. That was so very much a Russian view of luck: being glad that an innocent man had been given five years—after all, he could have been given ten or even the death penalty.

Krist and Miroliubov didn't meet in Kolyma. Kolyma is too big a place. But to judge from what Krist heard and from his inquiries, Dr. Miroliubov's luck was good enough to last all five years of his time in the camps. He was released during the war and worked as a doctor at the mines. He grew old and died in 1965.

1965

IVAN FIODOROVICH

IVAN FIODOROVICH Nikishev, wearing civilian clothes, met Henry Wallace.[10] The guard towers in the nearby camp had been sawed down and the convicts had been blessed with a day off. All under-the-counter supplies in the settlement shop had been put onto the shelves, so that trade went on as if there were no war.

Wallace took part in "volunteer" work harvesting potatoes on a Sunday. When he was taken to the vegetable garden, Wallace was pleased by being given a curved American spade, recently supplied by lend-lease. Ivan Fiodorovich was equipped with the same sort of spade, except that his had a long Russian handle. Pointing at this spade, Wallace asked a question; a man in civilian clothes standing next to Ivan Fio- dorovich said something, then Ivan Fiodorovich said something, and the interpreter kindly translated for Wallace what he had said: that in America, a country with such advanced technology, they had even given thought to the shape of spades, and then he touched the spade that Wallace was holding. It was a very good spade, but the handle didn't suit Russians because it was too short, not much of a clod-lifter. The interpreter had trouble with translating the term "clod-lifter." But he said that the Russians, who had made metal shoes for a flea (Wallace had read something about this when he was preparing for his trip to Russia), had made an improvement to the American tool: they'd put the spade blade onto a different handle, a long one. The best length for the spade handle and the spade itself is from the ground to the bridge of the digger's nose. The man in civilian clothes standing next to Ivan Fiodorovich demonstrated. Now it was time to start the shock work, harvesting potatoes, which grew rather well in the Far North.

Everything interested Wallace. How did cabbages or potatoes grow here? How were they planted? Were they transplanted? Like cabbages? Amazing. What was the yield per hectare?

From time to time Wallace would look at the men next to him. Young, rosy-cheeked, happy men were digging all around the bosses. They dug merrily and enthusiastically. Wallace took the opportunity of glancing at their hands, which were white, and their fingers, which had never touched a spade before; he laughed, since he realized that they were guards in disguise.

Wallace had seen it all: the towers, whether sawed down or not, and the clusters of prisoners' barracks surrounded by wire. He knew just as much about this country as Ivan Fiodorovich did.

They dug merrily. Ivan Fiodorovich soon wearied. He was a pudgy, heavily built man, but he wanted to keep up with the American vice president. Wallace was as lightweight as a boy, even though he was rather older in years than Ivan Fiodorovich.

"I'm used to this sort of work on my farm," Wallace said cheerfully.

Ivan Fiodorovich smiled; he was taking more and more frequent rest breaks.

"When I get back to the camp," Ivan Fiodorovich was thinking, "I'll definitely have a glucose injection." Ivan Fiodorovich was very fond of glucose. Glucose was excellent for maintaining the heart. He would have to take a risk, though, since he hadn't brought his personal doctor on this trip.

The shock Sunday was over: Ivan Fiodorovich had the health chief summoned. When the health chief came, he was pale, fearing the worst. Had there been denunciations about that damned fishing trip when the patients caught fish for the head of the sanatorium? After all, that was a tradition consecrated by the passage of time.

When he saw the doctor, Ivan Fiodorovich forced himself to smile as gracefully as he could.

"I need to have a glucose injection. I've got ampoules of glucose. My own."

"You? Glucose?"

"Why should that astound you?" said Ivan Fiodorovich, looking suspiciously at the chief of the medical service, who had become so jocular. "Well, give me an injection."

"Me? You?"

"You. Me."

"Glucose?"

"Glucose."

"I'll tell Piotr Petrovich, our surgeon. He'll do it better than me."

"What? Don't tell me you don't know how to!" said Ivan Fiodorovich.

"I know how to, sir. But Piotr Petrovich is even better at it. I'll give you my own personal syringe."

"I have my own syringe, too."

The surgeon was sent for.

"Reporting, sir. Krasnitsky, Piotr Petrovich, hospital surgeon."

"You're a surgeon?"

"Yes, sir."

"A former convict?"

"Yes, sir."

"Can you give me an injection?"

"No, sir. I don't know how to."

"You don't know how to do injections?"

"Sir," the head of the medical service interrupted, "we'll send you a paramedic straightaway. A convict. He'll do it so you won't feel a thing. Let me have your syringe. I'll boil it in your presence. Piotr Petrovich and I will keep an eye out in case there's any sabotage or terrorism. We'll keep the tourniquet tight. We'll roll up your sleeve."

The convict-paramedic came, washed Ivan Fiodorovich's hands, wiped them with alcohol and did the injection.

"May I go now, sir?"

"Go," said Ivan Fiodorovich. "Give him a packet of cigarettes from my briefcase."

"It's not worth it, sir."

That's how complicated a glucose injection turned out to be when traveling. For a long time Ivan Fiodorovich fancied he had a fever, that his head was spinning, that he had been poisoned by the convict-paramedic, but in the end he calmed down.

The next day, Ivan Fiodorovich saw Wallace off to Irkutsk; he was so pleased that he crossed himself. He ordered the guard towers to be put up again and the goods to be removed from the shop.

Recently Ivan Fiodorovich had felt he was a special friend of America, within the diplomatic boundaries of friendship, naturally. Just a few months ago the production of electric lightbulbs had been set up forty-seven kilometers from Magadan. You had to be a Kolyma inhabitant to realize the importance of that. Losing a lightbulb was a criminal offense; the loss of a lightbulb at the mines meant the loss of thousands of working hours. You couldn't get enough imported lightbulbs. And suddenly a run of luck: we'd created our own. We'd freed ourselves of "foreign dependency."

Moscow appreciated Ivan Fiodorovich's achievements, and he was given a medal. The factory manager, the head of the workshop where the lights were made, the laboratory assistants got rather smaller medals. Everyone got a medal, except the man who had set up the production, the atomic physicist from Kharkov, the engineer Georgi Georgievich Demidov. He was an "acronymic," a political prisoner sentenced by an NKVD troika for something like ASA, Anti-Soviet Agitation. Demidov thought he might at least be considered for early release, as the factory manager hinted, but Ivan Fiodorovich considered any application for such a reward to be a political mistake. You couldn't offer a fascist early release! What would Moscow say? No, he could just be content that he was working in a warm factory, not doing hard manual labor: that was better than any early release. And Demidov could not have a medal, of course not: medals were for faithful servants of the state, not for fascists.

"Well you could let him have twenty-five rubles or so as a bonus. For tobacco, sugar...."

"Demidov doesn't smoke," the factory manager said respectfully.

"If he doesn't, he doesn't.... He can swap it for bread or something else... if he doesn't want tobacco, then he'll need new clothes, not camp uniform, I mean, you know.... There are those boxes of American outfits we started to give you as bonuses. There's a suit, a shirt, a tie. One of the white boxes. So you can give him that as a bonus."

At a solemn session in the presence of Ivan Fiodorovich himself, each hero was presented with a box containing gifts from America. Each one bowed and said, "Thank you." But when Demidov's turn came, he approached the presiding committee's table, put the box on the table, and said, "I'm not going to wear Americans' hand-me-downs," before turning around and leaving.

Ivan Fiodorovich considered this act first and foremost from a political view as a gesture by a fascist against the Soviet-American bloc of freedom-loving countries: that very evening he rang the district NKVD department. Demidov was tried, given eight years "extra," removed from his job, and sent to do hard manual labor in a punishment mine.

It was now, after Wallace's departure, that Ivan Fiodorovich recalled the Demidov incident with real pleasure. Ivan Fiodorovich was always noted for his political astuteness.

After his recent marriage to the twenty-year-old Komsomol member Rydasova, Ivan Fiodorovich was taking special care of his heart. He had made her his wife and at the same time put her in charge of a large section of the camps. She decided matters of life and death for many thousands of people. The romantic Komsomol leader was quickly transmogrified into a beast. She exiled people, fabricated cases, handed out sentences, "extras," and was behind all kinds of plots that were as nasty as only a camp plot can be.

The theater gave Madame Rydasova a great deal of bother.

"We've had this denunciation from Kozin, who says that the director Varpakhovsky has been making plans for a May Day demonstration in Magadan with festive columns like processions of the cross, with banners and icons. And he says, of course, that this is subversive counterrevolutionary work."

At a committee meeting Madame Rydasova didn't think there was anything criminal about these plans. A demonstration: so what? Nothing worth commenting on. Then suddenly, church banners! Something had to be done; she consulted her husband. He, Ivan Fiodorovich, a man of experience, immediately took an extremely serious view of Kozin's report.

"He's probably right," said Ivan Fiodorovich. "And banners are not the only thing he's writing about. Apparently, Varpakhovsky is having an affair with one of the actresses, a Jewish girl, and is giving her the key parts—she's a singer. Anyway, who is Varpakhovsky?"

"He's a fascist, he's been moved here from the special zone. He's a theater director, I've just remembered he used to work for Meyerhold. Here, I've got it written down." Rydasova poked about in her card index, something that Ivan Fiodorovich had taught her to keep. "Some *Lady of the Camellias*. And he did *The History of a Town*, about Glupov, in the satirical theater. He's been in Kolyma since 1937. So you see. Kozin, on the other hand, is reliable. He may be a pederast, but he's not a fascist."

"And what has Varpakhovsky staged?"

"*The Abduction of Helen*. We've seen it. You remember, you even laughed. You even signed a recommendation for the actor to get an early release."

"Yes, yes, I think I remember. That *Abduction of Helen* wasn't by a Soviet author."

"Some Frenchman. I've got it on record here."

"Don't bother, don't bother, it's all straightforward. Send that Varpakhovsky off with a touring brigade, and as for his wife—what's her name?"

"Zyskind."

"The Jewess: keep her here. Theirs is a short-term love affair, not like ours." Ivan Fiodorovich made his graceful little joke.

He had commissioned a big surprise for his young wife. Rydasova was very fond of baubles, of any precious mementos. For two years, not far from Magadan, a prisoner who was a famous ivory carver had been carving an elaborate jewelry box from a mammoth's tusk: this was to be Ivan Fiodorovich's present to his young wife. To begin with, the ivory carver had been registered as a hospital patient, and then he had been put on the staff of a workshop, so that he could earn credits to count against his sentence. The credit he earned was a three-day reduction for each day worked, which was on the same scale as someone who overfulfilled the norm in the Kolyma uranium mines, where the credits, because of the damage to health, were even higher than the "gold" or "top metal" credits.

The carving of the box was nearly finished. Tomorrow that charade with Wallace would be over and Ivan Fiodorovich could get back to Magadan.

Rydasova gave the orders to have Varpakhovsky included in a traveling brigade, then passed the singer's denunciation on to the district headquarters of the Ministry of the Interior. She then started thinking. She had a lot to think about: Ivan Fiodorovich had aged and taken to drink. A lot of new young bosses had come onto the scene. Ivan Fiodorovich feared and loathed them. A Lutsenko had appeared as one of the deputies, had toured all of Kolyma, taking notes in the hospitals about patients suffering from trauma as a result of beatings. There were, he found, quite a lot of such patients. Naturally, Ivan Fiodorovich's informers told him about Lutsenko's notes.

Lutsenko delivered a report to the management committee.

"If someone in authority in the administration uses foul language, then what do you expect of the mine boss? The works clerk? The guard? What will be going on at the pit face? I'm going to read out to you the figures I have from my inquiries in the hospitals—and these are clear underestimates—for broken limbs and beatings."

Ivan Fiodorovich followed up Lutsenko's report with a major speech.

"We've had a lot of new people coming here," he said, "but they have all eventually realized that the conditions here are peculiar Kolyma conditions and that this has to be taken into account." He hoped that the younger comrades would understand this and work along with the rest.

Lutsenko's concluding remark was: "We have come here to work, and we shall: but we shan't work according to Ivan Fiodorovich's rules but according to the party's."

Everyone, the whole management committee and all Kolyma, realized that Ivan Fiodorovich's days were numbered. Rydasova shared their opinion. But the old man knew how things worked better than any Lutsenko did: it would take more than some commissar to deal with Ivan Fiodorovich. He wrote a letter. And Lutsenko, who was his deputy, the head of the political department, a hero of the Great Patriotic War, vanished like the morning dew. He was given an emergency transfer to somewhere. To celebrate his victory Ivan Fiodorovich got drunk and then caused an uproar in the Magadan theater.

"Chuck that singer out on his neck, I can't stand listening to the swine," he raged, sitting in his personal box.

And the singer vanished forever from Magadan.

But this was Ivan Fiodorovich's last victory. He was well aware that

Lutsenko was somewhere writing something, but he didn't have the strength to ward off the coming blow.

"Time I retired," he thought. "All I need is the jewelry box...."

"You'll get a big pension," his wife said, to comfort him. "Then we'll go. We'll forget it all. All the Lutsenkos and Varpakhovskys. We'll buy a nice little house near Moscow, with a garden. You'll be the chairman of the Civil Defense and a leading figure on the district council, eh? It's high time."

"How revolting," said Ivan Fiodorovich. "Chairman of Civil Defense? Ugh! And what about you?" he suddenly asked.

"I'll be with you."

Ivan Fiodorovich understood that his wife would wait two or three years for him to die.

"Lutsenko! Was he after my job, then?" he thought. "Sly bastard! We work differently, do we? He calls it 'smash and grab.' It's hard graft. Hard graft, my dear comrade Lutsenko, coming from the war, with government orders to increase gold production. As for the broken limbs, beatings, and deaths, there have always been lots and there always will be. This is the Far North, not Moscow. The law is like the taiga, the convicts say. A whole lot of supplies fell into the sea at the coast and three thousand men died. Ivan Fiodorovich Nikishev had Vyshnevetsky, the deputy in charge of camps, put on trial, and he got a prison sentence. How else could it have been dealt with? Is Lutsenko going to show us?"

"Get me my car!"

Ivan Fiodorovich's black ZIM limousine sped away from Magadan where plots and traps were being set up. Ivan Fiodorovich didn't have the strength to fight them.

He stopped for the night in the director's house. This was an institution he had created. In Berzin's day or in Pavlov's day there had been no such thing in Kolyma. "But," Ivan Fiodorovich reasoned, "once I'm entitled to have them, let's have them." Every five hundred kilometers on the enormous highway a building was erected, which had pictures, carpets, mirrors, bronze sculptures, an excellent buffet, a cook, a butler, and guards, where Ivan Fiodorovich, the director of Far East Construction could spend the night in suitable conditions. Once a year he actually did spend the night in one of his houses.

The black limousine was now speeding with Ivan Fiodorovich to Debin, the central hospital, where the nearest director's house was. They had already been telephoned, the head of the hospital had been woken up, and the whole hospital had been put on "combat alert." Everything was being washed, cleaned, scrubbed.

Suppose Ivan Fiodorovich visited the central hospital for prisoners and found dirt or dust? That would be the end of the chief. The chief would, however, accuse careless paramedics and doctors for underhanded sabotage; he'd say they neglected the cleaning in the hope that Ivan Fiodorovich would see this and dismiss the chief from his job. He'd say that was in the mind of every prisoner who was a doctor or a paramedic when they overlooked a bit of dust on a desk.

Everything in the hospital was trembling as Ivan Fiodorovich's black limousine sped along the Kolyma highway.

The director's house had no connection with the hospital; it happened to be built next to it, about five hundred meters away. But being so close was enough to cause all sorts of anxiety.

In the nine years he had been in Kolyma, Ivan Fiodorovich had never visited the central hospital for prisoners, a hospital of a thousand beds. Not once. But everyone was on alert while he had breakfast, lunch, and supper in the director's house. Only when the black limousine drove out onto the highway was the all clear given.

This time, the all clear was not timely. "He's there! He's drinking! Visitors have arrived!" That was the news from the director's house. Three days later, Ivan Fiodorovich's limousine approached the settlement for free hired workers; this was where the hospital's free doctors, paramedics, and support staff lived.

Everything was hushed. The hospital chief, panting as he went, clambered across the stream that separated the settlement from the hospital.

Ivan Fiodorovich got out of his limousine. His face was puffy and stale. He eagerly lit a cigarette.

"Hey you, what's your name?" Ivan Fiodorovich poked a digit into the hospital chief's gown.

"At your service, sir."

"Have you got children here?"

"My children? They're at school in Moscow, sir."

"Not yours. Children, you know, little ones. Have you got a nursery? Where's the nursery?" Ivan Fiodorovich barked.

"This building here, sir."

The limousine followed Ivan Fiodorovich to the nursery building. Nobody said a word.

"Bring the children out," Ivan Fiodorovich ordered.

The duty caregiver leapt out. "They're asleep."

"Shh...." The hospital chief pulled the caregiver to one side. "Get them all out, wake them. Make sure their hands are washed."

The caregiver dashed inside the nursery.

"I want to take the children for a ride in my limousine," said Ivan Fiodorovich, lighting another cigarette.

"A ride, sir. That's really wonderful." The children had by now come running down the steps to surround Ivan Fiodorovich.

"Get into the car," the hospital chief shouted. "Ivan Fiodorovich is going to take you for a ride. Don't all push."

The children got into the limousine; Ivan Fiodorovich sat next to the driver. The limousine took three trips to give all the children a turn.

"How about tomorrow, tomorrow? Will you come and get us tomorrow?"

"I will, I will," Ivan Fiodorovich assured them.

"Mind you, that's not bad," he thought as he made himself comfortable on his snow-white sheet. "Home, children, nice uncle. Like Joseph Stalin with a child in his arms."

The next day he was summoned to Magadan. He had been promoted to the minister of precious metals, but this was not the real reason for his summons.

The Magadan traveling theater brigade was making its way up and down the Kolyma highway, visiting one mine after another. It included Leonid Varpakhovsky. Dusia Zyskind, his camp wife, was left behind in Magadan, on the orders of Rydasova, who was the boss. A camp wife. But this was real love, real feelings. He was an actor, a professional at faking feelings, so he would know all about that. What could be done now, whom could they ask? Varpakhovsky felt a terrible weariness.

In Yagodnoye he was surrounded by the local doctors, free men, and prisoners.

In Yagodnoye. Two years earlier he was passing through Yagodnoye on his way to the special zone, and he had managed to "put on the brakes" in Yagodnoye and avoid ending up in the terrible Jelgala mines. The efforts that this had cost him. He had been forced to plumb the depths of his inventions, his skills, his ability to make the most of what little he had available to him in the north. So he mobilized all his resources; he would put on a musical show. Not Verdi's *Masked Ball*, which he was to put on for the Kremlin theater fifteen years later, nor Zapolska's *The Morality of Mrs. Dulska*, nor Lermontov in the Maly Theater, none of the director in chief's work in the Yermolova Theater. He would put on an operetta, *The Black Tulip*. No piano? It would have an accordion accompanist. Varpakhovsky himself would arrange the score, and he'd play the accordion. And he'd produce it. And he'd be victorious, and get out of Jelgala.

He is successful in getting a transfer from Magadan Theater, where he enjoys Rydasova's patronage. He's in the authorities' good books. Varpakhovsky is preparing auditions of amateur acts, he is putting on one show after another in the Magadan Theater, each more interesting than the last. And then he meets Dusia Zyskind, the singer, then there's love, Kozin's denunciation, and long-distance traveling.

Varpakhovsky knew many of the people standing around the truck that was transporting the Culture Brigade. There was Andreyev, with whom he had traveled from Neksikan to the Kolyma special zone. They met in the bathhouse, the winter bathhouse: darkness, filth, sweaty slippery bodies, tattoos, foul language, jostling, guards yelling at you, crowding. A smoking oil lamp on the wall, and underneath it the barber holding his razor, doing everyone in one session, wet underclothes, icy steam around your legs, one bowl of water to wash your body. Bundles of clothes fly into the air in complete darkness: "Whose is it, whose?"

And then the uproar and the noise suddenly stops for some reason. And Andreyev's neighbor, waiting his turn to have his fine head of hair removed, says in a resonant, calm voice, very much an actor's:

"It's rather different—a glass of rum,
Sleep at night, tea in the morning,
It's rather different, pals, at home."

They introduced themselves and got talking: they were both from Moscow. But only Varpakhovsky had managed to detach himself from the prisoners' group in Yagodnoye in the Far North's administrative area. Andreyev was neither a director nor an actor. He served a sentence at Jelgala, then he spent a long time in a hospital, and he was still in the district hospital at Belichya, working as support staff, about six kilometers from Yagodnoye. He didn't come to the theater brigade's show, but he was glad to see Varpakhovsky.

Varpakhovsky was left behind after the brigade moved on: he had been an emergency admission to the hospital. By the time the brigade had gone to Elgen, the women's farm, and come back, he would have thought things out and made a decision.

Andreyev and Varpakhovsky talked a lot and decided that Varpakhovsky should write a letter to Rydasova, explaining how serious his feelings were and appealing to Rydasova's nobler self. They took several days to compose the letter, polishing every phrase. A reliable doctor served as courier and took the letter to Magadan, so they had only to wait. The answer came after Andreyev and Varpakhovsky had parted and the theater brigade was on its way back to Magadan: Varpakhovsky was to be dismissed from the theater brigade and sent to do hard manual work at a punishment mine. Zyskind, his wife, was also to be sent to manual labor at Elgen, the women's farm.

"This was heaven's reply," as one of Jasieński's poems puts it.

Andreyev and Varpakhovsky met in a Moscow street. Varpakhovsky was now the director in chief at the Yermolova Theater. Andreyev was working at a Moscow magazine.

Rydasova had taken Varpakhovsky's letter from the mailbox of her Magadan apartment.

She found it disagreeable, and Ivan Fiodorovich disliked it even more.

"They really have gone beyond the pale. Any terrorist. . . ."

The corridor concierge on duty was immediately dismissed and sent to the guardhouse. Ivan Fiodorovich decided not to put the case in the hands of the criminal investigators: he sensed that his powers were somehow too weak now.

"My powers are weaker now," he told his wife. "You see, people can now get right into our apartment."

Even before the letter was read, the fates of Varpakhovsky and Zyskind were sealed. All that had to be decided was the punishment: Ivan Fiodorovich was in favor of severity, Rydasova of something a bit milder. They ended up choosing Rydasova's version.

1962

THE ACADEMICIAN

IT TURNED out that it was very difficult to print a conversation with a member of the Academy of Sciences. Not because the academician talked a load of rubbish, no. The academician was renowned and had a lot of experience with all kinds of interviews, and he was talking about a topic with which he was very familiar. The journalist sent out to talk to him was sufficiently well qualified: he was good at his job, and twenty years ago he had been very good. The problem was the high speed of scientific progress. A journalist's timelines, first proofs, printer's proofs, publisher's timetables have lagged hopelessly behind the speed of scientific progress. That autumn, on October 4, 1957, a satellite was launched. The academician knew a few things about the launch preparations; the journalist knew nothing. But after the satellite was launched the academician, the journalist, and the editor all saw clearly that not only did the boundaries of information have to be shifted but the tone of the article had to be changed. The first version of the article had to be imbued with expectations of great, unprecedented events. Now the events had happened. That was why a month after the interview the academician, who was in a sanatorium at Yalta, sent at his own expense some lengthy reply-paid telegrams to the editor. Skillfully lifting part of the veil covering his cybernetic secrets, the academician was trying his very best to be "on the level" and at the same time to avoid saying anything he shouldn't. The editorial board had the same concerns about what was appropriate to the times and what was not, and until the very last moment they kept making corrections to the academician's article.

The proofs of the article were sent to Yalta by special air courier; they came back to the editor covered in the academician's scrawled comments.

"Proofs corrected as Balzac would have done," said the chief editor in dismay. Everything was sorted out, fitted in, proofread again. The gigantic juggernaut of publishing technology rolled out onto its wide tracks. But by the time the printers had set it, Laika the dog had flown off into the cosmos; the academician was now at a peace congress in Romania, and from there he sent more telegrams, pleading and demanding. The editorial board booked urgent international telephone calls to Bucharest.

Finally the magazine appeared, and the editors lost all interest in the academician's article.

All that came later, however; at the moment Golubev, the journalist, was climbing a narrow marble staircase in an enormous building on the main street of the city where the academician lived. The building was the same age as the journalist: it had been put up during the building boom at the beginning of the twentieth century. These were apartments built for sale: they had baths, gas, telephones, sewerage, electricity.

There was a concierge on duty in the entrance. The electric light was placed so as to illuminate the face of anyone coming in. Somehow, this reminded one of a pretrial prison.

Golubev gave the academician's name, the concierge telephoned him and got a reply, then told the journalist, "Please go ahead," and flung open the elevator doors, which were decorated with a cast-bronze relief.

"Like the pass office," Golubev thought idly. Whatever else he'd seen, he'd certainly seen plenty of pass offices in his time.

"The academician is on the sixth floor," the concierge respectfully told him. His face expressed no surprise when Golubev walked past the open elevator doors and strode up the clean narrow marble stairs. After his illness, Golubev couldn't stand elevators, whether they were going up or down, but especially down, when he experienced a treacherous weightlessness.

Pausing to rest at each landing, Golubev reached the sixth floor. The hum in his ears quieted down a little, and his heartbeat became more regular and his breathing more even. He stood for a while outside the academician's door, stretched out a hand, and cautiously made a few gymnastic movements with his head, as recommended by the doctors who were treating him.

Golubev stopped turning his head, groped in his pocket for his handkerchief, fountain pen, and notebook, and then with firm pressure rang the doorbell.

The popular academician answered the door himself. He was young and fidgety; he had darting black eyes and looked far younger and in better health than Golubev. Before the interview Golubev had consulted the encyclopedias in the library and also some biographies, official and scientific. He now knew that he and the academician were the same age. Leafing through articles relevant to his forthcoming interview, Golubev noted that the academician hurled thunderbolts and lightning from his scientific Olympus at cybernetics, which he declared to be "a very harmful idealistic pseudoscience." "Pseudoscience on the warpath" is how the academician had put it about twenty years earlier. The interview that Golubev had come for was also meant to deal with the significance of cybernetics today.

The academician turned on the light, so that Golubev could take off his coat.

Both of them—the academician in a black suit with a black tie, black hair, black eyes, smooth face, agile, and Golubev's erect figure with a tired face and lots of wrinkles, more like deep scars—were reflected in the enormous, bronze-framed mirror. But Golubev's blue eyes sparkled and were, in fact, younger than the academician's lively shining eyes.

Golubev took a hanger and hung up his stiff new imitation leather coat, which he'd recently bought. Hanging next to his host's well-worn brown leather coat, lined with raccoon-dog fur, this coat looked quite respectable.

"Please come in," said the academician as he opened a door on his left. "And do excuse me. I'll be back in a minute."

The journalist looked around. A series of rooms stretched out in two directions, straight ahead and to the right. The doors were made of glass with a lower half of mahogany; somewhere in the distance, despite the utter silence, shadows of people kept appearing. Golubev had never lived in apartments with suites of rooms, but he did remember Arbenin's apartment in the film of Lermontov's play *Masquerade*. The academician reappeared somewhere in the distance, then vanished again before reappearing and once again vanishing, just like Arbenin in the film.

To the right of the big room, which was bright, thanks to the glass doors and the three picture windows, and which led to another suite of rooms, was an enormous grand piano. The piano lid was closed, and various porcelain figures were awkwardly crammed together on the lid. There were vases, big and small, statues, big and small, on magnificent pedestals. Plates and rugs were hanging on the walls. Two spacious armchairs were upholstered in white, to match the piano. Somewhere beyond the glass, human shadows were moving about.

Golubev entered the academician's study. The tiny little study was dark and narrow, more like a pantry. It was made even smaller by the bookshelves on all four walls. A little, toylike carved mahogany desk seemed to be bending under the weight of an enormous marble inkwell with a cover of gilded bronze. Three walls of the library were given over to reference books and the fourth to the academician's own works. Here too were the biographies and autobiographies with which Golubev was already acquainted. Into this same room a little black piano had been squeezed: it was gasping for air; next to it was a round desk for correspondence, covered with recent technical magazines. Golubev shifted a pile of magazines to the piano, moved up a chair, and put his pen and two pencils on the edge of the table. The academician had left the door to the lobby open.

"Just like 'those' offices," Golubev thought idly.

Everywhere, on the black piano, on the bookshelves, there were little jugs and porcelain or pottery figurines. Golubev picked up an ashtray shaped like Mephistopheles's head. A long time ago, he had been fond of porcelain and glass, he had been struck in the Hermitage by the miracles wrought by human hands, for instance a white porcelain figure called *Sleep*, where the face of a man sleeping in an armchair was covered with the finest of handkerchiefs, so it looked as if the museum curators had put a piece of muslin there to protect it from dust. But it wasn't muslin, it was a fine covering of porcelain. Golubev could remember many other miracles of human skill. But the Mephistopheles head, heavy and provincial, made no sense. Pottery sheep, pressed against the spines of books as if the latter were trees, were trumpeting from the shelves; there were hares with leonine faces sitting there. Were these personal mementos?

By the door were two solid leather suitcases plastered with stickers from foreign hotels. There were a lot of stickers, but the suitcases were new.

The academician materialized on the threshold; he caught Golubev's eye and immediately began to explain: "I am sorry. I'm flying off to Greece tomorrow. Please sit down."

The academician squeezed past, reached his desk and made himself comfortable.

"I've been thinking about your editor's proposal," he said, looking at the skylight. The wind was blowing a yellowing five-fingered maple leaf into the room: it looked like an amputated human hand. The leaf spun in the air and fell on the floor. The academician bent down, crumpled up the leaf in his fingers, and threw it into a wastepaper basket that was pressed against a leg of his desk.

"And I have accepted it," he went on. "I've made a note of three main points in my response, my reaction, my opinion, whatever you want to call it."

He deftly extracted a tiny piece of paper from under the inkwell; a few words were scrawled over it.

"My first point runs like this—"

"Please," said Golubev, turning pale. "Speak a little louder. I don't hear very well. Do forgive me."

"Of course, of course," the academician responded politely. "My first point runs like this.... Loud enough?"

"Yes, thank you."

"So, the first question...."

The academician's eyes, constantly moving, looked at Golubev's hands. Golubev realized, or rather he didn't realize, his whole body just sensed what the academician thought of him, namely that the journalist he'd been sent didn't know shorthand. The academician was a little bit offended. Of course, there are journalists who don't know shorthand, especially the older ones. The academician looked at the journalist's dark, wrinkled face. Of course there were. But in cases like this the editor would send another person as well, a shorthand typist. Or they could just send a woman who knew shorthand and dispense with the journalist: that would have been even better. The magazine *Nature and the Universe*, for instance, always sent him just a shorthand typist. The editorial board couldn't possibly think, after all, that by sending this aging journalist that the latter was capable of asking him, an academician, any crucial questions. Not that crucial questions were needed, and they had never been the point. Journalists are like diplomatic couriers, the academician thought, or just ordinary couriers. He, an academic, was wasting his time just because there was no shorthand typist. Sending a shorthand typist was the obvious thing to do, in fact politeness demanded the editorial board to do so. The editors had been rude to him.

In the West, on the other hand, every journalist knows shorthand and can type. But here things are no different from a century ago, you might as well be in Nekrasov's study. What magazines did they have a hundred years ago? Apart from *The Contemporary* he couldn't remember, but there must have been some.

The academician had a lot of self-esteem and was very sensitive. He sensed that the editorial board had acted disrespectfully. What's more, as he knew by experience, recording an interview live can't help changing the content. A lot of effort would have to be expended correcting the result. Now, for instance, an hour had been set aside for the interview; the academician couldn't spare any more time, he had no right to, his time was more precious than the journalist's or the editorial board's.

That's what he was thinking as he dictated his usual interview phrases. But he concealed his annoyance and amazement. "If you've poured the wine, you have to drink it," was a French proverb he recalled. The academician could think in French; of all the languages he knew he loved French most, for the best scientific journals in his field and the best detective novels were in French. The academician pronounced the French phrase out loud, but a journalist who had no shorthand would, as the academician expected, be unable to react.

"Yes, the wine is poured," the academician thought as he dictated, "the decision has been made, the job has been begun." He wasn't accustomed to stopping halfway, so he calmed down and went on talking.

When all was said and done, there was a peculiar technical problem: to fit everything into one hour without dictating too fast, so that the journalist had time to get it all down, and to speak loud enough, quieter than at a lectern in his institute, quieter than at a peace congress, but considerably louder than in his study, roughly at the same level as when working in the laboratory. Once he saw that these problems had been successfully resolved and that the annoying unexpected difficulties had been overcome, the academician cheered up.

"Excuse me," he said. "You wouldn't be the Golubev who used to publish a lot when I was a young man, when I was beginning my career in the early thirties? All the young scientists used to follow those articles at the time. I can remember as if it was yesterday the title of one Golubev article: 'The Unity of Science and Literature.' In those days," the academician smiled, showing the fine dental work he had undergone, "that sort of topic was fashionable. That article would fit very nicely today for a discussion of physicists and lyrical poets with Poletayev, the cybernetics man. That was all a long time ago," he said with a sigh.

"No," said the journalist. "I'm a different Golubev. I know the one you have in mind. He died in 1938."

Golubev stared unswervingly at the academician's quick black eyes.

The academician emitted a vague sound that was meant to be interpreted as sympathy, understanding, regret.

Golubev wrote without a pause. He needed a little time to understand the French proverb. He had known French but then had forgotten it a long time ago, and now the unfamiliar words crawled over his weary, withered brain. This phrase of double Dutch crawled slowly, as if on all fours, down the dark alleys of his brain, stopping to gather strength until it crawled into a patch of light, and Golubev understood, with pain and fear, what it meant in Russian. It wasn't the content but the fact that, by understanding it, he had been shown a new region of forgotten things, which also had to be reconstructed, strengthened, revived. But now he lacked the strength, moral or physical, and it seemed far easier not to remember anything new. His back broke out into a cold sweat. He badly wanted to smoke, but the doctors had forbidden him to do so, and he was someone who had smoked for forty years. Once they told him not to, he'd given it up: he had lost courage and he had decided to live. He didn't need willpower to stop smoking; he needed it to ignore the doctors' advice.

A woman poked her head, dressed in a hairdresser's helmet, through the door. "They get serviced at home," the journalist made a mental note.

"Excuse me," said the academician, clambering past the piano and slipping out of the room. He shut the door firmly behind him.

Golubev waved his arm—it had pins and needles. Then he sharpened a pencil.

He could hear the academician's voice in the lobby; it was energetic, brusque to a degree, not to be interrupted, brooking no objection.

"The driver," the academician explained when he reappeared in the room, "is incapable of working out when to bring the car.... Let's go on," he said, passing behind the piano and bending over it so that Golubev could hear better. "The second section is the success of information theory, electronic, mathematical logic—in a nutshell, of everything we now call cybernetics."

The inquisitive black eyes caught Golubev's, but the journalist was imperturbable. The academician cheerfully went on: "At first this was a new science where we lagged behind the West a little, but we've quickly caught up and now we are in the lead. We're thinking of setting up chairs of mathematical logic and game theory."

"Game theory?"

"Quite. It's still being called Monte Carlo theory," the academician drawled rather affectedly. "We're keeping up with the times. Though for you—"

"Journalists have never kept up with the times," said Golubev, "unlike you scientists...." Golubev moved the Mephistopheles head ashtray. "I've been very taken by this ashtray," he said.

"Nothing special," said the academician. "I happened to get it by chance. I'm no collector, no *amateur*, as the French say, I just find pottery relaxing to look at."

"Of course, of course, you do, it's an excellent pastime." Golubev meant to say "enthusiasm" but was afraid of the *u* sound, in case his new denture fell out; the denture couldn't stand the vowel *u*. "Well, many thanks," said Golubev as he got up and assembled his sheets of paper. "Have a good journey. We'll send proofs."

"Well, in case anything happens," said the academician, frowning, "the editors can add anything that needs to be added. I'm a scientist, I'm no judge of the matter."

"Don't worry. You'll see a proof of everything."

"All the best to you."

The academician showed the journalist into the lobby, turned on the light, and looked sympathetically as Golubev tugged his new, excessively stiff coat onto his body. He had trouble getting his left arm into the left sleeve, and the effort made his face flush red.

"The war?" the academician asked, politely considerate.

"Something like it," said Golubev. "Something like it." And he went down the marble stairs.

Golubev's shoulder joints had been torn apart under interrogation in 1938.

1961

THE DIAMONDS MAP

IN 1931 there were frequent thunderstorms on the Vishera River.

Straight, short flashes of lightning slashed the sky like swords. The rain glittered and rang out like chain mail; the rocks were like ruined castles.

"The Middle Ages," said Vilemson as he leapt off his horse. "Boats, horses, rocks.... Let's take a break at Robin Hood's."

On the hillside there was a mighty, two-trunked tree. Time and the wind had ripped the bark off two poplars that had grown into one: this barefoot giant in short trousers really did look like the English hero. Robin Hood was rustling as he waved his arms about.

"We're exactly ten kilometers from home," said Vilemson as he tied the horses to Robin Hood's right leg. We took shelter from the rain in a little cavern under the tree trunk and lit up.

Vilemson, the head of the geological expedition, was not a geologist. He was a marine, a submarine commander. His boat had gone off course and surfaced by the Finnish shores. The crew was allowed to go, but Marshal Mannerheim detained the commander for all of six months in a cell walled with mirrors. In the end, Vilemson was released and arrived in Moscow. The neurologists and psychiatrists insisted that he be demobilized so that he could work somewhere in the open, in the forest, in the mountains. So he became the chief of a geological prospecting expedition.

After leaving the last docking point, we had spent ten days going up the mountain river, carrying our boat, an aspen dugout, on poles along the riverbanks. On the fifth day we had gone on horseback, since the river had disappeared and there was only a stony riverbed. We spent another day on horseback following a packhorse trail through the taiga. The journey seemed unending.

Everything is unexpected, and everything is phenomenal in the taiga: the moon, the stars, wild animals, birds, people, fish. The forest began to thin out imperceptibly, the bushes were spaced apart and the path turned into a road: we were suddenly faced with an enormous brick building, windowless and covered in moss. Its round, empty window holes looked like embrasures.

"Where did they get the bricks?" I asked. I was struck by this anomalous old building in the depths of the taiga.

"Good for you," shouted Vilemson, reining in his horse. "You've spotted it! You'll know all about it tomorrow."

But the next day came and I still knew nothing. We were off again, galloping along a forest road that was surprisingly straight. Here and there young birch trees had sprouted in the road, and on either side fir trees were stretching out their shaggy old arms to each other. They had reddened with age, but at no point did their branches block out the blue sky. The axle of a railcar, rusted over time, was sticking out of the ground like a tree with no branches or leaves. We stopped the horses.

"This is the narrow-gauge line," said Vilemson. "It went from the ore-processing plant to the warehouse, that brick building you saw. Now listen. There used to be a Belgian iron-ore concession here back in the tsar's days. There was a plant with two furnaces, a light railway, a village, a school, women singers from Vienna. The concession ran out in 1912. Russian industrialists headed by Prince Lvov, who couldn't rest until he got his hands on the fabulous profits the Belgians were making, asked the tsar to transfer the business to them. They got what they wanted: the Belgians' concession wasn't renewed. The Belgians refused compensation for their expenditure. They just left. But when they went they blew everything up: the plant and the furnaces. There wasn't a stone left standing in the village. They even dismantled the light railway, down to the very last fishplate. Everything had to be rebuilt from scratch. Prince Lvov hadn't anticipated all that. Before they'd managed to get things going, the war broke out. Then it was the revolution and the civil war. And now, in 1930, we're here. Here are the furnaces." Vilemson pointed to somewhere on the right where I could see nothing but luxuriant greenery. "And there is the plant," said Vilemson.

We were standing opposite a large shallow ravine, fallen earth covered all over with young trees. There was a hump in the middle of the ravine: it reminded one vaguely of the skeleton of a destroyed building. The taiga had swallowed up the remains of the ore plant; a brown hawk was sitting on the stump of a chimney, as if it were the top of a rock.

"You have to know there was a plant here if you want to see it," said Vilemson. "A plant with nobody around. Superb work. Just twenty years. Twenty generations of vegetation: of alliums, reeds, willow herb.... And that's the end of civilization. With a hawk perched on the plant chimney."

"That process takes far longer for a human being," I said.

"Far shorter," said Vilemson. "You don't need so many generations of human beings." Without knocking, he opened the door of the nearest cabin.

An enormous, silver-haired old man, wearing gold-framed spectacles and an old-style black beaver-fur jacket, was sitting at a table made from rough-planed wood and scrubbed until it was white. His gouty bluish fingers were clutching the dark leather binding of a thick book with silver clasps. He was calmly looking at us with blue eyes, bloodshot with an old man's red veins.

"How are you, Ivan Stepanovich?" said Vilemson, as he approached the old man. "You see, you've got visitors."

I bowed.

"Still digging, are you?" rasped the bespectacled old man. "A waste of time, a waste of time. I'd offer you boys tea, but there's nobody about. The women and the kids have gone to pick berries, my sons are out hunting. So kindly forgive me. This is my special time." And Ivan Stepanovich tapped the thick book with his finger. "Not that you're in my way."

The clasp clicked and the book opened.

"What is the book?" I couldn't help asking.

"The Bible, son. I haven't had any other book in the house for the last twenty years. . . . I find it easier to listen than to read: my eyes are not what they were."

I picked up his Bible. Ivan Stepanovich smiled. The Bible was in French.

"I don't know French."

"Quite," said Ivan Stepanovich, crackling the pages as he flicked through them.

"Who is he?" I asked Vilemson.

"The bookkeeper, taking on the whole world. Ivan Stepanovich Bugreyev, who has decided to fight civilization. He's the only man who's stayed out here in the backwoods since 1912. He was the head bookkeeper for the Belgians. He was so shattered by the destruction of the ore plant that he became a follower of Jean-Jacques Rousseau. You can see what a patriarch he is. He must be about seventy. He's got eight sons. He hasn't got any daughters. His wife's an old woman. He's got grandchildren. His children can read and write; they learned while there was still a school here. The old man won't let his grandchildren learn to read and write. Fishing, hunting, a sort of kitchen garden, bees, and the French Bible as retold by grandfather: that's their life. There's a settlement with a school and a shop about forty kilometers from here. I try to keep in with him: there are rumors that he has stashed away a geological map of these parts—it was left by the Belgians. The rumors may be true. They did do some prospecting. I myself have come across someone's old prospecting shafts in the taiga. The old man won't let me see the map. He refuses to make our job quicker. So we'll have to do without it."

We spent the night in a cabin belonging to the man's eldest son, Andrei. Andrei Bugreyev was about forty.

"Why haven't you joined me as a shaft digger?" asked Vilemson.

"My father disapproves," said Andrei Bugreyev.

"You could earn yourself some money!"

"We've got all the money we need. There are lots of wild animals here. And timber to be felled and chopped, too. And a lot of work around the house. Granddad makes a plan for each one of us. A three-year plan," said Andrei, smiling.

"Here, have a newspaper."

"I mustn't. My father will find out. And anyway I've almost forgotten how to read."

"How about your son? He's getting on fifteen, isn't he?"

"Vania can't read or write at all. Talk to my father, there's no point talking to me." Andrei started furiously tugging off his boots. "But is it true that they're going to build a school here?"

"It's true. It'll be opened in a year's time. But here you are, refusing to work with the prospectors. I need every man I can get."

"Where are all your men, then?" asked Andrei, tactfully changing the subject.

"At Krasny spring. We're poking around in the old prospecting shafts. But Ivan Stepanovich has a map, doesn't he, Andrei?"

"He hasn't got any map. That's all idle talk. Rubbish."

Suddenly an alarmed and angry face appeared. It was Maria, Andrei's wife.

"No, there is a map. There is, there is!"

"Maria!"

"There is! There is! I saw it myself ten years ago."

"Maria!"

"Why the hell do we keep that damned map? Why can't Vania read or write? We live like wild animals. We'll be covered in grass, next thing."

"No, you won't," said Vilemson. "There'll be a settlement. Then a town. There'll be an ore-processing plant. There'll be life. There may not be any singers from Vienna, but there will be schools, theaters. And your Vania will be an engineer."

"He won't, he won't," said Maria, weeping. "Now it's time for him to get married. But what girl would marry a man who can't read or write?"

"What's all this noise about?" Ivan was standing on the threshold. "Maria, go back to your place, it's time you were asleep. As for you, my good fellows, don't bring quarrels into my family. I do have a map, and I'm not going to give it to you. We can live without any of that."

"We can manage without your map," said Vilemson. "A year's work and we'll draw up our own map. The natural wealth is for everyone. Tomorrow Vasilchikov is bringing the plans. We're going to fell the forest to build a settlement."

Ivan Stepanovich slammed the door as he left. Everyone went to bed as quickly as they could.

I was woken up by the presence of a lot of people. Dawn was cautiously making its way into the room. Vilemson was sitting on the floor by the wall, his dirty bare feet stretched out in front of him, while the whole Bugreyev family was noisily breathing around him: all eight sons, all eight daughters-in-law, twenty grandsons, and fifteen granddaughters. Actually, the grandchildren were breathing somewhere on the porch. The only person missing was Ivan Stepanovich and his elderly wife, the beak-nosed Serafima Ivanovna.

"Is that how it is to be?" Andrei's breathless voice was asking.

"Yes."

"How about him, then?" And all the Bugreyevs sighed deeply, then fell silent.

"What about him?" Vilemson asked firmly.

"Granddad will die," Andrei pronounced in a sorrowful voice, and all the Bugreyevs sighed again.

"Perhaps he won't," Vilemson ventured to say.

"And Granny will die, too." The daughters-in-law burst into tears.

"Your mother is certainly not going to die," Vilemson assured them, adding, "though she is getting on."

Suddenly everyone began to move about noisily. The younger grandchildren dove into the bushes, the daughters-in-law dashed back to their cabins. Grandfather Ivan Stepanovich was slowly approaching us from his cabin; he was clutching with both hands an enormous, dirty bundle of papers that smelled of earth.

"Here's the map." Ivan Stepanovich held on to the sheets of parchment. His fingers were trembling. Serafima Ivanovna was looking over his mighty back. "Here, I'm handing it over. It's been twenty years. Serafima, forgive me; Andrei, Piotr, Nikolai, all my flesh and blood, forgive me." Bugreyev burst out weeping.

"Come on, come on, Ivan Stepanovich," said Vilemson. "Don't be upset. You should be pleased, not distressed." He then told me to keep close to Bugreyev. The old man had no intention of dying. He quickly calmed down; he seemed to shake off old age and chatted from morning to evening, grabbing me, Vilemson, Vasilchikov by the shoulder, constantly telling us stories about the Belgians, what had happened, what used to be there, the profit the owners made. The old man's memory was very good.

The bundle of parchment that smelled of earth contained a geological map of the district, compiled by the Belgians. There were ores: gold, iron.... There were precious stones: topaz, turquoise, beryl.... There were semiprecious gems: agate, jasper, amethyst, malachite.... The only things missing were the stones that had brought Vilemson here.

Ivan Stepanovich had not handed over the map for diamonds. Only thirty years later were diamonds found on the Vishera.

1959

UNCONVERTED

I LOVINGLY hang on to my old portable stethoscope. It was a graduation present from Nina Semionovna, who ran the practicals for the internal diseases courses.

This stethoscope is a symbol marking my return to life, a promise of freedom, of liberty, a promise that was kept. Mind you, freedom and liberty are different things. I was never free, I was merely at liberty during my whole adult life. But all that came later, much later than the day when I accepted that gift with a hint of concealed pain, a hint of concealed sadness, as if the stethoscope, the symbol marking my main victory, my main success in the Far North, where the line runs between death and life, should have been presented to somebody else, but not to me. I felt this all acutely—I don't know whether I understood it, but I definitely felt it as I put the stethoscope away next to my body under the well-worn camp blanket: the blanket had been a soldier's blanket and was now serving its second or third term, issued to those taking the courses. My frostbitten fingers stroked the stethoscope, unable to work out whether it was made of wood or iron. Once, when I was taking things out of a bag, my own bag, without looking, I pulled out the stethoscope instead of a spoon. That was a very significant mistake.

Former prisoners who have been lucky enough to have an easy camp life—if anyone's life in the camps could ever be easy—consider that the hardest time in their life was the time after their release when they had no rights, when they wandered from one place to another, when it was impossible to find any permanence in life, the permanence that helped them survive in the camps. Such people somehow adapted to the camp, as the camp adapted to them, giving them food, a roof, and work. Now they were suddenly forced to change their habits. People saw their hopes, however modest, crushed. Dr. Kalembet, who had served five years of his camp sentence, couldn't cope with freedom after the camps. A year later, he killed himself, leaving a note: "The fools won't let me live." But the fools weren't the problem. Another doctor, Dr. Miller, spent an extraordinary amount of energy throughout the war trying to prove that he was a Jew, not a German: he shouted it from the rooftops and underlined it in every form he filled out. Dr. Miller knew that fate doesn't like to joke. He succeeded in proving that he wasn't a German. He was released when he had served his term. But after a year of life in freedom Dr. Miller was charged with being a cosmopolitan. Actually, Dr. Miller was not charged at first. A sophisticated boss, who read the newspapers and kept up with new fiction, invited Dr. Miller for a preliminary chat. Orders are orders, but guessing what the "party line" will be before the order comes gives sophisticated bosses great satisfaction. Whatever had begun in the center was bound eventually to reach Chukotka, Indigirka, Yana, and finally Kolyma. Dr. Miller understood all this very well. In the village of Arkagala, where he was working as a doctor, a piglet had drowned in a pit full of sewage. The piglet suffocated in excrement but was dragged out, and this led to one of the most bitter disputes, whose resolution was a matter for all the social organizations to take part in. The free settlement, about a hundred bosses and engineers with their families, demanded that the piglet be handed over to the refectory for free employees: this would be a rare find—pork chops, hundreds of them. The bosses were salivating. But Kucherenko, the camp chief, insisted on the piglet being sold to the camp. The whole camp, everyone behind the wire, spent several days discussing the fate of the piglet. Everything else was forgotten. There were meetings in the settlement: the party organization, the trade union organization, the soldiers in the guards detachment.

Dr. Miller, a former prisoner and now the chief of the medical services in the settlement and the camp, was obliged to decide this thorny question. And he did so, in the camp's favor. A document was drawn up, stating that the piglet had drowned in excrement but could be used for the camp cook pot. Such documents were quite common in Kolyma. Stewed fruit that stank of kerosene: "unfit for sale in the free workers' shop but may be filtered and sold for the camp cook pot."

It was the day before his chat about cosmopolitanism that Miller signed this document about the piglet. This is just a matter of chronology, something that sticks in the memory as an important, notable incident in life.

After his chat with the interrogator Miller didn't go home: he went into the zone, put on his overalls, opened his office, went to his cupboard, took out a syringe, and gave himself an intravenous injection of morphine solution.

What is the purpose of all this story about suicidal doctors, about a piglet that drowned in sewage, about the unbounded joy of the prisoners? Here is the purpose.

For us, for me and hundreds of thousands of others who worked in the camps and were not doctors, our time after the camps was nothing but joy, joy every day and every hour. The hell we had put behind us was so dreadful that none of the tiresome ordeals as we trailed from one "special department" or "personnel department" to another, none of the peregrinations, none of the deprivation of rights that article 39 of the internal passport system imposed could take away from us this feeling of happiness and joy, when we compared it with what we had seen in our yesterdays and in the days before yesterday.

It was a great honor for those taking a paramedic course to find themselves doing their practice sessions in the third therapeutic section. The third section was run by Nina Semionovna, a former lecturer in the Department of Diagnostic Therapy at Kharkov Medical Institute.

Only two people, two students out of thirty, could take a one-month practical course in the third therapeutic section.

Practice consisted of live observation of patients—that was an infinite distance from books, from the "course." You can't become a medic, whether a doctor or a paramedic, by reading books.

Just two male students, Bokis and I, were to pass into the third section.

"A couple of men? Why?"

Nina Semionovna was a hunched old woman with green eyes; she was gray-haired and wrinkled, and she was not kind.

"Nina Semionovna hates women."

"She hates them?"

"Well, she doesn't like them. Anyway, two men. Lucky people." The course monitor took me and Bokis to be inspected by Nina Semionovna's green eyes.

"Have you been here long?"

"Since thirty-seven."

"Well, I've been here since thirty-eight. I was at Elgen first. I did thirty childbirths there; before Elgen I hadn't done any. Then came the war. My husband died in Kiev. So did my two children. Boys. A bomb. More people have died around me than in any battle in war. They died when there was no war, before there was a war. All the same. Grief is like happiness: it comes in all forms."

Nina Semionovna sat on a patient's bed and pulled back the blanket.

"Right, let's start. Pick up the stethoscope, put it on the patient's chest and listen. . . . The French listen through a towel. But a stethoscope is the best, most reliable way. I don't think much of the phonendoscope, it's something the lordly doctors like to use because they can't be bothered to bend down over the patient. The stethoscope. . . . What I'm showing you is something you won't find in any textbook. So listen."

The skeleton upholstered in skin meekly obeyed Nina Semionovna's command. It obeyed mine, too.

"Listen to the boxy sound, the hint of muffling. Remember it for the rest of your life, as you remember the bones, dry skin, the shine in the eyes. You'll remember?"

"I will. For my whole life."

"Do you remember what it sounded like yesterday? Listen to the patient again. The sound has changed. Describe all this, write it down in his notes. Don't be shy. Write firmly."

There were twenty patients in the ward.

"There are no interesting patients at the moment. What you've been seeing is starvation, starvation, starvation. Sit down on the left. Over here, in my place. Take the patient by the shoulder with your left hand. Grip him, grip him. What can you hear?"

I described what I heard.

"Right, it's lunchtime. Off you go, you'll be fed in the serving room."

Shura, the kindly woman who did the serving, generously poured out our "doctor's" dinner. The chief's sister's dark eyes were smiling at me, but more at herself, at something deep inside her.

"Why are you like this, Olga Tomasovna?"

"Oh, you noticed. I'm always thinking about something else. About yesterday. I try not to see today."

"Today isn't so bad, it's not so terrible."

"Shall I give you more soup?"

"Yes, please."

I wasn't interested in dark eyes. Nina Semionovna's lesson, mastering the art of treatment, was more important than anything else in the world.

Nina Semionovna lived in her section, in a room that was called a "cabin" in Kolyma. Nobody except her ever entered it. She herself kept it tidy and clean. I don't know if she washed the floor herself. You could see, when the door was open, a hard hospital bed with minimal bedding, a hospital night table, a stool, whitewashed walls. There was a little office next to the "cabin," but its door opened onto the ward, not the lobby. The little office had a sort of desk, two stools, and a couch.

Everything was the same as in the other sections, but there was a difference: perhaps because there were no flowers here, not in the cabin, nor in the office, nor in the ward. Was this due to Nina Semionovna's strictness, her unsmiling severity? Her eyes used to flash a dark green emerald fire at times and places that seemed inappropriate, uncalled-for. Her eyes flashed regardless of what was being said or done. But those eyes didn't have an independent life; they cohabited with Nina Semionovna's feelings and thoughts.

There was no friendship in the section, not even the most superficial friendship of nurses and their assistants. Everyone came here to work, to do their job, their shift, and it was obvious that the real life of those who worked in the third section was in the women's barracks, after their job was done, after work. Usually, real life in camp hospitals is stuck, is glued to the workplace and to working hours, and people are happy to go to their section so as to get away as fast as they can from the accursed barracks.

There was no friendship in the third therapeutic section. The nurses and their assistants disliked Nina Semionovna. They merely respected her. They feared her. They were afraid of the terrible Elgen, the Kolyma farm where women prisoners worked in the forest and on the land.

Everyone was afraid, except Shura in the serving room.

"It's difficult bringing men in here," Shura would say as she noisily flung the bowls she had washed into the cupboard. "But, thank God, I'm in my fifth month and I'll soon be sent to Elgen. I'll be free. New mothers get released every year: it's the only chance for people like me."

"If you're article fifty-eight, you don't get released."

"I'm article ten. Article ten gets released, the Trotskyists don't. Last year Katiushka was working here, where I am; Fedia, her husband, is living with me now. Katiushka and her baby were released, she came to say goodbye. Fedia said, 'Remember it was me that got you released.' She got out and not because she'd served her sentence, or been amnestied, or made a run for it in summer. She did it her own way, the most reliable way. And it worked, he got her released. And I think he's gotten me released...."

Shura trustingly pointed to her belly.

"I'm sure he's gotten you your release."

"Quite right. I'll get out of this bloody section."

"What's going on here that I don't know about, Shura?"

"You'll see. I know what: tomorrow's Sunday, we'll make a medical soup. Though Nina Semionovna doesn't like these special dishes much.... But she'll still let us...."

Medical soup was made of medicines, all sorts of roots, meat cubes dissolved in saline: you don't need to add salt, as Shura told me with delight.... Blueberry and raspberry jellies, rosehips, pancakes.

Everyone approved of the medical dinner. Nina Semionovna finished her portion and then got up.

"Come and see me in my office."

I went in.

"I have a book for you."

Nina Semionovna dug about in her desk drawer and got out something that looked like a prayer book.

"The New Testament?"

"No, not the New Testament," she said slowly, and her green eyes began to shine. "No, not the New Testament. It's Blok. Take it." Reverently and shyly, I took hold of the little dirty-gray volume in the small-format Poet's Library series. I passed my fingers over the spine. My fingers were frostbitten—the skin still had a miner's coarseness, so I couldn't sense the shape or the size of the book. The volume had two paper bookmarks in it.

"Read those two poems out loud to me. Where the bookmarks are."

"'A Girl Was Singing in a Church Choir.' 'In a Distant Blue Bedchamber.' I used to know those poems."

"Oh did you? Recite them."

I began reciting but instantly forgot the lines. My memory refused to let me have the verses. The world I had left for the hospital had done without poetry. There were days in my life, quite a few, when I couldn't remember and didn't want to remember any poetry. I was glad of that, it was a liberation from a burden I didn't need, a burden that wasn't necessary for my struggle in life's lower stories, its cellars, its cesspits. Poetry was only a hindrance for me there.

"Read them from the book."

I read out both poems, and Nina Semionovna burst into tears.

"You understand that it was the boy who died, he died. Go away and read Blok."

I devoured Blok, rereading him all night and all during my shift. Apart from "A Girl" and "Blue Bedchamber" there was "Spell by Fire and Darkness," verses of fire dedicated to Volkhova. These verses aroused utterly new forces. Three days later I returned the book to Nina Semionovna.

"You thought I was giving you a New Testament. I do have one. Here...." A little volume that looked like the Blok volume, but was dark brown instead of dirty gray, was extracted from the desk drawer. "Read the apostle Paul. To the Corinthians.... Here it is."

"I don't have any religious feeling, Nina Semionovna. But of course I have the greatest respect—"

"What? You, a person who has lived a thousand lives? Who has been resurrected? You don't have religious feelings? Haven't you seen enough tragedies here?"

Nina Semionovna's face became wrinkled and dark; her gray hair became disheveled and stuck out from under her white doctor's bonnet.

"You will read books . . . magazines."

"The magazine of the Moscow patriarchate?"

"No, not the Moscow patriarchate, but from elsewhere. . . ."

She gave a wave of her white sleeve, which looked like an angel's wing as it pointed heavenward. . . . Where to? Beyond the wire of the zone? Beyond the hospital? Beyond the limits of the free settlement? Overseas? Over the mountains? Beyond the boundaries of earth and heaven?

"No," I said inaudibly, chilled by my inner devastation. "Is the only way out of human tragedies a religious one?" Phrases were turning in my brain, hurting my brain cells. I thought I had forgotten such words a long time ago. And now the words had reappeared: more important, they were submitting to my own will. This was something of a miracle. I repeated one more time, as if reading something written or printed in a book: "Is the only way out of human tragedies a religious one?"

"The only way, the only one. Go."

I left the room, putting the New Testament in my pocket, for some reason thinking about something quite different from the Corinthians, the apostle Paul, or the inexplicable miracle of the human memory. When I imagined what this "something else" might be, I realized that I had come back to the world of the camps, that the possibility of a "religious way out" was too fortuitous and too unworldly. After putting the New Testament in my pocket I was thinking about only one thing: was I going to get supper today?

Olga Tomasovna's warm fingers took hold of my elbow. Her dark eyes were laughing.

"Go, go," she said as she moved me toward the exit. "You're not converted yet. People like you don't get supper from us."

The next day I gave Nina Semionovna her New Testament back; with a brusque gesture she put the book away in the desk drawer.

"Tomorrow you finish your practical. Let me sign your card, your report book. And here's a present for you: a stethoscope."

1963

THE HIGHEST PRAISE

ONCE UPON a time there was a beautiful maiden: Maria Mikhailovna Dobroliubova. Blok wrote about her in his diary; the ringleaders of the revolution listened to her and obeyed. Had her fate been different, had she not perished, the Russian Revolution might have taken a different direction. If only it had.

Every Russian, and not only Russian, generation produces the same number of giants and nonentities. Of geniuses and talents. It is the job of time to give a genius or a talent a path to follow, or to kill them casually, or to suffocate them with praise and with imprisonment.

Maria Dobroliubova is no lesser a figure than Sofia Perovskaya, is she? But Sofia Perovskaya's name is on the signs attached to the streetlights, while Maria Dobroliubova is forgotten.

Even her brother, the poet and sectarian Aleksandr Dobroliubov, is less forgotten.

A beauty who was educated at the Smolny Institute, Maria Dobroliubova had a good understanding of her place in life. She was endowed with a very great sense of self-sacrifice, with a willingness to face life or death.

As a young girl she worked with the starving—as a nurse in the Russo-Japanese War.

All these tests merely heightened the demands, physical and moral, that she made on herself.

Between the 1905 and 1917 revolutions, Maria associated with the Socialist Revolutionaries. She didn't go in for propaganda. Minor activity didn't fit the temperament of a young woman who by now had experience of life's storms.

Terror, an "act," was what she dreamed of, what she demanded. She made the leaders agree. "A terrorist's life span is six months," as Savinkov[11] used to say. She was given a revolver and went out to commit her "act."

But she couldn't find the strength to kill. Her entire past life rebelled against this ultimate decision.

Her struggle to save the lives of those dying of starvation, her struggle to save the lives of the wounded.

But now she had to turn death into life.

Her living work with people and her heroic past were a hindrance in preparing herself to be an assassin.

You had to be too much of a theoretician, a dogmatist, in order to distance yourself from real life. Maria could see that she was being manipulated by someone else's will; this stunned her, and she felt ashamed of herself.

She couldn't summon the strength to fire a gun. And she was afraid of living in disgrace, in an acute state of mental crisis. Maria Dobroliubova put the barrel in her own mouth and fired.

She was twenty-nine.

I first heard this radiant, passionate Russian name in Butyrki prison.

Aleksandr Georgievich Andreyev, the general secretary of the society of prerevolutionary political prisoners, told me about Maria.

"There are rules in terror. If for any reason an assassination attempt has failed, if the bomb-thrower lost his nerve or the fuse didn't work, or anything else, then you don't make the same assassin try again. If you use the same terrorists as in the failed first attempt, you can only expect it to go wrong."

"How about Kaliayev?"[12]

"Kaliayev was the exception."

Experience, statistics, and underground activity tell us that it is possible only once to summon the self-sacrificial inner strength needed for such an act. Maria Dobroliubova's fate is the best-known example of this in the oral anthology of our underground world.

"He's the sort of man we used to recruit for active service," said the silver-haired, dark-skinned Andreyev, pointing brusquely at Stepanov, who was sitting on his bunk with his arms around his knees. Stepanov was a young electrician at the Moscow Power Station. He was taciturn and unremarkable, but his dark blue eyes had an unexpected fire in them. He took his bowl of food in silence, he ate in silence, he accepted an extra portion in silence, he spent hours sitting on the edge of his bunk with his arms around his knees, thinking his own thoughts. Nobody in the cell knew what Stepanov had been arrested for, not even the extrovert historian Aleksandr Filippovich Ryndich.

There were eighty people in a cell meant for twenty-five. The iron bunks fixed to the walls were covered with sheets of wood, painted gray to match the walls. There was a stack of sheets of wood around the piss pot and by the door, and these were laid as beds almost end to end over the passage between the bunks, leaving just two openings so people could dive down under the bunks, where there were more sheets of wood with people sleeping on them. The space under the bunks was called the "metro."

Opposite the door with its spy hole and "food flap" was an enormous barred window with an iron "muzzle." The commandant on duty, when he inspected the new twenty-four-hour shift, would check the state of the bars acoustically by running over them from top to bottom the key that was used to lock the cell. This particular sound was joined by the clank of the door lock, which took two turns of the key at night and one turn in the day, as well as the jingling of the key against a brass belt buckle, to remind us what buckles were for. The final sound was a warning signal by an escort guard to his colleagues when making a journey down the endless corridors of Butyrki. These were the three elements composing a symphony of concrete prison music, which you remembered for the rest of your life.

Those who lived in the metro spent the daytime sitting on the edge of the bunks, in other people's spaces, as they waited for one of their own. During the day about fifty people lay on sheets of wood. These were men waiting their turn to sleep and live in a real space. The first men to come to the cell got the best places. The best places were considered to be those by the window and farthest from the door. Sometimes the interrogations went quickly and the detainee didn't have time to move up to a window space, where he would get a draft of fresh air. In winter this visible stratum of breathable air shyly but quickly slid down the glass panes to somewhere below; in summer it was just as visible where it met the stifling sweaty sultry air of the crowded cell. It could take six months to get to these blissful places: from the metro to the stinking piss pot, from the piss pot to the stars!

When the winters were cold the experienced residents, preferring warmth to light, kept to the middle of the cell. Every day someone was brought in and someone was taken away. Having a turn for a place was not just a pastime. No, justice was the most important thing in the world.

In prison a man is sensitive. A colossal amount of nervous energy is spent on trivia, on an argument about a space, and the argument can develop into hysterics or a brawl. And think of the physical and mental strength, astuteness, intuition, risks expended and taken to get hold of and keep possession of a piece of metal, a pencil stub, a pencil lead—things forbidden by the prison rules and therefore all the more desirable. Such minor things become a test of your personality.

Nobody here buys a space or hires someone to clean the cell. That is strictly forbidden. There are no rich and no poor, no generals and no soldiers.

Nobody is allowed to decide for himself to occupy a space when it becomes free. An elected elder makes these decisions. He has the right to allot the best space to someone who has just arrived, if that person is elderly.

The cell elder has a talk with each newcomer. It is very important to reassure the newcomer, to keep his spirits up. It's always easy to tell who has been in a prison cell before: they are calmer, they have a livelier, firmer gaze; they examine their new cellmates with obvious interest, for they know that a common cell is not particularly threatening; they can distinguish faces and people immediately, at first sight. But those who have come for the first time need a few days before the prison cell stops being a faceless, hostile, and incomprehensible place....

At the beginning of February 1937, or it may have been the end of January, the door to cell sixty-seven opened: a man with silver hair, dark eyebrows, and dark eyes, wearing an unbuttoned winter coat with an old caracul lamb collar, stood on the threshold. He was clutching a canvas bag, what the Ukrainians call a *torba*. He was old, sixty. The cell elder showed the newcomer his place—not in the metro or near the piss pot but next to me in the middle of the cell.

The silver-haired man thanked the elder: he appreciated what he had done. His black eyes had a youthful sheen. He greedily inspected people's faces, as if he had spent a long time in solitary confinement and was at last filling his lungs with the pure air of the prison's common cell.

There was no fear, alarm, or mental pain. The worn collar of his coat, the crumpled jacket proved that their owner knew, and had known before, what prison was like, and that he had been arrested at his home.

"When were you arrested?"

"Two hours ago. At home."

"You're a Socialist Revolutionary, are you?"

The man burst into loud laughter. His teeth were shining white: perhaps dentures?

"You've all become face-recognition experts."

"That's what prison teaches you!"

"Yes, I'm an SR, and a right-wing one, too.[13] It's wonderful that you know the difference. People your age don't always have a proper grounding in such an important question." Then he added, looking straight into my eyes with his unblinking, burning black eyes, "Right, right-wing. A genuine one. I don't understand the left SRs. I have respect for Maria Spiridonova,[14] for Proshian,[15] but everything they did.... My name is Andreyev, Aleksandr Georgievich."

Aleksandr Georgievich had a good look at his neighbors and summed them up in brief, brusque, precise assessments.

He was perfectly aware of the real nature of the repressions.

We always washed our clothes together in the bathhouse, the famous Butyrki bathhouse that was covered in yellow tiles on which it was impossible to write or scratch anything. But the door served as our postbox; it was iron inside and wood outside. The door was covered in all sorts of carved messages. From time to time these messages were planed or scraped off, just as a blackboard is wiped clean; new boards were nailed up and the postbox was back in full operation.

The bathhouse was a great treat. In Butyrki prison all those who were still under investigation did their own washing: that was a long-standing tradition. There was no official "service" in this respect, and no laundry was allowed from home. Naturally, there was no "depersonalized" camp underwear here, either. You dried your clothes in the cell. We were given plenty of time to wash our bodies and our clothes. Nobody was in any hurry.

When we were in the bathhouse I took a good look at Andreyev's body. It was supple, dark-skinned, not at all elderly, yet he was over sixty.

We never missed a single exercise period. You were allowed to stay in your cell, lie down, say you were ill. But both I and Aleksandr Georgievich knew from personal experience that exercise periods must not be missed.

Every day, before dinner, Andreyev would walk up and down the cell, from the window to the door. He did this mostly before dinner.

"It's an old habit. A thousand paces a day is my norm. Prison rations. Two laws in prison: don't lie down too much and don't eat too much. A prisoner should be half starved, so he doesn't feel any weight in his stomach."

"Aleksandr, did you know Savinkov?"

"Yes, I did. I met him when I was abroad, at Gershuni's[16] funeral."

Andreyev didn't have to explain to me who Gershuni was. I knew the names of everybody he ever mentioned and had a good idea who they were. That pleased Andreyev greatly. His black eyes shone and he became animated.

The SR Party had a tragic fate. The people who lost their lives for it, whether terrorists or propagandists, were the best in Russia, the flower of the Russian intelligentsia. Their moral qualities made all these people who were sacrificing or had sacrificed their lives worthy successors to the heroic People's Will, made them successors of Zhelyabov, Perovskaya, Mikhailov, and Kibalchich.[17]

These people went through the fire of the most savage repressions—after all, according to Savinkov's statistics, a terrorist has a life expectancy of six months. They died as heroically as they had lived. Gershuni, Sozonov,[18] Kaliayev, Spiridonova, Zilberberg[19] were all personalities of the same stature as Vera Figner or Morozov,[20] Zhelyabov or Perovskaya.

The SR Party played a major part in overthrowing the autocracy, too. But history took another path, and there lies the profound tragedy of the party and its members.

These thoughts often occurred to me. Meeting Andreyev confirmed these thoughts.

"What do you consider to be the most memorable day in your life?"

"I don't even have to think before I answer, I've got a response ready-made. It's March 12, 1917. Before the war I'd been tried in Tashkent. Under article 102 of the code. I got six years' hard labor. The hard-labor prison was first Pskov, then Vladimir. March 12, 1917, I was released. Today is March 12, 1937, and I'm back in prison!"

The Butyrki prisoners moving about in front of us were in some ways familiar and in other ways alien to Andreyev. They aroused pity, hostility, and compassion in him.

Arkadi Dzidzievsky, the famous Arkasha of the civil war, was dreaded by all the *batkas*, the nationalist leaders in Ukraine. This was a surname cited by Vyshinsky when he was examining the accused in the Piatakov show trial. If the future corpse was cited by name, that meant that Arkadi Dzidzievsky was alive at the time. He was half insane after going through the Lubyanka and Lefortovo prisons. His puffy old man's hands smoothed some colored handkerchiefs on his knees. There were three of them. "These are my daughters: Nina, Lida, Nata."

Take Sveshnikov, an engineer from Chemical Construction, who was told by his interrogator, "Here's your fascist place, bastard." Or a high-ranking railwayman, Gudkov: "I had some records of Trotsky's speeches, and my wife informed on me...." Or Vasia Zhavoronkov: "The instructor in the politics circle asked me, 'If there was no Soviet power, Zhavoronkov, where would you be working?' I said, 'I'd be working in the depot, the same place as now....'"

There was another railwayman, a representative of the Moscow center of joke-tellers (I swear I'm not kidding). His friends and their families used to get together on Saturdays to exchange jokes. He got five years, Kolyma, death.

Misha Vygon was a student at the Communications Institute. "I wrote to Comrade Stalin about everything I'd witnessed in prison." Three years. Misha Vygon survived by an insane process of renouncing and reneging on all his former fellow students; he was present at executions by shooting and became the chief of a shift at the Partisan mine where all his comrades perished, were annihilated.

Siniukov, the personnel manager of the Moscow party committee, has today written a declaration: "I flatter myself with the hope that Soviet power has laws." Flatters himself!

Kostia and Nika, fifteen-year-old Moscow schoolboys who in the cell played soccer with a ball made from rags, were terrorists who had killed Khandjian.[21] Much later I learned that Khandjian had been shot by Beria in the latter's own office. The children who were accused of this murder, Kostia and Nika, perished in Kolyma in 1938. They perished even though they weren't actually forced to work—they just died of the cold.

Captain Schneider of Comintern: an inveterate orator, always cheerful, performs magician's acts at our cell concerts.

Lionka "The Malefactor," who unscrewed the bolts on the railway tracks: a resident of the Tuma district in Moscow Province.

Falkovsky, whose crime has been classified as article 58, paragraph 10: agitation. The material evidence is his letters to his fiancée and her letters to him. Correspondence implies two or more persons, so it's article 58, paragraph 11: organization—and that makes the case much more serious.

Aleksandr Georgievich said quietly, "There are only men here; there are no heroes.

"On one of my files there's a decision by Tsar Nicolas II. The minister of war reported to the tsar that there'd been a robbery on a destroyer at Sevastopol. We needed arms, so we took them off a naval ship. The tsar wrote in the margins of the report, 'A nasty business.'

"I began when I was a schoolboy in Odessa. My first mission was to throw a bomb in a theater. It was a stink bomb, quite harmless. You could say I was taking an exam. Then things got serious, bigger. I didn't go in for propaganda. All those circles, chats: it was very hard to see or feel any final outcome. I went in for terror. At least you get instant results!

"I was the general secretary of the society of prerevolutionary political prisoners, until the society was dissolved."

An enormous black figure dashed toward the window, grabbed hold of the prison bars, and howled. Alekseyev, a bearlike, blue-eyed epileptic, who had once been a chekist, was shaking the bars and shouting wildly, "Let me out, let me out!" before he slid off the bars in a fit. People bent over the epileptic. Some took hold of his hands, some his head, some his legs.

Aleksandr Georgievich, pointing at the epileptic, merely said, "The first chekist.

"My interrogator is just a boy, that's the trouble. He doesn't know a thing about revolutionaries, and SRs are dinosaurs, as far as he's concerned. All he does is yell, 'Confess! Think about it!'

"I tell him, 'You know what SRs are like?' 'Well?' 'If I tell you that I didn't do something, it means I didn't. And if I decide to lie to you, there's no threat that will alter my decision. You ought to know just a little bit of history....'"

The conversation had taken place after the interrogation, but judging by what Andreyev said, there was no sign of his being at all worried.

"No, he doesn't shout at me. I'm too old. All he says is 'Think about it!' So we sit there. For hours. Then I sign the statement and we say goodbye until the next day."

I had thought of a way of avoiding boredom during interrogations. I counted the patterns on the wall. The wall was covered in wallpaper: 1,462 identical drawings. That was my examination of the wall on that particular day. I switched off my attention. There always have been repressions and there always will be. As long as the state exists.

It seemed that you didn't need experience, not the heroic experience of prerevolutionary political prisoners, for this new life that was following a new path. Then suddenly you realized that the path wasn't at all new, and that you needed every bit of your experience: memories about Gershuni, knowing how to behave under interrogation, the art of counting patterns on the wallpaper while under interrogation. Then the heroic shades of your comrades, who had died long ago under the tsars, doing hard labor or on the gallows.

Andreyev was animated and excited, but his wasn't the nervous tension that afflicts almost anyone who finds themselves in prison. Prisoners in pretrial detention do in fact laugh more often than they need to and on the most trivial pretexts. This boisterous laughter is a prisoner's defensive reaction, especially when he is in company.

Andreyev's animation was of a different kind. It was, as it were, an inner satisfaction at finding himself once more in the same position that he had been in all his life, and which was his path, a path he had held dear, and it was receding into history. And yet it turned out that the times still needed him.

Andreyev was not interested in whether charges were true or false. He knew what mass repression was, and nothing could astonish him.

Lionka, the seventeen-year-old youth from a remote village in the Tuma district of Moscow Province, was in the cell. He was illiterate and considered that Butyrki prison was a great piece of luck for him. He was getting all the food he could eat, and what nice people were there! In six months of pretrial detention Lionka learned more than he had during all his previous life. Every day there were lectures in the cell and, although prison memory is bad at taking in what it hears or reads, nevertheless a lot of new and important things were drummed into Lionka's brain. Lionka was not bothered by his own "case." He was accused of doing what the Chekhov hero did in the story "The Malefactor": in 1937 he had unscrewed the bolts from the railway track to make weights for fishing. This was clearly article 58, paragraph 7: sabotage. But Lionka had another paragraph under article 58: paragraph 8, terror!

"What's this about?" Lionka was asked when people were chatting with him.

"A judge chased after me with a revolver."

A lot of people laughed when they heard that reply. But Andreyev said to me in a quiet, serious voice, "Politics doesn't know the concept of guilt. Of course, Lionka's just Lionka, but then, Mikhail Gots[22] was paraplegic."

This was the blissful spring of 1937, when there were still no beatings under interrogation, when "five years" was what was usually stamped on your sentence from the Special Tribunals. "Five years in distant camps," as the Ukrainian NKVD men put it. The people who worked in that institution were by now no longer called chekists.

People were overjoyed to get a "fiver": it is typical of a Russian to be overjoyed that he didn't get ten, or twenty-five, or death by shooting. The joy had real reasons: everything now lay ahead. Everyone was now eager to be free, to get some "pure air," to get credit against their sentence for days worked.

"How about you?"

"All of us old politicals get sent to Dudinka: exile, for life. I'm pretty old, after all."

Nevertheless, the interrogators were already using the "endurance test," where prisoners weren't allowed to sleep for several days and nights on end, and the "conveyor," where one interrogator after doing his shift would be followed immediately by another, and the prisoner under interrogation had to stay sitting on the chair until he lost consciousness.

"Method number three," however, was still to come.

I realized that the old political convict liked what I was doing in prison. I was no novice; I knew what methods to use to revive people's fallen spirits. . . . I was the elected cell elder; Andreyev saw me as a version of his younger self. He enjoyed my constant interest in and respect for his past and my understanding of his fate.

A day in prison was never wasted. The internal self-government of Butyrki pretrial prison had its own laws, and obeying those laws improved your character, reassured the newcomers, and was generally beneficial.

Lectures were given every day. Everyone who came into the prison was able to say something interesting about his work or life. I can still remember to this day a simple metalworker and electrician talking about his work on the Dnepr hydroelectric station.

Kogan, a lecturer from the Air Force Academy, gave several talks: "How Man Measured the Earth," "The World of the Stars."

Georgie Kosparov, the son of Stalin's first female secretary (who was sent into exile and to the camps and thus died at the hands of her Great Pilot and Chief), told us the story of Napoleon.

A guide from the Tretiakov art gallery talked to us about the Barbizon school of art.

The lecture schedule was endless. It was kept in the memory of the cell elder, our "culture organizer."

Every new arrival, every newcomer could usually be persuaded to tell us what had been in the newspapers that evening and what people in Moscow were talking about. Once a detainee had settled down, he would find the strength to give a lecture as well.

What's more, there were always a lot of books in the cell from the famous Butyrki prison library, which had not been purged yet. There were a lot of books here that you couldn't find in outside libraries. Iles's *History of the International*,[23] Masson's *Notes*,[24] books by Kropotkin. The holdings were made up of gifts by prisoners: that was an age-old tradition. After my time there, at the end of the 1930s, this library too underwent a purge.

Men in pretrial detention studied foreign languages and read foreign authors aloud—O. Henry, Jack London—while lecturers gave introductory talks about these writers' lives and works.

From time to time—once a week—we had concerts; the ocean-going Captain Schneider did magic tricks, and the German Khokhlov, a literary critic on the newspaper *Izvestiya*, read verses by Tsvetayeva and Khodasevich.

Khokhlov was an émigré, a graduate of the Russian University in Prague, and he had asked to be allowed back to his homeland. The homeland greeted him with arrest, interrogation, and a sentence to the camps. I never heard of Khokhlov again. He had tortoiseshell glasses, myopic blue eyes, and dirty fair hair.

Apart from general educational study, the cell was frequently the scene of arguments, discussions of very serious topics.

I remember Aron Kogan, an outgoing young man, asserting that the intelligentsia provided examples of revolutionary behavior, of revolutionary valor, and was capable of the greatest heroism, more so than the workers or the capitalists, even though the intelligentsia was a "wobbly" layer that didn't belong to any particular class.

Given that at the time I had a limited experience of the camps, I had a different idea about the behavior of the intelligentsia in times of difficulty. Religious people, sectarians were, according to my observations, the people who had fire and moral firmness.

In 1938 it was fully confirmed that I was right; by then Aron Kogan was no longer alive.

"False witness! My comrade! What have we come to?"

"We haven't come to anything yet. I assure you that if you meet such a bastard, you'll talk to him as if nothing were wrong."

And so it happened. During one of our "dry baths," which is what we called a search in Butyrki, several people pushed their way into the cell, among them Kogan's acquaintance, the false witness. Kogan didn't hit him, he talked to him. After the "dry bath" Kogan told me all about it.

Aleksandr Georgievich gave no lectures and took no part in arguments, but he listened very attentively to these debates.

Once, after I had my say and lay down on my bunk, Andreyev sat down nearby; we slept next to each other.

"I expect you're right, but let me tell you an old story.

"This isn't the first time I've been arrested. In 1921 I was deported to Narym for three years. I'll tell you a good story about exile in Narym.

"All exiles are arranged the same way, as Moscow dictates. Exiles are not entitled to communicate with the locals, they have to stew in their own juices. This destroys the weak morally, but it fortifies the strong; sometimes, though, you come across things that are very peculiar.

"I was assigned a place to live that was very remote, farther into the backwoods than anyone else. It was a long journey by sled and I had to spend a night in a little village where there was a whole colony of exiles, seven of them. Life was tolerable. But I was too big a fish, so I couldn't stay there: my village was another two hundred kilometers away. There was a touch of winter, then a burst of spring, then a wet snow blizzard, and no passage for a sled. So to my joy and the joy of my escort guards, I spent a whole week in the colony. Seven exiles were there. Two anarchists who were in the Komsomol, a married couple who were followers of Prince Kropotkin; two Zionists, husband and wife; two Socialist Revolutionaries, husband and wife. The seventh was an Orthodox theologian, a bishop and a professor of the Theological College, who had once given lectures in Oxford. So it was a very varied company. Everyone was at daggers drawn with everybody else. Endless discussions, ill-mannered ideological fanaticism. A terrible way to live. Petty quarrels that exploded into mad rows, mutual malevolence. Too much time on their hands.

"And all of them, each in their own way, were decent, good people who thought and read a lot.

"During the week I was there I thought about each one and tried to understand each of them.

"Finally, the blizzard died down. I left for two years in the depths of the taiga. Two years later I was allowed—before the end of my sentence—to go back to Moscow. I went back the same way I'd come. Over that long distance there was only one place where I knew anybody: where I had been held up by the blizzard.

"I spent the night in the same village. All the exiles were there, all seven, none of them had been released. But what I saw there was more than release.

"There had, after all, been three couples: Zionists, Komsomol, Socialist Revolutionaries. And one theology professor. Now listen: all six of the married people had converted to Orthodoxy. The bishop, that learned professor, had talked them into it. They were all praying to God together, living as an evangelical commune."

"That really is a strange story."

"I've thought a great deal about it. It speaks for itself. All these people, SRs, Zionists, Komsomol, all six had one thing in common. They were all absolutely convinced of the power of the intellect, they believed in reason and the word.

"People should make decisions on the basis of intuition and not trust reason too much. You don't need logic to make a decision. Logic is justification, shaping, explaining. . . ."

We found parting difficult. Aleksandr Georgievich was called out "with his things" before I was. We paused for a minute at the open cell door and were caught in a ray of the sun, which made us screw up our eyes. The guard, quietly jangling his key against the brass buckle of his belt, waited. We embraced.

"I wish you," said Aleksandr Georgievich in a muffled but cheerful voice, "I wish you happiness and good luck. Look after your health. Well," he gave me a particular smile, a kindly smile. "Well," he said, gently tugging at my shirt collar. "You are able to do time, you can do it. I mean every word of what I say."

Andreyev's praise was the highest, the most significant and authoritative praise I ever had in my life. It was prophetic praise.

A note from the magazine *Hard Labor and Exile*: "Andreyev, Aleksandr Georgievich, born 1882. Joined the revolutionary movement in 1905 in the Odessa student branch of the SR Party and in the general party; in Minsk in the city party. In 1905–6 in Chernigov and Odessa SR Party committees; in the Sevastopol SR Party committee; in 1907 in the southern provincial committee of the SR Party; in 1908 in the Tashkent active service squad attached to the central committee of the SR Party. Tried by military tribunal in Odessa in 1910, sentenced to one year imprisonment; 1913 tried by Tashkent military district court on article 102 charges and sentenced to six years hard labor. Served sentence in Pskov and Vladimir temporary hard-labor prisons. Spent ten years, three months in prison (Crimean section). Andreyev had a daughter, Nina."

1964

THE DESCENDANT OF A DECEMBRIST

A LOT OF books have been written about the first hussar, the famous Decembrist. In the chapter he destroyed of *Eugene Onegin*, Pushkin wrote: "A friend of Mars, of Bacchus, and of Venus...."

A knight, a great mind, a man of boundless knowledge, whose deeds always matched his words. And what a great cause there was.

As for the second hussar, the descendant, I'll tell all I know.

At Kadykchan, we went to work, hungry and weak, rubbing our chests into bloody blisters, turning the Egyptian circular winch[25] and dragging wagonloads of ore out of the slop—we were "carving out" a gallery, a gallery now famous throughout Kolyma. As for Egyptian slave labor, I happen to have seen and experienced it personally.

The winter of 1940–41 was approaching, a snowless, vicious Kolyma winter. Cold contracted your muscles and squeezed your temples like an iron hoop. Iron stoves were set up in the torn canvas tents where we lived in summer, but it was the free air that was heated by these stoves.

Our ingenious bosses were getting the men ready for winter. A second, smaller tent was built inside the first, allowing a layer of air about ten centimeters thick. This inner carcass was lined, except for the ceiling, with tarred paper and roofing felt, so that the result was a double tent slightly warmer than the canvas one.

The very first nights we spent in this tent showed that it meant certain death, and soon, too. We had to get away. But how? Who would help? Eleven kilometers away was a big camp, Arkagala, where there were miners working. Our team was part of this camp. That's where we had to go, to Arkagala!

But how?

Prisoners' traditions demand that in such cases the first person you turn to is the doctor. There was a paramedic clinic at Kadykchan, where, so it was said in our tent, there was a "quack," a doctor who had never graduated from his course at Moscow Medical Institute.

It takes a great effort of willpower to summon enough strength after a working day to get up and go to the outpatient clinic. You don't have to get dressed or put boots on, because you never take anything off between visits to the bathhouse, but you haven't got the strength. You are reluctant to spend your rest period on a "visit" that may well end with abuse or even a beating (that did happen). The main thing was the hopelessness, the unlikeliness of any good outcome. But if you are seeking a way out, then you can't overlook the smallest chance: that was what my body, my exhausted muscles, rather than my experience and reason, were telling me.

Willpower listens only to instinct, as is the case with wild animals.

The other side of the track from the tent was a cabin where prospectors and search groups, and sometimes "secret action squads," the endless patrols in the taiga, took shelter.

The geologists had left long ago, so the cabin had been turned into a clinic, a cabin with a trestle bed, a medicine cupboard, and an old blanket for a curtain. The blanket screened off the trestle bed where the "doctor" lived.

The queue for patients was outside, in the freezing cold.

I squeezed through into the cabin. The heavy door pressed on my innards. Blue eyes, a big forehead, a bald patch, and the inevitable haircut that marked your person. In the camp your hair testified to your situation. Everyone was shaved to the skin. Those whose heads weren't shaved were envied by everyone. Hair was a peculiar protest against the camp regime.

"From Moscow?" the doctor asked me.

"Moscow."

"Let's introduce ourselves."

I gave him my surname and shook the hand he offered. It was cold, slightly damp.

"Lunin."

"A famous surname," I said with a smile.

"I'm a direct great-grandson. In our family the eldest son is called either Mikhail or Sergei, in turn. The one Pushkin knew was Mikhail Sergeyevich."

"We know." This first conversation had something very untypical of the camps about it. I forgot what I had come to ask for, I was reluctant to alter the tone of this conversation with anything that would jar. But I was starving: I wanted bread and warmth. That hadn't, however, occurred to the doctor yet.

"Have a cigarette."

I rolled myself a cigarette with my pink frostbitten fingers.

"Take more tobacco, don't hesitate. I've got a whole library about my great-grandfather at home. I'm a student at the medical faculty, you know. But I haven't finished. I was arrested. Everyone in our family is in the military, but here I am, a doctor. And I have no regrets."

"So Mars must have been set aside. 'A friend of Aesculapius, of Bacchus, and of Venus.'"

"Not much hope of Venus in these parts. But all you can take of Aesculapius. It's just that I don't have my diploma. If I had my diploma, I'd show them."

"How about Bacchus?"

"We've got a bit of pure spirit, you know. But I only have to drink a glass and that's me done. I get drunk quickly. I look after the free workers' settlement too, you know. Come and see me."

I half opened the door with my shoulder and staggered out of the clinic.

"You know," the doctor continued, "Muscovites are people who more than any others, Kiev or Leningrad people, love to recall their city, its streets, skating rinks, houses, the Moscow River...."

"I'm not a Muscovite by birth."

"People like you recall even more, they remember even better."

I came for several evenings at the end of the reception time to smoke another roll-your-own: I was afraid to ask for bread.

Sergei Mikhailovich, like anybody who had an easy life in the camp, whether by luck or because of his job, didn't give much thought to others and had little understanding of the starving: his area, Arkagala, was at the time not yet starving. The miseries of the mines had passed Arkagala by.

"If you want, I'll operate on you. I'll cut the cyst off your finger."

"All right, then."

"But, God forbid, I can't let you off work. That would be awkward for me, you understand."

"How am I supposed to work with my finger operated on?"

"Well, you'll manage."

I agreed, and Lunin cut out my cyst quite skillfully, leaving a scar as a souvenir. Many years later I met the woman who was to become my wife, and she was captivated for the first minute of our meeting, squeezing my fingers, looking for this "Lunin" cyst.

I saw that Sergei Mikhailovich was simply very young, that he needed someone more sophisticated to talk to, that all his views of the camp and of "fate" were no different than those of any free man in authority, that he was inclined to find even the common criminals delightful, that the storm of 1937 had passed him by.

For me, on the other hand, every hour of rest, every day of rest was precious: muscles, permanently worn out by the gold mine, ached and begged for a respite. Every piece of bread, every bowl of soup was precious to me; my stomach demanded food, and my eyes couldn't help looking for bread on the shelves. But I forced myself to remember Moscow streets: Kitai-gorod, Nikita Gates, where the writer Andrei Sobol shot himself, where Shtern fired at the German ambassador's car—a history of Moscow streets nobody will ever write.

"Yes, Moscow, Moscow. Now tell me, how many women have you had?"

It was unthinkable for a half-starved man to carry on a conversation of this sort, but the young surgeon was listening only to himself, and he was not offended by my silence.

"Listen, Sergei. What has happened to us is a crime, the greatest crime of the century."

"Well, I don't know about that," said Sergei with annoyance. "It's the Jews who keep messing everything up."

I just shrugged.

Soon Sergei Mikhailovich managed to get his transfer to the main area, to Arkagala, and I thought, without sadness or resentment, that yet another person had left my life forever, and what a simple matter, actually, parting and separation were. But things turned out rather differently.

The man in charge of Kadykchan, where I was working on the Egyptian circular winch, was Pavel Ivanovich Kiseliov. He was an engineer, not a party member, and no longer young. Kiseliov used to beat prisoners every day. When the boss came out to the mine area this meant there would be beatings, punches, yelling.

Was it impunity? Bloodthirstiness that slumbered somewhere deep in his soul? A desire to make his mark in the eyes of the top authorities? Power is a strange business.

Zelfugarov, a boy who had been a counterfeiter, and who worked in my brigade, was lying in the snow, spitting out his teeth after a beating.

"You know, all my relatives were executed for counterfeiting, but I was a minor, so I got fifteen years in the camps. My father said to the interrogator, 'Take five hundred thousand in cash, real money, and stop the case....' But the interrogator wouldn't."

The four of us doing our shift on the winch lingered around Zelfugarov. Korneyev was a Siberian peasant, there was the gangster Lionia Semionov, the engineer Vronsky, and me. Lionia the gangster said, "Only in the camp can you learn to work a machine, you can take on any job you like, you don't have to answer for it if you break a winch or a crane. You gradually learn." That was a way of thinking which was also typical of the young surgeons in Kolyma.

Vronsky and Korneyev were more acquaintances than friends of mine, ever since Black Lake, a workplace where I had started coming back to life.

Zelfugarov didn't get up. He turned his bloodstained face and dirty swollen lips toward us.

"I can't get up, boys. He was hitting me in the belly. God, the boss, the boss."

"Go and see the paramedic."

"I'm afraid it'll be worse. He'll tell the boss."

"Listen," I said, "there'll be no end to this. There is a way out. When the head of Far East Construction Coal comes, or some other big boss, someone should step forward and punch Kiseliov in the face when the bosses are watching. The whole of Kolyma will know about it and he'll be fired, he'll definitely be transferred. The man who hits him will get a sentence. How many years would you get for hitting Kiseliov?"

We went to work, turned the winch, went back to barracks, had supper, and got ready to go to bed. I was called out to the office.

Kiseliov was sitting in the office, looking at the ground. He was no coward, and he didn't like threats.

"So that's it," he said cheerfully. "The whole of Kolyma will know about it, will it? Now I'm going to have you charged for an attempt on my life. Get out of here, you bastard!"

Only Vronsky could have informed on me, but how? We'd been together all that time.

After that, life got easier for me at the workplace. Kiseliov didn't even come near the winch. When he did come to work, he was carrying a small-caliber rifle, but he never went down the mine gallery, which had now been cut deep into the slope.

Someone came into the barracks.

"Go and see the doctor."

The "doctor" who had replaced Lunin was called Kolesnikov. He too was a medical student who hadn't finished his course, a tall young man and a prisoner.

Lunin, wearing a fur jacket, was sitting at the desk in the clinic.

"Get your things, we're going right now to Arkagala. Kolesnikov, write us a travel order."

Kolesnikov folded a sheet of paper several times and tore off a tiny piece, hardly bigger than a postage stamp. In the tiniest handwriting he wrote, "To the health center in Arkagala camp."

Lunin took the piece of paper. "I'll go and get Kiseliov to stamp it," and he ran off.

He came back crestfallen. "He won't let you, you know. He says you promised to punch him in the face. There's no way he'll agree."

I told him the whole story.

Lunin tore up the "travel order."

"It's your own fault," he told me. "What do you care about Zelfugarov and all those.... You weren't the one who got beaten up."

"I've been beaten before."

"Well, goodbye. I've got a truck waiting. We'll think of something."
Lunin got into the truck cabin.

Several days passed before Lunin reappeared.

"I'm off now to see Kiseliov. About you."

Half an hour later he came back.

"Everything's fine. He agreed."

"How come?"

"I have a way of taming shrewish hearts."

Sergei Mikhailovich replayed his conversation with Kiseliov.

"What brings you here, Sergei Mikhailovich? Do sit down. Have a cigarette."

"No, I won't. I don't have the time. Pavel Ivanovich, I've brought you the statements about beatings. The special-action people have passed them on for my signature. Well, before I sign them, I thought I ought to ask you whether all this is true or not."

"It's not true, Sergei Mikhailovich. My enemies are ready—"

"That's what I thought. I won't sign these documents. All the same, Pavel Ivanovich, things can't be put right, if you knock someone's teeth out, they can't be put back."

"True, Sergei Mikhailovich. Why don't you come to our house, my wife has made a very nice liqueur. I've been keeping it for the New Year, but for an occasion like this—"

"No, no, Pavel Ivanovich. One favor deserves another. Let Andreyev go to Arkagala."

"That's something I definitely can't do. Andreyev is someone I'd call—"

"Your personal enemy?"

"Yes, yes."

"Well, he's my personal friend. I thought you would give my request a bit more consideration. Take this and look at the statements about beatings."

Kiseliov fell silent.

"All right, he can go."

"Write him a reference."

"He can come personally for it."

I strode into the office. Kiseliov was staring at the ground.

"You're going to Arkagala. Take this reference."

I said nothing. The office clerk wrote out the reference and I went back to the clinic.

Lunin had gone by then, but Kolesnikov was waiting for me.

"You'll go this evening, about nine. Acute appendicitis." And he proffered me a paper.

I never saw Kiseliov or Kolesnikov again. Before long, Kiseliov was transferred somewhere else, to Elgen, where he was killed after a few months, accidentally. One night a thief got into the apartment, a small building, where he was living. Kiseliov heard footsteps, snatched his loaded double-barreled gun off the wall, cocked the trigger, and rushed at the thief. The thief dived through the window; Kiseliov struck the thief's back with the gun's butt, and the charges in both barrels exploded, hitting Kiseliov in the belly.

All the prisoners in all the coal-mining districts of Kolyma were overjoyed at this death. The newspaper carrying the announcement of Kiseliov's funeral was passed from hand to hand. In the coal mine, when work was apace, this crumpled piece of newspaper was lit up by a mining lamp attached to a battery. People read it, rejoiced, and shouted, "Hurrah! Kiseliov's dead! There is a God after all!"

And it was Sergei Mikhailovich who saved me from Kiseliov.

The Arkagala camp provided a labor force for the mine. For every hundred people working as miners underground there were a thousand providing all sorts of support.

Arkagala was being threatened with famine. And, naturally, the first to starve were the inhabitants of the barracks for people convicted under article 58.

Sergei Mikhailovich was getting angry.

"I'm not the sun: I can't keep everybody warm. You got yourself a nice job as the orderly in the chemistry laboratory, you should have lived, you should have known how to live. On camp terms, you realize?" Sergei Mikhailovich clapped me on the shoulder. "Before you came, Dimka used to work there. He sold all the glycerin—there were two barrels of it—at twenty rubles for a half-liter can: good as honey, he used to say, ha-ha-ha! If you're a prisoner, everything is good."

"That doesn't suit me."

"So what does suit you?"

An orderly's job was not secure. I was quickly transferred—there were strict orders to that effect—to the mine. I kept getting hungrier and hungrier.

Sergei Mikhailovich was rushing around the camp. He had a passion: any sort of authority just bewitched our doctor. Lunin was absurdly proud of having a friendship, or the shadow of a friendship, with the camp bosses and was always anxious to show how close he was to the bosses; he boasted of this phantom closeness and was capable of talking about it for hours on end.

I was sitting in his reception room, hungry, afraid to ask for a piece of bread, and listening to his unending boasting.

"What is authority? Authority, old man, is power. There is no power but of God: ha-ha-ha! You have to know how to give them what they need, and then everything will be fine."

"I would be very happy to give them a punch in their ugly faces."

"Well, so you see. Listen, let's make a deal. You can come and visit me. I expect you get bored in the prisoners' barracks, don't you?"

"Bored?!"

"Yes. So come and see me. You can sit and smoke for a bit. They won't let you smoke in the barracks, after all. I know that: everyone wants to get hold of your cigarette. But don't ask me to get you off work. I can't do that. Well, I can, but it's awkward for me. It's up to you. As for food, you realize, I can't get any for you, that's up to my male nurse. I don't fetch bread personally. So if you should ever need any bread, tell Nikolai, the nurse. But you're an old lag, so surely you can lay your hands on bread, can't you? Listen, this is what Olga Petrovna, my boss's wife, was saying. They invited me over for a drink—"

"I'm off, Sergei Mikhailovich."

A period of terrible starvation began. Once, unable to cope with the hunger, I somehow made my way to the clinic.

Sergei Mikhailovich was sitting on a stool, using Liston shears to remove the necrotic nails from the frostbitten toes of a man who was covered in dirt and convulsing. The toenails clattered one after the other into an empty bowl. Sergei Mikhailovich noticed me.

"Yesterday I filled half a bowl with toenails like these."

A woman's face looked from behind the curtain. We rarely saw women, and then only at a distance, not face-to-face. I thought she looked beautiful. I bowed and greeted her.

"How do you do?" she said in a wonderful low voice. "Sergei, is this your friend? The one you were telling me about?"

"No," said Sergei Mikhailovich, dropping the Liston shears into the bowl and retreating to the sink to wash his hands.

"Nikolai," he told the male nurse, who had just come in, "take the bowl and give him," he nodded in my direction, "some bread."

I waited until I got the bread and then went back to the barracks. That was the camps for you. But that woman, whose tender and charming face I can still remember, even though I never saw her again, was Edit Abramovna, a free worker, a party member, who'd signed a contract to work at the Olchan mine as a nurse. She had fallen in love with Sergei Mikhailovich, was living with him, and managed to get him transferred to Olchan and, during the war, got him an early release. She had made the trip to Magadan to see Nikishev, the head of Far East Construction, and put in a word for Sergei Mikhailovich; when she was expelled from the party for a relationship with a prisoner (the usual punitive measure in such cases), she had the case reviewed in Moscow and managed to get Lunin's conviction quashed, so that he could take his Moscow University examination and get his doctor's diploma and restoration of all his civic rights. She then married him legally.

But when the descendant of the Decembrist got his diploma, he abandoned Edit Abramovna and demanded a divorce.

"Like all Jews, she's got too many relatives. That's no good for me."

He may have abandoned Edit Abramovna, but he was not able to abandon Far East Construction. He had to go back to the Far North, if only for three years. His ability to get on with the authorities had won Lunin, a qualified doctor, an unexpectedly important appointment: chief of the surgical department of the central hospital for prisoners on the left bank, in the settlement of Debin. By then, 1948, I was the senior paramedic in the surgical department.

Lunin's appointment was as sudden as a thunderbolt.

The nub of the matter was that a surgeon called Rubantsev, the former chief of the department, was a wartime surgeon at the front, a major in the medical service, a capable and experienced worker who had come here after the war and meant to stay. Rubantsev had one major fault: he couldn't get on with the top bosses, hated sycophants and liars, and was treated as an outsider by Shcherbakov, the head of health services in Kolyma. Rubantsev had signed a contract and had come already warned to treat the prisoners as his enemies; but he was a clever, independent-minded man and very soon realized that his "political" preparation had been a deceit. Rubantsev's colleagues were self-serving, slanderous, idle swine, while the prisoners—of all professions, including the medical—were the people who kept the hospital, the treatments, and the business going. Rubantsev grasped the truth and refused to conceal it. He applied for a transfer to Magadan, where there was a secondary school: he had a school-age son. His application was refused, though not in writing. After a lot of trouble he managed a few months later to get his son a place in a boarding school about ninety kilometers from Debin. Rubantsev was by now confident about his job, and he was getting rid of the idlers and the thieves. These actions, which threatened the general peace, were immediately reported to Shcherbakov's headquarters in Magadan.

Shcherbakov disliked refinement in his dealings with others. Swearing, threats, criminal charges were all very well when talking to prisoners and former prisoners, but they didn't go down well with a contract worker, a surgeon from the front, with medals on his chest.

Shcherbakov dug up Rubantsev's old application and transferred him to Magadan. Even though it was the middle of the academic year, even though everything was now running smoothly in the surgical department, Rubantsev was forced to abandon it all and leave. . . .

Lunin and I met on the stairs. He had a habit of blushing when he was embarrassed. His cheeks now flushed with blood. But he did "treat" me to a cigarette, expressed pleasure at my success, my "career," and he told me about Edit Abramovna.

Aleksandr Aleksandrovich Rubantsev had left. Two days later a drunken party was organized in the treatment room: the surgical spirit was tried out by Kovaliov, the chief doctor, and by Vinokurov, the head of the hospital, who had both been rather afraid of Rubantsev and had avoided visiting the surgical department. Doctors' surgeries began to have drinking parties to which prisoners—female nurses and ward assistants—were invited: in short, all hell was let loose. Operations in the sterile department began to be done with wounds left unsutured, because nobody would use precious spirits to sterilize the operation area. The bosses were walking half drunk up and down the surgical department.

This hospital was my hospital. After I finished my courses at the end of 1946, I came here with the patients. I witnessed the hospital's expansion. It had been a building that belonged to the Kolyma regiment; after the war a specialist in military camouflage rejected the building because it could be seen among the mountains from ten kilometers away. It was given to the hospital for prisoners. Its owners, the Kolyma regiment, as they were leaving, ripped out all the water pipes and drainage pipes that could be ripped out of an enormous three-story building; they removed all the furniture from the auditorium and burned it in the boiler room. The walls were smashed, the doors broken down. The Kolyma regiment left in true Russian style. We carefully restored everything, screw by screw, and brick by brick.

We were a collection of doctors and paramedics who were trying to do the best we could. For very many of us this was our sacred duty, paying back our medical education by helping people.

All the idle scroungers raised their heads the moment Rubantsev left.

"Why are you taking spirits from the cupboard?"

"Go stuff yourself," a nurse replied. She went on: "There's no Rubantsev now, thank God. Sergei Mikhailovich said I could...."

I was struck, depressed by Lunin's behavior. The orgies continued.

During one of his five-minute pep talks, Lunin mocked Rubantsev: "He never did a single stomach ulcer operation, and he calls himself a surgeon?"

This was a familiar subject. True, Rubantsev didn't operate on stomach ulcers. The patients from the therapeutic department who had this diagnosis were prisoners, and they were emaciated, dystrophic; they had no hope of surviving an operation. "Bad background," Rubantsev used to say.

"Coward," yelled Lunin, accepting twelve of these patients from the therapeutic department. All twelve were operated on, and all twelve died. The hospital doctors had a reminder of Rubantsev's experience and mercy.

"Sergei Mikhailovich, we can't work like this."

"I'm not taking instructions from you!"

I submitted a request to summon a commission from Magadan. I was transferred to the forest, to serve a forestry brigade. They wanted to send me to a punishment mine, but the NKVD man in the district headquarters persuaded them not to: this was no longer 1938, it wasn't worth it.

A commission did come and Lunin was "dismissed from Far Eastern Construction." So instead of three years, he was forced to work for just eighteen months.

A year later, when the hospital's management was changed, I came back from my paramedic clinic in the forest and took over the hospital's reception room.

Once in a Moscow street I met the descendant of the Decembrist. We ignored each other.

It was sixteen years later when I found out that Edit Abramovna had managed a second time to get Lunin reinstated at Far Eastern Construction. She and Lunin came to the settlement of Pevek in Chukotka. This was where they had their last conversation and their last, fatal discussion. Edit Abramovna threw herself into the water and drowned.

Sometimes sleeping pills don't work, and I wake up in the middle of the night. I recall the past and I can see a charming female face and can hear a low voice say, "Sergei, is this your friend?"

1962

POORCOMS

ON RUSSIA'S tragic pages of 1937 and 1938 there are also some lyrical lines, written in very peculiar handwriting. A curious custom, a tradition that had been kept up for several decades, was current in the cells of Butyrki prison, that enormous organism with its complex life of a great many blocks, cellars, and towers, all packed to the gills, to the point of suffocation, with prisoners under investigation, and this custom continued, despite the maelstrom of arrests, the parties of prisoners departing without verdicts or sentences, in cells crowded with living human beings.

The constantly enforced vigilance, which had grown into spy mania, was a disease that had the whole country in its grip. To any trivial incident or slip of the tongue an ominous secret meaning was attributed, and this meaning was subjected to interpretation in the interrogators' offices.

One contribution made by the prison department was a prohibition on any gifts of things or food to prisoners under investigation. The wise men of the legal world asserted that any text, even an extract from *Anna Karenina*, could be communicated to the prison just by a combination of two buns, five apples, and an old pair of trousers.

Such "signals from the outside world," the fruit of the inflamed brains of the eager old hands of the Institution, were stopped without exception. From now on only money could be sent in, and no more than fifty rubles a month to each prisoner. The money transfer could only be in round figures—ten, twenty, thirty, forty, or fifty rubles—so as to make sure than no new coded "alphabet" of signals could be developed.

The simplest and most reliable action was to forbid all money transfers, but such a measure was left to the interrogator dealing with a particular "case." "In the interests of the investigation" he had the right to forbid all forms of money transfer. But there was also a commercial interest at play: the shop or "stall" in Butyrki prison increased its turnover by an enormous amount once parcels of food and other things were forbidden.

For some reason the administration hesitated to refuse all help from relatives and friends, even though it was confident that if it did take such action there would be no protest, either inside the prison or outside in the free world.

There was a severe limitation and restriction of the rights, vestigial as those were, of prisoners under investigation.

No Russian liked to be a witness at a trial. Traditionally, at a Russian trial there is little difference between being a witness and being the accused, and the former's "involvement" in the case is a definite black mark on his future reputation. The situation of prisoners under investigation is even worse. All of them are potentially "going down" for a long time, for it is considered that "Caesar's wife has no vices" and that the Ministry of Interior organs never make mistakes. Nobody is arrested without good reason. A guilty verdict is the logical outcome of an arrest; a prisoner under investigation may get a short sentence or a long one, depending either on his good fortune, his "lucky star," or on a whole agglomeration of reasons, including the bedbugs biting the interrogator the night before he wrote his report or the voting pattern in the American Congress.

There is, basically, only one exit door in the pretrial prison—into the Black Maria, the prison bus that takes sentenced prisoners to the railway station. At the station they are loaded into goods vans, and trains of endless prison carriages slowly proceed along the track until they finally reach one of the thousands of labor camps.

This sense of doom leaves its mark on the behavior of pretrial prisoners. Carefree self-assurance gives way to grim pessimism and a loss of moral strength. Under interrogation the pretrial prisoner has to battle with phantoms, phantoms of gigantic strength. The prisoner is used to dealing with real things, but now he is battling with a Phantom. But this "flame burns and it hurts when this pike strikes you."[26] Everything except the actual case is horribly real. His nerves tautened, his spirit crushed by struggling with fantastical visions, defeated by their extent, the prisoner loses his will. He signs everything that the interrogator has invented, and from that moment he himself becomes a figure in the unreal world he has been struggling against, he becomes a pawn in the terrible and obscure bloody game that is being played out in the interrogators' offices.

"Where has he been taken?"

"To Lefortovo. To sign."

Prisoners under investigation know they are doomed. The prison people on the other side of the bars, the administration, also know it. Commandants, duty wardens, sentries, escort guards have grown accustomed to regarding pretrial prisoners as actual, not just potential, convicts.

One pretrial detainee in 1937, during a check by the chief guard on duty, asked a question about the new constitution then being introduced. The chief guard retorted brusquely, "That doesn't apply to you. Your constitution is the Criminal Code."

Changes, too, were about to affect prisoners in the camps who were under investigation. The camps always had plenty of convicts under investigation, for being given a sentence did not in the least mean exemption from the effects of all the articles of the Criminal Code. The articles applied here as much as they did in the outside world, except that everything—denunciations, punishments, interrogations—was far more brazen, more coarse, and more fictional.

When parcels of food or other things were forbidden in the capital, a special "pretrial ration" was introduced on the periphery of the prison world, in the camps: it consisted of a mug of water and three hundred grams of bread a day. The solitary confinement conditions inflicted on prisoners under investigation quickly brought them to the edge of the grave. The pretrial ration was an attempt to extract the "best of proofs," a voluntary confession by the prisoner, the suspect, the accused under investigation.

In 1937 Butyrki prison permitted money transfers of not more than fifty rubles a month. For this sum anyone who had the money in his personal account could get food from the prison shop, being allowed to spend thirteen rubles four times a month: there was one shop day a week. If the prisoner had more money when he was arrested, then it was put in his personal account, but he was not allowed to spend more than fifty rubles.

Naturally, there was no cash. Receipts were issued and the account was run on the basis of these receipts, which the shop assistant made out by hand, invariably in red ink.

For any communication with the authorities and to keep up comradely discipline in the cell, there was the age-old institution of cell elders.

Every week, a day before the shop day, the administration would, during an inspection, let the cell elder have a slate and a piece of chalk. The elder had to write down on the slate a list of all the purchases that the prisoners in his cell wanted to make. Usually one side of the slate listed the total quantity of each food item, and the other side recorded whose orders these quantities corresponded to.

It normally took a whole day to draw up this list. Prison life was, after all, made up of a great variety of events, big and small, but all of them were equally important to every prisoner. On the morning of the following day the cell elder, accompanied by one or two other men, would go to the shop to fetch the purchases, which would be weighed out according to the "individual orders."

The prison shop had a range of groceries: butter, sausages, cheese, white bread, cigarettes, tobacco.

The weekly rations for the prison diet had been worked out on a permanent basis. If a prisoner ever forgot what day of the week it was, they would know by the smell of the soup served for dinner, or the case of the single-course supper. On Mondays it was always pea soup for dinner and oats porridge for supper; on Tuesdays millet soup and pearl-barley porridge. Over six months spent in pretrial detention each prison dish would be served exactly twenty-five times; food in Butyrki prison was always famous for its variety.

Anyone who had money could buy, if only four times a month at thirteen rubles a time, a few tastier and more nourishing, healthier items, to supplement the prison gruel and "shrapnel."

Those who had no money could not, of course, make any purchases. There were always people, and more than one or two, in the cell who didn't have a penny. Such a person might be from another town, arrested in the street and "top secretly." His wife would be rushing around to all the prisons and headquarters and police stations in town, trying without success to find out her husband's "address." The rule in all institutions was to decline to answer, to observe complete silence. A wife would carry a parcel from prison to prison—perhaps it would be accepted, which meant that her husband was still alive, and if it wasn't accepted, then she had nothing but anxious nights ahead of her.

Or the detainee might be the father of a family; immediately after his arrest, his wife, children, and other relatives would be forced to disown him. Tormenting him from the moment he was arrested with nonstop interrogations, his interrogator would try to extract from him a confession to something he had never done. As a method of persuasion, apart from threats and beatings, the detainee would have his money taken away.

Relatives and friends had very good reasons to be afraid to visit the prison with parcels or money. If you were persistent with your gifts or your search or your inquiries, you would frequently incur suspicion, resulting in undesirable and serious unpleasantness at your place of work, or even arrest: such cases did happen.

There was yet another sort of unfortunate detainee. In cell sixty-eight there was Lionka, a youth of about seventeen from the Tuma district in Moscow Province; in the 1930s Tuma was the backwoods.

Lionka was a fat, pasty-faced youth with unhealthy skin. He hadn't seen fresh air for a long time, but he thought life in prison was splendid. He was fed better than he had ever been fed before. Almost everyone treated him to luxuries from the prison shop. He had learned to smoke proper cigarettes, not roll-your-own. He was moved to wonderment by everything around him: how interesting it was here, what nice people—a whole new world was revealed to this illiterate boy from the Tuma district. He thought the case against him was some sort of game, a delusion: it didn't bother him in the least. All he wanted was for his life in pretrial prison, where he was so well-fed, where it was so clean and warm, to go on forever.

His case was an astonishing one. It was an exact repetition of the Chekhov story "The Malefactor." Lionka had been unscrewing the bolts on the railway track to make fishing weights and was caught in flagrante delicto and put on trial as a saboteur, under paragraph 7 of article 58. Lionka had never heard of Chekhov's story, and he tried to "prove" to the interrogator, just like Chekhov's classic hero, that he never undid two adjacent bolts, that he "understood" what he was doing....

On the basis of the statements given by the lad from Tuma, the interrogator built up extraordinary "concepts," the most innocent of which made Lionka liable to the death penalty. But the investigation failed to link Lionka to anybody at all, and that was why Lionka was now starting a second year in prison, waiting for the investigators to find that link.

People who had no money in their personal prison account had to survive on official rations with no supplements. Prison rations were dreary. Even the slightest variety in nourishment brightens up a prisoner's life and makes it somehow more cheerful.

The prison ration (unlike the camp ration) has probably had its calories, proteins, fats, and carbohydrates measured on the basis of theoretical calculations and experimental norms. These calculations are probably based on "scientific" works; scientists like working on such projects. It is equally likely that the Moscow pretrial prison administration's supervision of food preparation and provision of the number of calories a living consumer requires are sufficiently well organized. And, very likely, the test samples in Butyrki prison are not the cynical gesture that they are in the camps. An old prison doctor, looking for the place in the certificate where he had to put his signature to confirm the food distribution, might ask the cook to give him a bit more of the lentils, the dish with the most calories. The doctor would joke that the prisoners had no cause for complaint, as he, the doctor, enjoyed his bowl of lentils—though the doctor was given his test dish of today's lentils on a proper plate.

Nobody complained about the food in Butyrki prison. That wasn't because the food was good. A pretrial detainee is not, after all, interested in food. Even the most disliked prison dish, boiled beans, which was made here to taste astoundingly bad, beans that acquired the nickname of "gulp-it-down course," never gave rise to any complaints.

The sausages, butter, sugar, cheese, and fresh white bread from the shop were delicacies. Naturally, everyone liked to have them with tea, not the institutional boiled water with some raspberry cordial but real tea made in a mug with boiled water from an enormous copper kettle the size of a bucket: this was a kettle made in tsarist times, which political prisoners of the People's Will may have used.

The shop was, of course, a festive event in the cell's life. Being banned from the shop was a serious punishment, and it always led to arguments and quarrels; such deprivations were taken very badly by the prisoners. If the corridor guard thought there was too much noise, or if there was an argument with the chief guard on duty, such things could be considered insubordination and the punishment for that was deprivation of the prisoners' next shop day.

The dreams of eighty men squeezed into a cell meant to house twenty were shattered. This was a severe punishment.

For prisoners who had no money, deprivation of the shop day ought to have meant nothing. But this was not how it was.

Once the food was brought in, evening tea began. Each person had bought whatever they wanted. But those who had no money felt like strangers at this general feast. They alone were left out of the raised spirits that resulted on shop day.

Of course, they were all offered something to eat or drink. But you could have a mug of tea with someone else's sugar and someone else's white bread, and smoke somebody else's cigarette, one or two of them, without the slightest feeling of home comforts that you would have if you had bought them with your own money. Someone with no money becomes so tactful that he is afraid of eating more than he should.

The prison's ingenious collective brain found a way of alleviating the awkward position of its penniless comrades and of sparing their pride by giving everyone who had no money a quasi-official right to use the shop. Such a prisoner could spend his own money quite independently and buy whatever he wanted.

But where did this money come from?

This was where a famous term of temporary military communism was reborn, a term that comes from the first years of the revolution. The term is "poorcoms," committees for the poor. Some unknown person let this term drop in the prison cell, and by some miracle it caught on, took root, and started creeping from cell to cell, by someone tapping the walls or hiding a note under a bench in the bathhouse, or by even simpler means, when someone was transferred to another prison.

Butyrki prison is famous for its exemplary orderliness: an enormous prison built to hold twelve thousand, where there is a continuous, twenty-four-hour flow of a transient population. Every day prisoners are taken by regular buses to and from Lubyanka for interrogation, or to confrontations, or to court for trial, or to other prisons.

The prison's internal administration can put prisoners who have committed "cell" crimes in the Pugachiov, northern or southern towers where there are special punishment cells. There is also a solitary confinement block with cells where you can't lie down and have to sleep in a sitting position.

Every day a fifth of the cell's population is taken off somewhere—to be photographed according to all the rules, full-face and profile, with a number attached to the screen that the prisoner sits by; or to "play the piano," a compulsory finger-printing procedure that for some reason has never been considered demeaning; or to be interrogated, in the interrogation block, reached through the gigantic prison's endless corridors, where at every turn your guard jangles his key against his brass buckle to warn anyone there that a "secret prisoner" is coming. The guard won't let his prisoner proceed until he hears someone clap their hands (in Lubyanka a clap of the hands is the response to a click of the fingers rather than to a jangling of keys).

The movement is ceaseless and uninterrupted: the entrance doors are never closed for long, and there has never been an incident when two men involved in the same case end up in the same cell.

Once a prisoner has crossed the threshold of the prison, should he leave it if only for a second, his journey having been suddenly canceled, he is not allowed to return without having all his things disinfected. This is the rule, the sanitary law. People who are frequently taken to be interrogated at Lubyanka find that their clothes rapidly fall apart.

Your outer garments in prison wear out far faster in any case than they do outside, because you sleep in them, toss and turn on the sheets of wood placed over the bunks. These boards, combined with the frequent violent "louse killings" by steaming, quickly destroy the clothes of every pretrial prisoner.

However strict the control, the "warden thinks about his keys less than the prisoner thinks about escaping," as the author of *The Charterhouse of Parma* put it.

The poorcoms were an elemental phenomenon, prisoners' self-defense, like a mutual assistance society, all because someone recalled those committees of the poor. Who knows: perhaps the author who gave an old term new meaning had personally taken part in the real committees of the poor in the Russian countryside during the first years of the revolution. Mutual assistance committees are what the prison poorcoms really were.

The organization of poorcoms was no more than the simplest kind of mutual assistance. When ordering from the shop, everyone ordering groceries for themselves had to assign ten percent to the poorcom. The total sum was divided between all those in the cell who had no money, and each of them had the right to his own grocery order from the shop.

A cell holding seventy to eighty men would always have seven or eight penniless prisoners. More often than not, money would arrive and a debtor would try to pay back what his cellmates had given him, but this was optional. His only obligation was take his turn to set aside the same ten percent, once he was able to.

Every beneficiary of a poorcom got ten to twelve rubles to spend in the shop, thus spending almost the same amount as those who did have money. Poorcoms didn't expect thanks; they were seen as a prisoner's right, as an unassailable prison custom.

It took a long time, perhaps years, for the prison administration to become aware of this organization, perhaps because it failed to pay attention to the loyal information given by the snitches in the cell and by the prison's secret informants. It is hard to believe that the poorcoms were not mentioned in denunciations. Simply, the Butyrki administration was reluctant to repeat its deplorable experience of losing the battle against the notorious matches game.

All games are forbidden in prison. Chess pieces, made from bread chewed by everyone in the cell, were immediately confiscated and destroyed if the guard's vigilant eye spotted them when he looked through the spy hole. In prison the very expression "vigilant eye" took on its real, perfectly literal sense: this was the observant eye of the guard, framed by the spy hole.

Dominoes and drafts were all strictly prohibited in the pretrial prison. Books were allowed, and the prison library was a rich one, but a prisoner under investigation who reads gets no benefit from his reading other than a distraction from his own grave and acute thoughts. It's impossible to concentrate on a book in a pretrial cell. Books are a pastime, a distraction, a substitute for dominoes and drafts.

Card games are played in cells where there are common criminals, but in Butyrki there were no cards, and no games except for matches.

Matches is a game for two.

There are fifty matches in a box. The game needs thirty matches to play, and these matches are put in the lid, which is then placed vertically, on its end. The lid is shaken, then lifted, and the matches spill over the table.

The player who goes first picks up a match with two fingers and, using it as a lever, throws or pushes aside all the matches he can remove from the pile without disturbing the others. If he makes a match collide with another one, he loses his turn. The second player continues until he too makes a mistake.

Matches is just the most ordinary children's game of pickup sticks, merely adapted by a prisoner's ingenious mind to a prison cell.

The whole prison was carried away to the point of mania, playing matches from breakfast to lunch, from lunch to dinner.

Matches champions emerged, and sets of special quality matches, shiny from continuous use, came into use. These matches were never struck when lighting cigarettes.

This game saved the prisoners a lot of nervous energy and gave their troubled souls a measure of peace.

The administration was unable to stop this game or to forbid it. After all, matches were allowed. They were even issued, one at a time, and on sale in the shop.

The block commandants tried to break the matchboxes, but the game could be played without the box.

In its battle against a game of pickup sticks the administration was shamefully beaten: none of the steps it took led to any sensible outcome. The whole prison went on playing matches.

For the same reason, for fear of a shameful defeat, the administration turned a blind eye to the poorcoms as well. They had no wish to engage in an inglorious battle.

But unfortunately the rumors of the poorcoms went higher and higher, further and further until it reached the Institution itself, which then issued a dreaded decree: abolish the poorcoms, whose very name sounded like a challenge, some kind of appeal to revolutionary consciences.

There were countless moral lectures read out when the cells were checked. Countless incriminating pieces of paper were seized after an unannounced search with coded totals of expenditure and buying orders. Countless cell elders spent time in the Police and Pugachiov towers with their solitary confinement cells and punishment wards.

Nothing worked. The poorcoms existed despite all the warnings and sanctions.

It was in fact a violation very hard to check up on. In any case, a block commandant, a guard, after working for a long time in a prison, takes a rather different view of prisoners than his high-up superior, and there are times when he inwardly sides with the prisoner against his superiors. That doesn't mean he will help a prisoner. No, he just turns a blind eye whenever possible to minor infractions, he doesn't see what he doesn't have to see, he is less of a faultfinder. Especially if he is getting on in years. For a prisoner the best officer is someone who is no longer young but still low-ranking. The combination of these two qualities almost ensures that you get a relatively decent human being. If the officer also drinks, so much the better. Such people are not careerists: a guard's career in a prison, and even more so in a camp, is made with prisoners' blood.

The Institution, however, demanded that the poorcoms be abolished, and the prison administration made futile efforts to achieve this.

There was an attempt to "explode" the poorcoms internally: that

330 · KOLYMA STORIES

was, of course, the most cunning decision. Poorcoms were an illegal organization and any prisoner could refuse to set aside money, if he was being compelled to do so. A prisoner who didn't want to pay such "taxes," who refused to support the poorcoms could protest and, once he had refused, his protest would immediately be supported by the prison administration. What else would you expect? Collectively the prisoners were not a state that could impose taxes, therefore the poorcoms were extortion, a racket, robbery.

There's no dispute that any prisoner could refuse to set aside money. "I won't, so there! It's my money and nobody has the right to touch it, etc." If anyone made a declaration like that, then nothing was deducted and they got everything they had ordered in full.

But who would risk making such a declaration? Who would risk opposing the whole cell collective, people who are with you twenty-four hours a day, comrades from whose unfriendly, hostile looks only sleep would save you? Everyone in prison instinctively looks to his neighbor for moral support: to risk being boycotted is too frightening. That would be more frightening than the threats of your interrogator, even if no physical means of changing your mind were used.

A prison boycott is a weapon of nerve warfare. God forbid anyone should have to undergo his comrades' intense contempt.

But if an antisocial citizen is too thick-skinned and stubborn, then the cell elder has a weapon that is more hurtful and more effective.

Nobody (except interrogators, who occasionally find this necessary for "progressing the case") has the right to deprive a prisoner of his rations, so even the stubborn resister will get his bowl of soup, his portion of porridge, and his bread.

Food is distributed by the server as the cell elder indicates (that is one of his functions). The bunks along the cell walls are separated by a passage running from the door to the window.

A cell has four corners, and food is distributed from each corner in turn, each day a different corner. This alternation is necessary to prevent the prisoners' heightened sensitivity being disturbed by some trivial thing such as the tops of root vegetables or bits of crust in the Butyrki gruel, so that everyone has an equal chance of getting soup of the same thickness and temperature ... nothing in a prison is unimportant.

When the food is handed out the cell elder gives the command to start and adds, "Feed X (whoever it is) last," naming the person who refuses to acknowledge the poorcoms.

Such an unbearably demeaning humiliation can be inflicted four times a day in Butyrki, since tea is given in the morning and the evening, and soup is given for lunch and porridge for dinner.

When bread is issued, this pressure can be exerted for a fifth time.

It is risky to call on the block commandant to sort out such problems, since the whole cell will give evidence against the stubborn individual. In such cases the rule is to lie collectively, so that the block commandant won't find out the truth.

But a selfish, mean egotist is a determined man. He also thinks that he is the only innocent person to have been arrested and that all the others in the cell are criminals. He is pretty thick-skinned and stubborn. He finds it easy to put up with a boycott from his cellmates: the tricks that intellectuals get up to won't make him lose his patience and resolve. The time-honored method of persuasion, a "dark beating" (where the victim is covered with a blanket so he can't identify his attackers), might have been effective. But there are no dark beatings in Butyrki. The egoist is on the verge of celebrating victory, since the boycott doesn't have the expected effect.

But the cell elder and the other cellmates have one other effective measure available to them. Every day, at the evening roll call, when one shift of guards ends, the block commandant taking over the shift is required to put a question to the prisoners: "Are there any complaints?"

The cell elder then steps forward and demands that the man boycotted for his stubbornness be transferred to another cell. He doesn't have to offer any reasons for this transfer: he only has to demand it. In at most twenty-four hours, often earlier, the transfer is certain to be carried out, and this public warning relieves the cell elder of any responsibility for maintaining discipline in the cell.

If he isn't transferred, the stubborn man can be beaten up or, you never know, killed. A prisoner's soul is unfathomable; such happenings lead to the block commandant having to give unpleasant and repeated explanations to his superiors.

If there is an investigation into this prison murder, it will immediately be revealed that the block commandant had been warned. So it's better to do things nicely: move the man to another cell and give in to that sort of demand.

If a man arrives in another cell as the result of a transfer, instead of coming from "outside," things can get unpleasant. Suspicions will always be aroused, his new cellmates will be on the lookout in case he is a snitch. "Fine if he's been transferred to us only because he's refused to take part in the poorcom," the new cell elder will think. "But suppose it's something worse?" The elder will try and find out the reason for the transfer by leaving a note at the bottom of the rubbish bin in the washrooms, or by tapping the walls either by the Decembrist Bestuzhev's system[27] or in Morse code.

Until the cell elder receives a reply, the newcomer has no hope of getting any sympathy or trust from his new companions. After many days, when the reason for the transfer has been ascertained and passions have died down, even then the new cell, too, will have its own poorcom and its own deductions.

Everything then starts again—or it may not, since the obstinate newcomer may have learned from his experience and may behave differently in the new cell. His stubbornness will have been broken.

When parcels of food and other things were accepted and when use of the prison shop was practically unrestricted, there were no poorcoms in the pretrial cells at Butyrki.

Poorcoms arose in the second half of the 1930s as a curious form of "personal initiative" on the part of prisoners under investigation. It was a way in which a person with no rights could assert himself. This was a tiny area where the human community, united as it always is in a prison, unlike the free world or the camps, despite a total absence of rights, finds a point to which it can apply its spiritual strength to assert and insist on the age-old human right to live as one wishes. This spiritual strength is a counterforce to all prison and pretrial rules of every kind and it triumphs over them.

1959

MAGIC

SOMEONE was banging the window with a stick. I recognized the stick: it belonged to the section chief.

"Coming right away," I yelled through the window, then put on my trousers and buttoned up my tunic. At that very moment Mishka, the chief's courier, appeared on the threshold of my room and shouted out the usual formula that began my every working day: "To the chief!"

"His office?"

"The guardhouse."

I was already on my way.

Working for this boss was easy. He wasn't cruel to the prisoners, he was clever, and even though he invariably brought down all lofty concepts to the level of his own coarse language, he did understand what was what.

True, "rehabilitation" was then in fashion and in these unknown waters our boss simply wanted to keep his boat in a safe channel. That may be so. Maybe. At the time I didn't think about it.

I knew that my boss—Stukov was his name—had a lot of clashes with his superiors, and in the camp they were constantly devising cases to set him up, but I don't know the details or the basis of these cases, which never came to anything, or of the investigations, which weren't begun or which were terminated.

Stukov liked me because I didn't take bribes and didn't favor drunks. For some reason Stukov hated drunks. He probably also liked my boldness.

Stukov was a loner, and he was getting on in years. He was very fond of anything new in technology or science, and stories of the Brooklyn

Bridge made him ecstatic. But I couldn't tell him about anything like the Brooklyn Bridge.

But Miller, Pavel Petrovich Miller, a mining engineer, told Stukov all about it.

Miller was a favorite of Stukov's, for Stukov eagerly listened to any sort of scientific news.

I caught up with Stukov at the guardhouse.

"You're still asleep."

"I'm not."

"Do you know about the party of prisoners that's arrived from Moscow? Via Perm. As I said, you're asleep. Get your men and we'll select some people."

Our section was at the very edge of the free world, at the railhead, after which parties of prisoners were faced with a journey of many days on foot through the taiga. Stukov had the right to hold back the people he felt he needed.

This was astounding magic, tricks that probably belonged to the field of applied psychology. These tricks were performed by Stukov, a chief who had grown old working in prisons and camps. Stukov needed to have spectators, and I was perhaps the only person capable of appreciating his amazing talent, abilities that for a long time I considered to be supernatural, until the moment came when I felt that I myself possessed the same magical powers.

The top bosses gave the section permission to hold back fifty carpenters. The party of prisoners lined up, facing the boss not in single file but in lines of three or four.

Stukov slowly walked around the party, tapping his stick on his boots, which he hadn't cleaned. From time to time he raised his arm.

"You come out, you. And you. No, not you. Out—you!"

"How many does that make?"

"Forty-two."

"Well then, another eight."

"You . . . you . . . you. . . ."

We copied out the surnames and took their personal files.

All fifty knew how to use an ax and a saw.

"Thirty metalworkers!"

Stukov walked up and down the ranks, frowning slightly.

"You come out.... You ... you.... But you go back. You're one of the gangsters, aren't you?"

"Yes, sir, a gangster."

Thirty metalworkers had been chosen without a single mistake. Ten office clerks were needed.

"Can you choose them by looking at them?"

"No."

"Let's go, then.

"You come out ... you ... you...."

Six men stepped forward.

"There are no more bookkeepers in this party," Stukov said.

I checked their files and he was right: there were no more. We selected office clerks from the next parties of prisoners.

This was Stukov's favorite game, and it left me dumbfounded. Stukov himself was as pleased as a child at his magical abilities, and he suffered agonies if he ever lost self-confidence. He never made mistakes, but he did lose self-confidence, and then we would stop selecting people.

Every time I watched this game, which had nothing to do with cruelty or other people's blood, I felt pleasure.

I was struck by his insight into people. I was struck by this timeless connection between body and soul.

I had seen these tricks, these demonstrations of my boss's mysterious power, so many times. Their sole secret was his many years of experience working with prisoners. Prisoners' clothes smooth out the differences between them, which only makes the task easier, the task of reading a man's profession by his face and hands.

"Who are we going to select today, sir?"

"Twenty carpenters. I've just had a telegram from the administration: to pick out anyone who has previously worked in the secret police"—Stukov gave a laugh—"and has been convicted for nonpolitical crimes or crimes at work. That means they're going to get jobs as interrogators again. What do you think about that?"

"I don't think about such things. Orders are orders."

"Did you work out how I selected the carpenters?"

"Tell me. . . ."

"I just pick out peasants, peasants. Every peasant is a carpenter. And when I want conscientious workers I also choose peasants. And I don't get it wrong. As for knowing who worked in the secret police by looking at their eyes, I shan't say. Do you think they can't look you straight in the eye? Tell me."

"I don't know."

"Nor do I. Well, now I'm getting old, perhaps I'll find out. Before I retire."

The new party was lined up, as always, along the railway cattle cars. Stukov made his usual speech about work, about crediting working days, then he stretched out a hand and walked up and down the railway cattle cars twice.

"I need carpenters. Twenty of them. But I'll do the choosing. Don't move. You, come out . . . you . . . you. . . . That's all. Take their files."

The boss's fingers groped for a piece of paper in his service jacket.

"Stay in line. There's one more question."

Stukov raised the hand holding the piece of paper.

"Is there anyone here who has worked in the secret police?"

Two thousand prisoners stayed silent.

"I'm asking you, is there anyone among you who used to work in the secret police? In the Ministry of the Interior?!"

In one of the back rows, a lanky man, whose eyes really did avoid meeting anyone else's, used his fingers to fight his way to the front.

"I used to work as an informer, sir."

"Clear off!" said Stukov with contempt and satisfaction.

1964

LIDA

KRIST'S sentence, his last sentence in the camps, was coming to an end. The dead winter ice was being undermined by time's spring rivulets. Krist had trained himself to pay no attention to the working days he had credited against his sentence: these were a means of destroying a man's willpower, they were a treacherous phantom hope that did nothing but rot prisoners' souls. But time was passing more and more quickly, as it always does toward the end of a sentence. Blessed are those who are released suddenly, before the end of their sentence.

Krist tried not to think about the possibility of freedom, about what in his world was called freedom.

Being freed is very difficult. Krist knew this from experience. He knew how one is forced to relearn the rules of life, how hard it is to enter a life where the scales, the moral measures are different, how hard it is to revive concepts that used to be alive in a man's soul before he was arrested. Those concepts were no illusions, they were the laws of another, earlier world.

It was difficult to be freed, but it was also a time of joy, for forces appeared and arose in the soul, making Krist confident in his behavior, bold in his actions, and he was able to face the dawn of a new day with a firm gaze.

Krist was not afraid of life, but he knew that it was no joke, that life was a serious business.

Krist knew something else: that once free, he would become forever a "marked" man, forever "branded," forever a quarry for the hounds that at any moment might be set loose by the masters of life.

But Krist was not afraid of the hunt and the chase. He still had a lot of strength, even more moral strength, if a little less physical strength than before.

The hunt of 1937 had driven Krist into prison, to a new lengthened term, and when he had served that sentence, he was given another one, even longer. But there were still several steps between that and execution by shooting, several steps on the dreaded living escalator that connected the human being and the state.

Being freed was dangerous. A proper hunt was out for any prisoner whose sentence was ending or was in its last year. This hunt may well have been prescribed and arranged on orders from Moscow, for "not a hair falls," etc. The hunt consisted of provocations, denunciations, interrogations. The sounds of the terrible camp jazz band, a group of eight players where "seven blow and one man beats the drum,"[28] echoed in the ears of those awaiting release more loudly and more unmistakably every day. The tone became more and more ominous, and very few people could—by good luck—safely leap over this fish trap, this funnel, these lines of nets, and swim out into the open sea where there were no buoys to guide the newly released prisoner, no safe channels, no safe days or nights.

Krist knew this and understood it very well; he had long known it and taken all the precautions he could. But you couldn't guarantee your safety.

His third sentence, a ten-year one, was now ending, but the number of arrests, of charges brought, of attempts to hand out a new sentence from which Krist had in the end emerged unharmed—these were his victories and his good luck—were too many to count. Krist hadn't even tried to count them. In the camps counting brought bad luck.

A long time ago, when he was nineteen years old, Krist had received his first sentence. Selflessness to the point of self-sacrifice, a desire not to give orders but to do everything with his own hands, entered Krist's soul irrevocably and coexisted with a passionate feeling of insubordination to others' orders, others' opinions, others' will. In the depth of his soul Krist always preserved a desire to measure his strength against whoever was sitting at the interrogator's desk. This desire had been nurtured by his childhood, his reading, by the people he had seen in his youth and whom he had heard about. There were a lot of such people in Russia, at least in literary Russia, in the dangerous world of books.

Krist was linked to the "movement" in all the card indexes of the Soviet Union. When the signal came for yet another witch hunt, he left for Kolyma bearing the fatal brand KRTD (Counterrevolutionary Trotskyist Activity). This acronym made him a "letter man," someone with the most dangerous letter T, a Trotskyist. There was a thin piece of cigarette paper stuck in Krist's personal file. This thin transparent paper was a "special note" from Moscow, a very blurred text poorly printed off a duplicator, or possibly it was the tenth or so carbon copy of a typewritten document. Krist happened once to hold in his own hand this deadly piece of paper, where the surname was inserted in firm handwriting, the imperturbably clear hand of an office clerk, who apparently didn't need to read the text but wrote blindly, inserting the surname without looking, and underlining the necessary line in ink: "During imprisonment to be deprived of telegraph and postal communications, to be used only for heavy physical labor, behavior to be reported once a quarter."

The special note was an order to kill, not to release alive. Krist understood that. But he had no time to think about it. And he didn't want to.

All prisoners with special notes knew that this piece of cigarette paper compelled any future person in charge, from the escort guard to the chief of the camp administration, to keep an eye on them, to denounce them, to take measures, and if any lesser boss failed to take an active part in annihilating those who had a special note, he himself would be denounced by his own colleagues, his comrades in the service. A boss knew that he would meet with his superiors' disapproval, that he had no prospects of a career in the camps, if he didn't take an active part in carrying out Moscow's orders.

There were not many prisoners involved in prospecting for coal. The prospector's bookkeeper, who was also the boss's secretary, was a nonpolitical convict named Ivan Bogdanov. Bogdanov had a few conversations with Krist. It was a good job, working as a night watchman. The previous night watchman, an elderly Estonian, had died of a weak heart. Krist dreamed of getting this job. And he failed to get it. So he swore. Ivan Bogdanov listened.

"You've got a special note," said Bogdanov.

"I know."

"Do you know how that works?"

"No."

"There are two copies of your personal file. One follows you around, like your ID papers; the other is kept in the camp administration. That one you can't get hold of, of course, but nobody has ever been known to have been checked up on there. The important paper is the one that's here, that goes wherever you go."

Soon after this conversation Bogdanov was to be transferred somewhere. He came straightaway to say goodbye at Krist's workplace, the prospector's mine shaft. A small smoky bonfire was lit to keep the mosquitoes away from the open shaft. Ivan Bogdanov sat on the edge of the shaft and extracted from under his shirt a piece of paper, very thin and completely faded.

"I'm leaving tomorrow. Here are your special notes."

Krist read them and remembered them forever. Ivan Bogdanov took the piece of paper and burned it in the bonfire, not letting go of the paper until the last letter on it had been burned.

"I wish you—"

"Goodbye."

A new boss came—Krist had had a great many bosses in his life—and with him a new secretary.

At the mine Krist began to seriously tire, and he knew what that meant. There was a vacancy for a winch man. Krist, however, had never had anything to do with machinery; even when he looked at a radio-phonograph he felt doubt and uncertainty. But Semionov, a gangster who was leaving the winch-man's job for something better, reassured him: "You're a *freier*, you're such a sucker that you're beyond help. All you *freiers* are the same. All of you. What are you afraid of? No prisoner should be afraid of any machine. You learn on the job. You're not going to be held responsible. All you need is courage, that's all. Grab the handles, don't make me stay here, or I'll lose my chance. . . ."

Krist knew that a gangster was one thing, but a *freier*, especially one with the letters KRTD, was an utterly different thing when the word "responsible" was used. Nevertheless he was infected by Semionov's confidence.

The clerk of works was still the same man, and he slept close by, in a corner of the barracks. Krist went up to him.

"You've got a special note."

"How would I know?"

"The point is you wouldn't. Anyway, let's assume I haven't seen your file. Let's try."

So Krist became a winch man, switching the electric winch levers on and off, unwinding the steel cable, letting the wagons go down into the mine. He had something of a rest. He had a month's rest. Then an engineer with a nonpolitical conviction turned up and Krist was sent back down into the mine, pushing wagons, filling them with coal, and reflecting that the nonpolitical engineer wouldn't want to stay doing such petty work as a mine winch man, work with no prospect of making something on the side, and that a mine winch was paradise only for "letter men" like Krist, and that when the nonpolitical engineer left, Krist would again be moving those blessed levers and turning on the winch's knife switch.

Not a single day of his time in the camps was erased from Krist's memory. After the mine he was moved to the special zone, charged, and given a new sentence, which was now coming to an end.

Krist had managed to complete his paramedic course; he was still alive and, more important, had won independence, an important asset of the medical profession in camps in the Far North. Krist now managed the admissions room in the enormous camp hospital.

But there was no escaping the inevitable. The letter T in Krist's acronymic note was a mark, a brand, a stamp, a distinguishing feature that was used to hound him for many years, to keep him at the icy gold-mine pit faces in the minus sixty temperatures of Kolyma. They were killing him with hard labor, camp labor too heavy to be borne, labor glorified as a matter of honor, a matter of glory, a matter of valor and heroism;

killing him with the bosses' beatings, the guards' rifle butts, the foremen's fists, the barbers' rough handling, and his fellow prisoners' elbows; killing him with starvation, with the camp's "dumpling soup."

Krist knew, saw, and observed a countless number of times that no other article of the Criminal Code was as dangerous to the state as his, Krist's, acronym with the letter *T*. Betrayal of the motherland, terror, that terrible bouquet of paragraphs in article 58 was less dangerous. Krist's four-letter acronym was the mark of the beast that had to be killed, whose death was ordained.

All the guards of the entire country in the past, the present, and the future were hunting down this letter. Not a single boss in the world would have wanted to show any weakness in exterminating such an "enemy of the people."

At the moment Krist was a paramedic in a big hospital and he was waging a major struggle against the gangsters, the underworld, which the state had called on for help in 1937, so as to annihilate Krist and men like him.

Krist worked very hard in the hospital, sparing neither his time nor his strength. Several times, following Moscow's repeated orders, the authorities at the top had ruled that men like Krist were to be dismissed and sent off to do manual labor. But the hospital chief was an old Kolyma hand and he knew how valuable the energy of such men was. The chief understood very well that Krist would put, and was already putting, a very great deal into his work, while Krist knew the chief understood that.

And now his term of imprisonment was slowly coming to an end, just like the thawing of the winter ice in a country where there are no spring rains to transform life, where there is only the slow destructive work of a sun that shines now cold, now hot. His sentence was thawing, receding like the ice. Its end was near.

Something frightening was getting closer to Krist. His whole future would be poisoned by that crucial certificate of his criminal record, with the article 58 and the letters KRTD. Those letters would block his path in any future life, would block it for life in any place in the land, in any job. That *T* would not only deprive him of identity papers but would for all eternity stop him from finding work, from leaving

Kolyma. Krist had followed with careful attention the release of the very few who, like himself, had lived long enough to be freed, despite having a *T* in their Moscow sentence, in their camp identity documents, and in their personal file.

Krist tried to imagine the extent of this inert force that controlled people. He tried to assess it objectively.

At the very best, he would be left doing the same job in the same place when he was released. He wouldn't be allowed out of Kolyma. He would be left alone until the first signal, the first blast of the hunting horn.

What was he to do? Perhaps the simplest way out was the rope.... That was how many people settled this same question. No! Krist would fight to the end. Fight, like a wild animal, fight as he had been taught to in those many years in which the state had persecuted the human being.

Krist spent countless sleepless nights thinking about his imminent, irrevocable release. He wasn't cursing it, he wasn't afraid of it. He was seeking something.

Light dawned, as always, suddenly. Suddenly, but after a terrible period of tension, not mental tension, nor emotional, but a tension of his whole being. It dawned in the same way as the best verses or the best lines of a story emerge. You think about them day and night without any response, and then light dawns, like the joy of the right word, the joy of a decision. Not the joy of hope—there had been too many disappointments, mistakes, stabs in the back in Krist's path through life.

But light had dawned. Lida....

Krist had been working for a long time in this hospital. His unswerving devotion to the interests of the hospital, his energy, his constant interventions in hospital matters—always in the hospital's favor—had created a special position for him. Paramedic Krist was not the manager of the admissions room, for that was a post for a free hired employee. Nobody knew who the manager was; personnel questions were riddles that were solved every month by two persons: the hospital chief and the head bookkeeper.

All his conscious life Krist had liked actual power, rather than surface prestige. Even when he was a writer, Krist had, as a young man at the time, not been attracted by glory or fame; he was attracted by an awareness of his own strength and ability to write, to do something new, personal, which nobody else could do.

From a legal point of view, the doctors were in charge of the admissions room, but there were thirty of them on duty, so the priorities of orders, of the current camp "policies," and other laws of the prisoners' and guards' world were held only in Krist's memory. These questions were subtle and not everyone could cope with them. But they demanded attention and action, as the duty doctors understood only too well. In practice, the decision whether to admit any patient to the hospital was left up to Krist. The doctors knew this, and even had direct orders to this effect (oral, of course) from the hospital chief.

About two years previously a duty doctor, himself a prisoner, had taken Krist aside.

"There's a girl here."

"No girls."

"Wait. I don't know her myself. But this is what it's all about."

The doctor whispered in Krist's ear some coarse and ugly words. Essentially, the boss of the camp institution in the camp department was harassing his secretary, a nonpolitical prisoner, naturally. This convicted girl's camp husband had long been worked to death at a punishment mine on the boss's orders. But the girl refused to live with her boss. And now they were both passing through, escorting a party of prisoners, and the girl was trying to get into the hospital so as to escape harassment. When patients recovered, they were never sent back from the central hospital to where they had come from, they were sent somewhere else. Perhaps somewhere the boss's hands couldn't reach.

"So that's it," said Krist. "All right, bring the girl in."

"She's here. Come in, Lida."

A short blond woman stood before Krist; she boldly met his eyes.

How many people had passed before Krist's eyes in his lifetime. How many thousands of eyes had he understood and deciphered. Krist seldom made mistakes, very seldom.

"Good," said Krist. "Admit her."

The boss who had brought Lida rushed into the hospital to protest.

But he was a second lieutenant, too low a rank to frighten hospital supervisors. He wasn't allowed in. The lieutenant didn't even manage to see a colonel, the hospital chief; he only got as far as a major, the chief doctor. The chief doctor asked the lieutenant not to tell hospital doctors who was ill and who wasn't. And in any case, why was the lieutenant so interested in what happened to his secretary? He could ask for another girl from the local camp, and they'd let him have one. In short, the chief doctor had no time: "Next!"

The lieutenant went off, cursing, and vanished forever from Lida's life.

Eventually, Lida remained in the hospital, with a job in the office, taking part in the amateur dramatics. Krist never found out what she had been convicted of—he had never been interested in his fellow camp prisoners' convictions.

It was a big hospital. An enormous three-story building. Twice every twenty-four hours the guards supervised a change of shift in the staff from the camp zone, whether they were doctors, nurses, paramedics, or male nurses; the staff soundlessly took off their coats in the cloakroom and just as soundlessly spread out over all the hospital departments. Only when they got to their workplaces were they transformed into Vasili Fiodorovich, Anna Nikolayevna, Katia or Petia, Vaska or Zhenka, "the tall girl," or "the pockmarked woman," depending on their rank, whether they were doctors, nurses, attendants, or "outside" workers.

Krist never went into the camp during his round-the-clock work. Sometimes he and Lida saw each other and exchanged smiles. All that had happened two years previously. The bosses of every "part" of the hospital had been changed twice by then. Nobody even remembered how Lida came to be admitted to the hospital. Only Krist remembered. He needed to find out if Lida also remembered.

The decision was made, and Krist approached Lida when the staff was gathered.

The camp is no place for sentimentality, for protracted and unnecessary preliminaries or explanations, or any "beating around the bush."

Both Lida and Krist were old Kolyma hands.

"Listen, Lida. You work in the records department, don't you?"

"Yes."

"Do you type out the release documents?"

"Yes," she said. "The boss types them himself, too. But he does it badly and spoils the forms. So I always type those documents."

"You'll soon be typing my documents."

"Congratulations." Lida brushed an invisible speck of dust off Krist's overalls.

"You will be typing out old convictions, there's a section for that, isn't there?"

"There is."

"When you type KRTD leave out the letter *T*."

"I've got it," said Lida.

"If the boss notices when he signs it, just smile and say you made a mistake. That you spoiled the form—"

"I know what to say."

The staff was already lining up to leave the building.

Two weeks passed. Krist was summoned and handed a certificate of release with the letter *T* missing.

Two engineers he knew and a doctor went with Krist to the passport department to see what sort of identity papers Krist would be given. Or would be refused as a.... He handed his documents through a window; the answer would come in four hours. Krist had lunch with a doctor he knew; he wasn't worried. In any situation like this you had to know how to make yourself have lunch, dinner, breakfast.

Four hours later the window threw out a mauve-colored piece of paper, a one-year identity card.

"Just one year?" Krist asked. He was at a loss and his question was loaded with his own special meaning.

A shaved military face showed itself in the window.

"One year. We don't have any blank five-year identity papers at the moment. Which you're entitled to. Do you want to stay until tomorrow? They'll bring the papers and we'll redo yours. Or will you change this one-year one in a year's time?"

"I'd rather keep this one and change it in a year."

"Of course." The window was slammed shut.

Krist's friends were amazed. One engineer said it was Krist's good luck; the other saw this as a sign of a long-awaited relaxation of the regime, the first swallow that definitely, definitely heralded spring. The doctor saw it as God's will.

Krist never said a word of thanks to Lida. She didn't expect thanks, either. For a favor like that you don't get thanked. Gratitude is not the right word.

1965

AORTIC ANEURYSM

GENNADI Petrovich Zaitsev began his shift at nine in the morning; at half past ten a party of sick prisoners, all women, had arrived. Among them was a patient that Podshivalov had warned Gennadi about. Her name was Yekaterina Glovatskaya. She had dark eyes and a full figure and Gennadi took a liking to her, a great liking.

"Pretty?" asked the paramedic when the patients had been taken away to wash.

"Pretty...."

"It's...." The paramedic whispered something into Dr. Zaitsev's ear.

"So what, if she belongs to Senia?" the doctor responded in a loud voice. "Senia or Venia: nothing ventured, nothing gained."

"I wish you the best of luck. I really do!"

At the end of the day Gennadi set off to do his hospital rounds. The duty paramedics knew the doctor's habits, so they poured some unusual mixtures of tincture of absinthe and tincture of valerian into measuring glasses, as well as a liqueur they called "Blue Night," which was just methylated spirits. Dr. Zaitsev's face became redder and redder, his cropped gray hair not concealing his scarlet bald patch. Zaitsev got to the women's wards at eleven in the evening. The women's section had been closed off with iron bolts to prevent any raids by rapists among the gangsters in the men's section. There was a prison-type spy hole, a judas window, in the door and a button, which, when pressed, would ring a bell in the house where the hospital guards lived.

Dr. Zaitsev knocked, an eye blinked in the spy hole, and the bolts were drawn with a clang. The nurse on night duty unlocked the door. She was familiar enough with the doctor's weaknesses and her attitude to them had all the indulgence that one prisoner has for another prisoner.

The doctor went into the treatment room; the nurse gave him a measuring glass of Blue Night. He drank it.

"Bring me one of today's new patients, Glovatskaya."

"But you do know. . . ." The nurse shook her head reproachfully.

"None of your business. Call her in."

Katia Glovatskaya knocked on the door and came in. The duty doctor bolted the door shut. Katia sat on the edge of the couch. Dr. Zaitsev unbuttoned her gown, pulled the collar aside and whispered, "I have to examine you . . . your heart. . . . Your chief asked me to . . . I'll do it the French way, without a stethoscope. . . ."

Dr. Zaitsev pressed his hairy ear to Katia's warm breast. Everything proceeded as it had dozens of previous times with other women. The doctor's face turned bright red and all he could hear was the sound of his own heart beating. Then he embraced Katia. Suddenly he heard a strange but very familiar sound. It was as if a cat was purring or a mountain stream was burbling nearby. He was too much a doctor; after all, he had once been an assistant to the great Dr. Pletniov.[29]

His own heart was beating more and more quietly and evenly. He wiped his sweaty brow with a waffle towel and began to listen anew to Katia's heart. He asked her to take her clothes off, and she did so. She was alarmed by the change in his tone and the anxiety in his voice and eyes.

Gennadi Zaitsev listened again and again. The catlike purr was still there.

He paced the room, clicking his fingers, then undid the bolt. The night-duty nurse, with a conspiratorial smile, came in.

"Give me this patient's notes," said Dr. Zaitsev. "Take her away. Please forgive me, Katia."

He took the folder with Glovatskaya's medical notes and sat down at his desk.

"You see, Vasili Kalinych," the hospital chief was telling a new party organizer the next morning, "you're new to Kolyma, you're young, you don't know all the underhanded tricks these convicts can get up to. Here you are, read what the duty doctor has just concocted. This is Zaitsev's report."

The party organizer moved to the window, drew back a corner of the curtain to let in some light, which was refracted by the thick layer of ice on the windowpane, onto the paper of the report.

"Well?"

"This seems to be very dangerous. . . ."

The chief laughed out loud.

"I," he said gravely, "am not going to let Mr. Podshivalov pull the wool over my eyes."

Podshivalov was a prisoner who ran an amateur dramatics circle, a "serf theater," as the chief liked to joke.

"But what has he got to do with it?"

"I'll tell you, my dear Vasili. That girl, Glovatskaya, was in the Culture Brigade. Performers, as you know, enjoy a certain amount of freedom. She's Podshivalov's bit of skirt."

"So that's why—"

"Naturally, as soon as we found that out, we had her slung out of the brigade and sent to the women's punishment mine. In cases like hers, Vasili, we break the lovers up. The more useful and important one we keep, the other one goes to a punishment mine."

"That's not very fair. Both of them ought to be—"

"Quite wrong. The point is to keep them apart. The hospital keeps the useful one. So we have our cake and eat it."

"I see, I see. . . ."

"Now listen to what comes next. Glovatskaya went off to the punishment mine, and a month later she's brought back pale and ill. They know all the tricks there, so they swallow henbane or something, and she gets admitted to the hospital. I found out in the morning and ordered her to be discharged, to hell with her. She gets taken away. Three days later she's brought in again. Then I'm told she's an expert seamstress—all those western Ukrainian women are fine seamstresses—so my wife asked me to let her stay a week in the hospital, my wife's having a surprise present made for my birthday, something embroidered, I suppose, I don't know.

"Anyway, I call in Podshivalov and tell him: 'If you give me your word not to try to see Glovatskaya, I'll admit her for a week.' Podshivalov bows and thanks me."

"What happened? Did they meet?"

"No, they didn't. But Podshivalov is using other people as pawns. Take Zaitsev: he's not a bad doctor, there's no disputing that. He even used to be famous in his time. And now he's insisting, his report says: 'Glovatskaya has an aortic aneurysm.' Other doctors kept on diagnosing neurosis of the heart, stenocardia. They sent her here from the punishment mine on the grounds of a heart defect. It was a phony certificate, and our doctors saw through it right away. Now you see, Zaitsev is writing that 'any careless movement by Glovatskaya can have a lethal outcome.' They really have wound him up!"

"Ye-e-es," said the party organizer. "But we've got general practitioners, we could get others to look at her."

The hospital chief had already had Glovatskaya looked at by other doctors, before he received Zaitsev's report. These doctors had all examined her and pronounced her healthy, so the chief had ordered her to be discharged.

There was a knock at the chief's door. Zaitsev came in.

"You should at least comb your hair before you come to see your superiors."

"Fine," replied Zaitsev, running his fingers through his hair. "I've come to see you, sir, about something important. Glovatskaya is being sent away. She has an aortic aneurysm, a serious one. Any movement—"

"Get out of here!" yelled the chief. "These bastards will stop at nothing. They come into your office...."

Katia gathered her possessions after the traditional leisurely search, put them in a bag, and joined the ranks of the prisoners being led away. The guard called out her surname, she took a few steps, and the enormous hospital door pushed her outside. A truck, its platform covered with canvas, was parked by the hospital porch. The rear cover was folded back. A nurse sitting in the cab stretched out a hand to help Katia. Podshivalov emerged from the thick freezing fog. He waved his glove at Katia. She smiled back calmly and cheerfully, held out her hand to the nurse, and jumped into the truck.

That same moment Katia felt a burning sensation in her chest; as she lost consciousness, she saw for the last time Podshivalov's face, distorted by fear, and the hospital windows, covered in ice.

"Take her into the reception room," the duty doctor ordered.

"The morgue would be better," said Zaitsev.

1960

A PIECE OF FLESH

YES, GOLUBEV had brought this blood-soaked offering. A piece of flesh had been cut out of his body and thrown at the feet of the almighty god of the camps: to appease the god. To appease him, or to deceive him? Life repeats Shakespeare's plots more often than we think. Are Lady Macbeth, Richard III, King Claudius merely remote medieval figures? Is Shylock, who wanted to cut a pound of live human flesh out of the merchant of Venice, a fairy-tale figure? Of course, the wormlike bit of gut, an appendix, a rudimentary organ, weighs less than a pound. Of course, the blood-soaked offering was made under fully sterile conditions. Yet, all the same.... The rudimentary organ turned out to be not at all rudimentary. It was vital, active, and lifesaving.

The end of the year fills prisoners' lives with anxiety. Anxiety besets everyone whose place is insecure (and what prisoner could be sure that he was secure), especially if they are convicted under article 58, once they have managed, after many years' labor at the pit face, hungry and frozen, to win the illusory, uncertain good fortune of a few months, a few weeks working either in a job they were trained for or at some cozy idiot's job—as a bookkeeper, a paramedic, a doctor, a laboratory assistant—everyone who's won the fight for a job that is supposed to go to a free hired worker (except when there are no such workers available) or to a nonpolitical convict (and ordinary convicts look down on these "privileged" jobs, because they can always get one, and for that reason they spend their time getting drunk or worse).

Fifty-eighters can get permanent staff jobs, and they do them well. Very well indeed. And without hope. For a commission is bound to come, find them, and get them dismissed, and, what's more, give their boss a reprimand. No boss wants to spoil his relations with this powerful commission, so he acts in advance by getting rid of anyone who is not entitled to work at these "privileged" jobs.

A good boss waits until the commission has arrived. Let the commission do the hard work of deciding whom they can dismiss and send away. Those who are sent away won't be away for long, and those who aren't dismissed will stay for some time, for a year, until the next December. At the very least, six months. If the boss himself does the dismissing, without waiting for the commission to arrive so he can report that everything is in order, he'll do it worse and more stupidly.

The worst sort of boss, the least experienced, will conscientiously carry out his superiors' orders and not allow anyone with article 58 to do any job that doesn't involve pickax and wheelbarrow, saw and ax.

That sort of boss presides over the worst-run enterprises, and they are the ones who get dismissed quickly.

The flying visits by commissions always happen toward the end of the year. The top bosses have their own backlog of checks and control, and they therefore make an effort to catch up on the backlog by the end of the year. So they send out commissions. Sometimes they make personal visits. In person. That means they get travel expenses and their "hot spots" have not been left personally unsupervised. They can tick the boxes for fulfilling their duty, and they can simply relax, have a nice trip, or if they like, show what they're made of, display their strength and their importance.

Both prisoners and their bosses, from the lowest to the highest rank with big stars on their epaulets, know all this. It's an old game, a very familiar ritual. But it is still worrying, dangerous, and relentless.

A December flying visit can reverse the fate of many and quickly drive yesterday's children of fortune to an early grave.

After such visits nobody in the camp ever experiences any changes for the better. Prisoners, especially if they come under article 58, expect only the worst from such visits. For them there were no good expectations.

Ever since the previous evening there had been rumors, camp "grapevine" whispers, the kind that always turn out to be true. People said some important bosses had come, with a whole truckload of armed soldiers and a prison bus, a Black Maria, to take their captives to a hard-labor camp. Faced with those masters of life and death, the local bosses went into a panic; even the senior figures began to seem juniors, unknown captains, majors, and lieutenant colonels. Lieutenant colonels were hiding deep in their offices. Captains and majors were running around the courtyard holding various lists, lists that probably contained surnames, and among those surnames Golubev's was sure to be found. Golubev felt this, he knew it. But nothing had been announced and nobody had been summoned. Not one name in the zone had been listed yet.

About six months earlier, when a Black Maria had made its regular visit to the settlement and there had been another manhunt, Golubev, who was not on the lists then, was standing by the guardhouse next to a prisoner-surgeon. The surgeon was working in the hospital not just as a surgeon but as a general physician.

The new group of prisoners who had been caught, hunted down, or exposed were pushed into the Black Maria. The surgeon took his leave of a friend who was being sent away.

Golubev was then standing next to the surgeon. When the truck crawled off, raising a cloud of dust, and disappeared in the mountain ravine, the surgeon looked Golubev in the eyes and said, referring to his friend who had now gone to a certain death, "It's his own fault. If he'd had an attack of acute appendicitis, he'd still be here."

Golubev had committed those words to memory. It wasn't the thought or the reasoning he remembered. It was a visual memory: the surgeon's eyes, the mighty clouds of dust....

"The clerk of works is looking for you," said someone who had just run up to him. Golubev saw the clerk of works.

"Get your things!" The clerk was holding a paper list. It was a short one.

"Right away," said Golubev.

"Then come to the guardhouse."

But Golubev did not go to the guardhouse. He clutched the right side of his belly with both hands and groaned as he staggered in the direction of the clinic.

The surgeon came out onto the porch: it was the same surgeon. Something was reflected in his eyes, something he remembered. Perhaps it was the dust cloud that covered the truck that was taking his friend away forever. The examination was quick.

"Admit him. And call out the theater nurse. Call a doctor from the free village to assist. It's an urgent operation."

In the hospital, about two kilometers from the zone, Golubev was undressed, washed, and registered.

Two male nurses took him in and laid him on the operating table. They tied him to the table with canvas straps.

"The injection's coming," Golubev heard the surgeon say. "But I think you're brave enough."

Golubev said nothing.

"Answer! Nurse, talk to the patient."

"Does it hurt?"

"Yes."

"It's always like that with local anesthesia." Golubev heard the surgeon's voice explaining something to the assistant. "It's all talk, it doesn't really work. Here it is...."

"Hang in there just a bit longer...."

A sharp pain made Golubev's whole body jerk, but the pain stopped being acute almost immediately. The surgeons started talking, interrupting each other cheerfully and loudly. The operation was coming to an end.

"Well, we've removed your appendix. Nurse, show the patient his bit of flesh. Can you see it?" The nurse held a snakelike piece of gut, about half as long as a pencil, over Golubev's face.

"We have instructions to show patients that there was a good reason for an incision, that the appendix really has been removed," the surgeon explained to his assistant, who was a free worker. "Well, this gives you a little bit of practical experience."

"I'm very grateful to you," said the free doctor, "for the lesson."

"For a lesson in human kindness, a lesson in philanthropy," said the surgeon, speaking in metaphors as he took off his gloves.

"If you get anything else like this, be sure to call me in," said the free doctor.

"If we get anything else like this, I certainly shall," said the surgeon.

The male nurses, convalescent patients wearing patched white gowns, carried Golubev into the hospital ward. It was a small, postoperative ward, but there weren't many operations in the hospital and none of the patients there were surgical ones. Golubev lay on his back, cautiously touching the bandage wrapped around him, like an Indian fakir's or yogi's loincloth. When he was a child, Golubev had seen drawings of such people in magazines; for almost the whole of his adult life he hadn't known whether those fakirs and yogis really existed or not. But the thought of yogis slipped past and disappeared from his brain. The efforts of his will and his nervous tension weakened, and a pleasant feeling of having done his duty flooded his body. Every cell of that body was singing, purring a happy tune. This meant a break for a few days, a reprieve from being sent into the unknown realm of hard manual labor. For the time being Golubev was saved. This was a postponement. How many days did a wound take to heal? Seven or eight. So danger would return in a fortnight. Two weeks is a very long time, as good as a thousand years, long enough to prepare oneself for new ordeals. And in any case the time it takes for a wound to heal according to the textbooks, and for healing by primary intention, is seven or eight days, so the doctors said. And if the wound gets infected? If the plaster stuck over the wound should come off the skin too early? Golubev cautiously felt the plaster: it was a piece of gauze impregnated with gum arabic, and it was firm, already drying. He felt it through the bandaging. Yes.... This was an emergency exit, a reserve, a few extra days, possibly months if need be. Golubev recalled the big ward at the mine where he had been a patient a year ago. Almost all the patients there would undo their bandages at night and put in a bit of salutary dirt, real dirt picked off the floor, which they would rub in with their fingernails and thus reopen the wounds. Golubev was then a novice and these nighttime changes of dressing used to arouse his amazement to the point of contempt. But a year had passed and Golubev now understood why the patients had acted as they did. It was time for him to profit from what he had learned there. He fell asleep and woke only when somebody's hand pulled the blanket off his face. Golubev always slept as camp prisoners did, with his head under the blanket, trying above all to get warm and to protect his head. Someone's very handsome face was bending over Golubev. The face had a mustache and a haircut, which was either short on the back and sides or a crew cut. That meant the head was not a prisoner's head. Golubev opened his eyes and thought it must be the memory of the yogis or a dream, perhaps a nightmare, but perhaps just an ordinary dream.

"Just an ordinary *freier*," the man rasped in disappointment, putting the blanket back over Golubev's face. "An ordinary *freier*. No proper people about."

But Golubev's feeble fingers pulled his blanket down so that he could look at the man. That man knew Golubev, and Golubev knew him. There was no doubt about it. But he must not, must not be in any hurry to show he recognized him. He had to remember things properly. Remember everything. Golubev did remember. The crew-cut man was. . . . Any moment now the man would be taking off his shirt by the window and Golubev would see a cluster of intertwined snakes tattooed on his chest. The man turned around and the cluster of intertwined snakes appeared before Golubev's eyes. This was Kononenko, a gangster with whom Golubev had been in a transit camp a few months ago, a man who had served several sentences for murder, a prominent gangster who had been "taking a break" for several years in hospitals and pretrial prisons. Whenever the time came for him to be discharged, Kononenko would murder someone in a transit camp: he didn't care who, any *freier* would do, and he would suffocate them with a towel. A towel, a prison-issue towel was Kononenko's favorite murder weapon, it was his calling card. He would be arrested, a new case would be opened, he would be tried again and get an extra twenty-five years to add to the many hundreds of years he already had to serve. After the trial Kononenko would do his best to get into the hospital "for a rest," then he would murder again, and the whole process would start anew. At the time execution of common criminals by shooting had been abolished. The only people who could be executed were "enemies of the people" under article 58.

"Kononenko's in the hospital now," Golubev reflected calmly, every cell of his body singing for joy, afraid of nothing, confident of success. "Kononenko is in the hospital now. He's going through the hospital cycle of his horrible transformations. Tomorrow, or perhaps the day after tomorrow, Kononenko's well-known program will require yet another murder." Would that not make Golubev's efforts—his operation, his terrible effort of willpower—count for nothing? He, Golubev, would be the next victim whom Kononenko would strangle. Perhaps he shouldn't have tried to get out of being sent to hard-labor camps, where prisoners had the "ace of diamonds," a five-digit number, stitched to their backs and were issued striped uniforms. But at least you didn't get beaten there and they didn't strip the flesh off your bones. And there weren't all those Kononenkos there.

Golubev's bunk was by the window. Kononenko was lying opposite him. By the door, a third man lay, his feet close to Kononenko's feet. Golubev could see the third man's face clearly, he didn't even have to turn his head to see that face. Golubev knew that patient, too. It was Podosionov, a permanent inhabitant of the hospital.

The door opened and a paramedic brought the medicines in.

"Kazakov!" he shouted.

"Here," yelled Kononenko, getting up.

"Something for you to read," said the paramedic, handing a piece of paper folded over several times.

"Kazakov?" the name wouldn't stop pounding inside Golubev's brain. But this was Kononenko, not Kazakov. Suddenly Golubev realized what was going on, and his body broke out in a cold sweat.

Everything had taken a turn for the worse. None of the three men was mistaken. This was Kononenko, a "cold fish" as the criminals called him, who had taken somebody else's name and under that name, Kazakov's name, along with Kazakov's criminal record, had gotten himself admitted to the hospital as a "shift worker." This made things even worse, even more dangerous. If Kononenko was just Kononenko, his next victim might be Golubev or it might not. In that case there would still be a choice, a chance, a possibility of salvation. But if Kononenko was Kazakov, then Golubev had no hope of survival. The moment Kononenko suspected anything, Golubev would die.

"You, have we met before? Why are you looking at me like a boa constrictor looking at a rabbit? Or a rabbit looking at a boa constrictor? Which is the right expression, in your learned opinion?"

Kononenko was sitting on a bedside table in front of Golubev's bunk; he was crumpling up his message with his big, hard fingers, scattering crumbs of paper over Golubev's blanket.

"No, we haven't met," said Golubev hoarsely. He was turning pale.

"Well, it's a good thing we haven't," said Kononenko, taking a towel off a nail that was hammered into the wall over the bunk, and shaking the towel in Golubev's face. "Only yesterday I was going to strangle that 'doctor' over there," he said, nodding in the direction of Podosionov, whose face now expressed boundless horror. "After all, what is the bastard doing?" Kononenko went on cheerfully, pointing the towel at Podosionov. "He's mixing his own blood into his urine—look at the jar under his bunk. . . . He scratches his finger and puts a drop of blood in his urine. He knows what he's doing. He's as good as the doctors. The laboratory analysis results: blood in his urine. Our 'doctor' stays in the hospital. Well, tell me, does a man like that deserve to live or not?"

"I don't know," said Golubev.

"You don't? You do. And then you were brought in yesterday. You were in transit camp with me, weren't you? Before I was tried. I went under the name of Kononenko at the time."

"I've never seen your face before," said Golubev.

"You have. So I've decided. Instead of the 'doctor,' I'll finish you off. What has he done wrong?" Kononenko pointed to Podosionov's pale face, which was very slowly turning red as the blood began to circulate again. "What has he done wrong? He's trying to save his life. Like you. Or, if you like, me. . . ."

Kononenko paced the ward, tossing the crumbs of paper, all that was left of the message he'd received, from one hand to the other.

"And I would do you, I'd send you to the next world, and I wouldn't hesitate. Except the paramedic's just brought me a message, you see. I've got to get out of here as quick as I can. The bastards at the mine are trying to kill us. All the thieves in the hospital have been called on to help. You don't know what our life is like. . . . You stupid *freier*!"

Golubev said nothing. He did know what their life was like. As a *freier*, of course, by observation only.

After dinner Kononenko was discharged and he was out of Golubev's life forever.

While the third bunk was still empty, Podosionov managed to get himself to the edge of Golubev's bunk, where he sat at Golubev's feet and started whispering.

"Kazakov is going to strangle both of us, no doubt about it. We've got to tell the bosses—"

"Go fuck yourself," said Golubev.

1964

MY TRIAL

OUR BRIGADE had a personal visit from Fiodorov himself. As always, when the bosses are about to come, the wheels on the wheelbarrow start turning faster, the pickaxes are swung more frequently and loudly. Only a little faster, only a little louder, since old camp lags were working here and they didn't give a damn about any bosses, and they didn't have the strength, either. The speeding up of the work tempo was just a cowardly concession to tradition, possibly also a mark of respect to one's foreman, who would have been accused of conspiracy, dismissed from his job, and put on trial if the brigade stopped working. Even the weakest attempt at a pretext to take a break was taken to be a demonstration, a protest. If the wheelbarrow wheels were turning faster, it was more out of courtesy than fear.

Fiodorov, whose name was repeated on dozens of lips, burned and cracked by the wind and by starvation, was the district NKVD officer at the mine. He was approaching the pit face where our brigade was working.

There are few spectacles so telling as the juxtaposition of the camp bosses with the goners: the former figures are well-fed, portly, weighed down by their own fat, wearing smelly new sheepskin jackets that shine like the sun, ornate Yakut reindeer-fur boots, and brightly patterned long gauntlets, while the latter are skeletal and ragged, with "steaming" clots of cotton wool sticking out of their quilted jackets, all with the same dirty, bony faces and sunken eyes shining with hunger. Such composite spectacles could be seen every day, every hour in the Moscow-to-Vladivostok prison wagons and in the torn, plain tarpaulin camp tents in which prisoners lived at the Cold Pole, never taking their outer clothes off, never washing, where their hair froze and stuck to the tent walls and where there was no way to get warm. The tent roofs were torn; during the recent dynamiting at the pit face, rocks had hit the tents. One tent was hit by a rock so big that it remained in the tent forever—people used it as a place to sit, eat, and share their bread.

Fiodorov moved at a leisurely pace along the pit face. Other men in fur jackets accompanied him. I wasn't to know who they were.

It was spring, an unpleasant time, when icy water came to the surface everywhere, but you still hadn't been issued your summer rubber boots. We were all wearing winter footwear: coarse soft boots made of old quilted trousers with soles of the same material, which became soaking wet in our first ten minutes at work. Our toes, which were frostbitten and bleeding, were unbearably cold. Wearing rubber boots was no better for the first few weeks, since the rubber let in the coldness of the permafrost, and there was no escape from the throbbing pain.

Fiodorov walked the length of the pit face, asked a question, and our foreman, with a respectful deep bow, reported something. Fiodorov yawned, and his gold teeth, the result of good dentistry, reflected the sun's rays. The sun was now at its zenith. One's only conclusion was that Fiodorov had undertaken this trip after his "night work." He asked another question.

The foreman called me over. I'd just wheeled up an empty barrow with the skill of an experienced barrow man, holding the handles vertical so as to rest my arms, and the barrow tipped so that its wheel was in front. I went up to the boss.

"So you're Shalamov, are you?" asked Fiodorov.

That evening I was arrested.

Our summer clothes were being issued: a tunic, cotton trousers, foot bindings, rubber boots. This was one of the important days of the year in a prisoner's life. On another even more important day, winter clothing was issued. They handed out whatever they laid hands on; trying to sort out sizes for shoes and clothes took place later, in the barracks.

When my turn came, the quartermaster said, "Fiodorov wants to see you. When you get back, then you'll get them...."

At the time I didn't grasp the real meaning of what the quartermaster had said.

Some official, a stranger to me, led me to the edge of the settlement where the district NKVD man had a tiny cabin.

I was sitting in the twilight outside the dark windows of Fiodorov's cabin, chewing a piece of last year's straw, not thinking about anything. There was a solid bench on the mound of earth outside the cabin, but prisoners were not allowed to sit on the bosses' benches. I stroked and scratched my parchment-dry, cracked, dirty skin under my quilted jacket and I smiled. Whatever was ahead was bound to be something good. I was seized by an amazing feeling of relief, almost of happiness. Tomorrow and the next day I wouldn't have to go to work. I wouldn't have to swing my pickax to hit that accursed rock that makes your muscles, as thin as rope, quiver with each blow.

I knew that I was always at risk of getting a new sentence. I was very much aware of the camp traditions in that respect. In 1938, the year of dread in Kolyma, the first people to be framed with new charges were those who had short sentences, or whose sentences were coming to an end. That was what they always did. I had arrived here, however, in the Jelgala special zone, as an "overstayer." My sentence had ended in January 1942, but instead of being released, I was "detained in the camps until the end of the war," like thousands, tens of thousands of others. Until the end of the war! It was hard enough to get through a day, let alone a year. All the overstayers became the subject of the investigating authorities' intensive surveillance. They had made great efforts to frame me with a new case at Arkagala, too, where I was before I came to Jelgala. But they didn't succeed. All they achieved was to transfer me to a punishment zone, which was, of course, by its very nature an ominous sign. But why torture myself by thinking about something I could do nothing about?

I knew, of course, that I had to be doubly cautious about what I said, how I behaved. I wasn't a fatalist. And yet, what difference did knowing everything, foreseeing everything make? All my life I have been unable to make myself call a swine a decent human being. And

I believe it's better not to be alive at all if you can't say a word to anyone, or if you can only say the opposite of what you think.

"What's the point of *human experience*?" I was asking myself, as I sat on the ground under Fiodorov's dark window. What was the point of knowing, feeling, guessing, that one man was an informer, a snitch, and another a swine, and yet another a vindictive coward? I would be better off, safer, if I treated him as a friend rather than as an enemy. Or at least, if I kept my mouth shut. All you had to do was lie, to them and to yourself, and that was unbearably difficult, far harder than telling the truth. What was the point if I couldn't change my nature, my behavior? What did I need that accursed "experience" for?

A light came on in the room, the curtain was suddenly drawn back, the door of the cabin opened wide, and the orderly stood on the threshold, gesturing for me to come in.

An enormous office desk with lots of drawers, piled high with folders, pencils, notebooks, filled the tiny, low-ceilinged room. Apart from the desk two homemade chairs had somehow been squeezed into this room. One of them was painted; Fiodorov was sitting on it. The other was unpainted; it was polished by hundreds of prisoners' behinds, and it was reserved for me.

Fiodorov pointed to the chair, started rustling papers, and the "case" began....

There are three ways in which a prisoner in a camp can have his fate "broken," that is, changed: serious illness, a new sentence, and something extraordinary. There were quite a few extraordinary chance happenings in our lives.

As I grew weaker with every day at the Jelgala pit face, I hoped that I would end up in the hospital and die there, or recover, or be sent off somewhere. I was falling over with tiredness and weakness; when I walked, I shuffled my feet over the ground. Any unevenness, a pebble, a thin piece of wood were insuperable obstacles in my path. But every time I went to the outpatient clinic, the doctor would pour me a tin ladle full of potassium permanganate solution and croak out, without looking me in the eye, "Next!" They gave you potassium permanganate to drink as treatment for dysentery; they used it to anoint frostbitten digits, wounds, and burns. Permanganate was the camp's universal and unique medication. They never once gave me time off from work—the simpleminded male nurse explained that "the limit had been reached." In fact, every camp medical point and clinic had its target figures for category T: "temporarily let off work." Nobody wanted to exceed the limit: any doctors or paramedics who were also prisoners ran the risk of being sent to do manual labor if they were too softhearted. The "plan" was a Moloch that demanded human sacrifices.

In winter Jelgala had been visited by the top authorities. Drabkin, the head of the Kolyma camps, had come.

"Do you know who I am? I'm the one who is everyone's superior." Drabkin was a young man, who had only recently been appointed.

Surrounded by a mob of bodyguards and local bosses, he inspected the barracks. There were people in our barracks who still hadn't lost interest in having a conversation with the top bosses. Drabkin was asked, "Why are there dozens of people without sentences being kept here, when they finished serving their sentence a long time ago?"

Drabkin was fully prepared for this question. "Don't you know you do have a sentence? Weren't you read out a document saying you would be detained until the end of the war? That was your sentence. That means that you have to stay in the camp."

"Indeterminately?"

"Don't interrupt when someone in authority is speaking to you. Your release depends on the references you're given by the local camp authorities. Do you know the character references you're getting?" Drabkin made a vague gesture with his arm.

What an anxious silence ensued behind my back, how many conversations were broken off when I, a *doomed* man, approached, how many looks of sympathy—no smiles, of course, no mockery, for men in our brigade had long forgotten how to smile. Quite a few men in the brigade knew that Krivitsky and Zaslavsky had ratted me out. Quite a few sympathized with me but were afraid to show it in case I got them involved. I later found out that Fertiuk, an ex-schoolteacher whom Zaslavsky had called on as a witness, had refused outright, so that

Zaslavsky had to perform with his usual partner, Krivitsky. Two witness statements were the minimum required by the law.

When I'd lost my strength, when I'd become utterly feeble, I had an irresistible desire to fight. This feeling was an enfeebled man's perverse obsession, familiar to any prisoner who has ever been starved. Hungry people don't fight like other people. They take a run-up in order to deliver a punch, they try to hit with their shoulders, to bite, to trip their opponent up, to squeeze his throat. There are countless pretexts for a quarrel. Everything irritates a prisoner: the bosses, the work that lies ahead, the cold, the heavy tools, and his fellow prisoner next to him. A prisoner picks a fight with the sky, with his spade, with a rock, with any living creature nearby. The most petty argument can expand into a bloodletting battle. But prisoners don't write denunciations. Denunciations are written by the Krivitskys and Zaslavskys. That, too, was in the spirit of 1937.

"He called me a fool, so I wrote that he wanted to poison the government. We're quits! He quotes something at me, I get him exiled." But not just exile: prison or a bullet in his neck.

The experts at this sort of business, the Krivitskys and Zaslavskys, quite often end up in prison themselves, which means that someone else has been turning their own weapon against them.

In the past Krivitsky was a deputy minister of the defense industry, and Zaslavsky was a sketch writer for the newspaper *Izvestiya*. I had beaten up Zaslavsky several times. What for? For being underhanded, for picking up a beam by the top end instead of the heavy bottom end, for telling the foreman or the deputy foreman, Krivitsky, everything that the working team talked about. I never had a chance to beat up Krivitsky: we worked on different teams—but I loathed him for the special part he played as deputy foreman, for his constant inactivity at work, for the invariable "Japanese" smile on his face.

"How does the foreman treat you?"
"Well."

"Who are you on bad terms with in your brigade?"

"Krivitsky and Zaslavsky."

"Why?"

I did my best to explain.

"Well, none of that matters. Let's write: Krivitsky and Zaslavsky are on bad terms with me because I've quarreled with them while working."

I signed.

Late at night the escort guard and I were walking back to the camp, not to the barracks but to a squat building just outside the zone: the camp solitary confinement area.

"Have you got anything in the barracks?"

"No. It's all on me."

"So much the better."

It's said that interrogation is a battle between two persons: the interrogator and the accused. Probably that's true. Only you can hardly talk about willpower when a man has been worn out by many years of unremitting starvation, cold, and hard labor, when his brain cells are desiccated and have lost their properties. The effects of many years of prolonged hunger on the human will and soul is quite different from those of any prison hunger strike or torture by starvation that reaches the point when force-feeding is required. In the latter cases a man's brain still remains intact and his spirit is still strong. His spirit can still dominate his body. If Dimitrov[30] had been prepared for his trial by Kolyma interrogators, the world would not have known any Leipzig trial.

"Well, how are we going to proceed?"

The main thing is to gather what's left of your reason, to try to guess, understand, find out: only Zaslavsky and Krivitsky could have written statements against you. (At whose insistence? According to whose plan, to meet what target figures?) Look at how wary the interrogator became, how he made his chair creak as soon as you mentioned those names. Stand firm: announce that you challenge the witnesses. Challenge Krivitsky and Zaslavsky! If you win, you're "free." You're back in the barracks, in "freedom." This fairy tale, this joyful solitude, this cozy dark isolation cell where the only light and air you get comes through a gap in the door, will immediately stop, and the rest will start again: the barracks, the lining up to go to work, pickax, wheelbarrow, gray rock, icy water. Which is the right road? Where is salvation to be found? Where is luck?

"Well, how are we to proceed? If you like I can summon ten witnesses of your choosing from your brigade. Give me any names you like. I'll see them in my office and they'll all give evidence against you. I'm right, aren't I? I guarantee that's what will happen. You and I are grown-ups, aren't we?"

The punishment zones are distinguished by the musicality of their names: Jelgala, Golden.... Places for punishment zones are selected cleverly. Jelgala is on a high mountain: the mine pit faces are down below, in a ravine. That means that after many hours of exhausting work people have to climb ice-covered steps, carved out of the snow, and grab stumps of frozen willow; they have to climb, using up their last reserves of strength, carrying firewood with them, a daily portion of firewood to heat the barracks. The little boss who chose this place as a punishment zone was, of course, well aware of all this. He understood something else, too: that anyone who resisted, who refused or was unable to go to work, could be rolled or thrown down the camp's mountain, and they did this at the morning roll calls in Jelgala. Anyone who wasn't walking was grabbed by the arms and legs by big guards, swung in the air, and thrown downhill. At the bottom there was a horse waiting; it was harnessed to a sled. Resisters were tied by their feet to the sled and dragged to their workplace.

Man may have become man because he was physically stronger,

tougher than any other animal. And this is still true. People didn't die because they were made to bang their heads over the Jelgala roads for two kilometers: horses pulling sleds don't gallop, after all.

Thanks to the topographical features, it was easy at Jelgala to have what they called "roll calls minus one," when prisoners try to dash down by themselves, to roll down before the guards can throw them into the abyss. Roll calls minus one in other places were usually done with the help of dogs. The Jelgala dogs took no part in roll calls.

It was spring, and solitary confinement was not so bad. By then I had gotten to know the Kadykchan solitary confinement, with cells hacked out of the rock in the permafrost, and the Partisan isolation unit, where the guards had deliberately ripped out all the moss that filled the gaps between the beams. I was also familiar with the Spokoinoye mine's ice-covered, solitary confinement prison, made from logs of winter larch, surrounded by frozen fog, as well as the Black Lake solitary confinement unit, where icy water served as a floor and a narrow bench as a bunk. My prison experience was extensive: I could sleep on a narrow bench, dream, and yet not fall into the icy water.

Camp ethics allow you to deceive your bosses, to "stuff rubbish" in your measurements and calculations, so it appears as if you have fulfilled your norm. In any carpentry job you can cut corners and fake things. There is only one job where you are meant to be conscientious: when you build the camp solitary confinement prison. You can be careless when you assemble logs to make the bosses' barracks, but any prison for the prisoners must be warm and solid. "We're going to be the ones in it." Even though this is a tradition observed mainly by the gangsters, rationality is still at the core of this attitude. But it is all theory. In practice, wedges and moss are the main materials everywhere, and a camp solitary confinement prison is no exception.

The Jelgala solitary confinement prison had a special design: there was no window, so it brought back memories of the Butyrki "trunks." A gap in the door to the corridor was the nearest thing to a window. I spent a month here on solitary rations: three hundred grams of bread and a mug of water a day. Twice that month the solitary confinement orderly shoved a bowl of soup into my hands.

Covering his face with a perfumed handkerchief, interrogator Fiodorov deigned to have a conversation with me.

"Would you like to see the paper? Look, Comintern has been dissolved. That should interest you."

No, it didn't interest me. But I would like a cigarette.

"You'll have to pardon me. I don't smoke. You see, you're being accused of praising Hitler's armaments."

"What does that mean?"

"Well, that you reacted with approval to the German invasion."

"I know practically nothing about it. I haven't seen the papers for many years. Six years."

"Well, that's beside the point. Now, you once said that in the camps the Stakhanovite movement was fake and a lie."

Apart from the punishment, pretrial, and convoy rations, there were three other levels of rations in the camp: the prisoners' full pot, the Stakhanovite or shock workers' ration, and the normal production. These rations differed in the quantity of bread and the quality of the dishes. In the pit face next to ours the mining supervisor measured out a distance for each worker—his set task—and fixed a roll-your-own cigarette there. If you could barrow out the earth and rock as far as his mark, then the cigarette was yours and you were a Stakhanovite.

"So that's how things stand," I said. "I think that's monstrous."

"And then you said that Bunin was a great Russian writer."

"He really is a great Russian writer. Can you give me a prison sentence for saying that?"

"I can. He's an émigré. An embittered émigré."

The "case" was progressing nicely. Fiodorov was cheerful and lively.

"Well, look how well we're treating you. Not a single rough word. Pay attention: nobody's hitting you as they did in 1938. No pressure."

"How about the three hundred grams of bread a day?"

"Orders, dear man, orders. There's nothing I can do. Orders. Pretrial rations."

"And a cell with no window? I'll go blind, and there's no air to breathe."

"Really, no window? That can't be. Light must get in from somewhere."

"From the gap at the bottom of the door."

"Well, then, you see."

"In winter that would be covered in freezing fog."

"But it's not winter now."

"True. It's not winter anymore."

"Listen," I said. "I'm sick. I've got no strength left. I've been to the medical center many times, but they've never let me off work."

"Write a statement. That will have an impact on the court and the investigation."

I reached out for the nearest fountain pen; there were many of all sizes and brands lying on the table.

"No, no, an ordinary pen, please."

"All right."

I wrote that I had been to the outpatient clinics in the zone many times, almost every day. It was very hard to write, I hadn't had much practice in that area.

Fiodorov smoothed out the piece of paper.

"Don't worry. Everything will be done according to the law."

That same evening my cell's locks clanged and the door opened. A Kolyma lamp—a kerosene lamp made from a tin can, with four outlets—was burning on the duty guard's table in the corner. A man wearing a fur jacket and a hat with earflaps was sitting at the table.

"Come here."

I went over to him. He got up. It was Dr. Mokhnach, an old Kolyma hand, a victim of 1937. He had done manual labor in Kolyma, then he was allowed to practice as a doctor. He had been trained to fear authority. I had been to his surgery at the zone's outpatient clinics many times.

"Hello, doctor."

"Hello. Undress. Breathe. Don't breathe. Turn around. Bend over. You can put your clothes on."

Dr. Mokhnach sat down at the table and wrote in the light of the flickering lamp: "Prisoner Shalamov V. T. is to all intents and purposes healthy. During his time in the zone he has not sought treatment in the outpatient clinic. Head of Outpatients, Dr. Mokhnach."

That text was read out to me a month later at my trial.

The investigation was coming to an end, but I could not, try as I might, work out what I was being accused of. My hungry body ached but rejoiced that it didn't have to work. But suppose they suddenly let me out to go back to the pit face? I suppressed these alarming thoughts.

A Kolyma summer begins suddenly, hastily. During one of my interrogations I saw a burning sun and a blue sky, and smelled the subtle scent of the larch. Dirty ice still lay in the gullies, but summer couldn't wait for the dirty ice to thaw.

The interrogation had dragged on, we were trying to pin something down, so the guard had not yet taken me away, when another man was brought up to Fiodorov's cabin. He was my foreman Nesterenko. He took a step toward me and said in a muffled voice, "I was forced to, you understand, forced," before disappearing through the door to Fiodorov's cabin.

Nesterenko was writing a statement against me. The witnesses were Zaslavsky and Krivitsky. But I doubt whether Nesterenko had ever heard of Bunin. And if Zaslavsky and Krivitsky were bastards, it was Nesterenko who saved me from dying of starvation by taking me into his brigade. I was no worse, but no better than any other worker there. I had no grudge against Nesterenko. I had heard that this was his third term in the camp, that he used to be a Solovetsky Islands[31] prisoner. He was a very experienced foreman and he understood not just the work but hungry people, too; he didn't sympathize, he understood. Very few foremen have that gift. In every brigade seconds—a ladle of thin soup from whatever was left—were given out after supper. Usually foremen gave these ladlefuls to whoever had worked the best that day, which was the procedure officially recommended by the camp authorities. This issue of seconds was made a public, almost a ceremonial affair. Seconds were also used with a view to increasing production and educating the prisoners. The person who had worked most was not always the one who had worked best. And it wasn't always the best worker who wanted to eat more dumpling soup.

In Nesterenko's brigade seconds were given to the hungriest, in accordance with the foreman's orders, of course.

Once, in a prospecting shaft, I hammered out an enormous rock. It was obvious that I didn't have the strength to pull this rock out of the shaft. Nesterenko saw that, and without a word jumped down into the shaft, got his pickax under the rock, and jolted it up....

I didn't want to believe that Nesterenko had written a statement against me. But all the same....

It was said that a year earlier two people had been removed from that brigade and put on trial by a tribunal: Yozhikov and, three months later, Isayev, the former secretary of a Siberian provincial committee. The witnesses had been the same Krivitsky and Zaslavsky. I hadn't paid any attention to this talk.

"And now sign here. And here, too."

I didn't have long to wait. On June 20 the doors were flung open and I was led out onto the hot brown earth, into the blinding, burning sunlight.

"Here are your things: shoes, cap. You're off to Yagodnoye."

"You mean on foot?"

Two soldiers carefully looked me over.

"He won't make it," one said. "We won't take him."

"What do you mean you won't take him?" said Fiodorov. "I'm telephoning the special squad."

These soldiers weren't real escort guards, who would have been ordered and equipped beforehand. These two special operations men were going back to Yagodnoye—eighteen kilometers through the taiga —and were supposed to take me with them to the Yagodnoye prison.

"Well, what do you think?" said one of the operations men. "Will you make it?"

"I don't know." I was perfectly calm. I had no reason to hurry. The sun was too hot—it burned my cheeks, which were unused to bright light and fresh air. I sat against a tree. It was pleasant to sit outside for a while, breathing in the remarkable spring air, the scent of blossoming briars. My head started spinning.

"Right, let's go."

We went into the bright green forest.

"Can't you walk any faster?"

"No."

We went a countless number of steps. The willow branches were lashing my face. Stumbling over the tree roots, I somehow got through to a clearing.

"Listen," said the older operations man, "we need to get to the Yagodnoye cinema. It starts at eight. In the club. It's two now. This is our first day off this summer. It's the first time we'll be in a cinema in six months."

I said nothing.

The soldiers had a quick discussion.

"You take a break," said the younger one. He unbuttoned his bag. "Here's white bread for you. A kilo. Eat, have a rest, then we'll go. If it weren't for the cinema, we wouldn't give a damn. But it is cinema night."

I ate the bread, licked the crumbs off my hand, lay down by a stream, and cautiously drank my fill of delicious, cold stream water. And I lost the last ounce of my strength. It was hot, I just wanted to sleep.

"Right? You can walk?"

I said nothing.

Then they started beating me. They stamped on me, I yelled and covered my head with my hands. But they didn't hit my face, these were experienced men.

They beat me for a long time, and they took trouble over it. The more they beat me, the clearer it became that there was no way of speeding up our progress toward the prison.

For hours and hours we wandered through the forest and it was twilight when we came out onto the highway that stretched the length of Kolyma, a highway that ran across rocks and marshes, a road two thousand kilometers long, all built on "barrows and pickaxes," with no machinery at all.

I had almost lost consciousness and could barely move when I was delivered to the Yagodnoye detention center. The cell door was flung open and the duty guard's experienced hands *squeezed* me inside. All you could hear was people's rapid breathing. After about ten minutes I made an attempt to lower myself to the floor and lay against a pillar under the bunks. A short time after that thieves who were in the cell crawled over to search me and steal something, but their hopes to get something out of me were dashed. Apart from lice, I had nothing. I fell asleep to the irritated growls of the disappointed common criminals.

The next day, at three o'clock, I was summoned to my trial.

It was very stuffy; there was no air to breathe. For six years I had spent every day and night in the open air, and I found the tiny room of the military tribunal unbearably hot. The larger half of the twelve-square-meter room was set aside for a tribunal that sat behind a wooden barrier. The smaller half was for the accused, the guard, and the witnesses. I saw Zaslavsky, Krivitsky, and Nesterenko. There were rough unpainted benches along the walls and two windows with lots of small panes in the Kolyma fashion, like the windows in Menshikov's Berio-zovo hut in Surikov's painting.[32] Panes like these could be made from broken glass: that was the architect's idea, taking into consideration the difficulty of transporting glass, its fragility, and a lot of other factors, for instance the use of preserve jars that could be sawed in half lengthwise. All this, of course, was relevant only for the windows in the bosses' apartments and in official buildings. Prisoners' barracks didn't have any glass panes.

The light such windows gave was refracted and murky. The tribunal chairman's table had an unshaded electric lamp for illumination.

The trial was very short. The chairman read out a short charge, point by point. He questioned the witnesses, asking whether they affirmed their statements during the preliminary investigation. I was surprised by the fact that there were four witnesses, instead of three—a certain Shailevich had expressed the wish to take part in my trial. I had never met this witness and never spoken to him in my life; he worked in a different brigade. This didn't stop Shailevich from quickly rattling through his set speech: Hitler, Bunin. . . . I realized that Fiodorov had taken on Shailevich just in case I unexpectedly challenged Zaslavsky and Krivitsky. But Fiodorov needn't have worried.

"Do you have anything to ask the tribunal?"

"Yes. Why is this the third accusation to come from Jelgala mine under article fifty-eight, and yet the witnesses are the same?"

"Your question is irrelevant to the case."

I was sure the sentence would be a harsh one; killing people was a tradition in those years. And furthermore this trial was on June 22, the anniversary of the beginning of the war. The court deliberated for about three minutes, and the tribunal—there were three members—delivered a sentence of "ten years plus five years' deprivation of civic rights."

"Next!"

There was a commotion in the corridor. Boots stomped. The next day I was moved to the transit camp. The procedure of compiling a new personal file, one that I had experienced several times before, began again: endless fingerprinting, forms to fill in, photographing. I was now called "fill in name," article 58, paragraph 10, sentence ten plus five deprivation. I was no longer an acronym prisoner with the terrible *T* for Trotskyist in my file. That had important consequences and may well have saved my life.

I don't know what happened to Nesterenko, or Krivitsky. There were rumors that Krivitsky died. Zaslavsky, however, returned to Moscow and became a member of the Union of Writers, although he'd never written anything in his life except denunciations. I saw him from a distance. But the Zaslavskys and Krivitskys are not the point. Immediately after being sentenced I could have murdered informers and false witnesses. I would certainly have murdered them if I had returned to Jelgala after my trial. But camp procedures took care to see that men given new sentences never returned to the camp from which they had been brought to court.

1960

ESPERANTO

A TRAVELING actor, a prisoner-actor, reminded me of this story. After a show by the camp Culture Brigade, the main actor (who was also the director and set-builder) mentioned the name of Skoroseyev.

It was as if my brain had been burned: I recalled a transit camp in 1939, typhus quarantine, and the five of us who endured and came through all the many transfers, the various parties of prisoners, the hours spent standing in sub-zero temperatures, and who were caught in the net of camps and cast out into the boundless taiga.

The five of us learned nothing, knew nothing, and didn't want to know anything about one another until our party had reached the place where we were to work and live. In our party the news struck us in differing ways. One of us went mad, thinking that he was being taken off to be shot, when he was being taken off to live. Another tried to outwit his fate and almost succeeded. The third—that was me!—was a man who'd been "on the gold," a miner, who'd become a skeleton who didn't care. The fourth was a jack-of-all-trades, well over seventy. The fifth was—"Skoroseyev," he said, rising up on tiptoe to look each of us in the eye. "Score ... save ... get it?"

I didn't care. I'd lost forever any taste I had for puns. But the jack-of-all-trades kept the conversation going.

"What was your job?"

"Agronomist in the Ministry of Agriculture."

The chief of coal prospecting flicked through Skoroseyev's file when he took over our party.

"Sir, I can also—"

"I'll make you night watchman."

Skoroseyev was a very diligent night watchman for the prospecting team. He never left his post for a minute, fearing that a fellow prisoner might take advantage of any blunder he made to denounce him or sell him out, or to attract the boss's attention. It was better not to take risks.

Once a blizzard raged all night. Skoroseyev alternated shifts with a Galician called Narynsky, a somewhat fair-haired man who'd been a prisoner of war during World War I, and who had been sentenced for starting a conspiracy to restore the Austro-Hungarian Empire. He was just a tiny bit proud of having such a rare, unprecedented case file among the swarms of "Trotskyists" and "saboteurs." When Narynsky took over from Skoroseyev, he would laugh and point out that even when a blizzard was blowing Skoroseyev would not move from his post. Such devotion was noticed. Skoroseyev was securing his position.

A horse collapsed in the camp. That was not such a great loss; horses didn't do well in the Far North. But the meat! Meat! The horse had to be flayed, but the corpse had frozen in the snow. Nobody had the skills or the desire to do anything. Skoroseyev offered to take the job on. The boss was amazed and pleased: a skin and meat. The skin would have to be accounted for, but the meat would go into the pot. The whole barracks, the whole settlement was talking about Skoroseyev. Meat, meat! The horse's carcass was dragged into the bathhouse, and Skoroseyev thawed it out, flayed it, and gutted it. The skin was stiffened in the freezing air and then taken to the stores. But we were fated not to eat the meat: at the last minute the boss changed his mind—there was no veterinary surgeon about, and so no signature on a certificate. The horse's carcass was cut up with an ax, a statement was drawn up, and the carcass was burned on a bonfire in the presence of the boss and the works overseer.

The coal that our prospecting team was looking for was not there. Little by little, parties of men, five or ten at a time, began to be escorted away from the camp. These people climbed the mountain along a taiga path to disappear forever from my life.

It was still a prospectors' camp, not a mine, where we were living, and each one of us understood that. Each of us tried hard to hang on here as long as we could. Each "put on the brakes" in his own way. One began working with extraordinary diligence. Another began praying longer than usual. Anxiety had now crept into our lives.

Escort guards appeared. They had come from the other side of the mountains. To fetch people? No, the guards didn't take away a single person.

That night there was a search in the barracks. We had no books, we had no knives, we had no indelible pencils, newspapers, or paper. What was there to look for?

They took away our civilian clothes; many of us still had civilian clothes, since there were free workers in this prospecting team and the team was working without guards. Was this to prevent escape attempts? Was it just carrying out orders? Had there been a change in the regime?

Everything was taken away without any statements or record. It was taken, and that was all. There was no end to the outrage. I remembered the civilian clothes being taken from hundreds of parties, from hundreds of thousands of men, two years previously in Magadan. Tens of thousands of fur coats, which the wretched prisoners had brought with them when they went north, to the Far North, along with warm overcoats, sweaters, expensive suits (expensive, because somebody had to be bribed), in order to save their lives at a crucial moment. But this lifesaving way out was cut short in the Magadan bathhouse. Mountains of civilian clothing were stacked in the courtyard of the Magadan bathhouse. The mountains were higher than the water tower, higher than the roof of the bathhouse. Mountains of warm clothing, mountains of tragedies, mountains of human fate, suddenly and abruptly interrupted, thus dooming everyone who came out of the bathhouse to death. How hard all these people had fought to protect their possessions from the gangsters, from the open robbery that went on in the barracks, the railcars and transit camps. Everything that had been saved or hidden from the gangsters had now been taken by the state in the bathhouse. How simple! That had happened two years ago. And now it happened again.

The civilian clothes that filtered down to the mines took longer for the guards to catch up with. I remember being woken at night; there were searches in the barracks every day, and every day people were taken away. I would sit on the bunks and smoke. This was a new search for civilian clothes. I didn't have any: I'd lost everything in the Magadan bathhouse. But my fellow prisoners did have civilian clothes. They were precious things, symbols of another life; they might be rotting to pieces, torn, patched—we didn't have the time or the strength to mend things— but they were still close to our hearts.

Everyone was standing by their bunks, waiting. An interrogator was sitting near the lamp, writing documents, a certificate of search, of removal, as it was called in camp language.

I sat on the bunks, smoking, not anxious, not outraged. All I wanted was for the search to end as quickly as possible so that I could sleep. But I saw our orderly, a man called Praga, chopping up his suit with an ax, tearing sheets to bits, and crushing his boots to pieces.

"Only as foot bindings. I'll let them have them only as foot bindings."

"Take the ax off him," yelled the interrogator.

Praga flung the ax on the ground. The search stopped. The things that Praga had torn, cut, and destroyed were his own possessions. There had been no time to list them in the certificate. When Praga saw that he wasn't being grabbed by the arms, he turned all his civilian clothes into rags: I saw it with my own eyes. So did the interrogator.

That had happened a year earlier. And now it was happening again.

Everyone was upset, tense, and it took a long time to go to sleep.

"There's no difference between the gangsters robbing us and the state," I said. And everybody agreed with me.

Skoroseyev the night watchman was off to do his shift two hours earlier than us. Walking in pairs, which the taiga path allowed us to do, we got to the office: we were angry, we felt offended. A naïve feeling for fairness lies very deep, perhaps ineradicably deep, in men's hearts. You might think: What was there to be offended by, or angry at, or outraged by? This damned search was something that happened thousands of times. Something was seething deep in our souls, and it was stronger than our willpower or experience. The prisoners' faces were dark with wrath.

The boss himself, Viktor Nikolayevich Plutalov, was standing on the office porch. He too had a dark, wrathful face. Our tiny column of men stopped in front of the office, and I was now called in to see Plutalov.

"So you are saying," Plutalov looked askance at me, biting his lips.

He sat down with some difficulty and discomfort on the stool at his desk. "You say that the state is worse than the gangsters, do you?"

I remained silent. Skoroseyev! Mr. Plutalov was an impatient man and had failed to protect his snitch. He hadn't even waited for a couple of hours! Or was something else going on?

"I don't care about your talk. But if you are denounced to me, what do you think this is all about? Are they making trouble?"

"Making trouble, sir."

"Perhaps they are ratting you out?"

"They're ratting me out, sir."

"Get back to work. You yourselves are your own worst enemies. Plotters. The universal language. Everyone understands everyone else. I am the boss, after all. I have to do something when I get denunciations."

Plutalov was so furious that he spat.

A week later I left the prospecting team, the blessed prospecting team, with the next party of prisoners to go to a big mine. On my very first day there I did a horse's or Egyptian slave's job of turning the wooden beam of the winch, pressing my whole chest against the beam.

Skoroseyev stayed on with the prospectors.

There was a camp amateur show and, after the master of ceremonies announced the next item, a traveling actor ran into the performers' room (one of the hospital wards) and gave a pep talk to the inexperienced participants. "The show's going well! The show's going really well!" he whispered in each participant's ear. "The show's going really well," he announced at the top of his voice, wiping the sweat from his hot brow with a dirty rag as he walked the length and breadth of the room.

It was all just like a proper show, and the traveling actor had himself been a proper actor in the outside world. Someone whose voice sounded very familiar was onstage reciting Zoshchenko's story "Lemonade." The master of ceremonies bent down toward me.

"Give me a cigarette."

"Have one."

"You wouldn't believe it," the master of ceremonies suddenly said. "If you didn't know who was reciting, you'd have thought it was that son of a bitch Skoroseyev."

"Skoroseyev?" I realized whose intonations the voice onstage had reminded me of.

"Yes. I'm an Esperantist. Got it? The universal language. Not some 'Basic English' rubbish. And I got sentenced because of Esperanto. I'm a member of the Moscow Esperanto Society."

"Under article fifty-eight, paragraph six? For spying?"

"Obviously."

"Ten years?"

"Fifteen."

"How about Skoroseyev?"

"Skoroseyev was the deputy chairman of the society's committee. It was he who sold everybody else down the river, got them all criminal cases."

"That little fellow?"

"Well, yes."

"And where is he now?"

"I don't know. I'd like to strangle him personally. I'm asking you as a friend"—the actor and I had known each other for no more than a couple of hours or so—"if you see him, if you come across him, just punch him in the face. A punch in the face and half your sins will be forgiven."

"So just half my sins?"

"They'll be forgiven, they will."

But the man who had recited Zoshchenko's "Lemonade" was now climbing off the stage. He was not Skoroseyev; he was a thin, lanky man, like a grand duke from the Romanov family: a baron, Baron Mandel, Pushkin's descendant. After a closer look at Pushkin's descendant, I felt disillusioned. The master of ceremonies was by now bringing his next victim onto the stage. "Over the gray plains of the sea, the wind gathers storm clouds...."

"Listen," whispered the baron, bending down to me, "call that a poem? 'The wind howls, the thunder rumbles'? There are much better lines than that. It's terrible to think that this was written at the same time that Blok wrote 'A Spell by Fire and Darkness' and Bely wrote 'Gold in Azure'...."

I envied the baron his lucky gift: being able to distance himself, escape, hide, conceal himself in poetry. I was unable to do that.

Nothing was forgotten. Many years passed. After I had been released I arrived in Magadan. I was trying to free myself properly to sail across that terrible sea over which they had brought me to Kolyma twenty years earlier. And although I knew how hard life would be in my endless wanderings from place to place, I didn't want to stay of my own free will for even an hour on that accursed Kolyma ground.

I was desperately short of money. A truck that was going my way, for a ruble a kilometer, got me to Magadan in the evening. The town was wrapped in white darkness. I did have people I knew there. I must have. But in Kolyma you look for your friends in the daytime, not at night. At night nobody will open a door, even if they recognize the voice. I needed a roof, a bunk, sleep.

I stood at the bus station, looking at the floor, which was completely covered by bodies, possessions, bags, boxes. As a last resort. . . . Only it was just as cold here as outside, about minus fifty. The iron stove was stone-cold, and the door was constantly being banged open.

"I think we know each other, don't we?"

I was glad to see even Skoroseyev in that ferocious freezing cold. We shook each other's hands through our gloves.

"Come and spend the night at my place, I've got a house here. I was released a long time ago. I built it on credit. I've even gotten married." Skoroseyev burst out laughing. "Let's have some tea. . . ."

It was so cold that I agreed. We spent a long time clambering up the hills and over the gullies of nighttime Magadan, which was wrapped in cold, murky white mist.

"Yes, I built myself a house," Skoroseyev was saying as I paused to smoke. "Credit. State credit. I thought I'd make myself a nest. A northern nest."

I drank plenty of tea. I went to bed and fell asleep. But I slept badly, despite the long journey. There had been something bad about that day.

"Well, I'm off. I've got someone I know here."

"Why don't you leave your suitcase? You'll find your friends and then come back for it."

"No, it's not worth climbing the hill twice."

"You could stay with me. We're old friends, in a way."

"Yes," I said. "Goodbye." I buttoned my fur jacket, picked up my suitcase, and grabbed the door handle. "Goodbye."

"How about the money?" said Skoroseyev.

"What money?"

"For the bed, for the overnight stay. It doesn't come free, you know."

"I'm sorry," I said. "I didn't think." I put down my suitcase, undid my jacket, groped in my pocket for the money, paid him, and walked out into the whitish-yellow mist of the day.

1965

SPECIAL ORDER

AFTER 1938 Pavlov received a medal and a new post as the minister of internal affairs for the Tatar Republic. It was clear how things were shaping up: whole brigades were employed to dig graves. Pellagra and gangsters, escort guards and dystrophy from malnutrition contributed all they could. Belated medical intervention saved whomever it could, or rather whatever it could, for the people saved had ceased forever to be human. At that time at the Jelgala mine, of the three thousand men who were listed as working there, only ninety-eight actually lasted; the others were let off work, or sent to the countless convalescent centers or convalescent teams, or were temporarily exempted.

In the big hospitals they introduced improved nutrition, and Traut's words "patients have to be fed and kept clean if their treatment is to be successful" enjoyed great popularity. Special diets were also concocted in the big hospitals; these consisted of a number of different menus. True, the ingredients didn't vary much and one menu often was no different from any other, but all the same.....

Then there was the special order, which the hospital administration was authorized to provide for seriously ill patients. These special orders were distinct from the hospital menus and limited: only one or two could be authorized for a three-hundred-bed hospital.

There was just one drawback: any patient who was prescribed a special order—pancakes, meat rissoles, or something else equally fabulous—would already be in such poor condition that he couldn't eat anything and would turn his head away in a moribund state of exhaustion after the merest lick of a spoon from one of these dishes.

The tradition then dictated that these regal leftovers would go to the person in the next bed or to one of the patients who had volunteered to help the male duty nurse and care for the seriously ill.

To have a special order served when the patient was no longer strong enough to eat anything was a paradox, the antithesis of the dialectical triad. The only possible principle behind the introduction of the special order idea was that it should go to the most emaciated and most seriously ill.

The issue of a special order was therefore a dreaded omen, a symbol of the approach of death. Patients would have been afraid of special orders, were it not that their minds were so clouded by then that they were not the ones who were horrified; instead it was those who were receiving the first menu on the dietetic scale, those who still could reason and feel, who were horrified.

Every day the person in charge of a hospital department was faced with an unpleasant question—who should have a special order today?—to which all answers seemed equally dishonest.

In the bed next to mine was a young man of twenty, who was dying of dystrophy from malnutrition (in those days it was called polyavitaminosis).

The special order was turning into the final meal a man sentenced to death might request on the day of his execution, a last wish the prison administration had to carry out.

The young man was refusing food—oatmeal soup, pearl-barley soup, oat porridge, pearl-barley porridge. When he refused semolina, he was marked for a special order.

"They'll cook you anything you like, Misha, anything. Understand?" The doctor was sitting on the patient's bed.

Misha smiled faintly and happily.

"Well, what do you want? Meat soup?"

"No-o-o." Misha tossed his head from side to side.

"Meat rissoles? Meat pies? Pancakes with jam?"

Misha tossed his head from side to side.

"Well, tell us, tell us...."

Misha rasped something.

"What? What did you say?"

"Dumplings."

"Dumplings?"

Misha nodded to show agreement; smiling, he lay back on the pillow. Bits of hay and dust fell out of the pillow.

The next day they made dumplings.

Misha came to life, took the spoon, fished a dumpling out of the steaming bowl, and licked it.

"No, I don't want it, it doesn't taste nice."

By evening he had died.

The second patient on special orders was Viktorov, who was suspected of having stomach cancer. For a whole month he was given special orders, and other patients were angry at him for not dying, for then he could have given his precious rations to someone else. Viktorov didn't eat anything and finally he died. It turned out he didn't have cancer; it was just the usual emaciation, dystrophy from malnutrition.

When Demidov, an engineer who'd had an operation for mastoiditis, was given a special order, he refused. "There are people sicker than me in this ward." He refused outright, not because the special order was something frightening. No, Demidov considered that he had no right to take a ration that might have benefited other patients. The doctors had wanted to do something good for Demidov, using the official method.

That's what a special order was.

date unknown

MAJOR PUGACHIOV'S LAST BATTLE

A LOT OF time must have passed between the beginning and end of these events, for months in the Far North can be counted as years, so great is the experience, the human experience, that is to be had there. Even the state recognizes this fact, since it raises the salaries and increases the privileges of those who work there. In this country of hope, but inevitably also of rumors, guesses, conjectures, and hypotheses, every event takes on a legendary quality even before some courier manages to swiftly deliver a local chief's report about that event to some "higher sphere."

There was talk that when a visiting top boss deplored the fact that cultural work in the camp was in bad shape, the cultural organizer, Major Pugachiov, told the visitor, "Don't worry, sir, we're rehearsing a show that will be the talk of all Kolyma."

The story could begin with a denunciation from the surgeon Braude, who had been posted from the central hospital to a district of military action.

It could also begin with a letter written by Yashka Kuchen, a prisoner and male nurse who was a patient in the hospital. He had written the letter with his left hand, since he had been shot in the right shoulder and the bullet had gone right through him.

Or we could start with Dr. Potanina's story: she hadn't seen a thing or heard a thing, and she'd been away on a trip when the unexpected events happened. It was this trip that the interrogator called a "false alibi," criminal inertia, or whatever the term is in the language of the law.

In the 1930s arrests happened to people by chance. They were victims of a terrible and false theory that the class struggle would intensify as socialism became established. The professors, party workers, military officers, engineers, peasants, and workers who filled the overcrowded prisons had no particular virtues except, perhaps, personal honesty or perhaps naïvety—in short, qualities that made the punitive work of the "justice system" at the time easier rather than harder. The absence of any single idea that might unite them fatally weakened the moral defenses of the prisoners. They were neither enemies of the authorities nor state criminals, and when they died, they still didn't understand why they had to die. Their self-respect or their resentment had nothing to focus on. Alienated from one another, they died in Kolyma's white desert—from hunger, from cold, from many hours of labor, from beatings, and from diseases. They immediately learned not to intercede for one another. This was what the authorities were striving to achieve. The souls of those who remained alive were subjected to complete defilement, while their bodies lacked the qualities needed for physical labor.

After the war these people were replaced by one shipload after another of repatriated Soviet citizens—from Italy, France, Germany—who were sent straight to the Far Northeast.

Among them were many men with different mind-sets, with habits picked up during the war—boldness, the ability to take risks, a belief in armed strength alone. They were commanders and soldiers, pilots and reconnaissance men.

The camp administration was used to the angelic patience and servile meekness of the Trotskyists, so they weren't in the least worried and they didn't expect anything new.

The new arrivals asked those "aborigines" who were still alive, "Why do you eat your soup and porridge in the refectory, but take the bread back to the barracks? Why not eat the bread with your soup, like normal people?"

Smiling with the cracks of their blue mouths, so as to show how scurvy had removed all their teeth, the local inhabitants replied to the novices, "In two weeks every one of you will understand why, and will do the same."

How could you tell them that they had never yet in their lives known real hunger, hunger that goes on for many years, that saps your will, so that you can't fight the passionate, obsessive desire to prolong the process of eating for as long as you can, to finish eating, sucking your bread ration in the uttermost bliss in the barracks, with a mug of tasteless water made from "heated" snow.

But not all the new arrivals shook their heads in contempt before moving away.

Major Pugachiov understood quite a few things. He had no doubt that they had all been brought here to die, to replace these living corpses. They'd been brought here in autumn, with a view to winter, when there was no prospect of running away; whereas in summer, even if you couldn't get away for good, at least you would die a free man.

So there would be all winter to weave the net of this plot, the only one in twenty years.

Pugachiov realized that the only people capable of surviving the winter and then escaping would be those who didn't do manual labor at the pit face. After just a few weeks working in a brigade, nobody would be able to run away to anywhere.

Slowly, one by one, the plotters infiltrated the support jobs: Soldatov became a cook, Pugachiov became the culture organizer; there were a paramedic and two foremen, while Ivashchenko, who had been a mechanic, was repairing weapons in the guards' section.

But none of them was allowed "outside the wire" without a guard escorting them.

The dazzling Kolyma spring had begun: not a drop of rain, no cracks in the ice, no birds singing. The snow disappeared little by little, as it was burned up by the sun. Wherever the sun's rays could not reach, the snow still lay in the gullies and ravines, like silver ingots, until the following year.

The appointed day dawned.

There was a knock at the door of the tiny guardhouse by the camp gates: the guardhouse had doors leading both into and out of the camp, and the rules stated that two men always had to be on guard there. The duty guard yawned and looked at the pendulum clock. It was five in the morning. "Only five," he thought.

The duty guard lifted the hook and let in whoever was knocking. It was a prisoner, the camp cook Soldatov, who had come to get the keys to the pantry. The keys were kept in the guardhouse. Soldatov came three times a day to fetch them, and he would then bring them back.

The duty guard had to open the kitchen cupboard himself, but he knew that there was absolutely no point checking up on the cook, that no locks would stop a cook who intended to steal something. So he entrusted the cook with the keys, especially as it was five in the morning.

The duty guard had worked more than a dozen years in Kolyma; he had been getting double pay for a long time, and he had put the keys in the cook's hand thousands of times.

"Take them," he said, as he picked up a ruler and bent down to draw lines on his morning report.

Soldatov went behind the guard's back, took the key off the nail, put it in his pocket, and then seized the guard by the throat. That instant the door opened and Ivashchenko the mechanic came into the guardhouse from the camp side. Ivashchenko helped Soldatov strangle the guard and drag his corpse behind a cupboard. Ivashchenko stuffed the guard's revolver in his pocket. Looking out through the window, they could see that the other duty guard was coming back down the path. Ivashchenko hurriedly put on the murdered man's greatcoat and cap, buckled up his belt and sat at the desk, as if he were the guard. The second guard opened the door and strode into the dark, kennel-like guardhouse. Instantly he was seized, strangled, and thrown behind the cupboard.

Soldatov put on the second guard's clothes. The two plotters now had weapons and military uniforms. Everything was going exactly according to Major Pugachiov's plan. Suddenly the wife of the second guard turned up at the guardhouse. She had also come for the keys, keys her husband had accidentally taken with him.

"We shan't strangle the woman," said Soldatov. She was tied up, her mouth was stuffed with a towel, and she was placed in a corner.

One of the prisoner brigades was on its way back from work. This had been anticipated. As soon as their guard entered the guardhouse he was disarmed and tied up by the two "guardhouse" men. The fugitives now had his rifle. From then on Major Pugachiov took over command.

The area in front of the gates was a field of fire for two guard towers at each corner manned by sentries. The sentries didn't notice anything peculiar.

Slightly earlier than expected, another brigade lined up to go to work, but who can say in the north what is early and what is late? It seemed a little earlier but may have been a little later than expected.

The brigade of ten men moved off in twos down the road to the pit faces. As the rules dictated, the escort guards in their greatcoats, one of them holding a rifle, strode six meters ahead of and behind the prisoners.

The sentry in the guard tower saw the brigade turn off the road down a path that passed by the guards' section building. This was where the soldiers of the guard service lived; the squad consisted of sixty men.

The guards' sleeping quarters were at the back of the building, while the squad's duty guard's quarters and a pyramid of weapons were right by the front door. The duty guard was half asleep at his desk and dimly noticed an escort guard leading a brigade of prisoners down the path past the guards' house windows.

"It must be Chernenko," he thought, not recognizing the escort guard. "I'll definitely report him." The duty guard was an expert at causing trouble and would not miss a chance to do something nasty to somebody, as long as it conformed to regulations.

That was his last thought. The door was flung open and three soldiers ran into the barracks. Two of them rushed to the dormitory doors, while the third shot the duty guard point-blank. Prisoners came running in after the soldiers and all of them went for the pyramid: they now had rifles and automatic weapons. Major Pugachiov violently flung the barracks dormitory door open. The soldiers, barefoot and still in their underwear, tried to rush to the door, but they were stopped by two rounds of automatic fire aimed at the ceiling.

"Lie down," ordered Pugachiov; the soldiers crawled under their bunks. A man with an automatic guarded the threshold.

The "brigade" began without hurry to change into military uniform, to stack up groceries, and to supply themselves with weapons and ammunition.

Pugachiov ordered his men not to take any food except for biscuits and chocolate, but as much weaponry and ammunition as possible.

The paramedic slung a first-aid bag over his shoulder.

Those escaping now felt they were soldiers again.

The taiga lay ahead, but was that any more terrible than the Stokhod marshes in western Ukraine?

They walked out onto the highway, where Pugachiov raised an arm and stopped a truck.

"Get out," he said, opening the cab door.

"But I—"

"I told you to get out."

The driver got out. Georgadze, a tank regiment lieutenant, took the wheel, and Pugachiov got in next to him. The escaping soldiers climbed into the back of the truck and it sped off.

"There's supposed to be a turn here."

The truck turned onto one of....

"We're out of gas!"

Pugachiov swore.

They went into the taiga like ducks diving into water and vanished in the enormous silent forest. Using a map, they kept to the fateful path to freedom, striding straight on, through the amazing Kolyma morass of fallen timber.

Kolyma trees die lying down, like human beings. Their mighty roots resembled the giant talons of a predatory bird, caught in a rock. Thousands of fine, tentacle-like offshoots descended from these gigantic talons into the permafrost. Every summer the permafrost retreated a little, and a brown tentacle root would immediately find its way down and fix itself in each inch of newly thawed earth.

Trees here did not reach maturity until they were three hundred years old; they lifted their mighty, heavy bodies slowly on such weak roots.

Pushed over by storms, the trees fell on their backs, their crowns all facing the same way, and they died lying on a thick layer of moss, bright pink or green in color.

The men began to pitch camp for the night. They were practiced and quick.

Only Ashot and Malinin were unable to calm down.

"What are you up to?" asked Pugachiov.

"Ashot is trying to persuade me that Adam was expelled from paradise to Ceylon."

"What do you mean, Ceylon?"

"That's what the Muslims say," said Ashot.

"Are you a Tatar then?"

"I'm not, but my wife is."

"I've never heard of that," said Pugachiov with a smile.

"Quite, nor have I," Malinin joined in.

"Well, time to sleep!"

It was cold. Major Pugachiov woke up. Soldatov was sitting with his automatic over his knees, fully alert. Pugachiov lay on his back trying to catch sight of the polestar, the walker's favorite. In Kolyma the constellations had different positions from those of Europe, of mainland Russia; the map of the stars was slightly askew, and the Great Bear drifted off toward the horizon. The taiga was silent and severe. The enormous gnarled larches were widely spaced. The forest was full of a worrying silence, familiar to any hunter. But on this occasion Pugachiov was not a hunter but a wild animal being tracked down, which made the silence of the forest three times more worrying for him.

This was Major Pugachiov's first night of freedom, a first night of liberty after the long months and years of his terrible stations of the cross. As he lay there he recalled the beginning of the drama-packed film that was now being shown before his very eyes. It seemed as if Pugachiov had personally shot the film of all his twelve lives in such a way that events were flashing past with unbelievable speed instead of keeping to their slow daily unfolding. And now came the credits, the "end of film," for they were free. And it was the beginning of battle, of a game, of life.

Major Pugachiov remembered the German camp he had escaped from in 1944. The front was getting closer to the town. He worked as a sanitation truck driver inside the enormous camp. He remembered accelerating the truck to full speed and smashing through the single fence of barbed wire, ripping out the hastily erected support stakes. Shots fired by the sentries, shouts, furious driving through the town in various directions, abandoning the truck, making his way by night to the front line, and then the meeting: interrogation in the special department. Charges of spying, a sentence of twenty-five years imprisonment.

Major Pugachiov recalled the visits by emissaries of General Vlasov and he recalled Vlasov's "manifesto," his visits to starving, exhausted, tormented Russian soldiers.

"Your authorities abandoned you a long time ago. Every prisoner of war is a traitor in the eyes of your government," said Vlasov's men, who then showed them the orders and speeches in copies of the Moscow newspapers. The prisoners of war already knew about this. It was significant that Russian prisoners of war were the only ones not to be sent parcels. The French, American, English prisoners, like all the other nationalities, received parcels, letters, had their own compatriots' clubs and made friends with one another. The Russians had nothing except for starvation and angry resentment of everything in the world. No wonder that many prisoners of war left the German camps to join the Russian Liberation Army.

Major Pugachiov didn't believe Vlasov's officers until he himself reached the Red Army units. Everything Vlasov's men had said was true. The state didn't want him, the state was afraid of him.

Then came the cattle cars with their bars and escort guards, a journey of many days to the Far East, the sea, the hold of a steamship, and the gold mines of the Far North. And a hungry winter.

Pugachiov sat up. Soldatov waved an arm at him. It was Soldatov who took the credit for beginning this enterprise, although he was one of the last to be drawn into the plot. Soldatov hadn't had cold feet, he hadn't lost his head, he hadn't sold them down the river. A fine man, Soldatov!

Captain Khrustaliov lay at Pugachiov's feet. Their fate was similar. His plane had been shot down by the Germans, he'd gone through captivity, starvation, an escape, a tribunal, and the camps. Khrustaliov now turned onto his side: one cheek was redder than the other, he'd been lying on it too long. Khrustaliov was the first man that Major Pugachiov had talked to, a few months earlier, about escaping. They'd agreed that death was better than a prisoner's life, that it was better to die with a gun in your hands than to die of starvation or to die at work from the guard hitting you with a rifle butt or his boots.

Both Khrustaliov and the major were men of action, and the negligible chance of success, for which the lives of twelve men were now being gambled, had been discussed in the greatest detail. The plan was to seize an airfield and an aircraft. There were several airfields here, and they were now heading through the taiga for the nearest one.

Khrustaliov was also the foreman whom the escapees had sent for after attacking the guard squad; Pugachiov refused to leave without his closest friend. And now Khrustaliov was sleeping nearby, calmly and deeply.

Next to him was Ivashchenko, a weapons expert who had been repairing the guards' revolvers and rifles. Ivashchenko had found out everything they needed to know in order to succeed: where the weapons were kept; who of the guard squad was on duty and when; where the ammunition stores were. Ivashchenko had been a reconnaissance man.

Levitsky and Ignatovich, two pilots, Khrustaliov's comrades, were fast asleep, huddled against each other.

Poliakov the tank driver had flung both arms over the backs of his neighbors, the giant Georgadze and the bald joker Ashot, whose surname the major had momentarily forgotten. Sasha Malinin, a camp paramedic, formerly an army paramedic, and now the Pugachiov group paramedic, was asleep, with his first-aid bag under his head.

Pugachiov smiled. Each man probably had his own idea of what this escape entailed. But the fact that everything was going smoothly, that they all understood one another instantly, was, Pugachiov knew, not just down to the major. Each man knew that events were unfolding as they should. They had a commander and a goal. A confident commander and a difficult goal. They had weapons. They had freedom. They could sleep soundly, as soldiers should, even in this empty pale-lilac polar night with its strange sunless light where the trees cast no shadows.

He had promised them freedom, and they had received it. He was leading them to their death, but they didn't fear death.

"And nobody betrayed us," Pugachiov was thinking, "right to the final day." Naturally, many people in the camp had known about the plan to escape. The selection of men had been going on for several months. Many people with whom Pugachiov had spoken frankly had refused, but nobody had run to the guardhouse with a denunciation. This was a circumstance that reconciled Pugachiov with life. "Fine men, fine men," he whispered as he smiled.

They ate biscuits and chocolate, then set off in silence. They were following a barely noticeable path.

"A bear's path," said Selivanov, a Siberian hunter.

Pugachiov and Khrustaliov climbed to a pass, to the mapmaker's tripod, and began surveying the ground below them through binoculars: there were two gray stripes, a river and the highway. The river was just a river; the highway was full of trucks carrying people over a stretch of several dozen kilometers.

"Prisoners, I expect," Khrustaliov suggested.

Pugachiov took a closer look.

"No, soldiers. They're after us. We'll have to split up," said Pugachiov. "Eight men should spend the night in the haystacks, and the other four of us will follow that gully. We'll be back by morning if everything is all right."

Passing through the undergrowth, they came to a streambed. It was time to go back.

"Take a look: there are too many of them, let's go upstream."

Breathing heavily, they quickly climbed upstream, and stones flew down, rustling and rumbling, hitting the feet of the soldiers attacking them.

Levitsky turned around, swore, and fell. A bullet had hit him right in the eye.

Georgadze, stopped by a big rock, turned and fired an automatic round at the soldiers climbing the gully. It stopped them only for a short time. His automatic fell silent, and only his rifle was firing.

Khrustaliov and Major Pugachiov managed to climb much higher, right to the pass.

"Carry on alone," the major told Khrustaliov. "I'll shoot."

The major took his time, knocking out every soldier who showed his face. Khrustaliov came back, shouting, "They're coming!" and then fell. People ran out from behind the big rock.

Pugachiov dashed forward, fired at the soldiers running toward him; then he threw himself from the pass on the plateau into the narrow streambed. In midair he grabbed hold of a willow branch, clung on, and clambered to one side. The stones he had struck as he fell rumbled and crashed even before they hit the bottom.

Pugachiov walked through the pathless taiga until he was exhausted.

The sun rose over the forest clearing, and the men hiding in the haystacks could clearly see the figures in military uniform coming from all sides of the clearing.

"Is this the end?" asked Ivashchenko, jostling Ashot Khachaturian with his elbow.

"Why should it be?" replied Ashot, taking aim. A rifle shot rang out, and a soldier on the path fell.

Gunfire aimed at the haystacks then opened up from all sides.

On command, soldiers dashed across the marsh toward the haystacks; shots rang out, the wounded groaned.

The attack was beaten back. Several wounded men lay on the hummocks in the marsh.

"Stretcher-bearer, crawl forward," an officer ordered.

The stretcher-bearer, a male nurse and prisoner, Yashka Kuchen, from western Ukraine, had been brought from the hospital as a precaution. Without saying a word, Kuchen crawled to a wounded man, waving his first-aid bag as he went. A bullet hit him in the shoulder and he stopped halfway.

The guard squad officer leapt out, unafraid. He came from the squad that the escapees had disarmed. He yelled out, "Hey, Ivashchenko, Soldatov, Pugachiov, surrender, you're surrounded. You can't hide anywhere."

"Come and take my weapon," shouted Ivashchenko from his haystack.

Bobyliov, the guard squad officer, ran toward the haystacks, his boots squelching in the marsh.

When he had run half the distance, Ivashchenko's rifle crackled, and a bullet hit Bobyliov right in the forehead.

"Attaboy!" Soldatov said in praise of his comrade. "The reason the officer's so brave is that he doesn't care. He'll be shot, or he'll get prison for letting us escape."

The fugitives were fired on from all sides. Machine guns were brought up; they rattled away.

Soldatov felt both his legs burn, and then he felt Ivashchenko, who'd been killed, thrust his head into his shoulder.

No sound came from the other haystack. About a dozen corpses lay in the marsh.

Soldatov kept firing until something hit him in the head and he lost consciousness.

Nikolai Sergeyevich Braude, the hospital's senior surgeon, was sent orders by a telephoned telegram from Major General Artemiev, one of the four Kolyma generals and the head of the guards of all the Kolyma camps. Braude was told to go to the settlement of Lichan and bring, in the words of the telegram, "two paramedics, bandaging material, and instruments."

Braude made no attempt to guess what was afoot. He quickly got everything ready and the hospital's decrepit little one-and-a-half-ton truck moved off in the required direction. The hospital truck, once on the highway, was constantly overtaken by powerful Studebakers laden with armed soldiers. The distance was only forty kilometers, but because of the frequent stops and the pileup of trucks ahead of it, because of the constant checks on papers, Braude took all of three hours to get there.

Major General Artemiev was in the local camp chief's apartment, waiting for the surgeon. Both Braude and Artemiev were old Kolyma hands, and this was not the first time that they were fated to meet.

"What's going on here? War?" Braude asked the general after they exchanged greetings.

"Not exactly war, but twenty-eight men killed in the first battle. As for the wounded, see for yourself."

While Braude was washing his hands in a basin hung by the door, the general told him about the escape.

"Why didn't you call out aircraft?" asked Braude, lighting a cigarette. "Two or three squadrons, then you could bomb them and bomb them. Or just use one atom bomb."

"You think it's all a joke," said the major general. "I'm waiting for orders, and there's no joking about it. I'll be lucky if I'm just dismissed from command of the guards. I could be court-martialed. Anything could happen."

Yes, Braude knew that anything could happen. Some years previously three thousand men were sent on foot, in winter, to one of the ports, where the stores that lay on the shore had been destroyed by a storm. In the course of that journey, only three hundred men of the original three thousand survived. The deputy chief of administration who had signed the order for the party of prisoners to go was sacrificed; he was put on trial.

Braude and his paramedics were extracting bullets, amputating limbs, and bandaging wounds until evening. The only wounded men were soldiers of the guard: there was not a single escaped prisoner among them.

Toward evening on the next day more wounded men were brought in. Surrounded by officers of the guard, two soldiers carried in a stretcher, on which Braude saw his first and only escaped prisoner. The fugitive was wearing a military uniform and only his unshaven face differentiated him from the soldiers. He had gunshot fractures in both shins, a gunshot fracture of the left shoulder, and a head wound with damage to the skull. The fugitive was unconscious.

Braude carried out first aid and, at Artemiev's orders, admitted the wounded man, along with his escort guards, to the big hospital where Braude worked and where he had the right facilities for a serious operation.

Everything was over. A military truck, covered with a tarpaulin, was parked nearby, and in it the bodies of the escaped prisoners were stacked. Next to it was another truck with the bodies of the dead soldiers.

The army could have been demobilized after this victory, but for many more days truckloads of soldiers drove up and down all sections of the two-thousand-kilometer highway.

The twelfth escapee, Major Pugachiov, was missing.

Soldatov's treatment took some time, until he was well enough to be shot. Actually, his was the only death penalty out of the sixty cases—the number of the fugitives' friends and acquaintances—that were tried by a tribunal. The chief of the local camp was given ten years. The head of the health service, Dr. Potanina, was acquitted by the court, and as soon as the trial was over she found herself a new job somewhere else. Major General Artemiev seemed to have been clairvoyant: he was removed, dismissed from his post in the guard service.

Pugachiov managed with some difficulty to crawl down through the narrow opening of a cave; it was a bear's den, its winter quarters, but the bear had long since left it and was wandering about the taiga. There was bear fur here and there on the cave walls and on the stones on the ground.

"How very quickly it all ended," thought Pugachiov. "They'll bring dogs and find me. And capture me."

Lying in the cave, he recalled his life, a hard life, a man's life, which was coming to an end now on a bear's track in the taiga. He recalled people, everyone he had respected and loved, beginning with his mother. He remembered Maria Ivanovna, his schoolteacher, who wore a quilted jacket covered with black velvet that had faded to a rust color. He recalled many, many other people whom he had been destined to come across.

But best of all, finest of all were his eleven dead comrades. None of the other people in his life had endured so many disappointments, so much deceit, so many lies. Even in this northern hell they had found enough inner strength to believe in him, Pugachiov, and to reach out for freedom. And to die in battle. Yes, those were the best people in his life.

Pugachiov tore off a bunch of lingonberries: a clump of bushes grew on a rock right by the cave entrance. Last year's blue, wrinkled berries burst when his fingers touched them, and he licked his fingers. The overripe fruit had no more taste than melted snow. The skin of the berries stuck to his dried-out tongue.

Yes, they had been the best people. And he now knew Ashot's surname: Khachaturian.

Major Pugachiov remembered them all, one after the other, and smiled at each one of them. Then he put the barrel of his pistol in his mouth and, for the last time in his life, he fired.

1959

THE HOSPITAL CHIEF

"JUST you wait. You'll trip up one day and get it in the neck," the hospital chief threatened me, using gangster language. The chief was Dr. Doctor,[33] one of the most menacing characters in Kolyma. "Stand up straight, properly."

I was standing "properly," but I was calm. A trained paramedic with a diploma is not to be thrown to the wolves, or abandoned to the mercy of Dr. Doctor. It was 1947 now, not 1937, and I, who had seen things Dr. Doctor could not even have imagined, was calm, waiting for just one thing: for the chief to go away. I was the senior paramedic in the surgical department.

This persecution had begun only recently, after Dr. Doctor discovered from my personal file that I had been sentenced under the acronym of KRTD, Counterrevolutionary Trotskyist Activity. Dr. Doctor was a member of the secret police, a specialist in political cases who had sent quite a few KRTDs to their deaths. And now he had in his hands, in his hospital, a paramedic who had graduated from one of his courses and who was meant to have been liquidated.

Dr. Doctor tried to get help from the local NKVD officer. But the NKVD officer was Baklanov, a young military man who'd served at the front. He wasn't interested in Dr. Doctor's dirty little tricks. Baklanov had special fishermen bringing him fish, he had hunters killing game for him—at that time the bosses were looking after themselves as never before. So Dr. Doctor found Baklanov quite unsympathetic.

"But he's just graduated from your courses. You're the one who took him on."

"That was a blunder by personnel. There's been a cover-up."

"Well," said the NKVD officer, "if there are any infringements or wrong actions, we'll remove him, obviously. We'll help."

Dr. Doctor complained that things were going to the dogs, and he began to wait patiently. Bosses too can patiently wait for their subordinates to trip up.

The central hospital was big; it had a thousand beds. There were prisoner-doctors of every specialty. The bosses, who were free men, not prisoners, asked for and were granted permission to open two emergency postoperative wards—one for men, the other for women—for nonprisoner patients in the surgical department. My ward had a female patient who was brought in with appendicitis; she was not operated on but was given conservative treatment. She was a cheerful, active girl. I believe she was the secretary of the Komsomol in the mine administration. When she was admitted, the surgeon Braude, a ladies' man, showed the new patient around the surgical department, chatting to her about . . . fractures and cases of spondylitis, and then showed her around one department after another. It was minus sixty outside and there were no stoves in the blood transfusion station; frost had obscured all the windows, and you couldn't touch metal with your bare hands. But the gallant surgeon flung open the doors of the transfusion station, and everybody staggered back into the corridor.

"This is where we usually receive women."

"Without much success, I expect," said the girl, warming her hands with her breath.

The surgeon was taken aback.

It was this enterprising girl who began coming to see me in my ward office. We had some frozen lingonberries, a whole bowlful, and we talked late into the night. But once, about midnight, the ward office doors burst open and in came Dr. Doctor, wearing a leather jacket, not a white gown.

"Everything in the department is in order."

"So I see. And who are you?" Dr. Doctor addressed the girl.

"I'm a patient. In the women's ward here. I've come for a thermometer."

"You'll be gone tomorrow. I'm putting an end to this disgraceful mess."

"Disgraceful mess? Who is he?" the girl asked.

"It's the hospital chief."

"Ah, so that's Dr. Doctor. I've heard of him. Will you get into trouble because of me? Because of the lingonberries?"

"There won't be any trouble."

"Well, just in case, I'll go and see him tomorrow. I'll give him a talking-to and take him down a notch. And if they touch you, I promise you—"

"Nothing will happen to me."

The girl was not discharged; she had her meeting with the hospital chief and everything died down until the first general meeting, at which Dr. Doctor delivered a report on the collapse of discipline.

"For example, in the surgical department the paramedic was sitting in the operating theater with a woman"—Dr. Doctor had confused the ward office with the operating theater—"eating lingonberries."

"Who was she?" people in the audience started whispering.

"Who with?" one of the free workers shouted out.

But Dr. Doctor gave no names.

Lightning had struck, but I didn't understand anything. A senior paramedic is responsible for food; the hospital chief had decided to strike the simplest blow.

The kisel jelly was weighed and ten grams were found to be missing. With great difficulty I managed to prove that it was served with a small ladle, but shaken out onto a big plate, so that it was inevitable that ten grams of whatever "stuck to the bottom" would go missing.

The lightning was a warning to me, even though there was no thunder.

The next day there was thunder without lightning.

One of the ward doctors asked me to save a spoonful of something nice for a patient of his who was dying. I promised I would and I ordered the server to leave a half or quarter of a bowl of soup from the special diet menu. This was against the rules, but it was always done everywhere, in every department. At dinnertime a crowd of the top bosses, headed by Dr. Doctor, burst into the department.

"Who's that for?" Half a bowl of special diet soup was being kept warm on the stove.

"Dr. Gusegov asked for one of his patients to have it."

"The patient whom Dr. Gusegov is treating is not entitled to a special diet."

"Call in Dr. Gusegov."

Dr. Gusegov, a prisoner whose file listed him as article 58, paragraph 1a, as a traitor to the motherland, turned white with fear when he faced the chief's bright eyes. He had only recently been taken on by the hospital after many years of applications and requests. And now he had taken this unfortunate measure.

"I never gave such an instruction, sir."

"So, mister senior paramedic, that means you are lying. You are trying to mislead us," raged Dr. Doctor. "You've gone too far, admit it. You've tripped up."

I was sorry for Dr. Gusegov, but I could understand him. I said nothing. All the other members of the commission—the chief doctor, the chief of the camp—were silent, too. Dr. Doctor was the only one ranting.

"Take off your gown and go to the camp. Manual labor! I'll see you rot in solitary!"

"Yes, sir."

I took off my gown and was immediately transformed into an ordinary prisoner to be shoved in the back, to be shouted at. It was some time since I'd lived in the camp....

"And where is the barracks for support staff?"

"You're not going there. Off you go to solitary!"

"There hasn't been a warrant for that!"

"Lock him up, and get the warrant later."

"No, I won't take him without a warrant. The camp chief has forbidden that."

"I reckon the hospital chief is senior to the camp chief."

"He may be, but my only superior is the camp chief."

I didn't have to stay long in the support staff barracks. The warrant was quickly drawn up and I entered the camp solitary confinement block, a stinking cell, like dozens of other solitary cells I'd been in before.

I lay down on the bunk and stayed lying down until the next

morning. The supervisor came in the morning. We'd known each other earlier.

"You've been given seventy-two hours solitary, with manual labor outside. Come on out, you'll get gloves and you'll be barrowing sand in the foundation pit for the new guards' building. It's been quite a drama. The head of Special Camp Centers was telling me about it. Dr. Doctor was demanding that you be sent to a punishment mine for life. . . . To move you to a numbered[34] camp. 'All that for nothing much at all!' the others said. 'If you get a punishment or a numbered camp for such minor things, then everyone has to be sent there. And we've been deprived of a trained paramedic.'"

The whole commission knew of Gusegov's cowardice; so did Dr. Doctor, but he only became more rabid.

"What are you on about? If we don't have manual labor and the wheelbarrow, then we don't have any punishment. If it's only a matter of spending a night in solitary, then it's a mere formality."

"All right, then: twenty-four hours with manual labor outside."

"Seventy-two."

"All right, fine."

So, after many years, I had my hands on wheelbarrow handles, on the three-man Special Tribunal[35] machine, which has two handles and one wheel.

I was an old hand at barrowing in the Kolyma. I was trained in 1937 at the gold mines in all the finer points of wheelbarrowing. I knew how to press on the handles to let the shoulders take the strain, I knew how to wheel an empty barrow back, wheel in front, handles held high, to let the blood drain back. I knew how to tip the barrow in one movement, how to extract it from the pile and get it onto the gangway.

I was a professor of wheelbarrowing. I was happy to push a barrow and show my stylish skills. I was happy to spin it around and to smooth the gangway with shingle. Nobody got any lessons. You just had the barrow, your punishment, and that was it. Work done by a man in solitary was not accountable to anyone. For several months I hadn't left the central hospital building; I'd done without fresh air. I used to joke that I'd had all the fresh air I could take, twenty years' worth at the mines, and that I wasn't going to go outside. And now I was breathing fresh air, remembering my barrowing trade. I spent two nights and three days doing this job. On the evening of the third day I had a visit from the camp chief. In all his time working in the Kolyma camps he'd never come across such extreme punishment as Dr. Doctor had demanded for a minor infringement; the camp chief was trying to understand why.

He stopped by the gangway.

"Good morning, sir."

"Your hard labor ends today, you needn't go back to solitary."

"Thank you, sir."

"But do a full day's work today."

"Yes, sir."

Just before the end of work, signaled by an iron rail being struck, Dr. Doctor turned up. He was accompanied by two of his adjutants: the hospital commandant Postel and the hospital orthodontist Grisha Kobeko.

Postel used to work for the NKVD. He was a syphilitic who had infected two or three nurses who then had to be sent to the venereal isolation zone, where infected women, all syphilitics, worked outside in forestry. Grisha Kobeko, a handsome man, was the hospital snitch, informer, and fabricator. These were worthy companions to Dr. Doctor.

The hospital chief approached the foundation pit, and three men wheeling barrows stopped work, got up, and stood to attention.

Dr. Doctor examined me with great satisfaction.

"So that's where you are.... That's the sort of job you should be doing. Got it? That's your sort of job."

Had Dr. Doctor brought witnesses in the hope of provoking something, if only some small breach of the rules? Times had changed, definitely. Dr. Doctor understood that, and so did I. A chief and a paramedic were not the same as a chief and an ordinary laborer. Not in the least.

"I can do any work, sir. I can even be a hospital chief."

Dr. Doctor swore obscenely and left in the direction of the free workers' settlement. The iron rail was struck, and I went off to the hospital, not to the camp or the zone as I had for the last two days.

"Grisha, hot water!" I shouted. "And something to eat after my bath."

But I had underestimated Dr. Doctor. The department was snowed under by commissions and checks almost every day.

Dr. Doctor was going out of his mind as he waited for the senior bosses to come.

Dr. Doctor would have gotten his hands on me, but other free chiefs tripped him up, pushed him out of a good job, and wrecked his career.

Suddenly Dr. Doctor was given leave and sent to the mainland, although he'd never asked for leave. Another chief replaced him.

There was a farewell round of the wards. The new hospital chief was a portly, idle man who breathed heavily. The surgical department was on the second floor, and they were moving quickly and gasping for breath. When he saw me, Dr. Doctor could not help creating a diversion. "That's the counterrevolutionary I was telling you about downstairs," he said loudly, pointing a finger at me. "We kept trying to remove him, but never got around to it. I advise you to do so immediately, at once. The hospital air will be all the cleaner for it."

"I'll do my best," said the fat new chief offhandedly. I realized that he hated Dr. Doctor just as much as I did.

1964

THE SECONDHAND BOOK DEALER

I WAS TRANSFERRED from night to day—a notable promotion, an affirmation, a success in the dangerous but lifesaving career of a male nurse who had once been a patient. I didn't notice who had replaced me. At that time I didn't have the strength to be curious. I was wary of making any movement, physical or mental. Somehow I had managed to be resurrected, and I knew how much any unnecessary curiosity would cost me.

But out of the corner of my eye I did spot, in my nocturnal, half-asleep state, a dirty, pale face sprouting thick reddish bristles, with sunken eyes of an indeterminate color and crooked frostbitten fingers hooked into the handle of a soot-stained cooking pot. The night in that barracks hospital was so impenetrably dark that the flames of the kerosene lamp, seeming to sway and shake in the wind, were incapable of illuminating the corridor, the ceiling, the walls, the door, and the floor, and extracted only a small piece of the whole night from the darkness: a corner of the bedside table and a pale face bending over that table. The new duty nurse was wearing the same gown I had worn on my shift: a dirty, torn gown, an ordinary patient's gown. In the daytime this gown hung in the hospital ward; at night it was pulled over the quilted jacket of the male nurse on duty, who was also a patient. Its flannel cloth was extraordinarily thin: you could see through it. Yet it didn't tear. Patients were too afraid or too weak to make any sudden movements, so the gown didn't fall apart.

The semicircle of light swung to and fro, it swayed, it changed. It seemed that it was the cold—not the wind, not a draft, but the cold— that was making the light swing over the duty nurse's bedside table. The face, grimacing with hunger, swung in this spot of light; the crooked fingers were scraping the bottom of the pot for whatever couldn't be

411

extracted with a spoon. Fingers, although frostbitten and devoid of feeling, were better than a spoon, and I understood the purpose of their movement, the language of the gesture.

I didn't need to know any of this. I was the daytime duty male nurse, after all.

But a few days later—a hurried departure, an unexpected speeding up of my fate, thanks to a sudden decision—and there I was in the back of a truck, jolted by every surge it made as it crawled up the frozen bed of some nameless stream, following the taiga winter road that slowly wended its way south to Magadan. In the back of the truck two people were flying about and hitting the bottom with a wooden thump, rolling around like wooden logs. The escort guard was sitting in the cab; I didn't know if I was being struck by a tree or a man. At one of our stops to eat, my neighbor's greedy chomping seemed familiar to me, and I recognized the crooked fingers and the pale, dirty face.

We didn't talk. We were both afraid of jinxing our luck, our prisoners' luck. The truck was in a hurry; the journey had to end within twenty-four hours.

We were both going to take paramedic courses; we had been seconded by the camp. Magadan, hospital, courses: that was all fog, the white Kolyma fog. Were there any milestones, milestones on the road? Would they accept someone convicted under article 58? Only paragraph 10? How about my companion in the truck? He also had paragraph 10— ASA, Anti-Soviet Agitation, which came under paragraph 10.

A Russian-language examination. A dictation. You get your marks the same day. Excellent. Written mathematics—excellent. Oral mathematics—excellent. Future students are exempted from the subtleties of the Constitution of the USSR, as everyone knew in advance.... I was lying on my bunk, dirty, likely still louse-infested; working as a male nurse hadn't gotten rid of the lice, but perhaps I was imagining things. Louse infestation is a camp psychosis. The lice may be long gone, but you just can't get used to the thought (is it a thought?), the feeling that there are no lice left: that had happened to me two or three times in my life. As for the Constitution, or history, or political economy, none of that was for us. In Butyrki prison, when I was still being interrogated, the block warden on duty yelled at me, "Why are you asking about the Constitution? Your constitution is the Criminal Code." And he was right. Yes, the Criminal Code was our constitution. That had been so for some time. A thousand years. The fourth subject was chemistry. My grade was "fair."

How eager the prisoners in the course were for knowledge, now that their lives were at stake. Here, former professors of medical institutes were eager to drum the lifesaving science into the heads of ignoramuses, blockheads who had never shown any interest in medicine —from the store man Silaikin to the Tatar writer Min Shabai....

The surgeon would twist his thin lips and ask, "Who discovered penicillin?"

"Fleming!" It was not me but my neighbor from the district hospital. His reddish bristles had been shaved. He still had unhealthily pale puffy cheeks (he had gobbled up the soup too fast, I rapidly worked out).

I was struck by what this red-haired student knew. The surgeon looked this triumphant "Fleming" up and down. Who are you, night-shift male nurse? Who?

"What was your job before you were arrested?"

"I'm a captain. A captain in the army engineers. I was in charge of a fortified district at the start of the war. We built the fortifications in a hurry. In autumn 1941, when the morning mist lifted, we saw the German heavy cruiser *Graf von Spee* in the bay. It shelled our fortifications point-blank. Then it left. I was given ten years. If you don't believe me, treat it as a fairy tale."

I believed it. I knew the procedure.

All the students studied through the night, absorbing knowledge with all the passion of someone sentenced to death who has suddenly been given hope of a reprieve.

But Fleming, after some businesslike meeting with the people in charge, cheered up, and when it was study time in the barracks he would bring along a novel and, eating boiled fish, the leftovers of someone else's feast, he would casually leaf through a book.

Catching my ironic smile, Fleming said, "It makes no difference. We've been studying for three months now, and everyone who's stayed the course is going to be allowed to pass, everyone will get their diploma. Why should I drive myself insane? You must agree—"

"No," I said. "I want to learn how to treat people. I want to learn to do it properly."

"The proper thing is to live."

That was the hour when it turned out that Fleming's captain's rank was just a mask, yet another mask on that pale prison face. The captain's rank itself wasn't a mask, but the army engineering was. Fleming had been an NKVD interrogator with the rank of captain. Information had been sifted and accumulated drop by drop over several years. These drops were a measure of time, like water-operated clocks. Or these drops fell on the bare head of somebody being interrogated: the water clocks in Leningrad's prison cells in the 1930s. Sand-filled hourglasses measured the prisoners' exercise time, water clocks measured the time needed to extract a confession, the interrogation time. Hourglasses moved fast, water clocks were agonizing. Water clocks counted and measured out not minutes but human souls, human willpower, which they destroyed drop by drop, wearing it away as water does a rock, in the proverbial phrase. This interrogator folklore was very popular in the 1930s, even in the 1920s, too.

Captain Fleming's words were collected drop by drop, and the treasure turned out to be priceless. Fleming himself considered it priceless, too: of course he would!

"Do you know what the biggest secret of our time is?"

"What secret?"

"The trials of the 1930s. How they were set up. I was in Leningrad then, you know. With Zakovsky.[36] Setting up trials is chemistry, medicine, pharmacology. Suppressing people's will by chemical means. There are an awful lot of those chemicals. And you don't think, do you, that if there are means of suppressing people's will, they won't be used? Are the Geneva Conventions going to stop them?

"If you have in your possession chemical means of suppressing willpower and you don't use them under interrogation, fighting on the 'internal front,' that is being far too humane. In the twentieth century you can't take those humane ideas seriously. This is the only secret of the 1930s trials, trials that were open, even to foreign correspondents, Lion Feuchtwanger[37] and his ilk. No doubles were used at those trials. The secret of those trials was the secret of pharmacology."

I was lying on one of the uncomfortable short double bunks in the deserted students' barracks; it was shot through by the sun's diagonal rays, and I listened to these confessions.

"There had been experiments earlier, in the trials of the 'wreckers,' for instance. Pharmacology, however, was barely relevant to the Ramzin[38] farce."

Fleming's stories oozed out drop by drop. Was it his own blood dripping onto my memory, which had now been stripped bare? What were these drops—blood, tears, or ink? No, not ink, and not tears.

"There were cases, of course, when drugs didn't work. Or the solutions used hadn't been calculated properly. Or there was sabotage. Then you had to have a backup system. Following the rules."

"Where are those doctors now?"

"Who knows? Probably in the next world."

The interrogator's arsenal: the latest in science, the latest in pharmacology.

It wasn't in cupboard A, *venena*, "poisons," nor was it in cupboard B, *heroica*, "strong drugs" (apparently, the Latin word *hero* becomes a strong drug in Russian translation). Where, then, were Captain Fleming's drugs kept? In cupboard C for "crimes," or cupboard M for "miracles"?

It was only through a paramedic course that a man who had at his disposal cupboards C and M, containing science's greatest achievements, learned that a human being has only one liver, that livers don't come in pairs. He also found out about the circulation of the blood, three hundred years after Harvey.

The secret was hidden in laboratories, underground offices, stinking vivaria where the animals stank just like the prisoners in the filthy Magadan transit camp in 1938. Compared with that transit camp, Butyrki prison was as polished and clean as a surgeon's theater, and smelled of the operating theater, not of the vivarium.

All scientific and technological discoveries are first tested for their military implications, military, even if it's only for the future or just a possible conjecture. Only what the generals discard, what isn't needed for warfare, is returned for general use.

Medicine and chemistry, like pharmacology, have long been preserves of the military. All over the world institutes of the brain have always been accumulating the results of experiments and observations. The Borgia poisons have always been a weapon of practical politics. The twentieth century has brought us an extraordinary flowering of pharmacological and chemical means for controlling the psyche.

But if fear can be destroyed by medicine, then the reverse can be done thousands of times: you can suppress human willpower by injections, by pure pharmacology and chemistry, without any "physical" means such as crushing ribs and trampling bodies with your boots, or smashing teeth in, or stubbing out cigarettes on the body of the person you are interrogating.

There were the chemists and the physicists, as the two schools of interrogation were called. The physicists were those who gave priority to purely physical methods and saw beatings as a way of laying bare the moral essence of the world. Once the depths of human nature were laid bare, how vile and contemptible it would appear. Beatings were a method of obtaining more than any statement: use of the stick devised and revealed things that were new to science, it led to the writing of verse and novels. The fear of being beaten, rations based on measurement of the stomach: these things accomplished great deeds.

Beating was a pretty substantial psychological weapon, and it was quite effective.

A lot of benefit came too from the famous and ubiquitous "conveyor," the process by which one interrogator took over after another, but the prisoner was not allowed to sleep. Seventeen days and nights without sleep would drive a man insane; this scientific observation was surely drawn from the interrogation offices.

But the chemical school would not concede victory.

The physicists could supply the Special Tribunals or any other threesome with material, but the physical-methods school was no good for open trials. The physical-methods school (that seems to have been the same as Stanislavsky's) was unable to put on an open bloody theatrical spectacle, it couldn't stage the open trials that made all humanity tremble. The chemists, however, were capable of staging such spectacles.

Twenty years after that conversation I find myself inserting into a story some lines from a newspaper article: "By using certain psychopharmacological drugs it is possible, for example, to remove completely a person's feelings of fear. And, what is very important, this does not in the least affect his clarity of mind.

"Later even more surprising facts emerged. The state and the behavior of people whose beta-wave sleep was suppressed for long periods, in this particular case for up to seventeen days and nights continuously, began to show various psychological disorders."

What is this? Extracts from evidence given by a former boss in the NKVD administration during a trial of former judges? Is it a deathbed letter by Vyshinsky or Ryumin?[39] No, these paragraphs come from a scientific article by a full member of the Academy of Sciences of the USSR. But all this was a hundred times more familiar, better tested and applied in the 1930s when the "open trials" were being staged.

Pharmacology was not the only weapon in the interrogator's arsenal then. Fleming mentioned a name I knew very well.

Ornaldo!

Of course! Ornaldo was a well-known hypnotist, who had in the 1920s often performed in Moscow's circuses, and not just Moscow's. His specialty was mass hypnosis. There are photographs of his famous touring performances, there are illustrations in books on hypnosis. Ornaldo was, of course, a pseudonym. He was in fact N. A. Smirnov, a Moscow doctor. His photograph was on all the posters on the street pillars—in those days advertisements were pasted to round pillars. Svishchev-Paolo's[40] photography studio was then on Stoleshnikov Lane. Their shopwindow had a gigantic photograph of two eyes, titled *Ornaldo's Eyes*. I can still remember those eyes and the mental disturbance I suffered when I heard or saw Ornaldo's circus performances. The hypnotist performed until the end of the 1920s. There are photographs from Baku in 1929 of Ornaldo performing. After that he stopped.

"In the beginning of the 1930s Ornaldo began working secretly for the NKVD."

When that mystery was solved, a chill ran down my back.

Fleming often praised Leningrad, unprompted. In fact, he admitted that he wasn't born there. Actually, Fleming was summoned from the provinces by the aesthetes of the NKVD in the 1920s, as someone suitable to replace those aesthetes. He had acquired tastes rather broader than those you get from a normal school education. Not just Turgenev and Nekrasov but Balmont and Sologub, too; not just Pushkin but also Gumiliov.

"'And you, the king's hounds and freebooters, / who keep your gold in a dark port....'[41] Have I got it right?"

"You have, completely right."

"I don't remember what comes after. Am I a king's hound? A state hound?"

Smiling at himself and his past, Fleming talked with reverence, like a Pushkin specialist talking about having held the quill with which *Poltava* was written; he mentioned the folders of the "Gumiliov case," referring to his conspiracy as the "lycée boys" conspiracy. You'd have thought Fleming had touched the Kaaba stone, so great was the bliss and exaltation of his every facial feature. I couldn't help thinking that this, too, was a way of approaching poetry. An astonishing and very rare path by which you could grasp literary values in an interrogator's office. Of course, this was no path for grasping the moral values of poetry.

"What I read first in a book are the footnotes, the commentaries. I'm a footnotes man, a commentary man."

"What about the text?"

"Not always. If I have the time."

For Fleming and his colleagues, contact with culture could only happen, however sacrilegious this sounds, in their work as interrogators. Getting to know people whose lives lay in literature and the social sciences was, nevertheless, in some ways genuine, authentic knowledge, not concealed by thousands of masks, even though it was distorted.

Likewise, the chief informant on the creative intelligentsia of those years, a regular, thoughtful, and qualified author of all sorts of memoranda and surveys of writers' lives was—and the name is surprising only when you first hear it—Major General Ignatiev.[42] *Fifty Years in the Ranks*. Forty years in Soviet intelligence.

"I read that book *Fifty Years in the Ranks* when I had already read the surveys and had been introduced to the author, or he was introduced to me," Fleming said pensively. "It's not a bad book, *Fifty Years in the Ranks*."

Fleming was not very fond of newspapers or the news they printed, or of radio broadcasts. International events didn't interest him much. Internal events were quite a different matter. Fleming's predominant feeling was one of grim resentment at the dark forces that had promised him as a schoolboy that he would attain the unattainable and that raised him to great heights before unashamedly dropping him without a trace into the abyss: I've never been able to remember properly how the song, so famous in my childhood, "The Moscow Fire Roared and Burned," ended.[43]

It was an odd way of communing with culture. Some short courses, a guided tour of the Hermitage. As the man grew, the result was an aesthete of an interrogator, shocked by the rough forces that had poured into the "organs" in the 1930s and then been swept aside and annihilated by the "new wave," which believed only in rough physical strength and despised not just psychological subtleties but even the "conveyors" and "endurance tests." The new wave simply didn't have the patience for any scientific considerations or profound psychology. It turned out that it was simpler to get results by ordinary beatings. The aesthetes who took their time ended up themselves going to the next world. Fleming survived by mere chance. The new wave didn't have the time to wait.

The hungry glow in Fleming's eyes died down, and the voice of the observant professional made itself heard again....

"Listen, I've been watching you during lectures. You've been thinking about something else."

"I just want to remember everything, remember it and write it down."

Pictures were moving about in Fleming's brain, which had calmed down and was now resting.

In the neurological department where Fleming worked, there was a Latvian, a giant who was given, with full official permission, triple rations. Every time the giant started eating, Fleming, unable to conceal his delight at this gargantuan trencherman, sat opposite him.

Fleming was never parted from his cooking pot, one that he had with him when he arrived in the north. It was a talisman, a Kolyma talisman.

Gangsters in the neurological department caught, killed, and cooked a cat. They treated Fleming, since he was the paramedic on duty, to the traditional "paw," a Kolyma bribe, a gift to your seniors. Fleming ate the meat and never mentioned the cat. It was the surgical department's cat.

The paramedic students were afraid of Fleming, but then they were afraid of everybody. By now Fleming was working as a paramedic in the hospital, he was an official "quack." Everyone was hostile toward him, everyone feared him, sensing that he was not just someone who had worked in the secret police but that he possessed some unusually important and terrible secret.

The hostility grew and the mystery thickened after Fleming made a surprise trip to see a young Spanish woman. She was a real Spaniard, the daughter of a member of the Spanish Republican government. She was an intelligence agent who was caught in a net of provocations, given a sentence, and abandoned in Kolyma to die. But Fleming, it turned out, was not forgotten by his old and now faraway friends, his former colleagues in the service. There was something he had to find out from the Spanish woman, something that needed confirming. She was sick and couldn't wait. But the Spanish woman recovered and was sent with other prisoners to a women's mine. Out of the blue, Fleming took a break from his hospital work and went to meet her, spending forty-eight hours driving down the thousand-kilometer truck highway, where there was a constant flow of vehicles and at every other kilometer a checkpoint staffed by special operations men. Fleming was in luck and came back from his trip safe and sound. This action would have seemed romantic, had it been done because of some camp love affair, but, alas, Fleming didn't travel because of love and didn't carry out heroic exploits for love. This was a question of something far greater than love, it was a higher passion, a force that would see Fleming through all the camp's checkpoints unharmed.

Fleming recalled 1935 very often: the sudden torrent of murders. The death of Savinkov's family:[44] one son was executed, while the rest—Savinkov's wife, two other children, and mother-in-law—refused to leave Leningrad. They all left letters, deathbed letters, for one another. They all killed themselves, and Fleming's memory had preserved lines from a child's note: "Granny, we're going to die soon."

In 1950 Fleming's sentence for his part in the NKVD case ended, but he didn't go back to Leningrad. He wasn't given permission. His wife, who'd kept for many years the square meters of accommodation they were entitled to, left Leningrad for Magadan, but couldn't settle there and went home. Just before the Twentieth Congress of the Communist Party in 1956, Fleming returned to Leningrad, back to the room he had lived in before catastrophe struck.

Frantic applications. A pension of 1,400 rubles a month, reflecting his long service. But this connoisseur of pharmacology, now enhanced by a paramedical education, was not to go back to his old profession. Apparently all the old employees, all the veterans of these cases, all the aesthetes who had survived, had been compulsorily retired—right down to the most junior courier.

Fleming found himself a job as a book buyer in a secondhand-book shop on Liteiny Avenue. Fleming considered himself to be a Russian intellectual by inheritance, even though he had such a peculiar relationship to and way of dealing with the intelligentsia. Fleming refused to draw a line between his fate and that of the Russian intelligentsia, perhaps feeling that only contact with books could preserve the necessary intellectual qualifications, provided that he succeed in living long enough for better times to dawn.

In the times of Konstantin Leontiev,[45] a captain in the army engineers could end up in a monastery. But the world of books is both dangerous and exalted. Living to serve books has a touch of fanaticism about it, but, like any amateur's love of books, it does contain a moral element of purification. After all, a man who once worshipped Gumiliov and was an expert annotator of Gumiliov's verses and fate could not take a job as a janitor. Could he switch careers and become a paramedic, his new specialty? No, being a dealer of secondhand books was better.

"I campaign all the time, I keep campaigning. Let's have some rum!"

"I don't drink."

"Oh, what a pity, how awkward that you don't drink. Katia, he doesn't drink! Can you believe it? I campaign all the time: I'll get my old job back in the end."

"If you go back to your old job," his wife, Katia, announced, her lips blue, "I'll hang myself, I'll drown myself the very next day."

"I'm joking. I'm always joking. I campaign, I'm always campaigning. I hand in various applications, I take legal action, I travel to Moscow. They've reinstated me in the party, after all. But not properly."

Fleming pulled out piles of crumpled sheets of paper from under his jacket.

"Read. This is a reference from Drabkina.[46] She was with me on the Igarka."[47]

I ran my eyes over an extensive reference from the author of *Black Rusks*.

"As the chief of a camp area, he treated the prisoners well, for which he was arrested and convicted. . . ."

I leafed through the dirty, sticky statements made by Drabkina. They had been perused many times by the authorities' uncaring fingers. . . .

Meanwhile Fleming bent over my ear and, his breath smelling of the rum he had drunk, explained to me in a hoarse voice that in the camp he at least had been a "decent human being," as even Drabkina confirmed here.

"Do you really need this?"

"I do. This is how I fill my life. Just in case, you never know. Are we drinking?"

"I don't drink."

"Ah! For long service. Fourteen hundred rubles. But that's not what I want—"

"Shut up, or I'll hang myself," yelled his wife, Katia.

"My wife's got a bad heart," explained Fleming.

"Get a grip on yourself. Write. You have a way with words. And a story or a novel is as good as a power of attorney."

"No, I'm not a writer. I campaign. . . ."

Spattering my ear with saliva, he whispered something quite absurd, as if there had been no Kolyma, as if in 1937 Fleming himself had spent seventeen days and nights on the interrogation "conveyor" and his mind had noticeably begun to crack.

"A lot of memoirs are being published now. Reminiscences. For example, Yakubovich's *In the World of the Rejected*.[48] And why not?"

"Have you written your memoirs?"

"No. There is a book I'd like to recommend for publication: you know which. I went to the Leningrad publishing house: they told me it was no business of mine."

"What book then?"

"The *Notes* of Sanson,[49] the Paris executioner. That would be some memoir!"

"The Paris executioner?"

"Yes, I remember. Sanson cut off Charlotte Corday's head and struck her cheeks, and the cheeks on the severed head blushed. And another thing, they used to have 'victims' balls.'[50] Do we have victims' balls?"

"The victim's ball was to do with Thermidor, it wasn't just about the time after the Terror. And Sanson's *Notes* are a fake."

"Does it really matter if they were a fake, or not? The book existed. Let's have some rum. I've tried a lot of drinks, and rum is the best. Rum. Jamaican rum."

His wife was getting dinner ready: great piles of some fatty dish that the glutton Fleming devoured virtually in an instant. Unrestrained greed had become a permanent feature, just like his psychological trauma, a lifelong affliction of thousands of other former prisoners, too.

I thought about the power of life, concealed in a healthy stomach and gut, in a capacity to devour things: that had been a defensive reflex of Fleming's life in Kolyma, too. Indiscriminate greed. The indiscriminate nature of his soul, which derived from his work as an interrogator, was also a preparation, a peculiar shock absorber for that fall into Kolyma, where Fleming never discovered any abyss, for he had known about it before, which is why he was saved and why his moral torments were assuaged, if he ever had any such torments! Fleming had never had any further mental traumas. He had seen the worst and he looked without caring at everybody around him perishing. He was prepared to fight only for his own life. Fleming's life was saved, but his soul bore a heavy trace that needed to be erased and cleansed by repentance. Repentance in the form of a slip of the tongue, a half hint, talking to himself aloud, without regret and without condemnation. "Simply, I was unlucky." And yet what Fleming told me was repentance.

"Do you see that booklet?"

"Your party card?"

"Aha. A nice new one. But it was all very complicated, very complicated. The provincial committee considered rehabilitating me in the party six months ago. The party secretary, some Chuvash, was offhand and rude: 'All right, I see. Put down this decision: Reinstate, but with interrupted record.'

"That really stung me: 'with interrupted record.' I thought that if I didn't immediately declare that I wouldn't accept the decision, then I'd always be asked in the future, 'And why didn't you say anything when your case was being considered? After all, the reason you're summoned in person for the case to be investigated is so that you can declare things in good time and say—' I raised my hand.

"'Well, what have you got to say?' Offhand and rude.

"I said, 'I don't accept the decision. Anywhere I go, any job I get, I'll be told to explain the interruption.'

"'Well, you don't hang about,' says the first secretary of the provincial committee. 'The reason you're so full of yourself is that you're well off. How much do you get for your long service?'

"He was right, but I interrupt him and say, 'I want complete rehabilitation without any interruption in my record.'

"The secretary suddenly comes out with, 'Why are you pushing so hard? Why are you getting so heated up about it? You were up to your neck in blood!'

"I had a rush of blood to my head. I said, 'And you weren't?'

"The secretary says, 'We weren't here then.'

"I say, 'And wherever you were in 1937, you weren't up to your neck in blood?'

"The first secretary says, 'That's enough of your lip. We can take another vote. Get out!'

"I went out into the corridor and they came out and told me their decision: 'Rehabilitation in the party refused.'

"I spent six months in Moscow on the warpath. The decision was canceled. But they decided only on the first formula: 'Reinstated with interrupted record.'

"The man who reported on my case to the Committee of Party Control told me I shouldn't have had a go at the provincial committee.

"I'm still campaigning, taking legal advice, going to Moscow and trying to get something done. Drink up!"

"I don't drink."

"This is brandy, not rum. Five-star brandy. For you."

"Take the bottle away."

"I really will take it away, I'll take it when I go. Don't be offended."

"I shan't be."

A year later I had my last letter from the secondhand book dealer: "My wife died suddenly when I was away from Leningrad. I came back six months later, saw the mound over her grave, a cross, and an amateur photo of her in her coffin. Don't blame me for being weak, I'm mentally fine, but I can't do anything. I seem to be living in a dream, I've lost all interest in life.

"I know this will pass, but it will take time. What did she get out of life? Going around the prisons for information and with parcels? Contempt from society, a journey to see me in Magadan, a life of poverty, and now this ending. Forgive me, I'll tell you more when I next write. I may be healthy, but is the society I live in healthy?

"Greetings."

1956

ON LEND-LEASE

THE FRESH tractor marks in the marsh were like the tracks of some prehistoric animal, far less like the delivery of American technology on lend-lease.

We prisoners had heard of these gifts from abroad, which disconcerted the camp authorities. The well-worn knitted suits, secondhand pullovers and sweaters that had been collected on the other side of the Pacific for the Kolyma prisoners were grabbed, if not fought over, by the wives of the Magadan generals. These woolen treasures were described in the bills of lading as "secondhand," which is of course much more expressive than the adjective "worn" or any abbreviations like "p/u"—previously used—which sounded familiar only to the ear of someone in the camps. The word "secondhand" has a mysterious vagueness about it, as if it had been held in someone's hand or kept in somebody's wardrobe at home, so that a suit could become secondhand without losing any of its many qualities, qualities that would be out of the question if the word "worn" had entered into the documentation.

Lend-lease sausages were not at all secondhand, but we saw those fabulous cans only from afar. Lend-lease canned pork in bulging cans was, however, a dish we knew well. Lend-lease canned pork, counted and measured out according to a complicated table for substitute foods, looted by the bosses' greedy hands and then once more recounted and again measured out before being allowed into the cooking pot, was boiled down until it had turned into mysterious threads that smelled of anything but meat; only the sight, but not the taste, excited us. The canned pork that got as far as the camp cooking pot had no taste at all. Camp prisoners' stomachs preferred something Russian, like rotting old venison, which even seven camp cooking pots couldn't boil down. Venison didn't disappear and become ephemeral the way canned pork did.

Lend-lease porridge oats were something we approved of and ate, but all the same we never got more than two tablespoons of porridge as our portion.

But inedible technology also came through lend-lease: tomahawks, which were hard to handle; spades, very easy to use with un-Russian short handles that did not take so much effort when loading the wagons. The spades were instantly converted to the Russian kind with long handles and the blade was flattened out to dig and hold as much soil and rock as possible.

Barrels of glycerin! Glycerin! The very first night, the night watchman took a pot and ladled out a bucket of liquid glycerin to sell it that night to the camp's prisoners as "American honey." He made a fortune.

Lend-lease also brought gigantic black fifty-ton Diamond M20 trucks and trailers with steel sides, also five-ton Studebaker trucks that could easily climb any hill. There was nothing to match these machines anywhere in Kolyma. Day and night, these Studebakers and Diamonds carried American wheat in handsome white canvas sacks up and down the thousand-kilometer highway. Our bread rations, plump loaves with no taste, were made from this flour. This lend-lease bread had one remarkable quality. Anyone who ate lend-lease bread stopped going to the lavatory: just once every five days the stomach produced something that could not even be called excrement. The camp prisoner's stomach and gut absorbed this splendid white bread, with its admixture of maize, powdered bone, and something else—perhaps just human hope—absorbing it entirely. The time has not yet come to count up all the lives that were saved by this overseas wheat.

The Studebakers and Diamonds went through a lot of gasoline. But the gasoline also came through lend-lease: it was light-colored aviation fuel. Our Russian trucks, GAZs, had been converted to run on charcoal gas; they had two tubular stoves placed near the engine, which were fueled by offcuts of wood. The word "woodburner" came into use, and there were several plants to produce the raw fuel; these plants were run by contracted party members. The technological management of these wood plants was the responsibility of the chief engineer, an ordinary engineer, a quantity surveyor, a planner, and several bookkeepers. I don't remember how many manual laborers there were, perhaps two or three, it might have been three, per shift per wood plant. We had lend-lease machinery; we got a tractor and it brought into our language a new word: "bulldozer."

This prehistoric animal was unleashed, let loose on its caterpillar tracks: an American bulldozer with a broad blade, a suspended metal shield that shone like a mirror. It was a mirror that reflected the sky, the trees, and the stars, as well as the prisoners' dirty faces. An escort guard even approached this overseas miracle and said he could use the iron mirror to shave with. But we didn't need to shave, and such a thing would never have occurred to us.

The sighs and groans of the new American beast could long be heard in the frosty air. In sub-zero temperatures the bulldozer coughed and lost its temper. It would start panting, grumbling, and then boldly move forward, crushing the hummocks and easily passing over tree stumps: our help from overseas.

We no longer had to skid trunks of Dahurian larch, as heavy as lead: construction timber and firewood was scattered all over the forest on the hill slope. Dragging trees by hand up onto stacks—which is what the merry word "skidding" means—is unbearable work in Kolyma, too much for human beings. Skidding manually over hummocks, along narrow winding paths on a slope is more than anyone can put up with. In the distant past, before 1938, they used horses, but the horses are even worse than human beings at enduring the north, they turned out to be weaker, and, unable to cope with the skidding, they died. Now we had the blade of an overseas bulldozer to come to our aid (was it ours?).

None of us found it believable that we would be given light work instead of the hard, backbreaking skidding that we all hated. We would just get a higher lumberjacking norm, we would in any case be made to do something else just as demeaning, just as despicable as any form of camp labor. The American bulldozer wasn't going to heal our frost-bitten fingers. But American solidol might! Oh, solidol, solidol. The barrel that solidol came in was immediately besieged by a crowd of goners, who instantly used a rock to smash the bottom of the barrel.

Hungry men were told that solidol was lend-lease butter, and there was less than half a barrel left when a sentry was put over it and the authorities used gunshots to chase the crowd of goners away from the solidol barrel. The lucky ones were swallowing this lend-lease "butter," not believing that it was just solidol: after all, the American bread that was so good for them was also bland and had a strange aftertaste of iron. Everyone who managed to get hold of solidol spent several hours licking their fingers, swallowing the tiniest drops of this overseas manna from heaven that tasted like fresh stones. After all, a stone doesn't start off as a stone but as a soft butter-like substance. Substance, rather than material. Stone becomes a material when it is old. The sight of young liquid tufa in limestone strata used to bewitch escapees and geological prospectors. It required an effort of will to tear oneself away from these blancmange-like shores, these milky rivers of young fluid stone. But tufa was found among mountains, rocks, landslides, whereas here we had a lend-lease delivery, something manufactured.

Nothing bad happened to those who'd dipped their hands in the barrel. A Kolyma-trained stomach and gut could cope with solidol. But a sentry was assigned to guard what was left, since solidol was food for trucks, creatures infinitely more important to the state than people.

And now one of these creatures had come to us from the other side of the ocean: a symbol of victory, friendship, and something else.

Three hundred men couldn't stop envying Grinka Lebedev, the prisoner who took the wheel of the American tractor. There were prisoners who were better tractor drivers than Lebedev, but they were all politicals, article 58 with the initials for anti-Soviet or counterrevolutionary on their files, while Grinka Lebedev was a nonpolitical, or to be precise, just a man who had murdered his father. Every one of the three hundred could see his earthly bliss: chirring away, sitting at the wheel of a well-lubricated tractor, to rumble off and fell timber.

Timber to be felled was getting farther and farther away. Harvesting construction timber in Kolyma is done in streambeds where, if the gully is deep enough, the trees stretch out toward the sun, are sheltered from the wind, and can grow tall. If they are in the wind, in the light, or on the marshy hill slopes, the trees are dwarfs, broken and twisted, exhausted by constantly revolving to catch the sun, by their endless struggle for a bit of thawed soil. The trees on the slopes are more like monsters fit for a chamber of horrors than trees. Only in the dark ravines where the mountain streams flow do trees grow and strengthen. Extracting timber is like extracting gold and is done on the same gold-mining rivers with the same urgency and haste: a stream, a box, a gold-washing pan, temporary barracks, a fast-moving, predatory market that leaves the stream and the whole area treeless for three hundred years and without gold for all eternity.

Somewhere there was supposed to be a forestry nursery, but what hope was there of a nursery in wartime Kolyma, where larches took three hundred years to mature, and when the only answer to lend-lease was a violent outburst of gold fever, bridled, however, by the guard towers of the prisoner zones.

A lot of construction timber as well as ready-chopped firewood lay scattered wherever trees had been felled. A lot of butt ends that had fallen on the ground had been buried in the snow, being too big for the fragile bony shoulders of the prisoners to lift. The prisoners' weak arms, even dozens of them, couldn't lift a two-meter piece of trunk onto someone's shoulder (and there wasn't a shoulder strong enough), so as to drag this beam, as heavy as cast iron, several dozen meters over the hummocks, ruts, and potholes. A lot of timber was abandoned because it was far too heavy to skid, and we needed the help of the bulldozer.

We saw the chirring bulldozer turn to the left and begin climbing onto a terrace, a piece of jutting rock where an old road ran past the camp cemetery, a road that we had been made to walk along to work hundreds of times.

I had shown no curiosity as to why for the last few weeks we had been taken to work by another route, instead of being sent up the familiar path, trodden smooth by the guards' boot heels and the prisoners' rubber boots. The new route was twice as long as the old one. There were constant climbs and descents. We were growing tired just getting to our workplace. But nobody asked why we were being taken by this other route.

We just had to, those were the orders, so we clambered on all fours, grabbing hold of stones, which made our fingers bleed.

Only now did I see and realize what the reason was. And I thanked God for giving me the time and strength to see it all.

Timber-felling was going ahead. The hill slope was laid bare; the wind had blown away the snow, which was not yet deep. Every single tree stump had been pulled out: the big ones had a charge of ammonal explosive put under them, so that the stump flew up in the air. Smaller stumps were twisted out, using big levers. The smallest were just torn out by hand, like bushes of dwarf pine.

The hill had been laid bare and turned into a gigantic stage for a spectacle, a camp mystery play.

A grave, a prisoners' common grave, a stone pit packed to the top as long ago as 1938 with still-undecomposed corpses, had now spilled over. Corpses were crawling across the hillside, exposing a Kolyma secret.

In Kolyma bodies are consigned not to the earth but to the stones. Stone preserves and reveals secrets. Stones are more reliable than earth. Permafrost preserves and reveals secrets. Every one of those close to us who perished in Kolyma, everyone who was shot, beaten to death, exsanguinated by starvation, can still be identified, even after decades. There were no gas ovens in Kolyma. The corpses wait in the stones, in the permafrost.

In 1938 in the gold mines there were whole brigades standing by to dig such graves. They were constantly drilling, exploding, and deepening enormous gray, hard, cold stone pits. Digging graves in 1938 was easy work; there was no minimum amount, no norm set for each dead person and each fourteen-hour working day. It was easier to dig graves than to stand with rubber boots on your bare feet in the icy waters of the gold-mine pit face, doing "basic production" of "metal number one."

These graves, enormous stone pits, were packed to the top with corpses. Undecomposed corpses, bare skeletons covered in dirty skin that had been scratched to pieces and bitten by lice.

Stone and the north resisted man's handiwork with all their strength. They did not want to let corpses into their depths. Stone, once it had given way, had been defeated and degraded, promised that it would forget nothing, that it would wait and keep its secret. The harsh winters and hot summers, the winds and rain had in six years taken the corpses away from the stone. The earth had opened and shown its underground stores, for the Kolyma's underground stores contain not just gold, not just lead, not just wolfram, not just uranium but undecomposed human bodies.

These human bodies were crawling down the slope, perhaps about to be resurrected. I had seen before, from a distance, on the other side of the stream, these moving objects that had gotten caught up by fallen branches or rocks; I'd seen them through a forest that had been thinned by loggers, and I had thought they were tree trunks that had not yet been skidded out.

Now the hillside was stripped bare and the mountain's secret revealed. The grave had burst open, and the dead were crawling down the stony slope. Right by the tractor road an enormous new mass grave had been hammered or drilled out. By whom? Nobody from the barracks was taken out to do that sort of job. It was a very big grave. If I and my comrades should freeze and die, there'd be room for us in this new grave, there'd be a corpse's housewarming.

The bulldozer was scraping out these stiffened corpses, thousands of them, thousands of skeletal dead men. Nothing had rotted: the twisted fingers, the toes with their infected sores, the stumps after frostbitten digits had been removed, the dry skin that had been scratched until it bled, and the eyes burning with the luster of starvation.

My tired, exhausted brain tried to understand the origins of such a gigantic grave in this region. There hadn't, I thought, been a gold mine here: I was an old Kolyma hand. But then it occurred to me that I knew only a small piece of this world that was bounded by a barbed-wire zone and guard towers that reminded one of the tented stages when Moscow's cityscape was being built. Moscow's tall buildings were the guard towers watching over Moscow's prisoners, that is what those buildings looked like. And who had priority? The Kremlin guard towers, or the camp towers that served as the model for Moscow's architecture? A camp zone tower was the main idea of the times, brilliantly expressed by the architectural symbolism.

It occurred to me that I knew only a small piece of this world, a negligible, tiny piece, that there might be only twenty kilometers away a cabin full of geological prospectors looking for uranium, or there might be a gold mine with thirty thousand prisoners. In the folds between the mountains a great deal could be hidden.

Later I remembered the eager fire of the willow herb, the furious flowering of the taiga in summer, when it tries to cover up any human activity, good or bad, in grass and foliage. I remembered that grass is even more oblivious than humanity. And if I forgot, so would the grass. But stone and permafrost wouldn't.

Grinka Lebedev the parricide was a good tractor driver and was managing the well-lubricated overseas tractor well. Grinka Lebedev was doing his job very thoroughly. He was scraping corpses toward the grave with his shiny bulldozer blade, pushing them into the pit, and then coming back to do some skidding.

The authorities had decided that the lend-lease bulldozer's first trip, its first job would not be forest work but a far more important task.

The job was done. The bulldozer had scraped up a pile of stones and rubble over the new grave, and the corpses had been covered by stone. But they had not vanished.

The bulldozer was coming toward us. Grinka Lebedev, the nonpolitical prisoner and parricide, didn't look at us politicals, 58ers with letters signifying our crimes. Grinka Lebedev had been entrusted with an assignment on behalf of the state, and he had carried it out. His stony face was etched with pride, an awareness of duty done.

The bulldozer rumbled past us. There wasn't a single scratch or stain on its mirrorlike blade.

1965

MAXIM

for Nadezhda Yakovlevna Mandelstam

PEOPLE were arising, one after the other, out of nonexistence. Someone I didn't know was lying next to me on my bunk, slumping at night against my bony shoulder, passing on his warmth, or drops of it, and getting my warmth in return. There were nights when no warmth reached me through the fragments of our pea jacket and quilted body-warmer; in the morning I would look at my neighbor as if he were a corpse and be just a little amazed that the corpse was alive, got up when called, dressed itself, and meekly obeyed a command. I had little warmth of my own. Not a lot of flesh was left on my bones. This flesh sufficed only for malice, the last human feeling to go. Not indifference but malice was the last human feeling, it was the closest to the bone. The human being that had surfaced from nonexistence vanished in daytime—there were a lot of sites in the coal-prospecting area—and vanished forever. I didn't know the people who slept next to me. I never asked them anything, and not because I was observing the Arab saying, "Ask no questions, hear no lies." I didn't care at all whether I would be lied to or not; I was beyond truth and lies. For such occasions the gangsters had a harsh, colorful, coarse saying, imbued with profound scorn for any questioner: "If you don't believe it, take it as a fairy tale." I didn't question or listen to fairy tales.

What did I retain until the very end? Malice. By hanging on to this malice, I counted on dying. But death, which had very recently been so near, began to recede little by little. It wasn't life that displaced death but a half-conscious state, an existence that couldn't be formulated or even called life. Every day, every time the sun rose, there was a new danger of a fatal jolt. But the jolt never came. I was working as the boiler man, the easiest of all jobs, easier than being a night watchman, but I could never chop enough firewood to keep up with the Titan boiler—Titan was the name of the hot-water system. I could have been thrown off the job, but where to? The taiga was a long way away, our settlement, our "posting," to use the Kolyma term, was like an island in the taiga world. I could barely drag one foot after the other, the two hundred meters from tent to workplace seemed endless to me and I had to sit down and rest several times. I can still remember all the gullies, the potholes, the ruts on that deadly path, the stream where I lay down on my belly to lap its cold, tasty, curative water; the two-man saw that I either lugged on my shoulder or dragged along the ground, holding it with one hand, seemed to me an unbelievably heavy load.

I could never get the water boiled in time or manage to have the Titan boiling by lunch.

But none of the workmen—they were all free men, only recently released from the camp—were bothered if the water wasn't boiling. Kolyma had taught us all to identify drinking water only by temperature. We could tell hot and cold apart, but not boiled and unboiled.

We didn't care about the dialectical leap between quantity and quality. We weren't philosophers. We were manual laborers, and our hot drinking water didn't have the important qualities needed for a dialectical leap.

I ate without any interest, trying to consume everything I caught sight of: trimmings, crumbs of food, last year's berries in the marsh, yesterday's or the day before yesterday's soup from the free workers' cooking pot. In actual fact, our free men never left any of yesterday's soup uneaten.

There were two guns, shotguns, in our tent. The ptarmigans weren't afraid of people and in the early days the birds could be shot from the tent entrance. The game was baked whole in bonfire ash or it was boiled, in which case it was carefully plucked. The feathers and down went to make pillows: that was a form of commerce, good money that boosted the earnings of those who owned the guns and the taiga birds. Ptarmigans, once gutted and plucked, were boiled in three-liter cans suspended over campfires. I never found any remains of these mysterious birds. Hungry, free stomachs hacked up, ground down, and sucked dry all the bird bones, leaving nothing. That was another miracle of the taiga.

I never even tried a piece of these ptarmigans. What I got were berries, grass roots, and the bread ration. And I wasn't dying. I began looking with less and less interest, without malice, at the cold red sun, the mountains, the bare stony heights where everything—rocks, the bends in the streams, the larches and poplars—was angular and hostile. In the evening a cold mist rose from the river and there was not an hour in the taiga day or night when I felt warm.

My frostbitten fingers and toes throbbed with pain. The bright pink skin on my fingers never lost its pink color and was easily damaged. My fingers were always wrapped in dirty rags, which protected my hands from further injury and from pain but not from infection. Pus oozed from both of my big toes, and there was no end to the pus.

I was woken up by an iron rail being struck. The same sound marked the end of the working day. After I'd eaten I lay down right away on the bunk, without undressing, of course, and fell asleep. I could only see the tent I slept and lived in through a mist: somewhere people moved about, loud obscene swearing broke out, fights started, there was an instant silence anticipating a dangerous blow. The fights soon died down—by themselves, for nobody restrained anybody or pulled people apart: it's just that the fight's engine stalled. Then the cold silence of the night would set in, with the pale high sky visible through the holes in the tarpaulin ceiling, with the snores, rasping, groans, coughs, and delirious swearing from the sleeping men.

One night I sensed that I could hear these groans and rasping sounds. The sensation was as sudden as a revelation; it gave me no joy. Later, recalling that minute of astonishment, I realized that the need for sleep, oblivion, and unconsciousness had decreased; I'd slept my full, as Moisei Kuznetsov, our blacksmith, used to say. He was an exceptionally clever man.

Real pain appeared in my muscles. I don't know if what I then had could be called muscles, but they hurt; the pain annoyed me and wouldn't allow me to think of anything but my body. Then something appeared other than malice or spite, but it coexisted with malice. What appeared was indifference and fearlessness. I realized that I didn't care whether I was going to be hit or not, whether I was going to get my dinner and my bread ration or not. And although I wasn't beaten while out prospecting, on a posting without guards (beatings only occurred at the mines), I remembered the mine and measured my courage by mine measures. This indifference and fearlessness formed a sort of bridge leading away from death. The awareness that I wouldn't be, wasn't being, or never would be beaten here gave rise to new strength and new feelings.

Indifference was followed by fear, but not a very strong fear, a fear of being deprived of this lifesaving life, the lifesaving job of a boiler man, or of being deprived of the high cold sky and the throbbing pain in my worn-out muscles. I realized that I was afraid of leaving here and going back to the mine. I was afraid, that was all. All my life I had always been satisfied with whatever was tolerable. With every day, there was more and more flesh on my bones. Envy is the right word for the next feeling to come back to me. I envied my dead comrades, men who had perished in 1938. I also envied my living neighbors who were chewing something and had something to smoke. I didn't envy the boss, the clerk of works, the foreman: theirs was another world.

What didn't come back to me was love. Oh, how distant love is from envy, fear, and malice. What little need people have of love. Love only comes when all other human feelings have returned. Love is the last to come, the last to return, if it can return at all. But indifference, envy, and fear were not the only proofs that I was coming back to life. Pity for animals came back before pity for humanity did.

As the weakest man in this world of open shafts and prospecting ditches, I worked with the topographer, hauling his measuring rod and his theodolite for him. Sometimes, to speed up our journey, the topographer would strap the theodolite to his back, so that all I had to carry was the lightweight rod with its painted numbers. The topographer was a former prisoner. To keep up his courage—there were a lot of fugitives in the taiga that summer—he carried around a small-caliber rifle that he had asked his bosses to let him have. But the rifle only got in our way. And not just because it was yet another thing to be carried on our difficult travels. Once we sat down for a rest in a clearing; the topographer was playing with his small-caliber rifle and aimed at a red-breasted bullfinch that had flown near to take a closer look at the danger and to draw it away. If necessary, the bird would sacrifice its life: the female bullfinch was hatching eggs somewhere, that was the only explanation for the bird's crazy boldness. The topographer raised his rifle, but I pushed the barrel aside.

"Put the gun away!"

"What's wrong with you? Are you mad?"

"Leave the bird alone, that's all."

"I'll report this to the boss."

"To hell with you and your boss."

However, the topographer didn't want a quarrel; he said nothing to the boss. I realized that something important had come back to me.

For several years I hadn't seen a single newspaper or book, and I'd trained myself a long time ago not to regret the loss. All fifty of my neighbors in the tent, that torn tarpaulin tent, felt the same way; not a single newspaper or book had ever appeared in our barracks. Our superiors—the clerk of works, the chief of the prospecting team, the guard—had descended into our world without books.

My language, my coarse miner's language, was as impoverished as the feelings that still survived around my bones. Reveille, lining up for work, dinner, end of work, time to sleep, please sir, may I speak, spade, shaft, yes sir, drill, pickax, it's cold outside, rain, cold soup, hot soup, bread, ration, leave me a cigarette end: for some years I had made do with about two dozen words. Half of these words were swear words. When I was a young man, a child in fact, there used to be a story about a Russian getting by when he traveled abroad with just one word repeated in different intonations. The wealth of Russian swear words, their inexhaustible offensiveness was not revealed to me in my childhood or youth. Here, that story about the single swear word sounded like a girl from a nice boarding school talking. But I wasn't searching for any other words. I was happy not to have to search for other words. I didn't know if they even existed. That was a question I couldn't answer.

I was frightened, overwhelmed when my brain—right here, I clearly remember, under the right temple bone—gave birth to a word that was utterly unsuitable for the taiga, a word that neither I nor my comrades could understand. I got up on my bunk and yelled out this word to the heavens, to infinity: "Maxim! Maxim!"

And then I burst into loud laughter.

"Maxim!" I roared straight into the northern sky, the double dawn; I roared it without yet understanding the meaning of the word that had been born within me. If this was a word that had returned, that had been found again, so much the better, so much the better! A great joy filled all my being.

"Maxim."

"Listen to that psycho!"

"He really is a psycho! Are you a foreigner, or what?" Vronsky the mining engineer asked me sarcastically, the same "three flakes of tobacco" Vronsky.

"Vronsky, give me something to smoke."

"No, I haven't got any."

"Well, just three flakes of tobacco."

"Three flakes? All right."

His dirty fingernail extracted three flakes from a pouch that was full of tobacco.

"A foreigner?" That question transferred our fate into the world of provocations and denunciations, interrogations and extra sentences.

But I didn't care about Vronsky's provocative question. What I'd discovered was too enormous.

"Maxim!"

This really was a psycho talking.

Malice is the last feeling a man takes with him into oblivion, into the world of the dead. Was it really a dead world? Even a stone, let alone grass, trees, a river, didn't seem to me to be dead. A river was not just an incarnation or a symbol of life, it was life itself. Its constant movement, its never silent burbling, its form of conversation, its business of making water run down with the current against a contrary wind, smashing through rocks, cutting through plains and meadows. A river, which transformed a bare riverbed that the sun had dried out, and with a barely visible thread of water made its way over the stones, submitting to its age-old duty, a stream that has lost hope of any help from the sky, hope of any lifesaving rain. The first thunderstorm, the first downpour, and the water has transformed the banks, broken rocks, thrown trees up, and is rushing madly down along its same eternal path.

Maxim! I couldn't trust myself, I was afraid as I went to sleep that the world that had come back to me would vanish overnight. But the word did not vanish.

Maxim. That could be a new name for the little river that ran by our settlement, our posting: the Rio Rita. In what way was that a better name than Maxim? The bad taste of the master of the earth, the topographer, had put the name Rio Rita on the maps of the world, and that couldn't be changed.

There is something Roman, firm, Latin about the word "maxim." In my childhood, ancient Rome was a story of political struggles, of people's struggles, while ancient Greece was the kingdom of art, even though there were politicians and murderers in ancient Greece too, and ancient Rome had its fair share of people of the arts. But my childhood years differentiated these two very different worlds sharply, simply, and narrowly. Maxim is a Roman word. It took me a week to understand what maxim meant. I whispered it, shouted it out, frightening and amusing my neighbors with it. I demanded a solution, an explanation, a translation from the world, from the heavens.... A week later I understood it, and quivered with fear and joy. With fear, because I was frightened of any return to a world I had no way of returning to. Joy, because I could see life returning to me against my will.

Many days passed until I learned to summon more and more new words, one after the other, from the depths of my brain. Each word found it hard to come, each one arose suddenly and separately. Thoughts and words did not come back in a flow. Each one came back on its own, not escorted by other familiar words, and it came back to my tongue before it came back to my brain.

Finally the day came when everyone, all fifty workmen, abandoned their work and ran off to the settlement, toward the river. They clambered out of their open shafts, their ditches, they abandoned trees they were sawing and soup half cooked in its pot. They were running faster than me, but I managed to hobble there in time by using my hands to run down the mountain.

A boss had arrived from Magadan. It was a clear, hot, dry day. There was a phonograph on the enormous larch stump by the entrance to the tent. It was playing something symphonic, the music drowning out the hiss of the needle.

Everyone, murderers and horse thieves, gangsters and *freiers*, foremen and manual laborers, stood around the phonograph. The boss was standing next to us. His facial expression suggested that he had composed this music for us, for our remote posting in the backwoods of the taiga. The shellac disc revolved and hissed, even the stump was revolving, wound up for three hundred revolutions, like a taut spring wound up for three hundred years....

1965

BOOK THREE
The Spade Artist

A HEART ATTACK

THE WALL rocked, and a familiar sweet sense of nausea swept through my throat. There was a burned match on the floor; for the thousandth time it flashed past my eyes. I stretched out a hand to grab this tiresome match. It disappeared and I couldn't see anything. The world hadn't entirely abandoned me; on the boulevard outside there was still a voice, the nurse's distant, insistent voice. Then I had glimpses of medical gowns, a corner of a building, a star-studded sky. An enormous gray tortoise loomed into being, its eyes shining with indifference. Someone pulled a rib out of the tortoise, and I crawled into a hole, clinging to whatever I could and pulling myself along with my hands, trusting only my hands.

I recalled other people's insistent fingers, skillfully bending my head and shoulders toward a bed. Everything went quiet; I was alone with someone as gigantic as Gulliver. I was lying on a board, like an insect, and someone was examining me carefully under a magnifying glass. When I turned over, this terrible magnifying glass followed my movements. I writhed under its monstrous lens. Only when the male nurses moved me onto a hospital bed and I felt the blissful peace of solitude did I understand that Gulliver's magnifying glass was no nightmare; it was the duty doctor's glasses. That gave me more joy than I could express.

My head ached and the slightest movement made me dizzy. I couldn't think, I could only remember, and frightening images from the distant past began to appear as black-and-white figures, like frames from a silent film. The sweet nausea, like anesthesia under ether, wasn't going away. Now I'd solved the mystery of that familiar feeling. I remembered the first time that a day off work was announced, many years ago, in

445

the north, after six months without a break. Everyone wanted to stay lying down, just lying down, without mending their clothes, without moving.... But we were all forced to get up in the morning and sent out to fetch firewood. Eight kilometers from the settlement there was a wood mill, and we had to choose as big a log as we could carry and bring it back. I decided to make a detour; about two kilometers further there were some old wood piles where you might find a suitable log. The climb was hard work and when I reached the pile, the only logs there were heavy ones. Further up, I could see the dark shapes of a once neat stack of wood that had fallen apart, so I started making my way there. Here the logs were not so thick, but the ends were trapped in the stack and I wasn't strong enough to pull one out. I tried several times, but only exhausted myself completely. Going back without any firewood, however, was out of the question, so I gathered my last reserves of strength and clambered even higher up the stack, which was lightly covered with snow. I spent a long time scraping away the porous squeaky snow with my feet and hands. Finally, I pulled out one of the logs. But it was too heavy for me. I unwrapped the dirty towel that served me as a neck scarf, tied it to the top of the log, and dragged it down. It bounced and hit my legs. Or it may have freed itself and was running downhill faster than me. The log kept getting stuck in dwarf pine bushes or jamming itself in the snow. I had to crawl up to it and make it move again. I was still high up on the hill when I saw that darkness had fallen. I realized that many hours had passed, and the path to the settlement and the zone was still a long way away. I gave my scarf a tug and the log again started bouncing and rushing downhill. I dragged it onto the path. When I looked at the forest it was swaying to and fro, and a sweet nausea swept through my throat. I came to my senses in the winch operator's cabin. He was rubbing down my face and hands with snow, and it stung.

I now visualized all this on the hospital wall.

But it wasn't the winch operator who was holding my hand, it was the doctor. There was a Riva-Rocci blood-pressure manometer nearby. I realized with joy that I wasn't in the north.

"Where am I?"

"In the neurology institute."

The doctor was asking questions. I found it hard to respond. I wanted to be alone. I wasn't afraid of my memories.

1960

A FUNERAL SPEECH

THEY HAD all died.

Nikolai Kazimirovich Barbé, one of the organizers of Communist Youth in Russia, a foreman and comrade who'd helped me drag a big rock out of a narrow open-pit mine, was shot for failing to fulfill the plan for the area his team was working on. Barbé had been reported on by the area boss, a young communist called Arm who got a medal in 1938, became a mining chief in charge of administration, and had a brilliant career. Nikolai Barbé had one thing he treasured: a camel-hair scarf, blue, long and warm, made of real wool. Thieves stole it in the bathhouse. They just took it when Barbé's back was turned. The next day Barbé had frostbitten cheeks, so badly frostbitten that the sores hadn't healed by the time he was shot.

Ioska Riutin died. He was my work partner, and good workers didn't want to have me as a partner. But Ioska did. He was far stronger and more nimble than I was. But he understood perfectly why we'd been brought here. And he didn't resent the fact that I was bad at the job. Eventually, the senior warden (that was what officials in the mines were called in 1937, just as they were under the tsars) ordered a "personal allotment" for me. What that means will be explained later. Meanwhile, Ioska worked with a different partner. But we were still next to each other in the barracks. Once I was awoken by an awkward movement; it was someone wearing leather and smelling of sheep. This person had his back to me in the narrow gap between the bunks. He woke my neighbor: "Riutin? Get dressed."

Riutin hurriedly started dressing, while the man who smelled of sheep began searching his meager possessions. Among them were chess pieces, which the man in leather set to one side.

448

"They're mine," Riutin said hastily. "My property. I've paid money for them."

"So what?" said the sheepskin.

"Leave them alone."

The sheepskin burst out laughing. When it was tired of laughing it wiped its face with its leather sleeve and announced, "You won't be needing them any more...."

Dmitri Nikolayevich Orlov, a former adviser to Sergei Kirov, died. He and I used to saw wood on the night shift at the mine and, still with our saws, we worked days in the bakery. I can remember well the tools store man giving us a critical look as he issued the saw, an ordinary two-handed cross-saw.

"Listen, old man," said the tools store man—in those days we were called "old men," unlike twenty years later. "Can you sharpen a saw?"

"Of course I can," Orlov said hurriedly. "Have you got a setting tool?"

"You can set it with your ax," said the store man, who had concluded that we knew what we were doing, unlike the other intellectuals.

Orlov went down the path, his back bent double, his hands stuffed up his sleeves. He was carrying the saw under his arm.

"Listen, Dmitri," I said bounding along to catch up with him. "I don't know how to do this. I've never sharpened a saw before."

Orlov turned to face me, stuck the saw into the snow, and put on his glove.

"I think," he said in a pedantic tone, "that it is the duty of anyone who has been to university to know how to sharpen and set a saw."

I agreed with him.

The economist Semion Alekseyevich Sheinin died. He was a kind man. It took him a long time to understand what was being done to us, but he understood in the end and began to wait calmly for death. He had the necessary courage. Once I received a parcel—it was very rare for a parcel to arrive—and all it contained was a pair of pilot's felt boots. Our relatives really had no idea of the conditions we were living under. I was only too aware that the boots would be stolen. They'd be taken from me the very first night. So I sold them before I even left the commandant's office; I got a hundred rubles for them from Andrei Boiko, the guard. The boots were worth seven hundred, but I'd gotten a good price. After all, I could now buy a hundred kilos of bread, or butter and sugar instead. The last time I had eaten butter and sugar was in the pretrial prison. So I bought a whole kilo of butter in the shop. I remembered how good it would be for me. That butter cost me forty-one rubles. I bought it in the daytime (we were working at night) and ran to see Sheinin—we were in different barracks—to celebrate the parcel's arrival. I'd also bought some bread....

Semion was both perturbed and happy.

"But why me? What right do I have?" he mumbled in his extreme anxiety. "No, no, I can't...."

But I managed to persuade him and, full of joy, he ran off to fetch hot water.

That very moment I was felled to the ground by a terrible blow to the head.

When I got back on my feet, the bags with the butter and bread were gone. A meter-long larch log, which I had been hit with, was lying by my bunk. Everyone around me was laughing. Sheinin came running with the hot water. For many years afterward I couldn't recall this theft without a terrible, almost traumatic anxiety.

Semion, however, died.

Ivan Yakovlevich Fediakhin died. We'd come here on the same train and the same ship. We ended up at the same mine, on the same brigade. He was a philosopher, a peasant from Volokolamsk, the organizer of the first collective farm in Russia. As many will know, it was the Socialist Revolutionaries who set up the first collective farms in the 1920s, and the Chayanov-Kondratiev[1] group lobbied the "people on top" about the advantages of collective farms.... Ivan Fediakhin was another rural Social Revolutionary, one of the million who voted for that party in 1917. He was sentenced to five years in prison for organizing the first collective farm.

In our very first Kolyma autumn of 1938 we found ourselves working together on the ore barrows by the notorious mine conveyor. There were two of these ore barrows, which had couplings. In the time it took the horse man to take one barrow to the ore-washing machine, it was all that two men could do to fill the other barrow up. There was no time for a cigarette, not that the guards would have let us smoke. But the horse man did smoke—an enormous roll-up made with almost half a packet of tobacco (tobacco was still available then)—and he left us enough at the edge of the pit face for us to take a puff or two.

The horse man was Mishka Vavilov, who used to be the deputy chairman of the Industrial Import Trust; Fediakhin and I just worked at the pit face.

While we threw the soil and stones into the barrow, we didn't hurry. We talked. I told Fediakhin about the norm the Decembrists were given at Nerchinsk, according to Maria Volkonskaya's *Notes*, fifty kilos of ore per man.

"And how much does our norm weigh, Vasili?" Fediakhin asked.

I calculated it as about six and a half tons.

"Well, the norms really have gone up, Vasili. . . ."

Later, when it was winter and we were starving, I got hold of some tobacco, begged, hoarded, or bought, and exchanged it for bread. Fediakhin disapproved of my "business dealings."

"It's not like you, Vasili. You shouldn't be doing it. . . ."

The last time I saw him was in winter by the refectory. I gave him six dinner coupons I had gotten that day for copying out documents in the office at night. I had good handwriting and that was a help sometimes. The coupons would only have been wasted; they were already date-stamped. Fediakhin got the dinners. He sat at table, pouring dumpling soup from bowl to bowl. The soup was extremely watery and didn't have a single piece of fat floating in it. Six coupons' worth of "shrapnel" porridge didn't amount to enough to fill a half-liter bowl. . . . Fediakhin didn't have a spoon; he licked the porridge with his tongue. And he wept.

Derfel died. Derfel was a French communist who had served time in the quarries of Cayenne. He was tormented not just physically, by the cold and by hunger, but morally. He refused to believe that he, a member of the Comintern, could have ended up here doing hard labor in the Soviet Union. His horror would have been lessened if he had seen that he was not the only one. Everyone he'd arrived with, and with whom he was living and dying, was in the same situation. He was a feeble little man, and beatings were now the fashion. . . . Once he was struck—just punched—by his foreman to keep him in his place, as it were, but Derfel fell down and didn't get up. He was one of the first to die, one of the lucky ones. In Moscow he had worked as an editor for TASS, the news agency. He spoke good Russian.

"Things were bad in Cayenne, too," he once told me. "But here they're very bad."

Fritz David died. He was a Dutch communist, working for the Comintern, and had been accused of espionage. He had beautiful wavy locks, deep-set blue eyes, and a child's lips. He knew virtually no Russian. I met him in a barracks that was so overcrowded that you could sleep standing up. We stood next to each other. Fritz smiled at me and closed his eyes.

The space between the bunks was packed tight with people. You had to wait if you wanted to sit down or squat, then you had to lean against some bit of the bunks, such as a pillar, or against someone else's body, to get some sleep. I was waiting, with my eyes shut. Suddenly something next to me collapsed. It was my neighbor Fritz David. He got up, embarrassed.

"I fell asleep," he said. He was frightened.

This Fritz was the first man in our party of prisoners to receive a parcel. It had come from his wife in Moscow. It contained a velvet suit, a nightshirt, and a big photograph of a beautiful woman. When he was squatting next to me he wore the velvet suit.

"I'm hungry," he said, smiling and blushing. "I'm very hungry. Bring me something to eat."

Fritz David went mad and he was taken away somewhere.

His nightshirt and his photograph were stolen on the very first night. Later, whenever I told people about him, I was always puzzled and indignant: who would want someone else's photograph, and why?

"Even you don't know everything," some knowing person I was talking to remarked. "That's an easy question to answer. The gangsters stole it for what they call a 'session.' For masturbating, my naïve friend. . . ."

Seriozha Klivansky died. He was a fellow student during our first year at university, and we met again ten years later in the Butyrki prison cell where prisoners were assembled for deportation. He was expelled from the Komsomol in 1927 for his lecture to a current politics circle on the Chinese revolution. He managed to graduate, and then worked as an economist for the State Planning Department, until circumstances changed there and he was forced to leave. He later won a place as a second violinist in the orchestra of the Stanislavsky Theater, until he was arrested in 1937. He was a sanguine person, a wit who never stopped being ironic. And he never stopped taking an interest in life and in events.

In the cell for deportees everyone walked around almost naked, pouring water over themselves, sleeping on the floor. Only a hero could have put up with sleeping on the bunks. Klivansky used to joke, "This is torture by steaming. Afterward, in the north, we'll be tortured by freezing."

The prediction was accurate, but Klivansky was no moaning coward. He was cheerful and outgoing at the mine. He enthusiastically tried to master the gangsters' vocabulary and was as happy as a child when he could use their expressions with the right intonation.

"Any moment now I'll blow my top," Seriozha would say as he climbed onto the top bunks.

He loved poetry and in prison often recited poems by memory. Once he was in the camps he stopped doing that.

He would share his last piece of bread, or rather, he was still sharing. . . . Which means that he didn't survive to the times when nobody had a last piece and nobody shared anything with anyone.

Diukov the foreman died. I never knew his first name. He was a nonpolitical: his crime had nothing to do with article 58. In the camps on the mainland he was a so-called collective chairman, fond of "playing his part," even if he was no romantic. He had arrived in winter and made an amazing speech at a meeting. The nonpoliticals used to have meetings—after all, men who had committed ordinary crimes or misdemeanors at work, just like professional thieves, were considered "friends of the people" who deserved rehabilitation, not castigation. They were unlike us "enemies of the people" who were condemned under article 58. Later, when the recidivists started to be sentenced under paragraph 14 of article 58, "sabotage (for refusing to work)," all of paragraph 14 was removed from article 58 and exempted from various punitive measures, inevitably leading to lengthy sentences. Professional criminals were always considered friends of the people, right up to and including the famous Beria amnesty of 1953. Many hundreds of thousands of unfortunates were sacrificed in order to justify Krylenko's "rubber-band" theory and the notorious "reforging" idea.[2]

At that first meeting Diukov suggested that he should take charge of article 58 prisoners, at a time when political prisoners usually had a foreman who was also political. Diukov was a good man. He knew that peasants were the best workers in the camp, excellent in fact, and he remembered that there were many peasants convicted under article 58. This is a reason to consider both Yezhov and Beria as especially wise, for they understood that intellectuals had a very low value as a work-force, and that the productive aims, unlike the political aims, of the camps couldn't be realized by the intellectuals. Diukov didn't go in for such arcane speculations: he was unlikely ever to have thought of anything except people's working capacities. The brigade he selected was composed solely of peasants, and he set them to work. This was in spring 1938. Diukov's peasants managed to get through the hungry winter of 1937–38. He never accompanied them to the bathhouse, otherwise he would immediately have realized what was actually going on.

They worked quite well; they just had to get the food they needed. But when Diukov asked for the food, the authorities refused outright. By extreme exertions, the starving brigade heroically fulfilled its norm. Then the surveyors, the bookkeepers, the guards, and the work clerks began cheating Diukov. He started to complain and protest more and more sharply, as the brigade's official production figures fell further and further and their food got worse and worse. Diukov tried to appeal to the top bosses, but they advised the appropriate employees to put Diukov's brigade and Diukov himself on the notorious "lists." This was done and they were all executed by shooting at the famous Serpantinnaya.[3]

Pavel Mikhailovich Khvostov died. The most terrifying thing about men who are starving is their behavior. They seem to be entirely healthy, but they are nevertheless half insane. The starving are always furious defenders of justice, as long as they are not too hungry and not excessively emaciated. They argue constantly, they brawl desperately. Normally, only one in a thousand quarrelers, even when extremely provoked, ends up in an actual fight. The starving, however, are always fighting. Quarrels arise for the most absurd and surprising reasons: "Why have you taken my pickax, why have you taken my turn?" A man who is shorter uses his feet to try and trip up his opponent. The taller man will fall on his enemy and fell him with his physical weight, then scratch, punch and bite. . . . All this is too minor to hurt anyone. It isn't lethal and far too often it happens in order to draw the attention of those around them. Nobody tries to break up a fight.

Khvostov was one such man. Every day he would brawl with somebody in the barracks and in the deep drainage trench that our brigade was digging. I'd gotten to know him in winter, so I had never seen his hair. His hat had earflaps and it was made of torn white fur. His eyes were dark, the shining eyes of a starving man. I would sometimes recite poetry and he would look at me as if I were an idiot.

Suddenly he began desperately to hit the trench rock with his pickax. The pickax was heavy, and Khvostov was swinging it from over his head, hardly stopping between blows. I was astounded by his strength. We had been together, both starving, for a long time. Then the pickax fell with a ringing sound to the ground. I turned around and looked. Khvostov was standing there swaying, his legs apart. His knees were bending. He rocked once and then fell facedown. His arms were stretched out before him; he was wearing gloves he darned every evening. His arms were now bared and both upper arms turned out to be tattooed. Pavel Khvostov had been an oceangoing captain.

I watched Roman Romanovich Romanov die. At one time he had been a sort of squad commander for us. He was the one who'd issued parcels and enforced cleanliness in the camp. Simply put, he had a privileged position that none of us, article 58 and "acronym" politicals (the common criminals called us "letter men," the senior camp officials' version was "literals"), could even dream about. The most we ever dreamed of was a job doing the laundry in the bathhouse or making repairs in the nighttime tailor shop. Moscow's "special instructions" forbade us everything but stone. Every one of us had a file with a special paper to say so. And yet Roman Romanov had this unattainable job. And, what's more, he had quickly learned all the ins and outs: how to open a box so that the sugar spilled onto the floor, how to smash a jar of jam, how to roll rusks and dried fruit under the trestle table.

Roman Romanov learned all this very quickly and avoided any acquaintance with us. He was strictly official and behaved like a polite representative of a higher authority with which we could have no contact. He never gave us advice. He would only specify that one letter a month could be sent, that parcels were issued from eight to ten in the evening in the camp commandant's office, and so on. Roman Romanov aroused astonishment, not envy, in us. Obviously, he owed his position to some lucky personal connection. In any case, he wasn't squad commander for long: a couple of months at most. Whether there had been one of the periodic checks on employees (these checks took place from time to time, and always on the eve of the New Year), or whether somebody had grassed him up, to use the picturesque camp expression, one day Roman Romanov vanished. He had served in the military, as a colonel, apparently. Then four years later I found myself on a vitamin expedition, where we were collecting dwarf pine needles, dwarf pines being the only evergreen tree in the region. The needles were taken hundreds of kilometers away to a vitamin factory, where they were boiled down and the needles turned into an astringent brown mixture that smelled and tasted awful. It was poured into barrels and distributed to the camps. At the time, the local medical authorities considered it to be the most easily available and indispensable means of preventing scurvy. There was an epidemic of scurvy, as well as pellagra and other vitamin-deficiency diseases. But anyone who happened to swallow even a drop of this horrible preparation would prefer to die rather than follow a course of such hellish medication. Orders were orders, however, and food was not issued in the camps until a portion of this medicine had been swallowed. The duty server would stand there with a special tiny ladle. You couldn't get into the refectory without passing the dwarf pine distributor: so what the prisoner most treasured—dinner, food—was irreparably ruined by this compulsory preliminary dose. This went on for more than ten years.... The better informed doctors had their doubts: how could this sticky ointment preserve vitamin C, which is extremely sensitive to any changes in temperature? This treatment was utterly useless, but the extract was distributed all the same. In the same area, near all the settlements, there were a lot of briar roses. But the authorities were reluctant to collect rose hips: they hadn't been mentioned in orders. Only much later, in 1952 I believe, was a document received from the local medical authorities, containing a categorical prohibition on issuing the extract of dwarf pine needles, because of the damage it did to the kidneys. The vitamin factory was closed down. But at the time I met Romanov, collecting dwarf pine needles was all the rage. They were collected by the goners—the slag from the mine, the rubbish from the gold-mine pit face—chronically starving semi-invalids. The gold-mine pit face took three weeks to turn healthy men into invalids: hunger, sleeplessness, hard labor for many hours on end, beatings. . . . New people were taken into the brigade, and Moloch chewed them up. . . . By the end of the season, Ivanov was the only man left on the brigade of which he was the foreman. The rest had ended up in the hospital, under the "mound," that is, buried, or sent on vitamin expeditions where they were fed once a day and couldn't get more than 600 grams of bread. That autumn Romanov and I weren't gathering dwarf pine needles. We were doing "construction" work. We were building ourselves a winter house (in summer we lived in torn tents).

The area was marked out by pegs driven into the ground, and we drove in two rows of spaced-out fence poles. The gaps between the poles were filled with clumps of frozen moss and peat. Inside, we made single-story bunks out of laths. There was an iron stove in the middle. We were given a daily ration of firewood, calculated by guesswork to last the night. Yet we didn't have a saw or an ax. Such sharp tools were kept by the soldiers guarding us, who lived in a separate tent that was heated and insulated with plywood. Saws and axes were given out only in the morning when we were lined up to go off to work. The reason was that the foreman of a neighboring vitamin expedition had been attacked by a group of common criminals. Such men were very prone to theatrical gestures, which they acted out so well that they would have made the director Yevreinov jealous. They had decided to murder the foreman and a suggestion by one of the criminals that they should saw his head off was greeted with delight. The foreman's head was sawed off with an ordinary cross-saw. That was why an order was issued forbidding prisoners to keep saws and axes overnight. Why just overnight? Nobody, however, expected to find any logic in orders.

How could you cut firewood up to fit the logs into the stove? The thinner pieces could be smashed with your feet, while the thicker pieces were just fed, starting with the thinner end, through the stove door as a whole bundle and burned up gradually. Someone would use their foot to push them in further; there was always someone keeping a lookout. The light from the open stove door was the only illumination in our house. Until the first snow fell the house was full of drafts, but then we raked the snow up against the walls and poured water over it to make proper winter quarters. We hung a piece of tarpaulin over the doorway.

It was in this shed that I met Roman again. He didn't recognize me. He was dressed like a "flame," to use the common criminals' expression, apt as always: tufts of cotton wool stuck out of his quilted jacket, his trousers, and his hat. Very likely, Roman had often been forced to run and get a "burning coal" to light some criminal's cigarette. His eyes shone with famine; his cheeks were as ruddy as ever, but they no longer reminded you of balloons, for they were now stretched tight over his cheekbones. Roman lay in a corner, noisily breathing in the air. His chin rose and fell.

"He's going," said his neighbor Denisov. "He's got good foot wrappings." Deftly pulling the dying man's boots off, Denisov unwrapped the foot wrappings, which were made from green blanket material and were still strong. "That's what you have to do," he said, giving me a menacing look. But I didn't care.

Roman's corpse was carried out when we were being lined up to be led off to work. His hat had also gone. The hems of his unbuttoned jacket dragged along the ground.

Did Volodia Dobrovoltsev, the steamer, die? Was steaming a job, or a personality trait? It was a job that aroused only envy in the barracks of article 58 prisoners. Having separate barracks for politicals in a general camp where there were barracks for nonpoliticals and professional criminals, all surrounded by the same barbed wire, was, of course, a mockery of the law. Nobody got any protection from attacks by gangs and the gangsters' gruesome score-settling.

The steamer controlled an iron pipe emitting hot steam. The steam was used to heat the rock ore and small stones that had frozen together. The workman would regularly scrape out the warmed-up stone with a metal spoon the size of a human hand, attached to a three-meter-long handle.

This was considered skilled work, since the steamer had to open and close the hot valves that led to the pipes from a booth where there was a primitive boiler. Being the boiler attendant was even better than being the steamer. Few engineers or mechanics convicted under article 58 could dream of getting a job like this, and not merely because it was skilled work. It was by pure chance that Volodia was chosen from a thousand others to do this job. It transformed him, however. He no longer had to think the eternal thought about how to get warm....The icy cold no longer permeated his whole being, no longer stopped his brain from working. The hot pipe saved him. That was why everyone envied Dobrovoltsev.

There was talk that he had gotten the steamer's job unfairly; the job was viewed as sure proof that he was an informer, a spy. Naturally, the gangsters always said that anyone who had a job in the camp as a male nurse was drinking the workers' blood. People knew what could come of this sort of reasoning: envy leads people to do bad things. Volodia immediately acquired immeasurable status in our eyes, as if we had discovered we had a remarkable violinist among us. The fact that Dobrovoltsev, because his job dictated it, left the barracks on his own and left the camp through the guardhouse, opening the guardhouse window and shouting out his number "twenty-five" in a loud, happy voice, was an anomaly we couldn't get used to.

Sometimes he worked near our pit face. Using our rights as acquaintances, we took turns running up and warming ourselves on his pipe. The pipe was four centimeters in diameter, so that when you held it in your clenched fist you could feel the warmth spreading from your hands to your body. It was impossible to tear yourself away and go back to the pit face, to the subzero cold.

Volodia, unlike other steamers, never drove us away. He never said a word to us, although I knew that steamers were forbidden to let people like us warm themselves by the pipes. He stood there, surrounded by clouds of thick white steam. His clothes were iced up. Every fiber on his pea jacket shone like a crystal needle. He never talked to us. The job was, obviously, far too precious for that.

That Christmas Eve we were sitting around the stove. Because of the holiday, its iron sides were redder than usual. You immediately sensed the difference in temperature. Sitting around the stove, we felt sleepy, we felt lyrical.

"It'd be good, pals, to go back home. Miracles do happen...." said Glebov the horse man, who used to be a professor of philosophy and was notorious in our barracks for having forgotten his wife's name a month previously. "Only, let's have the truth...."

"Home?"

"Yes."

"I'll tell you the truth," I replied. "I'd rather go back to prison. I'm not joking. I wouldn't like to go back to my family now. They'll never understand me, they can't possibly. I know that whatever they think is important is actually nothing. What's important to me, what little I've got left, they can't possibly understand or feel. I'll just inflict more fear on them, one more fear to add to the thousands that their lives are full of. What I've seen here no person should see or even know about. Prison is quite different. It's the only place I know where people aren't afraid to say what they think. Where they get some spiritual rest. They get physical rest, too, because they don't work. In prison every hour of your existence makes sense."

"What nonsense you're talking," said the former professor of philosophy. "It's because you weren't beaten under interrogation. Anyone who was subjected to method number three[4] will have a different opinion...."

"Piotr Ivanych, what do you say to that?"

Piotr Ivanovich Timofeyev, who used to be the manager of a government company in the Urals, smiled and winked at Glebov.

"I'd go home to my wife, Agnia. I'd buy a loaf of rye bread. I'd make myself some millet porridge: a couple of gallons of it. And another couple of gallons of dumpling soup! And I'd eat the lot. For the first time in my life I'd eat my fill of the stuff and I'd make Agnia eat the leftovers."

"How about you?" Glebov turned to Zvonkov, the getter in our mine, who in his former life had been a peasant in the provinces, Yaroslavl or Kostroma, or somewhere similar.

"Home," Zvonkov said gravely, without a smile. "I think I'd go there and not move an inch from my wife. Wherever she goes, I go, wherever she goes, I go. The trouble is I've been made to forget my work here, I've lost my love for the land. Well, I'll find some job somewhere...."

"How about you?" Glebov touched our orderly's knee with his hand.

"First thing, I'd go to the Party District Committee. I remember there used to be masses of cigarette butts on the floor."

"Don't joke, please...."

"I'm not joking."

Suddenly I realized that only one person hadn't answered yet: it was Volodia Dobrovoltsev. He raised his head, not waiting to be asked. The light of the glowing coals came from the open stove door and shone into his eyes, which were alive and deep.

"As for me," his voice was calm and unhurried, "I'd like to be a stump. A human stump, you know, with no arms or legs. Then I'd find the strength to spit in their ugly mugs for everything they've been doing to us."

1960

HOW IT BEGAN

HOW DID it begin? On what winter day did the wind change and everything become frightening? In autumn we were still work—

How did it begin? Kliuyev's brigade was detained at work. Such a thing was unheard-of. The pit face was surrounded by the guards. It was a cross section, a gigantic pit, and the guards took up position around its edges. The inside of the pit was seething with people who were in a hurry to catch up with each other. Some did so with concealed alarm, others with the firm belief that today, this evening, were chance events. When dawn and morning came, it would all go away, things would be clearer and life would go on as before, albeit in camp fashion. Being detained at work: why? Before the day's allotted work was finished. The blizzard screeched at a high pitch; the fine dry snow felt like sand hitting your cheeks. In the triangular beams of the floodlights that illuminated the pit faces at night, the snow swirled like specks of dust in a sunbeam, reminding me of the specks of dust in a sunbeam by the doors of my father's shed. Except that in my childhood everything was small, warm, alive. Here everything was enormous, cold, and antagonistic. The wooden boxes, in which the earth and stones were carted out to the dump, screeched. Four men would take hold of a box, pushing, pulling, rolling, shoving, and dragging it to the edge of the dump, where they turned it around and tipped it over to pour the frozen stones into the ravine. The stones rolled down without much noise. There was Krupiansky in one place, Neiman in another, the foreman Kliuyev in yet another. All of them were in a hurry, but the work was never-ending. The siren had sounded at five, the mine siren had hooted and shrieked at five, when the brigade was allowed "home," but it was about eleven at night now. "Home" meant barracks. Tomorrow at five in the morning it would be reveille and a new working day and a new target for the day. Our brigade had taken over from Kliuyev's at this pit face. Today we'd been set to work at a neighboring pit face; only at midnight did we take over from Kliuyev's brigade.

How did it begin? A large number, a very large number of soldiers had suddenly come to the mine. Two new barracks, which the prisoners had built of logs for themselves, were handed over to the guards. We were left to spend the winter in tents, torn tarpaulin tents, pierced by stones from the explosions in the pit face. The tents were insulated: pillars were rammed into the earth and tarred paper was stretched over laths. Between the tent and the tarred paper there was a layer of air. We were told we could stuff the space with snow. But all that came later. Our barracks were handed over to the guards—that was the key fact. The guards didn't like these barracks: they were made of unseasoned timber: larch is a treacherous wood, it doesn't like people, and the walls, floors and ceilings still hadn't dried out after a whole winter. Everyone knew that before: those whose flanks were supposed to dry out the barracks, and those who found themselves taking the barracks over. The guards accepted their misfortune as just another inconvenience of the north.

Why were there guards at the Partisan mine? It was a small mine, which had no more than two or three prisoners in 1937. The Partisan's neighbors, the Storm mine and the Berzin mine (its name was changed to Upper At-Uriakh when Berzin was shot), were towns with a population of between twelve and fourteen thousand prisoners. Of course, the maelstroms of death in 1938 made big changes to those numbers. But all that came later. Why did Partisan have to have a guard now? In 1937 the Partisan mine had just one soldier, always on duty, armed with a revolver. He had no trouble maintaining order in this peaceful kingdom of "Trotskyists." And the gangsters? The duty guard turned a blind eye to their robbery expeditions and tours, and made sure he was diplomatically absent when things got especially critical. Everything was "quiet." Yet now there was suddenly a horde of guards. Why?

Suddenly a whole brigade of objectors, men who refused to work, was taken away: they were "Trotskyists" who in those days were not yet classified as objectors, but far less harshly as "non-working." They lived in a separate barracks in the middle of the settlement, a prisoners' settlement that was not enclosed and did not yet have the terrible name it would soon, very soon, have—"the zone." Trotskyists received what was then their legal due: six hundred grams of bread a day and whatever hot food was specified. Their exemption from work was completely official. Any prisoner could join them and move to a non-working barracks. In autumn 1937 there were seventy-five men in that barracks. All of them suddenly vanished, the door swung open in the wind, and inside there was a dead, black emptiness.

It suddenly turned out that there was a shortage of official rations, of the bread ration, that however much you wanted to eat you couldn't buy anything, or ask a fellow prisoner for anything. You might still ask a comrade for a herring or a piece of herring, but bread? Suddenly things got so bad that nobody gave anyone anything to eat, everyone began eating, chewing something furtively, hurriedly, in the dark, groping about in their pockets for crumbs of bread. Searching for crumbs became an almost automatic action whenever a person had a free moment. But there were fewer and fewer free moments. An enormous barrel of cod-liver oil had always stood in the cobbler's workshop. The barrel was waist-high, and anyone who wanted to could dip dirty rags into the barrel and grease their boots. It took me some time to realize that cod-liver oil was edible: it was an edible fat, it was nutritious, you could eat this boot grease. The moment of illumination was like Archimedes's "Eureka!" I rushed, or rather, staggered off to the workshop. Alas, the barrel had been emptied a long time ago. Other people had gone down the road I had only just set off on.

Dogs, German shepherds, were brought to the mine. Dogs?

How did it begin? The pit face getters weren't paid for November. I remember the first months working at the mine, August and September, when a mine warden (the term must have survived from the times of Nekrasov, from the 1870s) stopped to look at us toiling away and said, "Bad work, boys, bad. If you work like that you'll have nothing to send home." After a month we would find out that each man had earned something. Some mailed the money home to reassure their families. Others used the money to buy cigarettes, canned dairy products, white bread in the camp shop, or rather stall. All that stopped suddenly, out of the blue. A rumor spread like a gust of wind through the grapevine that no more money would be paid. This grapevine news, like everything else on the camp grapevine, turned out to be completely true. Any payment would be made only in food. The same went for the camp employees, whose name was legion, as well as the production bosses, whose numbers had multiplied plenty of times. The armed camp guards, the soldiers, would be supervising fulfillment of the plan.

How did it begin? A heavy blizzard raged for several days, blocking the roads with snow and closing the pass over the mountains. The very first day that the snow stopped falling—during the blizzard we stayed at home—we were not taken home after work. Surrounded by guards, we slowly walked at our casual prisoners' pace for several hours over unfamiliar paths toward the pass, climbing higher and higher. Fatigue, the steep ascent, the rarefied air, hunger, resentment—everything slowed us down. The guards urged us on with shouts that were like lashes from a whip. It was now getting completely dark—there were no stars shining—when we saw the lights of many campfires on the roads near the pass. The deeper the night, the brighter the bonfires burned; they burned with a fire of hope, hope of resting and eating. But no, the bonfires had not been lit for us. They were for the guards. A great number of fires when the temperature was forty or fifty below zero. The fires stretched out like a snake for about thirty kilometers. Somewhere at the bottom of snow-embanked pits stood men, clearing the road with spades. The snow-covered sides formed a narrow trench with walls five meters high. The snow was flung up in terraces, having to be tossed up two or three times. When all the men had been put in position and were surrounded by guards and a serpentine chain of campfire lights, the workers were left to their own devices. Two thousand men could choose not to work, to work badly, or to work desperately: nobody cared. The pass had to be cleared and until it was cleared, nobody would be allowed to move. We stood for many hours in this snow pit, swinging our spades to avoid freezing to death. That night I understood something terrible, I observed something that was later confirmed many times. The tenth and eleventh hour of such extra work is hard, agonizingly hard and difficult, but after that you stop noticing the time, and you are overwhelmed by the Great Indifference: hours flow like minutes, even faster. We returned home after working for twenty-three hours, and we had no appetite at all. We ate our twenty-four-hours' ration of cooked food with an unusual lack of interest. It was very difficult to get to sleep.

In the winter of 1937–38 three maelstroms of death coincided and swirled in the snow-covered pit faces of the Kolyma gold mines. The first maelstrom was the "Berzin case" when Eduard Berzin, the director of Far East Construction, the pioneer of the Kolyma camps, was shot as a Japanese spy at the end of 1937. He was summoned to Moscow and shot. His closest assistants, Filippov, Maisuradze, Yegorov, Vaskov, Tsvirko, the whole "Vishera River" guard that had come in 1932 with Berzin to colonize the Kolyma region, perished with him. Ivan Gavrilovich Filippov had been the boss of the Administration of the Northeast Corrective Labor Camps, Berzin's camp deputy. An old chekist, a member of the Collegium of OGPU, Filippov had at one time been the chairman of the "disposal" (i.e., execution) trio in the Solovetsky Islands camps in the Arctic. There is a documentary film from the 1920s called *Solovetsky Islands*. In that movie Filippov was filmed in his role as chief. Filippov died in the Magadan prison; his heart failed.

The prison that was built in Magadan at the beginning of the 1930s was called the Vaskov Building. When the wooden structure was later rebuilt in stone it retained its original name. Vaskov was the surname of its chief. Vaskov was a solitary man and always spent his days off in the same way on the Vishera River, sitting on a bench in the garden, or the copse that stood as a garden, firing his .22 rifle into the leaves. Aleksei Yegorov, "Lioshka the redhead" as they called him on the Vishera, was in charge of production in Kolyma, administering several gold mines belonging to the Southern Administration. Tsvirko was the boss of the Northern Administration, which included the Partisan mine. In 1929 Tsvirko had been chief of a border guards division, and had gone on leave to Moscow. After an orgy in a restaurant, Tsvirko opened fire on the statue of Apollo's chariot over the entrance to the Bolshoi Theater and ended up in prison. His epaulets and buttons were ripped off. In spring 1929 Tsvirko arrived with a party of prisoners on the Vishera to serve his three-year sentence. When Berzin arrived on the Vishera at the end of 1929, Tsvirko's career took a sharp upturn.

While still a prisoner he became the chief of the Parma expedition. Berzin took a great liking to him and had him accompany him to Kolyma. They say Tsvirko was shot in Magadan. Aleksandr Maisuradze was the chief of the accounting and distribution section. He had once served a sentence for "inflaming ethnic hostility," was released while still on the Vishera, and also became one of Berzin's favorites. He was arrested in Moscow when he was on leave and executed there and then.

All these dead people came from Berzin's close circle. Many thousands of people, free contract workers and prisoners—mine bosses and camp bosses, chiefs of various camp centers, political instructors, party secretaries, guards and clerks of works, barracks elders and foreman—were shot or "rewarded" with sentences in connection with the "Berzin case." How many thousands of years did the sentences to prison and camps amount to? Who knows … ?

In the suffocating smoke of provocations at the time, the Kolyma version of the sensational Moscow trials looked quite respectable.

The second maelstrom that shook all of Kolyma consisted of endless camp executions, the so-called Garanin policy of finishing off enemies of the people, finishing off Trotskyists.

For many months the morning and evening roll calls involved the reading out of countless death sentences. In temperatures of minus 50, musicians who were nonpolitical prisoners would play a flourish before and after the announcement of each death order. The smoking gas lanterns failed to disperse the darkness; they merely drew hundreds of eyes to the frosted sheets of thin paper on which those terrible words were typed. At the time this didn't seem to apply to us. It all seemed alien, too terrible to be real. But the flourish was real, and it was as loud as thunder. The musicians' lips froze as they pressed them to the mouthpieces of the flutes, the silvery saxtubas, the cornets. The cigarette paper was covered in hoarfrost, and some boss or other would shake the snowflakes off it with his sleeve, trying to read and then yell out the surname of the next man to be shot. Every list ended with the same words: "The sentence has been carried out. Head of the Administration of Northeast Corrective Labor Camps, Colonel Garanin."

I saw Garanin some fifty times. He was about forty-five, broad-shouldered, potbellied, balding, with energetic dark eyes. He rushed between the northern mines day and night in his black ZIS-101 car. Later I heard that he personally executed people. Garanin was the chairman of the death-sentence troika. Orders were read out day and night: "The sentence has been carried out. Head of the Administration of Northeast Corrective Labor Camps, Colonel Garanin." Given the Stalinist traditions of those years, Garanin could not have had long to live. In fact he was seized, arrested, condemned as a Japanese spy and shot in Magadan.

Not one of the numerous Garanin death sentences was ever annulled by anyone. Garanin was one of the many Stalin hangmen to be killed by other hangmen when the time came.

A cover story was spread to explain his arrest and death. The real Garanin was alleged to have been killed on his way to work by a Japanese spy, and it was Garanin's sister, who had come to stay with her brother, who exposed the spy.

That legend was one of hundreds of thousands of fairy tales with which Stalin's era stuffed the ears and brains of ordinary men and women.

What did Colonel Garanin execute people for? What did he murder them for? "For counterrevolutionary agitation" was one of the headings in Garanin's orders. Nobody needs to be told what constituted counterrevolutionary agitation outside the prisons in 1937. If you praised a Russian novel published abroad, ten years for ASA (anti-Soviet agitation). If you said that the queues for liquid soap were extremely long, five years for ASA. And, following Russian custom and in keeping with the Russian character, anyone who got five years was happy not to have gotten ten. If he got ten, he was happy not to get twenty-five, and if he got twenty-five he would dance for joy because he wasn't going to be shot.

The camps didn't have that ladder of five, ten, twenty-five. You only had to say out loud that the work was too hard and that was enough to get shot. For any remark about Stalin, even the most innocent: shooting. To stay silent when others were shouting "Hurrah" for Stalin was also enough to get yourself shot. Silence, as everyone by now knows, is a form of agitation. Interrogators at every mine would compile lists of future corpses, tomorrow's corpses, based on the reports of their "grasses," informers, and a great number of volunteers, players in the well-known camp octet ensemble where "seven blow their instruments, and one bangs his drum." The sayings of the gangster world are aphorisms. But there was no actual case file. And there was no investigation. Statements by a troika, that well-known Stalin-era institution, were enough to lead to death.

Punched cards had not yet come into use, but the camp statisticians tried to make things easier for themselves by producing "formulars" with special markings. A "blank" with a diagonal blue stripe was used for the personal files of Trotskyists. Green (or mauve?) stripes were used for "recidivists," political ones, of course. Filing is filing, and you can't color a blank form with each individual's blood.

What else would you be shot for? "For insulting a camp guard." What was that? It meant verbal offense, a response that was insufficiently respectful, any talking back in response to a beating, punches, kicks. Any gesture by a prisoner that was too casual when talking to a guard was treated as "attacking a guard."

"For refusing to work." A great number of men perished without ever understanding the lethal danger of their action. Feeble old men, hungry, exhausted people, didn't have the strength to take a step outside the gates when we were led off to work in the morning. Such a refusal was documented. "Given footwear and clothes appropriate to the season." The forms for such documents were printed on a duplicator, and in mines that had the money blank forms were even ordered from the printers, and on these forms all that had to be entered were the surname and such data as year of birth, article of criminal code and sentence. . . . Three refusals meant execution. According to the law. Many people were unable to understand the main law of the camps— what the camps were invented for—that you couldn't refuse to work, that a refusal would be treated as the most monstrous crime, worse than any form of sabotage. You had to at least summon your last reserve of strength and somehow crawl to the workplace. A guard had to sign for each "unit," for each "unit of labor," and then the production people would sign their "acceptance." And you'd be saved. From being shot, at least for today. Once you were at work you needn't actually work, and in any case you wouldn't be able to. Endure the agony of the day until it ends. You will do very little as far as production is concerned, but you're not an "objector," so they can't shoot you. They say that the authorities have no such "right" in such cases. Whether they do have a right or not, I don't know, but many times over many years I had to struggle to stop myself from refusing to work and halting at the gates when the camp was led out to work.

"For stealing metal." Anyone on whom "metal" was found was shot. Later on, they spared your life and just gave you an extra sentence of five or ten years. A lot of metal nuggets passed through my hands—the Partisan mine was very "nuggety"—but the only feeling gold aroused in me was one of the profoundest revulsion. You needed skill to spot a nugget, to distinguish it from stone. Experienced workmen taught the novices this important skill, so that they didn't throw gold into the barrow and have the warden watching over the sizing trommel yell at them, "Hey you, you slobs, you've sent nuggets down to be washed again!" Prisoners were paid a bonus for gold nuggets: a ruble a gram for anything fifty-one grams or over. There were no scales at the pit face. Deciding whether the nugget you'd found was forty or sixty grams could only be done by the warden. We never told anyone more senior than the foreman when we found one. I found a lot of nuggets that had been rejected and I was twice put up for payment. One nugget weighed sixty grams, the other eighty. Naturally, I never got any actual cash. All I got was a "Stakhanov card," which gave me a shock worker's ration for the next ten days, and a pinch of tobacco from both the guard and the foreman. And I was grateful for that.

The most frequent "heading" under which a great number of men were shot was "for failing to fulfill the norm." Whole brigades were executed for this camp crime. It too was based on theoretical consid-erations. At the time the state plan was "brought down" all over the country to every machine-tool in all the factories and plants. In prisoner country, in Kolyma, the plan was implemented down to each pit face, each barrow, each pickax. The state plan was the law! Failure to fulfill the state plan was a counterrevolutionary crime. Anyone who failed to fulfill the norm was off to the next world!

The third lethal maelstrom, which took away more prisoners' lives than the first two combined, was mass death from starvation, beatings, and disease. The gangsters, the common criminals, those "friends of the people," played an enormous part in this.

In all of 1937, of the two or three thousand listed as working at the Partisan mine, just two men, one free worker and one prisoner, died. They were buried next to each other at the bottom of a hill. Each grave was marked by something like an obelisk: the free man's was a bit higher, the prisoner's was a bit lower. In 1938 there was a whole brigade standing by to dig graves. Rock and permafrost refuse to accept the corpses. The ground had to be drilled, blown up, and the stones and earth had to be excavated. Digging gravel and "smashing out" prospector shafts were jobs that required very similar techniques, as far as tools, materials, and "labor force" were concerned. A whole brigade was assigned solely to dig graves, just common graves for nameless corpses. Actually, they were not entirely nameless. The procedures specified that the labor supervisor, as a representative of the camp authorities, had to tie a plywood label to the corpse's left ankle, with the number of the corpse's personal file. Everyone was buried naked. What else would you expect? Gold teeth were knocked out, again as the protocol dictated, and listed in a special burial document. The pit, once it was full of corpses, was filled by dumping stones over them, but the ground still refused to accept the corpses. They were doomed to be imperishable in the Far North's permafrost.

Doctors were afraid to put down the true cause of death on their certificates. New diagnoses appeared: polyavitaminosis, pellagra, dysentery, APE, or acute physical emaciation, which was at least a step in the direction of the truth. APE was as cryptic an acronym as the initials NFI, the secret beloved of the poet Lermontov, finally deciphered by the critic Andronikov. Such diagnoses were made only by the bravest doctors, those who weren't themselves prisoners. The formula "alimentary dystrophy" was pronounced by the Kolyma doctors later, during the war, after the Leningrad blockade, when it was now deemed possible to give the true cause of death, albeit using Latin terminology. The Leningrad poet Vera Inber wrote, "The burning of a guttered candle, all the dryly listed symptoms of what doctors call in learned language alimentary dystrophy: things that anyone who isn't a philologist specializing in Latin would define by the Russian word for hunger." I used to repeat those lines quite often. People I knew who liked poetry had vanished long ago. But Inber's words had a resonance for every Kolyma inhabitant.

Everyone beat the workmen: the orderly, the hairdresser, the foreman, the political instructor, the supervisor, the escort guard, the barracks elder, the office manager, the labor manager—all of them. When you can beat people up and murder them with impunity, your soul is depraved and corrupted. I saw and knew all of those who did this.... The escort guard was then responsible, thanks to the wisdom of some top bosses, for the plan being fulfilled. That was why the guards used their rifle butts as enthusiastically as they could to beat the plan into fulfillment. Other guards behaved even worse; they put the responsibility onto the common criminals, who were always insinuated into brigades of article 58 men. The criminals didn't work. They merely ensured that the plan was fulfilled. They walked around the pit face with a stick, which they called their "thermometer," and beat up the mute and helpless *freiers*. They could beat you to death. The foremen, who had been appointed from the ranks of ordinary prisoners, tried their very hardest to prove to the bosses that they, the foremen, were on the side of the authorities, not the prisoners. Foremen tried to forget that they too were political prisoners. Not that they had ever been politicals. Nor had, in any case, any of the article 58 men at the time. The reason that it was possible to dispatch millions of people so successfully was that these people were innocent.

They were martyrs, not heroes.

1964

HANDWRITING

LATE ONE night Krist was summoned to go "behind the stables."
That was what the camp called a cottage that was right at the base of
a hill on the edge of the settlement. It was inhabited by the interrogator for especially important cases. The joke in the camp was that there
were no cases that were not especially important, since any infringement
or even the appearance of an infringement was punishable by death.
Either death, or complete acquittal. Not that anyone could say they'd
been fully acquitted. Ready for anything, indifferent to everything,
Krist followed the narrow path. A light came on in the kitchen building. It was probably the bread cutter starting to cut up the bread rations
for breakfast. For breakfast tomorrow. Would Krist live to see tomorrow and its breakfast? He didn't know and was very happy not to know.
Krist's feet trod on something not like snow or ice fragments. He bent
down, picked up a frozen crust and immediately recognized it as a
clump of frozen turnip peelings. The ice had already thawed in his
hands, and he thrust the crusty peelings into his mouth. There was
obviously no need to hurry. Krist walked the length of the path, starting from the last barracks, and he realized that he was the first to walk
this long, snow-covered path, that today nobody had trodden it before,
along the settlement edge, to see the interrogator. Pieces of turnip
had frozen to the snow all along the way. They looked as if they were
wrapped in cellophane. Krist found ten pieces, some bigger, some
smaller. It was a long time since Krist had seen anyone who would
throw turnip peelings into the snow. It must have been a free contract
worker, not a prisoner, of course. Perhaps it was the interrogator himself. Krist chewed up and swallowed all the crusts. He could taste in
his mouth something he had long forgotten: his native earth, fresh

vegetables. In a happy mood, Krist knocked at the door of the inter-rogator's cottage.

The interrogator was a short, skinny and unshaven man. All he had here was his office and an iron bunk covered with a soldier's blanket and a crumpled dirty pillow. The desk was a roughly made piece of furniture with crookedly placed drawers, packed tight with papers and folders. There was a box of index cards on the windowsill. The set of shelves was also packed tight with folders. Half of an empty can served as an ashtray. The clock showed half past ten. The interrogator was lighting the iron stove with paper.

His skin was white, he was pale, like all interrogators. He didn't have an orderly, or a revolver.

"Sit down, Krist," he said, addressing the prisoner politely and moving an old stool for him to sit on. He was sitting on a chair, another homemade item, with a high back.

"I've looked through your file," said the interrogator, "and I have a proposition for you. I don't know if you'll find it acceptable."

Krist froze in expectation. The interrogator said nothing for a while.

"I need to know a few more things about you."

Krist raised his head and, although he tried not to, belched. It was a pleasant belch with an insistent taste of fresh turnip.

"Write an application."

"An application?"

"Yes, an application. Here's a sheet of paper, here's a pen."

"An application? What about? To whom?"

"To anyone you like! All right, if not an application, then a poem by Blok. It makes no difference. Do you get it? Or Pushkin's 'Bird':

> Yesterday I opened the prison
> Of my ethereal captive,
> I returned the songster to the woods,
> I gave her back her freedom,—"

the interrogator declaimed.

"That's not Pushkin's 'Bird,'" Krist whispered, straining every fiber of his desiccated brain.

"Whose is it then?"

"Tumansky's."

"Tumansky's? That's the first I've heard of it."

"Aha, you need a handwriting sample for an expert opinion, do you? To see if I'm a murderer? Or if I wrote a letter to the outside? Or forged a shop voucher for the gangsters?"

"Not at all. We don't have any problem getting samples of that sort." The interrogator smiled, exposing his swollen bleeding gums and small teeth. However slight this flashed smile was, it added a little light to the room. And also to Krist's soul. He couldn't help looking into the interrogator's mouth.

"Yes," said the latter, catching Krist's gaze. "Scurvy, scurvy. Even free men aren't exempt from scurvy here. There are no fresh vegetables."

Krist thought about the turnip. It was Krist who had gotten the vitamins, since there were more vitamins in the peelings than in the inside. Krist wanted to keep the conversation going, to tell the interrogator how he had sucked and stroked the turnip peelings that the interrogator had thrown away. But he held back, fearing that this boss would punish him for being excessively familiar.

"Well, have you got it, or not? I need to take a look at your hand-writing."

Krist still failed to understand a thing.

"Write!" dictated the interrogator. "'To the chief of the mine. Prisoner Krist, date of birth, article, sentence, application. I ask to be transferred to lighter work....' That will do."

The interrogator took Krist's half-written application, tore it up and threw it into the fire.... For a moment the stove burned more brightly.

"Sit at the desk. At the end."

Krist had a professional calligrapher's handwriting, which he liked a lot, although all his comrades laughed at it, saying that it wasn't like the hand of a professor or someone with a doctorate. It wasn't a scholar's, a writer's or a poet's hand. It was a storekeeper's hand. People joked that Krist could have had a career as the tsar's clerk, as in the story by Aleksandr Kuprin.

But Krist wasn't embarrassed by these jokes. He had gone on having his beautiful fair-copy manuscripts typed. The typists approved of him, but made fun of him in secret.

Fingers that are used to handling a pickax or a spade handle have enormous trouble holding a pen, but in the end they managed.

"Everything here's a mess, chaos," the interrogator was saying. "I realize that. But you can help me to put things in order."

"Of course, of course," said Krist. The stove was now burning well and the room was warm. "I'd like a cigarette."

"I don't smoke," the interrogator said curtly. "And I don't have any bread either. You're not going to work tomorrow. I'll tell the labor manager."

So it was that for several months Krist came once a week to the camp interrogator's badly heated, uncomfortable accommodation to copy papers and stitch them into folders.

The deadly winds of the snowless winter of 1937–38 had now got into the barracks in full force. Labor supervisors ran every night around the barracks with some list or other, looking for people to wake up and join a party to be sent out. Even before this terrible winter happened, nobody had ever come back from these "parties," and now prisoners had stopped even thinking about these nighttime actions. A deportation party was a deportation party, and work was so hard that you couldn't think about anything.

The working hours were extended, escort guards were introduced, but the week passed and Krist, barely alive, would wend his way to the familiar place, the interrogator's office, to endlessly stitch papers. Krist stopped washing, he stopped shaving, but the interrogator seemed not to notice that Kris was starving, nor that his cheeks were sunken and his eyes inflamed. Krist just kept writing, and stitching. The quantity of papers and folders kept on growing, and there was no hope of ever putting them in order. Krist was copying out endless lists that showed only surnames, while the top of the list was bent back and he never even tried to get at the secret of this office, although all he had to do was bend back the sheet of paper in front of him. Sometimes the interrogator picked up a batch of "case files" that had appeared out of nowhere in Krist's absence, and he would then hurriedly dictate lists for Krist to write down.

Dictation used to end at midnight, and Krist went back to his barracks and slept and slept. He was exempt from the next day's roll call for work. Week after week passed, as Krist kept getting thinner and kept writing.

Then one day, picking up the next batch of papers to read the next surname, the interrogator stumbled, looked at Krist and asked him:

"What's your first name and patronymic?"

"Robert Ivanovich," Krist replied with a smile. If the interrogator started calling him by his first name or any other polite way, he wouldn't have been surprised. The interrogator was young enough to be Krist's son. Still holding on to the folder and not uttering anyone's surname, the interrogator turned pale. He went on turning pale until he was whiter than snow. The interrogator's quick fingers leafed through the thin sheets of paper stitched into the folder—there were neither more nor fewer pages than in any other folder in the pile lying on the floor. Then the interrogator took decisive action. He opened the stove door, and the room at once became bright, as if his soul had been fully illuminated and something very important and human had been discovered at the bottom of it. The interrogator tore the folder into pieces and pushed the pieces into the stove. The light became even brighter. And, without looking at Krist, the interrogator said.

"Bureaucratic nonsense. They don't understand what they're doing, they're not interested." He looked at Krist with a firm gaze. "Let's continue writing. Are you ready?"

"I am," said Krist. Only years later did he realize that the folder has been his, Krist's.

By then many of Krist's fellow prisoners had been shot. The interrogator too had been shot. But Krist was still alive and sometimes, at least once every few years, he would remember that burning folder, the interrogator's decisive fingers as he tore up Krist's "case file": a present to one doomed man from another.

Krist wrote in a lifesaving calligraphic hand.

1964

THE DUCK

THE MOUNTAIN stream was by now in the grip of ice; in the rapids there was no flowing water at all. The stream began to freeze at the rapids and a month later there was nothing left of the summer water that roared so menacingly. Even the ice was trampled down, crushed to pieces and squashed by hooves, by tires, and by felt boots. But the stream was still alive and water still breathed in it. White mist would rise over the pools of unfrozen water and the thawed patches of ground.

An exhausted tufted duck slipped with a splash into the water. The flock had long before flown south, but this duck stayed behind. It was still light out, and snowy. The snow covering the naked forest made it exceptionally light all the way to the horizon. The duck wanted to rest, if only for a little, and then take off and fly where the flock had gone.

It didn't have the strength to fly. Its wings weighed a ton and forced it to the ground, but in the water it felt support and salvation. The unfrozen pool water seemed to be a living river.

Hardly had the duck looked around and rested than its sharp hearing caught the sound of danger. Not so much a sound as a rumble.

From the snowy crust above, breaking his descent on the frozen hummocks that became even colder toward the evening, a man was running down. He had seen the duck some time before and had been tracking it with secret hopes. Now his hopes had come true and the duck was sitting on the ice.

The man crept up to the duck, but missed his footing. The duck noticed him, and then the man ran without trying to hide; the duck was unable to fly, it was too tired. All it had to do was to rise up and then nothing but angry threats would have menaced it. But to rise skyward its wings needed strength, and the duck was too tired. All it could manage was to dive and vanish in the water, while the man, armed with a heavy branch, stopped by the pool where the duck had disappeared and waited for it to surface. After all, the duck would have to breathe.

Twenty meters away there was another pool of water, and the man cursed as he saw the duck had swum under the ice to emerge in the next pool. But it was no more able to fly from there. It spent seconds resting.

The man tried to smash and crush the ice with his feet, but his footwear, made of rags, was of no use.

He struck the blue ice with his stick. The ice crumbled a little, but didn't break. The man exhausted himself and, breathing heavily, sat down on the ice.

The duck swam on the pool. The man ran toward it, cursing and throwing stones, and the duck dove down and reappeared in the first pool.

They went on running back and forth like this, man and duck, until darkness fell.

It was time to abandon the failed hunt and go back to the barracks. The man regretted wasting his strength on this crazy pursuit. He was too hungry to think properly, to make a rational plan and trick the duck. Impatience, caused by hunger, had suggested the wrong path to take, a bad plan. The duck remained on the ice, in its unfrozen patch of water. It was time to go back to the barracks. The reason the man tried to catch the duck was not to cook and eat it. True, a duck was a bird and therefore meat, wasn't it? To be boiled in a tin pot or, even better, put in a clay pot buried in burning hot violet-colored ash or just chucked into a bonfire. The fire would burn out and the clay the bird was baked in would break open. Inside there would be hot, slippery fat. The fat would flow over his hands and solidify on his lips. No, the man was trying to catch the duck for quite a different purpose. Shaky plans were arising and taking a vague, foggy shape in his brain. To take this duck and offer it to the foreman as a gift, so that the foreman would cross the man's name off the ominous list which was being compiled at night. The whole barracks knew about this list, and the man was trying hard not to think about the impossible, the incomprehensible, about somehow getting out of the deportation party, so as to stay here on this expedition. The starvation here could be endured a little longer, somehow, and this man knew that a bird in the hand was always best.

But the duck was still there on its unfrozen patch of water. It was very hard for the man to take the necessary decision, to act, to do something that his everyday life had not taught him to do. He had never been taught how to hunt duck. That's why his movements were useless and clumsy. He'd never been taught to think about the possibility of such hunting. His brain was unable to solve the unexpected quandaries that life posed. He had been taught how to live in such a way that no personal decision was needed, so that somebody else's will determined events. It was extraordinarily difficult to intervene in one's own fate, to turn it around.

Perhaps it was for the best if the duck died on the pool, and the man in the barracks.

It was hard to warm his fingers, frozen and scratched by the ice, by putting them against his chest. First he put each hand, then both hands at the same time under his clothes, quivering at the throbbing pain in his permanently frostbitten fingers. His hungry body held little warmth, and he went back to the barracks, pressed himself close to the stove, and yet still could not get warm. His body was shaking with severe and unstoppable convulsions.

The foreman looked in through the barracks door. He too had seen the duck and seen this corpse hunting down a dying duck. The foreman had no desire to leave this settlement. Who knew what was waiting for him in a new place? The foreman had set his hopes on a generous gift—a live duck and free-man's trousers—to soften the heart of the clerk of works, who was still asleep. When he woke up, the clerk of works could cross the foreman off the list, him instead of the workman who had caught the duck.

The clerk of works was lying down, crumpling a Rocket cigarette with practiced hands. He had been looking through the window and had also seen the start of the hunt. If the duck was caught, the carpenter would make a cage and the clerk would take the duck to the big boss, or rather the big boss's wife, Agnia. And the clerk's future would be assured.

But the duck stayed on its unfrozen patch of water where it was to die. Everything went on as if the duck had never appeared.

1963

THE BUSINESSMAN

THERE were a lot of men called Handyman in the hospital. Handyman was the nickname given to someone who had injured his hand, not who had had his teeth knocked out. Which Handyman? The Greek? The lanky man from ward seven? That's Kolia Handyman, the businessman.

The right hand: Kolia's hand was shot off by an explosion. Kolia was a self-shooter, a self-mutilator. In the medical accounts self-shooters are listed under the same heading as men who chop their feet off with an ax. It was forbidden to accept them into the hospital if they didn't have a high "septic" temperature. Kolia Handyman did have that temperature. For two months he struggled to stop the wound healing, but his youth won the battle and Kolia did not have long to stay in the hospital.

It was time to go back to the mine. But Kolia was not afraid. What could a gold-mine pit face do to a one-armed man like him? The times had passed when one-armed men were forced to "trample a road" for men and tractors in the forestry areas, spending a working day in deep, porous crystal snow. The authorities did what they could to combat self-shooters, prisoners who blew up their feet, inserting a percussion cap into their boot and lighting a safety fuse by their knee. The fuse method was the most convenient. They stopped sending the one-armed to trample a road. Would they make him wash gold in a sieve—with one arm? Well, you could go and do it for a day or so in summer. If it didn't rain. Kolia's mouth opened in a broad grin showing his white teeth. The scurvy hadn't affected his teeth yet. Kolia Handyman had already learned how to roll a cigarette with just his left hand. Almost well-fed, and rested in the hospital, Kolia just kept on smiling. Kolia

Handyman was a businessman. He was always swapping something, taking forbidden herring to those who had diarrhea and getting bread from them in exchange. Those who had diarrhea also needed to get kept back, to put on the brakes in the hospital. Kolia swapped soup for porridge, and porridge for two portions of soup and he knew how to cut any bread ration he was entrusted with to exchange for tobacco. He got the bread from the bedridden patients, swollen scurvy sufferers, those who had serious fractures and were in the trauma wards or, as the paramedic Pavel Pavlovich used to pronounce it, "drama" wards, not suspecting the bitter irony of his malapropism. Kolia Handyman's luck began the day he shot his hand off. Almost well-fed, almost warm. As for the foul curses of the bosses and the threats from the doctors, Kolia considered all that to be of no importance. And he was right.

Several times during those blissful months that Kolia spent in the hospital strange and terrible things happened. The hand that had been blown off by the explosion, although it didn't exist, hurt as it had at the start. Kolia could feel all of it: the permanently bent fingers, still in the same frozen position as they had been at the mine, curved exactly to fit around a spade handle or a pickax handle. It was hard to hold a spoon with a hand like that, but you didn't need a spoon at the mine: anything edible could be drunk "overboard" from the bowl, soup or porridge, milk pudding or tea. These permanently bent fingers could hold your bread ration. But Handyman had amputated them, blasted them off to hell. So why then could he feel these bent fingers just as he had at the mine, when they'd been shot off? His left hand, after all, had begun a month ago to unbend and bend right back, like a rusty hinge after it has had a touch of grease applied. That had made Handyman weep for joy. Even now, as he lay with his belly over his left hand, he was unbending the hand, and doing so freely. But the amputated right hand wouldn't unbend. All this happened mainly at night. Handyman grew cold with fear, he would wake up, weep and not dare to ask even the men in the nearby beds about it. Perhaps it meant something? Perhaps he was going mad.

Pain from the missing hand came more and more seldom, the world was becoming normal. Handyman was pleased at his luck. And he kept on smiling, as he remembered how neatly he'd managed to do it.

Pavel Pavlovich the paramedic emerged from his cubbyhole, holding a fat roll-up that he hadn't yet lit. He sat down next to Handyman.

"Do you want a light, Pavel Pavlovich?' Handyman said, bending over the paramedic. "Just a moment."

Handyman dashed to the stove, opened the door, and used his left hand to throw a few burning embers onto the floor.

Deftly tossing up a smoldering coal, Handyman caught it in his hand and rolled the coal, which was now black, but still had a flame, desperately blowing on it to keep the fire going. Then, with a slight bow, he offered it right up to the paramedic's face. The paramedic drew in the air hard, holding the roll-up in his mouth, and finally had his light. Puffs of blue smoke drifted over his head. Handyman flared his nostrils. Patients are woken up in the wards by this smell and desperately try to breathe in the smoke, not smoke, but a receding shadow of smoke....

Everyone realized that it was Handyman who would get the stub to smoke.

Handyman meanwhile was working out that he would have a couple of draws and then take it to the surgical ward to a *freier* with a fractured spine. A nice dinner ration was waiting for Handyman there, and that was no small matter. If Pavel Pavlovich left more of his roll-up, then the butt could be turned into a new cigarette that would be worth more than a dinner ration.

"You'll be off soon, Handyman," Pavel Pavlovich was saying casually. "You've had a good break here, you've really put on weight, so it's got to come to an end.... Tell me, how did you have the guts to do it? That might be something to tell my children. If I ever see them again...."

"I'm not trying to hide anything, Pavel Pavlovich," said Handyman, still working out what to do. Pavel had clearly rolled his cigarette carelessly. Look at how he draws on it, takes the smoke in so that the flame moves and the paper gets burned. The paramedic's roll-up wasn't smoldering, it was burning like a safety fuse. Like a safety fuse. So he had to tell the story quickly.

"Well?"

"I got up one morning, got my bread ration, and put it in my secret pouch under my shirt. I go and see Mishka the Dynamite man. 'How's things?' he says. 'Got it,' I say. I give him all my eight-hundred-gram ration and get a percussion cap and a length of fuse in exchange. I go and join the people from my parts in our barracks. They're not really from my parts, we just say so. Fedia and Petro or somebody. 'Ready?' I ask them. 'Ready,' they say. 'Hand it over.' They give me their bread rations. I put the two lots in my secret pouch under my shirt and we toddle off to work.

"At the workplace, while our brigade is getting its tools, we take a burning coal from the stove, go behind the earth mound. We stand as close as we can, each of us holding a percussion cap in the right hand. We light the fuse, bang and fingers are flying in all directions. The foreman yells, 'What are you doing?' The senior guard, 'Quick march to the camp, to the medical center!' We were bandaged at the medical center, but I had a temperature so I ended up in the hospital."

Pavel Pavlovich had nearly finished his cigarette, but Handyman was so carried away by his story that he nearly forgot about it.

"How about those bread rations that you had left over. Did you eat them?"

"Of course I did. As soon as I was bandaged, I ate them. My fellow countrymen came up and asked me to break off a piece. 'Go to hell,' I told them. This is my profit."

1962

CALIGULA

A NOTE was delivered to the punishment barracks even before the twilight siren sounded.

The commandant lit the kerosene lamp, read the paper and hurried off to give orders. Nothing struck the commandant as strange.

"He's not off his head, is he?" asked the duty guard, putting a finger to his forehead.

The commandant gave the soldier a cold look, which frightened the soldier and made him wonder if he had been too frivolous. The soldier turned his eyes to the road.

"They're bringing it," he said. "Ardatiev's coming in person."

Two escort guards with rifles loomed up in the mist. They were followed by a drover leading an emaciated gray horse. Behind the horse a big, heavily built man was striding over the snow. His white sheepskin jacket was unbuttoned, his Siberian sheepskin hat was tipped back over his neck. He was holding a stick and mercilessly beating the horse's bony, dirty, sunken flanks. The horse jerked at every blow, but, too weak to change pace, it went on meandering.

At the checkpoint hut the guards stopped the horse. Ardatiev staggered ahead. He was breathing like an overheated horse, and fumes of alcohol came over the commandant, who was standing to attention.

"Ready?" Ardatiev rasped.

"Yes, sir!" replied the commandant.

"Drag it away!" roared Ardatiev. "Take it and do what's necessary. I punish people, so I'm not going to let horses off. I'll make it do its job. It hasn't worked for three days," he mumbled, poking the commandant's chest with his fist. "I was going to lock up the drover. After all, the plan's being wrecked. The pla-a-an...."

The drover swore on his honor, "It's the horse, not me, that's stopped work."

"I kn-now," Ardatiev hiccupped, "I b-believe you.... I tell them, give me the reins. I took the reins, it wouldn't move. I hit it, it still doesn't move. I offer it sugar—I deliberately took some from home—it won't take it. So, I think, you bloody swine, how am I going to make up for the working days you've lost? Go on and join the other layabouts, all those enemies of humanity: to solitary. Nothing but water. Seventy-two hours to begin with."

Ardatiev sat down in the snow and took off his hat. His wet tangled hair was falling over his eyes. He tried to get up, swayed, and fell over onto his back.

The guard and the commandant dragged him into the booth. Ardatiev was asleep.

"Do we take him home?"

"No. His wife doesn't like it."

"How about the horse?"

"We've got to take it away. If he finds out when he wakes up that we haven't locked it up, he'll kill us. Put the horse in number four, with the intellectuals."

Two prisoners who worked as night watchmen brought some firewood for the night into the hut and started stacking it around the stove.

"What do you say, Piotr," said one of them, his eyes on the door to the room where Ardatiev was snoring.

"I'd say there's nothing new about it . . . Caligula. . . ."

"Yes, yes, just like Derzhavin's verses," responded the other. Straightening his back, he recited with feeling:

Caligula, your horse in the Senate
Could not shine, however radiant its gold:
Only good deeds are radiant.

The old men lit up and the blue tobacco smoke drifted around the room.

1962

THE SPADE ARTIST

AFTER work on Sunday, Krist was told that he was being moved to Kostochkin's brigade, to make up numbers on a gold-mine brigade that was rapidly losing men. This was an important piece of news. Whether it was good or bad news was not for Krist to consider, since it was ineluctable news. Krist had heard a lot about Kostochkin at that mine, but there were not even rumors about him in the mute barracks, insulated as it was from the outside world. Like every other prisoner, Krist didn't know where the new people in his life had come from: some came for a short while, others for a long time, but in both cases people vanished from Krist's life without saying a thing about themselves. Their departures were like deaths, their deaths were like departures. Bosses, foremen, cooks, quartermasters, the men in the next bunk, your wheelbarrow partner, your pickax team....

Krist never grew tired of this kaleidoscope, this movement of countless persons. He simply never gave it a thought. Life didn't give him the time for such thoughts. "Don't get worked up, don't think about new bosses, Krist. You're just one man, but you'll have a great number of bosses," was what a joker and philosopher had told him. Krist had forgotten who the man was. He couldn't remember the surname or the face, or the voice of the man who'd uttered these important jocular phrases to him. The reason they were important was because they were said in jest. There did exist a few people who dared to make jokes, to smile, if only a well-hidden, very secret smile, but still a smile, an unmistakable smile, though Krist was not one of them.

The foremen that Krist had had.... Either they were article 58 politicals, like himself, who had taken on a job far too weighty for themselves and would soon be dismissed, dismissed before they had time to turn into murderers. Or they'd be another article 58 like him, *freiers*, but beaten *freiers*, knocked about and with experience, so that they could not only give orders at work, but organize the work and even get on with the norm-setters and other various bosses, give bribes, talk people round. But these men too, article 58 prisoners like Krist, refused even to contemplate the fact that giving orders for camp work was the worst sin in the camps. In a place where scores were settled in blood, where men had no rights, to take on the responsibility of determining others' lives and deaths at the whim of the authorities—all that was too great a mortal sin, a sin that was unforgivable. There were foremen who died with their brigade. There were also foremen who were immediately corrupted by this horrible power over someone else's life—they wielded a pickax or a spade handle in order to facilitate any conversations with their comrades. And when they remembered such occasions, they would repeat, as if it were a prayer, the gloomy camp saying, "You die today, I die tomorrow." Many times Krist's foremen were not article 58 prisoners. More often than not, and always in the most terrible years, his foremen were nonpolitical prisoners sentenced for murder or employment crimes. These were normal people, and you could blame only the power of authority, as well as heavy pressure from above, a torrent of lethal instructions, for forcing these people to commit actions they would, perhaps, never have consented to in their former lives. The boundary between a crime and "a non-punishable act" in the articles of the law regarding employment was very subtle and sometimes indistinguishable. People were tried today for acts that they would not have been tried for yesterday, not to mention pretrial detention and the legal scale of nuances between an action and a crime.

The nonpolitical foremen were beasts because they were ordered to be. But the foremen who were gangsters were beasts regardless of orders. A gangster foreman was the worst thing that could happen to a brigade. Kostochkin, however, was neither a gangster nor an ordinary nonpolitical criminal. He was the only son of some major employee, either in the party or in a soviet, of the Chinese-Eastern Railway,[5] who was tried on the "Chinese-Eastern Railway case" and put to death. Kostochkin junior, who had been studying at Harbin and knew no other city, was at the age of twenty-five sentenced to fifteen years as an FM, family member. Brought up to a foreign life in Harbin, a life where innocent people were jailed only in novels, and those largely translated from a foreign language, young Kostochkin was not convinced at the bottom of his heart that his father had been wrongly convicted. His father had brought him up to believe in the NKVD's infallibility. Young Kostochkin was very ill-prepared for any other belief. When his father was arrested and he himself was convicted and deported from the Very Far East to the Very Far North, young Kostochkin's anger was directed at his father for ruining his life by some mysterious crime. What did Kostochkin know about adult life? He had studied four foreign languages, two European, two Asian, and was the best dancer in Harbin; he had learned every sort of blues and rumba from visiting professionals. He was the best boxer in Harbin, a middleweight who could also be a light heavyweight; he'd learned his uppercuts and hooks from a former European champion. What could he know about big politics? So if his father was shot, there must have been a reason. Perhaps the NKVD had overdone things, perhaps his father should have had ten or fifteen years. In that case, as Kostochkin junior, he should have had five, not fifteen years, if he had to be sentenced.

Kostochkin would repeat four words, putting them in a different order—in each case, they sounded bad and worried, "So there was something. . . . So something was there."

The interrogators had achieved a major success by making Kostochkin hate his executed father and by giving him a passionate desire to free himself of the slur, of the curse on his father. Not that the main interrogator was aware of this. That interrogator, the one who had been in charge of Kostochkin's case, had long before been executed after being named in yet another "NKVD case."

But foxtrots and rumbas were not all Kostochkin had learned in Harbin. He had graduated from Harbin Technical Institute and had a degree in mechanical engineering.

When Kostochkin was brought to the mine he had been assigned to, he managed to get an interview with the mine chief, in which he asked for a job that matched his qualifications. He promised to work conscientiously, he cursed his father, he pleaded with the local bosses. "He can write labels for the canned food," the mine chief responded curtly, but the local NKVD officer who was present at this conversation detected certain familiar tones in the young Harbin engineer's voice. The bosses had a private chat, then the NKVD man had a talk with Kostochkin, and the pit-face brigades suddenly learned that one of their foremen would be a novice, a fellow article 58 political prisoner. The optimists interpreted this appointment as a sign that things would soon change for the better; the pessimists muttered something about new brooms. But both optimists and pessimists were amazed, apart from those who had long ago learned to be amazed by nothing. Krist was not amazed.

Each brigade has its own life, its own section of the barracks with a separate entry, and they meet other people from the same barracks only in the refectory. Krist had often come across Kostochkin, who was noticeably red-faced, broad-shouldered and powerfully built. His long-sleeved gloves were made of fur. The poorer foremen had gloves made of rags from quilted trousers. Kostochkin's hat was also a "free" one, fur with earflaps, and his felt boots were genuine, not camp-issue string boots. All this made Kostochkin stand out. He worked as foreman for one winter month, which meant that he'd fulfilled the plan, or a percentage of it—you could find out from the board by the guardhouse, not that an old hand like Krist took any interest.

Krist assembled his future foreman's life story mentally, while lying on his bunk. But he was sure he had got it right, that there could be no mistakes. There were no other ways that a lad from Harbin could have got a foreman's job.

Kostochkin's brigade was melting away, as were all the brigades working at a gold-mine pit face. From time to time—and that had to mean on a weekly, not a monthly basis—reserves were sent to Kostochkin's brigade. Today the new man was Krist. "Kostochkin probably knows who Einstein is," Krist thought, as he fell asleep in his new place.

As a new man, Krist was given a place well away from the stove. The first men to join the brigade had the best places. That was the normal way of doing things, and Krist was perfectly familiar with it.

The foreman was sitting by a table in the corner, near the lamp, reading a book. Even though a foreman, being the master of his workmen's lives and deaths, could for his convenience put the only lamp on his table and deprive everyone else in the barracks of light, they wouldn't do so to read or talk.... You could talk just as well in the dark, not that there was any time to talk, or anything to talk about. But Kostochkin had moved up to the common lamp and he was reading, reading, sometimes arranging his chubby childlike lips in a smile, screwing up his big, handsome gray eyes. Krist was so taken by this peaceful scene, something he had not seen for ages, a foreman and his brigade all relaxing, that he quietly made up his mind definitely to stay in this brigade and to devote all his strength to his new foreman.

The brigade had a deputy foreman, too, who was the orderly, the short Oska, old enough to be Kostochkin's father. Oska swept the barracks, fed the brigade, helped the foreman; everything was as it should be. As he fell asleep, Krist recalled that his new foreman probably knew who Einstein was. The thought made him happy and, warmed up by the cup of boiled water he'd just drunk, he fell asleep.

The new brigade made no noise at all when taken out to work. Krist was shown to the tool store and got his tools. He adapted the spade, as he had done a thousand times before, by knocking away the hateful short handle with a crossbar that had been fixed onto the American spade, then he used the back of his ax and a stone to make the blade a little bit wider, and chose himself the longest possible haft from the many hafts in the corner of the shed. He put the haft into the opening on the blade and fixed it firmly. Then he placed the spade at an angle, with the blade at his feet, measured it and made a mark, "notched" the haft at chin height and hacked it off at the notch. Using his sharp ax, Krist shaved and carefully smoothed the butt end of the new handle. He stood up and turned around. Kostochkin was standing in front of him, paying full attention to the new man's actions. Krist had been expecting this. Kostochkin didn't say a word, and Krist realized that the foreman was postponing judgment until work, pit-face work.

The pit face wasn't far; work had begun. The spade handle quivered, Krist's back ached, both his hands took up their usual position as his fingers gripped the haft. It was a little bit too thick, but Krist would put that right in the evening. And he would sharpen the spade with a file. His arms swung the spade again and again, and the melodic screech of metal against rock was accompanied by an accelerated rhythm. The spade screeched and rustled, the stone fell off the spade with each swing and fell to the bottom of the barrow, and the barrow responded with a wooden thump, and the stone replied to stone. Krist knew all this pit-face music well. The same barrows were all around, the same spades were screeching, the stones were rumbling as they fell off the lumps of rock undercut by the pickax, and the spades screeched again.

Krist put down his spade and tabbed the handles, then took over from his partner on "OGPU's court of appeal: Just two handles and one wheel," which meant wheelbarrow in Kolyma prisoners' language. Not quite gangster slang, but something like it. Krist placed the body of the barrow on the board of the ramp, with the handles facing away from the pit face. Then he quickly filled it up, after which he arched his back, tensed his stomach muscles and, once he had his balance, wheeled the barrow to the sizing trommel, the ore-washing machine. When he came back Krist followed all the rules for barrowing that had been bequeathed by convicts in tsarist times: handles pointing up, wheel in front. Krist rested with his hands on the barrow handles, and then put the barrow back and picked up the spade again. The spade began to screech.

Foreman Kostochkin, the Harbin engineer, was standing, listening to the pit-face symphony and observing Krist's movements.

"Well, I see you're a spade artist," he said, bursting into loud laughter. His laughter was as uninhibited as a child's. The foreman wiped his lips on his sleeve. "What category were you getting where you came from?"

This meant the category of food, the "stomach scale," which was meant to urge prisoners to work harder. Krist knew that these categories had been invented on the White Sea canal, where prisoners were "reforged." The slobbery romanticism of reforging had a basis in calculations that were cruel and ominous, as was this stomach scale.

"The third," Krist replied, his voice emphasizing as clearly as he could how much he despised his previous foreman for failing to value a spade artist's talent. Because he understood the advantages, Krist was accustomed to a certain amount of deceit.

"I'll see you get the second. Starting today."

"Thank you," said Krist.

The new brigade was in fact a little quieter than the others in which

Krist had found himself living and working. The barracks were a little cleaner and there was slightly less foul language. Krist wanted to toast a piece of bread, left over from supper, on the stove. It was a habit he had acquired years ago. But the man next to him, whose name Krist didn't know and never was to know, pushed him and said that the foreman didn't like people toasting bread on the stove.

Krist went up to the iron stove, which was burning merrily, and spread his hands over the current of heat, sticking his face into a stream of hot air. Oska, the deputy foreman, got off the bunk nearby and, with his mighty arm, pulled the new man back from the stove: "Go back to your place. Don't hog the stove. Let everyone get some heat." On the whole, that was fair, but it was very hard to restrain one's body when it longed for the fire. Prisoners in Kostochkin's brigade had learned to restrain themselves. Krist would have to learn to do that. He went back to his place and took off his pea jacket. He stuck his feet into its sleeves, adjusted his hat, curled into a ball and fell asleep.

As he was falling asleep, he could still see someone come into the barracks and give orders. Kostochkin, not moving away from the lamp, swore, and went on reading his book. Oska jumped up to meet the man who had come in, and in a series of deft, quick movements grabbed him by the elbows and pushed him out of the barracks. In his previous life Oska had been a history teacher in some institute.

For many days that followed, Krist's spade screeched, as the sand rustled. Kostochkin soon realized that the polished technique of Krist's movements had long concealed a total lack of strength. However hard Krist tried, his barrows were always slightly less full than they should have been. This technique had nothing to do with his own will, it was dictated by some inner feeling that controlled Krist's muscles—all of them, whether healthy or feeble, young or worn-out and exhausted. It always turned out that in the pit-face allocation where Krist was working, less was achieved than the foreman expected from the professionalism in the spade artist's movements. But Kostochkin never picked on Krist; he swore at him no more than he swore at the others. Kostochkin never swore for the sake of swearing and never lectured anyone. Perhaps he realized that Krist was working to the maximum of his strength and holding back only what could not be squandered for the sake of any foreman in any camp in the world. Or Kostochkin sensed, if he didn't understand, that our feelings are far richer than our thoughts, and a prisoner's exsanguinated tongue reveals only some of his inner feelings. Feelings also become pallid and weak, but long after thoughts do, long after human speech does. Krist was, in fact, working harder than he had for a long time, and although what he achieved was not enough to get the "second category," he still received it. For diligence, for effort....

After all, the second category was the maximum that Krist could have. The first category was for record-breakers who fulfilled the plan by 120 percent or more. There were no record-breakers in Kostochkin's brigade. The brigade did have third category men who fulfilled the norm, and fourth category men who failed to fulfill the norm, but managed just 70–80 percent. But these were not the obvious bone-idle who deserved the punishment rations of the fifth category: in Kostochkin's brigade there were no such men.

The days passed. Krist was getting weaker and weaker; the submissive peace and quiet in the barracks appealed to him less and less. One evening, however, Oska, the history teacher, took Krist to one side and told him quietly, "The cashier is coming today. The foreman's ordered some money for you, so...." Krist's heart was pounding. Kostochkin had appreciated his efforts, his skill. That Harbin foreman who knew who Einstein was did have a conscience, after all.

In the brigades Krist had worked in earlier, he was never issued any money. In every brigade there were inevitably men who were more deserving, or actually physically stronger and better workers, or else friends of the foreman: Krist had never gone in for such futile reflections, he just considered every dinner voucher—the categories changed every ten days, when the percentage of the norm achieved was calculated—to be the finger of fate, good luck or bad, success or failure, which would pass, would change, and could not last forever.

The news about the money Krist was to receive that evening filled his body and soul with a burning, uncontrollable joy. So he did have enough strength to feel joy. How much might he be paid...? It could be as much as five or six rubles, which meant five or six kilos of bread. Krist was prepared to worship Kostochkin as a saint; it was all he could do to wait for the working day to end.

The cashier came. He was the most ordinary of men, but he was a free contract worker wearing a good-quality leather jacket. He was accompanied by a guard who either had a revolver or pistol concealed on his body, or else had left his gun at the guardhouse. The cashier sat down at a table, opened his briefcase a few inches: the briefcase was stuffed with well-worn banknotes of different colors, looking like washed rags. The cashier pulled out a document that was covered with closely packed lines and bore all sorts of signatures from people who were pleased or disappointed at the money allocated to them. The cashier summoned Krist and showed him a line marked by a tick.

Krist looked closely and sensed there was something special about this payment, this disbursement. Nobody but him had come up to the cashier. There was no queue. Perhaps the men in the brigade had been trained to stand back by their solicitous foreman. Well, no point thinking about it! The money had been ordered, the cashier was paying. So Krist was in luck.

The foreman wasn't in the barracks at the time. He hadn't yet left the office, and the deputy foreman, Oska the history teacher, stood in as a guarantor of Krist's identity. Oska's index finger showed Krist where to sign.

"And ... how much?" Krist rasped, as he gasped for breath.

"Fifty rubles. Are you satisfied?"

Krist's heart sang as it pounded. This really was luck. He hurriedly signed the document, tearing the paper with the sharp nib and nearly overturning the non-spill inkwell.

"Lucky lad!" said Oska, approvingly.

The cashier slammed his briefcase shut.

"Nobody else in your brigade?"

"No."

Krist still couldn't understand what had happened.

"How about the money? The money?"

"I handed Kostochkin the money," said the cashier. "Earlier today." Oska was short, but his iron hand, which had more strength than that of any pit-face getter in the brigade, tore Krist away from the table and flung him into the darkness.

Nobody in the brigade said a word. Not a single man gave Krist any support or asked any questions. Krist wasn't even sworn at for being a fool. . . . That horrified Krist more than the beast Oska and the grip of his iron hand. It was more terrifying than foreman Kostochkin's child-like chubby lips.

The barracks door was flung wide open and Kostochkin strode in, with quick and light steps, to the table and the light. The rough boards of the barracks floor barely bent under his light, elastic footsteps.

"Here's the foreman, have a talk with him," said Oska, stepping back. Oska then explained to Kostochkin, pointing to Krist: "He wants the money!"

But the foreman had understood the situation the moment he entered. Kostochkin immediately felt as if he were in a Harbin boxing ring. With a practiced, elegant boxer's gesture, he stretched out his arm from the shoulder at Krist, and Krist fell stunned to the ground.

"Knockout, knockout," croaked Oska, pretending to be a referee in the ring, and dancing around Krist who was only half-alive. "Eight . . . nine . . . Knockout."

Krist didn't get up off the floor.

"Money? Money for him?" asked Kostochkin, as he slowly lowered himself onto a chair at the table and took a spoon from Oska's hand, so as to begin eating his bowl of peas.

"Now these Trotskyists," Kostochkin said slowly, as if lecturing, "are destroying you and me, Oska." Kostochkin raised his voice: "They've ruined the country. And they're ruining you and me. So that spade artist wanted money, did he? Hey, you lot," Kostochkin was shouting at his brigade. "You fascists! Listen! You're not going to cut my throat. Oska, dance!"

Krist was still lying on the floor. The enormous figures of the fore-man and the orderly blocked out the light. But suddenly Krist saw that Kostochkin was drunk, very drunk: that was the fifty rubles which had been ordered for Krist. . . . How much alcohol you could "redeem" for fifty rubles, alcohol which was meant for, and actually issued for the brigade. . . .

Oska, the foreman's deputy, obeyed and started dancing, reciting as he danced:

"I bought two troughs, two liters,
And my other half Rochita's. . . .

"That's one of our Odessa songs, foreman. It's called 'From the Bridge to the Slaughterhouse.'" A history teacher in a metropolitan institute, the father of four children, Oska started dancing again.

"Stop, pour us a drink."

Oska groped for a bottle under the bunks and poured something into a tin can. Kostochkin drank and washed down the last of his peas, peas that his fingers were picking out of the bowl.

"Where's that spade artist?"

Oska lifted Krist off the floor and pushed him into the light.

"What, no strength left? You get the bread ration, don't you? Who else gets category two? Isn't that enough for you, you Trotskyist scum?"

Krist said nothing; the brigade said nothing.

"I'll strangle the lot of you. Damned fascists," Kostochkin raged.

"Get back to your place, spade artist, or the foreman will give you another one," Oska advised, as if making peace. He put his arms around the drunken Kostochkin and maneuvered him into a corner, tipping him onto the foreman's luxurious single trestle bed, the only one in the barracks, where all the bunks were double ones in two stories, like a second-class railway sleeper. Meanwhile Oska, the deputy foreman and orderly, who slept on a bunk at the end, was now taking on his third set of important and completely official duties as bodyguard and night watchman, ensuring that the foreman had sleep, peace, and a good life. Krist groped his way to his own bunk.

But neither Kostochkin nor Krist could get to sleep. The barracks door was opened, letting in a current of white mist, and someone came in. He was wearing a white hat with earflaps and a dark winter overcoat with a lamb's fur collar. The overcoat was thoroughly crumpled. The lamb's fur was badly worn, but it was still a genuine overcoat and genuine lamb's fur.

The man walked the length of the barracks toward the light and Kostochkin's trestle bed. Oska greeted him respectfully and started shaking the foreman awake.

"Minia the Greek wants to talk to you." Krist knew the name. He was the foreman of a brigade of gangsters. "Minia the Greek wants to talk to you." By now Kostochkin had woken up properly; he sat on the trestle bed, facing the light.

"You still on a bender, lion tamer?"

"Well, look...see for yourself what the bastards have driven me to...."

Minia the Greek grunted in sympathy.

"One day you'll be blown sky-high, lion tamer. Eh? They'll put some ammonite under your bunk, light the fuse and that's you gone...." The Greek pointed to the sky. "Or you'll get your head sawed off. You've got a thick neck, it'll take a long time to saw through it."

Kostochkin took some time to come to his senses. He waited to hear what the Greek had to say.

"Why don't I pour you a little drink? Just say the word, and we'll rustle some up in a second."

"No. Our brigade's got lots of that alcohol, and you know it. I've got something more important to discuss."

"Happy to be of service."

"'Happy to be of service,'" Minia the Greek laughed. "So that's how you were taught to speak to people in Harbin."

"I didn't mean anything by it," Kostochkin hurriedly replied. "It's just that I still don't know what you want."

"It's this...." The Greek said something very quickly, and Kostochkin nodded in agreement. The Greek drew some diagram on the table, and Kostochkin nodded to show he understood. Oska was following the conversation with some interest. "I've been to see the norm-setter," Minia the Greek was saying, in a voice that was neither sullen nor animated, but couldn't have been more ordinary. "The norm-setter said 'It's Kostochkin's turn.'"

"But I had cubic meters taken off me last week, too."

"What can I do about it...." The Greek's voice was getting more cheerful. "Where else are our lot going to get their cubic meters? I told the norm-setter, and he said it was Kostochkin's turn."

"But, look...."

"What's the point? You know our situation...."

"All right then," said Kostochkin. "You go to the office and count it up, and tell them to take the meters off us."

"Keep your hair on, *freier*," said Minia the Greek, clapping Kostochkin on the shoulder. "You've helped me out today, tomorrow it'll be my turn. You can rely on me. Today you help me, tomorrow I help you."

"Tomorrow we'll both be kissing each other," Oska said, breaking into a dance. He was so pleased by the decision that had finally been reached, and he was afraid that the foreman's hesitation could only ruin things.

"Well, so long, lion tamer," said Minia the Greek as he rose from the bench. "The norm-setter says, 'Just go and have it out with Kostochkin, the lion tamer. There's a touch of the crook about him.' Don't be afraid, don't lose your nerve. Your boys will be all right. You've got those spade artists...."

1964

RUR

But we weren't robots, were we? Robots from Čapek's play *R.U.R.* ("Rossum's Universal Robots")? Nor did it mean we were miners from the Ruhr coal basin. Our RUR could be deciphered as Regiment under Ultra-strict Rules, a prison within a prison, a camp within a camp. No, we weren't robots. There was something human about the metallic insensitivity of robots.

In any case, who among us in 1938 gave a thought to Čapek or to the Ruhr coal district? Only twenty or thirty years later did we find the strength to make comparisons, to attempt to resurrect time, and time's colors and feelings.

Back then all we experienced was a vague, aching joy in our bodies, in muscles that had been desiccated by starvation, which would get relief from the gold-mine pit face, from the accursed work and the hateful toil, at least for a moment, for an hour, for a day. Toil and death were synonyms, and not just for prisoners, for the doomed "enemies of the people." Toil and death were synonyms for the camp bosses, as well, and for Moscow. Otherwise they would not have written in their "special instructions," in those Moscow warrants for a journey to death: "to be used only for heavy physical labor."

We were put into the RUR as skivers, as idlers, for not fulfilling the norm. But not for refusing to work. Refusing to work in the camp was a crime punishable by death. You were shot if you refused to work, or failed to appear three times. Three recorded offenses. When we left the camp zone, we would crawl to our workplace. There was no more strength for work. But we weren't objectors.

We were led off to the guardhouse. The guard on duty poked his arm at my chest; I swayed and could barely stay on my feet; a blow from a revolver butt on my chest had broken a rib. For years the pain gave me no peace. Actually, it wasn't a fracture, as specialists later explained to me, just a tear of the periosteum.

We were led off to the RUR, but there was no RUR there. I saw a living piece of ground, black stony earth, covered with the charred roots of trees, the roots of bushes polished by human bodies. I saw a black rectangle of burned earth: the rectangle stood out, whether it was among the luscious green of the short, passionate Kolyma summer, or in the dead and white infinity of the winter. A black pit made by fires, a trace of warmth, a trace of human life.

The pit was alive. People were turning over beams, rushing around, swearing, and I saw a rejuvenated RUR arise before my eyes: the walls of the punishment barracks. It was then explained to us: the day before, a drunken storekeeper, a nonpolitical criminal, had been put in the RUR communal cell. Naturally, he had dismantled the RUR, the whole prison, log by log. The sentry had failed to shoot him. He had been in a frenzy, but the sentries had a thorough understanding of the legal code, of camp policies, and even of the whims of the bosses. The sentry had failed to shoot. The storekeeper was taken away and put in solitary with a squad of guards over him. But even the storekeeper, the "nonpolitical," obviously a hero, had lacked the courage to leave this black pit. He had merely dismantled the walls. And now a hundred men with article 58 convictions, who had been packed in the RUR, were carefully and hurriedly reconstructing their prison, putting up walls, terrified of crossing the edge of the pit or carelessly stepping onto white snow, not yet stained by human beings.

The article 58 men were in a hurry to restore their prison. There was no need to urge them on or to threaten them.

A hundred men huddled on bunks, on the frames of broken bunks. There were no intact bunks: all the boards, all the bunks' joists were put together without nails. In Kolyma nails cost money, and the gangsters, when put in the RUR, had burned the bunks. The 58ers wouldn't have dared to break off even a fragment of their bunks to warm their frozen bodies, or their withered muscles, which looked like pieces of rope.

Not far from the RUR was the guards' building, just as burned and sooty. The guards' barracks did not look any different from the prisoners' accommodation; even inside there wasn't much difference. Dirty smoke, sacking instead of glass in the windows. All the same, it was the guards' barracks.

Those assigned to RUR would go out to work, not to the gold-mine pit face, but to cut and fetch firewood, to dig ditches, to trample roads smooth. Everyone in the RUR got the same food, which was another source of joy. The RUR working day finished earlier than the pit face. How many times, lifting our eyes from our barrows, from the pit face, from our pickaxes and spades, we enviously watched the ragged columns of RUR prisoners moving off for their night's rest. Our horses would neigh when they saw the RUR men. The horses demanded that work should stop. Perhaps they knew the time rather better than people did, and they didn't need to see the RUR for that. . . .

Now I myself was breaking into a trot, trying, sometimes managing, to march in time with the others, at the same pace, sometimes moving ahead, sometimes lagging behind. . . .

I wanted just one thing: for the RUR never to end. I didn't know for how many days I had been "imported" into the RUR—ten, twenty, thirty.

"Imported" was a prison term I was very familiar with. Apparently the verb "import" was used only in places of detention, while the opposite "deport" took on a broad career in diplomacy, "to deport beyond the frontiers," et cetera. The intention was to give the verb a subtext of threat and mockery, but life changes the scales and "to import" sounded to us almost the same as "to rescue."

Every day after work the RUR prisoners were "herded out" to gather firewood "for themselves," as the bosses put it. In fact, the pit-face brigades were also herded out. There were trips by sled, when the harness straps were adapted for human beings, with wire loops into which you stuck your head and shoulders, and then adjusted the harness, and then you pulled and pulled. The sled had to be hauled uphill for about four kilometers to the stack of dwarf pine that had been piled up in summer. The wood was black, crooked, and lightweight. The sleds were loaded up and then released downhill. The gangsters—those who still had the strength—used to ride the sleds and roar with laughter as they sped downhill. We, however, just crawled down; we didn't have the strength to run. But we slid down quickly, grabbing hold of frozen, broken branches of willow or alder when we needed to brake. It was a happy time because the day was ending.

Each day we had to go further to fetch firewood, the stacks of dwarf pine covered with snow. We didn't grumble, for riding out to fetch wood was something like the banging of the iron rail or the sound of the siren: a signal that food and sleep were coming.

We unloaded the wood and joyfully began forming rank.

"A-bout turn!"

Nobody turned round. I saw mortal anguish in everybody's eyes, the uncertainty of people who don't believe they can come out on top, for they would always be cheated, deceived, and given less than their due. But at least firewood was better than stones, and sleds better than wheelbarrows....

"A-bout turn!"

Nobody turned around. Prisoners are extremely sensitive to breaches of promise, although you wouldn't think that fairness could possibly be expected.

Two men, the camp chief (a lieutenant no longer young) and the head of the guards unit (a younger lieutenant), came out onto the guards' barracks porch. There is nothing worse than what two bosses of roughly equal rank do when they are standing next to each other, in sight of one another. Anything human in them dies; each one wants to demonstrate his "vigilance," not to "betray any weakness," to carry out the state's orders.

"Get harnessed to the sleds."

Nobody turned around.

"This is an organized demonstration!"

"It's sabotage!"

"Let's do it the nice way: will you go?"

"We don't care if you're nice, or not."

"Who said that? Step forward!"

Nobody stepped forward.

A command was given and several escort guards came running out of the barracks, their rifle bolts clicking. They surrounded us, although they found the snow heavy going. They gasped with anger at men who were depriving guards of rest time, interfering with their shifts and work timetable.

"Lie down!"

We all lay down in the snow.

"Get up!"

We got up.

"Lie down!"

We lay down.

"Get up!"

We got up.

"Lie down!"

We lay down.

I had no trouble getting into this simple rhythm. And I remember well that I didn't care one way or the other. As if all this was being done to somebody else.

There were a few shots and bolt clicks, warning shots.

"Get up!"

We got up.

"Those who are willing to go, move to the left."

Nobody moved.

The camp chief came up close, eyeball to eyeball with the anguish in those crazed eyes. He went up to the nearest man and banged his chest.

"Are you going?"

"Yes."

"Move to the left!"

"Are you going?"

"Yes."

"Get harnessed! Guard, take over and count the men."

The wooden sled runners moved off, squeaking.

"Off you go!"

"That's how to do it," said the older lieutenant.

But not everyone left. Two men stayed behind: Seriozha Usoltsev and I. Seriozha was a gangster. All the young nonpoliticals had for some time been running their sleds along the same track as the 58ers.

But Seriozha could not stand seeing some scabby *freier* holding out while he himself, a hereditary criminal, retreated.

"Any moment they'll send us back to barracks....We'll just stand here for a while," Usoltsev said, smiling grimly. "Then it's the barracks, and we'll get warm."

But we weren't allowed back to barracks.

"A dog!" ordered the older lieutenant.

"Take this," said Usoltsev without turning his head. The criminal's fingers put something very thin and almost weightless into my hand. "Got it?"

"Got it."

I was holding a piece of a razor blade, which I showed to the dog without the guards noticing. The dog saw it and understood. The dog growled, yelped and pulled at the lead, but it didn't try to tear either me or Seriozha to bits. Usoltsev was clutching another piece of a razor blade.

"That dog's just a puppy!" said the camp chief, the older lieutenant, a very experienced know-it-all.

"To the barracks."

The door was unlocked, the heavy iron bolt was moved back. Any moment we'd be warm, warm.

But the older lieutenant said something to the duty guard, who then threw the glowing coals out of the iron stove into the snow. The coals hissed, then were covered with blue smoke, and the duty guard then threw snow over them, raking it up with his feet.

"Get into the barracks."

We sat on the framework of the bunks. We felt nothing but the cold, the sudden onset of the cold. We stuck our hands in our sleeves, and bent double.

"Never mind," said Usoltsev. "Any moment the lads will come back with some firewood. Until they do, let's dance." And we started dancing.

The sound of voices, the joyful sound of voices getting nearer, was interrupted by someone's brusque command. Our door opened, but there was no light outside, just the same barracks darkness.

"Come on out!"

"Bat" torches could be seen flashing in the guards' hands.

"Form ranks!"

It took a little time for us to see that the ranks of those who'd come back from work were right there. Why was everyone standing in line waiting? Who were they waiting for?

Dogs were howling in the white haze of the darkness; torches were moving, as they lit up the path of people who were quickly getting nearer. The movement of the light told us that these were no prisoners.

The man who was quickly striding ahead of them, ahead of his bodyguards, was the potbellied but agile colonel. I recognized him straightaway. He had often inspected the gold-mine pit faces where our brigade worked. It was Colonel Garanin. Breathing heavily, unbuttoning his tunic collar, Garanin stopped in front of the ranks and, poking a soft, manicured finger into the dirty chest of the nearest prisoner, said, "What are you inside for?"

"I've got a conviction."

"I don't give a damn what you were convicted of. Why are you in the RUR?"

"I don't know."

"You don't know? Hey, chief!"

"Here's the book of orders, Colonel."

"What the hell do I want your book for? Ugh, you reptiles."

Garanin moved on, looking each man in the face.

"And you, old man, how did you end up in the RUR?"

"I'm still under investigation. We ate a fallen horse. We're night watchmen."

Garanin spat.

"Listen to orders! All of you, back to barracks! To your own brigades! And tomorrow you go to the pit face."

The ranks broke and everyone ran down the path that led over the snow to the barracks, to their brigades. Usoltsev and I also meandered off.

1965

BOGDANOV

BOGDANOV was a dandy. He was always close-shaven and well-scrubbed, and smelled of perfume—God knows what the perfume was—and he wore a luxurious deerskin hat with earflaps, which he tied to his chin with an elaborate system of black moiré ribbons. He also wore a Yakut embroidered jacket and soft, decorative, Siberian deerskin boots. His nails were polished, his collar was starched and a brilliant white. Bogdanov worked as an NKVD officer in one of the Kolyma administrations. Bogdanov had been hidden away by his friends at a coal prospecting expedition at Black Lake when the Ministry of the Interior thrones were overturned and the bosses' heads rolled, as they were replaced one after the other. This new boss with his polished nails turned up in the remotest taiga where there had never been any dirt since the world was created. He appeared with his family, a wife and three little children, none of them much more than babies. The children and the wife were forbidden to leave the house where Bogdanov lived, so that I saw his family only twice: the day they arrived and the day they left.

The store man would bring groceries to the boss's house every day, and workmen rolled a two-hundred-liter barrel of alcohol over a wooden road, laid across the taiga for such purposes. Alcohol, after all, is the main thing to be looked after, as Bogdanov had been taught in Kolyma. A dog? No, Bogdanov didn't have a dog. No dog, and no cat.

The prospecting expedition had an accommodation barracks and tents for the workmen. Everyone lived together, free contract workers and prisoner-workers. There was no difference between them as far as trestle beds or household goods were concerned: the free men were yesterday's prisoners and hadn't yet managed to get themselves suitcases, those homemade prisoners' suitcases that every prisoner was familiar with.

There was no difference in the "regime," the order of the day, either. The previous boss, who had opened up a great number of mines that had been waiting there in Kolyma since the world was created, couldn't for some reason stand hearing the words "Yes, sir" or "I wish to report." When Paramonov, as the first boss was called, was in charge, we had no roll calls; in any case, we got up with the sun and we went to bed with the sun. Actually, the polar sun stopped setting in spring and early summer, so there was no question of a roll call. The taiga nights are short. And we weren't trained to "greet" the boss. Anyone who had been trained was very happy to forget quickly that degrading training. That was why, when Bogdanov came into the barracks, nobody shouted "Attention!" One of the new workmen, Rybin, went on mending his torn tarpaulin cape.

Bogdanov was outraged. He yelled that he would bring these fascists to order; that there were two sides to Soviet authority, the corrective and the punitive; that he, Bogdanov, promised to try out the second side in full; that having no guards wouldn't help us. The prisoners living in the barracks, whom Bogdanov was addressing, were five or six men—five would be more accurate, since two night watchmen took turns to be the sixth.

As he left, Bogdanov grabbed hold of the wooden door of the tent. He meant to slam it, but the submissive tarpaulin merely rippled noiselessly. The next day we five prisoners, plus the absent night watchman, were read an order: the new boss's first order.

The boss's secretary read in a loud, measured voice the new boss's first literary composition, "Order number one." It turned out that Paramonov hadn't even possessed a book of orders, so Bogdanov's schoolgirl daughter's new exercise book was turned into a book of orders for the coal district.

"I have noticed that prisoners in this district have become slack. They've forgotten camp discipline, a fact expressed by their failure to get to their feet for roll call and their failure to greet their chief.

"In view of the fact that this is a violation of Soviet law, I categorically propose. . . ."

The rest was an "order of the day," which Bogdanov's memory had preserved from his previous work.

This same order instituted the post of barracks elder and appointed an orderly who had to take on this responsibility in addition to his basic job. The tents were partitioned with a tarpaulin curtain to separate the clean from the unclean. The unclean weren't bothered by this, but the clean (yesterday's unclean) would never ever forgive Bogdanov for his action. The order sowed enmity between free workers and the boss.

Bogdanov didn't understand anything about the work. He handed over everything to the clerk of works, and all the administrative enthusiasm of this bored forty-year-old boss was directed against six prisoners. Every day some misdemeanor or other was noticed, infringements of camp rules that almost amounted to crimes. A solitary confinement prison was hastily erected in the taiga, and an iron bolt for this prison was ordered from the blacksmith Moisei Moiseyevich Kuznetsov, while the boss's wife contributed her own personal padlock. The padlock came in handy. Every day one of the prisoners was locked up. Rumors began to circulate that a squad of guards would soon be brought in to watch over us.

We were no longer issued vodka as part of our polar rations. Norms now restricted the sugar and tobacco.

Every evening one of the prisoners was summoned to the office to begin an interview with the district boss. I too was summoned. Leafing through my swollen case file, Bogdanov read out extracts from numerous memorandums, and showed exaggerated delight in their tone and style. Sometimes it just seemed that Bogdanov was afraid of forgetting how to read and write. Apart from a few battered children's books, there was not a single book in the boss's quarters.

Suddenly I was amazed to see that Bogdanov was simply very drunk. The smell of cheap perfume was mingled with the smell of alcohol on his breath. His eyes were clouded and dim, although his speech was clear. Everything he said, however, was so ordinary.

The next day I asked the free worker Kartashov, the boss's secretary, if this could be so.

"What's wrong with you—have you only just noticed? He's always drunk. By morning. He doesn't drink a lot at a time, but whenever he feels he's beginning to sober up he takes another half glass. If he starts sobering up, then another half glass. He beats his wife, the bastard," said Kartashov. "That's why she never lets herself be seen. She's too ashamed of her bruises."

It wasn't only his wife that Bogdanov beat. He struck Shatalin, he struck Klimovich. He hadn't gotten around to me yet. But one evening I was invited again to the office.

"Why?" I asked Kartashov.

"I don't know," replied Kartashov, who served not just as secretary, but as messenger and manager of solitary confinement.

I knocked at the door and entered the office.

Bogdanov was combing his hair and trying to look handsome in a big dark mirror that had been hauled into the office. He was sitting at his desk.

"Ah, the fascist," he said as he turned to look at me. I didn't have time to pronounce the regulation response.

"Are you going to work, or not? You're a real deadbeat." "Deadbeat" was a gangster expression. The usual approach and way of talking.

"I do work, sir." And that was the usual response.

"Some letters have arrived for you, see?" I hadn't been in touch with my wife for two years, I had no way of contacting her, I knew nothing of her fate or of the fate of my eighteen-month-old daughter. And suddenly here was her writing, her hand, her letters. Not one, but several letters. I stretched out my trembling hand to take them.

Bogdanov did not let go of the letters. He raised the envelopes toward my dry eyes.

"Here are your letters, you fascist scum!" Bogdanov tore them into shreds and threw the letters from my wife into the burning stove. I had waited over two years for these letters, gone through blood, executions, and beatings at the Kolyma gold mines while I waited.

I turned around and left without uttering the customary formula "Permission to leave, sir." Bogdanov's loud drunken laughter is still, even now after many years, ringing in my ears.

The plan was not being fulfilled. Bogdanov was no engineer. The free workers loathed him. The drop that made the cup overflow was a drop of alcohol, as the main source of conflict between boss and workers was that the barrel of alcohol had migrated to the boss's apartment and was quickly being emptied. Bogdanov could have been forgiven anything—his ridiculously cruel treatment of the prisoners, his hopelessness at his job, his lordly manners. But once the fair sharing of alcohol was abolished, the inhabitants of the settlement began to make war, both openly and covertly, on their boss.

One moonlit winter night a man dressed in civilian clothes turned up in the district: he was wearing a modest hat with earflaps and an old winter coat with a black lambskin collar. The district was twenty kilometers from the main highway, and he had walked that distance along a frozen river. Taking his coat off in the office, the stranger asked for Bogdanov to be woken up. Bogdanov sent an answer: he would get up tomorrow. But the stranger was insistent and asked him to get up, get dressed and come into the office. He explained that a new chief of the coal district had arrived and that Bogdanov had to hand over everything within twenty-four hours. He asked Bogdanov to read the order. Bogdanov got dressed, came out, and invited the stranger to his quarters. The visitor refused and said he would begin the handover of the district immediately.

The news spread instantaneously. The office began to fill with men in a state of undress.

"Where have you put the alcohol?"

"In my apartment."

"Have it brought here."

Kartashov the secretary and the orderly brought a jerry can.

"What about the barrel?"

Bogdanov mumbled something that made no sense.

"Fine. Put lead seals on the jerry can." The visitor sealed the jerry can. "Give me some paper to draw up a statement."

On the evening of the following day Bogdanov, freshly shaved, perfumed, merrily waving his decorated fur gloves, left for the "center." He was completely sober.

"Isn't that the Bogdanov who used to be in the river administration?"

"Probably not. Don't forget, in this job they change their surnames."

1965

THE ENGINEER KISELIOV

I COULDN'T understand what was going on inside the mind of engineer Kiseliov, a young thirty-year-old engineer, an energetic worker, who had just graduated and arrived in the Far North to do his compulsory three-year practical stint. He was one of the few bosses who had read Pushkin, Lermontov, Nekrasov, or so his library card suggested. Above all, he was not a party member, so he couldn't have come to the Far North on higher orders to check up on anything. Before he came to the Far North Kiseliov had never met a prisoner in his life, yet he outdid all the hangmen in his devotion to the trade.

Kiseliov used to beat up prisoners personally, thus setting an example for all his guards, foremen, and the escort guards. After work, Kiseliov went from barracks to barracks and couldn't rest until he'd found someone he could humiliate, hit, beat up with impunity. He had two hundred men at his mercy to choose from. This murky sadistic thirst for murder lay deep inside Kiseliov. The Far North's despotism and lawlessness let him release, develop, and increase it. It wasn't just a question of knocking men to the ground: there were a lot of major and minor bosses in Kolyma who were fond of doing that. They had itchy hands, which, after they had let off steam, would forget a minute later about a tooth they had knocked out, or a prisoner whose face was covered in blood, a prisoner who would remember all his life a blow that the boss had forgotten. Kiseliov didn't just hit you, he knocked you to the ground then stamped his steel-tipped boots again and again on your semi-corpse. Quite a few prisoners had seen the steel tips on the soles and heels of Kiseliov's boots next to their faces.

Who was lying under Kiseliov's boots today, who was sitting in the snow? Zelfugarov: my neighbor in the bunk above me in the train that was going direct to hell, an eighteen-year-old boy with a weak constitution and worn-out muscles, prematurely worn-out. Zelfugarov's facial features were drowned in blood and it was only his thick bushy eyebrows that enabled me to recognize my neighbor. He was a Turk, a forger. The fact that someone had forged money, an offense under article 58, paragraph 12, and was still alive, was something that no prosecutor and no interrogator could believe. The state had only one response to forging money—death. But Zelfugarov was a boy of sixteen when this happened.

"We were making quality money, you couldn't tell it from real money," Zelfugarov, worked up by his memories, whispered to me in the barracks (an insulated tent with a plywood carcass inside the tarpaulin). "There are ways of doing that." His father and mother and two of his uncles had been executed, but the boy survived. Not that he'd live long, as Kiseliov's boots and fists would guarantee.

I bent over Zelfugarov; he spat out his broken teeth onto the snow. His face was swelling before my eyes.

"Go away, go away. If Kiseliov sees you he'll lose his temper," said the engineer Vronsky, pushing me in the back. Vronsky was a Tula miner, born in Tver, and he was the latest specimen from the trials of coal miners. He was an informer and a swine.

We used to climb up narrow steps, hacked into the mountain, to get to our workplace. These were "cross-cut" shafts. There was a gallery tunneled through the mountainside. A lot of rock had already been hauled out by cable—the rails went deep inside. Inside they were drilling, hacking away, and exposing the ore.

Vronsky and I, along with Savchenko, a postal worker from Harbin, and Kriukov, a locomotive driver, were all too weak to be getters, even to be allowed the honor of access to a pickax, a spade, and the "intensified" rations that apparently differed from our ordinary worker's rations by an additional portion of porridge. I knew very well what the camp nutrition scale meant, what horrors were latent in this inducement by food rations, and I wasn't complaining. The others, the novices, heatedly discussed the crucial question: Which category of nutrition would they be given in the next ten days (rations and vouchers changed every ten days). Which one indeed? We were too weak to get the intensified ration, our arm and leg muscles had long ago turned into rope, even string. But we still had muscles in our backs, in our chests, and we still had skin and bones, so we acquired calluses on our chests by carrying out engineer Kiseliov's wishes. All four of us had chest calluses and white patches on our dirty, torn quilted jackets; the calluses on our chests made us look as if we were all wearing the same prison uniform.

Rails had been laid down the gallery, and we would roll a wagon over the rails, using an ordinary rope or hemp cable. At the bottom it would be loaded and we would haul it back up. Naturally, we couldn't haul the wagon up by hand, even if all four of us pulled together, as troikas of draft horses do in Moscow. In the camps every man hauls with all his strength, or with 50 percent more than full strength. Nobody knows how to haul together in the camps. But we had a mechanism, the same one that existed in ancient Egypt and made the construction of the pyramids possible. Pyramids, rather than some shaft, some lousy little shaft. That mechanism was a horse-drawn capstan, except that here we, humans, were harnessed to it instead of horses, and each one of us would press his chest against his own beam, pressing hard until the wagon slowly crawled out of the gallery. Then we left the capstan and rolled the wagon to the dump, unloaded it, hauled it back, put it on the rails, and pushed it down the black maw of the gallery.

The bleeding calluses on our chests, the patches on everyone's breasts were the marks of the horse capstan—or rather Egyptian capstan—beam.

Here we found engineer Kiseliov, hands on hips, waiting for us. He was checking that we took our places in the harness. After finishing his cigarette and stubbing it out thoroughly with his boot, rubbing away any remaining tobacco, Kiseliov would leave. Although we knew that Kiseliov was being deliberately petty by scrubbing away the remains of his cigarette so we wouldn't get a single flake of tobacco, for the clerk of works could see our inflamed, hungry eyes, our prisoners' nostrils, breathing in from afar the smoke of his cigarette, we still couldn't control ourselves as all four of us ran to the stubbed-out, destroyed cigarette, trying to gather at least a flake, a crumb of tobacco. Of course, it was impossible to find even a wisp or a speck. There were tears in our eyes as we went back to our working positions, to the worn beams of the horse capstan, to that revolving winch.

It was Kiseliov, Pavel Dmitriyevich Kiseliov,[6] who resurrected at Arkagala the icy solitary cell of 1938, a cell hacked out of a rock in permafrost, an icy solitary confinement cell. In summer people were stripped to their underwear—following the Gulag instructions for the summer season—and were put in this cell barefooted, hatless, without gloves. In winter you kept your clothes when you were put there—those were the winter-season instructions. Many prisoners had their health permanently destroyed after just one night in this cell.

Kiseliov was discussed a lot in the barracks and tents. His methodical lethal daily beatings seemed to many, who had not been schooled in 1938, too horrible, too unbearable.

Everyone was struck or amazed or even hurt to the quick by a boss who personally took part in the daily reprisals. Prisoners could easily forgive being struck or pushed by the escort guards, the senior guards, and they even forgave their own foremen, but they felt that the area boss, this non-party engineer, was behaving shamefully. Kiseliov's activity outraged even those whose feelings were blunted after many years of imprisonment, who had seen everything, who had learned to be profoundly indifferent, a quality that the camp brings out in people.

The sight of the camps is horrible, and nobody in the world should have to know the camps. Camp experience is entirely negative, every single minute of it. A human being becomes only worse. And it cannot be otherwise. There is a lot in the camps that no man should see, but to see the lower depths of life is not the most terrible thing. The most terrible is when a man begins to feel, forever, that lower depth in his own life, when his moral criteria are borrowed from his camp experience, when the morality of professional criminals is applied to life in the outside world. When a man's mind is not only employed in justifying these camp feelings, but serves the feelings. I know many educated people, and not only educated people, who made the criminal's limits the secret limits of their own behavior when they were freed. In the battle between these people and the camp, the camp won. This meant that they adopted the morals of "better to steal than to ask"; this meant making a false criminal distinction between a person's rations and government rations; this meant too liberal an attitude to anything belonging to or coming from the state. There are many examples of depravity. The moral boundary, the line that one must not cross, is very important for a prisoner. The crucial question in his life is whether he has remained human or not.

The distinction is very subtle, and what you should be ashamed of is not memories of having been a goner, a "malingerer," of having run around like "a whore with a cooking pot," rummaging in rubbish heaps. You should be ashamed of having acquired a gangster's morals, even if they allowed you a chance of surviving as the gangsters did, ashamed of pretending to be a nonpolitical and behaving so that God forbid that either the boss or your fellow prisoners find out that you had a conviction under article 58 or article 162, or some employment crime, such as embezzlement or negligence. In a word, the intellectual tries to be a Zoya Kosmodemianskaya,[7] to be a gangster with gangsters, a criminal with the criminals. He thieves, drinks, and is even pleased to get a sentence for a nonpolitical offense, because the stigma of being a "political" is finally erased. Not that there ever was anything political about him. There were no politicals in the camps. They were imaginary, invented enemies with whom the state was settling scores—shooting them, murdering them, starving them to death—as if they were genuine enemies. Stalin's deadly scythe mowed down without distinction everyone, matching the allocations, the lists, the plan to be fulfilled. The percentage of scoundrels and cowards among those who perished in the camp was the same as in the free world. They were all people who happened to be there, indifferent people or cowards, philistines or even hangmen, who were by chance turned into victims.

The camp was a powerful test of a human being's moral strength, of everyday human morality, and 99 percent of the men failed that test. Those who passed it died alongside those who failed, although these men tried to be better and firmer than everyone else: what they were doing was purely for their own sake.

In the middle of autumn there was a raging blizzard. A young duck that had put off migration too long, was losing its strength, unable to struggle with the snow. A floodlight was lit on the flat clearing and, deceived by its cold light, the duck rushed toward it, flapping its wings weighed down by the wet snow. It thought it was heading for the sun, for warmth. But the search lamp's cold light was not the burning, life-giving sun: the duck gave up its battle with the snow. It landed on the clearing in front of the mine gallery, where we—skeletons dressed in ragged quilted jackets—were pressing our chests against the beam of the capstan, to the sound of the guard's sarcastic whooping. Savchenko caught the duck with his hands. He kept it warm under his jacket, against his bony belly, drying its feathers with his cold, hungry body.

"Shall we eat it?" I asked. Using the plural was utterly pointless. This was Savchenko's game and booty, not mine.

"No. I'll give it away instead."

"Who to? The guard?"

"To Kiseliov."

Savchenko took the duck to the building where the area chief lived. The chief's wife brought out to Savchenko two pieces of bread, about three hundred grams, and poured a cooking pot full of liquid from a barrel of fermented cabbage. Kiseliov knew how to pay off prisoners and had taught his wife to do the same. Disappointed, we devoured the bread. Savchenko took the larger piece, I took the smaller one. We drank the soup and licked the pot clean.

"We'd have done better to eat the duck ourselves," Savchenko said sadly.

"We shouldn't have taken it to Kiseliov," I concurred.

It was by sheer luck that I was still alive after the exterminations of 1937. I had no intention of dooming myself to those familiar torments. To doom yourself to daily, hourly humiliations, to beatings, to taunts, to fights with the guard, the cook, the bathhouse attendant, the fore-man, to anyone in power: an endless struggle for a piece of something edible, so as not to die of hunger, so as to live to see a tomorrow that would be just the same.

You had to gather the last remnants of your shattered, exhausted, tormented will if you were to put an end to the taunts, possibly at the cost of your life. Life was not such a big stake in the camp gamble. I knew that everyone thought the same way, although they didn't say so. I devised a way to get rid of Kiseliov.

One and a half million tons of semi-soft coking coal, as high in calories as coal from the Don basin, was what Arkagala, the coal district of Kolyma, had in its reserves. Here it took non-coniferous trees, twisted by the cold in their crowns and the permafrost at their roots, three hundred years to reach maturity. Given forests of this kind, the importance of coal reserves was obvious to any boss in Kolyma. That was why the very top bosses were often seen at the Arkagala mine shafts.

"The moment any top boss comes to Arkagala, punch Kiseliov in his ugly mug. In public. They'll be touring the barracks and definitely the mine shaft. Step out of the line and give him a slap on the cheek."

"Suppose they shoot you the moment you step forward?"

"They won't. They won't be expecting it. Kolyma bosses don't have a lot of experience in getting their cheeks slapped. After all, you'll be going up to your own clerk of works, not to a visiting boss."

"They'll give us a sentence."

"They'll give you two years or so. They won't give you more for a son of a bitch like him. And you have to take your two years."

None of the old Kolyma hands anticipated coming back from the north alive, so a sentence had no significance for us. As long as we weren't executed, weren't murdered. And even that. . . .

"What's clear is that after he's been slapped, Kiseliov will be removed, he'll be transferred, dismissed. In top boss circles being slapped is considered a disgrace. We prisoners don't think like that, nor, probably, does Kiseliov. A slap like that will echo all over Kolyma."

After daydreaming about the most important thing in our lives, as we sat around the stove, around the cooling hearth, I climbed up to my place on the top bunks, where it was warmer, and fell asleep.

I slept without dreaming. The next morning we were taken to our workplace. The office door opened, and the area chief strode across the threshold. Kiseliov was no coward.

"Hey, you," he yelled. "Come here."

I approached.

"So it will echo all over Kolyma, will it? Eh? Well, wait for it. . . ."

He didn't hit me, he didn't even make a gesture of swinging a punch, which would have been in accordance with his dignity as a boss. He turned around and went away. I had to wait it out very cautiously. Kiseliov never approached me and never told me off again, he just shut me out of his life, but I realized that he wouldn't forget a thing, and sometimes I felt piercing my back the hate-filled gaze of a man who hadn't yet worked out how to take his revenge.

I had thought a great deal about the great camp wonder: the wonder of grassing, of denunciation. When was I denounced to Kiseliov? It meant that the grass hadn't slept that night, but had run off to the guardhouse or to the boss's apartment. Worn out by his daytime work, this loyal grass had stolen his own nighttime rest, had gone through agonies, had suffered so that he could "report." Who was it then? There were four of us present at that conversation. I myself hadn't grassed, I was certain of that. There are situations in life when a man doesn't know himself if he has grassed on his comrades, or not. Take for example the endless declarations of penitence from all the deviationists in the party. Were those denunciations, or not? I'm not talking about the mindless state in which statements are made after a hot soldering iron has been used. That also happened. Even today there is a professor in Moscow, a Buryat Mongol, who bears the scars on his face from a soldering iron used in 1937. Who else? Savchenko? Savchenko was sleeping next to me. Vronsky the engineer? Yes, it was Vronsky. Him. I had to move quickly, so I wrote a note.

On the evening of the next day a doctor, a prisoner called Kunin, traveled the eleven kilometers from Arkagala. I knew him slightly; we'd met in a transit camp years before. After inspecting the sick and the healthy, Kunin winked at me and set off to see Kiseliov.

"Well, how was the inspection? Everything in order?"

"Yes, nearly, nearly. I have a request, Pavel Dmitriyevich."

"Happy to be of service."

"Let Andreyev go to Arkagala, will you? I'll sign the transfer."

Kiseliov flared up.

"Andreyev? No, Sergei Mikhailovich, anyone else, but not Andreyev." He laughed. "How can I put it in printable words? He's my personal enemy."

There are two schools among camp bosses. Some consider that any prisoner, and not just a prisoner, anyone who has personally annoyed a boss, should be sent as quickly as possible somewhere else, transferred, thrown off the site.

The other school considers that all offenders, all personal enemies must be kept close to you, where you can see them and personally check up on the effectiveness of punitive measures that the boss has devised to satisfy his own ego, his own cruelty. Kiseliov subscribed to the second school's principles.

"I wouldn't dare insist," said Kunin. "To be frank, that's not the reason I'm here. Here are some statements, and there are quite a lot of them." Kunin undid the clasps of his battered canvas briefcase. "Statements about beatings. I haven't signed them yet. You know, I hold the simple 'popular' view of such things. You can't resurrect the dead, you can't glue broken bones together. Not that there are any corpses in these statements. I'm just talking figuratively about the dead. I have nothing against you, Pavel Dmitriyevich, and I could tone down some of the medical conclusions. I can't destroy them, I can just tone them down. I can set out what happened in an understated way. But now I see the state your nerves are in, I don't want to bother you with a personal request."

"No, no, Sergei Mikhailovich," said Kiseliov, putting restraining hands on the shoulders of Kunin, who had risen from his stool. "Why not? Couldn't you just tear up these idiotic statements? Word of honor, I did it in the heat of the moment. And anyway, they're such rogues. They'd drive anyone to hit them."

"If you're saying that these rogues would drive anyone to hit them, I have my own opinion about that, Pavel Dmitriyevich. As for the statements.... Of course they can't be torn up, but they can be toned down."

"Then do so!"

"I'd be only too willing," Kunin said coldly, looking Kiseliov straight in the eyes. "But I have asked you to transfer one lousy prisoner to Arkagala, that goner Andreyev, and you refuse even to listen. All you did was laugh...."

Kiseliov stayed silent for a while.

"You're all scum," he said. "Write that transfer order to the hospital."

"That's the job of your area paramedic, on your instructions," said Kunin.

That same evening I was driven away to Arkagala, the main camp zone, with a diagnosis of "acute appendicitis." I never saw Kiseliov again. But within six months I did hear about him.

People were rustling a newspaper and laughing in the dark mining drifts. The paper had printed an announcement of Kiseliov's sudden death. For the hundredth time, the story was told in all its details and people were choking with joyful laughter. One night a burglar got through a window into the engineer's apartment. Kiseliov was no coward; he always had a loaded double-barreled shotgun hanging by his bed. When he heard the noise, Kiseliov leapt off his bed, cocked the triggers, and ran into the next room. When the burglar heard the owner's footsteps, he rushed to the window, and was delayed for a short time as he tried to squeeze out of the narrow opening.

Kiseliov struck the burglar from behind with the butt of his gun, as one does in defensive hand-to-hand battle—following all the rules that the free men had been taught during the war, when they were instructed in outdated methods of hand-to-hand combat. The double-barreled gun went off. The whole charge hit Kiseliov in the belly. Two hours later he was dead. The nearest surgeon was forty kilometers away, but Kunin, being a prisoner, was not authorized to perform an emergency operation.

The day when news of Kiseliov's death reached the mine shaft was a holiday for the prisoners. Apparently, the plan, too, was fulfilled that day.

1965

CAPTAIN TOLLY'S LOVE

THE EASIEST job in a gold-mine pit-face brigade is the gangway maker's: he's the carpenter who extends the wooden ramp by nailing together boards over which the barrows full of "sand" are pushed to the sizing trommel, the ore-washing equipment. These wooden "whiskers" lead to each pit face from a central ramp. Seen from above, from the sizing trommel, it looks like a gigantic centipede that has been squashed, dried out, and nailed forever to the bottom of the gold-mine cross section.

The gangway carpenter's job—a "breeze"—is easy work compared to that of a getter or a barrow man. The gangway carpenter doesn't have to hold barrow handles, or a spade, or a crowbar, or a pickax. An ax and a handful of nails is his equipment. The foreman usually gives each workman a turn to do this vital, necessary, and important work, thus letting them have at least a short break. Of course, fingers that have lost their feeling, after endlessly gripping a spade haft or a pickax handle, need more than a day of easy work to unbend. They need a year or more of rest. But there was a grain of fairness in this alternation of light and heavy labor. Work was not allocated just in turn: the weaker the worker, the better his chance of getting at least a day as a gangway carpenter. You didn't need to be a joiner or a carpenter to hammer in nails and to hack boards into shape. People with university degrees could cope very well with the job.

In our brigade this "breeze" wasn't allocated by turn. The job of gangway carpenter in our brigade was always given to the same man, Isai Rabinovich, a former director of Soviet Union State Insurance. Rabinovich was sixty-eight years old, but he was a strong old man and hoped to survive his ten-year sentence in the camps. Work is what kills people in the camps, so anyone who praises camp labor is either a scoundrel or a fool. Twenty-year-olds and thirty-year-olds died one after the other—which was why they'd been brought to this special zone—but Rabinovich the gangway man went on living. He had some acquaintances among the camp bosses, secret connections, for Rabinovich would get a temporary job in the accounts department or as an office clerk. Rabinovich understood that every day and hour not spent at the pit face was a promise of life, of salvation for an old man, whereas the pit face meant only perdition and death. People of pensionable age were not supposed to be taken to special zones. The information in Rabinovich's file was what had gotten him into the special zone, to die.

Then Rabinovich dug his heels in and refused to die.

One day we were locked up together, "isolated," on May 1, as happened every year.

"I've been keeping an eye on you for a long time," said Rabinovich, "and I found it extraordinarily pleasant to know that someone was keeping an eye on me, studying me, and not someone whose job it is to keep an eye open." I smiled my crooked smile, ripping open my injured lips, and tearing up my scurvied gums. "I'm sure you're a good person. You never talk foully about women."

"I've never kept an eye on myself, Isai Davydovich. Anyway, who talks about women here?"

"I'm told you're the only one who doesn't join in that sort of conversation."

"To tell you the truth, Isai Davydovich, I consider women to be better than men. I understand the unity of a couple, of husband and wife, and so on. All the same, motherhood is labor. So women work better than men."

"That's utterly true," said Rabinovich's neighbor, Beznozhenko the bookkeeper. "Whenever you have a day of shock work or a working Saturday, you'd better not work next to a woman. She'll drive you mad and chase you away. If you want a cigarette she gets angry."

"Yes, there's that, too," said Rabinovich, not paying attention. "Probably, probably."

"Take Kolyma. A great number of women follow their husbands here—a horrible fate, you have the bosses making passes at you, all those louts who are infected with syphilis. You know that just as well as I do. Yet not a single man has ever come here to be with a wife who's been deported and condemned."

"I was a manager in State Insurance for a very short time," said Rabinovich. "But long enough to 'get a tenner.' For many years I was in charge of the external agents of State Insurance. Do you understand what this means?"

"I do," I said without thinking, for I didn't understand.

"Apart from State Insurance work abroad—" at this point Rabinovich suddenly looked me in the eyes, sensing that none of it interested me, at least until I'd had dinner.

After a spoonful of soup, we went on with the conversation.

"If you like, I'll tell you about myself. I've spent a lot of my life abroad, and now, in the hospitals I've been in, or the barracks I've lived in, I keep getting asked about just one thing. What I ate, where, and how. Gastronomical subjects. Gastronomical nightmares, fantasies, and dreams. Do you want to hear this sort of story?"

"Yes, I do, too," I said.

"Right. I'm an insurance agent from Odessa. I worked for the Russia, which was an insurance company at the time. I was young, I tried to do things for the boss as conscientiously and as well as I could. I studied languages. I was sent abroad. I married the boss's daughter. I lived abroad right until the revolution. My boss wasn't particularly frightened by the revolution—like Savva Morozov,[8] he was betting on the Bolsheviks.

"During the revolution I was abroad with my wife and daughter. My father-in-law died unexpectedly, not because of the revolution. I knew a lot of people, but none of them had any use for the October 1917 revolution. Do I make myself clear?"

"Yes."

"Soviet power was only just getting to its feet then. People came to see me. Russia, the Russian Soviet Federal Socialist Republic, was making its first purchases abroad. They needed credit. But promissory notes from the State Bank were not enough to get credit. A note and a recommendation from me, however, was. So I put Kreuger, the match king, in touch with the RSFSR. After a few more operations of that sort I was allowed to go back home, where I was busy with certain sensitive deals. Have you heard anything about the sale of Spitsbergen and the way payment was made after that sale?"

"I've heard a little."

"Well then: I was reloading Norwegian gold in the North Sea onto our schooner. So, apart from our external agents, I had a number of missions like that. Soviet power was my new boss. I worked just as I had in the insurance company: conscientiously."

Rabinovich's intelligent, calm eyes were looking at me.

"I'm going to die. I'm an old man now. I've seen life. I'm sorry for my wife. And for my daughter in Moscow. They haven't yet been swept away in the roundup of members of the family.... Clearly, I'll never see them again. They write to me often. They send parcels. Do you get any parcels? Do your people send any?"

"No. I wrote and told them not to. If I survive, then it will be without any outside help. I shall be obliged only to myself."

"There's something chivalrous about that. My wife and daughter wouldn't understand."

"There's nothing chivalrous about it. You and I are not just beyond good and evil, we're beyond everything human. After what I've seen, I don't want to be in anyone's debt, even to my own wife."

"That's confusing. I just write and ask for things. Parcels mean getting work for a month in the accounts department. I handed over my best suit to get that job. I expect you think the boss felt sorry for an old man...."

"I thought you had some special relationship with the camp bosses."

"Do you think I'm a grass? Well, who needs a seventy-year-old grass? No, I simply gave a bribe, a big one. And I'm still alive. I've never shared the result of that bribe with anyone, not even with you. I get something, I write and I ask."

After our May Day imprisonment we came back to the barracks together and chose neighboring bunks. The bunks were on the railway sleeping car system. It's not that we'd become friends; it's impossible to make friends in the camp. It's just that we respected each other. I had a lot of experience of the camps, while old Rabinovich had a young man's curiosity about life. He saw that there was no way of suppressing my anger, and he began treating me with respect, but no more than respect. Perhaps it was just an old man's nostalgia for the sleeping car habit of telling the first person you meet all about yourself. A life you wanted to leave behind on earth.

Lice didn't frighten us. At the same time I got to know Isai Rabinovich, my scarf was stolen: it was cotton, of course, but still, it was a real knitted scarf.

We were going out together to line up for work, a lineup "minus the last man," as such lineups are called, so colorfully and frighteningly, in the camps. A lineup "minus the last man." The bosses would grab hold of men, the escort guard would jostle them with his rifle butt, beating and herding the crowd of ragged men off the ice-covered mountain, sending them downhill: anyone who lagged behind or was late was led to what was called a lineup "minus the last man," because this man would be grabbed by the arms and legs, swung to and fro and then hurled down the icy mountain. Rabinovich and I did our best to leap now as fast as we could, then line up and reach the clear space where the guard was now waiting and lining men up for work, punching them in the mouth. Mostly, we managed to roll down safely and reach the pit face alive, to confront whatever was waiting for us there.

The last man, who had been late and was thrown off the mountain, would be tied by the feet to the horse-drawn drays and dragged along to the pit face where he worked. Rabinovich and I were both lucky enough to escape this lethal ride.

The camp zone was sited where it was for a special reason: we had to return uphill from work, clambering over steps, grabbing the remains of the bare, broken bushes as we crawled up. After a working day at a gold-mine pit face, you'd have thought that a man wouldn't find the strength to climb. And yet we did. It may have taken half an hour, but we reached the guardhouse gates, the zone, the barracks, our living quarters. There was the usual inscription over the pediment of the gates: "Labor is a matter of honor, a matter of glory, a matter of valor and heroism." We went to the refectory, downed something from the bowls, went to the barracks, and lay down to sleep. In the morning it all began again.

Not everyone starved here—but why they didn't, I never found out.

When it got warmer, as spring approached, the white nights began, and so did terrible games of "catch alive." A bread ration was laid on a table, then men hid in the corner, waiting for a hungry victim, some goner, to come up, bewitched by the bread, and touch and grab the bread ration. Then everyone would rush out from their dark ambush in the corner, and a thief or a living skeleton would start to get a fatal beating. This was a new sport I only ever saw at Jelgala. The organizer of these amusements was Dr. Krivitsky, an old revolutionary, the former deputy People's Commissar of the Defense Industry. Together with Zaslavsky, the journalist from *Izvestiya*, Krivitsky was the main organizer of these bloody "manhunts," these terrible lures.

I had a scarf, cotton, of course, but knitted, a real scarf. The hospital paramedic had given it to me as a present, when I was being discharged. When our party of prisoners was unloaded at Jelgala, an unsmiling gray face with a northerner's deep-cut wrinkles and the marks of old frostbite scars loomed up toward me.

"Let's swap!"

"No."

"Sell it."

"No."

All the local men—and about twenty of them had run up to our truck—looked at me with amazement, astonished by my impetuousness, stupidity and pride.

"He's the elder, the camp elder," someone informed me, but I shook my head.

The eyebrows on his toothless face moved upward. The elder nodded to someone, pointing to me.

But in this zone people hesitated to commit robbery. There was a much simpler way, and I knew what it would be. I knotted the scarf around my neck and never took it off again, not in the bathhouse, nor at night, never.

It should have been easy to keep the scarf, but the lice made it hard. There were so many lice in the scarf that it moved when I took the scarf off for a minute, laid it out by the table lamp, and tried to shake them off.

I fought for about two weeks with shadowy thieves, telling myself that they were shadows, not thieves. Just once in two weeks I hung the scarf on the bunks where I could see it, turned around to pour myself a mug of water, and the scarf, grabbed by an experienced thieving hand, instantly vanished. I was so tired of fighting to keep this scarf, and the prospect of this theft, which I knew, sensed, and almost saw, demanded so much intensive effort, that I was even glad I no longer had anything to hang onto. For the first time since my arrival at Jelgala I fell into a deep sleep and had a pleasant dream. That could be, of course, because thousands of lice had vanished and my body instantly felt relieved.

It was with some sympathy that Isai Rabinovich observed my heroic struggle. Naturally, he didn't help me to hang on to my lousy scarf—everyone looks after himself in the camps, and I didn't expect any help.

When Isai Rabinovich had a few days' work in the bookkeeper's office, however, he did slip me a dinner voucher, which consoled me for my loss. And I thanked him.

After work everyone immediately went to bed, using their dirty work clothes as a mattress.

Isai Rabinovich said, "I want your advice about something. Nothing to do with the camp."

"About General de Gaulle?"

"No, there's no need to laugh at me. I've received an important letter. At least, important to me."

I fought off the sleepiness that was overcoming me by tensing my whole body; I shook myself and began listening.

"I told you earlier that my daughter and wife are in Moscow. They've been left alone. My daughter wants to get married. I've had a letter from her. And from her fiancé, too—here it is," Rabinovich took a bundle of letters from under his pillow. It was a packet of beautiful sheets of paper, written in precise and quick handwriting. I took a closer look: the letters were Latin ones, not Russian.

"Moscow has given permission for these letters to be sent on to me. Do you know English?"

"Me? English? No."

"They're in English. From her fiancé. He's asking for my consent to marry my daughter. He writes, 'My parents have already given their consent, all I now need is the consent of my future wife's parents. I ask you, my dear father....' And here's my daughter's letter. 'Daddy, my husband, the naval attaché of the United States of America, Captain Tolly, is asking for your consent to our marriage. Daddy, please reply as soon as you can.'"

"What sort of madness is this?" I asked.

"It's not mad at all, it's Captain Tolly's letter to me. And my daughter's letter. And my wife's letter."

Rabinovich slowly groped for a louse under his shirt, pulled it out and squashed it against the bunk.

"Your daughter is asking for consent to a marriage?"

"Yes."

"Your daughter's fiancé, the naval attaché of the United States, Captain Tolly, is asking for your consent to marrying your daughter?"

"Yes."

"Well, run and see the camp boss and make an application for permission to send an express letter."

"But I don't want to give my consent to her marriage. That's what I wanted your advice about."

I was simply stunned by these letters, these stories, this action.

"If I agree to the marriage, I'll never see her again. She'll leave with Captain Tolly."

"Listen, Isai Davydovich. You'll soon be seventy. I consider you to be a reasonable man."

"It's just a feeling, I haven't yet given it proper thought. I'll send my reply tomorrow. It's time we went to sleep."

"Let's celebrate this event tomorrow. We'll eat the porridge before we eat the soup. And the soup after the porridge. We can still toast some bread. We can dry some rusks. We can boil bread in water. How about it, Isai Davydovich?"

Even an earthquake wouldn't have stopped me sleeping, from seeking the oblivion of sleep. I shut my eyes and forgot about Captain Tolly.

The next day Rabinovich wrote a letter and dropped it in the post-box by the guardhouse.

Soon I was taken off to be tried; I was tried and a year later brought back to the same special zone. I had no scarf, and the former barracks elder was there no more. I came as an ordinary camp goner, a walking ghost with no particular distinguishing features. But Isai Rabinovich recognized me and brought me a piece of bread. He had found his niche in the bookkeeping department and he had learned not to think about the next day. The pit face had finally taught Rabinovich that.

"I think you were here when my daughter was getting married, weren't you?"

"I was, of course I was."

"The story continues."

"Tell me."

"Captain Tolly did marry my daughter—I think that's where I left off," Rabinovich began telling me. His eyes were smiling. "He spent about three months with her. He spent three months dancing, then Captain Tolly was given command of a battleship in the Pacific and went off there to serve. My daughter, Captain Tolly's wife, was forbidden to leave the country. Stalin then viewed such marriages to foreigners as a personal insult, so someone in the Foreign Ministry whispered to Captain Tolly, 'Go on your own, you've had your fun in Moscow— you're an eligible young man, what's holding you back? Get married again.' In a word, that was the final answer—this woman stays at home. Captain Tolly left and for a whole year there were no letters from him. But a year later my daughter was sent to work in Stockholm, in the embassy in Sweden."

"As a spy, do you mean? Doing secret work?"

Rabinovich gave me a disapproving look. He didn't approve of my idle chatter.

"I don't know, I don't know what work. She went to work in the embassy. My daughter worked there for a week. Then an airplane came from America, and she flew off to join her husband. Now I shall expect letters from somewhere other than Moscow."

"How about the bosses here?"

"The people here are afraid, they don't dare to have their own opinions about such matters. An interrogator came from Moscow and questioned me about it. Then he left."

That wasn't the end of Rabinovich's happiness. The miracle that excelled all others was the miracle of completing his sentence, right to the very last day, with no credit given for working days.

The former insurance agent's constitution was so strong that Rabinovich went on working as a free worker in Kolyma, as a tax inspector. He wasn't allowed back to the mainland. Rabinovich died about two years before the Twentieth Party Congress.[9]

1965

THE CROSS[10]

THE BLIND priest crossed the yard, his feet feeling for the narrow board, like a ship's gangway, laid over the ground. He walked slowly, almost without stumbling or missing the board, treading on the wooden path with the rectangular toes of his son's enormous, badly worn boots. The priest held in both hands buckets of steaming swill for his goats, which were locked in a dark, low shed. There were three goats, Mashka, Ella, and Tonia—the names were cleverly chosen, with different vowel sounds. Usually only the goat whose name he called would respond. But in the morning, when food was being given out, the goats' heart-rending voices bleated in a disorderly way, as they took turns poking their noses through the crack in the shed door. Half an hour previously, the priest had milked them and had taken the steaming milk home in a big churn. In his eternal darkness he often made mistakes when milking: a fine stream of milk might spout silently and miss the churn. The goats would look anxiously at their own milk, when it was squeezed out straight onto the ground. But perhaps they didn't even look.

The reason he made mistakes was not because he was blind. His thoughts were just as great a hindrance and, as his warm hand rhythmically squeezed the goat's cool udder, he often forgot himself and what he was doing, as he thought about his family.

The priest had gone blind shortly after the death of his son, a Red Army man in the chemical squad. His glaucoma, the "yellow water," became acute and he lost his sight. The priest had other children, two more sons and two daughters, but this middle son was his favorite and was like an only son.

The work involving the goats—milking them, caring for them, feeding them, cleaning out their shed—was all done by the priest, and this desperate and unnecessary work was a measure of ensuring his place in life. The blind priest had been accustomed to being the breadwinner for a large family, to having his own place in life, to being independent of everybody, of society, and of his own children. He told his wife to keep a careful record of the expenditure on the goats and of the income received from selling goat's milk in summer. People in town were happy to buy goat's milk, it was considered especially good for those with tuberculosis. The medical value of this opinion was slight, no greater than the well-known diet of black puppy meat recommended by some authorities for those suffering from tuberculosis. The blind priest and his wife each drank two glasses of the milk every day, and the priest also had the value of these glassfuls recorded. The very first summer it turned out that the goats' food cost far more than the value of the milk given, and the taxes on "small cattle" were by no means small. But the priest's wife hid the truth from her husband, telling him that the goats were profitable. And the blind priest thanked God that he had found the strength to help his wife, no matter in how small a way.

Everyone in town used to call the priest's wife "Mother," since she was a priest's wife, until 1928, and in 1929 they stopped doing so. Nearly all the town churches were then blown up, and the "cold" cathedral, in which Ivan the Terrible had once prayed, was turned into a museum. The priest's wife used to be so stout and fat that her own son, who was then six, made a fuss and wept, insisting, "I don't want to walk with you, I'm embarrassed. You're so fat." Later, some time ago, she lost her fat, but her body's stoutness, the unhealthy stoutness of someone with a bad heart, remained. She could barely walk across the room, it was hard for her to get from the kitchen stove to the living room window. At first the priest used to ask her to read him something, but his wife never had the time: there were always a thousand household chores, food had to be cooked for themselves and for the goats. The priest's wife never went to the shops: the neighbors' children did her modest shopping, and she paid them with some goat's milk or gave them a boiled sweet or something similar.

There was a cauldron, a "cast-iron" as such pots are called in the north—on the hearth of the Russian stove. The edge of the cast-iron had been broken off, which happened in their first year of marriage. The boiling goat swill poured out from the cast-iron's broken lip and dripped off the hearth onto the floor. Next to the cast-iron was a small pot of porridge—dinner for the priest and his wife. People needed far less food than animals did.

But people did need something.

There wasn't a lot to do, but the woman moved too slowly around the room, her hands holding on to the furniture, and by the end of the day she grew so tired that she couldn't find the strength to read. So she fell asleep, which annoyed the priest. He slept very little, although he tried to make himself sleep and sleep. When their second son came to stay with them, he was dismayed by his father's hopeless state. He asked anxiously, "Dad, why do you sleep day and night? Why do you sleep so much?"

"You're a fool," the priest replied. "When I'm asleep, I can see...."

And his son could not forget these words until the day he died.

Radio broadcasting was then in its infancy. Amateurs had quartz receivers that used to crackle, and nobody had the courage to attach the earth wire to the heating radiator or to the telephone. The priest had only heard of radio receivers, but he understood that his children, who were scattered all over the world, would not be able to get together enough money even for a set of earphones for him.

The blind man found it hard to understand why a few years previously they were forced to move out of the room that they had lived in for over thirty years. His wife whispered something that made no sense, and was full of anxiety and anger, with her enormous, toothless and chomping mouth. His wife never told him the truth about the policemen carrying out of the wretched room their broken chairs, old chest of drawers, box of photographs, daguerreotypes, cast-iron and clay pots, a few books—the remains of what had been an enormous library—and a trunk where they kept their last valuable, a golden pectoral cross. The blind man was utterly puzzled; he was taken off to new quarters, and he said nothing, just quietly praying to God. The bleating goats were led off to their new quarters, and a carpenter he knew settled them in there. One goat went missing in the confusion, the fourth goat, Ira.

The new tenants of that apartment on the riverbank were a young town prosecutor and his fashion-conscious wife. They stayed in the Central Hotel until they were told that the flat was free. The couple installed in the main room a metalworker and his family, who had been living in an apartment opposite, while the metalworker's two rooms went to the prosecutor. The town prosecutor had never seen, and would never see, the priest or the metalworker whose living quarters he had taken over.

The priest and his wife seldom recalled their previous room: he, because he was blind, she, because she had seen too much grief, far more grief than joy, in the old apartment. The priest never found out that his wife, for as long as she was able, baked pies that she sold at the market and kept writing letters to her various friends and relatives, begging them to contribute something, however small, to support her and her blind husband. Occasionally, money did come in, not much, but enough to buy hay and oil-cake for the goats, to pay their taxes and to pay the shepherd.

The goats should have been sold long ago: they were only a hindrance—but she was afraid even to think of it, for this was the only job her blind husband had. Remembering what a lively, energetic man he was before his terrible illness, she couldn't bring herself to talk to him about selling the goats. So everything went on as before.

She also wrote to her children, who had long ago grown up and had their own families. The children replied to her letter; they all had their worries, their own children. In fact, not all the children replied.

A long time ago, back in the 1920s, the eldest son had renounced his father. It was then the fashion to renounce your parents, and quite a few writers and poets who would later become well-known began their literary careers with declarations of that kind. The eldest son was neither a poet nor a scoundrel; he was simply afraid of life and sent his declaration to a newspaper when people began to come at him at work with talk about his "social origins." The declaration did him no good, and he carried his mark of Cain to the grave.

The priest's daughters had married. The elder lived somewhere in the south, she had no control over money in her new family and was afraid of her husband, but she often wrote tearful letters home, full of her woes. Her old mother replied to her, weeping over her daughter's letters and consoling her. Every year the elder daughter sent her mother a parcel of several tens of kilos of grapes. It took a long time for a parcel to arrive from the south. Her mother never told her daughter that the grapes arrived every year completely spoiled: she could pick out for herself and her husband only a few berries out of the whole consignment. Each time she thanked her daughter and did so humbly, too embarrassed to ask for money.

The second daughter was a paramedic, and after she married she had the intention of setting aside her wretched salary to send to her blind father. Her husband, a trade union worker, approved of this intention, and for about three months the paramedic contributed her pay to her parents' house. But after she gave birth, she stopped working and spent all day and all night busy with her twins. Soon it emerged that her husband, the trade union worker, was a binge drinker. His career quickly took a downward turn, and three years later he became a supply agent, a job he was unable to keep for long. His wife and two small children ended up destitute, so she went back to work and struggled as best she could to keep two small children and herself on a nurse's salary. How could she have helped her old mother and blind father?

The youngest son was unmarried. He should have lived with his father and mother, but he decided to try his luck on his own. The middle brother had left an inheritance: a hunting rifle, an almost new turn-bolt Sauer. His father told his mother to sell the rifle for ninety rubles. For twenty rubles they had two new satin Tolstoy-style tunics made for their son, and he left to live with an aunt in Moscow, taking a job as a factory worker. The younger son sent money home, but not much at a time—five or ten rubles a month. But soon, he was arrested for taking part in an underground meeting and he was exiled. They could not trace him.

The blind priest and his wife always got up at six in the morning. The old mother would stoke the stove, while the blind priest went to milk the goats. There was no money at all, but the old woman managed to borrow a few rubles from the neighbors. These rubles had to be paid back, however, but they now had nothing to sell: all their portable things, their tablecloths, linen, chairs, had long been sold or swapped for flour for the goats, or for pearl barley for soup. Both their wedding rings and a silver neck chain had been sold to the hard-currency shop a year ago. Only on major holidays did they have meat with their soup, and the old couple bought sugar only for special occasions. Someone might drop in and let them have a sweet or a bun, which the old mother would take away into her room and thrust into her blind husband's dry, nervous, constantly fidgeting fingers. Then both of them would laugh and kiss each other, the old priest kissing his wife's swollen, cracked and dirty fingers, which were mutilated by heavy domestic work. The old woman would weep as she kissed the old man's head, and they thanked each other for all the good they had brought and were still bringing into each other's lives.

Every evening the priest would kneel before the icon and pray ardently, thanking God again and again for his wife. He did this every day. Sometimes he didn't face the icon, and then his wife would clamber out of her bed, put her arms around his shoulder, and turn him so he faced the image of Christ. This annoyed the blind priest.

The old woman tried not to think of the morrow. But the morning came when there was nothing to feed the goats with, and the blind priest woke up and started to get dressed, his feet feeling for his boots under the bed. Then the old woman started yelling and weeping, as if it were her fault that they had nothing to eat.

The blind man put his boots on and sat on his armchair, which was covered with patched oilcloth. The rest of the furniture had been sold a long time ago, but the blind man didn't know: his wife had told him that she gave it to their daughters.

The blind priest sat, leaning against the chair back, and said nothing. But his face did not betray any bewilderment.

"Give me the cross," he said, stretching out both hands and moving his fingers.

His wife waddled to the door and fastened the hook. Together they lifted up the table and pulled the chest out from under it. The priest's wife fetched a small key from a wooden thread box and unlocked the chest. The chest was full of things, but what things! Children's shirts that their sons and daughters had worn, bundles of yellowing letters they had written to one another forty years ago, wedding candles with wire decoration, on which the wax had long fallen off the wire pattern, various-colored balls of wool, bundles of rags for patching. At the bottom of the chest were two small drawers, which usually contained medals, watches, or valuables.

The woman sighed heavily and proudly, stood up straight and opened a box in which a pectoral cross with a small sculpture of Christ lay on a still-new satin cushion. The cross was reddish, made of red gold.

The old priest felt it.

"Bring me an ax," he said quietly.

"You mustn't, you mustn't." she whispered, embracing him, trying to take the cross out of his hands. But the blind priest ripped the cross from his wife's gnarled, swollen fingers, badly bruising her hand.

"Bring it," he said. "Bring it.... Do you think God is in this?"

"I shan't: do it yourself, if you want to."

"Yes, yes. Myself, myself."

The priest's wife, half crazed with hunger, waddled to the kitchen where there was an ax and a dry log, which they used to make kindling to light the samovar.

She brought the ax back, put the door on the hook, and wept with no tears, just wailing.

"Don't watch," said the blind priest, as he placed the cross on the floor. But she couldn't help watching. The cross lay there with the figure of Christ face down. The blind priest felt the cross and swung the ax. He struck a blow, and the cross bounced aside, making a quiet ringing sound on the floor; the blind priest had missed. He felt for the cross and put it back where it had been, and again lifted the ax. This time, the cross bent, and he could break off a piece with his fingers. Iron was harder than gold, so it turned out quite easy to hack the cross up into pieces.

The priest's wife had stopped weeping and yelling, as though the cross, once hacked to pieces, had stopped being a holy thing and had turned into mere precious metal, like a nugget of gold. Hurriedly, yet very slowly, she wrapped the pieces of the cross into rags and placed them back in the box of medals.

She put on her glasses and carefully examined the blade of the ax, in case any specks of gold were left on it.

When everything had been put away and the trunk was back in its place, the priest put on his canvas cape and hat, took his milking pail and crossed the yard over the long boardwalk to milk the goats. He was late milking them. It was now daylight and the shops had been open for some time. The hard-currency shops that traded in gold objects opened at ten in the morning.

1959

COURSES: FIRST THINGS FIRST

PEOPLE don't like recalling bad things. This fact of human nature makes life easier. Test it on yourself. Your memory strives to retain whatever is good and bright, and to forget whatever is grim and black. No friendships are forged in life's more difficult circumstances. Human memory refuses to "issue" indiscriminately the entire past. Instead, it selects what makes life happier and easier. This is a kind of defense reaction by the organism. This fact of human nature is, essentially, distortion of the truth. But what is truth?

Of the many years I spent in Kolyma the best times were the months spent taking paramedical courses at the camp hospital near Magadan. All the prisoners who spent time, if only a month or two, at kilometer twenty-three on the Magadan highway will have the same opinion.

The students had come there from every part of Kolyma, from the north and the south, from the west and the southwest. The most southerly point was far to the north of the settlement on the shore to which they had come.

Students from distant areas tried to occupy the lower bunks, not because it was now spring, but because they couldn't retain their urine, a condition that almost every prisoner who'd been in the mines suffered from. The dark patches on their cheeks, signs of old frostbite, were like some official branding, a seal which Kolyma had marked them with. The faces of these provincials all bore the same sullen, mistrustful smile of ill-concealed resentment. All the "miners" had a slight limp, for they had been near the Cold Pole and had reached the Hunger Pole. Being sent to take paramedical courses was an ominous adventure for them. Each one of them felt that he was a mouse, a half-dead mouse, which fate, the cat, had released from its claws so as to prolong the game a little. What of it? Mice don't have anything against this game, either, and they don't care if the cat knows it.

The provincials greedily finished off the "city boys'" roll-up cigarettes: they still didn't have the courage to let everyone see them rush to pick up a cigarette butt, even though the frank pursuit of them had been perfectly worthy behavior for a true camp inmate in the gold and lead mines. Only when he saw there was nobody about did a provincial quickly grab a cigarette end and stick it in his pocket, crushing it in his fist so as to roll a "separate" cigarette later, when he had the time. Many "city boys" had only just arrived from across the sea; they had come straight off the ship's gangway and still had their civilian shirts, ties, and caps.

Every other minute Zhenka Katz would take a tiny soldier's mirror out of his pocket and carefully comb his thick curls with a broken comb. To the provincials, whose heads were shaven, Katz's behavior seemed like dandyism, but nobody made any comments, they didn't "tell him how to live," such a thing being forbidden by the unwritten law of the camps.

The students were housed in a fairly clean barracks like a sleeping car; it had two-story bunks with a separate place for each man. Apparently, these bunks were more hygienic and looked better in the authorities' eyes—see, everybody has his own place. But the louse-ridden veterans who had come from the remote areas knew they didn't have enough flesh on their bones to get warm on their own, while fighting the lice would be just as hard whether they slept on sleeping car bunks or communal ones. The provincials badly missed the communal bunks of the barracks in the distant taiga, just as they missed the stench and stifling comfort of the transit camps.

The students were fed in the same refectory as the hospital staff. The dinners were much more nutritious than at the mines. The "miners" used to come up for seconds, and they were given them. If they came back yet again, the cook would calmly fill the bowl through the window he tended. Such things never happened at the mines. Thoughts slowly crossed their drained brains, and an ever more clear and categorical decision was formed: they had at all costs to keep taking these courses, to become "students," to see to it that the next day was like this day. The next day meant exactly that. Nobody was thinking about working as a paramedic or getting a medical qualification. They were afraid to speculate about something so far ahead. No, just the next day with the same cabbage soup for dinner, with boiled plaice, with millet porridge for supper, as the pain of their osteomyelitis was dulled by sticking their toes into torn foot wrappings stuffed in soft, homemade, quilted boots.

The students were fatigued by the rumors, each one more alarming than the previous, that came through the camp grapevine. Either they heard that prisoners older than thirty, or forty, would not be allowed to take their examinations. The barracks for aspiring students had men from nineteen to fifty years old. Or they heard that there would be no courses, that the authorities had changed their minds, or that there were no funds, and tomorrow the students would be sent to do manual labor. The most terrible rumor was that they would be *sent back* to their previous place of residence, to the gold mines and to the lead-ore mines.

These fears were confirmed when the next day the students were awoken at six in the morning, lined up outside the guardhouse, and made to walk about ten kilometers to mend the road. A road worker's job in the forest, which every prisoner in the mine dreamed of, now seemed to everybody to be extraordinarily heavy, humiliating, and unjust. The students did the job so badly that the next day they weren't sent back again.

There was a rumor that the boss had forbidden men and women to be taught together, that those with convictions under article 58, paragraph 10 (anti-Soviet agitation), which had previously been recognized as completely nonpolitical, would not be allowed to take their examinations. Examinations! That was the key word. There had to be entry examinations. The last entry examinations I had taken in my life were those for university. That had been a very, very long time ago. I couldn't remember a thing. My brain cells hadn't had any training for years on end, my brain cells had been starved, they had lost forever any capacity to take in and then reissue knowledge. Examination! My sleep was disturbed. I couldn't come to any solution. An examination "at the level of the seventh class." That was unbelievable. That had nothing to do with working outside prison or with life as a prisoner. Examination!

Fortunately, the first examination was the Russian language. The dictation was a page from Turgenev, read out to us by the local connoisseur of Russian literature, a prisoner-paramedic called Borsky. My dictation was given the highest mark by Borsky, and I was exempted from the oral Russian language test. It was exactly twenty years since I had sat in the ceremonial hall of Moscow University and produced a written work, my entrance examination, which exempted me from taking oral tests. History was repeating itself: once as tragedy, the second time as farce. In my case, it couldn't be called a farce.

Slowly, feeling physical pain, I activated my memory cells: something important and interesting had to be revealed to me. Together with the joy of my first success came the joy of recollection; I had long forgotten my life, the university.

The next examination was mathematics, a written examination. To my own surprise I quickly solved the problem posed in the examination. It was clear my nerves were now collected, what was left of my strength had been mobilized, and by some inexplicable, miraculous means they produced the required solution. An hour before and an hour after the examination I couldn't have solved such a problem.

In every conceivable educational establishment in this country there is one compulsory examination subject, "The Constitution of the USSR." But considering the nature of their batch of examinees, the bosses of the Cultural-Educational Section in the camp administration completely removed this tricky subject, to everyone's satisfaction.

The third subject was chemistry. The examination was conducted by a doctor of chemistry, a former researcher of the Ukrainian Academy of Sciences, A. I. Boichenko, who was now the director of the hospital laboratory, a conceited wit and pedant. But Boichenko's personal qualities were irrelevant. Chemistry had always been a subject I found personally insuperable. It was studied in secondary school. My secondary schooling happened during the Civil War. It so happened that our school chemistry teacher, a former officer, was executed when the Noulens[11] conspiracy in Vologda was being dismantled, so I was permanently deprived of chemistry. I didn't know the composition of air, and I only remembered the formula for water from the old student song:

> My leather boots are far too old,
> They're letting through the H_2O.

Subsequent years proved that you could live without chemistry, and I had begun to forget about all these events, and now suddenly in my fortieth year it turned out that a knowledge of history was essential, and of chemistry according to the secondary school syllabus.

How was I going to explain to Boichenko, when I had written in my application form that I had completed secondary education, but not tertiary education, that chemistry was one thing I hadn't studied?

I didn't turn to anyone, fellow students or bosses, for help: my life in prison and in the camps had taught me to rely only on myself. "Chemistry" began. I still remember the whole examination.

"What are oxides and acids?"

I started a confused and incorrect explanation. I could have told him about Lomonosov's escape to Moscow, about Lavoisier the tax farmer being executed,[12] but not about oxides.

"Tell me the formula for lime...."

"I don't know."

"And for soda?"

"I don't know."

"Why have you turned up to the examination? After all, I'm writing down the questions and answers for the record."

I said nothing. But Boichenko was not a young man; he had some understanding. He looked with displeasure at the list of my previous marks: two A's. He shrugged.

"Write the symbol for oxygen."

I wrote a capital H.

"What do you know about Mendeleyev's periodical table of elements?"

I told him. My story had very little to do with the elements, but a lot to do with Mendeleyev. I knew a few things about him. After all, he was the father-in-law of the poet Blok!

"You can go," said Boichenko.

The next day I found out that I had gotten a C for chemistry and that I was registered, registered for paramedical courses at the central hospital of the Northeastern Administration of the NKVD camps.

I did nothing for the next two days. I just lay on my bunk, breathing in the barracks stench, looking at the soot-stained ceiling. A very important, extraordinarily important period was beginning in my life. I could sense that with my whole being. I now had to prepare for life, not for death. And I didn't know which was harder.

We were given paper—enormous sheets with burned edges, the trace of a fire last year, when an explosion had demolished the whole city of Nakhodka. We stitched exercise books out of this paper. We were issued pencils and pens.

Sixteen men and eight women! The women sat on the left in the classroom, nearer the light, while the men sat on the right, which was darker. A meter-wide corridor divided the class. We had new, narrow desks with lower shelves—exactly the same desks I had when I was in secondary school.

Later I happened to find myself in the fishing settlement of Ola. Outside the Ola Evenki school was a school desk. I spent a long time examining its enigmatic construction, until I finally realized that it was an Erismann[13] desk.

We had no textbooks at all, and our only visual aids were a few anatomy posters.

To learn, you had to be a hero, but to teach, you needed to be a saint.

Let's start with the heroes. None of us, men or women, had thought of becoming paramedics just for the sake of a carefree life in the camps or in order to turn as quickly as we could into "quacks."

For some of us, including me, the courses were lifesaving. Although I was nearly forty, I drew on all my resources and studied as hard as my physical and mental strength would allow me. Moreover, I had hopes of being able to help certain people, and to settle ten-year-old scores with others. I hoped to become a human being again.

For other people the courses were offering a lifelong profession, widening their horizons. The courses had substantial general educational value and they promised a firm social position in the camps.

Min Garipovich Shabayev, the Tatar writer Min Shabai, a victim of 1937, sentenced on a charge of Anti-Soviet Agitation (ASA), sat at the first desk right by the hallway.

Shabayev had a good command of Russian, he took lecture notes in Russian, although, as I found out many years later, he wrote his prose in Tatar. Many people concealed their past in the camps. That was logical and made sense, not just for former interrogators and prosecutors. A writer, as an intellectual, as a man who worked with his mind, was a "four-eyes," which in places of imprisonment always aroused his fellow prisoners' and his bosses' hatred. Shabayev had realized that long ago, so he pretended he had been a petty trader, and never took part in conversations about literature: that was the best and the least troublesome way out, in his opinion. He smiled at everyone and was always chewing something. As one of the leading students he began to acquire a fatherly appearance, swelling up. The years in the mines had left their mark on Min. He was absolutely enthralled by the courses.

"You realize, I'm forty, and I've just found out for the first time that a man has only one liver. And I thought he had two, two of everything."

The presence of a spleen in human beings aroused complete ecstasy in Min.

When he was released, Min did not start working as a paramedic. He went back to a job close to his heart, as a supply agent. Becoming a supply agent offered even more dazzling prospects than a medical career did.

Next to Shabayev sat Bokis, a Latvian of enormous dimensions, and the future Kolyma ping-pong champion. He had "landed" in the hospital several years earlier, first as a patient, then as a patient serving as a male nurse. The doctors had promised to ensure Bokis got a diploma. Once he had his paramedic's diploma, Bokis went out to the taiga, and saw the gold mines. For him the taiga was a frightful hallucination, but what he most feared there was not what he should have feared: having his own soul become depraved. Being indifferent is not as bad as being a scoundrel.

The third place was occupied by Buka, a soldier who had lost an eye in World War II and had been convicted of looting. It took the mine three months to throw Buka back into a hospital bunk. Buka's combination of seven years of education, an easygoing nature, and a touch of Ukrainian slyness, ensured that he was accepted into the courses. Buka's one eye had seen at the mine as much as many people's two eyes, and he saw the main thing, that he could sort out his destiny by keeping well away from article 58 and all its many subsections. There was nobody in the courses more secretive than Buka.

After a couple of months, Buka replaced his black eye-patch with an artificial eye. But the hospital assortment turned out to have no brown eyes, so he had to choose a blue one. That made a strong impression, but everyone soon got used to his differently colored eyes, sooner than Buka did.

I tried to comfort him by telling him about Alexander the Great's eyes. Buka politely heard me out—Alexander the Great's eyes seemed to be somehow "political," so he mumbled something noncommittal and moved away.

The fourth man in the corner by the wall was Labutov, like Buka a World War II soldier. He was an outgoing radio man with a lot of self-esteem. He had built a miniature receiver on which he listened to fascist broadcasts, but he told a comrade and was found out. The tribunal gave him ten years for ASA. Labutov had a full ten years' education, he loved drawing all sorts of schemes that looked like gigantic military staff maps, with arrows, signs, and the names of the subject, say, in anatomy: "Operation," "Heart." He didn't know Kolyma. The spring day when we were herded out to work, Labutov decided to take a dip in the nearest drainage ditch, and we had some difficulty in stopping him. He became a good paramedic, especially later, when he mastered the secrets of physiotherapy, which for someone like him, an electrician and a radio expert, was not difficult. He finally found a permanent job in an electrotherapy clinic.

The second row consisted of Chernikov, Katz, and Malinsky. Chernikov was a self-satisfied lad, always smiling; he too was a frontline soldier who had been convicted of some criminal act or other. Like Labutov, he had not had even a sniff of Kolyma; he had come to the courses straight from Maglag, the Magadan camp section. He was literate enough to study and he rightly supposed that he wouldn't be chased out of the courses even if he broke the rules and quickly struck up a relationship with one of the women students.

Zhenka Katz, Chernikov's friend, was a lively nonpolitical who was inordinately fond of his luxurious curls. As the class monitor, he was without any spite and had no authority. When the courses were over and he worked at outpatient admissions, he heard a doctor who was examining a patient call out "Permanganate!" Zhenka, instead of putting gauze soaked in a weak solution of kalium hypermarganicum on the wound, sprinkled dark violet crystals of full-strength permanganate over it. The patient knew very well how burns should be treated, but didn't move his arm away, didn't protest, didn't blink an eye.[14] The patient was an old Kolyma hand. Zhenka Katz's carelessness got the patient exempted from work for almost a whole month. Luck comes seldom in Kolyma and has to be grabbed firmly and held onto for as long as you have the strength.

Malinsky was the youngest in the class. Called up in the last year of the war, he was nineteen. He'd been brought up in wartime and had rather loose morals. Kostia Malinsky was convicted of looting. By chance he ended up in the hospital where his uncle, a Moscow general practitioner, was working. His uncle helped get him onto the courses, but they didn't interest Kostia very much. His character defects, or perhaps just his youth, constantly led him into various shady camp enterprises: getting butter with a forged voucher, selling footwear, taking trips to Magadan. He was always being called in by the NKVD officers because of this (and perhaps for other things too?). Someone had to be an informer.

Thanks to the courses, Kostia got a profession. A few years later I met him in the settlement of Ola. Kostia was presenting himself there as a paramedic who had completed the wartime two-year course. I might have been, unintentionally, the reason that his lies were exposed.

In 1957 Kostia and I were riding the same bus in Moscow. He was wearing a velour hat and a soft overcoat.

"What are you up to?"

"I've taken up medicine, medicine," Kostia shouted as we parted.

The other students were people from the mine areas, people with very different fates.

Orlov was a "letter man," convicted of a crime with an acronym, thus convicted by a troika or a special tribunal. Orlov was a Moscow mechanical engineer and on three occasions he came near his end at the mines. The Kolyma machine discarded him, as if he were slag, into the local hospital, and it was from there that he got into the courses. His life was at stake. Orlov knew nothing except studying, no matter how hard he found it to understand medicine. Gradually, he got the hang of his studies and began to believe in the future.

The secondary-school teacher, the geographer Sukhovenchenko, being over forty, was older than Orlov. He had served eight years of his ten-year sentence and had little more to serve. He too was one of those who came through, who hung on. He now had an undemanding job and could survive. He had gone through the stage of being a goner, and had stayed alive. He was working as a geologist, a sample collector, as an assistant to the party chief. But all these good things might suddenly vanish like smoke; all it took was a change of boss. Sukhovenchenko had no degree, while the memory of his years in the mines was only too fresh. He had a chance of getting a permit to attend the courses. They were supposed to be eight-month courses, and he had only a short term left to serve. He could have acquired a good profession for the camps. Sukhovenchenko abandoned his geological group and got a paramedic's education. But he never became a medic. The times weren't right, or his personal qualities were the wrong ones. After he finished the courses, Sukhovenchenko sensed that he couldn't treat people, that he didn't have the willpower to make a decision. After working for a short time as a paramedic, he returned to his profession as a geologist. So he was one of the people on whom the teaching was wasted. His decency and good nature were beyond doubt. He feared "politics" like fire, but would never have gone and denounced anyone.

Silaikin hadn't had seven years of education: he was getting on in years, and he found learning very hard. While Kundush, Orlov, and I felt more and more confident with every day, Silaikin found things harder and harder. But he went on studying, relying on his memory, which was excellent, on his ability to outwit other people, and not only to outwit but to understand them. Silaikin's observations told him that there were no criminals here except for the professional ones. All the other prisoners had behaved in the outside world like anyone else, they'd stolen no more from the state, they'd made no more mistakes, they'd broken the law no more often than those who had not been convicted under various articles of the Criminal Code and who were carrying on with their work. The year 1937 had especially emphasized that fact by eliminating every legal right a Russian had. Prison became something nobody could in any way avoid.

The only criminals inside or outside the camps were the gangsters. Silaikin was clever, he knew what people felt and thought, and, although convicted of fraud, he was in his own way an honest man. There is honesty that is sentimental, sincere. And there is honesty that is rational. What Silaikin lacked were not honest convictions, but honest habits. He was truthful, because he realized that this was now to his advantage. He never did anything that breached the rules, because he knew that he mustn't. He had no faith in people and considered that the main motive force of social progress was personal advantage. He was witty. In our general surgery classes, when the very experienced teacher Meyerson was quite unable to get the students to understand "supination" and "pronation," Silaikin stood up and asked if he might speak. Then he stretched out his hand, palm upward and said, "Soup, please," then turned his palm over and said, "No, mate." Everyone, including Meyerson, remembered, probably for the rest of their lives, Silaikin's grim mnemonic and appreciated his Kolyma wit.

Silaikin passed his final examinations with no difficulty and worked as a paramedic—at the mine. He probably did a good job, because he was clever and "understood life." "Understanding life" was, in his opinion, the most important thing.

His desk partner, Iliusha Logvinov, was just as sophisticated. Logvinov had been convicted of robbery and, although he wasn't a gangster, he fell deeper and deeper under the influence of the criminal recidivists. He saw clearly how strong the gangsters were in the camps, strong in both moral and material senses. The bosses kowtowed to the gangsters, they were afraid of them. For the gangsters the camps meant "home." They hardly ever worked, they enjoyed all sorts of privileges and although lists of prisoners for deportation were secretly compiled behind the criminals' backs and, from time to time, a Black Maria full of guards would turn up and take away the gangsters who had gone too far, that was life—and the gangsters were just as well off in their new place of residence. Even in punishment zones they were in charge.

Logvinov came from a hardworking family; his crime was committed during the war, when he saw he had no alternative. The camp boss who read Logvinov's file persuaded him to enroll in the courses. Somehow he managed to pass the entrance examination and began studying passionately, but hopelessly. Medical subjects were just too complex for Iliusha. But he found the inner strength to hold on, to finish the courses, and for several years he worked as a senior paramedic in a big therapeutic department. He was released, got married, and had a family. For him the courses had opened up a path in life.

Once there was an introductory lecture on general surgery. The teacher listed the names of those most prominent in world medicine.

"... And in our time one scientist made a discovery that revolutionized surgery and all medicine. ..."

"Fleming."

"Who said that? Stand up."

"I did."

"Surname?"

"Kundush."

"Sit down."

I felt strongly offended. I myself had no idea who Fleming was. I'd spent almost ten years, since 1937, in prison or the camps, without newspapers or books, and I knew nothing except that there had been a war and that it was over, that penicillin or something existed, and so did streptocide. Fleming!

"Who are you?" I asked Kundush, speaking to him for the first time. The two of us both came from the Western Administration at the same time on the same list, we were both sent on these courses by our common savior Andrei Maksimovich Pantiukhov. We had starved together—he less, I more—but we both knew what the mines were. We knew nothing about each other.

Kundush told me an astounding story.

In 1941 he was appointed the commander of a fortified district. The builders were putting up, in a leisurely way, concrete pillboxes and timber gun emplacements, until one July morning the mist in the bay lifted and the garrison saw the German heavy cruiser *Admiral Scheer* facing them at the roadstead. The cruiser approached as close as it could and fired point-blank at the unfinished fortifications, turning them all into ashes and piles of stones. Kundush got ten years. The story was interesting and instructive, except for one thing, Kundush's article of conviction, ASA. That could not be applied to cases of negligence, such as the one that the *Admiral Scheer* took advantage of. When we got to know each other better, I found out that Kundush had been convicted under a notorious NKVD case, one of the mass open or closed trials in Lavrenti Beria's time, such as the Leningrad case or the NKVD case, or the Rykov and Bukharin trials, or the Kirov case—these were all stages in the "great path." Kundush was an excitable, impulsive person, not always able to control his flare-ups, even in the camps. He was an absolutely straightforward person, especially after he witnessed for himself the "practices" in the prisons and camps. He now had a true, proper understanding of his own work in the recent past as a deputy NKVD chief under Zakovsky[15] in Leningrad. Having kept his interest in books, knowledge, and the news, able to appreciate a joke, Kundush was one of the most appealing of the students. He did work as a paramedic for a few years, but after his release he became a supply worker, then worked as a stevedore in Magadan port, until he was rehabilitated and could return to Leningrad.

Being a booklover who was especially fond of footnotes and commentaries and never skipped over anything set in small print, Kundush had a wide, if dissipated, knowledge of the world, enjoyed chatting about all sorts of abstract topics, and had his own views on all questions. His entire nature protested against the camp regime and against violence. He would prove his personal courage later when he made a daring trip to see an imprisoned Spanish girl, the daughter of one of the members of the Madrid government.

Kundush was a rather pudgy man. All of us, naturally, ate cats, dogs, squirrels, crows, and dead horses, too, if we could get hold of them. But once we were paramedics, we stopped doing that. When Kundush was working in the neurological department, he cooked a cat in the sterilizer and ate it on his own. It was very difficult to hush up the scandal. Kundush had met Mr. Hunger at the mines and knew his face.

Was Kundush revealing everything about himself? Who knows? And why should we? "If you don't believe it, take it as a fairy tale." In the camps you don't ask about people's past or their future.

On my left sat Barateli, a Georgian, convicted of some crime committed as an employee. He had a poor command of Russian. He found a compatriot in the courses, the pharmacology teacher, and he received both moral and practical support from him. Coming late in the evening to the "hut" next to the hospital department, where it was as dry and warm as a conifer forest in summer, to drink sugared tea or have a leisurely meal of pearl-barley porridge with big blobs of sunflower oil, to feel a throbbing, relaxing joy in all his revived muscles: wasn't that the ultimate miracle for a man who'd come from the mines? And Barateli had been at the mines.

Kundush, Barateli, and I sat at the fourth desk. The third desk was shorter than the others, since room had to be made for the tiled stove, and it had only two occupants, Sergeyev and Petrashkevich. Sergeyev was a nonpolitical who had worked as a supply agent while a prisoner, so that he had no great need to become a paramedic. He studied in an offhand way. At the first practical classes in anatomy at the morgue—whatever else was lacking, there was no shortage of corpses for the students—Sergeyev fainted and was removed from the course.

Petrashkevich would never have fainted. He'd come from the mines and he had a political conviction with an acronym, KR, a counter-revolutionary one. This acronym was quite common in 1937: "convicted as a member of the family," which was how children, fathers, mothers, sisters, and other relatives of the convicted got their sentences. Petrashkevich's grandfather (his grandfather, not his father!) was a prominent Ukrainian nationalist. That was enough reason in 1937 to shoot Petrashkevich's father, a teacher of Ukrainian, while Petrashkevich himself, a sixteen-year-old schoolboy, got "ten years as a member of the family."

I had often noticed that imprisonment, especially in the north, somehow arrests people's moral growth, so that their abilities don't develop any further than the level at which they were arrested. This state of anabiosis lasts until they are released. A man who has spent twenty years in a prison or a camp misses out on the experience of normal life: the schoolboy remains a schoolboy; the wise man remains just a wise man, but does not become a sage.

Petrashkevich was now twenty-four. He ran around the classroom, he shouted, he would stick pieces of paper to Shabayev's or Silaikin's back, he would release pigeons, he would laugh. His answers to teachers had all the qualities of a schoolboy's, but he wasn't a bad kid and he made a good paramedic. He avoided "politics" like the plague and was afraid of reading newspapers.

The boy's constitution was not strong enough for Kolyma. Petrashkevich died of tuberculosis a few years later before he could get away to the mainland.

There were eight women. The class monitor was Muza Dmitriyevna, who used to be a party or, rather, a trade union worker; that sort of work leaves an indelible mark on a person's habits, manners, and interests. She was about forty-five, and she was always trying to win the trust of the authorities. She wore a sort of velvet jacket and a good-quality woolen dress. During the war American charities sent an enormous amount of woolen goods for the people of Kolyma. Naturally, these gifts never got as far as the depths of the taiga or the mines, and even on the seashore the local bosses did their best to grab them, by either asking or forcing prisoners to hand over the sweaters and jerseys. But a few Magadan inhabitants managed to hang on to these "rags." Muza had kept hers.

She didn't get involved in anything to do with the courses, limiting her authority to the other women in the group. Muza was friends with the youngest female student, Nadia Yegorova, and protected her from the temptations of the camps. Nadia didn't find this protection much of an obstacle, and Muza couldn't hinder the stormy progress of Nadia's affair with a camp cook.

"The way to a woman's heart is through her stomach," Silaikin repeated with amusement. Nadia and her desk partner Muza found themselves being given special-diet dishes: all sorts of meatballs, breaded rump steak, pancakes. They got double, even triple portions. The barrage didn't last long: Nadia surrendered. A grateful Muza went on protecting Nadia, not from the cook, but from the camp authorities.

Nadia was a poor student. But she found an outlet in the amateur dramatics club. It was the only place in the camp where men and women were allowed to meet one another. But the beady eye of camp supervision made sure that relations between men and women never overstepped the permitted boundary—the local custom was that adultery had to be proved as solidly as it was by the police commissioner in Maupassant's *Bel Ami*. Guards observed and tried to catch people out. Their patience was not always enough, for, as Stendhal remarked, a prisoner thinks more about his bars than a warden thinks about his keys. The surveillance slackens.

Even if members of the amateur dramatics club couldn't count on love in its most ancient and eternal form, rehearsals nevertheless seemed to a prisoner to be another world, more like the world they used to live in. This was quite an important consideration, even though camp cynicism didn't allow people to admit to such feelings. There were palpable gains, if only petty advantages, for participants in amateur dramatics: an unexpected issue of tobacco and sugar. Permission not to have one's hair cut was no small matter in the camps. Haircuts caused real brawls and arguments in which the people who took part were neither actors nor thieves.

The fifty-year-old Yakov Zavodnik, once a Civil War commissar on the Siberian front against Admiral Kolchak (and a close comrade of Zelensky, the secretary of Moscow Communist Youth, who was executed after the Rykov trial) used to fend off the camp barbers with a poker: thanks to his hair, he ended up at a punishment mine. What was that all about? Surely, the story of Samson's hair was only a legend, wasn't it? Why get so worked up about it? Obviously, the mind is damaged by the desire to assert oneself, if only in a small, petty matter: yet another example of the great displacement in scales of value.

The distortions of prison life—the separate lives of men and women—were somehow smoothed over in the amateur dramatics club. In the final analysis, this too was an illusion, but it was still preferable to "low truths."[16] Anyone who could squeak or sing, anyone who recited poems or who had performed in shows at home, anyone who could twang a mandolin or do a tap dance had "their chance" of getting into the club.

Nadia Yegorova used to sing in a choir. She couldn't dance, she was clumsy onstage, but she went to rehearsals. Her stormy personal life took up a lot of her time.

Elena Melodze, a Georgian, was another "member of the family": her husband had been executed. Deeply disturbed by his arrest, she naïvely thought that he must have been guilty of something, and only calmed down when she herself ended up in prison. It all became clear, logical and simple: there were tens of thousands in her position.

The difference between a scoundrel and a decent person is this: when a scoundrel ends up in prison for no good reason, he considers that he is the only innocent one, and all the others are enemies of the state and the people. A decent person, once in prison, considers that if he, an innocent man, could be put behind bars, then the same thing could have happened to the persons on the neighboring bunks.

> This is the Hegelian philosophy
> This is the deepest sense of books![17]

... as far as the events of 1937 are concerned.

Melodze recovered her mental balance, her placid, cheerful moods. When she was at Elgen, the women's outpost in the taiga, she had escaped heavy manual labor. And here she was in the paramedical courses. She didn't become a medic. After her release—her term ended at the beginning of the 1950s—she was, like everyone released at that time, "attached," and had to become a lifelong resident of Kolyma. She got married.

Next to Melodze sat a vivacious, fun-loving young girl, Galochka Bazarova, who had been convicted for some offenses during the war. She was always laughing, even guffawing, which did not suit her, for she had enormous teeth with big gaps between them. But this did not deter her. Thanks to the courses, she became an operating theater nurse, and after her release she worked for a number of years in the Magadan hospital, where she spent her first earnings on stainless steel crowns for her teeth, which immediately improved her looks.

Behind Bazarova was a white-toothed Finnish girl called Aino. Her sentence had begun in the war winter of 1939–40. As a prisoner she learned Russian and, as a hardworking girl, with her Finnish conscientiousness, she attracted the attention of one of the doctors and ended up taking the courses. She found the studying hard, but she managed and became a qualified nurse.... She liked the life of a paramedical student.

Next to Aino sat a small woman, whose name and surname both escape me. She may have been a spy of some sort, or she may really have been the shadow of a human being.

Marusia Dmitriyeva occupied the next desk. She and her close friend Tamara Nikiforova were friendly with Chernikov. Both women had nonpolitical convictions, neither had been in the taiga, and both were eager students.

Next to them sat Valia Tsukanova, a black-eyed Cossack girl from the Kuban. She was a patient from the hospital and was still wearing her hospital gown when she came to the first practicals. She had spent time in the taiga and she was a very successful student. It took some time for her face to lose the marks of hunger and illness, and when it did she turned out to be a beauty. Once she got her strength back, she began her "love life," without waiting for the courses to end. Many men courted her, with no success. She became intimate with a blacksmith and used to run off to the forge to see him. After she was released, she worked for a number of years as a paramedic in a separate area.

We wanted to learn, and our teachers wanted to teach. They had badly missed animated speech, passing on knowledge, which they had been forbidden to do. Passing on knowledge was the whole point of their lives before their arrest. Professors and lecturers, people with PhDs in medicine, teachers for doctors' continuing education, they had, for the first time in many years, found an outlet for their energy. Apart from one man, all the teachers in the courses were politicals, convicted under article 58.

The authorities had suddenly come to the realization that a knowledge of the mysteries of the circulation of the blood might not always be connected with anti-Soviet propaganda, so the quality of the courses was assured by the high qualifications of the teachers. True, students were supposed to be nonpoliticals. But how could you find enough nonpoliticals with seven years' schooling? In any case, nonpoliticals served their sentences doing privileged jobs and had no need of any courses. The top bosses didn't want even to hear of article 58ers being brought into the courses. In the end, a compromise was found. Those convicted of ASA—anti-Soviet agitation—and paragraph 10 of article 58, crimes that were virtually nonpolitical, were allowed into the entry examinations.

A timetable was compiled and displayed on the wall. A timetable! Everything as in normal life. A vehicle, which looked like a heavy-goods truck, an elderly taiga-goods vehicle, was somehow put in working order and lumbered over the gullies and marshes of Kolyma.

Our first lecture was on anatomy. This subject was taught by the hospital anatomical pathologist David Umansky, an old man of seventy.

An émigré in tsarist times, Umansky had received his medical degree in Brussels. He lived and worked in Odessa, where he had a successful medical practice, at least for a few years. He owned a great number of properties, but the revolution proved that houses were not the most reliable investments. He went back to medical practice. By the mid-1930s he sensed which way the wind was blowing and decided to retreat as far as he could by getting a job with Far East Construction. That didn't save him. He was picked up "on the lists" for Far East Construction, and in 1938 arrested and sentenced to fifteen years. Since then he had been in charge of the hospital morgue. He was hindered from working properly by his contempt for people, his resentment at what had been done to his own life. He had enough wit not to quarrel with the doctors who were treating patients; he could have made things very unpleasant for them at autopsies. But perhaps it was not so much his wits as his contempt, a simple feeling of scorn, which allowed him to give way in arguments over postmortems.

Dr. Umansky had a crystal-clear mind. He was a pretty good linguist—that was his hobby, his favorite pastime. He knew a lot of languages. In the camps he studied Asian languages and tried to deduce laws on their formation, spending all his free time in his morgue, where he lived with his assistant, the paramedic Dunayev.

In conjunction with anatomy, Umansky taught, as if it were a mere joke, a course in Latin for future paramedics. I don't know what kind of Latin it was, but I stopped having trouble with the genitive case when writing prescriptions.

Dr. Umansky was a lively man who reacted to every political event and who had a well-considered opinion on any question of international or domestic matters. "The main thing, my dear friends," he used to say in private conversations, "is to hang on and outlive Stalin. Stalin's death is what will bring us freedom." Alas, Umansky died in Magadan in 1953,[18] just before the event he had awaited for so many years.

He was quite a good lecturer, albeit a somehow casual one. He was the least involved of all our teachers. From time to time there would be questions about what we'd learned, repeated lessons, or the replacement of general anatomy by the anatomy of a particular part. There was just one section of his science that Umansky refused outright to lecture on: the anatomy of the genital organs. Nothing could persuade him otherwise, so that the students finished their training without gaining any knowledge of this section, just because of their Brussels professor's excessive prudery. What were Umansky's reasons? He felt that the moral, cultural, and educational level of his students was so low that such topics would arouse an unhealthy interest. Such an unhealthy interest was aroused in schools, for example by anatomical atlases, and Umansky remembered this fact. He was wrong. The "provincials" would have had a completely serious attitude toward the question.

He was a decent man and long before many other teachers he saw his students as human beings. Dr. Umansky was a convinced geneticist.[19] He would tell us about the splitting of chromosomes and, in passing, mention that there was another theory of the splitting of chromosomes, but that he didn't know the new theory and had decided to tell us what he knew well. So we were brought up to be believers in genetics. The full triumph of geneticists, once the electron microscope was invented, came too late for Dr. Umansky. That triumph would have given the old doctor real joy.

We learned by heart the names of bones and muscles, in Russian, not Latin, of course. Carried away, we memorized them enthusiastically. There is always a democratic element in rote learning; we were all equals in the eyes of the science of anatomy. Nobody made an effort to understand anything. We tried just to memorize. Bazarova and Petrashkevich, recent schoolchildren (if you omitted the time spent in incarceration, which in Petrashkevich's case amounted to nearly eight years), had the most success.

As I carefully memorized the lesson, I remembered hostel number one—Cherkaska—at Moscow University in 1926, where medical students, drunk from their practice classes, walked the corridors at night, memorizing, memorizing, with their fingers stuck in their ears. The hostel was full of loud noise, laughter and life. The special faculty[20] students, the literature students, the historians all laughed at the unfortunate rote learners of the medical faculty. We despised a subject where rote learning, not understanding, was required.

Twenty years later I was learning anatomy by rote. Over those twenty years I had come to realize what specialization was, what applied sciences were, what medicine and engineering were. And now I had a God-given chance to study them myself.

My brain was still able to take in and to reproduce knowledge.

Dr. Blagorazumov lectured us on "The Foundations of Sanitation and Hygiene." It was a dreary subject, and Blagorazumov was reluctant, or perhaps unable for reasons of political discretion, to liven up his lectures with any witticisms. He remembered 1938, when all specialists, doctors, engineers, accountants, were forced to work with barrows and pickaxes, following the "special instructions" sent from Moscow. For two years Blagorazumov had pushed a wheelbarrow, and three times he had been near death from hunger, cold, scurvy, and beatings. The third year he was permitted to practice as a paramedic at a clinic under a doctor who was a nonpolitical prisoner. Many doctors had died that year. Blagorazumov survived and never forgot: no chatting, not with anyone. Friendship only on "a drink and a bite" basis. Blagorazumov was much liked in the hospital. His binge drinking was covered up by the paramedics, and when it couldn't be covered up, he was dragged off to solitary confinement, the punishment block. He would emerge from there to go on with his lectures. Nobody thought it strange.

He was a thorough lecturer who made us take down his dictation on important points and then systematically checked our notes and our understanding. In short, Blagorazumov was a conscientious and prudent teacher.[21]

Pharmacology lectures were given by the hospital paramedic Ghoghoberidze, who had been the director of the Transcaucasian Pharmacological Institute. He had a good command of Russian and his speech had no more of a Georgian accent than Stalin's did. He had once been a prominent party member: his signature was on Sapronov's "The Platform of 15."[22] From 1928 to 1937 Ghoghoberidze was in exile, then in 1937 he was given a new sentence: fifteen years in the Kolyma camps. Now he was approaching sixty and tormented by high blood pressure. He knew he would die soon, but he wasn't afraid. He hated all scoundrels and, when in his own department he caught Dr. Krol taking bribes and contributions from prisoners, he beat up the doctor and made him hand back someone's patent-leather boots and striped trousers. Ghoghoberidze never left Kolyma. He was released into permanent exile at Narym, but got permission to exchange Narym for Kolyma. He lived in the settlement of Yagodny, where he died in the early 1950s.

The only nonpolitical convict among our teachers was Dr. Krol from Kharkov, a specialist in venereal and skin diseases. All our teachers worked to instill in us moral decency and portrayed, in lyrical digressions from their lectures, an ideal of moral purity, as they tried to develop a powerful sense of responsibility in those who would have the great task of helping the sick, sick prisoners, and, most of all, Kolyma prisoners. They repeatedly stressed, as best they could, what they had been inculcated with in their youth by medical institutes and faculties, by the Hippocratic oath. All of them except Krol. Krol sketched out different prospects for us, he approached our future jobs from a different angle, which he knew better. He never tired of painting a picture of the paramedic's material prosperity. "You'll earn enough for butter," he would giggle, smiling in his carnivorous way. Krol had never-ending dark dealings with thieves, who would visit him even in the intervals between lectures. He was always selling, buying, or swapping something, and the presence of his students didn't bother him. Treating the bosses for impotence gave Krol a substantial income and kept him safe during his term of imprisonment. Krol would undertake mysterious treatments involving herbal medicines. There was nobody to discipline him, and he had powerful connections.

The two slaps on the face that Ghoghoberidze the paramedic had given him left Krol unmoved. "You went too far, pal, a bit too far," he told Ghoghoberidze, who had turned green with anger.

Krol was the object of general contempt from both his fellow teachers and the students. Moreover, his course was chaotic, for he had no talent for teaching. Diseases of the skin was the one section that I was compelled, after the courses were over, to read carefully for myself, with pencil and paper to hand.

Olga Stepanovna Semeniak, once a lecturer in the diagnostic therapy faculty of the Kharkov Medical Institute, didn't give any lectures in our courses. But she supervised our practicals. She taught me how to tap a patient's chest and back, how to listen to his breathing. When our practicals were nearly over she gave me an old stethoscope, which is one of my few Kolyma mementos. She was about fifty and her ten-year sentence was not yet over. She had been convicted of counter-revolutionary agitation. Her husband and two children had stayed behind in the Ukraine, where they had all perished during the war. The war ended, and so did Olga Semeniak's sentence, but she had nowhere to go. She stayed on in Magadan after she was released.

Olga Semeniak had spent several years at the women's camp at Elgen. She had found the strength to cope with her terrible grief. She had a gift for observation and saw that only one group of people kept their humanity in the camps, the believers, whether Orthodox or sectarians. She would pray twice a day in her "hut," she read the Gospels, she tried to do good deeds. Doing good deeds was not difficult. Nobody can do more good deeds than a camp doctor can, but her temperament—stubborn, quick-tempered, and domineering—was an obstacle. Semeniak paid no attention to self-improvement in this respect.

She was a strict, pedantic manager and ruled her staff with a rod of iron. She was always considerate to patients, though.

After the working day was over, she would give her students dinner in the hospital cafeteria. She would usually sit there, drinking tea.

"What are you reading?"

"Nothing, except the lecture notes."

"Well, here's something to read," she passed a small book to me. It looked like a prayer book. It was a small volume of Blok, in the little series of the Poet's Library.

Two or three days later I gave her back the poetry.

"Did you like it?"

"Yes," I felt too embarrassed to tell her that I knew—or had known—these verses well.

"Read me 'A Girl Was Singing in a Church Choir.'"

I recited it.

"Now, 'O Faraway Mary, Bright Mary'... good. Now this...."

I recited "In a Distant Blue Bedchamber."

"You realize that it was the boy that died...."

"Yes, of course."

"The boy died," Olga's dry lips repeated, as she wrinkled her taut white forehead. She said nothing for a while, and then: "Shall I give you something else?"

"Please do."

She opened her desk drawer and took out a little book, like the Blok volume. It was a New Testament.

"Read it, read it. Especially this bit: the apostle Paul's letter to the Corinthians."

A few days later I gave the book back. The agnosticism I had upheld throughout my conscious life had not made me a Christian. But in the camps I had not seen better people than the believers. Depravity affected everyone's souls; only the believers held out. That was true, whether fifteen or five years previously.

In Olga Semeniak's hut I got to know Vasia Shvetsov, a foreman builder and former prisoner. He was a handsome twenty-five-year-old man who had enormous success with all the women in the camp. In Olga's department he used to pay visits to Nina, a server in the kitchens.

He was a sensible, able young man, had seen a lot of things clearly and could explain clearly, but I remembered him for one particular reason. I told him off because of Nina, who was pregnant.

"She was asking for it," said Shvetsov. "What can you do about it? I grew up in the camps. I was a boy when I was put in prison. As for all the women I've had, believe it or not, I've lost count. And you know what? I never ever slept with any of them in a bed. It was always somehow in the lobby, in a shed, everywhere except actually walking. Would you believe it?" That was Vasia's story, the story of the most handsome young man in the hospital.

Nikolai Sergeyevich Minin, a gynecologist and surgeon, was in charge of the women's department. He didn't give us lectures, but supervised our practical classes, in which there was no theory.

When there were major snowstorms, snow covered the hospital settlement to the roof, and the smoke from the chimneys was the only way to tell where you were. Each department had steps cut into the snow, leading down to the entrance. We would climb upward out of our hostels, then run to the women's department and enter Minin's office at half past eight, put on our gowns, and, opening the door just a few inches, slip into the room. The usual five-minute procedure was taking place, as the nurse handed over the night shift. Minin, an enormous gray-bearded old man, sat at a tiny desk, frowning. When the night shift report was finished, he waved a hand and everyone started talking again. . . . Minin turned his head to the right. The senior nurse had brought a glass of a bluish liquid on a small glass tray. It smelled familiar. Minin took the little glass, drank it and smoothed down his gray mustache.

"Blue Night liqueur," he said, winking at the students.

I was present several times at his operations. He always operated when he'd had one too many, but he assured us that his hands weren't going to shake. The theater nurses backed him up. But after the operation, when he was washing up, rinsing his hands in a big basin, he would sadly examine his uncontrollably trembling hands.

"You're past it, Nikolai, you're past it," he would quietly tell himself. But he went on operating for several years.

Before Kolyma he had worked in Leningrad. He was arrested in

1937 and wheeled a barrow for two years in Kolyma. He was the coauthor of a major textbook on gynecology. The other author was Serebriakov, and after Minin was arrested the textbook began to be published with Serebriakov as the only named author. After he was released, Minin didn't have the strength to bother with litigation. Like everyone else, he was released without the right to leave Kolyma. He began drinking even more heavily; in 1952 he hanged himself in his room in the settlement of Debin.

As an old Bolshevik, during the revolution Minin conducted negotiations with the American Relief Agency on behalf of the Soviet government. He met Nansen. Later, he gave radio lectures on antireligious themes.

Everyone was very fond of him. Somehow it always turned out that Minin wished everyone well, but did nothing for anyone, good or bad.

Dr. Sergei Ivanovich Kulikov lectured on tuberculosis. In the 1930s citizens of the mainland were eagerly assured that the climate of Kolyma and of the Far East were identical, that the Kolyma mountains were good for treating tuberculosis and, at the very least, stabilized the condition of those with lung diseases. The enthusiasts for these views forgot that the bare hills of Kolyma were covered with marshes, that the Kolyma forested tundra was the very worst of places for those with bad lungs. They forgot about the almost 100-percent tubercular morbidity among the Evenki, Yakuts, and Yukagir peoples of Kolyma. No tuberculosis sections were planned for the prisoners' hospitals. But Koch bacillus is Koch bacillus, and very extensive tuberculosis sections finally had to be set up.

Sergei Kulikov looked gray and decrepit, and he was decidedly deaf, but he was lively in body and soul. He considered this subject to be of primary importance and was angry if he was contradicted. He tended to keep silent but, if he heard of any major news item in the papers, he would give a curt laugh and his eyes would blaze.

Dr. Kulikov was serving ten years under some paragraph of article 58. When he was released, he was prohibited for life from moving away. His family, an elderly wife and a daughter, who was also a tuberculosis doctor, came to be with him.

The chemistry teacher Boichenko was in charge of the students' laboratory practicals. He remembered me well and treated me, as a person who knew no chemistry, with utter contempt.

The neurological illness lectures were given by Anna Izrailevna Ponizovskaya. By then she was a free woman, allowed even to take her doctorate. For some years, while still a prisoner, she happened to work with a major neurologist, Professor Skoblo, who helped her a great deal in formulating her topic, or so they said in the hospital. She met Professor Skoblo some time after I got to know him. In the spring of 1939 we had washed floors together in Magadan transit camp. It was a small world. Anna Izrailevna was a lady who took herself extremely seriously. She kindly agreed to give a few lectures to the paramedic students. The actual lectures were given in such a solemn way that all I remembered of them was the rustling black silk dress she wore and the sharp tang of her perfume, a perfume that none of our women students had. True, the cook did give Nadia Yegorova a tiny little bottle, but Nadia sniffed it so cautiously and meanly during our classes, that no smell spread even two rows behind her. Perhaps that was because of the constant cold I had caught in Kolyma.

I remember some posters being brought into class. They must have been diagrams of conditioned reflexes, but I don't know if they made any sense to anyone.

It was decided not to give us any lectures at all on mental illness, thus curtailing further a program that was short enough as it was. But the teachers did exist: the chairman of the admissions committee for the courses, Dr. Sidkin, was the hospital psychiatrist.

Lectures on diseases of the ear, nose, and throat were given by Dr. Zader, a pure-blooded Hungarian. A real oil-painting of a man, with sheep's eyes, Zader's Russian was very bad, so that he was almost unable to get anything across to his students. He volunteered to lecture so he could practice his Russian. His classes were a sheer waste of time.

We kept pestering Meerzon, who by then had been appointed chief doctor in the hospital: "How on earth are we going to know what Zader is lecturing about?"

"Well, if that's the only subject you're not going to know, then it doesn't matter," Meerzon replied in his usual manner.

Zader had only just been sent to Kolyma. In 1956 he was rehabilitated, but this came at the end of the year, so he decided not to return to Hungary, but, having received a large sum of money in his settlement with Far East Construction, he ended up somewhere in the South. Shortly after taking all the students' tests, Dr. Zader was involved in an incident.

Dr. Janos Zader, the ear, nose, and throat specialist, was a Hungarian prisoner of war and, consequently, must have been a follower of the fascist Ferenc Szálasi. His term was fifteen years. He quickly learned Russian,[25] he was a doctor, and the time when doctors were made to do manual labor had passed (in any case, this instruction affected only those with T for Trotskyist in their file). Moreover, there was a particular shortage in his specialization. He was successful at operating on and treating patients. When abdominal surgery was required he usually assisted the chief of the surgical department, the surgeon Meerzon. In short, Dr. Zader was in luck: he had clients even among the free workers, he dressed in civilian clothes, he wore his hair long, he was well-fed and he could have gotten drunk, except that he never touched a drop of alcohol. His fame kept spreading, until the incident happened that deprived our hospital of otolaryngology for a long period.

The point is that an erythrocyte, that is, a red blood cell, survives for twenty-one days. A living human's blood is constantly being renewed. But once blood is taken out of the human being, it cannot survive longer than twenty-one days. The surgical department, as it was meant to, had its own transfusion station, which received donors' blood from free workers and from prisoners—the free workers received a ruble per cubic centimeter, the prisoners just ten kopecks. For anyone with high blood pressure this was a source of basic income, and they gave 300–400 ccs a month. You were encouraged to give blood, it was good for your treatment, and you also got extra rations as well as money. The prisoner-donors were the nonmedical staff of the hospital (porters and so on), who were kept on the premises because they provided blood for the patients. There was a greater demand for transfusions here than on the mainland, but transfusions were prescribed not by general medical criteria, emaciation for instance, but only in cases when a transfusion was needed in preparation for an operation, or because of a particularly serious condition in the therapeutic departments.

There was always a supply of already donated blood in the transfusion station. The presence of this supply was a matter our hospital took pride in. In all the other hospitals, if blood was transfused, it was done directly from one person to another. Donor and recipient lay on adjacent tables during this procedure.

Blood whose shelf life had expired was thrown away.

Not far from the hospital was a pig farm, where, when a pig was slaughtered, the blood was collected and brought to the hospital. Here a solution of trisodium citrate was added to the blood to stop it curdling, and it was then given to the patients to drink, as a sort of homemade hematogen. It was very nutritious and the patients, whose nourishment consisted of various dumpling soups and pearl-barley porridges, loved it. Issuing hematogen to patients was nothing new. Once, when Meerzon, the head of the surgical department, went off on a mission, the management of the department was taken over by Dr. Zader.

As he did the rounds of the department, he deemed himself obliged to visit the transfusion station, too. Here he found that a substantial amount of the blood supply was past its expiration date, and he listened to the nurse telling him she intended to throw this blood away. Dr. Zader was astounded. "Does this blood really have to be thrown away?" he asked. She replied that this was what they always did.

"Pour the blood into kettles and give it to the seriously ill patients *per os* (by mouth)," ordered Zader. The nurse did so, and the patients were very pleased. "In future," said the Hungarian, "any blood that is too old is to be dealt with the same way."

So began the practice of issuing donors' blood to the wards. When the department chief returned he raised as loud an outcry as he could that the fascist Zader was doing no more or less than feeding patients on human blood. The patients immediately found out about this, for rumors spread even faster in hospitals than in prisons, and those who had at any time drunk this blood started to feel nauseated. Zader was suspended without any explanation, and a detailed report, accusing him of all kinds of crimes, winged its way to the health administration. Zader was bewildered. He tried to explain that there was no difference in principle between intravenous transfusion and ingestion by mouth, that this blood was a good supplementary food, but nobody would listen to him. Zader's head was shaved, his free man's jacket was removed, and, dressed in prisoner's garb, he was sent to the Lurié brigade to do forestry work. Dr. Zader had managed to make it to the forest region's Board of Honor as a shock worker, when a commission arrived from the health administration, worried not so much by the actual fact of such blood transfusion, but that the patients needing an ear and throat specialist had been left with no doctor. By a lucky coincidence, this commission was headed by a major in the medical service, who had just been demobilized from the army and who had spent the whole war working in surgical departments of the medical battalions. When he had familiarized himself with the material charges, he completely failed to understand what it was all about. Why was Zader being persecuted? When it was explained that Zader had issued human blood to the patients, that "he gave them blood to drink," the major shrugged and said, "I did that for four years at the front. Why, can't you do it here? I wouldn't know, I've only arrived recently."

Zader was brought back from the forests and reinstated in the surgical department, despite a written protest from the forestry fore-man, who considered that he was being deprived of his best lumberjack on someone's whim.

But Zader had lost interest in his work and stopped making any proposals for rationalizing the use of blood.

Dr. Doctor was an utter swine. In Kolyma he was said to be a bribe-taker and to misappropriate state property, but that was normal for bosses in Kolyma. Even his vindictiveness and love of troublemaking were forgivable by Kolyma standards.

Dr. Doctor hated prisoners. It wasn't just that he treated them badly or distrusted them. He tyrannized them, he humiliated them at any time of day or night, he found fault with them, he insulted them and made extensive use of his unlimited power (within the hospital walls) to fill the solitary confinement cells of the punishment area. He did not consider former prisoners to be human, and several times he threatened, for example the surgeon Traut, that he wouldn't hesitate to get them new sentences. Every day a fresh fish was delivered to Dr. Doctor's apartment—a brigade of "patients" were sent out to fish with nets—or greenhouse vegetables were brought in or meat from the pig farm: all this in quantities sufficient to feed Gulliver. Dr. Doctor had a servant, an orderly who was a prisoner and who helped him turn all offerings into money. Parcels of tobacco, Kolyma's hard currency, kept arriving from the mainland. He was in charge of the hospital for a great many years until he was finally felled by another gangster. Dr. Doctor's boss found that his "rake-off" was too small.

But all that happened later. During the courses Dr. Doctor was king and god. Meetings were arranged every day, where Dr. Doctor made speeches with a strong bent toward the cult of personality.

Dr. Doctor was also a very skilled fabricator of slanderous memorandums and could stitch up anyone.

He was a vindictive chief, vindictive in a petty way.

"You didn't bow when you met me, so I'm going to write a denunciation, not just a denunciation, but an official memorandum. I'll write that you're 'a regular Trotskyist and an enemy of the people' and, you needn't have any doubts, you're guaranteed to get the punishment mines."

The courses, which were his own brainchild, dismayed Dr. Doctor. There were, it turned out, too many politicals with article 58 convictions, and this made him worried about his career. A typical bureaucrat of 1937, Dr. Doctor was briefly retired from Far East Construction at the end of the 1940s, but when he saw that everything was staying the same, and that if he went to the mainland, he'd have to work, he went back to his Kolyma job. Even though he now had to earn his percentage bonuses all over again, he at least found himself back in familiar surroundings.

After inspecting the courses before the final examinations, Dr. Doctor amiably listened to a report about the students' progress, then ran his bright blue, glassy eyes over all the students and asked, "And does everyone know how to do cupping?"

He was answered by respectful laughter from the teachers and students. Unfortunately, cupping was the one thing we hadn't learned to do, as none of us thought that there were any secrets to this elementary procedure.

Dr. Fiodor Yefimovich Loskutov taught eye diseases. I was fortunate enough to know and to work with him for a number of years. He was one of the most remarkable people in Kolyma. He was a commissar in charge of a battalion during the Civil War, and a bullet from Admiral Kolchak's side had lodged permanently in his left eye. He received his medical education in the early 1920s and worked as a military doctor in the army. A casual joke about Stalin ended with him facing a military tribunal. He came to Kolyma to serve a sentence of three years and spent the first year as a metalworker at the Partisan mine. Then he was allowed to practice medicine. His three-year sentence was coming to an end. This was a period that Kolyma and all Russia knew as the Garanin times, although it would have been more accurate to call it the Pavlov times, after the then head of Far East Construction. Colonel Garanin was only the deputy to Pavlov, who was head of the camps, although Garanin chaired the troika that issued death sentences and signed the endless lists of those to be shot throughout 1938. For someone convicted under article 58, it was terrifying to be released in 1938. Everyone who was completing their sentence was threatened with the creation, the stitching and organization of a new case. You would feel more at ease with a sentence of ten or fifteen years than with one of three or five. You could breathe easier.

Loskutov was condemned all over again by the Kolyma troika under Garanin—to ten years. A capable doctor, he specialized in eye diseases, performed operations, and was a highly valued specialist. The health administration kept him near Magadan at the twenty-third kilometer, and, when he was needed, he would be brought under guard to Magadan for consultations and operations. One of the last country doctors in Russia, Loskutov could turn his hands to anything: he could do simple abdominal operations, and he knew gynecology, as well as being an eye specialist.

In 1947, when Loskutov's second sentence was ending, the NKVD officer Simonov fabricated a new case. Several paramedics and nurses at the hospital were arrested and sentenced to various terms. Loskutov got another ten years. This time the authorities tried to insist that he be removed from Magadan and transferred to Berlag, a new strict-regime camp for political recidivists in the interior of Kolyma. For a few years the hospital bosses succeeded in keeping Loskutov out of Berlag, but eventually he ended up there *for his third sentence*! After credit for working days he was released in 1954, and in 1955 was completely re-habilitated on all three counts.

When he was released he owned just one set of spare underclothes, a tunic, and a pair of trousers.

A man of the highest moral qualities, Dr. Loskutov devoted his entire medical practice, all his life as a camp doctor, to one task: actively and constantly helping people, mainly prisoners. This help was far from restricted to medicine. He was always helping someone settle down, recommending someone for a job after they were discharged from the hospital. He was always feeding somebody, taking parcels for somebody— a pinch of tobacco for one, a piece of bread for another.

Patients thanked their lucky stars if they ended up in his department (he worked as a general practitioner).

He spent all his time interceding, going to see people, writing.

And this was every day not just for a month or a year, but for twenty full years, while all the authorities gave him were additional terms of punishment.

History tells us of a similar figure: the prison doctor Fiodor Petrovich Gaaz,[24] about whom A. F. Koni wrote a book. But Gaaz's times were different: those were the 1860s, a time when Russian society was experiencing a moral resurgence. The 1930s had no such resurgence. In an atmosphere of denunciations, slander, punishments, arbitrariness, when you received prison sentences one after the other for charges based on provocations, it was far harder to do good deeds than in Gaaz's times.

Loskutov would arrange for one man to be allowed to travel to the mainland as an invalid, and he would find easy work for another man. Without asking anything of his patient, he would arrange his future wisely and for the best.

Fiodor Yefimovich Loskutov was not particularly literate, in the schoolboy sense of the word, and had entered the medical institute with only an elementary education. But he read a lot, he had observed life carefully and had thought a lot, he had his own judgment on the most varied subjects, so that he was a widely educated person.

An extremely modest man, never rushing to judgment, he was a remarkable figure. He had one fault: his help was, in my view, far too indiscriminate, which was why the gangsters tried to "saddle" him, once they sensed his notorious weakness. But as time went on he became well aware of this, too.

Three sentences to the camps, an anxiety-ridden Kolyma life, with threats from the bosses, with humiliations, and no certainty as to what the next day would bring, had failed to make Loskutov either a skeptic or a cynic.

When he emerged as a wholly free man, after being rehabilitated and paid a lot of money, he went on as before, handing out money to anyone who needed it. As a result of helping people, he still didn't have a spare set of underwear, even though he now received several thousand rubles a month.

This was our teacher of eye diseases. When I finished the courses it was under Loskutov that I had to work for a few weeks—my first weeks as a paramedic. The first evening ended in the treatment room. A patient with a throat abscess was brought in.

"What is it?" Loskutov asked me.

"A throat abscess."

"Treatment?"

"To release the pus, making sure the patient doesn't choke on the fluid."

"Put the instruments in the sterilizer."

I put the instruments in the sterilizer, boiled them, and summoned Loskutov.

"Ready."

"Bring in the patient."

The patient sat on a stool with his mouth open. A lamp lit up his throat.

"Wash your hands, Fiodor Yefimych."

"No, you wash yours," said Loskutov. "You're the one who's going to do this operation."

My back broke out in a cold sweat. But I knew, I knew very well, that until you did something with your own hands, you couldn't say that you knew how to do it. Something easy suddenly seems to be beyond you, while the complicated seems unbelievably simple.

I washed my hands and with a firm step approached the patient. His wide-open eyes were looking at me reproachfully and fearfully.

I took aim, and lanced the ripe abscess with the blunt end of the knife.

"His head, his head!" Fiodor Yefimych shrieked.

I managed to bend the patient's head forward, and he spat out the pus straight onto the skirts of my gown.

"Well, that's it. Now change your gown."

The next day Loskutov sent me off to the "semi-outpatient" clinic where the invalids lived, entrusting me with taking everyone's blood pressure. Taking my Riva-Rocci manometer with me, I took all sixty men's pressures and recorded them on paper. They all suffered from high blood pressure. I spent a whole week measuring blood pressure, ten times for each person. Only after that did Loskutov show me the patients' cards.

I was glad to be taking these measurements on my own. Many years later I realized that this was a deliberate way of letting me learn my job calmly. My first case, which demanded quick decisive action and a bold hand, had required me to behave differently.

Fiodor Yefimovich never exposed malingerers or exaggerators.

"They only think," he said sadly, "that they're exaggerating or malingering. They are far more seriously ill than they themselves believe. Malingering and exaggerating when you have the dystrophy and dementia that come from camp life are problems that have not been described, just have not been described."

Aleksandr Aleksandrovich Malinsky, who lectured us on internal disease, was a well-scrubbed, well-fed, sanguine man, a cheerful man who was clean-shaven, gray-haired, and beginning to put on weight. His lips were dark pink and heart-shaped. On his bright-red back he had an aristocrat's long-stemmed moles, and they shook—we sometimes saw him in the sauna of the hospital bathhouse. He was the only Kolyma doctor, and I think the only Kolyma inhabitant, to sleep in a specially tailored long nightshirt that went down to his ankles. This was revealed when there was a fire in his department. The fire was successfully extinguished right away and soon forgotten about, but Dr. Malinsky's nightshirt was a subject of gossip in the hospital for many months.

Formerly a lecturer in Moscow giving postgraduate courses for doctors, Malinsky found it hard to adapt to the level of the students' knowledge.

There was always a chill of alienation between the lecturer and his audience. Malinsky would have liked to break down this barrier, but he didn't know how to do it. He devised a few rather vulgar jokes, but this did not make his subject matter any easier to take in.

Visual aids? But even in anatomy lectures we dispensed with skeletons. Umansky used the blackboard and chalk to draw the bones we needed to know about.

Malinsky gave his lectures, trying his hardest to give us as much information as possible. He knew the camps very well, having been arrested in 1937, and his lectures gave us a lot of important advice about medical ethics in their distorted camp version. "Learn to trust the patient," Malinsky passionately urged us, as he bounced up and down by the blackboard, tapping the chalk. He was talking about bullet wounds, lumbago, but we understood that this appeal was about more important matters, about the way *real* medicine should be carried out in the camp, telling us that the monstrosity of camp life must not divert medicine from its proper paths.

We owed a lot—information, knowledge—to Dr. Malinsky and, although his constant instinct to keep a significant distance between himself and us unfortunately left us out of sympathy with him, we did recognize his merits.

Dr. Malinsky put up well with the Kolyma climate. Even after being rehabilitated he voluntarily stayed on and lived for the rest of his life in Seimchan, one of the Kolyma vegetable farms.

Dr. Malinsky regularly read the newspapers, but never shared his opinions with anyone: that was because of his experience, experience.... The only books he read were medical ones.

The course director was a free contract worker, Dr. Tatiana Mikhailovna Ilyina, the sister of Sergei Ilyin, the famous soccer player, as she personally liked to introduce herself. She was a lady who tried in every small detail to adopt the top bosses' mannerisms and tone. She had had a great career in Kolyma. Her moral sycophancy had almost no limits. Once she asked for something decent to read. I brought her something valuable: a volume of Hemingway with *The Fifth Column* and *48 Stories*. Ilyina turned over the cherry-colored volume and leafed through it.

"No, take it back. This is fancy stuff, and we need black bread."

Those were obviously someone else's words, the words of a sancti-monious hypocrite, but she enjoyed uttering them, even though they didn't quite fit the occasion. After such an affront I abandoned my role as literary adviser to Dr. Ilyina.

She was married. She had come to Kolyma as a wife following her husband, bringing her two children with her. Her husband was an army officer who signed a contract after the war with Far East Con-struction and brought his family to the northeast. Here he kept his officer's rations, ranks, and privileges: having two children meant that he had a big family. He was appointed chief of the political section of one of Kolyma's mine administrations, quite a major post, almost a general's, and with promotion prospects, too. But Nikolayev, Dr. Ilyina's husband, was a keen observer, conscientious and not in the least a careerist. When he had seen for himself the arbitrariness, speculation, denunciations, thieving, scheming, self-serving, bribe-taking, and em-bezzlement, and all the cruel acts committed by the Kolyma bosses at the expense of the prisoners, Nikolayev took to drink. He understood and condemned deeply and irrevocably the demoralizing effect of people's cruelty. The most terrible pages of life, far more terrible than his years at the front, were revealed to him. He wasn't a bribe-taker, he wasn't a scoundrel. He took to drink.

He was very soon removed from his post as head of the political section. In a very short period, no more than two or three years, his career went into reverse and he ended up with a sinecure, the badly paid and unimportant job of inspector of the Culture and Education Center of a prisoners' hospital. He was compelled to make fishing his passion. On the banks of a river deep in the taiga he felt better and calmer. When his contract period was over, he left for the mainland.

Dr. Ilyina did not follow him. On the contrary, she joined the party and laid the foundations for her career. They split the children between them: the daughter went to her father, the boy to his mother.

But all that happened later. At this time Dr. Ilyina was a caring and tactful director of our courses. She was a little apprehensive of prisoners, and tried to have as little to do with them as she could. Apparently she wouldn't even have prisoners as servants.

General and specialized surgery was the subject taught by Meerzon, who had studied under Spasokukotsky, and he was a surgeon with a great future and a major place in science. But Meerzon was married to a relative of Zinoviev, so that in 1937 he was arrested and sentenced to ten years as the head of some terrorist anti-Soviet organization of wreckers. In 1946, when the paramedic courses started, he had only just been released. (He had gotten away with doing less than a year of manual labor, and was a surgeon throughout his imprisonment.) At that time, "lifelong restricted residence" had begun to be fashionable, and Meerzon too was forced to stay on for life. Having been released very recently, he was extremely cautious and extremely formal and extremely unapproachable. His great career had been smashed to smithereens, and his resentment needed an outlet, which he found in jokes and sarcasm. . . .

He was a superb lecturer. For ten years he had been deprived of his beloved teaching work—casual chats with the operating theater nurses did not, of course, compensate. For the first time he could face an audience, students in these courses, eager for medical knowledge. Even though the students were a very mixed bunch, Meerzon was not dismayed. To begin with, his lectures were entertaining and fiery. But his first test was a bucket of ice-cold water poured onto an overheated lecturer. His audience was too primitive: words like "element" and "form" needed to be explained, and explained in detail. Meerzon realized this and he was extremely disappointed, but he hid his feelings and tried to adapt to the students' level. He had to put himself at the level of the worst, the Finnish girl Aino, the shop manager Silantiev, and so on.

"A fistula forms," said the professor. "Who knows what a fistula is?"

Silence.

"It's a hole, a hole like this...."

The lectures became less exciting, but they never lost their useful content.

As befits a surgeon, Meerzon treated all other medical specializations with open contempt. He took the staff's concerns for sterility in his department virtually to metropolitan levels, demanding that the requirements of surgical clinics be scrupulously met. But in other departments he behaved with deliberate casualness. When he attended a consultation, he never took off his jacket and hat, and he would sit on the patient's bed wearing them, regardless of what therapeutic department he was in. This was done on purpose, and it looked insulting. The wards were, in fact, all clean, and the grumbling hospital porters had to spend a lot of time mopping up the wet traces of Meerzon's felt boots after he had gone. This was one way in which Meerzon amused himself: he had the gift of the gab and was always ready to let a general practitioner have the benefit of his bile, his resentment at and dissatisfaction with the world.

He didn't let himself do this in his lectures. He expounded everything clearly, exactly, and exhaustively. He was able to find examples that anyone could understand, live illustrations, and if he saw that the audience was taking it in, he was pleased. He was the hospital's chief surgeon and later became its chief doctor. His opinion had a decisive role whenever there was a question affecting our courses. Every action of his that we observed, and all of his conversations, were carefully thought out and to the point.

The first time we witnessed a real operation we were crowded into a corner of the operating theater, wearing sterile gowns and fantastical gauze half-masks, and it was Meerzon who was operating. His permanent operating theater assistant nurse, Nina Dmitriyevna Kharchenko, was helping him. She was a contract worker, the secretary of the hospital's Komsomol. Meerzon gave curt orders: "Kocher forceps ...! Needle!"

Kharchenko snatched the instruments from a little table and gingerly placed them into the surgeon's hand, which was stretched out to one side. He wore tight-fitting bright yellow rubber gloves.

Suddenly she handed him the wrong instrument. Meerzon swore

coarsely and, with a wave of his hand, threw a pair of tweezers onto the floor. The tweezers clanged, Nina Dmitriyevna blushed and meekly handed him the right instrument.

We felt offended on her behalf, and angry with Meerzon. We considered that he shouldn't have behaved like that. At least for our sake, even if he was such a ruffian normally.

After the operation we offered Nina some words of sympathy.

"Guys, the surgeon is responsible for the operation," she confided to us gravely. There was no embarrassment or resentment in her voice.

As if he had understood everything that was going on inside the minds of his neophytes, Meerzon devoted his next class to a particular topic. It was a brilliant lecture about a surgeon's responsibility, his willpower, about the need to overcome the patient's will, about the psychologies of doctor and patient.

This lecture delighted us all, and afterward we gave Meerzon a higher rating than any other doctor.

Just as brilliant, in fact outright poetic, was his lecture on "A Surgeon's Hands," in which his discussion of the essence of the medical profession, the concept of sterility, became incandescent. Meerzon delivered the lecture as if for himself; he barely looked at his audience. The lecture contained a lot of stories. They included the panic that came over Spasokukotsky's clinic when patients mysteriously became infected after clean operations—thanks to a wart, finally discovered on an assistant's finger. This was a lecture about the structure of skin and on a surgeon's intolerance of imperfection. It explained why no surgeon, theater nurse, or paramedic in a surgical department had the right to take part in camp "shock work" or in any manual labor. This revealed to us Meerzon's many years of passionate battling, as a surgeon, with the ignorant camp bosses.

Sometimes, on days devoted to testing what we had taken in, Meerzon managed to finish the questioning earlier than he had anticipated. The rest of the time was devoted to very interesting stories apropos of prominent Russian surgeons: Oppel, Fiodorov, and especially Spasokukotsky, whom Meerzon idolized. It was all witty, clever, useful, and it was all completely authentic. Our view of the world was changing. Thanks to Meerzon we were becoming medics. We were learning to think like doctors, and we were learning well. Every one of us was different after these courses that condensed a two-year syllabus into eight months.

Afterward, Meerzon moved from Magadan to Neksikan in the western region of Kolyma. In 1952 he was suddenly arrested and taken off to Moscow. An attempt was made to stitch him up in the "Doctors' Case."[23] Together with the other doctors, he was released in 1953. He returned to Kolyma and worked for a short time, afraid to stay any longer in such an unstable and dangerous area. He left for the mainland.

The hospital had a club, but the students didn't go there, except for the girls, Zhenka Kats and Borisova.

We thought it was a sacrilege to spend even an hour of our free time on anything but study. We studied day and night. At first I tried to make a fair copy of all my notes in a new exercise book, but there was not enough time or paper to do this.

The camp hospital was now overcrowded with people who were there because of the war—Russian émigrés from Manchuria, Japanese prisoners of war, who were given rice instead of bread, and many hundreds of people condemned as spies by military tribunals. But none of this had yet taken on the enormous dimensions that came with the repressions a little later, toward the end of the shipping season in 1946, when five thousand prisoners, brought over on the steamship *KIM*, were hosed down with water from the ship's fire pumps during a sea journey that had taken longer than it should have. The work of transporting these people and amputating their frostbitten fingers and toes was something we carried out as fully qualified paramedics, and not only in Magadan.

Every day we were tormented by doubts: were the courses going to be closed down? The rumors, each one more frightening, stopped me from sleeping. But our classes continued, little by little, and finally the day came when even the worst moaners and unbelievers could breathe more easily and feel relieved.

Three months had passed, and the courses were still going on. New doubts appeared: would we pass the final examination? After all, the courses were an official initiative, and they gave one the right to treat people. True, in 1953 the health administration of Far East Construction explained to the town health authorities in Kalinin (Tver, today) that those who had taken these courses could treat people only in Kolyma, but local authorities paid no attention to such strange limitations on the use of medical knowledge.

What disappointed us greatly was that the program was curtailed and gave its graduates only the rights of a qualified nurse. But that was a matter of secondary importance. The worst aspect was that no certificates were handed out to us. "Certificates will be inserted into your personal files," Ilyina explained. It turned out that there was not a single trace of our medical education in our personal files. After we were released, quite a few of us had to collect testimony, which was certified by teachers in the courses.

After three months of study, time began to move very, very fast. The approach of the examination day gave us no joy. The examination would be the final summary of our wonderful life at kilometer twenty-three, and we knew that life would get no better than that. So we were anxious and we were sad, even if only moderately so, for Kolyma had taught us not to count on the future more than one day ahead.

The examination day loomed. People were now saying openly that the hospital would be moved five hundred kilometers deeper into the taiga to the settlement of Debin on the left bank of the Kolyma River.

A month before the courses ended, a mock examination in all subjects was staged. I didn't think this occasion was important and only after the final examination did I realize that all the questions that the students had to answer at the real examination were, in all subjects, a repetition of the questions at the preliminary examination. Of course, the members of the examination board, the top bosses from the health department of Far East Construction, were able to ask, and did ask, supplementary questions. But the basis for an examinee's confidence and the basis for the impressions formed by the examiner were already there in an auspicious, familiar, question paper. I remember my question for surgery was on the "varicose widening of veins."

Even before the examination there was a reassuring rumor that everyone, absolutely everyone, would pass, that nobody would be deprived of their modest medical rights. This made everyone happy; the rumor turned out to be true.

Gradually our circle of acquaintances grew stronger and wider. We were no longer outsiders, we were initiates, members of the great Order of Medicine. Both doctors and patients saw us in this light.

We had stopped being ordinary people. We had become specialists.

For the first time in Kolyma, I felt I was needed—by the hospital, by the camp, by life, by myself. I felt I was a person with full rights, whom nobody could shout at or taunt.

Although many bosses put me in solitary confinement for infringements, real or imaginary, of the camp rules, even in solitary I remained a human being whom the hospital needed. When I came out of solitary, I went back to being a paramedic.

My smashed self-esteem now had the necessary glue and cement to make it possible to restore what had been shattered to pieces.

The courses were coming to an end, and the young men found themselves girlfriends: everything was as it should be. But the older men would not allow any feelings of love to interfere with their future. Love was too cheap a stake in the camp game. We had been taught over the years to restrain ourselves, and the lessons were not wasted.

I developed a supersensitive self-esteem. If anyone else gave an excellent answer in any class, I took it as a personal insult, I was offended. It was I who should be able to answer any question put by a teacher.

Our knowledge gradually increased, but, more importantly, our interests broadened, and we kept asking the doctors more and more questions—even if they were naïve, or stupid questions. But the doctors didn't consider a single one of our questions to be naïve or stupid. Everything was answered, always with a sufficiently categorical response. Answers called forth new questions. We didn't yet have the courage for medical arguments between ourselves. That would have been too arrogant.

Yet... once I was summoned to correct a dislocated shoulder. The doctor gave Rausch anesthesia, and I put back the shoulder with my foot, using the Hippocratic method. Something clicked softly under my heel, and the shoulder bone went back where it should go. I was happy. Tatiana Ilyina, who was present during the manipulation of the dislocated shoulder, said, "See how well you've been taught," and I couldn't help agreeing with her.

Naturally, I never once went to the cinema or to the amateur dramatics performances that were perfectly professional in Magadan and in the hospital, even though they were exceptionally inventive and in good taste, inasmuch as they could get through the censorship barriers of the Cultural and Educational Section. At that time the Magadan drama group was directed by L. V. Varpakhovsky, who later became the chief director of the Yermolova Theater in Moscow. I had no time, and anyway the secrets of medicine, as they were slowly revealed, interested me far more.

Medical terminology stopped being hocus-pocus. I started reading medical articles and books. I had lost my old helplessness and fear.

I was no longer an ordinary person. It was my duty to be able to provide first aid, to assess the condition of a seriously ill patient, if only in general terms. It was my duty to identify any danger that threatened people's lives. This gave me both joy and anxiety. I was afraid of not being able to carry out my exalted duties.

I knew how to carry out a siphon enema, how to use Bobrov's apparatus for an intravenous injection, how to use a scalpel or a syringe....

I knew how to change a seriously ill patient's bedding and could teach hospital porters the technique. I could explain to the same men the reasons for disinfection and cleaning up.

I learned thousands of things I hadn't known before, things that were necessary, vital, useful to humanity.

The courses were over, and the new paramedics began to be dispatched, one by one, to new workplaces. A list would appear, a list held by the escort guard, and my surname would be on it. But I would be the last person to get into the truck. I was taking patients to the Left Bank hospital. The truck was packed tight, and I would sit right at the end, my back against the side. While I was settling down, my shirt became untucked and the wind blew through a gap in the side of the truck. I was holding a folding bag full of vials: valerian, tincture of lily of the valley, iodine, liquid ammonia. At my feet was a tightly packed bag containing exercise books with my paramedic's course notes.

For several years those exercise books were my best support, until the day I finally left, when a bear got into the taiga clinic and tore all my notes to shreds, after piercing all my jars and vials.

1960

THE FIRST SECRET POLICEMAN

BLUE EYES tend to fade. Over the years a child's cornflower-blue eyes become the cloudy, dirty, bluish-gray little eyes of the man in the street, or else they turn into the glassy tentacles of interrogators and janitors, or the "steely" eyes of soldiers. There are a lot of different shades. Only very rarely do eyes preserve the color they had in childhood. . . .

A bundle of the sun's red rays was split up by the grid of the prison bars into several smaller bundles. Somewhere in the middle of the cell they combined again into a constant red-gold flow. In this stream of light, specks of dust made a thick golden cloud. Flies that flew into the zone of light also became as golden as the sun. The rays of the setting sun struck the door, which was framed in shiny gray iron.

The lock clanged: a sound that anyone in a prison cell, whether he is awake or asleep, will hear at any time. No conversation in the cell could blot out that sound. No sleep in the cell is deep enough to distract you from it. There is no thought in the cell that could—nobody can concentrate on anything so much that they would miss the sound or fail to hear it. Everyone's spirit drops when they hear the sound of the lock, fate knocking at the door of the cell, knocking at souls, hearts, and minds. Everyone is alarmed by this sound. And there is no way it can be confused with any other sound.

The lock clanged, the door opened, and the current of rays escaped from the cell. Once the door was open the rays could be seen to cut across the corridor and rush for the window, before flying across the prison yard and breaking up against the window panes of another prison block. All sixty inhabitants of the cell managed to take this in during the short time that the door was open. The door slammed shut with a melodious ringing sound, like that of an ancient trunk when the lid is banged shut. All the prisoners who had eagerly watched the spurt of light, the movement of the beam, as though it were a living creature, their brother and comrade, immediately understood that the sun had once more been locked up with them.

Only then did everyone see that a man, his eyes screwed up in the penetrating light, was standing by the door, letting his broad, black chest absorb the flow of the sunset's golden rays.

The man was middle-aged, tall and broad-shouldered, with a thick, full head of fair hair. Only a closer look could tell you that this straw-colored hair had for some time been mixed with gray. His wrinkled face, which looked like a relief map, was covered with a great number of pockmarks, like lunar craters.

He was dressed in a black fabric tunic; he had no belt, and the tunic was unbuttoned; he wore black cloth riding breeches and boots. His hands were crumpling a black, very worn greatcoat. His clothes only hung on him: all the buttons had been ripped off.

"Alekseyev," he said quietly, raising his large, hairy hand and putting it to his chest. "How do you do."

People were already going up to him, trying to encourage him with their tense, abrupt prisoner's laughter, clapping him on the shoulder, shaking his hand. The cell elder, the elected authority, was now approaching to show the newcomer his place. "Gavriil Alekseyev," the bearlike man repeated. Then he said, "Gavriil Timofeyevich Alekseyev." The man in black moved to the side, and the ray of sunlight now revealed his eyes to be large, children's eyes, the color of cornflowers.

The cell soon learned the details of Alekseyev's life: he was the chief of the fire brigade in a Naro-Fominsk factory, which is why he wore the black official suit. Yes, he had been a party member since 1917. Yes, he had been an artillery man and took part in the October battles in Moscow. Yes, he had been expelled from the party in 1927. He had been readmitted. And expelled again, a week ago.

Prisoners behave differently when they are first arrested. It is a very difficult business to break down the mistrust of some. By degrees, day by day, they get used to their fate and begin to understand things.

Alekseyev was different. He seemed to have stayed silent for many years, and then came arrest, and the prison cell gave him back his gift for speech. Here he found an opportunity to understand the crucial thing, to sense the movement of time, of his own fate, and to understand why. To find an answer to the enormous, gigantic "why" that loomed over all his life and fate, and not only his, but over the lives and fates of hundreds of thousands of others.

Alekseyev told his story without trying to absolve himself, without asking questions. He was just trying to understand, to compare, to solve the mystery.

This enormous, bearlike man, in an unbelted black tunic, would from morning to evening pace up and down the cell. He would put his enormous paw around somebody's shoulders and ask, ask.... Or he would tell his story.

"Why were you expelled, Gavriil?"

"Well, you understand. There was a class for our political circle. The topic was October in Moscow. After all, I was a soldier in Muralov's[26] artillery and was wounded twice. I personally aimed the cannon at the tsarist cadets at the Nikita Gates. My instructor at the political circle asks me, 'Who was in command of the Soviet troops in Moscow during the revolution?' I say, 'Muralov, Nikolai Ivanovich.' I knew him well, personally. What else could I say? What could I say?"

"That question was a provocation, Gavriil. After all, you know that Muralov has been declared an enemy of the people, don't you?"

"But what else can you say? It's something I know from life, not political instruction. That same night I was arrested."

"How did you end up in Naro-Fominsk? In a fire brigade?"

"I was a heavy drinker. I was demobilized from the Secret Police as far back as 1918. Muralov had gotten me a job there, as an especially reliable man.... And that's where my illness started."

"What illness, Gavriil? You're a great healthy bear of a man."

"You'll see in time. Even I don't know what sort of illness I've got.... I can't remember its name. I don't remember what happens to me. But something does happen.... I get worked up, I turn angry, and then It comes...."

"Is it the vodka?"

"No, it's not the vodka. It's life. Vodka's a separate thing."

"You could have gone back to school.... All the doors were open."

"How could I? Some people can go to school, others have to defend their schooling. Am I putting it simply enough, pal? Anyway, it's been years. I can't go to workers' evening classes. All I'm left with is that damned military site guarding. And the vodka. And It."

"Do you have any children?"

"A daughter by my first wife. She left me. Now I'm living with a weaving worker. Well, she'll be half-dead with fright, if not dead, now that I've been arrested. But I find being arrested a relief. You don't need to think about anything. Everything will be decided by someone else. Other people will do the thinking. About what Gavriil Alekseyev's future is going to be."

A few days, only a few, passed. It came.

Alekseyev gave a pathetic yell, swung out his arms, and fell supine on the bunk. His face had turned gray, bubbling foam was coming out of his blue mouth and flaccid lips. Warm sweat broke out on his gray cheeks and hairy chest. His neighbors grabbed him by the arms and piled onto his legs. His body shook with violent convulsions.

"Look out for his head, take care of his head," said someone, shoving the black greatcoat under Alekseyev's sweating head and disheveled hair.

It had come. The epileptic fit was very prolonged, the powerful lumps of his muscles kept swelling, his fists were striking at someone, and his neighbors' awkward fingers tried to unclench these mighty fists. His legs were trying to run, but the weight of several men piled onto him held him down on the bunk.

His muscles all gradually relaxed, his fingers unclenched. Alekseyev was asleep.

All this time the cell orderlies were knocking at the door, furiously calling for a doctor. There had to be a doctor somewhere in Butyrki prison. Some version of Fiodor Petrovich Gaaz. Or just a military doctor in charge of any rank, a lieutenant in the medical service.

It turned out to be difficult to get hold of a doctor, but one did come. He came wearing white overalls over his officer's uniform, accompanied by two hefty assistants who seemed to be paramedics. The doctor climbed up onto the bunks and examined Alekseyev. By now the attack had receded and Alekseyev was asleep. Without saying a word or answering any of the questions that the prisoners surrounding him fired, the doctor left, followed by his silent assistants. The lock clanged, calling forth an explosion of outrage. When the first wave had died down, the food flap in the prison door opened and the duty warden bent down to take a look. He said, "The doctor's said there's no need to do anything. It's epilepsy. Just see he doesn't swallow his tongue.... If there's another attack, don't call for him. There's no treatment for it."

So the cell stopped asking for a doctor for Alekseyev. But he had many more epileptic attacks.

Alekseyev, complaining of headaches, would sleep off his attacks. After a day or two the enormous bearlike figure in its black cloth tunic and black cloth riding breeches would crawl out again and stride up and down the cell's cement floor. Once again his blue eyes would sparkle. After two prison disinfections, or "roastings," Alekseyev's black clothes had turned brown and no longer seemed black.

But he kept on pacing and pacing, naïvely telling us about his past life, before his illness. He was in a hurry to set out for whomever he was now talking to in order to tell them what he hadn't yet said in this cell.

"...They say that nowadays there are special executioners. But do you know how things were done under Dzerzhinsky?"

"How?"

"If the Secret Police Collegium gave out a death sentence, then the sentence had to be carried out by the interrogator who had been dealing with the case.... By the man who had been advocating and demanding capital punishment. You demand a death sentence for this man? You're convinced of his guilt, you're sure that he's an enemy and should get death? Kill him with your own hand. There's a very big difference between signing a piece of paper to confirm a sentence and killing the man yourself."

"A big one."

"Also, every interrogator had to find his own time and place for these jobs of his.... It varied. Some did it in their offices, others in the corridor, or in some basement. Under Dzerzhinsky the interrogator arranged it all himself.... You'd think it over a thousand times before asking for a man's death...."

"Gavriil, have you seen executions?"

"I've seen them. Who hasn't?"

"Is it true that when the man is shot he falls facedown?"

"It's true. When he's looking at you."

"And if you shoot from behind?"

"Then he falls backward, on his back."

"Have you ever had to.... You know...."

"No, I wasn't an interrogator. I don't have any education. I was just in the squad. I fought banditry, and so on. Then I got this thing and I was demobilized. As an epileptic. Anyway I started drinking. They say that isn't treatable, either."

Prison doesn't like devious people. Everyone in the cell spends twenty-four hours a day under the eyes of everyone else. Nobody has the strength to conceal his true character, or to pretend he is different from what he really is in a prison pretrial cell, in minutes, hours, days, weeks, months of tension and nervousness, when anything superfluous or false peels off people, like the peel off a fruit. All that's left is the truth, which may not be created by the prison, but is proven and tested by it. Willpower is not yet broken or crushed, as it almost inevitably will be in the camps. But who was then thinking about the camps, about what they were? A few people may have known and been glad to talk about the camps and warn the newcomers. But people believe what they want to.

Among the prisoners was the black-bearded Weber, a Silesian communist, a member of the Comintern, who'd been brought from Kolyma for "further investigation." He knew what the camps were. Or take Aleksandr Georgievich Andreyev, the former general secretary of the society of tsarist political prisoners, a right-wing Social Revolutionary who had known penal servitude under the tsars and exile under the Soviets. Andreyev knew certain truths that the majority didn't know. But such truths can't be told. Not because they are a secret, but because they are beyond belief. That is why both Weber and Andreyev stayed silent. Prison is prison, and pretrial prison is pretrial prison. Everyone has their own case, their own battles, their own behavior, which can't be dictated to them, their own duty, character, soul, reserve of moral strength, experience. Human qualities are tested not as much in a prison cell as they are outside the cell, in some interrogator's cramped office. Fate depends on a chain of fortuitous events or, more often, not on anything fortuitous at all.

Even a pretrial prison, and not just a short-term prison, prefers people who are straightforward and frank. The cell had a benevolent attitude toward Alekseyev. Were they fond of him? Can you be fond of anyone in a pretrial cell? After all, this is for investigation, transit prior to deportation. The cell had a benevolent attitude toward Alekseyev.

Weeks and months passed, yet Alekseyev still wasn't being summoned to interrogation. And he just kept pacing and pacing.

There are two schools of interrogation. The first school considers that an arrested man must immediately be dazed and stunned. This school's success is based on a speedy psychological attack, on pressure, on suppressing the willpower of the prisoner under investigation, before the latter can come to his senses, take a good look at his surroundings, and gather his moral strength. Interrogators of this school begin their interrogations on the night of the arrest, and prolong them for many hours, using every possible threat. The second school considers that the prison cell will just exhaust and weaken the arrested person's will to resist. The longer he stays in his pretrial cell before encountering his interrogator, the greater the advantage to the interrogator. The prisoner prepares for interrogation, the first interrogation in his life, by harnessing all his strength. But there is no interrogation. For a week, a month, two months, there's nothing. All the work of suppressing the prisoner's psyche is done on the interrogator's behalf by the prison cell.

I don't know how such an effective tool as torture is applied by the first and second schools. This story is set at the beginning of 1937, but torture began only in the second half of that year.

Gavriil Alekseyev's interrogator adhered to the second school.

By the end of the third month of Alekseyev's pacing the cell, a girl wearing a military tunic came running up and summoned Alekseyev—"with his initial," but without his things—which meant for interrogation. Alekseyev combed his fair curls with his five fingers and, adjusting his tunic, which was now brown, strode out of the cell.

He soon came back from interrogation. That meant he had been interrogated in a special block and not driven off anywhere. He was amazed, depressed, stunned, shaken, and frightened.

"Did anything happen, Gavriil?"

"Yes, it did. Something new at the interrogation. I'm accused of conspiring against the government."

"Don't worry, Gavriil. Everyone in this cell is charged with conspiring against the government."

"They say I was planning a murder."

"That often happens, too. What were you accused of before?"

"It was after my arrest in Naro-Fominsk. I was in charge of a fire brigade at the textile factory. So I couldn't have ranked high."

"Nobody cares about rank here, Gavriil."

"Well, they were interrogating me about the political circle classes. For praising Muralov. But I was in his squad in Moscow. What could I say? But now Muralov has nothing to do with it."

His pockmarks and wrinkles now stood out. He was smiling as if he was forcing himself to look calm, and yet uncertain at the same time, and his blue eyes were flashing less and less. But, oddly enough, his epileptic fits happened less often. Imminent danger, the need to fight for his life had apparently pushed the attacks aside.

"What am I to do? They'll be the death of me."

"There's no need to do anything. Just tell the truth. Give them true statements as long as you have the strength."

"So you think it will be all right?"

"Not at all. It certainly won't be all right. Nobody leaves here without something happening to them, Gavriil. But shooting's worse than getting ten years. And ten years is worse than five."

"I get it."

Gavriil started singing more often. His singing was wonderful. He had such a pure, bright tenor voice. He sang quietly, in the corner furthest from the spy hole in the door:

> How good that blue night was,
> How gently the pale moon shone....

More and more often, it was a different song:

Open the window, open it,
I haven't got long to live.
So let me out to go free,
Don't stop me from suffering and loving.

Alekseyev would break off in midsong, leap up, and pace and pace.

He often picked quarrels. Prison life, especially pretrial life, makes people quarrel. You have to be aware of this and keep yourself in hand all the time, or find a way of distracting yourself. Gavriil didn't know these finer points about prison life, and was easily provoked to quarrelling and brawling. Someone would say something that he couldn't take, or would insult Muralov. Muralov was a god to Alekseyev, the god of his youth, the god of his entire life.

When Vasia Zhavoronkov, a locomotive driver from Saviolovo depot, said something about Muralov in the style of the latest party textbooks, Alekseyev threw himself at Vasia, grabbing the copper urn the cell poured tea from.

This tea urn, which had been in Butyrki prison since tsarist times, was an enormous copper cylinder. It was cleaned with brick dust and shone like the setting sun. The tea urn was brought in on a pole, and it took the two duty prisoners, when they poured out tea, to hold it.

A strongman, a Hercules, Alekseyev boldly grabbed the urn handle, but couldn't move the urn. It was full of water, as it was well before supper, when the urn was taken away.

So everything ended in laughter, although Vasia Zhavoronkov turned pale and prepared to receive a blow. Vasia was virtually Alekseyev's fellow accused; he too had been arrested after a class in his political circle. The class leader had asked him, "What would you do, Zhavoronkov, if suddenly Soviet power disappeared?" The simple-minded Zhavoronkov replied, "What? I'd work as a train driver as I do now. I've got four children." The next day he was arrested, and the investigation was now over. The locomotive driver was waiting for his sentence. Their cases were similar, and Gavriil had asked for Vasia's advice: they had been friends. But when the circumstances of Alekseyev's case changed and he was accused of conspiring against the government, the rather cowardly Vasia shunned his friend. And he made sure to repeat that remark about Muralov.

No sooner had Alekseyev been calmed down after this half-comic grappling with Zhavoronkov, than a new quarrel flared up. Alekseyev once more called someone a schemer. Again he had to be pulled off someone. Now the whole cell understood and knew that It was about to come. His comrades walked along by his side, holding him by the arms, ready at any moment to grab his arms and legs, to hold up his head. But Alekseyev suddenly tore himself free, leapt onto the windowsill, clutched the prison bars with both hands and shook and shook them, swearing and roaring. His black body hung from the grid like a great black cross. The prisoners detached his fingers from the bars, bent back his hands. They were in a hurry, because the sentry in the tower had already noticed the jostling by the open window.

Then Aleksandr Andreyev, the general secretary of the society of tsarist political prisoners, said, pointing to the black body that was sliding off the bars:

"The first secret policeman...."

But there was no vicious mockery in Andreyev's voice.

1964

THE GENETICIST

THERE were fresh bear tracks on the ground just by the door of the outpatient's clinic. The lock, a cunning screw lock used to keep the door closed, was lying in the bushes; it had been ripped out from the door and the doorframe with the wood.

Inside the hut, vials, bottles, and jars had been swept off the shelves and turned into a mess of broken glass. The rough smell of valerian drops still lingered in the air.

The exercise books with lecture notes from Andreyev's paramedic courses had been torn to shreds. Andreyev spent several hours of hard work trying to reassemble, page by page, his precious notes, for there had been no textbooks in the paramedic courses. These exercise books were Andreyev's only weapon in his battle with disease in the depths of the taiga. One exercise book had come off worse than the others: the anatomy notes. Its very first page, where there was a diagram of the parts of a cell, the elements of the nucleus, the mysterious chromosomes, had been drawn by Andreyev's clumsy hand, which had never been taught to draw. But the bear's claws had ripped this drawing, and the whole exercise book in its cellophane cover, in such fury that it had to be thrown into the stove, the iron stove. This was an irreplaceable loss, because those were Professor Umansky's lectures.

The paramedic courses had been at the prisoners' hospital. Umansky was an anatomical pathologist, the dissector in charge of the morgue. An anatomical pathologist does the ultimate, posthumous, as it were, check on the work of the doctors treating a patient. During an autopsy, a dissection opening the corpse, a judgment can be made about whether the diagnosis was correct and the treatment appropriate.

But a prisoners' morgue is not a normal morgue. You might think that death, the great democratizer, should not be interested in who is lying on the morgue's dissecting table and should speak the same language to all corpses.

Treating a patient who is a prisoner, especially if the doctor is a prisoner, is no easy task, if the doctor is a decent person.

Both in the hospital and in the morgue everything is done for prisoners, following the formalities that should be observed in any hospital in the world. But the scales have been altered, and the real content of a prisoner's hospital notes differs from that of a free worker's.

The point is not only that death's representative, the anatomical pathologist, is still himself alive, with living passions, resentments, merits, and faults, and varying experience. The point is something greater, for the official dryness of an autopsy conclusion is not enough for either the living or the dead.

If a patient with a diagnosis of cancer died and the autopsy revealed no signs of a malignant tumor, but only very profound, neglected physical emaciation, Umansky would be outraged and unable to forgive the doctors for not having saved a prisoner from starvation. But if it was obvious that the doctor had understood what was wrong, but did not have the right to make the true diagnosis of "alimentary dystrophy"—hunger, feverishly searching for synonyms: avitaminosis, polyavitaminosis, severe scurvy, pellagra, its name is legion—Umansky would help the doctor with his firm judgment. And he'd do more. If the doctor wanted to limit himself to a perfectly respectable diagnosis of influenza-like pneumonia or heart failure, then the anatomical pathologist's finger would point out for the doctors' attention the camp peculiarities of any illness.

Umansky's doctor's conscience also had its bonds and fetters. The first diagnosis of "alimentary dystrophy" was made after the war, after the Leningrad blockade, when starvation even in the camps could be called by its real name.

An anatomical pathologist ought to be a judge, but Umansky was complicit. The reason he was both judge and doctor was that he could also be complicit. However tightly he was bound by an instruction, a tradition, an order, or specific clarifications, Umansky looked deeper, further, and in a more principled way. He saw it as his duty not to catch out doctors in petty details, but to see—and point out to others!—the more important factor that lay behind these petty details, the "background" to emaciation from starvation, which changed the picture of a disease the doctor had studied in textbooks. No textbook of prisoners' illnesses had been written yet. It never was.

Frostbitten limbs in the camp were a phenomenon that shattered the frontline surgeons who came from the mainland. The treatment of fractures had to be done against the patients' will. To get admitted to a tuberculosis department, patients would bring with them somebody else's "gobs" and put into their mouths what was clearly a bacteria-infected poison before a preadmission analysis was done. Patients would stir blood into their urine, if only from a scratch on their finger, so as to get into the hospital, be it just for a day or an hour, to save themselves from the worst fate that exists for a prisoner: murderous and degrading labor.

Umansky, like all the doctors who were old Kolyma hands, knew all this: he approved of it and forgave it. No textbook of prisoners' diseases had been written.

Umansky had received his medical education in Brussels and during the revolution had returned to Russia, where he lived in Odessa and practiced medicine....

In the camps he understood that his conscience would be easier if he cut up the dead and didn't treat the living. He became director of the morgue, an anatomical pathologist.

A seventy-year-old man, not yet decrepit, but with ill-fitting upper and lower dentures, and silver hair, cut short like a prisoner's—a wit with a snub nose entered the classroom.

His lecture was particularly important for the students. Not because it was the first lecture, but because, starting with the first word Professor Umansky said, the courses came alive and began to exist as a serious reality, however much a fairy tale they had seemed. The time of anxiety had passed. The decision to start the courses had been taken. For many people this meant the end of exhausting labor at the gold-mine pit faces, an end to their daily struggle to live. Studies began with Professor Umansky's course of lectures: "Anatomy and Human Physiology."

The silver-haired old man in an unbuttoned fur jacket, a black, well-worn jacket, not the quilted pea jacket that we wore, went up to the board and took an enormous piece of chalk in his little fist. The professor flung his crumpled hat with earflaps onto the desk: it was April, and still cold.

"I shall begin my lectures by telling you about the structure of the cell. These days there are many arguments in science...."

Where? What arguments? The past life of all thirty persons in the class, from a former interrogator to a shop assistant in a village shop, had very little to do with the life of any science.... The students' past lives were further away from them than the next world. Every student was convinced of this. What did they care about arguments in any science? And what science was this? Anatomy? Physiology? Biology? Microbiology? Not a single student could have said that day what "biology" meant. Those who were a bit better educated had experienced enough starvation to have lost any interest in arguments in any sort of science....

"... There are many arguments in science. Today it is usual to set out this part of the course differently, but I shall be telling you what I consider to be true. I have an agreement with your administration that I may expound this section in my own way."

Andreyev tried to imagine the administration with which a Brussels professor had come to an agreement. The hospital chief who had pierced each student at the entrance examination with the sharp eye of a janitor. Or the red-nosed acting head of the health administration who smelled of alcohol, who hiccupped. That was all the top administration that Andreyev could think of or imagine.

"I shall expound this section in my own way. And I shan't conceal my opinion from you."

"Conceal his opinion," Andreyev repeated in a whisper. He was delighted by these unusual words in an unusual science.

"I don't want to conceal my opinion. I'm a geneticist, my dear friends...."

Umansky paused, so that we could appreciate his boldness and his tact.

A geneticist? That meant nothing to the students.

None of the thirty persons knew, and never did find out, what mitosis was, or nucleoprotein threads, chromosomes, which contain deoxyribonucleic acid.

Nor was the hospital administration interested in deoxyribonucleic acid.

But after a year or two passed, the dark rays of biological discussion penetrated social life in various directions, and the word "geneticist" became sufficiently intelligible to interrogators with an average legal education and to ordinary people subjected to the storms of political repressions. "Geneticist" started to sound menacing, to sound ominous, like the very familiar words "Trotskyist" and "cosmopolitan."

It was then, a year after the biological controversy, that Andreyev recalled and appreciated old Umansky's boldness and tact.

Thirty pencils drew imaginary chromosomes in thirty exercise books. It was this exercise book with the chromosomes that had aroused the bear's particular fury.

Andreyev remembered Umansky not just because of his mysterious chromosomes or his obliging and clever "sections."

At the end of the course, when the new recruits to medicine were already getting used to wearing a paramedic's white gown, something that separated the medics from ordinary mortals, Umansky again came out with a strange declaration: "I am not going to lecture you on the anatomy of the sexual organs. I've come to an agreement with your administration. This part of the course was included for previous students. Nothing good came of it. It will be better if I use the hours for therapeutic practice—at least you'll learn how to use cupping jars."

Thus the students got their diplomas without taking an important aspect of anatomy. But was that the only thing that the future paramedics didn't know?

About two months after the courses started, when they had managed to overcome, fight back, and drown out the hunger that had been gnawing at them all the time, and when Andreyev no longer rushed to pick up every cigarette end he saw on the path or the street or the ground or the floor, and when new—or old?—human features began to appear on Andreyev's face, he was invited by Professor Umansky to tea.

The tea was just tea. There wasn't meant to be any bread or sugar, and Andreyev didn't expect that sort of tea. This was an evening conversation with Professor Umansky, a conversation in the warmth, face-to-face.

Umansky lived in the morgue, in the morgue office. There were no doors between the office and the autopsy room, and the dissecting table, covered with oilcloth, could be seen from every corner of Umansky's room. There may have been no door between him and the dissection room, but Umansky was thoroughly used to every smell in the world and he behaved as if there were a door. It took Andreyev some time to grasp what made this room a room, and then he realized that the floor of the room was set half a meter higher than that of the dissecting room. Work was coming to an end, and Umansky was putting a photograph of a young woman on his desk. The photograph was roughly framed in tin and glazed with uneven greenish window glass. This well-practiced, habitual action was the start of Professor Umansky's private life. His right-hand fingers took hold of the drawer wood, pulled the drawer out until it touched his belly. His left hand picked up the photograph and put it on the desk facing him.

"Your daughter?"

"Yes. If I had a son, it would be far worse, wouldn't it?"

Andreyev was well aware of the difference between a daughter and a son for a prisoner. The professor opened a desk drawer—the desk had a lot of drawers—and took out countless sheets of paper cut from a roll, creased, worn-out, covered in columns, a great number of columns and lines. Each cell had a word written by Umansky in tiny handwriting. Thousands, tens of thousands of words, written in indelible pencil, words that had faded with time and in places had been rewritten. Umansky probably knew twenty languages. . . .

"I know twenty languages," said Umansky. "I knew them before I came to Kolyma. I know ancient Hebrew very well. That is the root of all things. Here, in this morgue, next to the corpses, I have studied Arabic, Turkic languages, and Farsi. . . . I've created a table—a summary of a unified language. Do you understand what it's about?"

"I think I do," said Andreyev. "Mother is 'Mutter,' brother is 'Bruder.'"

That's right, but everything is far more complex and important. I've made a few discoveries. This dictionary will be my contribution to science, it will give my life meaning. You're not a linguist?"

"No, professor," said Andreyev, a piercing pain running through his heart, for he so much wanted at that moment to be a linguist.

"Pity." The shape of Umansky's facial wrinkles altered slightly, and he then resumed his usual ironic expression. "Pity. This work is more interesting than medicine. But medicine is more reliable and more salutary."

Umansky had studied in Brussels. After the revolution, back in Russia, he had worked as a doctor and treated people. Umansky had gotten to the essence of 1937. He understood that his residence abroad for so long, his knowledge of languages, his freethinking were sufficient cause for repressions, so the old man had tried to outwit fate. He had made a bold move by getting a post with Far East Construction, by being recruited for Kolyma, for the Far North, as a doctor, and he had arrived in Magadan as a free contract worker. He treated people and lived. Unfortunately, Umansky didn't take into account the universal nature of the instructions that applied: Kolyma could not save him any more than the North Pole could. He was arrested and tried by a tribunal, and got a sentence of ten years. His daughter renounced this enemy of the people and vanished from his life; all he had left was the photograph on his desk that had survived by chance. The ten-year sentence was now coming to an end. Umansky was regularly credited with his working days, credits he was very interested in.

Finally the day came when Andreyev was again invited to have tea with Professor Umansky.

A scratched enamel mug of hot tea was waiting for Andreyev. Next to the mug was the host's glass, made of real glass, greenish, clouded and unbelievably dirty, even to Andreyev's practiced eye. Umansky never washed his glass. That, too, was a revelation, Umansky's contribution to the science of hygiene, a principle that Umansky applied to life with all his firmness, insistence, and pedagogical impatience.

"In our circumstances an unwashed glass is cleaner and more sterile than a washed one. This is the best, perhaps the only hygiene.... Do you understand?"

Umansky clicked his fingers.

"There's more infection in a towel than in the air. Ergo: glasses shouldn't be washed. I have an old believer's personal glass. And it shouldn't be rinsed. There's less infection in the air than in the water. The ABC of sanitary practice and of hygiene. Do you understand?" Umansky screwed up his eyes. "That's a discovery that goes further than the morgue."

After this tea drinking and more linguistic spell casting, Umansky, almost gasping, whispered in Andreyev's ear, "The main thing is to outlive Stalin. Everyone who outlives Stalin will survive. Do you understand? It isn't possible for the curses of millions of people not to materialize and strike him. Do you understand? He is bound to die of this universal hatred. He'll get cancer or something! Do you understand? We'll survive."

Andreyev said nothing.

"I understand your caution and I approve of it," Umansky said, no longer whispering. "You think I'm some sort of provocateur. But I am seventy years old."

Andreyev said nothing.

"You're right to say nothing," said Umansky. "Even seventy-year-old men can be provocateurs. Everything can happen...."

Andreyev said nothing. He was delighted by Umansky, he was unable to overcome himself and respond. This silence, instinctive and all-powerful, was part of the behavior that Andreyev had grown accustomed to during his life in the camps where there were so many accusations, investigations, and interrogations. These were inner rules it was not so easy to break or set aside. Andreyev shook Umansky's hand, a small, dry, hot old man's hand with hot, clutching fingers.

When the professor's sentence was over he was forbidden to leave Magadan for the rest of his life. He died on March 4, 1953, carrying on to the very last minute his linguistic work, which was not to be continued by anyone or bequeathed to anyone. So the professor never found out that the electron microscope had been invented and that experiments had confirmed chromosome theory.

1964

TO THE HOSPITAL

KRIST was a tall man. The paramedic was even taller, and broad-shouldered, fat-faced.

For a long time, for many years, all bosses had seemed fat-faced to Krist. Making Krist stand in the corner, the paramedic looked at his quarry with undisguised approval.

"So you say you were a hospital porter?"

"I was."

"That's good. I need a hospital porter. A real one. To keep things in order." With a wave of his arm the paramedic indicated the enormous outpatient clinic, which looked more like a stable.

"I'm sick," said Krist. "I need to go to the hospital."

"Everyone's sick. There'll be time. First let's get things shipshape. Make use of this cupboard here," the paramedic knocked on the door of an enormous empty cupboard. "Well, it's getting late. Wash the floors, and then go to bed. You can wake me up at reveille."

Krist had only begun pushing the icy water around all the corners of the cold, frosted outpatient's clinic, when his new boss's sleepy voice interrupted his work.

Krist went into the next room, which was just as stable-like. A trestle bed had been squeezed into a corner. Covered with a pile of torn blankets, fur jackets, rags, the sleepy paramedic was calling for Krist.

"Take my felt boots off, porter."

Krist pulled the stinking felt boots off the paramedic's legs.

"Put them up as high as you can by the stove. In the morning you can hand them to me when they're nice and warm. I like nice warm boots."

Krist used a rag to wash the dirty icy water into a corner of the clinic; the water curdled and turned into the sludge you get when a river starts to freeze over. Krist wiped the floor clean, lay down on his trestle bed, and immediately found oblivion in the shallow sleep he always had here. It seemed only a moment later that he woke up. The paramedic was shaking his shoulder: "What are you up to? Reveille was sounded long ago."

"I don't want to be a hospital porter. Admit me to the hospital."

"To the hospital? You have to earn that. So, you don't want to work as a porter?"

"No," said Krist, making his usual gesture to ward off any blows to his face.

"Get out of here and go to work!" The paramedic pushed Krist out of the clinic and strode with him through the fog to the guardhouse.

"Here's a shirker, a malingerer. Chase him out, chase him," the paramedic yelled to the escort guards, who were leading the next party of prisoners through the barbed wire. The guards were very experienced. They poked Krist with their bayonets and butts, but didn't hurt him.

Flotsam was being carried into the camp; this was easy work. The flotsam had to be carried two kilometers from the spring oxbows of a mountain river that had frozen down to the riverbed. Once debarked, washed, dried by the wind, the trunks were hard to pull out of the oxbow, where they were held down by waterweeds, branches, and stones. There was a lot of flotsam. None of the trunks were too heavy to carry. Each prisoner chose one that he could lift. A two-kilometer journey took up nearly a whole working day. This was a job for invalids: it was a settlement and there wasn't a lot of demand. It was a separate camp for vitamin collection. Long live vitamins! But Krist didn't understand, refused to understand this terrible irony.

Day after day passed, but still Krist was not admitted to the hospital. Others were, but not him. Every day the paramedic would come to the guardhouse and, pointing his glove at Krist, yell to the escort guards, "Chase him off, chase him off."

And it would all begin again.

The long-desired hospital was just four kilometers from the settlement. But to get there you needed a prescription, a piece of paper. The paramedic knew that he was the one who decided whether Krist lived or died. So did Krist.

From the barracks where Krist slept—they called it "lived"—to the guardhouse was just a hundred yards. The vitamin settlement was one of the most neglected, which made the paramedic seem taller, fatter, and more dreadful, while Krist seemed even more of a nonentity.

On that hundred-yard journey Krist met somebody; he couldn't remember whom. The man had already passed, vanishing in the mist. Krist's weakened, starving memory couldn't suggest anything. Yet. . . . Krist thought day and night, trying to overcome the subzero temperatures, hunger, and the pain of his frostbitten hands and feet: who was it? Whom had he met on the path? Or was he going mad? Krist knew that man who'd vanished into the mist: two years ago he had been a camp chief, but of a camp that was not a vitamin camp, but a gold mine, where Krist came face-to-face with the real Kolyma. He was a boss, the camp NKVD man, a "spook-sucker," as the gangsters called them. He was a free contracted boss, and he'd been tried when Krist was there. After his trial he'd disappeared, and it was said he'd been shot. Yet here he was, meeting Krist on the path of a vitamin-collecting expedition. Krist found his former boss in the camp office. It wasn't clear what job the boss had, but it was certainly clerical. The former boss had, of course, an article 58 conviction, but without any damning initial letter in his file, so he was allowed to work in an office.

Naturally, Krist could have known and recognized the boss, but the boss wouldn't be able to remember Krist. All the same. . . . Krist went up to the screen that cuts off clerks all over the world.

"What, trying to nail me, are you?" the former camp boss said, talking like a gangster, as he turned to face Krist.

"Yes. I've come from the mine, you see," said Krist.

"Glad to see someone from there." Understanding Krist perfectly, the former boss said. "Come and see me in the evening. I'll get you a herring."

Neither knew the other's name or surname. But the brief and insignificant link that had once united them had suddenly become a force strong enough to change a man's life. The boss, by giving up his herring to Krist who had been at the gold mine with him, rather than to his starving comrades on the vitamin expedition, knew that gold and vitamin collection were different things. But neither of them mentioned this. They both understood and sensed something: Krist—his subterranean rights; the former boss—his duty.

Every evening the former boss would bring Krist a herring. Every evening it was a bigger herring. The camp cook wasn't amazed by the clerk's sudden whim, even though the clerk had never ever taken his share of herring before. Krist ate the herrings in the way he ate at the mine: skin, head, bones and all. Sometimes the former boss brought a half-eaten piece of bread, already bitten into. It occurred to Krist that it was dangerous to go on eating this tasty herring. They might decide not to admit him to the hospital, his body might lose the condition needed for hospitalization. His skin wouldn't be dry enough, his sacrum wouldn't be angular enough. Krist told his former boss that he was going to be admitted to the hospital, but that the paramedic was using his authority to keep him out, so. . . .

"Yes, the paramedic here is a real son of a bitch. I've been here more than a year, and nobody has had a good word to say about that quack. But we'll pull the wool over his eyes. People get sent to the hospital here every day. And I draw up the lists." The former boss smiled.

That evening Krist was summoned to the guardhouse. Two prisoners were already standing there, each of them holding a small plywood suitcase.

"There's no guard to escort you," said the duty officer coming out onto the porch. "We'll send you off tomorrow."

For Krist that was lethal—the next day everything would be discovered. The paramedic would have Krist herded off to some hell. Krist didn't know the name of the hell where he might end up, or that it would be worse than what he'd already seen. But he had no doubt that there were places where things were even worse. Now he could only wait and stay silent.

The duty officer came out again.

"Go to the barracks. There's not going to be a guard."

Then a prisoner holding a suitcase stepped forward.

"Give me an authorization on paper, sir. I'll take everyone there.

I'm better than any soldier. You know me, don't you? This is something that's been done before. I don't need an escort, I'm a trustee, and as for the others—where would they run off to? It's night, it's below zero. . . ."

The officer went into the guardhouse and came straight back, giving the man with the suitcase an envelope made from a sheet of newspaper.

"Have you got your things?"

"What things. . . ."

"All right, off you go."

The iron bolt was drawn and three prisoners were released into the white frosty haze.

The trustee walked ahead. He was running, in Krist's opinion. Here and there the mist parted, letting through the yellow light of the electric streetlamps.

What seemed an age passed. Drops of hot sweat were streaming down Krist's shrunken belly and his bony back. His heart was pounding and pounding. But Krist kept running and running after his fellow prisoners, who were slipping off into the mist. At the corner of the settlement was the main highway.

"Do we have to wait for you?"

Krist was frightened of being abandoned and left behind.

"Listen, you," said the trustee. "Do you know where the hospital is?"

"I do."

"We'll go ahead, and we'll wait for you there."

The prisoners vanished in the darkness, and Krist, once he had his breath back, staggered along a drainage ditch, stopping every minute, before rushing ahead again. He had lost his gloves, but didn't notice the snow, ice, and stone scratching his bare hands. He growled and sniveled as he scraped the earth. He couldn't see anything ahead of him apart from white haze. Through the white haze, sounding their horns furiously, enormous trucks loomed up before vanishing immediately in the mist. But Krist didn't stop to let the trucks pass before he staggered on to the hospital. He was clutching at the drainage ditch, at its sidewalls—it seemed to be an enormous cable stretched across an icy abyss—as he crawled, crawled and crawled toward warmth and salvation.

The haze thinned a little, and Krist saw the turning to the hospital and the tiny buildings of the hospital settlement. About three hundred yards, no more. Uttering another growl, Krist crawled further.

"We'd begun to think you'd croaked," said the trustee, who was standing on the porch of the hospital barracks. His voice was indifferent, but not spiteful. "They're not admitting us now, not without you."

Krist wasn't listening or responding. The most important and difficult part was coming: would they admit him, or not.

The doctor came; he was a young, clean-looking man in an unbelievably white gown; he recorded all their names in a book.

"Get undressed."

Krist's skin was peeling, thin patches were dropping off his body, looking like the fingerprints in his case file.

"That's what we call pellagra," said the man who needed no guard.

"I had something like that," said the third man. Those were the first words Krist had heard him speak. "They took the skin off both my hands like a glove, and sent it to Magadan for the museum."

"The museum?" said the trustee scornfully. "As if there weren't enough hand skins in Magadan."

But the third prisoner wasn't listening to the trustee.

"You," he said, jerking Krist's hand. "Listen to this. With that illness you'll be prescribed hot injections, for sure. I was prescribed them, and I swapped them with the gangsters for bread. That's how I got better."

Forms for the patients' notes were now taken out of the cupboard. Three forms. All of them would be admitted. A hospital porter came in.

"Ward two for now."

A washdown with warm water, linen with no lice. A corridor where the wicks of the smoking lamps still burned on the orderly's table. The lamps were fueled by cod-liver oil, dripped onto a saucer from an old food can. A door to an empty ward, from which came the smell of frost, the street, ice. The porter went to fetch firewood to stoke the iron stove, which had gone out.

"I know what," said the trustee. "Let's all lie down together, or we'll all end up in a coffin."

They all lay down on the same bunk, their arms around one another. Then the trustee slipped out from under three blankets, collected all the mattresses and blankets in the ward, made a great pile on the bunk where the prisoners had lain down, and dove into Krist's bony embrace. The patients went to sleep.

1964

JUNE

ANDREYEV came out of the mine gallery and went to the lamp room to hand over his Wolf Safety lamp, which had gone out.

"They'll be pestering us again," he thought idly about the security service. "The wire's been torn."

Despite the prohibition, people were smoking in the mine. You could get a sentence for smoking, but nobody had been caught yet.

Not far from the ore slag heap Andreyev met Stupnitsky, a professor from the artillery academy. Stupnitsky worked in the mine as a surface foreman, even though he had a conviction under article 58. He was an efficient, conscientious, agile serving man, despite his age. The mine bosses couldn't have dreamed of a better foreman.

"Listen," said Stupnitsky. "The Germans have bombed Sebastopol, Kiev, and Odessa."

Andreyev listened politely. This information sounded like news of war in Paraguay or Bolivia. What did Andreyev care? Stupnitsky had plenty to eat, he was a foreman, so he could take an interest in things like war.

Grisha the Greek, a thief, came up to them.

"What are automatics?"

"I don't know. Something like machine guns, I expect."

"A knife is much more frightening than any bullet," Grisha said in a didactic tone.

"True," said Boris Ivanovich, a prisoner, but a surgeon. "A knife in your belly is sure to start an infection, there's always a danger of peritonitis. A firearm wound is better, it's cleaner...."

"The best thing is a nail," said Grisha the Greek.

"Li-i-ine up!"

They lined up and left the mine for the camp. The escort guard never went into the mine: the darkness underground protected people from his beatings. Free men who were foremen were also on their guard. God forbid a big lump of coal should fall on your head from the "stove." However ready Nikolai Antonovich, the senior man, might be with his fists, even he had almost given up his old habits. The only one to hit prisoners was Mishka Timoshenko, a young warden who'd been a prisoner and was now on the make.

Mishka Timoshenko was thinking as he walked, "I'll apply to go to the front. They won't actually send me, but it'll do me some good. Otherwise, you can beat people up here, but you don't earn anything by a sentence." The next morning he went to see the camp boss Kosarenko, who was not a bad type. Mishka did all the right things.

"Here's an application to go to the front, sir."

"There's a surprise.... All right, let's have it. You'll be the first.... Only, they won't take you...."

"Because of what I was sentenced for, sir?"

"Of course."

"What am I supposed to do about it?" asked Mishka.

"You'll be all right. You're artful enough," Kosarenko rasped. "Tell Andreyev to come and see me."

Andreyev was amazed to be summoned. He'd never been asked to appear before the actual camp boss in person. But his usual indifference, fearlessness, and lack of interest prevailed. He knocked at the plywood door to the office.

"I've come as you ordered. Prisoner Andreyev."

"Are you Andreyev?" asked Kosarenko, examining the newcomer with curiosity.

"Andreyev, sir."

Kosarenko raked through the papers on his desk, found something, and began reading it quietly. Andreyev waited.

"I have a job for you."

"I'm working as a barrow man on the third site...."

"In whose brigade?"

"In Koriagin's."

"Tomorrow you'll stay behind. You'll be working in the camp. Koriagin doesn't need a barrow man that badly."

Kosarenko stood up, shaking the piece of paper, and rasped, "You'll be taking down the zone. Rolling up barbed wire. Your zone."

Andreev realized that Kosarenko was talking about a zone for article 58ers. Unlike many camps, the barracks where the "enemies of the people" lived was surrounded by barbed wire within the actual camp zone.

"On my own?"

"With Maslakov."

"It's the war," thought Andreyev. "Must be the mobilization plan."

"May I go, sir?"

"Yes. I have two reports about you."

"I work just as well as anybody else, sir—"

"Go, will you. . . ."

They straightened rusty nails and removed barbed wire, rolling it up on a stick. Ten rows, ten iron threads, and diagonal threads as well, at intervals. It was a whole day's work for Andreyev and Maslakov. This job was in no way better than any other job. Kosarenko was wrong: prisoners' feelings had become coarser.

At dinner Andreyev found out something else that was new: the bread ration was reduced from a kilogram to five hundred grams, and that was dreadful news, for the cooked food made no difference in the camp. Bread was what decided things.

The next day Andreyev went back to the mine.

It was, as usual, cold and dark in the mine. Andreyev went down the miners' approach to the lower drift. No empty barrows had yet been sent down from the surface, and Kuznetsov, the second barrow man on this shift, was sitting in the light not far from the lower turntable, waiting for the wagons.

Andreyev sat down next to him. Kuznetsov was a nonpolitical, a rural murderer.

"Listen," said Kuznetsov. "I've been summoned."

"Where to?"

"Over there. The other side of the bridge."

"So?"

"I've been ordered to write a statement about you."

"About me?"

"Yes."

"What did you say?"

"I've done it. What else could I do?"

True, thought Andreyev, what can you do?

"So what did you write in it?"

"Well, I wrote what they told me to. That you praised Hitler. . . ."

He's not a bastard, really, thought Andreyev. He's just a wretch.

"So what are they going to do to me?" asked Andreyev.

"I don't know. The NKVD man said it was just a formality."

"Of course," said Andreyev. "Of course, just a formality. After all, my sentence ends this year. They'll manage to stitch on a new one."

The little wagons came thundering down the slope.

"Hey you!" yelled the man in charge of the turntable. "Dreamers! Take the empty wagon!"

"If you don't mind, I'll refuse to work with you," said Kuznetsov. "After all, I'll be summoned again, and I'll say 'I don't know, I don't work with him.' That's what—"

"That's the best thing to do," Andreyev agreed.

Starting with the very next shift Andreyev had a new partner, Chudakov, also a nonpolitical. Unlike Kuznetsov, who was so talkative, Chudakov was silent. Either he was born silent or he had been warned by "the other side of the bridge."

After a few shifts, Andreyev and Chudakov were set to work at the top turntable in the ventilation drift, where they had to send empty wagons thirty meters downhill and haul up the loaded ones. They turned the wagon around on the turntable, set its wheels onto the rails that went down the slope, fixed a steel hawser to the wagon, and, coupling it by its shaft to the winch hawser, sent the wagon rolling down. They took turns attaching the wagons. It was now Chudakov's turn. The wagons kept coming and coming, one after the other, and the working day was at its busiest when suddenly Chudakov made a mistake and sent a wagon down before he had attached it to the hawser. "Watch out!" A mine accident! They heard the far-off noise like thunder, then the screech of steel and the sound of props cracking, while clouds of white dust filled the sloping tunnel.

Chudakov was arrested there and then, but Andreyev went back to barracks. That evening he was summoned to see Kosarenko, the boss.

Kosarenko was nervously pacing his office.

"What have you done? What have you done, I'm asking you? Saboteur!"

"You're off your head, sir," said Andreyev. "It was Chudakov who accidentally—"

"You told him to, you reptile! Saboteur! You've stopped the mine!"

"What have I got to do with it? Nobody has stopped the mine. The mine's working.... Why are you yelling at me?"

"He doesn't know! Look at what Koriagin's written.... He's a party member."

An extensive report in Koriagin's tiny handwriting was actually lying on the boss's desk.

"You'll answer for this!"

"That's up to you."

"Get out, reptile."

Andreyev left. There was a noisy conversation going on in the barracks, in the foremen's hut. It stopped the moment Andreyev arrived.

"Who do you want to see?"

"You, Nikolai Antonovich," said Andreyev, turning to the senior foreman. "Where am I supposed to go to work tomorrow?"

"See if you survive until tomorrow," said Mishka Timoshenko.

"That's none of your business."

"It's thanks to eggheads like him that I've been sentenced, honestly, Nikolai," said Misha. "All because of these four-eyes."

"Well, you can join Mishka," said Nikolai Antonovich. "That's what Koriagin has ordered. If you're not arrested. Mishka will give you something to whine about."

"You should realize where you are," said Timoshenko severely. "You bloody fascist."

"You're the fascist, fool," said Andreyev and went off to give a few things to his workmates—spare foot wrappings, and an old, but still wearable cotton scarf, so that if he was arrested he wouldn't have anything he didn't need.

The man on the bunk next to Andreyev's was Tikhomirov, who had once been the dean of a mining faculty. He worked at the mine as the timberman. The chief engineer was trying to get this professor promoted, if only to foreman, but Svishchev, the boss of the mining district, refused outright and gave his deputy a nasty look.

"If you appoint Tikhomirov," Svishchev told the chief engineer, "then there's no reason for you to work at the mine. Got it? And I don't want to hear that kind of talk again."

Tikhomirov was waiting for Andreyev.

"Well, what's up?"

"It'll all go away," said Andreyev. "There's a war going on."

Andreyev wasn't arrested. It turned out that Chudakov refused to lie. He was kept for a month on solitary rations: a mug of water and three hundred grams of bread, but they couldn't make him write any statements. Chudakov had been in prison before and he knew what all this really amounted to.

"Why are you telling me what to do?" he told the interrogator. "Andreyev hasn't done anything wrong. I know how things are done. You can't see any point in putting me on trial. You want to put Andreyev away. Well, as long as I'm alive, you won't, we didn't arrive in the camps yesterday."

"Right," Koriagin told Mishka Timoshenko. "We're relying on you now. You can deal with this."

"Of course I can," said Timoshenko. "First we'll get him through the belly, we'll cut his rations. And if he blabs—"

"Fool," said Koriagin. "What's blabbing got to do with it? Were you born yesterday, or something?"

Koriagin took Andreyev off work underground. In winter it gets no colder than minus twenty deep down in the mine shaft, when outside it can be minus sixty. Andreyev spent the night shift on the high slag heap, where the ore was piled up. Wagons full of ore came up there from time to time, and Andreyev had to unload them. There weren't a lot of wagons, but the cold was terrible and even the slightest wind turned the night into a living hell. For the first time since he had come to Kolyma, Andreyev burst into tears. This had never happened to him before, except in his youth, when he received letters from his mother and he was unable to read them or recall them without tears in his eyes. But that had been a long time ago. But why was he weeping here? Helplessness, loneliness, cold—he had gotten used to that and trained himself in the camp to remember verses, to whisper something, to repeat something under his breath, but thinking in subzero temperatures was impossible. The human brain cannot operate below zero.

After a few icy shifts, Andreyev was back in the mine, rolling wagons, with Kuznetsov as his workmate.

"I'm glad you're here!" said Andreyev joyfully. "I've been taken back into the mine. What happened with Koriagin?"

"Well, they say they've already got evidence against you. Enough." said Kuznetsov. "They don't need any more. So I was allowed back. It's good to work with you. And Chudakov's been let out, too. They put him in solitary. He's like a skeleton. He'll be working in the bathhouse for the time being. He won't be working in the mine again."

This was important news.

The prisoner-foremen went back to camp after their shift without an escort guard, once they had produced the reports required of them. Mishka Timoshenko decided to do as he always did, pay a visit to the bathhouse before the workers came from the camp.

An unfamiliar attendant, all skin and bones, undid the hook and opened the door.

"Where are you going?"

"I'm Timoshenko."

"I can see that."

"Less of your lip," said the foreman. "You haven't had a taste of my 'thermometer' yet: you'll get one. Go and get some steam up." Pushing the bath attendant aside, Timoshenko went into the bathhouse. A moist black darkness filled the miners' bathhouse. Black, soot-stained ceilings, black tubs, black benches along the walls, black windows. The bathhouse was dark and dry, like the mine, and a miner's Wolf Safety lamp with cracked glass hung there from a hook on a pillar in the middle of the bathhouse, just as it hung from a shaft pillar.

Mishka quickly got undressed, chose a half-full barrel of cold water and put the steam pipe into it. The bathhouse had its own boiler, and the water was heated by hot steam.

The skeletal attendant stood on the threshold looking at Timoshenko's pink, chubby body. He said nothing.

"The way I like it," said Timoshenko, "is for the steam to keep on coming. You can warm up the water a bit, I'll get into the barrel, and then you let the steam in gradually. When it's right, I'll knock on the pipe, and then you switch off the steam. The old attendant, the one-eyed one, knew just how I liked it. Where is he?"

"I don't know," replied the skeletal attendant. The attendant's collarbones could be seen through his tunic.

"Where are you from?"

"I've been in solitary."

"Are you Chudakov, then?"

"Yes."

"I didn't recognize you. Lucky you." The foreman gave a laugh.

"It's the solitary that's made me look like a goner, that's why you don't recognize me. Listen, Mishka," said Chudakov, "but I've seen you...."

"Where?"

"The other side of the bridge. I heard you'd been singing to the NKVD man."

"It's every man for himself," said Timoshenko. "The law of the taiga. There's a war on. And you're a fool. You're a fool, Chudakov. You're a fool, and you're wet behind the ears. You brought all that on yourself just for that devil Andreyev."

"Well, that's my business," said the attendant as he left. The steam gushed forth and made the barrel seethe, and the water warmed up. Mishka knocked, and Chudakov switched the steam off.

Mishka climbed onto a bench and then flopped into the tall, narrow barrel.... There were lower barrels and wider ones, but the foreman liked to take a sauna in this particular one. The water came up to Mishka's neck. Screwing up his eyes with pleasure, the foreman knocked on the pipe. The steam immediately made the water seethe. It grew warmer. Mishka gave the attendant the signal, but the hot steam went on spurting into the pipe. The steam was burning his body, and Timoshenko felt scared: he knocked again, he tried to clamber out, to jump out of the barrel, but it was too narrow, and the iron pipe stopped him climbing out. The white, spurting, thickening steam made it impossible to see anything in the bathhouse. Mishka cried out in a wild voice.

There was no bath for the workmen that day.

When the doors and windows were opened, the thick, turbid white mist dispersed. The camp doctor came. Timoshenko was no longer breathing: he had been boiled alive.

Chudakov was transferred to a different job, and the one-eyed attendant came back—he hadn't been taken off the job, it was just that he spent a day in group T, temporarily released from work because of illness. He had a temperature.

1959

MAY

THE BOTTOM of a wooden barrel had been knocked out and replaced with a grid made from iron bars. Kazbek the dog lived in the barrel. Sotnikov fed him raw meat and asked anybody who passed by to poke a stick at the dog. Kazbek would growl and gnaw the stick into splinters. Sotnikov, a clerk of works, was training his future chained dog to be vicious.

Throughout the war the gold had been panned. This was a method used to get gold out of difficult places, and formerly it had been forbidden. Before, only a panner who was working with the prospectors was allowed to wash gold. The daily plan before the war was set in cubic meters of ore, but during the war it was set in grams of metal.

A one-armed panner deftly used a scraper to rake the earth into the pan, and, when he had rinsed it with water, he would carefully shake the pan over the stream to get rid of the stones that were left. At the bottom of the pan, once the water was gone, there would be a speck of gold. Putting the pan on the ground, the worker would use a fingernail to catch hold of the speck and place it on a piece of paper. The paper was then folded, as if it contained powders from the chemist. A whole brigade of one-armed men, who'd mutilated themselves, washed gold in winter and in summer. Then they handed over the specks of metal, the gold grains, to the mine's till. That's what the one-armed men were fed for.

The interrogator Ivan Vasilievich Yefremov had caught a mysterious murderer. A week ago, in the geology prospectors' hut, about eight kilometers from the settlement, four dynamiters had been hacked to death. Bread and tobacco had been stolen, but no money had been found. One week later, a Tatar from Ruslanov's carpentry brigade had been in the workmen's refectory and had swapped a boiled fish for a pinch of tobacco. There had been no tobacco at the mine since the war began. Green "ammonal," an incredibly strong wild herb, had been brought in, and an attempt to grow tobacco had been made. Only the free workers had tobacco. The Tatar was arrested. He confessed to everything and even showed where in the forest he had thrown the bloodstained ax into the snow. Yefremov was going to get a big bonus.

It so happened that the Tatar slept on the bunk next to Andreyev's. He was the most ordinary, starving lad, a living ghost. Andreyev was also arrested. After two weeks he was released. During that time a lot of new things had happened: Kolka Zhukov had hacked to death the hated foreman Koroliov. That foreman had beaten Andreyev every day in front of the whole brigade. The beatings were done in cold blood, slowly, and Andreyev was afraid of him.

Andreyev felt in the pocket of his pea jacket for a piece of his ration of white American bread, left over from dinner. There were a thousand ways to prolong one's enjoyment of it. You could lick the bread until it vanished from your palm, you could nibble crumbs off it, and move it around your mouth with your tongue. You could toast it on the stove, which was always lit, and eat the dark brown, slightly burned pieces of dry bread—not yet rusks, but no longer bread. You could cut the bread with a knife into very thin slices, and then dry them. You could put the bread in hot water then boil it and turn it into a hot soup, a floury mix. You could crumble up pieces in cold water and salt them, which made a sort of bread soup. Any of that had to be done in the quarter of an hour that was left of Andreyev's lunch break. He had his own way of finishing his bread. In an old tin can he boiled water, fresh melted snow, which was dirty because of the tiny bits of coal or dwarf pine needles that got into the can. Into this white boiling water Andreev would put his bread and wait. The bread would swell up like a sponge, a white sponge. Andreyev used a stick or a splinter to break off hot pieces of this sponge and put them into his mouth, where the soaked bread vanished instantly.

Nobody paid any attention to Andreyev's tricks. He was one of hundreds of thousands of Kolyma ghosts, goners whose minds had long become unbalanced.

The porridge came by lend-lease—American oats with sugar. The bread, too, was lend-lease, from Canadian flour with the addition of bonemeal and rice. The bread when it was baked rose unusually well, and none of the bread servers would risk getting the bread ration ready the day before, for every two-hundred-gram piece would lose ten or fifteen grams of weight overnight, and even the most honest bread cutter might turn out to have unintentionally cheated. The white bread left virtually nothing to excrete; the human organism disposed of any surplus just once every few days.

Soup, the first course, was also lend-lease. Everyone's dinner bowls had the smell of tinned pork and meat fibers, which looked like tuberculosis bacilli under the microscope.

There was said to be sausage, too, tinned sausage, but as far as Andreyev was concerned, it was mythical, like the Alpha condensed milk many remembered from their childhood, when it was sent by the American Relief Agency. The Alpha company still existed.

Red leather boots with thick glued-on soles also came by lend-lease. These leather boots were issued only to the bosses, and not every mining engineer could get this imported footwear. The mine bosses got sets of clothes in boxes too—suits, jackets, shirts, and ties.

Woolen items, collected by the American people, were also said to be available, but they never reached the prisoners. The wives of the bosses were experts when it came to quality material.

But the prisoners did get a good supply of working tools. These too came by lend-lease: curved American spades with short, painted handles. The spades lifted a lot of earth; someone had thought hard about the shape. The painted hafts would be knocked out of the spade blades and new ones, straight and long, would be made to fit each man, since the end of the haft had to reach your chin.

The blacksmiths straightened the spade edge very slightly and then sharpened them. The result was an excellent tool.

The American axes were very bad. They were hatchets, not axes, like tomahawks from a Mayne Reid novel. They were no good for serious carpentry. Our carpenters were amazed by the lend-lease axes. Clearly, a thousand-year-old tool was dying out.

The cross-saws were heavy, thick, and awkward to handle.

But the solidol grease was splendid. It was as white as butter, and it had no smell. The gangsters attempted to sell it as butter, but there was nobody at the mine who could afford it.

The Studebakers that came through lend-lease traveled up and down the steep Kolyma hills. They were the only trucks in the Far North that could easily cope with the gradients. The enormous Diamond trucks, which also came through lend-lease, could haul a load of ninety tons.

Our medicines were lend-lease. The drugs were American, so we had our first sight of the early miracle drug, sulphidine. The laboratory glassware was also a gift from America. So were the X-ray machines, the hot water bottles, and the vials....

Last year, after the Kursk Salient battle, people were already saying that the white American bread would soon be stopped. But Andreyev didn't listen to the news on the camp grapevine. Whatever would be, would be. Another winter passed. He, a man who never tried to guess the future, was still alive.

Soon there'd be good old black bread, black bread. Our men were getting close to Berlin.

"Black bread is better for you," said the doctors.

"The Americans must be idiots."

At this site that was going to be a working mine there wasn't a single radio.

"Infectious murders," as Voronov used to say. Andreyev remembered the term. Murder was infectious. If a foreman was murdered somewhere, then immediately there'd be imitators, and the foremen would find people to stay on duty and guard them while they slept. But none of that helped. One foreman was hacked to death, another had his head smashed in with a crowbar, a third had his neck sawed through with a two-man saw.

Only a month previously, Andreyev had been sitting by a bonfire. It was his turn to get warm. The shift was ending, the fire was going out, and it was the turn of four prisoners to sit around the fire, bending over it and stretching their hands to the dying flames, the departing warmth. Each man almost touched the glowing coals with his bare hands and frostbitten fingers that had lost their feeling. A white haze loomed behind them, their shoulders and backs shivered with cold, which made them want to press even closer to the fire. It was too frightening to straighten up and look around. They didn't have the strength to get up and go to their places, each to his open pit, where they were drilling and drilling...They didn't have the strength to stand up and get away from the foreman who was now approaching.

Andreyev idly considered what the foreman would hit him with, if he decided to use violence. Probably a piece of burning wood or a stone.... the burning wood was more likely....

The foreman was now only ten meters from the bonfire. Suddenly a man carrying a crowbar appeared from the open pit, near the path the foreman was taking. The man caught up with the foreman, and waved the crowbar at him. The foreman fell down, face forward. The man threw the crowbar down on the snow and walked past the bonfire where Andreyev and the three other workmen were sitting. He went on to the big bonfire where the escort guards were warming themselves.

During the murder Andreyev didn't move a muscle. None of the four men got up. They didn't have the strength to move away from the fire and the vanishing warmth. Each man wanted to sit there until the end, until the minute when they were chased off. But there was nobody to chase them off, because the foreman had been murdered. Andreyev was happy, as were his comrades that day.

With a final effort from his poor, starving brain, his desiccated brain, Andreyev realized that he had to find a way out of this. He didn't want to share the fate of the one-armed gold panners. He had once sworn never to be a foreman, not to try and save himself by taking on dangerous camp jobs. His path was a different one: no thieving, no beating up his workmates, no reporting on them. Andreyev waited patiently.

This morning the new foreman had sent Andreyev to fetch ammonite, a yellow powder the blasters poured into paper packets. Women prisoners worked at the big ammonite plant where the shipping and packing of explosives from the mainland was done. The work was considered easy. The ammonite plant left its mark on its workers: their hair became golden, as if they'd used hydrogen peroxide.

The little iron stove in the blasters' hut was fueled with yellow pieces of ammonite.

Andreyev showed his warden's note, unbuttoned his pea jacket, and unwound his ragged scarf.

"I need new foot wrappings, men," he said. "Give me a sack."

"Our sacks won't do," a young blaster began to say, but his elbow was jolted by an older man, and he fell silent.

"We'll give you a sack," said the older blaster. "Here you are."

Andreyev took off his scarf and gave it to the blaster. Then he ripped up the sack to make foot wrappings and wrapped them around his legs, in the peasant way, for there are three ways of "turning" foot wrappings: peasant, army, and city.

Andreyev wrapped them the peasant way, throwing the wrapping onto the foot from above. It was hard to press his feet into his soft boots, but he did and got up, took the box of ammonite, and left. His feet were hot, his throat was cold. He knew that neither feeling would last for long. He handed the ammonite to the warden and went back to the bonfire. He had to wait for the warden to reappear.

Finally, the warden came up to the bonfire.

"Let's have a smoke," several voices quickly said.

"Some of you will, some of you won't," said the warden, hitching up the heavy hem of his fur jacket and taking out a tin of tobacco.

Only now did Andreyev unwrap the rags that kept his boots on, and take his boots off.

"Good foot wrappings," said someone, who was wrapped in rags. as he pointed to Andreyev's feet, which were wrapped with pieces of solid, shiny sackcloth. The remark was without envy.

Andreyev made himself as comfortable as he could, moved his legs, and yelled out. A yellow flame flared up. His foot wrappings, soaked in ammonite, were burning slowly, but brightly. His trousers and quilted jacket had caught fire and were smoldering. His neighbors dashed to one side. The warden rolled Andreyev onto his back and piled snow over him.

"How did you do that, you reptile?"

"Send for a horse. And fill in an accident form."

"It'll be dinner soon, perhaps you can hang on...."

"No, I can't," Andreyev lied, shutting his eyes.

In the hospital Andreyev's legs were washed down with warm

permanganate solution and, without any bandaging, he was put on a bunk. The blanket was stretched over a frame, so that it all looked like a tent. Andreyev was guaranteed a hospital bed for a long time.

Toward evening the doctor came into the ward.

"Listen, you convicts," he said. "The war's over. It ended a week ago. A second courier has come from the administration. They say the first courier was murdered by escaped prisoners."

But Andreyev wasn't listening to the doctor. He was coming down with a fever.

1959

IN THE BATHHOUSE

IN THE unkindly jokes that are unique to the camps, the bathhouse is often called "unfair." "The *freiers* are yelling 'Unfair'—the boss is making them go to the bathhouse" is the usual, traditional as it were, irony that stems from the gangsters, who don't miss a thing. There is a bitter truth behind this jocular remark.

For prisoners the bathhouse is always a negative event that makes their lives even harder. This observation is yet another proof of the distortion of values, a distortion that is the most important and basic quality the camp instills in anyone who ends up there to serve their punishment, or "term," as Dostoevsky put it.

You might wonder how this can be. Avoiding the bathhouse was a constant puzzle to doctors and all the authorities, who saw absenteeism from the bathhouse as a kind of protest, a disciplinary offense, a challenge to the camp regime. But facts are facts. For years, making people go to the bathhouse was an event in the camp. The escort guards were mobilized and given instructions. All the bosses, not to mention the doctors, took a personal part in catching those who tried to refuse. Seeing that men went to the bathhouse and disinfecting their underwear in the disinfection chamber were outright obligations in the sanitary department service. All the lower orders of the camp administration, prisoners such as the elders and labor supervisors, also abandoned all other things to devote their attention to the bathhouse. Lastly, the bosses in charge of production were inevitably involved in this major question. On bath days (there were three a month) a whole series of measures were taken affecting production.

On such days everyone was on their feet from early morning to late at night.

What was at stake? Surely anyone, no matter how destitute his state, would not refuse to wash in the bathhouse, to sluice off the dirt and sweat that covered his skin, a skin eroded by diseases, so as to feel cleaner, if only for an hour?

There is a Russian saying: "Happy, as if straight from the bathhouse." This saying is accurate, and it reflects exactly the physical bliss that a man with a clean, freshly washed body feels.

Could people have lost their reason so completely that they don't understand, or refuse to understand, that it's better to be louse-free than lousy? And there were a lot of lice, and it was almost impossible to exterminate them without the disinfection chamber, especially for those living in tightly packed barracks.

Of course, louse infection is a concept that needs defining. Just a dozen or so lice in your underwear is not considered something worth worrying about. Louse infection begins to worry your workmates and doctors when they can be shaken off your clothes, when a woolen sweater moves around by itself, as the lice nesting there shake it around.

So would anyone, whoever he may be, not want to be rid of this agony, an agony that keeps you from sleep and, in trying to fight it, makes you scratch your filthy body until it bleeds?

Of course not. But the first "but" is the fact that you do not get a day off work when you go to the bathhouse. You are taken there after work, or before work. After many hours working in subzero temperatures (not that it is any easier in summer), when all your thoughts and hopes are focused on the desire to get back somehow, as fast as you can, to your bunks, to your food, and to get to sleep, the delay in the bathhouse is almost unbearable. The bathhouse is always a considerable distance from your living quarters. That's because it serves not just the prisoners but the free workers from the settlement, which is why it is in the free settlement, not the camp.

Delays in the bathhouse are far more than the hour or so assigned for washing and disinfecting clothes. There are a lot of people using it, one group after another, and all those who arrive late (they are taken to the bathhouse straight from work, without stopping in the camp, where they would scatter and find some pretext or other to get out of bathing) have to wait their turn in the freezing cold. When the temperature is very low, the bosses try and reduce the time the prisoners spend outside, so they are allowed into the changing room, which has room for ten to fifteen men, and yet about a hundred men wearing their outer clothing are herded in there. The changing room is unheated, or heated very badly. Everything gets mixed up there: naked men and men wearing fur jackets, all jostling, cursing, and making an uproar. Thieves, and people who are not thieves, exploit the noise and packed conditions to steal their workmates' things (after all, other brigades, which live separately, have arrived, so that it is never possible to retrieve anything stolen). There is nowhere safe to leave your things.

The second, or rather the third, "but" is the fact that the staff is obliged, while a brigade is taking a bath, to carry out a cleanup in the barracks, under the supervision of the sanitary department. They have to sweep it, wash it, and throw out anything not needed. But in the camps every rag is precious, and you have to use up a lot of energy to get hold of spare gloves, spare foot wrappings, not to mention less portable things, and of course, food. All this disappears without a trace, and perfectly legally, while the bathhouse is in operation. It is pointless to take your spare things with you and then to the bathhouse: the gangsters' sharp practiced eyes will quickly spot them. Any thief is desperate for a cigarette, which he can get in exchange for gloves or foot wrappings.

It is human nature, whether a beggar's or a Nobel laureate's, rapidly to acquire small objects. Every time they move somewhere new (not necessarily prisons), everyone finds they have so many small objects that they are astounded how and from where they accumulated so much. These things get given away, sold, thrown out, until with great difficulty they are reduced to the point that the suitcase lid can be slammed shut. Prisoners accumulate things in the same way. They are, after all, workers. They need to have a needle, cloth for patching, and an old spare bowl, perhaps. All that would get thrown away, and after every visit to the bathhouse people had to start collecting their "household goods" again, unless they had managed first to bury it all somewhere deep under the snow, and then pull it out twenty-four hours later.

In Dostoevsky's times you were given just one tub of hot water (the *freiers* had to buy anything else), and this norm still applies today. A wooden tub of not very hot water and an unlimited amount of stinging pieces of ice, which are thrown into the barrel and which stick to your hand. Just the tub—you get no second full jug to mix with the water—that's the complete ration of water with which a prisoner has to wash his head and his body. In summer, instead of ice, you are given cold water, but at least it's water, not ice.

You could say that a prisoner should know how to wash himself regardless of the amount of water, from a spoonful to a tankful. If he only gets a spoonful, then he will wash his eyes, which are stuck together with pus, and will consider he has completed his toilet. If he gets a whole tank, then he'll splash the people around him and change the water every minute, so that he can somehow contrive to use his ration in the time allotted. There are also ways and unwritten technical instructions for using a jug, a ladle, or a basin full of water.

All that shows the ingenuity with which such everyday questions as the bathhouse are dealt with. But, of course, that doesn't solve the problem of keeping clean. The dream of washing yourself in the bathhouse is an unattainable dream.

In the actual bathhouse, which is characterized by the same noise, smoke, shouts, and lack of space ("shouting as in the bathhouse" is a much-used expression), there's never any spare water, and nobody can buy any extra. But not only water is in short supply. There's a lack of warmth. The iron stoves are not always stoked to burn red-hot, and in the bath (in the overwhelming majority of cases) it's just cold. This feeling of cold is made much worse by the thousands of drafts coming from the doors and the cracks in the walls. The buildings are, like any wooden structure, caulked with moss, which quickly turns dry and crumbly, so that holes to the outside appear. Every bath day brings the risk of catching a chill, and everyone (including, of course, the doctors) knows that. After each bath day the number of prisoners let off work because of illness, the number of really ill people, increases, and all the doctors know it.

Let us not forget that the bathhouse firewood is brought the evening before, on the shoulders of the brigade that is going to the bathhouse, and that again delays any return to the barracks by a couple of hours and doesn't lessen people's dread of the bathhouse.

But there's much more. The most terrible thing is the disinfection chamber, which is officially compulsory every time prisoners wash.

Underwear in the camps can be "individual" or "general." These are bureaucratic, officially accepted expressions, together with such linguistic pearls as "bedbugization" and "lousification," etc. Individual underwear is if anything a bit new, a bit above average, reserved for the camp staff, prisoners who are foremen, and similarly privileged persons. This underwear is not assigned to any particular single prisoner, but it is washed separately and more carefully, and is replaced more often by new underwear. But "general" underwear is general. It is issued right there in the bathhouse after washing, in exchange for the dirty clothes that have been collected and counted, a job that is done earlier and separately. There's no question of choosing your washed underwear according to your size. Clean underwear is just a lottery, and I found it odd and so painful that I was moved to tears when I saw adults weeping with resentment when they received something clean, but in tatters, in exchange for something dirty, but intact. Nothing can give you distance from the unpleasant things that make up life: neither the clear realization that you only have to wear this until the next bath day, or that, in the final analysis, your whole life has been ruined, so why bother about a set of underwear, since, after all, any intact underwear you received was a matter of luck. Yet people argue and weep. Of course, that is a phenomenon of the same order as those psychological shifts away from the norm that are typical of almost every action of a prisoner: the same dementia that one neurologist called a universal disease.

In his mental sufferings, a prisoner is reduced to such a state that getting his underwear returned to him through the dark window that leads to the mysterious depths of the bathhouse buildings is a nerve-wracking event. Long before their underwear is reissued, the freshly washed prisoners crowd around that window. They argue and make a fuss about what underwear was issued the last time, what was issued five years ago in the Baikal-Amur railway camp, and as soon as the board that covers the window from inside is removed, they all rush toward it, pushing each other with their slippery, dirty, stinking bodies.

The washed underwear is not always dry when it is issued. Far too often it is given out still wet, for there was no time to dry it, or there wasn't enough firewood. Putting on wet, damp underwear after a bath is something few would find pleasant.

Curses rain down on the heads of the bath attendants, who are used to anything. Those who put on wet underwear begin to freeze irrevocably, but they have to wait for their outer clothing to be disinfected.

What is a disinfection chamber? It's a pit in the ground, covered with a boarded roof, and lined with clay. It is heated with an iron stove, which is stoked in the lobby. Here the pea jackets, quilted jackets, and trousers are hung on sticks, the door is shut tight, and the disinfector starts to "put on the heat." There are no thermometers, no bags of sulphur to determine the right temperature. Success depends on luck, or on a conscientious disinfection worker.

At the very best, the things that hang close to the stove will be nicely warmed up. The rest, protected from the heat by the first, will only get more damp, while whatever is hung in the far corner will come out still cold. This chamber kills no lice. It is merely a formality and a means of creating additional torments for the prisoner.

The doctors are well aware of this, but the camp can't be left without a disinfection chamber. So, after waiting for an hour in the big "changing room," the attendants begin to pull out armfuls of things, completely identical sets: they are thrown onto the floor, and everyone is supposed to use his own strength to find his clothes. Steaming pea jackets, still wet, quilted jackets, and trousers are pulled on by a cursing prisoner. That night, depriving himself of the little sleep he has left, he will dry his quilted jacket and trousers on the barracks stove.

No wonder nobody likes bathhouse day.

1955

DIAMOND SPRING

THE TRUCK stopped by the river ferry, and people started getting out, slowly and awkwardly throwing their stiffened legs over the side of the Studebaker. The left bank of the river was flat, the right was rocky, as they should have been according to the theory of the academician Behr.[27] We left the road headed straight for the bed of a mountain river and walked about two hundred paces over the polished dry stones, which rattled under our feet. A dark stream of water, which had seemed so narrow from the banks, turned out to be a wide and fast-running mountain river. A flat-bottomed boat was waiting for us, and the ferryman, holding a pole instead of oars, punted the boat, taking just three passengers at a time to the opposite bank, and then coming back alone. The crossing took until evening. Once on the other bank, we clambered for a long time up a narrow stony path, helping one another, like mountain climbers. The narrow path, barely noticeable in the yellowing, flattened grass, led to a ravine, where the mountain peaks closed in from the right and the left. The stream in this ravine was called Diamond Spring.

This was an amazing expedition, to the very Diamond Spring we had for so long tried, in vain, to reach from the gold-mine pit faces. We had heard so many unbelievable things about it. They said that there were no escort guards here, no constant roll calls, no barbed wire, no dogs.

We were used to the clicking of rifle bolts, we had learned by heart the guard's warning: "A step to the left, a step to the right, I consider an escape attempt: march!" And we marched, and there would be some clown—there always were in any setting, even the worst, for irony is the weapon of the disarmed—who would repeat the familiar camp joke, "A leap in the air I consider agitation." This malicious joke was spoken so that the guard couldn't hear it. It brought a certain amount of cheer, gave a second's tiny relief. We received the warning four times a day: in the morning, when we went off to work; in the middle of the day, when we went to lunch; and then after lunch; and in the evening, as a farewell before we returned to barracks. And every time after the familiar formula someone would utter the remark about a leap, and nobody got bored or irritated by it. On the contrary, we were prepared to listen to that joke a thousand times.

And now our dreams had come true. We were at Diamond Spring and without an escort guard. All we had was a young man with a black beard, which he had obviously grown to look more serious, who was armed with an Izhevsk rifle, watching over our river crossing. We had already had it explained to us that he was in charge of the forest region, that he was our boss, a free contract foreman.

At Diamond Spring pylons were being made for a high-voltage power line.

There are not many places in Kolyma where trees grow tall. We were going to carry out selective clearing, the best sort of work for people like us.

A gold-mine pit face is a murderous place to work, and it kills men quickly. The rations there are bigger, but bigger rations, not smaller ones, are what kill you in the camps. The truth of this camp saying was something we had long ago been able to convince ourselves of. No amount of chocolate could save a pit-face getter who had become a goner.

Selective forest clearing was better than complete clearing, for the forest was thin and low, the trees grew in marshes and there were no giants. Skidding—hauling the timber into stacks on your own shoulders over the porous snow—was agonizing. But twelve-meter pillars for a power line couldn't be skidded manually; they required a horse or a tractor. So life was bearable. And the fact that this expedition was without escort guards meant that there would be no solitary confinement, no beatings. The area boss was a free contract worker, an engineer or technician. So we were undoubtedly in luck.

We spent the night on the riverbank and in the morning we went up the path to our barracks. The sun had not yet set when we reached a low, long taiga log cabin with a roof plugged with moss and covered with stones. Fifty-two men lived in the barracks, and we new arrivals were twenty. The bunks of unplaned boards reached high up, and the ceiling was low, so that you could only stand up straight in the passage between the bunks.

The boss was an energetic, agile man. He surveyed the ranks of his new workmen with young eyes, but an experienced gaze. He was immediately interested in my scarf. It was, naturally, cotton, not woolen, but it was still a scarf, the sort worn by free men. I had been given it the year before by a hospital paramedic, and since then I hadn't taken it off my neck, winter or summer. I washed it as best I could in the bathhouse, but I never ever handed it over to be deloused. The hot disinfection chamber wouldn't have killed the lice, of which there were a lot in the scarf, and the scarf would immediately have been stolen. My neighbors, whether in the barracks, outside, or at work, were hunting, following the rules, for my scarf. There were those who hunted for it against the rules: anyone who happened to pass by, for who would refuse to earn money to buy tobacco or bread? And any free man would buy this scarf, for it would be easy to steam out the lice. Only a prisoner finds it hard to get rid of lice. But I heroically kept the scarf knotted around my neck when I went to sleep, although I suffered from the lice, which are as impossible to get used to as the cold.

"Won't you sell it?" asked the black-bearded boss.

"No," I answered.

"It's up to you. You don't need a scarf."

I didn't like the way this conversation was going. The other bad thing was that we were fed only once a day, after work. In the morning all we got was hot water and bread. But I had put up with that before. The bosses paid little attention to feeding the prisoners. Every one of them tried to make things as easy as they could for themselves.

All the food supplies were kept by the free foreman. He and his Izhevsk rifle lived in a tiny log cabin ten yards from the barracks. Keeping food like this was also something new, as food was usually kept with the prisoners, not with the people in charge of production. Things were apparently better ordered at Diamond Spring. It was dangerous and risky to let hungry prisoners keep the food supplies, and everybody knew of the risk.

We had a long way—about four kilometers—to get to work, and it was clear that with each day the selective clearance of trees would recede further and further into the depths of the ravine.

A long walk, even under armed escort, is more a good thing than a bad thing for a prisoner: the more time spent walking, the less spent on work, whatever the norm-setters and foremen calculate.

The work was no worse and no better than any prisoners' work in the forest. We felled the trees that the foreman had marked with his ax, we debarked them, we cleared off the side branches and collected them into a pile. The heaviest job was felling the tree, so that the bottom end fell on the stump and thus didn't fall into the snow, but the foreman knew that hauling it out was urgent, that tractors would arrive. He knew that in early winter the snow would not be deep enough to cover the trees we had felled, and he didn't always insist that we lift the trunk onto the stump.

Something astounding was awaiting me in the evening.

Supper at Diamond Spring was breakfast, lunch, and dinner in one: it didn't look any richer or more satisfying that any lunch or supper at the mine. My stomach kept insisting that the total calories and nutritional value were less than at the mine, where we got less than half the rations we were supposed to get, since all the rest was diverted to the bowls of the bosses, the support staff, and the gangsters. But I didn't believe my stomach, which had been so badly starved in Kolyma. Its reactions were exaggerations or underestimates; it wanted too much, it demanded too insistently, it was far too biased.

After supper, for some reason, nobody went to bed. They were all waiting for something. For a roll call? No, there were no roll calls here. Finally the door opened and in came the inexhaustible black-bearded foreman, holding a piece of paper. The orderly took the kerosene lamp from the upper bunks and put it on the table, dug into the middle of the barracks. He sat down by the light.

"What's this going to be?" I asked the man next to me.

"Percentages for today," he replied. In his tone of voice I detected something very frightening: I'd heard that tone in extremely serious circumstances, when the victims of 1938 had their work at the gold-mine pit face measured every day by an "individual allocation." I could not possibly be mistaken. There was something here that even I didn't know about, some dangerous innovation.

The foreman didn't look at anyone. In an even, bored voice he read out to each worker a surname and the percentage of the norm that had been fulfilled, then he carefully folded the piece of paper and left. There was silence in the barracks. All we could hear was the heavy breathing of several scores of men in the dark.

"Anyone with less than 100 percent," explained the man next to me, who had cheered up, "will get no bread tomorrow."

"None at all?"

"None at all."

I'd really never ever come across anything like that before.

In the mines your ration was determined by the brigade's production over ten days. At the very worst, you got punishment rations: three hundred grams, but you weren't wholly deprived of bread.

I thought very hard. Bread was our basic food here. We got half our calories from bread. The cooked food was something hard to define, its nutritional value depended on thousands of different things, on the honesty of the cook, on his hard work, for an idle cook gets help from "workmen" to whom he gives extra food. It depended on energetic and vigilant supervision, on the honesty of the bosses and the degree to which the escort guards were well-fed and decent. It depended on the absence or presence of gangsters. Finally, and this was a matter entirely of chance, it depended on the ladle used by the server, who might ladle out one dumpling and thus reduce the nutritional value of a soup to virtually zero.

Our versatile foreman was, of course, making up the percentages as he went along. And I promised myself that if I had my bread ration stopped as a way of affecting production, then I wouldn't hang around.

A week passed, during which I realized why the food was kept under the foreman's bunk. He hadn't forgotten about the scarf.

"Listen, Andreyev, sell me your scarf."

"It was a present, sir."

"Don't try and be funny."

But I refused outright. That evening I was on the list of those who had failed to reach the norm. I wasn't prepared to argue about it. In the morning I unwound my scarf and took it to our cobbler.

"Just make sure you steam it properly."

"We know, we weren't born yesterday," the cobbler replied merrily, pleased by his unexpected acquisition.

The cobbler gave me a five-hundred-gram bread ration. I broke off a piece and hid the rest under my shirt. I drank my fill of hot water and went to work with the rest of the workers, but I lagged further and further behind, before turning off the road into the forest. I made a wide detour around our settlement, then followed the same way I had come a month before. I walked about half a kilometer away from the path. Snow had fallen, but not enough to make walking difficult. The black-bearded foreman had no bloodhounds. Only later did I learn that he had managed to ski down to the ferryman's booth, for the mountain river takes a long time to freeze here, and had sent a message with a guard who was going that way to say I had escaped.

I sat down on the snow and stuffed some rags down my soft boots, below the knee. This sort of footwear was a boot only in name. It was a local model, an economical product for wartime. Hundred of thousands of soft boots were made from old, worn-out quilted trousers. The soles were made of the same material, stitched in several layers and equipped with ties. Flannel foot wrappings were issued with these boots, and that was the footwear for workmen hacking gold in temperatures of minus fifty or sixty. These boots fell apart after a few hours' work in the forest—they tore on branches and twigs—as well as after work at the gold-mine pit face. Holes in boots were repaired in night-time cobblers' workshops, and were crudely stitched. By the morning the repair would be finished. Layer after layer was stitched onto the soles, until the boots finally became utterly shapeless, more like the banks of a mountain river, laid bare after a landslide.

Wearing these boots, stick in hand, I headed for the river, a few kilometers above the ferry crossing. I clambered down steep stony slopes, and the ice crackled under my feet. A long patch of unfrozen water blocked my path, and I could see no end to it. The ice had broken in places, and I easily strode into the pearly steaming water, and my quilted soles could feel the stones that poked up from the bottom. I lifted one leg as high as I could: my iced-over boots shone, and I strode in even deeper, above the knee, and using the stick, managed to get to the other side. Once there, I carefully beat my boots with the stick and scraped off the ice from my boots and trousers: my feet were dry. I felt for the piece of bread under my shirt and moved off along the riverbank. After about two hours I came out onto the highway. It was pleasant walking without my louse-infected scarf: my throat and neck seemed to be resting, now that they were covered with an old towel, a "change" which the cobbler had given me for my scarf.

I was traveling light. It is very important for long journeys, both in winter and in summer, to have your hands free. Your hands take part in your movements and warm up as you walk, just like your feet. The main thing is not to carry anything in your hands. Even a pencil will seem an unthinkable burden after twenty or thirty kilometers. I had known that well for a long time. I knew a few other things: if a man is capable of carrying a burden in one hand for several paces, then he can do so indefinitely, because he will get a second, a third, a tenth wind. I, a goner, could get to wherever I wanted. Along an even road. Walking in winter is easier than in summer, if the freezing temperatures are not too low. I didn't think about anything, and anyway, thought is impossible below zero: low temperatures take away your thoughts, and quickly and easily turn you into a wild animal. I walked without any purpose other than a desire to get out of the damned expedition with no guards. About thirty kilometers from the camp, on the highway, some lumberjacks lived in a hut, and I was counting on warming myself up there and, if I was lucky, spending the night.

It was dark when I reached that hut, opened the door, and, stepping through the frozen mist, entered a barracks. A man got up from behind a Russian stove to meet me: it was the lumberjack foreman Stepan Zhdanov, whom I knew. He had been a prisoner, of course.

"Take your jacket off, sit down."

I immediately took off my jacket and boots, and hung them around the stove.

Stepan opened the stove door and, putting on a glove, pulled out a pot.

"Sit down and eat." He gave me bread and soup.

I lay down to sleep on the floor, but it took time to fall asleep. My feet and hands ached.

Stepan didn't ask where I was going or where I'd come from. I would appreciate his tact for the rest of my life. I never saw him again. But even now I can remember the hot millet soup, the smell of porridge that had burned a little, a smell that reminded one of chocolate, the taste of a clay pipe that Stepan offered me, after wiping it on his sleeve, when we were saying goodbye, so that I could have a puff for the road.

On a turbid winter evening I reached the camp and sat down in the snow not far from the gates.

Any moment I would go in and it would all be over. Those wonderful two days of freedom, after many years of prison—and now again there would be lice, icy stone, white haze, hunger, beatings. Just then an actor from the Culture Brigade—a man trusted to go around on his own, unescorted—walked past through the guardhouse into the camp. I knew him. Now the workers came back from the timber works, stamping their feet so as not to freeze, while the escort guard went up the steps to the guardhouse, into the warmth. He wasn't in a hurry. Now the camp boss, Lieutenant Kozychev, went in, dropping a Kazbek cigarette end in the snow, and the woodcutters standing by the guardhouse immediately made a dash for it. It was time. I couldn't sit there all night. I had to try to see my plan through to the end. I pushed the door and went into the entrance. I was holding a statement for the camp boss about all the procedures on an expedition with no guards. Kozychev read my statement and sent me off to solitary. There I slept, until I was summoned to see the interrogator, but, as I had foreseen, they didn't charge me with anything. My sentence was enough. "You'll be going to a punishment mine," said the interrogator. A few days later that's where they sent me. They didn't hold people very long at the central transit point.

1959

THE GREEN PROSECUTOR

HERE THE scale of values was completely reversed, and any human concept, while still keeping its spelling, its pronunciation, and its usual set of letters and sounds, now meant something quite different, for which the mainland had no name. Here there were different measures, particular customs, and habits, and the sense of any word was altered.

Whenever a new event, feeling, or concept can't be expressed by the usual human words, a new word is born, borrowed from the language of the professional criminals who legislate the fashions and tastes of the Far North.

These metamorphoses of meaning affect more than just concepts like Love, Honor, Work, Virtue, Vice, Crime. They also affect words that are almost exclusive to this world, that have their origin in it, for example: "Escape"....

In my early youth I happened to read about Kropotkin's escape from Petropavlovsk fortress: a fast cab drawing up at the prison gates, a woman wearing a disguise in a light carriage, carrying a revolver, working out the number of paces to the guards' door, the prisoner fleeing while the guards fired at him, the clattering of the trotting horse's hooves over the cobbles.... That was, without a doubt, a classic escape.

Later I read the recollections by exiles of escapes from Yakutia, from Verkhoyansk, and I was bitterly disappointed: no disguises, no pursuit! Riding a horse-drawn sled (the horses harnessed in single file) in winter, just as in Pushkin's *Captain's Daughter*, arriving at a railway station, buying a ticket at the ticket office.... I just could not understand why this was called an escape. That sort of escape used to be classified as "willful absence from place of residence" and, in my view, such a formula is a more accurate definition of what was happening than the romantic word "escape."

Even the escape by the Social Revolutionary Zenzinov[28] from Providence Bay, when an American yacht approached the rowboat in which Zenzinov was fishing and took the refugee on board, doesn't look like a real escape, not like Kropotkin's.

There were always many attempted escapes in Kolyma, and none of them were successful.

The reason was the peculiar nature of the harsh polar region, where the tsar's government decided not to settle prisoners, as they had settled them in Sakhalin in order to populate and colonize the region.

The distances to the mainland were thousands of kilometers. The narrowest place, the taiga vacuum, the distance between Aldan and the inhabited areas, where Far East Construction had its mines, was about a thousand kilometers of uninhabited taiga.

True, if you headed for America, the distances were far shorter: the Bering Strait at its narrowest point is only just over a hundred kilometers, but the guards in this area are reinforced by border troops, and it is absolutely impenetrable.

The very first route took you to Yakutsk, and from there you progressed either by horse or by river. There was no airplane service at the time, and, in any case, there is nothing easier than to keep airplanes safely locked up.

It's understandable why no escapes took place in winter: to get through the winter anywhere with a roof and an iron stove is the passionate dream of every prisoner, and not just prisoners.

Captivity becomes unbearable in spring: that is a universal fact. Here, apart from the meteorological factor, which has an imperative effect on a man's feelings, there was also the consideration that came from cold intellectual logic. Traveling across the taiga is possible only in summer when, if your food runs out, you can eat herbs, mushrooms, berries, roots, and bake cakes of reindeer moss ground into flour, catch mice and voles, chipmunks, squirrels, nutcrackers, hares. . . .

However cold the northern summer nights are, in a country of permafrost, an experienced man will avoid catching a chill if he spends the night on a rock. He will turn over from side to side in good time, he won't sleep on his back, he'll put grass or branches under his side. . . .

It's impossible to run away from Kolyma. Whoever chose the sites for the camps was a genius. Nevertheless, the power of illusions, for which people pay with terrible days in solitary confinement, extra sentences, beatings, starvation and, very often, death, is just as strong here as anywhere else at any time.

A lot of escape attempts are made. The moment the larch tree buds turn emerald, fugitives are on the move.

Almost always the fugitives are novices in their first year. They still have some willpower and pride left in their hearts, and their reason has not yet taken in the conditions of the Far North, which are nothing like the mainland world they knew hitherto. The novices are offended to the bottom of their hearts by what they have seen: beatings, tortures, taunts, human depravity. . . . The novices make a run for it: some do it better, some worse, but they all end up the same way. Some are caught in a couple of days, others in a week, others in two weeks. There are fairly light sentences for fugitives who wander off with a "directive" (a term we will explain later).

The enormous resources of the camp guards and special troops with thousands of German shepherds, combined with border detachments and army groups stationed in Kolyma, concealed under the name of "the Kolyma Regiment," are more than enough to catch all potential escapees.

But how is an escape attempt possible, and would it not be simpler for the special troop forces to focus on guarding people in the first place, on guarding instead of trying to catch them?

Economic considerations show that keeping a large detachment of "skull hunters" costs the country less than having an intensive guard system as in prisons. It is extraordinarily difficult to stop the actual escape attempt. Even the gigantic network of informers among the prisoners, who are paid by the bosses with cigarettes and bowls of soup, is of no use.

This is a matter of human psychology, its nooks and crannies, and it is impossible to predict who will decide to escape, and when or how. What actually happens is not at all as you might suppose.

Of course, there are prophylactic measures meant to counter escape: arrests, imprisonment in punishment zones, which are prisons within prisons, transfers of suspicious persons to new places. A lot of measures have been devised that may have some effect in reducing escape attempts. Possibly there would be more escapes were it not for the punishment zones, sited in the remotest areas, with their reliable and numerous guards.

But there are escape attempts from punishment zones, too, whereas nobody tries to get away from expeditions where there are no guards. Anything can happen in the camps. Stendhal's subtle observation in *The Charterhouse of Parma* that "the warden thinks less about his keys than the prisoner about his bars" is fair and true, and it applies here:

> Kolyma, o Kolyma,
> Wonderful planet.
> Nine whole months of winter,
> All the rest is summer.

That is why special preparations are made for spring. The guards and special troops increase their numbers and the numbers of their dogs. Men are dragged in, dogs are trained. Prisoners also prepare, by hiding canned food and rusks and recruiting partners....

There is just one case of a classic escape from Kolyma, carefully thought out and prepared, and carried out with ingenuity and without haste. This is the exception that proves the rule. But even this escape left a loose end that looked insignificant, and at first sight trivial, but the loose end was a blunder that made it possible to trace the fugitive in exactly two years. Clearly, the pride of the Vidocqs and Lecoqs[29] was badly hurt, and the case was given far more attention than was usual for such events.

It is curious that the man who "went on escape" and brought it off with fabulous energy and cleverness was not a political prisoner at all and certainly not a gangster (specialists in such matters), either. He had been sentenced to ten years for fraud.

That's understandable. A political prisoner's escape is always a reflection of mood and willpower and, like a prison hunger strike, its strength lies in the willpower used. You need to know, and know well and beforehand, why you're escaping, and where to. What political prisoner could in 1937 answer such a question? People who got caught up in politics by chance don't try to run away from prison. They could escape back to their families, their friends, but in 1938 that meant subjecting anyone whom such an escapee even looked at in the street to severe repressive measures.

This was not just a matter of getting away with fifteen, twenty years in prison. To jeopardize the lives of your nearest and dearest was the only possible outcome of such an escape by a political. After all, someone would have to shelter, hide, and help the fugitive. There were no such people among the politicals in 1938.

The very few men who returned after serving their sentences found that their own wives were the first to check up on the correctness and the legality of a husband's documents when he got back from the camps and, in order to inform the authorities of his arrival, they would run to the police station as fast as they could together with the apartment's responsible householder.

The punishment meted out to people who got innocently involved by chance was very simple. Instead of being given a reprimand, or a warning, they were tortured and after the torture were given ten or twenty years in "distant camps," or hard labor, or prison. Death was what they now faced. And they died, not thinking about escape, they died, showing yet again the national characteristic of endurance, which was celebrated long ago by Tiutchev and which has been brazenly remarked on by politicians at all levels.

Gangsters didn't try to escape, because they didn't believe they could succeed, they didn't believe they would make it to the mainland. In any case, investigators and camp staff were highly experienced at recognizing gangsters. They had a sixth sense, and would assure you that gangsters bore a mark of Cain that could not be concealed. The most striking "exegesis" of this sixth sense was the case of a hunt for an armed robber and murderer along the Kolyma roads, when an order was issued to shoot him as soon as he was identified.

A special forces man, Sevastianov, stopped a stranger wearing a sheepskin jacket near a gas pump at one of the gas stations on the highway. When the man turned around, Sevastianov shot him straight through the forehead. Even though Sevastianov had never seen this robber's face before, even though it was winter and the fugitive was wearing winter clothes, even though the distinguishing features that the special forces man had been told of were as vague as they could be (you are not going to examine everyone you meet for tattoos, and the bandit's photograph was very bad and blurred), nevertheless Sevastianov's intuition had not let him down.

A sawed-off shotgun fell out of the dead man's coat, and a Browning revolver was found in his pockets.

That was more than enough documentation.

How should one assess such a decisive deduction, suggested by somebody's sixth sense? Another minute, and Sevastianov would himself have been shot.

But suppose he had shot an innocent man?

The gangsters had neither the strength nor the desire to attempt to escape to the mainland. After weighing all the pros and cons, the criminal world decided not to take the risk, but to limit themselves to settling down nicely in the new places fate had brought them to. That, of course, was sensible. To the criminal world, running away from here seemed too bold an adventure, an unnecessary risk.

Then who was going to escape? A peasant? A priest? I've only happened to meet one priest who tried to escape, and this escape happened before the famous meeting between Patriarch Sergius and Ambassador Bullitt, when the first American ambassador was handed a list of all the Orthodox priests serving sentences of imprisonment and exile throughout the Soviet Union. When he was a metropolitan bishop, Patriarch Sergii had personally become familiar with the cells of Butyrki prison. After Roosevelt's intercession every single one of the clerics was released from imprisonment and exile. A concordat with the church, which was vital in view of the approach of war, was being anticipated.

It would never make sense for a person sentenced for a nonpolitical crime—a child rapist, someone who stole state funds, a bribe-taker, a murderer—to try to escape. Their sentence, their "term," to use Dostoevsky's word, was usually not very long, and while imprisoned they enjoyed all sorts of advantages, and worked as camp support staff, in the camp administration, and in any one of the "privileged" jobs. They had good credits for days worked, and above all, when they got home, whether to the country or the city, they were met with the most friendly reception. Not because this friendliness was a quality of the Russian people, who used to pity "the unlucky wretch": such pity for unlucky wretches had long vanished into the world of legends, and had become a nice literary fairy tale. Times had changed. The highly disciplined nature of society told "ordinary people" to look and see how the authorities viewed the subject. The view was very benevolent, for the authorities were not bothered by this contingent of criminal. Only Trotskyists and enemies of the people were singled out to be hated.

There was a second and equally important reason for ordinary people not to be worried about those who'd come back from prison. So many people had spent time in prisons that there was probably not a family in the whole country whose relatives or friends had not been subjected to persecution and repressions. After the "wreckers" it was the turn of the "kulaks," the rich peasants; after the kulaks, the Trotskyists; after them, people with German surnames. The declaration of a crusade against the Jews was just over the horizon.

All this led to people not caring in the least. It instilled in the people a complete indifference to those who'd been singled out by any part of the Criminal Code.

In the past, a man who had been in prison and then come back to his native village aroused either caution or hostility, or contempt, or sympathy (open or secret). Now, however, no attention was paid to such people. The moral isolation of the "branded," of convicts who had served hard labor, had long ago fallen into oblivion.

Provided that their return was sanctioned by the authorities, people coming from prison were met with the greatest hospitality. In any case, any gang rapist like Chubarov,[30] who raped his child victim and infected her with syphilis, could, after he had served his sentence, count on having complete "spiritual" freedom in the same circle in which he had overstepped the limits of the Criminal Code.

The way literary figures treated legal categories has had a part in all this. For some reason, writers and playwrights put themselves forward as theoreticians of the law. But the prison and camp realities are still a book with seven seals, and no serious, fundamental deductions have been made from all the reports that come from those who have served in the criminal world....

But why should nonpoliticals try to escape from the camps? They didn't. They fully entrusted themselves to the care of the authorities.

All of which makes the escape attempt by Pavel Mikhailovich Krivoshei all the more amazing.

He was a squat man, with short legs and a thick scarlet neck. His name, appropriately, means "crooked neck."

He was a chemical engineer at a Kharkov plant and had a perfect command of several foreign languages. He read a lot and also had a good knowledge of art and sculpture, and he had a big collection of antiques.

A prominent figure among Ukrainian collectors, Krivoshei, as a non-party member and engineer, utterly despised politicians of all hues. Being a clever and cunning man, he had ever since his youth been brought up with a passion for enjoying life, as far as he understood it, but not for accumulating possessions, which would have been too coarse and stupid for Krivoshei. All this meant relaxation, vices, art.... He had no taste for loftier pleasures. His culture and his advanced knowledge opened up big opportunities for him, not just for material prosperity but also for sating his needs and desires for lower and baser pleasures.

The reason Krivoshei learned all about art was to make himself more prestigious, to rank higher among connoisseurs and dilettantes, so as not to disgrace himself because of his other, purely sensual infatuation with someone, either female or male. Art in itself didn't excite or interest him at all, but he considered himself obliged to have an opinion even about the square hall in the Louvre.

The same applied to literature, which he read mainly in French and English and predominantly to practice his languages. Literature in itself held little interest for him, and he could spend an eternity on one novel, reading a page a night before going to sleep. It was of course unthinkable that Krivoshei would ever find a book that he could read all night until dawn. He was very protective of his sleep, and no detective novel could have disturbed Krivoshei's carefully measured regime.

As for music, Krivoshei was a complete ignoramus. He had no ear, and even Blok's kind of understanding of music was beyond him. But he had realized a long time ago that lacking a musical ear was "a misfortune, not a vice," and he had come to terms with it. In any case, he had enough patience to listen to a fugue or a sonata and thank the performer, preferably female.

His health was excellent, his body was endomorphic, with a certain tendency to stoutness, which, by the way, was no danger to him in the camps.

Krivoshei was born in 1900.

He always wore tortoiseshell or rimless glasses with round lenses. Slow-moving, inept, with a high, round, balding forehead, Krivoshei was an extremely imposing figure. There was something deliberate about this. His grave manners had an effect on the bosses, which must have made his fate in the camps easier.

Alien to art, to the artistic excitement of a creator or a consumer, Krivoshei found his métier in collecting, in antiques. He devoted himself to this activity with passion; it was both profitable and interesting, and it brought him new acquaintances. All in all, this hobby made the engineer's desires less base and more noble.

An engineer's salary, even the "special rates" of the times, became insufficient for living on the grand scale that Krivoshei, the amateur antiquarian, required.

He needed the means, means that the state possessed, and whatever you might say about Krivoshei, you couldn't deny that he was determined.

He got a death sentence, commuted to ten years—a sentence that was very heavy for the mid-1930s. It meant his fraud had been in the millions. His property was confiscated and auctioned, but Krivoshei had, of course, already anticipated such an outcome. It would have been odd if he hadn't managed to hide away a few hundred thousand. The risk was small, the advantages were obvious. Krivoshei was a nonpolitical, he would serve his sentence as a "friend of the people." After serving half his sentence or even less, he would be released on the basis of credited working days or an amnesty, and he could then live off the money he had hidden.

But Krivoshei wasn't kept for long in a mainland camp; he was moved, as a long-term prisoner, to Kolyma. That complicated his plans. True, his reliance on his crime's status in the Criminal Code and on his lordly manners proved to be fully justified, and he didn't spend a single day at any mine's pit face. He was soon assigned, as a specialist engineer, to the chemical laboratory in the Arkagala coal district.

This was the time when the famous Chai-Uryinsky gold had not yet been discovered and when old larch trees and six-hundred-year-old poplars were still standing where one day there would be dozens of settlements and thousands of inhabitants. This was the time when nobody thought that the supply of gold nuggets in the At-Uriakh valley would ever be exhausted or superseded. Life had not yet shifted toward the northwest, in the direction of what was then the Cold Pole, Oymiakon. Old mines were worked until they were exhausted and new ones were being opened. Life in the mines was always temporary.

The Arkagala coal, the future Arkagala basin, was an outpost for gold prospectors, and was the new source of fuel for the region. Around a small mine gallery where, if you stood on the rail, you could touch the roof, the gallery ceiling—it was a gallery dug out on the cheap, in the taiga style, as the bosses said—there were other galleries, dug by hand with pickax and spade, just like all the thousand-kilometer roads in Kolyma. Those roads and the early mines were hand-dug: the only mechanical aid was the "three-man special tribunal machine: two handles and a wheel."

Prison labor is cheap.

The geological search parties were still choking in the gold of Susuman and the gold of At-Uriakh.

But Krivoshei was well aware that the geologists' paths would extend to the surroundings of Arkagala and then move on toward Yakutsk. The geologists would be followed by carpenters, miners, guards....

He had to make haste.

A few months passed and Krivoshei was visited by his wife, who'd come from Kharkov. She hadn't come just to see him, no—she had followed her husband, repeating the heroic selfless acts of the wives of the Decembrists. Krivoshei's wife was not the first or the last of these "Russian heroines." The geologist Faina Rabinovich's name is well-known in Kolyma. But Faina Rabinovich was a prominent geologist. Her fate was an exception.

Wives who followed their husbands were dooming themselves to the cold, to the ceaseless torments of following their husbands wherever the latter had gone, and husbands were constantly being transferred somewhere: the wife would then have to abandon her place of work, where she had had so much trouble finding a job, and travel to regions where it was dangerous for a woman to travel, where she might be the victim of rape, robbery and abuse.... Quite apart from the peregrinations, such martyrs could expect coarse advances and harassment from the bosses, from the very top man to the average escort guard who had already got into the swing of life in Kolyma. An invitation to share the company of drunken bachelors was the invariable fate of all women. While a female prisoner was just given the order, "Get undressed and lie down!" with no reference to Pushkin or Shakespeare or anything like that, after which she would be infected with syphilis, wives of prisoners were treated even more licentiously. If a man raped a female prisoner, he always risked being denounced by a friend or a rival, a subordinate or a boss, but "love" with prisoners' wives, who were, legally speaking, independent persons, was not classified as a crime anywhere in the Code.

The main thing, however, was that this journey of thirteen thousand kilometers turned out to be utterly pointless. The poor woman was not allowed to have any meetings with her husband, and any promise to allow a meeting was turned into a weapon when the boss made his own advances.

Some wives brought permits from Moscow for monthly meetings, conditional on exemplary behavior and fulfilling the production norms. These meetings would not include a night together, naturally, and had to take place in the presence of the camp authorities.

Wives almost never succeeded in finding work in the same settlement as the one where their husbands were serving their sentences.

Even if, against all expectations, a wife managed to find a job near her husband, he would immediately be transferred elsewhere. This was not just a whim of the bosses, it was the fulfillment of official instructions: "orders are orders." Moscow had already provided for such cases.

No wife ever succeeded in passing anything edible to her husband. There were orders to deal with this, too: norms, contingencies depending on the results of labor and behavior.

Could she pass her husband bread with the help of the guards? They'd be too afraid, they were forbidden to do that. Via one of the bosses? He might agree, but he would want payment in kind—her body. He didn't need money, he was rolling in money, he'd been a "100-percenter" for a long time now, in other words he got a quadruple salary. In any case, women like her were unlikely to have the money for bribes, especially on the Kolyma scale. So that was the hopeless position in which wives of prisoners found themselves. And if the wife was also the wife of an enemy of the people, then nobody would even give her the time of day: any abuse of her was considered the right thing to do, a good deed, and, in any case, would be regarded positively from a political point of view.

Many wives came on three-year contracts and, once caught in this trap, had to wait for a ship home. Those who were strong in spirit—and they needed more strength than even their imprisoned husbands— waited for their contracts to expire and then traveled home without ever having seen their husbands. Those who were weak in spirit remembered how they were persecuted on the mainland and were afraid to go back. They lived in an atmosphere of debauchery, fumes of alcohol and tobacco, drunkenness, big sums of money, and they got married again and again, had children, and washed their hands of their prisoner-husbands and of their own selves.

As you might expect, Krivoshei's wife couldn't find work at Arkagala. After spending a short time there, she left for the local capital, the town of Magadan. When she got work there as an accountant— Angelina Grigorievna had no qualifications, she'd been a housewife all her adult life—she found somewhere to live and settled in Magadan, where life was at least less dismal than at Arkagala in the taiga.

From Arkagala, through secret channels, to the same Magadan, addressed to the head of the criminal investigation department, an institution that was on the same street (almost the only street) in the town, where there was a barracks partitioned by screens for people with families, a coded official communication came flying: "Prisoner Pavel

Mikhailovich Krivoshei, born 1900, convicted under article 168, sentence ten years, number of personal file ... has escaped."

They thought he was being hidden by his wife in Magadan. They arrested her, but couldn't get anything out of her. "Yes, I've been there, I've seen him, I left, I now work in Magadan." Lengthy surveillance and observation produced no results. Checks on departing ships and aircraft were strengthened, but it was all in vain. There was no trace of Angelina's husband.

Krivoshei had left not for the sea, but in the opposite direction, heading for Yakutsk. He was traveling light. Apart from a canvas cape, a geologist's hammer, a bag with a small quantity of geological ore "samples," and a supply of matches and of money, he had nothing.

He walked without hiding or hurrying along the packhorse roads, reindeer tracks, keeping to herders' camps and workers' settlements, never deviating deep into the taiga, always spending the night under the roof of a wooden cabin, a yurt, or a hut.... In the very first Yakut settlement he hired workmen who dug trial shafts, or ditches as he directed. In short, he did all the jobs that he had occasion to do for real geologists. Krivoshei had enough technical knowledge to pose as a collector. Arkagala, where he'd spent about a year, was the latest base camp for many geological expeditions, and Krivoshei had studied geologists' manners and ways of doing things. His leisurely movements, his tortoiseshell glasses, his daily shave, his nicely filed fingernails all inspired limitless trust in people.

Krivoshei was in no hurry. He would fill his journal with mysterious signs that had some similarity to geologists' field journals. Making haste slowly, he was moving relentlessly toward Yakutsk.

Sometimes he even backtracked, or made a detour, or stopped off: all that was necessary for "surveying the Pocked Spring basin," to make his trip look genuine, to cover up his tracks. Krivoshei had nerves of steel, and he never stopped smiling a welcoming, extroverted smile.

After a month he crossed the Yablonovy range. Two Yakuts, assigned by a collective farm for important government work, were carrying his bags of "samples."

They were getting closer to Yakutsk. Once in Yakutsk, Krivoshei left his stones in a luggage storage office at the steamship dock and set off for the local geological administration, with a request for help in sending some important packages to Moscow, to the Academy of Sciences. Krivoshei went to the bathhouse, the hairdresser's, bought an expensive suit, a few colored shirts, underwear and, combing his thinning hair, presented himself to the top academic authorities, smiling amiably.

The top academic authorities received him benevolently. The knowledge of foreign languages that he demonstrated produced the effect required.

The academic authorities saw the new arrival as a major cultural force, something that Yakutsk then badly lacked, and they begged Krivoshei to stay as long as he could. When Krivoshei responded with embarrassed phrases that he had to hurry off to Moscow, they promised to arrange his travel at state expense as far as Vladivostok. Keeping up his dignity, Krivoshei thanked them calmly. But the academic authorities had their own plans for Krivoshei.

"Of course you won't say no, dear colleague," they said in a fawning tone, "to giving our scientists two or three lectures. . . . About . . . well, you're free to choose, it's up to you, of course. Something about the coal reserves in the Central Yakutia plateau, perhaps?"

Krivoshei had a sinking feeling.

"Oh, of course, with great pleasure. Within the limits, as it were, of what I'm allowed to say. . . . You'll understand that this information, without Moscow's say-so. . . ."

Krivoshei then showered the scientific resources of Yakutsk with compliments.

No interrogator could have posed a question more cunningly than did the Yakut professor, despite his liking for their learned visitor, for his bearing, his tortoiseshell glasses, and his desire to serve his homeland as best he could.

A lecture took place and even attracted an audience of a respectable size. Krivoshei smiled, quoted Shakespeare in English, drew a few things on the board, and listed dozens of foreign surnames.

"Those Muscovites don't know all that much," said a man sitting next to the Yakut professor, once they were in the buffet. "Everything that was geological in that lecture was really at the level of a secondary schoolboy, wasn't it? As for the chemical analysis of coal, that's nothing to do with geology, is it? The only thing brilliant about him is his glasses."

"You mustn't say that," the professor said, frowning. "It's all very useful, and our colleague from the capital certainly has a gift for popularization. We'll have to ask him to repeat his lecture to our students."

"Well, perhaps for first-year students," the professor's neighbor said, not backing down.

"Be quiet. Anyway, it's a favor, it's very good of him. You don't look a gift horse...."

Krivoshei very graciously repeated his lecture to the students, who responded with interest all around and completely positive approval.

At the expense of Yakutsk's scientific organizations, their guest was dispatched to Irkutsk.

His collection—a few boxes packed with stones—had been sent off in advance. The "leader of the geological expedition" managed in Irkutsk to mail the stones to Moscow, addressing them to the Academy of Sciences, where they were received and where they lay for several years in the storage rooms, a scientific enigma whose nature nobody ever guessed at. It was assumed that this mysterious present, collected by some crazy geologist who had lost his knowledge and forgotten his own name, was the outcome of some as yet undiscovered tragedy in the polar regions.

"The most amazing thing," Krivoshei used to say, " is that throughout my three months' travels almost nobody anywhere—not in the nomads' village councils, not at the top scientific institutions—ever asked me for my papers. I did have papers, but I never ever had to show them anywhere."

Naturally, Krivoshei avoided Kharkov. He settled down in Mariupol, bought a house there, and used forged papers to get a job.

Exactly two years later, on the anniversary of his "crusade," Krivoshei was arrested, tried, sentenced to another ten years, and sent back to Kolyma to serve his punishment.

Where had he made the blunder that completely nullified this truly heroic action, this exploit that had demanded so much self-control, so much ingenuity, and physical strength—every human quality simultaneously?

This escape was unique in the care with which it was prepared, in the subtle and profound ideas behind it, in the psychological calculations that underlay the whole enterprise.

It was astounding in that almost nobody else was involved in organizing it, which was the main reason for its success.

The escape was also remarkable because a solitary man had personally taken on the whole state, with its thousands of men armed with rifles, in a region populated by the descendants of the first Russian settlers and by Yakuts, who had become accustomed to receiving ten kilos of white flour for every fugitive they caught (this was a tariff from tsarist times that was later incorporated into law). True, the man was forced, and rightly so, to see everyone he met as a possible informer or coward, but he had fought, he had done battle, and he had won!

So where and of what nature was the blunder that destroyed his brilliantly devised and splendidly realized task?

His wife was detained in the north. She was forbidden to leave for the mainland. The necessary papers for permission would have to be issued by the very same institution that dealt with her husband's case. But all that had been anticipated; she settled down to wait. The months dragged on. As before, she was met with refusals, with no explanation as to why. She made an attempt to leave Kolyma from the opposite side, by plane over the same taiga rivers and side valleys that her husband had crossed on foot some months before. But this, too, ended with her being refused permission. She found herself locked up in an enormous stone prison one-eighth the size of the Soviet Union, and she couldn't find a way out.

She was a woman, and she was tired of an endless struggle with someone whose face she couldn't see, a struggle with someone far stronger than her, stronger and more cunning.

The money she'd brought with her ran out. Life in the north is expensive—one apple at the Magadan market costs a hundred rubles. Angelina found herself a job, but people who were hired locally and not recruited from the mainland were paid different salaries, which were much the same as those paid in Kharkov province.

Her husband had often told her, "Wars are won by whoever has the strongest nerves." During her sleepless polar white nights, Angelina often whispered these words, a German general's. She felt that her nerves were beginning to crack up. She was exhausted by the white silence of nature, the blank wall of uncaring humanity, the complete lack of any information and the worries, worries about her husband's fate. He might have simply died of hunger during his journey, he could have been killed by other fugitives, he could have been shot by special forces. It was only the Institution's unfailing attention to her and to her personal life that led Angelina to the happy conclusion that her husband had not been caught, that he was still a wanted man and, therefore, that her sufferings were not in vain.

She wanted to confide in someone who might understand her and give her some advice. She knew so little about the Far North. She would have liked to lighten the terrible weight on her mind, a weight that she felt was growing every day, every hour.

But whom could she confide in? She saw and suspected every man or woman as a spy, an informer, an observer, and her feelings were no illusion, for everyone she knew in all the settlements and towns of Kolyma had been summoned and warned by the Institution. All her acquaintances were eagerly waiting for her to open up.

After her first year there she made several attempts to contact her Kharkov friends by post. All her letters were copied and sent to the Institution in Kharkov.

By the end of the second year of her forced seclusion, she was almost destitute and she nearly despaired. All she knew was that her husband was still alive. Trying to get in touch with him, she sent letters addressed to Pavel Mikhailovich Krivoshei to the "poste restante" in every major city.

She got a reply in the form of a money transfer, and thereafter she received money every month. It wasn't much: five hundred to eight hundred, from various places, and from various persons. Krivoshei was too clever to send money from Mariupol, while the Institution was too experienced not to understand this. There was a geographical map used in similar circumstances to mark out "war operations," like the military's headquarter maps. The flags put on it marked the places from which money had been sent to an addressee in the Far North: they were all at places with a railway station near and to the north of Mariupol, and each place was used only once. The detectives now had only to make a small effort to find out the surnames of persons who had taken up residence in Mariupol over the last two years and then to compare the photographs.

That was how Krivoshei was arrested. His wife had been a bold and loyal helpmate. She had brought him, when he was in Arkagala, ID papers and more than fifty thousand rubles in cash.

As soon as Krivoshei was arrested, she was given permission to leave. Morally and physically exhausted, Angelina left Kolyma on the very first steamship.

Krivoshei served his second sentence as the manager of the chemical laboratory in the central hospital for prisoners. He enjoyed some small privileges allowed by the authorities, and he went on, as before, despising and fearing the politicals, being extremely cautious about whom he spoke to, cowardly and sensitive when others were talking. . . . This cowardice and extreme caution was not like the cowardice of the average citizen. It had a different basis. For Krivoshei anything political was alien and of no interest at all. He knew that it was this sort of criminality that cost the most in the camps and he refused to sacrifice his everyday, material, if not mental, peace, which was so dear, too dear, to him.

Krivoshei lived as well as worked in the laboratory, not in the camp barracks; privileged prisoners were allowed to do so.

His bunk, clean government-issue, was tucked away behind cupboards full of acids and alkalis. There were rumors that he enjoyed a particular, special form of debauchery in his cave, and that even the Irkutsk prostitute Sonechka, who would stop at nothing, was struck by his abilities and knowledge in this area. But all that may have been untrue, a camp put-up job.

There were quite a few free ladies who wanted to have an affair with Krivoshei, a man in his prime. But Krivoshei the prisoner was careful and strong-willed: he curtailed all the offers that the ladies so generously made. He didn't want any illicit, excessively risky connections that were likely to be punishable. He wanted peace and quiet.

Krivoshei was credited regularly with working days. They may not have amounted to much, but after a few years he was released, though prohibited from leaving Kolyma. That didn't bother him in the slightest. The very next day after he was released, it turned out that he had an excellent suit, and a coat that looked as if it had been tailored abroad, as well as a fine velour hat.

He found a job to match his qualifications as a chemical engineer in one of the plants: actually, he was a specialist in "high pressure." After working one week, he took leave "for family reasons," as his papers stated.

"I'm off to find a woman," said Krivoshei with a faint smile. "A woman . . . ! I'm off to the bride fair at Elgen. I intend to get married."

That same evening he returned with a woman.

Near Elgen, a state farm for women, there was a filling station at the edge of the settlement, in the country. All around, next to the barrels of gasoline, were bushes of willow and alder. This was where all the Elgen women, once released, used to gather. And the "bridegrooms," former prisoners in search of a mate, would drive up. Matchmaking didn't take long, like everything in Kolyma except a camp sentence; the trucks would drive back with the newlyweds. If necessary, they first got to know each other in the bushes, which were thick and tall enough for the purpose.

In winter, all this business moved to private apartments or cabins, and naturally the initial bride inspections took longer in the winter months than in summer.

"And what about Angelina?"

"I'm not in contact with her any more."

It wasn't worth inquiring whether this was true or not. Krivoshei was capable of responding with the splendid camp saying, "If you don't believe me, take it as a fairy tale!"

Once upon a time in the 1920s, at the dawn of the "misty youth" of the camp institutions, in the few zones known as concentration camps, escape attempts were not punished by any additional sentences and seem not to have been considered crimes. It was thought natural for a convict, a prisoner, to run away, but the guards were obliged to hunt him down, and that constituted a completely understandable and normal relationship between the two groups of people who occupied different sides of the prison bars and who were linked to each other by those bars. Those were romantic times, when, to use de Musset's words, "the future had not yet dawned, and the past no longer existed." In the mid-1920s, Ataman Krasnov, taken prisoner, had been released on parole.[31] But above all, this was a time when the limits of a Russian's patience had not yet been tested and had not been infinitely expanded, as happened in the second half of the 1930s.

The Criminal Code of 1926 with its notorious article 16 ("in correspondence")[32] and article 35, which designated a whole social group in society as "35ers,"[33] had not yet been written or devised.

The first camps were opened on a very dubious legal basis. There was a lot of improvisation, or what is best called local arbitrariness. The notorious Kurilka of the Solovetsky Islands, who tied prisoners to tree stumps in the taiga so that the mosquitoes would devour them was, of course, an empirical man. The empirical nature of camp life and of camp rules was bloody: after all, experiments were being conducted with people, with live material. The top authorities might approve of Kurilka's or someone similar's experiments, and then his actions would have been put in the camp rule books, in the orders and instructions. Or his actions might have been condemned, and then Kurilka himself would have been put on trial. In any case, there were no long sentences then. In the whole of the fourth sector of the Solovetsky Islands there were only two prisoners who had ten-year sentences, and they were considered celebrities. One was a former colonel of the gendarmerie, Rudenko, and the other was Mardzhanov, an officer who had served under the White Russian general Kappel. A five-year sentence was serious, and most sentences were for two or three years.

It was in those years, before the beginning of the thirties, that escape was not punishable with any sentence. If you escaped, good luck to you; if you were caught alive that, again, was your good luck. People were not often caught alive: a taste for human blood fired the guards' hatred for prisoners. A prisoner feared for his life, especially when he was being moved, or taken to camp in a group, when a careless word spoken to the escort guard could have you sent to the next world, "the moon," as the slang put it. Stricter rules applied to escorted parties of prisoners, so that the escort guards could get away with a lot. When prisoners in transit were taken from one officer's command to another's they used to demand that the authorities tie their hands behind their backs, for they saw this as some sort of guarantee for their lives. They hoped that then they would not be "written off," not listed under the sacramental formal cliché, "killed while attempting to escape."

Such killings were always investigated in a very slipshod way and, if the killer was intelligent enough to fire a second shot into the air, the matter always ended happily for the guard. His instructions prescribed a warning shot before aiming at a fugitive.

On the Vishera, in the fourth department of the Special Purpose Camps—the Urals branch of the Solovetsky Island camps—Nesterov, commandant of the administration, would come out to meet fugitives who had been caught. Nesterov was a stocky, squat man with pale white hands, stubby fingers thickly covered with black hair (he seemed to grow hair even on his palms).

The fugitives, dirty, hungry, badly beaten, tired, covered head to toe with gray dust from the road, were hurled down at Nesterov's feet.

"Right, come up, come nearer."

A fugitive would come nearer.

"So you decided to have some fun! That's good, that's good."

"Please forgive me, Ivan Spiridonych."

"I forgive you," Nesterov would say in a solemn lilting voice, as he got up from the porch. "I forgive you. But the state will not...."

His blue eyes turned cloudy and were covered by thread-like red veins. But his voice remained benevolent and kindly.

"Well, choose," said Nesterov idly. "A slapping or solitary...."

"A slapping, Ivan Spiridonych."

Nesterov's hairy fist flew over the fugitive's head, and the happy fugitive bounced away, wiping off his blood and spitting out his smashed teeth.

"Go to the barracks."

Nesterov could knock anyone to the ground with one blow, one slap. This was what he was famous for and took pride in.

The prisoner came off well, too. Nesterov's slapping absolved him from further punishment.

If the fugitive refused to settle things privately, and instead insisted on official retribution, on being held legally responsible, then he could expect the camp's solitary confinement, a prison with an iron floor, where one, two, or three months on solitary rations would seem far worse than Nesterov's slapping.

If the fugitive then survived, his escape attempt had no particularly nasty consequences, except possibly during selections for release, when prisons were "unloaded," and a former fugitive could no longer count on being successful.

As the camps grew, so did the number of escapes. Increasing the number of guards did not achieve anything: it was too expensive, and in those times there were very few people who wanted to work as camp guards.

The question of answering for escapes had been settled in an unsatisfactory, unreliable way. The decisions taken seemed childish.

Soon a new clarification from Moscow was read out: the days that a fugitive was on the run, and the days he was serving in solitary for trying to escape, would not be included in the calculation of days served toward his basic sentence.

This order aroused considerable dissatisfaction in the camp's accounting departments. They had to increase their staff, and the camp accountants were not always capable of such complicated arithmetic.

The order was implemented and read out to all the camp's inmates during roll calls.

Unfortunately, it didn't put off future escapees.

Every day, in the brief reports by squad commanders the figures for "on the run" increased, and the camp chief who read these summaries daily would frown more with each day.

After the camp boss's favorite, Kapitonov, a musician in the camp's wind band, hung his cornet on the branch of the nearest pine tree and ran away, the boss became mentally unbalanced. When Kapitonov had left the camp, he had been carrying his shiny instrument as if it were a pass.

Late that autumn three prisoners were killed while escaping. After they had been identified, the camp boss ordered their corpses to be exposed for three days and nights next to the camp gates through which the prisoners all went out to work. But even an official step as dramatic as this didn't reduce the number of escapes.

This was at the end of the 1920s. Then came the "reforging" of the White Sea canal. Concentration camps were renamed "corrective labor camps," the numbers of prisoners rose by hundreds of thousands, and escapes were now treated as separate crimes. The 1926 code had article 82, prescribing a sentence of an extra year as a punishment for escape.

This all happened on the mainland, not in Kolyma, where a camp had existed since 1932 but the question of escape did not arise until 1938. From that year on, the punishment for escape was increased: the prisoner's term would be extended by three whole years.

Why are the Kolyma years from 1932 to 1937 missing from the chronicle of escapes? This was the time when Eduard Petrovich Berzin was working there. The first Kolyma boss with the same rights as the highest party, Soviet and trade union authority over the district, the founder of Kolyma, who was shot in 1938 and rehabilitated in 1965, was once Felix Dzerzhinsky's secretary, and a commander of a division of Latvian sharpshooters. He was the one who exposed the famous Bruce Lockhart conspiracy. Berzin tried, with great success, to solve the problem of colonizing a district with harsh conditions and, simultaneously, to solve the problem of reforging and isolation. There were work credits, which allowed men to return home after two or three years of a ten-year sentence. There was excellent food, clothing, a working day in winter of four to six hours, and in summer of ten hours, there were colossal salaries for prisoners, which allowed them to help their families and to return to the mainland, fully provided for after their sentence. Berzin didn't believe that professional criminals could be reforged. He was too familiar with this elusive and vile human material. In the early years it was hard for thieves to get sent to Kolyma; those who succeeded in getting there had no regrets afterward.

The prisoner cemeteries dating from that time are so few that you might think Kolyma inmates were immortal.

Nobody actually escaped from Kolyma; that would have been crazy, pointless.

Those few years were the golden age of Kolyma, which that unmasked spy and genuine enemy of the people Nikolai Yezhov spoke of with such indignation at a session of the Central Executive Committee of the USSR, just before the Yezhov terror began.

In 1938 Kolyma was transformed into a special camp for recidivists and for Trotskyists. Escape attempts were now punishable by three years.

"But how did you escape? You didn't have a map or a compass."

"We just escaped. Aleksandr promised to lead us out...."

We were waiting to be sent off on a transit party. There were three failed escapees: Nikolai Karev, a twenty-five-year-old fellow who used to be a journalist in Leningrad; Fiodor Vasiliev, the same age, a book-keeper from Rostov; and Aleksandr Kotelnikov, a Kamchadal. Aleksandr was a Kolyma aborigine, a native Kamchadal, by profession a reindeer herder, who had been condemned in Kolyma for stealing a load belonging to the state. He was about fifty, but could have been much older; it's very hard to tell a Yakut's, a Chukchi's, a Kamchadal's, or an Evenk's age just by their looks. Aleksandr spoke Russian well, it was just the sound "sh" that he could never pronounce—he replaced it with an "s," as in all the dialects of the Chukotsk peninsula. He had some idea who Pushkin and Nekrasov were, he'd been to Khabarovsk. In short, he was an experienced traveler, but he was a romantic at heart, and his eyes blazed in a way that was far too youthful, even childlike.

It was he who offered to lead his new young friends out of imprisonment.

"I told them: get nearer to America, let's go to America, but they wanted to go to the mainland, so I led them to the mainland. You have to get to the Chukchi, to the Chukchi nomads. The Chukchi used to be here, they left, as soon as Russians came to them.... It was too late."

The fugitives were on the run for just four days. They escaped at the beginning of September, wearing shoes, summer clothes, certain they would reach Chukotka settlements where, Aleksandr had assured them, they would find help and friendship.

But it snowed, thick and early snow. Aleksandr went to an Evenki settlement to buy reindeer-skin boots. He bought them, and by evening a squad of special operations men had caught the fugitives.

"Tungus people are enemies, traitors," said Aleksandr, spitting.

The old reindeer herder had offered to lead Karev and Vasiliev out of the taiga without any payment. He wasn't downcast at getting an extra three-year sentence.

"When spring comes, they'll let me go to the mines to work, and I'll leave again."

To pass the time he taught Karev and Vasiliev the Chukot language, Kamchadal. Karev was, of course, the instigator of this escape that was doomed to failure. His whole figure, which his modulated velvet voice made theatrical even in this prison-camp setting, gave off an air of frivolity that didn't really amount to risk-taking. Each day taught him better how hopeless such attempts were, and he was more and more often plunged in thought as he grew weaker.

Vasiliev was simply a good comrade, ready to share any fate his friend suffered. They had all tried to escape in their first year of imprisonment, while they still had their illusions . . . and physical strength.

One white summer night twelve cans of meat disappeared from the kitchen tent of a geologists' nomadic settlement. This loss was extremely mysterious. All forty workmen and technicians were free people, making decent money. They were unlikely to need such things as canned meat. Even if it had been fabulously valuable canned food, there was nowhere they could sell it in this remote, endless forest. The bear explanation was also immediately excluded, since nothing in the kitchen had been displaced. It might have been thought that someone had done this on purpose, to spite the cook who was in charge of kitchen supplies, although the cook, a very easygoing man, denied that there could be an enemy of his hiding among his forty comrades so as to taunt him. But if that assumption was wrong, only one explanation was left. To test that, the expedition's clerk of works, Kasayev, took two of his most energetic workmen with him, arming them with knives, and grabbing for himself the only firearm: a small-caliber rifle. They set off to inspect their surroundings, which were grayish-brown ravines without a trace of greenery, leading up to an extensive limestone plateau. The geologists' settlement seemed to be in a pit, on the green banks of a river.

It didn't take long to solve the mystery. About two hours later, when they had slowly climbed up to the plateau, one of the more sharp-sighted workmen stretched out a hand: he had seen a moving point on the horizon. They moved along the edge of a patch of precarious young tufa, stone that was not yet fully petrified and was like white butter, tasting unpleasantly salty. Their feet got stuck in it, as if in a bog, and their boots, which had sunk into the semi-liquid, oleaginous stone, seemed to be covered in white paint. It was easy to go around the edge, and about an hour and a half later they caught up with a man. He was dressed in rags that were once a pea jacket and in torn quilted trousers with his knees showing through. Both trouser legs had been cut short to make footwear, which had now become torn and worn out. For the same reason he had at an earlier point cut off and worn out the sleeves of his pea jacket. Any leather shoes or rubber boots he had worn had long since been ruined by the stones and branches; he had apparently thrown them away.

He was bearded, hairy, pale after his unbearable suffering. He had a desperate form of diarrhea. There were eleven untouched cans of food lying there on the stones. One had been smashed open on the rocks and consumed the day before.

He had been walking for a month, heading for Magadan, circling in the forest like an oarsman on a lake in thick fog and, once astray, losing all sense of direction. He had been walking at random until he stumbled on the expedition, at a time when he had lost all his strength. He had been catching field mice and voles and eating grass. He had managed to keep going until the previous day. He had then noticed smoke, waited for night to fall and in the morning crawled onto the plateau. He had taken the matches from the kitchen, but he had no need for them. He ate the canned meat, and a terrible thirst and his dried-out mouth had forced him to come down another narrow valley to a stream. Once there, he drank and drank the delicious cold water. Twenty-four hours later his face swelled up and his intestines, now that they were upset, deprived him of his last ounce of strength.

He was glad of any end to his journey.

The other fugitive, whom special operations men dragged out from the taiga to the same outpost, was an important person. He had taken part in a group escape from a nearby mine after the mine boss had been robbed and murdered; he was the last of the ten who had escaped. Two had been killed, seven had been caught, and this last man was hunted down on the twenty-first day. He had no footwear, and his cracked soles were bleeding. In his words, he had eaten in the course of a week just one tiny fish from a dried-up stream, a fish that took him several hours to catch, as he was weak with hunger. His face was swollen and drained of blood. The guards took great care of him, his diet and his recovery: they called in the paramedic on the expedition and ordered him without fail to see that the fugitive was looked after. The fugitive lived in the expedition's bathhouse for three whole days and finally, his hair cut, his face shaved, himself washed and well-fed, he was taken away by the operations squad for an interrogation that could only end with execution by shooting. The fugitive was aware of this, but he didn't care, for he was an experienced prisoner who had long before crossed the boundary of life in the camps, after which everyone becomes a fatalist and just lives, following the current. He was accompanied all the time by escort guards, by soldiers, who wouldn't let him talk to anyone. Every evening he sat on the bathhouse porch and watched the enormous cherry-colored sunset. The fire of the evening sun was reflected in his eyes, and his eyes seemed to be on fire: it was a very beautiful spectacle.

In Orotukan, a Kolyma settlement, there is a monument to Tatiana Malandina, and the Orotukan club also bears her name. She was a contract worker, a member of the Komsomol, who fell into the clutches of criminals on the run. They robbed and gang-raped her, in the revolting criminal expression "choir-raped" her, then murdered her in the taiga a few hundred meters from the settlement. This happened in 1938, and the authorities tried, but failed, to spread rumors that she had been murdered by Trotskyists. Slander of that kind was far too absurd. It outraged even the murdered girl's uncle, Lieutenant Malandin, for whom the death of his niece completely altered his attitude to thieves and to other kinds of prisoners, so that he hated the former and made allowances for the latter.

Both these fugitives were caught when they were running out of strength. Another fugitive, detained by a group of workmen on a path near some trial mining pits, behaved differently. Heavy rain had been falling constantly for three days, and a group of workmen, protecting themselves with special tarpaulin clothing—jackets and trousers—set off to see if their little tent had been damaged by the rain. The tent housed a kitchen with their crockery and food, a portable forge with an anvil, a portable kiln, and a supply of drilling tools. The forge and kitchen were on the dried-up bed of a mountain stream in a ravine about three kilometers from their living quarters.

Mountain rivers swell up very violently after rain, and the rain could be expected to play some dirty tricks. But what the men saw took them utterly aback. There was nothing there. There was no forge where the tools—drills, drill bits, pickaxes, spades, blacksmith's equipment—for a whole area had been kept. There was no kitchen and their supply of food for the whole summer was gone. There were no pots, no crockery, there was nothing. The ravine was quite changed: all the stones had been rearranged or brought down from somewhere by the furious waters. Everything that was there before had been swept away by the stream, and the workmen walked along the banks of the stream all the way to the river into which the stream fell—about six or seven kilometers, and didn't find a single piece of iron. Much later, when the water level went down, they found an enamel bowl from the settlement refectory, which had been crushed and turned inside out, on the riverbank in the willows, which were half-buried in sand. That was the only thing left after the rainstorm and the high water.

On their way home the workmen came across a man in jersey-lined boots, wearing a cape that was soaking wet and carrying a big shoulder bag.

"Are you a fugitive?" Vaska Rybin, one of the prospectors' ditch-diggers, asked.

"Yes," the man asked, half affirmatively. "I'd like to get dry...."

"All right, come to our place. We have a hot stove." In summer the iron stoves were kept stoked all the time in the big tent where all forty workmen lived.

The fugitive took off his boots, hung his foot wrappings around the stove, took out a tin cigarette case, sprinkled some tobacco in a piece of newspaper, and lit up.

"Where are you going in rain like this?"

"Heading for Magadan."

"Are you hungry?"

"What have you got?"

Soup and pearl-barley porridge didn't tempt the fugitive. He undid his bag and took out a piece of sausage.

"Well, pal," said Rybin. "You're not a real escapee."

An older workman, Vasili Kochetov, the deputy foreman, got up.

"Where are you off to?" Rybin asked him.

"To take a leak." Then he stepped over the board that was the tent's threshold.

Rybin laughed.

"I'll tell you what, pal," he said to the fugitive. "Get your things together now and go wherever you were going. He," and he meant Kochetov, "has run off to tell the authorities. To see you get detained, in other words. Well, we haven't got any armed guards, so don't be afraid, just keep on going. Here's some bread for you to take, and a packet of tobacco. The rain's not so heavy now, luckily for you. Head straight for the big hill, you can't go wrong."

The fugitive said nothing. He wrapped the dry ends of his still-wet foot wrappings around his feet, pulled on his boots, flung the bag over his shoulder and left.

Ten minutes later the piece of tarpaulin that served as a door was flung back and people in authority pushed in. It was Kasayev, the clerk of works, with a small-caliber rifle over his shoulder, two guards, and Kochetov, who was the last to enter the tent.

Kasayev stood there silently until he had gotten used to the darkness in the tent, then he looked around. Nobody paid attention to the newcomers. Everyone got on with what they were doing: sleeping, mending clothes, carving strange figures—the usual erotic studies—out of dead branches with a knife—or playing snap with homemade cards. . . .

Rybin was putting a soot-stained pot made from a tin can onto the burning coals in the stove; it was something he had boiled up.

"Where's the fugitive?" yelled Kasayev.

"He's gone," Rybin said calmly. "He took his things and left. What was I supposed to do—hold onto him?"

"But he didn't have a coat," shouted Kochetov. "He was thinking of going to sleep."

"But you were going to take a leak, too, and where did you run off to in that rain?" replied Rybin.

"Go home," said Kasayev. "And you, Rybin, watch out. This is going to end badly."

"What can you do to me?" asked Rybin, moving closer to Kasayev. "Put a spell on me? Or cut my throat when I'm asleep? Is that it?"

The clerk of works and the guards left.

This was a short lyrical episode in a monotonously murky tale of Kolyma fugitives.

The head of an expedition, alarmed by constant visits by fugitives—three within a month—tried in vain to get the authorities to organize a post with armed soldiers for his expedition. The administration wouldn't go to the expense of doing this for free workers, and they left the expedition chief to deal with any fugitives with whatever means he had at hand. Even though by now, apart from Kasayev's small-caliber rifle, the settlement also had at its disposal two double-barrel breech-loading shotguns, with cartridges containing bullets made of lead, like those used to shoot bears, everyone nevertheless realized that if they were attacked by desperate, starving escaped prisoners, those bullets were not going to be much help.

The expedition chief was an experienced man. Suddenly two guard towers were built on his site, looking just like the towers placed at every corner of real camp zones.

This was clever camouflage. The fake guard towers were meant to convince escaped prisoners that the expedition had armed guards.

The chief's assumptions were evidently right. No more fugitives visited this expedition, which was only two hundred kilometers from Magadan.

When mining of metal number one, gold, was moved to the Chai-Uryinsky valley along the path that Krivoshei had once taken, dozens of fugitives took this route. This was the shortest way to the "mainland," but then the authorities knew that too. The number of "secret sites" and armed posts was increased sharply. The hunt for fugitives was in full flow. Flying squads combed the taiga and blocked every "release by the green Prosecutor" as escapes were called. The green Prosecutor was releasing fewer and fewer, until finally he was releasing nobody.

Fugitives, when caught, were usually killed on the spot, and quite a few corpses lay in the Arkagala morgue, waiting to be identified, which was done when the recordkeepers came to take the corpses' fingerprints.

In a forest ten kilometers from the Arkagala coal mine, in the Kadykchan settlement, famous because of the mighty layers of coal—eight, thirteen, and twenty-one meters thick—that rose here almost to the surface, a special armed post was set up where soldiers slept and ate, a post that was in fact a base.

In summer 1940 the head of this flying squad was a young lance corporal, Postnikov, a man with a strong thirst for killing, who did his job with eagerness, enthusiasm, and passion. He personally captured five fugitives in one go and got a medal for it as well as the monetary award usual in such cases. The award was given whether the escaped prisoners were alive or dead, so that it made no sense at all to deliver a captive alive.

On a pale August morning Postnikov and his soldiers came across an escaped prisoner walking toward a stream where an ambush was waiting.

Postnikov fired his Mauser and killed the fugitive. It was decided not to drag him to the settlement, but to abandon him in the taiga: there were too many lynx and bear prints around.

Postnikov took an ax and cut off both of the fugitive's hands, so that the recordkeepers could take the fingerprints, then he put the two severed hands in his bag and set off home to compose his usual report on a successful hunt.

This report was sent off the same day—one soldier took the package, while Postnikov gave the others the day off to celebrate his success....

That night the corpse got up and, pressing the bloody stumps of his arms against his chest, followed their footprints out of the taiga and somehow got as far as the tent where the prisoner-workmen were staying. He stood by the door, his face white and bloodless, his blue eyes uncannily crazed, his body bent double, slumped against the doorframe. Looking sullen, he mumbled something. He was extremely feverish and trembling. His quilted jacket, his trousers, and rubber boots were stained black with blood. They gave him some hot soup, bandaged his horrible arms with rags, and led him off to the outpatients' clinic. But by now soldiers were running from the checkpoint's hut, and Lance Corporal Postnikov was running up too.

The soldiers led the fugitive off somewhere, but not to any hospital or clinic. Nobody heard any more about the escapee whose hands had been hacked off.

Postnikov and all his men operated until the first snow. After the first frosts, when there was less detective work needed in the taiga, the group was moved away from Arkagala.

Escaping is a great test of character, of self-control, of willpower, of physical and mental endurance. Conceivably, it's easier to choose the right comrades for even a winter at the North Pole or any expedition, than for an escape attempt.

What's worst is the hunger, the acute hunger, a constant menace to the fugitive. If you take into account that it is hunger that makes someone attempt to escape and that, therefore, he isn't afraid of it, then there is another unspeakable danger that the escaped prisoner may have to face: he may be eaten by his own comrades. Cases of cannibalism among fugitives are, of course, rare. But they do occur and I suspect that there isn't a single Kolyma old hand, if he's been in the Far North for ten years or so, who hasn't come across cannibals who have gotten a sentence for murdering their fellow escapees, for eating human flesh.

In the central hospital there was a patient called Soloviov, who stayed for a long period with chronic osteomyelitis of the hip. Osteomyelitis, an inflammation of the bone marrow, occurred after a bullet wound to the bone, a wound that Soloviov himself had artfully prevented from healing. Condemned for attempting to escape and for cannibalism, Soloviov was putting on the brakes to stay in the hospital. He was happy to tell people how he and a comrade, preparing to escape, deliberately invited a third man "in case we got hungry."

The escapees were on the run for a long time, about a month. When the third man had been killed and partially eaten, partially "roasted for the road," the two murderers went off in different directions, each afraid of being killed one night or another.

One also met other cannibals. They were the most ordinary of men. There is no mark of Cain on a cannibal and, until you know their biography in detail, everything looks fine. But even if you find out about the cannibalism, you are not put off, you don't feel outrage. There just isn't the physical strength for revulsion or indignation; there is just no room for such fine feelings to flourish. In any case, the story of normal polar expeditions in our times is not without similar actions. The mysterious death of the Swedish scientist Malmgren, who took part in Nobile's expedition,[34] is still fresh in our memory.

All the escape attempts we have been describing are attempts to get back home, to the mainland, the goal being to break free of the taiga's sticky paws and get to Russia. They all end the same way: nobody could get out of the Far North. The failure and hopelessness of such enterprises, on the one hand, and, on the other hand, the irresistible nostalgia for freedom, the hatred and revulsion aroused by forced labor, forced manual labor—these are the only things that the camp can induce in a prisoner. On the gates of every camp zone was the mocking slogan: "Labor is a matter of honor, a matter of glory, a matter of valor and heroism," together with the name of the author[35] of these words. The inscription was made according to special instructions and it was obligatory for every section of the camps.

It was this longing for freedom, this burning desire to find oneself in a forest where there was no barbed wire, no guard towers with rifle barrels shining in the sun, no beatings, no endless workdays without sleep or rest, that gave rise to a special kind of escape attempt.

A prisoner senses that he is doomed. In a month or two he will die, as his comrades are dying before his eyes.

He will not escape death, but he would like to die free, not at the pit face, in a ditch, after collapsing from tiredness and hunger.

In summer the mine work is harder than in winter. Sand is washed in summer. The prisoner's weakened brain suggests a way out that would make it possible to hold out for the summer and spend the winter warm and in a building.

That is how the idea of "leaving for the ice" is born, as these escapes along the highway are so colorfully called.

Two, three, or four prisoners run into the taiga, into the mountains, and settle in some cave or bear's den a few kilometers from the main highway, which is an enormous route stretching two thousand kilometers and cutting through the whole of Kolyma.

The fugitive has a supply of matches, tobacco, food, and clothing: whatever he can get together for his escape. However, it is almost never possible to collect things in advance, and if it were, that would attract suspicion and thus would wreck the escape plans.

Sometimes, the night before the escape, they rob the camp shop, or stall, as it's called in the camp, and leave for the mountains with their stolen food. Mostly, though, people run away with nothing, to live off the land. Living off the land, however, does not mean eating grass, roots, mice, and chipmunks.

Trucks move up and down the enormous highway day and night. Many of these trucks are carrying food supplies. In the mountains the road is one of constant changes in gradient, and trucks crawl slowly up to a pass. To leap onto a truck carrying flour and throw off a couple of sacks gives you a food supply for the whole summer. And flour is not the only thing being transported. After the first robberies trucks carrying food began to be sent off with armed convoys, but not every truck had this protection.

Apart from daylight robbery on the highway, fugitives would rob the settlements nearest to their den, small roadside outposts where two or three people lived and maintained the highway. The bigger and bolder groups of fugitives would stop trucks and rob both the passengers and the loads.

If they were lucky these escapees recovered both physically and "spiritually" in the course of the summer.

If they laid their bonfires carefully, and the traces of their loot were thoroughly eliminated, for the guards were vigilant and sharp-sighted, the fugitives could live until late autumn. Subzero temperatures and snow would force them out of the bare, inhospitable forest. The aspens and poplars lost their leaves, the larches dropped their rust-colored needles onto the cold, dirty moss. The fugitives no longer had the strength to hold out, and they came out onto the highway and surrendered at the nearest checkpoint. They were arrested and tried, not always quickly, for winter had set in some time before, and they were given a sentence for escaping. Then they joined the ranks of the workmen at the mine where (if they happened to go back to the same mine they had fled) they found their former brigade workmates were no longer there. They'd either died or, as semi-corpses, had gone to join invalid squads.

In 1939 the first "relief teams" and "sanatorium points" were set up for debilitated workmen. But since it would have required several years, not several days, to "recover," these innovations did not have the desired effect of restoring working strength. On the other hand, Kolyma's inhabitants, who believed that as long as a prisoner kept his sense of irony, he would remain human, learned by heart a sly rhyme:

> First Convalescent Centers, then the Teams,
> A tag on your ankle, and now sweet dreams!

A tag with the number of the case file was tied to the left leg of a prisoner when he was buried.

The fugitive, however, remained healthy and alive, even if he got five extra years (unless the interrogator managed to stitch him up for robbing trucks), for it made no real difference whether you had a sentence of five, ten, fifteen, or twenty years, because it was impossible to work at a pit face even for five years. Five weeks was the limit for a mine pit face.

These "spa holiday" escapes became more common, as did the robberies and the murders. But it wasn't the robberies or the murders that irritated the top authorities, who were used to dealing with paper and figures, not with living people.

The figures told them that the value of what was lost to robbery and murder was not worth counting, for it was far less than the value of lost working hours and days.

"Spa holiday" escapes were what the authorities were most frightened by. Article 82 of the Criminal Code was now wholly forgotten and was never applied again.

Escape attempts were now to be treated as crimes against good order, against the administration, the state: as political acts.

Fugitives began to be charged under article 58, no more and no less, on the same level as traitors to the motherland. And the paragraph of article 58 that was chosen was widely known to the judiciary, for it had earlier been used in the Mines' Trial of wreckers.[36] This was paragraph 14 of article 58: "counterrevolutionary sabotage." An escape was a refusal to work, and refusal to work was counterrevolutionary sabotage. Fugitives were now to be tried under this article and paragraph. Ten years for attempting to escape became the minimum additional sentence. A second escape was punishable by twenty-five years.

That didn't put anyone off and didn't reduce the number of escapes or of robberies.

At the same time any avoidance of work or refusal to work was also interpreted as sabotage, and the punishment for refusing to work, the worst camp crime, kept on being increased. "Twenty-five years imprisonment, plus five years' deprivation of civic rights" was the formula applied for many years during and after the war in sentencing those who refused work and those who tried to escape.

The specific features that distinguish Kolyma escapes from more ordinary escapes do not make them any less difficult. It may be easy, in the overwhelming majority of cases, to overstep the limit that turns absence without leave into an escape, but the difficulties increase with every day, with every hour that a man moves across the inhospitable environment of the Far North, hostile to anything that lives. The extremely short periods for escaping, the very brief seasons, force the fugitive to make hurried preparations, and to cover, in a short time, distances that are enormous and difficult. Bears and lynxes pose little danger to a fugitive. He perishes because of his own helplessness in this harsh region where he has very few ways to struggle for his life.

The local terrain is agonizing for anyone traveling on foot. One mountain pass comes after the other, ravine after ravine. The animal paths are barely noticeable, the ground in the thin, ugly taiga forest is just unstable wet moss. It is risky to sleep without a campfire: the underground cold of the permafrost doesn't allow the rocks to get warm during the day. There is no food on the journey except for dry reindeer moss, which can be ground up and mixed with flour and then baked into flat bread. It is no easy task to kill a ptarmigan or a nutcracker with a stick. Mushrooms and berries are not very nourishing on a journey, and in any case they are only found at the end of the short summer season, which means that the fugitive must take his entire supply of food with him from the camp.

The taiga paths are hard enough for a fugitive, but the preparations for escape are even harder. Any day, any hour the would-be fugitive may be unmasked and betrayed to the authorities by his fellow prisoners. The main danger is not the guards or the wardens, but fellow prisoners who live alongside the would-be fugitive for twenty-four hours a day.

Every fugitive knows that not only will nobody help him if they notice anything suspicious, but that they will take notice of anything they see. A prisoner may be on his last legs, starving and exhausted, but he will crawl or stagger to the guardhouse in order to denounce and unmask a comrade. This is done for a reason: the boss may reward him with tobacco, may praise him, may say thank you. The informer portrays his own cowardice and vileness as something like his duty. The only people he won't denounce are the gangsters, because he is afraid of getting stabbed with a knife or being strangled with a piece of rope.

A mass escape where there are more than two or three taking part, unless it is something as elemental and sudden as a mutiny, is almost unthinkable. It would be impossible to plan, given the people who fill the camps, depraved, mercenary, starving, and full of mutual loathing.

It is significant that the only mass escape ever prepared in advance, however it was to end, succeeded because that part of the camp where the escapees came from had none of the old Kolyma hands who were so poisoned and degraded by their experience, so debased by hunger, cold, and beatings—and therefore there was nobody who might have betrayed the fugitives to the authorities.

In *One-Story America* Ilf and Petrov point out, half jokingly, half seriously, a Russian national characteristic, something that is innate to Russian nature: an irresistible urge to complain. This national feature, when distorted by the crooked mirror of camp life, finds its outlet in denouncing one's fellow man.

An escape can suddenly flare up as an improvisation, like a natural catastrophe or a forest fire, which makes the fate of those involved—casual, peaceful bystanders, swept into the vortex of action almost against their own will—even more tragic.

None of them had yet formed a proper idea of the treachery of a Kolyma autumn, not realizing that the scarlet blazing of the leaves, the grass, and the trees lasts for no more than two or three days, and then from a high, pale-blue sky, just slightly brighter than usual, fine, cold snow can suddenly start to fall. None of the fugitives knew what to make of the green branches of dwarf pine that suddenly flatten themselves to the ground, clinging to the earth before the fugitives' eyes, or what to make of the sudden flight of the fish downstream.

Nobody knew whether there were any settlements in the taiga or, if so, what they might be like. Those who came from the Far East or from Siberia made the mistake of relying on their knowledge of the taiga and their hunting skills.

At the end of a postwar autumn an open truck carrying twenty-five prisoners was making its way to a hard-labor camp. A few dozen kilometers from their destination, the prisoners hurled themselves at the guards, disarmed them and went on the run, all twenty-five of them.

It was snowing, and the snow was mercilessly icy. The fugitives had no warm clothes. The dogs quickly caught their scent: they had split into four groups. The group armed with guns taken from the guards was shot dead. Two groups were caught a day later, and the last group on the fourth day. The latter were sent straight to the hospital; they all had fourth-degree frostbite on both hands and feet. The Kolyma sub-zero temperatures and Kolyma nature were always on the side of the authorities and always hostile to any solitary fugitive.

The fugitives spent a long time in a separate hospital ward, with a guard by the door. The hospital was for prisoners, but not for hard-labor ones. All five men were amputees, losing a hand or a foot; two of them lost both feet.

That was how the Kolyma cold dealt with hasty and naïve novices.

Lieutenant Colonel Yanovsky understood this very well. He had, in fact, been a lieutenant colonel in the war. Here he was just prisoner Yanovsky, the cultural organizer of a big camp section. This section was set up right after the war and included only new prisoners, war criminals, men who had served under General Vlasov and ex-prisoners of war who had served in German units or as policemen under German occupation, or those who had lived in villages occupied by the Germans and were suspected of collaboration.

They included men who had recent experience of war, of confronting death every day. They were used to risk, to using their animal instincts in fighting for their lives. They were experienced killers.

They included men who had already escaped from German, Russian, and British captivity... people who were used to staking their lives on a card, people whose boldness was nurtured by example and training. They were scouts and soldiers who were trained to kill. They continued the war in these new circumstances, a war for themselves against the state.

The authorities were used to dealing with submissive Trotskyists and did not suspect that they were now dealing with men of deeds, of action above all.

A few months before the events we are about to describe, this camp had been visited by a top boss. When he found out more about the life the new arrivals were leading and their work in production, the boss felt indignant that cultural work, amateur shows in the camp, left much to be desired. But former Lieutenant Colonel Yanovsky, the camp's cultural organizer, respectfully reported: "Don't worry, we are rehearsing for a concert all Kolyma will be talking about."

That was a very risky thing to say, but nobody paid any attention at the time, and, in fact, Yanovsky had been sure they would not.

All that winter the participants in the escape planned for spring slowly, one by one getting promoted to jobs in the camp support staff. The labor organizer, the barracks elder, the paramedic, the hairdresser, and the foreman—all the staff posts for prisoners were taken by men chosen by Yanovsky himself. They included pilots, drivers, scouts: all the men who could make a daringly planned escape succeed. The Kolyma conditions were studied, nobody overlooked the difficulties, and nobody made any mistakes. Their aim was freedom, or the good fortune to die in battle with weapons in their hands, rather than in the camp bunks, from starvation or beatings.

Yanovsky realized how important, how vital it was for his comrades to keep up their physical strength and endurance, as well as their moral and spiritual strength. If you had a job on the camp support staff, you could be fed well enough not to grow weaker.

The usual silent Kolyma spring came. No birds sang, not a drop of rain fell. The larches put on their bright-green young needles, the thin bare forest seemed to get thicker, the trees grew closer to one another, hiding people and animals in their branches. The white, or rather, pale-lilac nights began.

The guardhouse by the camp gates had two doors, one leading out of, and one leading into the camp: such were the architectural specifications of this sort of building. Two guards were on duty on each shift.

At precisely five in the morning, there was a knock on the guardhouse window. The duty guard looked through the glass and saw that the camp cook Soldatov had come for the key to the pantry. The key was kept in the guardhouse, on a hook hammered into the wall. For the last few months the cook had come here every day at precisely five in the morning to fetch the keys. The duty guard unhooked the door and let Soldatov in. The second guard was not there: he had just left by the outer door. The apartment where he and his family lived was about three hundred meters from the guardhouse.

Everything had been worked out in advance, and the author of this show was watching through the little window the first act of a spectacle he had planned long ago. He saw everything that had been rehearsed a thousand times in his imagination and reason become living flesh and blood.

The cook went toward the wall where the key was hanging, and there was another knock at the door. The guard knew the man who was knocking. It was prisoner Shevtsov, a mechanic and weapons expert who had often repaired machine guns, rifles, and pistols for the squad; he was one of their men.

At that very moment Soldatov rushed the guard from behind and strangled him, with the assistance of Shevtsov, who had now come into the guardhouse. They threw the corpse under a trestle bed in the corner of the guardhouse, and hid it behind a pile of firewood. Soldatov and Shevtsov pulled off the dead man's greatcoat, hat, and boots. Then Soldatov, dressed in a guard's uniform and armed with a revolver, sat at the duty desk. The second guard now returned. Before he could figure out what was happening, he too was strangled. Shevtsov put on his clothes.

Suddenly, the wife of the second guard came into the guardhouse. They didn't kill her: they just bound her hand and foot, gagged her, and placed her next to the dead guards.

An escort guard had now brought a brigade of workmen, and he came into the guardhouse to sign for the people he had been entrusted with. He too was killed. Another rifle and another greatcoat were thus obtained.

People were now moving around the yard by the guardhouse, as was to be expected when they were lined up for work. Lieutenant Colonel Yanovsky took over command.

The area around the guard towers at the nearest corners of the zone was in the field of fire. There were sentries in both towers, but in the murky morning light after a white night the sentries saw nothing suspicious in the clearing by the guardhouse. As usual, the duty guard opened the gates, counted the men, as he always did, and two escort guards came out to take over the brigade. Now the guards lined up a small brigade of just ten, no, nine men, and led them off. . . . The fact that this brigade turned off the road onto a path didn't alarm the sentries either. The path led past the guards' squad, and guards had sometimes taken workmen that way before, if the lineup for work was delayed.

The brigade walked past the guards' squad. When the sleepy duty guard saw them through the open door, he only had time to wonder why the brigade was being led down the path in single file, and not in the usual lines along the road, before he was knocked out and disarmed, and the "brigade" then rushed to the pyramid of rifles standing right in front of the duty guards, in the entrance to the barracks.

Armed with an automatic, Yanovsky flung open the door to a room where forty guards, young professionals in the escort-guard service, were sleeping. A round of automatic fire aimed at the ceiling made them all lie down on the floor under their bunks. Handing his automatic to Shevtsov, Yanovsky went out into the yard where his men had broken into the guard squad's stores and were now pulling out supplies of food, weapons, and ammunition.

The sentries in the towers decided not to open fire. Later, they said that it was impossible to see or understand what was happening in the guards' squad. Nobody believed their statements, and the sentries were consequently punished.

The fugitives took their time getting ready. Yanovsky ordered them to carry only weapons and ammunition, as many cartridges as possible, but as far as food was concerned, only biscuits and chocolate. Nikolsky the paramedic stuffed his bag with individual Red Cross packets. Everyone put on their new military uniforms and chose the right size of boots from the squad's storeroom.

While they were leaving the camp in a line, like prisoners, while they were raiding the guards' squad, they realized that not everyone who was to take part was there. Lieutenant Colonel Yanovsky's friend Piotr Kuznetsov, a foreman, was missing. He had unexpectedly been transferred to the night shift instead of the regular foreman, who had fallen ill. Yanovsky wouldn't leave without his comrade. They had been through a lot and planned a lot together. The foreman was summoned. Kuznetsov came and changed into a soldier's uniform. The commander of the squad that had been raided and the chief of the camp stayed in their apartments until they were told by their orderlies that the fugitives had left the camp's territory.

The telephone cable had been cut, and a message about the escape could be sent to the nearest camp department only after the fugitives had reached the main highway, Kolyma's central road.

As they emerged onto the highway, the fugitives stopped the first empty truck. The driver, threatened with a revolver, got out of the cab, and Kobaridze, a fighter pilot, took over the wheel. Yanovsky got into the cab next to Kobaridze and unfolded on his lap a map taken from the guards' squad. The truck sped off to Seimchan, the nearest airfield. To hijack a plane and fly away!

Second, third, fourth left turn. Fifth turn!

The truck turned left off the main highway and sped over a seething river, along a precarious rocky cornice, on a narrow, stony, winding road that crackled under the wheels. Kobaridze slowed down. It wouldn't have taken a second to fly off at an angle into the water seventy feet below. They could see the tiny, toylike houses of an expedition down below, by the stream. The road bent, as it made its way around rock after rock, and then went downhill as it came down from the pass. Settlement houses loomed up out of the taiga. They were now quite near, and Yanovsky saw through the cab's windshield a soldier running toward the truck with his rifle cradled in his hands.

The soldier leapt to one side, the truck rushed past him, and immediately afterward a short round of shots could be heard, fired at the departing fugitives. The guards had now been warned.

Yanovsky had already made his decision: ten kilometers or so down the road Kobaridze put on the brakes. The fugitives abandoned the truck, and, striding across the moss-covered drainage ditch, entered the taiga and vanished. It was still about another seventy kilometers to the airfield. Yanovsky decided to head across country.

They spent the night all together in a cave not far from a small mountain stream; they warmed themselves on each other's bodies and put out sentries.

The next morning, no sooner had the escapees set off than they came across special operations men: a local detachment was combing the forest. Four special operations men were killed by the fugitives' first shots. Yanovsky ordered his men to set fire to the forest: the wind was blowing in the direction of their pursuers. The fugitives moved on.

By now truckloads of soldiers were speeding up and down the Kolyma roads. An invisible army of regular troops had rushed to help the camp guards and the special operations men. Dozens of military vehicles were patrolling the central highway.

For scores of kilometers the road to Seimchan was crowded with military units. The top Kolyma authorities were personally directing this unusual operation.

They had guessed what Yanovsky's plan would be and had mobilized such a quantity of regular troops to guard the airfield that they had trouble finding room for them all on the approaches to it.

By the evening of the second day, Yanovsky's group had been discovered again: they joined battle. The troops left ten dead on the battlefield. Yanovsky exploited the direction of the wind and again set fire to the taiga and got away, this time by crossing a large mountain stream. The fugitives' camp for the third night, when they still hadn't lost a single man, was chosen by Yanovsky. It was in a marsh, with haystacks in the middle.

The fugitives spent the night in the haystacks, and when the white night was over, when the taiga sun lit up the crowns of the trees, they could see that the marsh was surrounded by soldiers. Without really bothering to take cover, soldiers were running from tree to tree.

The commander of the squad the fugitives had attacked at the beginning of their campaign waved a rag and shouted, "Surrender, you're surrounded. You've got nowhere to hide...."

Shevtsov stuck his head out of a haystack. "You're right. Come and take my weapon...."

The squad commander jumped onto the track in the marsh and ran toward the haystacks. He rocked from side to side, dropped his cap and fell facedown into a puddle in the marsh. Shevtsov's bullet had hit him in the forehead.

Chaotic fire then broke out everywhere. Commands could be heard, soldiers rushed the stacks from all sides, but the ring of defenders, invisible fugitives hidden in hay, cut the attack short. The wounded groaned, those that were unharmed lay down in the marsh. From time to time a rifle was fired, and a soldier's body convulsed before stretching out.

Again, the haystacks came under fire. This time there was no response. After an hour's shooting, a new attack was mounted, and again it was stopped by the fugitives' gunfire. Again, there were corpses in the marsh, and the wounded groaned.

A prolonged burst of fire began again. Two machine guns were set up and after a few rounds there was yet another attack.

The haystacks were silent.

As the soldiers raked each haystack apart, they found that only one fugitive was still alive: the cook, Soldatov. Both his calves had been hit, as had his shoulder and forearm, but he was still breathing. All the others were dead of gunshot wounds. But there were only nine, instead of eleven of them.

Yanovsky wasn't there, nor was Kuznetsov.

That evening, twenty kilometers further upstream, an unknown person dressed in military uniform was detained. Surrounded by soldiers, he killed himself with a pistol shot. The dead man was immediately identified. It was Kuznetsov.

The only one missing was the leader, Lieutenant Colonel Yanovsky. His fate remained unknown. The search for him went on for a long time, many months. He couldn't have swum down the river nor gotten away on mountain paths; everything had been very thoroughly blocked. Very likely he had committed suicide after hiding first in a deep cave or bear's den where his corpse was eaten by the beasts of the taiga.

The best surgeon and two free contract paramedics (they had to be free ones, not prisoners) were summoned from the central hospital to deal with the wounded from this battle. It was almost evening by the time the hospital pickup truck got as far as the Elgen collective farm where the active squad's headquarters were. There were so many military Studebakers on the road that its journey had been delayed.

"What's going on here? A war?" the surgeon asked the chief boss, the man who had been leading the operation.

"War or no war, so far we've got twenty-eight dead. And you can count the wounded for yourself."

The surgeon was bandaging and operating until the evening.

"How many escapees?"

"Twelve."

"You should have called for aircraft to bomb them, bomb them. With atom bombs."

The boss gave the surgeon a sidelong glance.

"You're always clowning, I've known you for a long time. But you'll see. I'll be dismissed and forced to retire early." The boss gave a deep sigh.

He was prescient. It was because of this escape that he was transferred from Kolyma and dismissed.

Soldatov recovered and was sentenced to twenty-five years. The camp boss got ten years, the sentries who had been in the towers each got five. As a result of this case a great number of people at the mine— more than sixty—were convicted: anyone who knew something and said nothing, anyone who helped or thought of helping, but didn't get around to it. The commander of the squad would have received a long sentence, but Shevtsov's bullet had spared him the inevitable punishment.

Even Potapova, the doctor and the head of the health section, on whose staff the escaped paramedic Nikolsky had worked, was held accountable, but the authorities managed to save her by quickly transferring her somewhere else.

1959

THE FIRST TOOTH

THE PARTY of prisoners being moved was the party I had dreamed of in my long boyhood years: blackened faces, blue lips, burned by the April sun of the Urals. Gigantic escort guards leaping onto moving sleds and the sleds flying up into the air; the one-eyed guard with the scar of an ax wound right across his face; the chief guard's bright blue eyes. By the afternoon of the first day of the prisoners' journey we knew his surname: Shcherbakov. We prisoners—there were about two hundred of us—now knew our boss's surname, by something of a miracle that I couldn't take in or comprehend. The prisoners pronounced this name all the time, as if our journey with Shcherbakov would go on forever. And he became a permanent feature of our life. That was how it was for many of us. Shcherbakov's enormous, agile figure would suddenly turn up here or there, now running ahead to meet us and watch with his own eyes the last wagon in the party passing, and only then chasing up to the front and overtaking us. Yes, we had wagons, classic wagons, on which the local Russian settlers were transporting their baggage. The convoy continued its five-day journey, the prisoners walking in ranks, without luggage. Whenever they stopped or were checked, they reminded one of the ragged lines of new recruits at a railway station. But all the railway stations were far behind where we were going to spend our lives. It was morning, a cheerful April morning. It was not yet light at the gradually lifting semidarkness of the monastery yard where our party was lining up, yawning and coughing, before setting off on a distant journey.

It was in the cellars of the Solikamsk police station, which used to be a monastery, that we spent the night after being handed over by caring and taciturn Moscow guards to those commanded by the blue-eyed Shcherbakov: a horde of tanned fighting men who yelled at us. The previous evening we had poured down into a cold, chilled cellar. The church was surrounded by ice and snow that thawed just a little in the daytime, but refroze at night. Blue and gray snowdrifts covered the whole yard and, to get to the real white snow, you had to break the hard crust of ice that cut your hands, then dig a pit, and only then could you haul out of the pit the thick-grained, crumbly snow, which thawed so joyfully in your mouth and, burningly fresh, revived you a little.

I was one of the first to go into the cellar and so I could choose a spot where it was a bit warmer. The enormous icy vaults frightened me. I was an inexperienced youth and my eyes looked for something like a stove, if only the sort that Vera Figner and Morozov[37] had in their cells. I couldn't find anything. But by chance I had a comrade, if only for a moment while I entered the prison-church cellar. He was a squat gangster, Gusev, and he pushed me against the wall to the only window, which was covered with bars and had double glazing. The window was semi-circular and rose about a meter from the floor; it was like an embrasure. I was thinking of choosing somewhere warmer, but the crowd of people kept pouring in through the door and there was no way of turning back.

Just as calm as before, not saying a word to me, Gusev struck the glass with the toe of his boot and smashed first the inner frame, then the outer one. Cold air, burning me like boiling water, rushed through the hole. Caught by this stream of air, I shivered with cold. I was in any case already frozen by the long wait and the endless roll call in the yard. It took me some time to understand Gusev's wisdom. All night we two were the only ones out of two hundred prisoners who could breathe fresh air. People were so packed, so crammed into the cellar that sitting or lying down was impossible: you could only stand.

A dirty, stifling white fog of men's breath filled the cellar halfway up the walls. People began to faint. Those gasping for breath tried to break through toward the door where there was a crack and a spy hole. They tried to breathe through the spy hole. But the guard standing outside would every now and again stick the bayonet on the end of his rifle through the spy hole, so that any attempts to breathe fresh air through the prison spy hole were abandoned. Obviously, no paramedics or doctors were called to help those who had fainted. Just Gusev and I were lucky enough to be holding out by the panes that Gusev had so wisely smashed. It took a long time to line us up....We were the last to come out. The mist had dispersed and we could see the ceiling, a vaulted ceiling: the sky of the prison and church was so near you could touch it. On the vaults of the Solikamsk police station I found letters drawn in charcoal, enormous letters covering the entire ceiling: "Comrades, we have been dying for three days and nights in this grave, but we're not dead yet. Courage, comrades!"

Orders were yelled out and the party of prisoners crawled out beyond the boundaries of Solikamsk and set off for the plains below. The sky was bright blue, like the chief guard's eyes. The sun burned our faces, the wind cooled them; they turned brown by the first night of the journey. Our overnight stay, prepared in advance, always involved the same fixed procedure. Two huts, one tidier and one more wretched and shedlike, sometimes an actual shed, were rented from the peasants to accommodate the prisoners for the night. You had to try and get in the "tidy" one, of course. But that didn't depend on choice: every evening we were sent past the chief guard who showed with a wave of his arm where the next prisoner would spend the next night. At the time I thought Shcherbakov was the wisest of the wise, because he didn't poke around in various papers and lists to look for "data" on your criminal conviction, but just waved an arm to separate a following prisoner the moment the party of prisoners came to a halt. Later it occurred to me that Shcherbakov was observant. On all occasions his choice, made by some unfathomable principle, turned out to be correct. All the article 58 prisoners were kept together, as were all the 35ers. Some time later, a year or two, I realized there was nothing miraculous about Shcherbakov's wisdom. The knack of guessing the crime by a prisoner's looks could be acquired by anyone. In our party there could have been additional signs, such as baggage, suitcases. But luggage was transported separately, on peasant carts and sleds.

On our journey's first night an event occurred which is the subject of this story. Two hundred men were standing, waiting for the chief guard to appear, when on the left we heard yells, bustles, people gasping, roaring, swearing, and, finally an articulate shout: "Dragons! Dragons!"

A man was flung down onto the snow in front of the ranks of prisoners. His face was smashed and bloody, somebody had rammed a lambskin hat over his head, but the head stuck out and could not conceal a narrow wound that was oozing blood. The man was wearing a homemade garment of brown woven cloth: a Ukrainian of some sort. I knew him. It was Piotr Zayats, a sectarian. He'd been brought from Moscow in the same railway car as me. He spent all his time praying and praying.

"He refuses to stand for roll call," a guard reported, panting and heated by the fuss.

"Make him stand up," ordered the chief guard.

Two enormous guards made Zayats stand up, supporting his arms. But Zayats was a head taller than them; he had a bigger build, he was heavier.

"Are you going to stand, or won't you?"

Shcherbakov punched Zayats in the face. Zayats spat into the snow.

Suddenly I felt a burning heat in my heart. I suddenly understood that everything, all my life was now facing a decisive moment. If I didn't do anything—but what, I did not know—it meant that my journey with this party was pointless, that my twenty years of life were pointless.

Burning shame at my own cowardice drained from my cheeks. I felt my cheeks turning cold and my body becoming light.

I stepped forward from the ranks and said in a cracking voice, "Don't dare hit that man."

Shcherbakov examined me with great amazement. "Get back into line."

I got back into line. Shcherbakov gave the order, and the party, divided between two huts, obeying the movement of Shcherbakov's finger, started dispersing in the darkness. Shcherbakov's finger pointed out the "dirty" hut for me.

We lay down to sleep in damp year-old straw that stank of mold. The straw was spread over bare smooth earth. We lay down in a heap for warmth, and only the gangsters, settling around a lantern that hung from a beam, played their eternal game of snap or poker. Soon, however, even the gangsters went to sleep. So did I, as I contemplated what I had done. I had no older comrade or example to follow. I was alone in this party, I had no friends or comrades. My sleep was interrupted. A lantern shone in my face, and one of my neighbors, a gangster, woken up by this, was repeating confidently and servilely, "It's him, him. . . ."

A guard was holding the lantern.

"Come outside."

"I'll get my coat on."

"Come out as you are."

I went out. I was shaking with nerves, and I didn't understand what would happen next.

Two guards and I came out onto the porch.

"Take off your underclothes!"

I did so.

"Kneel in the snow."

I knelt. I looked at the porch and saw two rifles pointed at me. How much time passed that night in the Urals, my first night in the Urals, I don't remember.

I heard an order: "Get dressed."

I put on my underclothes. I was struck on the ear and I fell onto the snow. A blow from a heavy heel got me straight in the teeth. My mouth was filled with warm blood and quickly swelled up.

"Get back to the barracks."

I went into the barracks, got to my place where another body had already taken over. Everyone was asleep or pretending to be asleep. . . . The salty taste of blood lingered on. There was something else in my mouth, alien, unwanted, so I grabbed it with my fingers and, with an effort, pulled it out of my mouth. It was a tooth that had been knocked out. I threw it out on the rotten straw, on the bare earth floor.

I embraced my fellow prisoners' dirty, stinking bodies and fell asleep. I fell asleep. I hadn't even caught a chill.

In the morning the party of prisoners set off, and Shcherbakov's imperturbable blue eyes surveyed the rows of prisoners in his usual way. Piotr Zayats was standing in line, he wasn't being beaten, and he wasn't shouting anything about dragons. The gangsters gave me hostile and wary looks. Everyone in a camp has to learn to fend for himself.

Another two days and nights on the journey, and we reached the administration building, a new log cabin on the banks of a river.

Commandant Nesterov, a boss with hairy fists, came out to take over the party. Many of the criminals who had walked with me knew this Nesterov and praised him highly.

"When they bring along people who've tried to escape, Nesterov comes out and says, 'Ah, so you fellows have turned up. Well, choose: a slapping, or solitary.' But solitary here is a cell with iron floors, and people can't take more than three months there, then there's interrogation and an extra sentence. 'Slapping, please sir.' He swings around, and they're on the floor. He swings around again, and they're down again. He was an expert. 'Go to barracks!' And that's it. No more interrogation. A good boss."

Nesterov walked up and down the ranks, carefully examining people's faces.

"Any complaints against the guards?"

"No, no," came a ragged chorus of voices.

"And you," the hairy finger touched my chest. "Why can't you answer properly? You're mumbling something."

"He's got a toothache," the men next to me answered.

"No," I replied, trying to make my smashed mouth pronounce the words as clearly as I could. "No complaints against the guards."

"It's not a bad story," I told Sazonov. "It's literate and it makes sense. But it won't get printed. And the end is sort of vague."

"I've got a different ending," said Sazonov. "A year later I was a big boss in a camp. At that time we had reforging, and Shcherbakov was about to get the job of junior NKVD man in the section where I worked. I was in charge of a lot of things there, and Shcherbakov was afraid I'd remember the business with the tooth. Shcherbakov hadn't forgotten the incident either. He had a big family, and the job was well-paid and well-regarded. He was a straightforward sort of man and came to see me to find out whether I had any objections to his being appointed. He brought a bottle with him to make peace the Russian way, but I wouldn't drink with him. I assured him that I wouldn't do anything bad to him.

"Shcherbakov was very pleased. He apologized at length and hung around in the doorway, digging at the carpet with his heel the whole time. He couldn't bring the conversation to an end. 'You know,' Shcherbakov said, 'it was on the road, a party of prisoners. We had fugitives with us.'"

"That ending is no good, either," I told Sazonov.

"Then I do have another one.

"Before I was appointed to work in the section where Shcherbakov and I met again, I met the hospital porter Piotr Zayats in the camp settlement. He was no longer the young giant with black hair and black eyebrows. Instead I saw a limping, gray-haired old man, who was coughing blood. He didn't even recognize me, and when I took him by the arm and spoke his surname, he tore himself free and went his own way. I could tell by his eyes that he was thinking his own thoughts, which I couldn't penetrate, and whatever I did was irrelevant or offensive to a man conversing with less earthly beings."

"That version's no good either," I said.

"Then I'll let the first version stand. Even if you can't get it into print, it's easier when you've written it. If you write it down, you can let go of what happened...."

1964

AN ECHO IN THE MOUNTAINS

In the records department they were quite unable to choose a senior clerk. Later, when business expanded, this job required the work of a whole separate department, "the release group." The senior clerk issued documents certifying a prisoner's release. He was an important figure in a world where prisoners' whole lives centered around the minute they received a document giving them the right to stop being a prisoner. The senior clerk himself had to be an ex-prisoner: that was what the economical staffing department had specified. Of course, you might be able to get a vacant job like this by being seconded from the party or through some trade union organization, or an army commander about to retire might have been talked into it, but those were different times. It wasn't that easy to find people who were willing to work in the camps, no matter how high the polar bonuses were. Volunteering to work in the camps was still considered rather demeaning, and in the whole of the records office, which dealt with all prisoners' affairs, there was only one free contract worker, Inspector Paskevich, a quiet binge drinker. He didn't come to the office often; most of his time was spent traveling as a courier, for the camp was, as it was meant to be, placed a long way from any place where it could be seen.

And now they were quite unable to find a senior clerk. Either a newly appointed employee had links to the world of gangsters and was doing their dirty work, or the clerk was releasing currency speculators from the south for money, or the fellow was honest and unshakable, but incompetent and chaotic, releasing people who shouldn't be released.

The senior authorities used all their energy to search for the person they needed. After all, any mistakes in release procedures were considered the worst form of criminality and could bring about the sudden end of a camp veteran's career, "dismissed from the OGPU troops" or even ending up as the accused in court.

The camp was one that a year previously had been called the fourth department of the Solovetsky Island camps. Now it was an important autonomous camp in the Northern Urals.

All this camp lacked was a senior clerk.

Then a specially guarded prisoner arrived from the actual Solovetsky Islands. This was something that seldom happened at Vishera. There was almost nobody who needed to be brought there under special guard: the authorities used red horse and cattle wagons with bunks inside, or the familiar hard-class passenger cars with their windows barred, so that it looked as if the carriages were ashamed of their bars. In the south, householders protected themselves from burglars by fitting bars in the most whimsical shapes—flowers or sunbeams. The southerners' lively imagination devised these shapes for bars, shapes that didn't offend a passerby's eyes, and yet were still bars. Thus a hard-class passenger car stopped being an ordinary car when iron veils covered its eyes.

In those days the famous "Stolypin"[38] wagons still ran along the long-distance lines in the Urals and in Siberia. The prisoners' cars would keep the name Stolypin for many decades after they had ceased to be Stolypin's.

A Stolypin wagon had two small square windows on one side and several large ones on the other. The windows, which were barred, did not let anyone outside see what was going on inside, even if they put their eyes against them.

Inside, the wagon was divided into two sections by massive bars with heavy, creaking doors; each half of the wagon had its own little window.

At both ends there were compartments for the guards, and there was also a corridor for the guards.

Specially guarded prisoners did not travel in Stolypin wagons. Escort guards took them individually in ordinary trains, booking an end compartment—everything was done in a "family" way, simply, as before the revolution. They had not yet gathered enough experience.

A specially guarded prisoner arrived from the Island (as the Solovetsky Islands were then called, just as the island of Sakhalin was called the

Island). When he was handed over, he turned out to be a short, elderly man on crutches, wearing the obligatory Solovetsky pea jacket made from greatcoat material and the Solovetsky hat with ear flaps.

This man was calm and gray-haired. He moved jerkily, and it was obvious that he was still learning the art of walking with crutches, that he'd only recently become an invalid.

The general barracks with double bunks was close-packed and stifling, even though the doors were kept wide open at both ends of the building. The wooden floor was strewn with sawdust, and the orderly who sat by the door would look, by the light of the seven-inch-wick kerosene lamp, at the fleas jumping up and down in the sawdust. From time to time he would lick a finger and start hunting these persistent insects.

A place was assigned to the newcomer in these barracks. The night orderly for the barracks vaguely gestured with a hand to point out a dark, stinking corner where people were sleeping, dressed, in a heap and where there was no space for a cat, let alone a man.

But the new arrival calmly pulled his hat over his ears and, laying his crutches on the long dinner table, climbed up to join the people sleeping there. He closed his eyes and did not move. Using his own weight, he squeezed himself in between the other bodies and, if his sleepy neighbors made any movement, the new man's body immediately filled the tiny bit of space that was freed. Feeling with his elbow and hip for the bunk's board, the newcomer relaxed his muscles and fell asleep.

The next morning it turned out that this newly arrived invalid was in fact the long-awaited senior clerk whom the camp administration had been so eager to see.

At lunchtime he was summoned to see the bosses, and by evening he had been transferred to another barracks for administrative support staff; this building was where all the camp officials who were ex-prisoners lived. It was a barracks of amazing and almost unique construction.

It had been built when the camp chief was a former sailor who had sunk the Black Sea fleet when the famous midshipman Raskolnikov[39] arrived there.

This sailor made his career on dry land, running the camps, and the building of a barracks for the support staff was his idea, a tribute to his naval past. The two-story bunks in these barracks were suspended from the ceiling on steel hawsers. The bunks hung in clusters, each for four men, like those for sailors in their crew's quarters. For additional strength the construction was reinforced from the side by a thick, long steel cable.

Thus the bunks swung together if just one man lying in the barracks made the slightest movement.

Since several men moved at the same time, the hanging bunks were in constant motion, and they creaked and squeaked audibly, if quietly. The rocking and creaking never stopped for a minute at any time of the day or night. Only during the evening roll calls did the moving bunks hold still, like a weary pendulum, and fall silent.

It was in these barracks that I got to know Stepanov, Mikhail Stepanovich Stepanov. That was the new senior clerk's name, not one of the aliases that were so widespread here.

In fact, twenty-fours earlier I had seen a packet containing his personal file, which the special escort guard had brought. It was a thin file in a green folder, beginning with the usual questionnaire and supplemented with two numbered photographs, full-face and profile, and a square space containing his fingerprints, something that looked like a cross section of a miniature tree.

The questionnaire gave his date of birth, 1888. I remember well those three eights, and his place of work: Moscow, People's Commissariat, Workers' and Peasants' Inspectorate. Member of the Bolshevik party since 1917.

An answer to one of the final questions ran: "I have been subject to.... I was a member of the Social Revolutionary party from 1905...." The answers were recorded, as usual, in an official hand, as briefly as possible.

His sentence was ten years, or to be exact, the death penalty, commuted to ten years.

His camp employment: he had been senior clerk at the Solovetsky Islands for over six months.

Our Stepanov didn't have a very interesting file. The camp had a lot of commanders who'd served Admiral Kolchak or General Annenkov;

we had a commander of the notorious Wild Division;[40] there was a con woman who claimed to be the daughter of Tsar Nikolai Romanov; we had the famous pickpocket Karlov, nicknamed the Contractor—he really did look like a contractor—bald, with an enormous belly and puffy fingers. He was one of the deftest pickpockets, an artist whose skills were demonstrated to the bosses.

There was a man called Mayerovsky, a burglar and an artist who never stopped drawing on things—a board or a piece of paper—one and the same subject, naked women and men intertwined in every possible unnatural position of intercourse. That was all Mayerovsky could draw. He was the black-sheep son of very well-off parents working in the world of scholarship. The gangsters considered him to be a total outsider.

There were several counts, a few Georgian princes from Tsar Nicholas II's suite.

Stepanov's personal file was placed in a new camp folder and put on the shelf with all the letter S's.

I wouldn't have known his remarkable history, were it not for a chance conversation in the records office one Sunday.

For the first time I saw Stepanov without his crutches. He was holding a stick, very easy to use, which he had evidently ordered long ago from the camp carpentry workshop. The stick had a hospital-type handle, bent inward, instead of being curved like an ordinary walking stick.

I said, "Oho!" and congratulated him.

"I'm getting better," said Stepanov. "I haven't got any fractures. It's scurvy."

He rolled up a trouser leg and I saw a lilac-blue stripe that went up his skin. We were silent for a while.

"Mikhail, why are you in prison?"

"How could I not be?" he smiled. "I'm the one that let Antonov go free...."

As a seventeen-year-old schoolboy, Stepanov, the son of a grammar school teacher, joined the party just before the 1905 uprising. He felt God himself had ordered him to do so, as was the fashion for young highly educated Russians at the time. Inspired by the aura of the legendary People's Will, the newly created Socialist Revolutionary party was divided into many factions, big and small. Among these factions a prominent role was played by the Union of Socialist-Revolutionary Maximalists, a group led by a well-known terrorist, Mikhail Sokolov. Family ties led Stepanov to join this group, and he soon was carried away enough to join the world of underground Russia: secret meetings, safe houses, learning to shoot, learning to use dynamite.

They always had a bottle of nitroglycerin in their laboratories, just in case they were arrested or searched.

Seven armed party men were surrounded by police in their safe house. The Maximalists responded with gunfire, until they ran out of cartridges. Stepanov had been firing too. They were arrested, tried, and all of them were hanged, except for Stepanov, who was underage. Instead of a noose, Stepanov got penal servitude for life and ended up not far from Petersburg in Shlisselburg fortress.

Penal servitude is a regime that varies according to the surroundings and the character of the autocrat. "Penal servitude for life" in tsarist times amounted to twenty years' labor, with two years in handcuffs and four years in shackles.

In Stepanov's time Shlisselburg applied an effective innovation: they shackled the hard-labor convicts in pairs, the most reliable method of making them quarrel with each other.

There is a story by Henri Barbusse demonstrating the tragedy of lovers who are shackled together and start to heartily loathe each other.

This had been done to hard-labor convicts for some time. Choosing a partner for shackling was a splendid device of the experts in these matters. The prison authorities could play their best jokes: shackling a tall man to a short one, a sectarian to an atheist, and their specialty was making political "bouquets" by shackling an anarchist to a Socialist Revolutionary, or a Social Democrat to a land redistributor.

If you didn't want to quarrel with the man shackled to you, you both had to have the greatest self-restraint, or the blind submission of the younger to the elder, and a passionate desire on the part of the elder man to impart the very best of his inner self to his comrade.

Occasionally human willpower, faced with a new and very powerful test, became even stronger. Characters and spirits were tempered.

That was how Stepanov's shackled period passed, wearing handcuffs and fetters.

The years passed as penal servitude years did: you got used to the number, the ace of diamonds on the back of your prison garb, and didn't even notice them.

It was during that period that Stepanov, now a young man of twenty-two, met Sergo Orjonikidze in Shlisselburg. Sergo was a prominent propagandist, and he and Stepanov spent many days talking in Shlisselburg prison. Being befriended by Orjonikidze made Stepanov turn from a Maximalist to a Bolshevik Social Democrat.

He began to adopt Sergo's faith in Russia's future and his own future. Stepanov was still young. Even if he had to serve every day of his "life" sentence, he would return to freedom before he was forty and would still be able to serve under a new banner. He would wait out those twenty years.

But he had a far shorter time to wait. February 1917 opened the doors of the tsar's prisons, and Stepanov found himself free much earlier than he had expected or been ready for. He sought out Orjonikidze, joined the Bolshevik Party, and took part in the storming of the Winter Palace. After the October Revolution, completing his military training, he went to the front as a Red commander and climbed the military ladder higher and higher as he went from front to front.

On the Tambov front, fighting against Antonov, Brigade Commander Stepanov was in command of a combined force of armored trains, and had considerable success.

The Antonov movement was now on the wane. Very mixed forces were ranged in the Tambov rebellion against the Red Army. The local villagers had suddenly been transformed into a regular army with its own commanders.

Unlike many other leaders during the Civil War, Antonov looked after the morale of his units and inspired his soldiers through his political commissars, an institution that he copied from the commissars of the Red Army.

Antonov himself had some time before been condemned by a revolutionary tribunal, sentenced to death in his absence, and declared an outlaw. All units of the Red Army received an order from the Supreme

Command demanding that he be shot as an enemy of the people immediately after capture and identification.

The Antonov movement was now on the wane. Suddenly Commander Stepanov was informed that an operation by a regiment of the Cheka had achieved complete success and that Antonov himself had been taken prisoner.

Stepanov ordered the prisoner to be brought to him. Antonov came in and stopped in the doorway. The light of a storm lantern hanging by the door fell on an angular, hard, and inspired face.

Stepanov ordered the guard to leave the room and wait outside the door. Then he approached and nearly touched Antonov—Stepanov was almost a head shorter—and said, "Sasha, is that you?"

They had been shackled together in Shlisselburg for a whole year without ever quarreling.

Stepanov embraced his prisoner, whose hands were bound, and they kissed.

Stepanov thought for a long time, pacing the railway carriage in silence, while Antonov smiled sadly as he looked at his old comrade. Stepanov told Antonov about the order, not that this was news to the prisoner.

"I can't shoot you and I'm not going to," said Stepanov, when he seemed to have hit on a solution. "I'll find a way to let you go. But you must, in turn, give me your word that you'll disappear, stop fighting against Soviet power—in any case your movement is doomed to perish. Give me your word, your word of honor."

It was easier for Antonov, who understood only too well what moral torments his comrade had suffered doing hard labor. He gave his word of honor. Antonov was then led away.

The tribunal was to meet the next day, but that night Antonov escaped. Instead of Antonov, whom the tribunal was due to try a second time, it was the chief guard who was tried for not stationing sentries properly and thus letting such an important criminal escape. The tribunal members included Stepanov and his brother. The chief guard was found guilty and given a suspended sentence of a year in prison for his negligence.

How was it possible for Stepanov not to know that Antonov was a former political prisoner doing hard labor? New to the Tambov front, he had not had time to familiarize himself with one of Antonov's most important leaflets, in which Antonov had written, "I am an old member of the People's Will and have spent many years under the tsars doing hard labor. Unlike your leaders Lenin and Trotsky who've never experienced anything except exile, I was kept in shackles...." and so on. Stepanov had occasion to familiarize himself with this leaflet much later.

At the time, it seemed that the matter was over and Stepanov's conscience was clear, as far as he was concerned, for he had saved Antonov—and as far as Soviet power was concerned, Antonov was going to vanish and that was the end of the his rebellion.

But things turned out differently. Antonov had no intention of keeping his word. He appeared to inspire his "green" troops and battles flared up with new intensity.

"That's when my hair turned gray," said Stepanov. "Not later."

Soon Tukhachevsky took over the general command. His energetic measures to liquidate the Antonov rebellion were completely successful. The most pernicious villages were annihilated with artillery fire. The Antonov rebellion was coming to an end. Antonov himself had typhus and was in a military hospital. When the hospital was surrounded by Red Army cavalry, Antonov's brother shot him in his hospital bed and then shot himself. That was how Aleksandr Antonov died.

The Civil War ended, Stepanov was demobilized, and began working under Orjonikidze, who was then the People's Commissar of the Workers' and Peasants' Inspectorate. As a member of the party since 1917, Stepanov got the job of head of the administration of the Inspectorate.

This happened in 1924. He worked in the Inspectorate for one, then two, then three years, but by the end of the third year he began to notice something like surveillance: someone was going through his papers and correspondence.

Stepanov had many sleepless nights. He tried to recall every step he had taken, every day of his life—everything was completely above board, except for that Antonov business. But Antonov was dead. Stepanov had never confided anything to his brother.

Soon he was summoned to the Lubyanka, and the high-ranking secret policeman interrogating him asked him casually whether Stepanov, as a Red Army commander, had in military circumstances released the prisoner of war Aleksandr Antonov.

Stepanov told the truth. Then all his secrets were revealed.

It turned out that Antonov was not the only man to have escaped that summer night in Tambov. He had been caught together with one of his officers. The officer had, after Antonov's death, fled to the Far East and crossed the border to join Ataman Semionov in China. Several times he had returned as a saboteur. He was caught and, imprisoned in the Lubyanka, had "decided to confess." Writing a detailed confession in his solitary cell, he mentioned that in such-and-such a year he had been captured by the Reds together with Antonov and escaped the same night. Antonov hadn't told him anything, but as a military specialist and a tsarist officer, he thought that this had been a case of treachery on the part of the Red commanding officers. These few lines from the chronicle of a murky and chaotic life were checked up on: records were found of the tribunal at which the chief guard Greshniov was given a suspended sentence of one year for stationing sentries improperly.

Where was Greshniov now? The army archives were searched. He'd been demobilized long ago, he was living as a peasant where he'd been born. He had a wife and three small children in a village near Kremenchug. He was suddenly arrested and brought to Moscow.

If Greshniov had been arrested during the Civil War, he might have gone to his death without betraying his commander. But times change: what did he care about the war or his commander Stepanov? He had three children, all tiny infants, a young wife, his whole life before him. Greshniov revealed that he had carried out Stepanov's request, or rather a personal order, which said that Antonov's escape was necessary for the good of the cause and that the commander promised that Greshniov would not be punished for obeying.

Greshniov was left in peace, and they went for Stepanov. He was tried, sentenced to be shot—a sentence then commuted to ten years in the camps—then he was sent to the Solovetsky Islands....

In the summer of 1933 I was crossing Strastnaya Square. Pushkin's monument had not yet been moved across the square, and I was standing at the end, or, to be exact, the start of Tverskoi Boulevard, which was where Opekushin had put Pushkin, since he understood what architectural harmony of stone, metal, and sky was. Someone poked me with a stick from behind. I looked around: it was Stepanov! He had been released some time ago and was working as the chief of the airport. The stick was the same.

"Do you still limp?"

"Yes. The aftereffects of scurvy. The medics call it a 'contraction.'"

1959

AKA BERDY

A FUNNY story that has been transformed into a mystical symbol. . . .
An actual reality, for people also treated Second Lieutenant Kijé[41] as
a real person. For a long time I couldn't take Yuri Tynianov's fine story
to be a record of real events. This striking story of the times of Tsar
Paul was a brilliantly witty malicious joke, as far as I was concerned,
made by some grandee of the period with too much time on his hands,
a joke that changed into a testimony to a remarkable reign. The sentry
invented by Leskov is the same sort of story: it proves that the autocracy's customs were hereditary. But until 1942 I had my doubts about
whether this "misstatement" by the tsar was an actual fact.

At Novosibirsk station Lieutenant Kurshakov discovered that someone had escaped. All the prisoners were led out of the wagons and
counted in the cold drizzle, then recounted according to a list of their
articles of conviction and their sentences: all this proved futile. Lined
up in fives, there were thirty-eight full rows, while in the thirty-ninth
row there was only one man, not two, as when they had been dispatched.
Kurshakov cursed the moment when he had agreed to take over the
party of prisoners without the personal files, in which the missing
prisoner was number sixty. The list he had was half-erased, as there was
no way to protect the paper from the rain. Kurshakov was so worried
that he could hardly make out the surnames: the letters were in fact
blurred. There was no number sixty. Half the journey had been covered.
The punishments for losing a prisoner were severe, and Kurshakov was
now saying goodbye to his epaulets and his officer's rations. He was
also afraid of being sent to the front. The war was now in its second
year, but Kurshakov had been happy serving as an escort guard. He
had made himself valued as an efficient and conscientious officer. He

had taken dozens of parties of prisoners, both large and small, by rail. He had been in charge of whole trainloads, he had carried out special escort duties, and he'd never had an escape. He'd even been awarded a medal "For Merit in Combat." Those medals were awarded to men even a long way from the front.

Kurshakov sat in the guards' wagon. His trembling fingers, slippery because of the rain, turned over the contents of his ill-fated packet: a certificate for the food supplies, a letter from the prison to the camps where he was taking the party, and the list, the list, the list. In all the papers and all the lines all he could see was the number 192. But 191 prisoners were locked in the tightly sealed wagons. The men were soaked through and cursing. They took off their jackets and overcoats, trying to dry their clothes in the draft that came through the wagon doors.

Kurshakov was bewildered and depressed by the escape. The guards, now off duty in a corner of the wagon, were frightened and silent. The face of Kurshakov's assistant, Sergeant Major Lazarev, reflected in turn whatever his senior officer's face expressed: helplessness, fear....

"What do we do?" asked Kurshakov. "What do we do?"

"Let me see the list...."

Kurshakov handed Lazarev a few crumpled sheets of paper, held together by a pin.

"Number sixty," Lazarev read. "Aka Berdy, article of conviction one hundred and sixty-two, sentence ten years."

"A thief," said Lazarev with a sigh. "A thief. A beast."

Frequent contact with the world of thieves had taught the escort guards to use criminals' slang, in which "beasts" was the term for people from Central Asia, the Caucasus, and Transcaucasia.

"A beast," Kurshakov concurred. "And I expect he can't speak Russian. He probably just grunted at roll calls. You and I, pal, are going to be flayed alive for this...." Kurshakov lifted the sheet of paper close to his eyes and read, with hatred in his voice, "Berdy...."

"They might not skin us alive," Lazarev responded in a suddenly firm voice. He raised his shining, darting eyes. "I have an idea." He quickly whispered something in Kurshakov's ear.

The lieutenant shook his head in doubt:

"Nothing will come of it...."

"It's worth a try," said Lazarev. "Otherwise it's the front. Otherwise it's the war."

"Go ahead," said Kurshakov. "We're going to be stuck here for two days, that's what they told me at the station."

"Give me some money," said Lazarev.

He was back by evening.

"He's a Turkmen," he told Kurshakov.

Kurshakov went to the wagons, opened the door of the first one and asked the prisoners whether there was anyone who knew at least a few words of Turkmen. The reply was negative; Kurshakov went no further. He moved a prisoner and his baggage to the wagon from which a prisoner had escaped, and the guards pushed into the first wagon some bedraggled person, who had gone hoarse shouting something important and terrible in an incomprehensible language.

"The bastards have caught him," said a tall prisoner as he cleared a space for the fugitive. The latter embraced the tall man's legs and burst into tears.

"Stop it, do you hear, stop it," rasped the tall prisoner.

The fugitive was saying something very quickly.

"I don't understand, pal," said the tall man. "Have some soup, I've got some left in my pot."

The fugitive sipped the soup and fell asleep. In the morning he was shouting and weeping again. He leapt out of the wagon and fell at Kurshakov's feet. The escort guards chased him back to the wagon, and right until the end of the journey the fugitive lay under the bunks, crawling out only when food was being handed out. He wept silently.

The handover of the party proceeded perfectly well for Kurshakov. After a few expletives addressed to the prison that had sent a party of prisoners without their personal files, the duty commandant came out to take over the party and used the list to begin a roll call. Fifty-nine men moved to one side, but there was no sixtieth.

"It's an escapee," said Kurshakov. "He got away from me in Novosibirsk, but we found him. In the market. That was a load of trouble. I'll show him to you. A beast: not a word of Russian."

Kurshakov took Berdy by the shoulder and brought him out. Rifle bolts clicked, and Berdy entered the camp.

"What's his surname?"

"Here it is," said Kurshakov, pointing it out.

"Aka Berdy," the commandant read. "Article one hundred and sixty-two, sentence ten years. A beast, but a fighting one. . . ."

The commandant firmly wrote down opposite Berdy's name: "Tends to escape, tried to escape while under interrogation."

An hour later Berdy was summoned. He leapt up joyfully, believing that everything would now be cleared up, that he would be free any minute now. He happily ran ahead of the guard.

He was led to a corner of the yard, toward a barracks fenced off with a triple row of barbed wire; he was pushed through the nearest door into stinking darkness from which came the roar of many voices.

"A beast, pals."

I met Aka Berdy in the hospital. By then he spoke a little Russian and told me that three years ago a Russian soldier, he thought part of a patrol, spent some time trying to talk to him. The soldier took the Turkmen off to the station to verify his identity. The soldier tore up Berdy's identity papers and pushed him into a prisoners' wagon. Berdy's real surname was Toshayev, he was a peasant from a remote Asian village near Chardzhou. He and a fellow countryman were looking for bread and work, and had got as far as Novosibirsk: his comrade had gone somewhere in the market.

Toshayev told me that he had already made several applications, but still had no reply. No case file for him ever arrived, and he was listed in a group of "unrecordeds"—persons kept in prison without any documentation. He said he had gotten used to responding to the name Aka, but that he wanted to go home, that it was cold here, that he was often ill, that he'd written home, but not gotten any letters, perhaps because he was constantly being transferred from one place to another.

In three years Aka Berdy had learned to speak Russian well, but he still hadn't learned to use a spoon. He took a bowl with both hands— the soup was never more than lukewarm, and the bowl wouldn't burn your fingers or lips. . . . Berdy drank the soup and used his fingers to pick out whatever was left on the bottom of the bowl. He ate porridge with his fingers, too, leaving the spoon on one side. This was an amusement for the entire ward. After chewing a piece of bread, Berdy would turn it into dough and roll it in ash before raking it out of the stove. After mixing it into taut dough, he rolled it into a ball and sucked it. This was "hashish," "grass," "opium." Nobody laughed at this ersatz: they had often found themselves having to crumble up dry birch leaves or blackcurrant roots to smoke instead of tobacco.

Berdy was amazed that I immediately understood what had really happened. It was a typist's mistake: she had given a new number to a continuation of nicknames belonging to the man who was number fifty-nine. Added to that were the chaos and confusion when prison parties were sent off in wartime, not to mention Kurshakov and Lazarev's servile fear of their bosses.

But there had been a real live person, number fifty-nine. Wasn't he the one who could have said that the nickname Berdy was his? Of course he could have. But everyone amuses themselves as best they can. Everyone is happy to see the bosses embarrassed and panicking. The bosses can be put on the right path only by an ordinary *freier*, not by a thief. And number fifty-nine was a thief.

1959

ARTIFICIAL LIMBS, ETC.

THE CAMP solitary confinement block was old and decrepit. It looked as if a wall might fall down, the whole block crumble, and the beams collapse, if you just knocked against a wooden cell wall. But the solitary confinement block wasn't going to fall, and the seven cells went on doing their job. Of course, any word spoken loudly would be heard in the neighboring cell. But those who were imprisoned there were afraid of being punished. If the duty warden took a piece of chalk and marked a cell with a cross, it meant the cell got no hot food. If he drew two crosses, then it didn't get bread, either. This was solitary for camp crimes; those suspected of anything more dangerous would be driven away to the main administration.

This time all the heads of camp institutions, all the managers, who were also prisoners, had suddenly been arrested for the first time. Some big case was being stitched together, some camp trial was being convened. On someone's orders.

So all five of us were standing in the solitary block's narrow corridor. We were surrounded by guards. We felt and understood only one thing: that once again we'd been caught up by the cogs of the same machine as several years previously, and that we wouldn't know why until tomorrow at the earliest. . . .

We were made to undress down to our underclothes and each led to a separate cell. The store man recorded the things we handed over for keeping, and then shoved them into bags, to which he tied labels, before writing on them. An interrogator, whose name I knew—Pesniakevich—was overseeing the operation.

The first man was on crutches. He sat down on the bench next to the light, put his crutches on the floor, and started undressing. That revealed a steel corset.

"Do I take it off?"

"Of course."

The man started unlacing his corset, and Pesniakevich the interrogator bent down to help him.

"Have you nailed me, old pal?" asked the man in gangster slang, giving the word "nailed" its inoffensive gangster sense.

"I have, Pleve."

The man in a corset, Pleve, managed the tailor's shop in the camp. This was an important post, for he had twenty skilled men under him. They took customers' orders, even from free men, if the bosses permitted.

The naked man curled up on the bench. The steel corset lay on the floor while it was recorded in the list of objects that had been removed.

"How do I record this thing?" the solitary block's store man asked Pleve, kicking the corset with the toe of his boot.

"Steel prosthesis, corset," replied the naked man.

Pesniakevich moved aside somewhere. I asked Pleve, "Did you really know that cop before you were locked up?"

"Of course I did," he replied harshly. "His mother used to run a brothel in Minsk, and I used to go there. That was in Tsar Nicholas the Bloody's time."

Pesniakevich emerged from the far end of the corridor with four guards. The guards took Pleve by the feet and hand and carried him into the cell. The lock clicked shut.

The next man was Karavayev, manager of the horse stables. He had served under Marshal Budionny in the Red Cavalry, and in the Civil War he had lost an arm. Karavayev banged his iron arm on the duty warden's desk: "You sons of bitches!"

"Take off your bit of iron. Give us the arm."

Karavayev took off his arm and swung it in the air, but the guards flung themselves on the Red cavalryman and shoved him into a cell. We heard the sound of his elaborate curses.

"Listen, Ruchkin," the chief of the solitary block started speaking, "any noise and we take away your hot food."

"You can stuff your hot food."

The solitary chief took a piece of chalk from his pocket and marked Karavayev's cell with a cross.

"Well, who's going to sign for his arm?"

"Nobody is. Just put a tick or something," ordered Pesniakevich.

It was now the turn of the doctor, our Dr. Zhitkov. He was a deaf old man, and he handed over his ear trumpet. Then came Colonel Panin, who managed the carpentry workshop. The colonel's leg had been torn off by a shell somewhere in East Prussia during World War I. He was a superb carpenter and told me that the gentry always had their children taught a craft, some manual craft. Old Panin unbuttoned his artificial leg and hopped on one leg into his cell.

Only two of us were left: Shor, Grisha Shor, the senior foreman, and I.

"Look at the way he moves: neat!" said Grisha, who had been overcome by the merriment that comes with arrest. "He gave his leg, the other man gave his arm. So I'll hand in my eye." And Grisha deftly removed his right eye, which was made of porcelain, and showed it to me when it was in his hand.

"I didn't know you had an artificial eye," I said with amazement. "I'd never noticed."

"You're no good at noticing things. But it was a good choice of eye, very successful."

While they were recording Grisha's eye, the chief of the solitary block suddenly became merry and couldn't stop giggling.

"So one man gives me an arm, another a leg, another an ear, another his back, and this one his eye. We'll collect a complete body. And how about you?" He carefully looked over my naked body. "What are you going to hand over? Your soul?"

"No," I said, "I won't let you have my soul."

1965

CHASING THE LOCOMOTIVE'S SMOKE

YES, THAT used to be my dream: to hear the whistle of a locomotive, to see its white smoke spreading down the slope of the railway embankment.

I used to wait for the white smoke, the living steam engine.

We crawled until we were exhausted, reluctant to throw off our pea jackets and fur jackets: we had only fifteen kilometers to go before we got home, to the barracks. But we were afraid to leave our jackets lying on the road, or in the ditch, to run, walk, crawl, to get rid of the terrible weight of our clothing. We were afraid to drop our pea jackets: it took only a few minutes in a winter night for your clothes to turn into a frozen bunch of pine branches, into an icy stone. At night we would never find our clothes, they'd be lost in the winter taiga, just as a quilted jacket would be lost in summer in the dwarf pine bushes, if you didn't tie it like a marker, a marker of life, to the very top of the bushes. We knew that without pea jackets and fur jackets we would be doomed. So we crawled on, our strength draining away. We had only to stop moving to feel the deadening cold creeping over our enfeebled bodies, which had lost their main function: to be a source of warmth, the simple warmth that arouses anger, if not hope.

We crawled along together, free men and prisoners. The driver, who had run out of gas, had stayed behind to wait for the help we would summon. He stayed behind, making a bonfire out of the only dry timber that was available, the guideposts. By saving himself, the driver was perhaps threatening other truckers with death, since all the guideposts had now been collected, broken up, and put on the bonfire, which burned with a small, but lifesaving flame. The driver bent over the fire and the flames, every now and again shoving another stick, another splinter on it. He wasn't even thinking of getting warm or warming himself. He was just trying to protect his life.... If the driver had abandoned his truck and crawled away with us over the sharp cold rocks of the mountain highway, he would have been sentenced to the camps. The driver was waiting, and we crawled on to get help.

I crawled, trying not to think any unnecessary thoughts—thoughts were like movements, and energy was not to be spent on anything other than getting abrasions, rolling, and dragging one's body further along the road on a winter night.

And yet our breath in that minus-fifty cold seemed like the smoke from a locomotive. The taiga's silver larches seemed like a burst of locomotive smoke. The white haze covering the sky and filling our night was also locomotive smoke, the smoke that I had dreamed of for so many years. In this white silence I could hear not the sound of the wind, but a musical celestial phrase, and a clear, melodious, resonant human voice sounded out in the frosty air over us. The musical phrase was a hallucination, a sound mirage, and it had something about it of the locomotive smoke that filled my valley. The human voice was just a continuation, a logical continuation of this winter musical mirage.

I saw that I wasn't the only one to hear that voice. All of us, as we made our way, could hear it. We were getting colder, but too weak to move. The celestial voice had something in it bigger than hope, bigger than our tortoise-like progress toward life. The celestial voice was repeating: "Here is a message from TASS news agency: fifteen doctors...." They'd suddenly been charged, they were entirely innocent, their confessions had been obtained by the use of impermissible torture and by interrogation methods that were strictly forbidden by Soviet law.

The doctors had been released. That was spectacular! What about Lidia Timashuk's[42] letters and medal? What about the journalist Yelena Kononenko, who glorified vigilance and was the heroine of vigilance, the personification of vigilance, as demonstrated before the whole world?

Stalin's death had not made the appropriate impression on us. We were too experienced.

Celestial music had been playing for some time now, as we crawled on. Nobody said a word. Everyone digested the news as best he could.

The lights of the settlement were now glimmering. The crawling men were greeted by their wives, subordinates, and bosses, who'd come out to meet them. Nobody came out to meet me: I had to crawl on my own to the barracks, to the room, the bunk, to light and stoke the iron stove. When I had gotten warm and had drunk some hot water, heated in a mug placed on the burning wood in the stove, I stood up straight in front of the fire and felt the warm light run over my face. Not all the skin on my face had been frostbitten earlier: there were still intact patches, segments, and areas. I then made a decision.

The next day I applied to be released from my job.

"Release is in the hands of God," the district chief said sarcastically. But he accepted the application, and it was dispatched by the next courier post.

"I have been in Kolyma for seventeen years. I request to be released. As a former prisoner, I have no rights as a long-serving employee for additional payments. It will cost the state virtually nothing to release me. This is my request." Two weeks later I received a refusal but no explanation whatsoever. I then immediately wrote in protest to the prosecutor, demanding his intervention, and so on.

The gist of it was that, if there was any hope, all the legal shackles had to be removed or smashed, so that the formalities and the papers would not be held up. Very probably, all my correspondence was a waste of time. But you never knew....

The portraits of Beria were torn down in the club, but I kept on writing and writing. Beria's arrest didn't make me more hopeful. Events seemed to be unfolding of their own accord, and any secret connection with my fate was intangible. I had to think about something other than Beria.

The prosecutor replied two weeks later. This prosecutor once held important positions in the neighboring administration. He had been removed from his post and transferred to somewhere in the backwoods. His wife had been trading in sewing machines, selling them at ten times the original price, and an article about this had even gotten into the newspapers. The prosecutor tried to defend himself, using the most predictable weapon: he denounced the administration boss's orderly, Azbukin, for selling prisoners tobacco at ten rubles per roll-up. Parcels of tobacco came from the mainland by air, virtually by diplomatic post in the special baggage allowances, with higher limits or no limits at all, for the top bosses. The boss of the administration had twenty people to lunch every day, so that no polar bonuses, no seniority pay increases could cover the expense of the wine and fruit. The administration boss was a loving family man, the father of two children. He covered all his expenses by selling tobacco at ten rubles per homemade cigarette. Eight matchboxes full of tobacco made sixty cigarettes from a two-ounce packet. At six hundred rubles for two ounces, the game was worth the candle.

For daring to attack this method of getting rich, the prosecutor was immediately dismissed and moved to our backwoods. He made sure the law was being observed, and he answered letters quickly, for he was inspired by hatred of his superiors and fired by his battle with them.

I wrote a second application: "I was refused a release. Now, sending you a certificate from the prosecutor...."

Two weeks later I received a refusal. There were no explanations. It was as if I'd asked for a foreign passport, something for which a refusal is given without explanations.

I wrote to the prosecutor of the province, of Magadan province, and had a reply: I was entitled to be released and allowed to leave. This battle of higher powers was reaching a new stage. Every turn of the wheel was leaving traces in the form of numerous orders, clarifications, and decisions. One could vaguely sense some sort of connecting logic in them. My applications were getting, as the criminals put it, "in line." In line with the times?

Two weeks later I received a refusal, again with no explanations. And although I repeatedly wrote pleading letters to my boss, the head of the health department of the administration, Tsapko, a paramedic, I never had a reply from him.

It was three hundred kilometers from my sector to the administration, where the nearest medical sector was.

I realized that I needed to meet Tsapko in person. And he arrived in the company of the new head of the camps, promising me a lot of things, everything, even release.

"I'll take it up as soon as we get back. Just stay on here for the winter. You can go in spring."

"No. Even if I don't get a release, I'll certainly leave your administration."

We parted. August turned into September. The fish stopped returning down the rivers. But I wasn't interested in trapping or dynamiting them, a practice which resulted in the various types of salmon and other fish bobbing about, their white bellies up, on the waves of the mountain streams, and then being swept away into the backwaters and rotting until they were unfit to eat.

Something had to happen. And it did. Our district was visited by an engineer, Colonel Kondakov, head of the roads administration. He spent the night in the district chief's cabin. I was in a hurry to catch Kondakov before he went to sleep, so I knocked on the door.

"Come in."

Kondakov was sitting at the desk, his tunic unbuttoned, rubbing a red mark left by the collar all round his white, round neck.

"District paramedic. May I discuss a personal matter with you?"

"I never talk to anyone when I'm traveling."

"I foresaw that," I said coldly and calmly. "I've written an application for you. Here's the envelope: it explains everything. Please will you read it whenever you think the time is right."

Kondakov felt embarrassed and stopped fiddling with his tunic collar. Whatever else he was, Kondakov was an engineer, a man with a university degree, albeit a technical one.

"Sit down and tell me what it's about."

I sat down and told him.

"If it's all as you say, then I promise to have you released as soon as I get back to headquarters. In about ten days' time."

Kondakov wrote my surname down in a tiny little notebook.

Ten days later I had a telephone call from the administration: from friends there, if I had any. Or perhaps they were just curious bystanders, rather than spectators who could look on for many hours without stopping, over many years, at a fish tearing free from a hole in the fish trap, at a fox gnawing off its paw so as to escape from a snare. They look on and make no attempt to undo the snare and let the fox go. They just watch the struggle between wild animal and human being.

A telephoned telegram was sent at my expense from my district to the administration. I had to beg the local boss for permission to send this telegram.... No reply.

A Kolyma winter was setting in. Ice was covering the streams, and only at a few places in the rapids was the water still flowing and running, still alive, throwing up mist like locomotive smoke.

I had to make haste, make haste.

"I'm sending a seriously ill patient to the headquarters," I reported to my boss. The patient had an inflamed stomach ulcer, due to malnutrition, avitaminosis; it was a stomach ulcer that was too easily confused with diphtheria. We had the right to send patients on in such cases: in fact, we were obliged to do so. It was an order, it was the law, it was a matter of conscience.

"And who's going to accompany him?"

"I am."

"Yourself?"

"Yes. We'll shut the clinic down for a week."

This sort of thing had happened before, and my boss knew it.

"I'll draw up an inventory. So that nothing gets stolen. And the cupboard can be sealed with a police seal."

"That's the right thing to do." My boss was reassured.

We left on a truck that was going our way. We froze and stopped every thirty kilometers to get warm. On the third day, when it was still light, we reached the administration building in the yellowish-white haze of a Kolyma day.

The first man I saw was Tsapko the paramedic, the head of the health sector.

"I've brought a seriously ill patient," I reported. Tsapko, however, was not looking at the patient, but at my suitcases—I had suitcases, plywood, homemade ones for my books, my cheap cotton suit, my linen, cushion, and blanket. Tsapko understood everything.

"I won't authorize you to leave unless the boss does."

We went to see his boss. He was a little man, compared to Colonel Kondakov the engineer. Judging by his wavering tone and his hesitant answers, I realized that some new orders, new clarifications had been received.

"Don't you want to stay the winter here?" It was the end of October, and winter was in full swing.

"No."

"All right. If he doesn't want to, don't detain him. . . ."

"Yes, sir!" Tsapko stood to attention in front of the camp chief, clicked his heels and we walked out into the filthy corridor.

"Well then," said Tsapko with satisfaction. "You've got everything you wanted. We are releasing you. You're free to go wherever you want. You can go to the mainland. Paramedic Novikov has been given your job. Like me, he was at the front, in the war. You can go back to your place with him and do the handover properly. Then you can come and get your final pay."

"What, three hundred kilometers? And then come back here. That will be a month spent traveling. At least."

"I can't do any more for you. I've done everything."

I realized that my chat with the camp chief was a ruse that had been planned in advance.

There was nobody in Kolyma to ask for advice. Prisoners and ex-prisoners don't have friends. The first person you ask for advice will run off to a boss to tell him, to betray a comrade, to demonstrate their vigilance.

Tsapko had gone some time ago. I was still sitting on the floor in the corridor, smoking and smoking.

"And who's this Novikov? A paramedic from the front?"

I found Novikov. He was a man who had been crushed by Kolyma. His loneliness, sobriety, and timid look testified that for Novikov Kolyma had turned out to be quite different from what he expected when he started chasing after the extra ruble bonuses. Novikov was too much of a novice, too much a frontline soldier.

"Listen," I said. "You're fresh from the front. I've been here for seventeen years. I've served two sentences. I'm being released now. I'll be seeing my family. My paramedic clinic is all in order. Here's the inventory. It's all been sealed. Sign the receipt without having to inspect the inventory."

Novikov didn't ask anyone's advice: he signed.

I didn't go to see Tsapko and report that the handover document had been signed. I went straight to the accounts office. The accountant took a look at my papers with all the certificates and other documents.

"All right, then," he said. "You can have your back pay. But there's one drawback. We had a telegram by phone from Magadan yesterday: all releases are to be stopped until spring, until the shipping season opens."

"What do I care about the shipping season! I'm going by plane."

"The order applies to everyone, as you well know. You weren't born yesterday."

I sat on the office floor and smoked and smoked. Tsapko passed by.

"Haven't you gone yet?"

"No, not yet."

"Well, stay then...."

I wasn't, for some reason, all that disappointed. I was used to such stabs in the back. But it was essential now that nothing go wrong. My entire body and all my willpower were still active, striving, fighting. It was just that not everything had been thought through. Fate had made a mistake in its cold calculations, in the game it was playing with me. I now found the mistake. I went to see Colonel Kondakov's secretary: the boss himself was again away traveling.

"Was there a telegram yesterday about releases being stopped?"

"There was."

"But I was...." I felt my throat dry up and I could barely get the words out, "... but I was released a month ago, on order number sixty-five. So yesterday's telegram can't apply to me. I've already been released. A month ago. I'm on my way, I'm in transit...."

"Yes, that seems to be right," the lieutenant agreed. "Let's go and see the accountant."

The accountant agreed with us, but said, "Let's wait for Kondakov to get back. Let him decide."

"Well," said the lieutenant, "I wouldn't advise that. It was Kondakov who signed the order. It was his decision. Nobody tricked him into signing. He'll flay you alive for not obeying."

"Fine," said the accountant, giving me a sidelong glance. "Only," he said, "you're paying for the journey out of your own pocket."

A plane and train ticket to Moscow cost three and a half thousand rubles, and I was entitled to have it paid for by Far East Construction, which had been my employer for fourteen years when I was imprisoned and three years when I was a free man, or rather a freely contracted worker.

Judging by the accountant's tone, I realized that he wasn't going to make me the slightest concession.

My pay book, that of a former prisoner, had no long-service bonuses, but over three years it had accumulated six thousand rubles.

The hares I had caught, stewed or roasted, and eaten, the fish I had caught, stewed or roasted, and eaten had helped me save up this amazing sum of money.

I paid the money at the till, got a credit note for three thousand, the necessary papers, and a pass to the Oymiakon airport. I started to look for a truck heading in that direction. I soon found one. It was two hundred rubles for two hundred kilometers. I sold my blanket and pillow—what would I want them for in a plane? I sold my medical books to Tsapko at the official price. He could then sell the textbooks and encyclopedias for ten times as much. But I didn't have time to think of that.

There was something worse. I'd lost my talisman, a homemade knife that I'd had for many years.

I had been sleeping on sacks of flour and it had apparently fallen out of my pocket. If I was going to find it, I would have to unload the truck.

We arrived at Oymiakon early in the morning. I'd been working at Tumor, near the Oymiakon airport, a year before, in a nice little post office, where I sent and received so many letters. I got off the truck at the airport hotel.

"Listen," said the truck driver. "Have you lost anything?"

"I lost my knife lying on all that flour."

"Here it is. I pulled up a board at the back and a knife fell onto the road. It's a nice little blade."

"Have it. As a souvenir. I don't need a lucky charm any more."

But my joy was premature. There were no regular flights at Oymiakon airport, and about ten truckloads of passengers had been waiting since autumn. There were lists, each of fourteen passengers, and a daily roll call. Like life in a transit camp.

"When was the last plane?"

"A week ago."

So I would be stuck here until spring. I shouldn't have given my talisman to the truck driver.

I went to see Suprun, the clerk of works at the camp where I had been a paramedic a year before.

"Are you trying to get to the mainland?"

"Yes. Help me to get away."

"Let's go and see Veltman tomorrow."

"Is Captain Veltman still in charge of the airport?"

"Yes, except he's a major now, not a captain. He's just got his new stripes."

The next morning the clerk of works and I went to Veltman's office and said hello.

"Look, our guy is trying to get away."

"Then why didn't he just come and see me? He knows me just as well as he does you, the clerk."

"Just to make sure, sir."

"All right. Where are your things?"

"I've got everything with me," I pointed to my little plywood suit-case.

"Excellent. Go to the hotel and wait."

"But I...."

"Shut up! Do as you're told. Clerk, you're to take out a bulldozer tomorrow and clear the airfield, or ... if there's no bulldozer...."

"I'll do it, I will," said Suprun with a smile.

I said goodbye to both Veltman and the clerk of works, entered the hotel corridor and, stepping over people's legs and bodies, found myself a space by the window. It was a little bit colder there, but later, after a few planes and a few more queues, I moved to the stove, the actual stove.

An hour or so passed, and people who were lying down leapt to their feet, listening eagerly to a roar in the sky.

"A plane!"

"A Douglas cargo plane."

"It's not a cargo plane, it's a passenger one."

The duty officer of the airport was dashing up and down the airport in his hat with earflaps and a cockade. He had a list in his hand, the list of fourteen persons he had learned by heart several months before.

"Everyone whose name I call, quickly buy your tickets. The pilot's having dinner, and then you'll be off."

"Semionov!"

"Here."

"Galitsky!"

"Here."

"Why has my name been crossed off?" raged the fourteenth man. "I've been waiting in line now for over two months."

"Don't talk to me about it. It's the airport chief who's crossed you off. Veltman himself, personally. Is that enough for you? If you want to argue, there's Veltman's office. He's there, and he'll explain why."

But the fourteenth man was reluctant to have it out. You never know what might happen next. Veltman might not like his face. And then he'd not only not catch the next plane, he'd be removed from all the lists. Things like that had happened before.

"Who's been written in?"

"I can't make it out," said the duty officer with the cockade as he stared at the new surname and suddenly shouted out my name.

"Here I am."

"Go to the ticket office, quickly."

I decided I wouldn't play the gentleman, I wouldn't refuse, I'd get away, away. I had seventeen years of Kolyma behind me. I rushed to the ticket office. I was the last man. I pulled out my papers, which were in disarray. I crumpled up my money and dropped things on the floor.

"Run quickly," said the cashier. "Your pilot's had his dinner, and the weather reports are bad. He's got to get ahead of the weather and reach Yakutsk."

I barely breathed as I listened to this unearthly conversation.

When he'd landed, the pilot had steered the plane as near as he could to the cafeteria door. Boarding had finished some time ago. I took my plywood suitcase and ran to the plane. I hadn't put on my gloves, I was clutching my ticket, covered in hoarfrost, in my freezing fingers, and I was out of breath from running.

The airport office checked my ticket, and pushed me through the plane's hatch. The pilot shut the hatch and went to the cabin.

"Air!"

I reached my seat. I was too weak to think of anything, or to understand anything.

My heart pounded for all seven hours of our flight, until the plane suddenly landed. It was Yakutsk.

My new companion, the man sitting next to me in the plane, and I hugged one other as we slept at Yakutsk airport. I had to work out the cheapest way of traveling to Moscow. Even though my travel documents were only valid as far as Jambul in Kazakhstan, I realized that Kolyma laws probably did not apply in the mainland. It was probably possible to find a job and have a life somewhere other than Jambul. I still had time to think about that.

Meanwhile, the cheapest way was to take a plane to Irkutsk, and a train to Moscow. That would be five days and nights. Or I could fly as far as Novosibirsk and reach Moscow from there by rail. Whichever plane was the first to leave. . . . I bought a ticket to Irkutsk.

The plane wasn't going to leave for a few hours, and that gave me time to walk to Yakutsk and look at the frozen Lena River and the silent, single-storied city, which looked like a big village. No, Yakutsk wasn't a city, it wasn't the mainland. It had no locomotive smoke.

1964

THE TRAIN

At irkutsk station I lay down under the sharp, bright light of an electric lamp. Just in case, I'd sewn all my money in my belt, a linen belt that had been made for me in the tailor's shop two years before and which now, finally, would have to do its job. Carefully stepping over people's legs, choosing a path through filthy, stinking, bedraggled bodies, a policeman was patrolling the station. Even better, there was a military patrol with red armbands and automatic weapons. No policeman, naturally, could cope with the gangs of thieves, and that had probably been ascertained long before I turned up at the station. It wasn't that I was afraid of having my money stolen; I hadn't been afraid of anything for a long time. It was just that having money was better than not having money. The light got in my eyes, but I'd had the light get into my eyes a thousand times before, and I'd learned to sleep very well with the light on. I turned up the collar of my pea jacket, which the official documents called a short overcoat, shoved my hands as deep as I could up my sleeves, loosened my felt boots a little. My toes felt free, and I went to sleep. I wasn't afraid of drafts. Everything was what I was used to: locomotives whistling, carriages moving, the station, the policeman, the market outside the station—it was like having a recurring dream, and then I woke up. I was frightened, and cold sweat broke out on my skin. I was frightened by that terrible human strength, the desire and ability to forget. I saw I was ready to forget everything, to erase twenty years from my life. And what years they were! When I realized this, I mastered myself. I knew that I wouldn't let my memory wipe out all that I had seen. And I calmed down and went back to sleep.

I woke up, redid my foot wrappings so the dry side was against my skin, and washed in the snow, as black water splashed off me in all directions. Then I set off into town. This was the first proper city I had seen in eighteen years. Yakutsk had been just a big village. The Lena River had receded a long way from the town, but the inhabitants were afraid of it coming back and overflowing. Its sandy bed was an empty field, filled with nothing but a raging blizzard. Here in Irkutsk there were big buildings, people running around, shops.

I bought a set of knitted underwear, something I hadn't worn for eighteen years. It gave me indescribable pleasure to stand in line, to pay, to hand over the receipt. "Size?" I forgot my size. "The biggest." The sales girl shook her head disapprovingly. "Fifty-five?"—"That's right." She wrapped up my underwear, which I never got to wear, since my size was fifty-one, as I found out when I got to Moscow. All the shop assistants wore identical blue dresses. I also bought a small brush and a penknife. These wonderful objects were fabulously cheap. In the north things like that were homemade: small brushes and penknives.

I went in to a bookshop. In the secondhand section Soloviov's *Russian History* was on sale for 850 rubles for the set. No, no, I wouldn't buy books until I got to Moscow. But holding books, standing by the bookshop counter was as good as a good meat soup . . . as a glass of fresh running water.

In Irkutsk my path separated from my companions. Only the day before, we had walked around the town and bought our plane tickets together. The four of us waited in line together, because it never occurred to us to entrust our money to anyone. That wasn't done in our society. I walked to the bridge and looked down at the seething, green Angara River, a mighty, clean river that was so clear you could see the riverbed. My freezing hand touched the cold dark-brown railings, I breathed in the smell of gas and the dust of the wintry city, I looked at the scurrying pedestrians, and I realized how much of a townsman I was. I realized that the most precious and important thing for a man is the time when his homeland becomes his homeland, before family feeling or love are born, and that time is childhood and early youth. And it touched my heart. I greeted Irkutsk with all my soul. Irkutsk was my Vologda, my Moscow.

As I was approaching the railway station, someone clapped me on the shoulder.

728 · KOLYMA STORIES

"Somebody wants a chat with you," said a fair-haired boy in a quilted jacket. He led me aside into a dark place. Immediately, a short man loomed out of the murk and looked at me intensely.

I could tell by the way he was looking at me whom I was facing. Cowardly and brazen, ingratiating and full of hatred as they were, I didn't have to know their identity: they would appear in their own time with knives, nails, stabbing instruments in their hands. For the time being I was facing just one person, with pale, earthy skin and swollen eyelids, with tiny lips that seemed to be glued onto his twisted shaven chin.

"Who are you?" He stretched out a filthy hand with long fingernails. An answer was required. No military patrol or policeman could have come to my help here. "You're from Kolyma!"

"Yes, from Kolyma."

"What did you do there?"

"I was a paramedic for prospectors."

"A paramedic? A quack? So you were sucking the blood of people like us. We need to talk."

I had the new penknife I'd just bought in my pocket: I clutched it and said nothing. All I could hope for was a chance, a chance of some sort. Patience and luck, the two whales on which the prisoner's world stands, were what used to save us, and still would. And a chance turned up.

The darkness parted.

"I know him," A new figure, a complete stranger to me, appeared. I had a very good memory for faces, but I had never seen this man.

"You do?" a finger with the long fingernail described a semicircle.

"Yes, he worked at Kudyma," said the stranger. "They said he was all right. He helped our people. They had nothing but good to say about him."

The finger and its fingernail vanished.

"All right, go," said the thief angrily. "We'll think about it."

I was in luck. I didn't have to spend the night at the station. The Moscow train was departing that evening.

In the morning the light of the electric lamps was oppressive: it was a cloudy light that refused to switch off. Whenever the doors banged, you could see Irkutsk's cold and bright daylight. Thick crowds of people blocked all the passages and filled every square centimeter of the concrete floors, and the grease-stained benches, too, if anyone stood up, moved, or left. There was an endless line at the ticket counter: a ticket to Moscow, to Moscow, and we'll take it from there.... Not to Jambul, the destination indicated in my papers. At last it was my turn at the window. I made convulsive movements to get my money and push a pile of shiny banknotes through to the till, where they would vanish, vanish irretrievably, as had my life until this minute. But the miracle continued working, and the window threw out a rough-surfaced, hard and thin object, like a lump of happiness: a ticket to Moscow. The woman behind the counter yelled out something to the effect that it was a mixed train, that the reservation for a hard seat was for a mixed train, that there would be a proper passenger train only the next day or the day after that. But I didn't understand any of that, except the words "today" and "tomorrow." Today, today. Clutching my ticket tightly, trying to feel all its edges with my unfeeling frostbitten skin, I pushed my way through and found a free space. I'd come by plane and I had the minimum of luggage: just a small plywood suitcase. I was from the Far North, I had the minimum of luggage, only the small plywood suitcase that I had tried and failed to sell in Adygalakh when I was getting the money together to go to Moscow. They hadn't paid my travel costs, but that wasn't important. The main thing was the hard piece of cardboard: a train ticket.

I got my breath back in a corner of the station. My place under the bright lamp had, of course, been taken. I walked across the city and returned to the station.

Boarding had started. A toy train stood on a raised track. It was unbelievably small, as if a few cardboard boxes had been lined up among the hundreds of others where the track maintenance workers and railway employees lived, their frozen washing hung out to dry and flapping in the gusts of wind.

My train was just like those lines of carriages that had been turned into hostels.

The train was not like the sort of train that leaves at such-and-such a time for Moscow. It was more like a hostel. Like a hostel, it had people coming down the steps from the carriages, while here and there things were being passed through the air over the heads of people moving around. I realized that this train lacked the essential thing: life, a promise of movement—there was no locomotive. And in fact, none of the hostels had a locomotive.

My train was like a hostel. And I wouldn't have believed that these carriages could take me to Moscow, but boarding was in progress.

A battle, a terrible battle was being waged at the carriage entrance. It was as if work had suddenly stopped two hours earlier than it should have, and everyone had run home to the barracks, to a warm stove, and they were rushing through the doors.

Where were the conductors? Everyone looked for their places, reserved them, and defended them. My reserved middle bunk was of course occupied by a drunken lieutenant who never stopped belching. I dragged the lieutenant onto the floor and showed him my ticket.

"I've got a ticket for that place, too," the lieutenant explained amicably, then hiccupped, slipped onto the floor, and fell asleep.

The carriage continued being packed with people. Enormous bundles and suitcases kept being lifted up to vanish somewhere on top. There was a penetrating stench of sheepskin jackets, human sweat, filth, and carbolic acid.

"Transit, transit," I kept repeating as I lay on my back, squeezed into the narrow space between the middle and the upper bunks. The lieutenant climbed up past me; his collar was unbuttoned, his face was red and crumpled. The lieutenant clung to something above me, pulled himself up by his arms, and vanished....

In the chaos and the shouts of transit I didn't hear the main thing that I wanted and needed to hear, what I had dreamed of for seventeen years, what had become for me a symbol of the mainland. I couldn't hear a locomotive whistle. I hadn't given it a thought while I was battling for my place in the carriage. I hadn't heard any whistle. But the carriages shuddered and rocked, and our carriage, our transit, began to move somewhere, as if I was beginning to go to sleep and the barracks was drifting before my very eyes.

I forced myself to understand that I was traveling—to Moscow.

At a stretch where there was a railroad switch, right by Irkutsk, the carriage shook and the figure of the lieutenant rolled out above me and hung over me, even though he was clinging to the upper bunk that he was sleeping on. The lieutenant belched, and vomit spattered straight onto my bunk and onto my neighbor's as well. My neighbor removed his fur coat—not a quilted jacket or a pea jacket, but a real coat, a Moscow-style one with a fur collar. Cursing furiously, he started cleaning off the vomit.

My neighbor had an endless quantity of woven baskets, covered in matting, some stitched, some not. From time to time women would emerge from the depths of the carriage. They were wrapped in rural headscarves and short fur coats, and they had the same woven baskets on their shoulders. The women were shouting something at my neighbor, and he gave them a friendly wave of the hand.

"My sister-in-law! She's off to see her relatives in Tashkent," he explained to me, although I hadn't demanded any explanations.

My neighbor was happy to open his nearest basket and show me what was in it. Apart from a battered two-piece suit and a few other things, there was nothing but a lot of photographs, family and group portraits on enormous framed boards. Some of the photographs were daguerreotypes. He would take one of the larger ones out of the basket and happily explain in detail who was standing where, who was killed in the war, who got a medal, who was training to be an engineer. "And that's me," he would never fail to put a finger somewhere on the middle of a photograph. Everyone he showed these photographs to nodded meekly, politely, and sympathetically.

On the third day of our communal life, shaken about in the carriage, my neighbor, who had formed a full, clear, and utterly correct idea of who I was, even though I'd told him nothing about myself, said to me rapidly, while the attention of our other neighbors was distracted by something: "I'm changing trains in Moscow. Will you help me to drag one of the baskets through the exit? Past the scales?"

"But someone's meeting me in Moscow."

"Ah, yes. I'd forgotten you were being met."

"What are you carrying?"

"What? Sunflower seeds. And we'll take galoshes from Moscow...."

I didn't get out at any of the stops. I had food. I was afraid that the train would be sure to move off without me, that something bad would happen. My luck couldn't go on forever.

On the middle bunk opposite me there was a man in a fur coat, hopelessly drunk, without hat or gloves. He'd been put in the carriage by his drunken friends, who had given his ticket to the conductor. He stayed on the train for a day and a night, then got off somewhere and came back with a bottle of some dark-colored wine, drank it from the bottle, and threw the bottle on the floor. The conductor deftly grabbed it and carried it off to her conductor's lair, which was piled up with blankets that nobody took in a mixed carriage, and sheets, which nobody needed. Behind a barricade of blankets in the conductor's compartment, there was a prostitute who had established herself on the top bunk. She had come all the way from Kolyma. Perhaps she wasn't a prostitute, but had been turned into one by Kolyma.... This lady was sitting not far from me on the lowest bunk, and the dim carriage candle's rocking light every now and again would fall on her infinitely weary face and her lips, which were painted with something that was not lipstick. Later, someone would come up to her and say something; then she would disappear to the conductor's compartment. "Fifty rubles," said the lieutenant, who had now sobered up and turned out to be a very pleasant young man.

The lieutenant and I played a very interesting game. Whenever a new passenger got on, each of us tried to guess his profession, age, and occupation. We exchanged observations, then he would sit next to the new passenger, start a conversation, and come back to me with the answer.

That was how we decided that the lady with the painted lips, but the unvarnished fingernails, must be a medical worker, while the leopard-patterned coat she was wearing, which was obviously artificial fur, told us that its wearer was more likely to be a nurse or a paramedic than a doctor. No doctor would have worn fake fur. Nobody had yet heard of nylon or other synthetics then. Our conclusion turned out to be true.

From time to time a two-year-old child would run past our compartment. His legs were crooked, he was dirty, dressed in rags, and blue-eyed. His pale cheeks were covered with sores of some sort. A minute or two later his young father would come striding along, confident and firm. The father was wearing a quilted jacket and his fingers were heavy and strong, like a workman's. He would try and catch the boy. The infant laughed and smiled at his father, the father smiled at the boy and, happy and delighted, took him back to his place in another compartment of our carriage. I found out their story. A usual Kolyma story. The father was a nonpolitical convict who had just been released and was going back to the mainland. The child's mother refused to return, so the father was traveling with his son, having firmly decided to tear the child, and perhaps himself, away from Kolyma's sticky embrace. Why wouldn't the mother come? Perhaps that was the usual story, too.

She had found another man, and had grown to love living free in Kolyma: she was a free woman now and didn't want to return to the mainland as a second-class citizen. . . . Or perhaps she had lost her youth. Or love, Kolyma love, was over. Anything could have happened. Perhaps it was something even more terrible. The mother had served a sentence under article 58, the most nonpolitical of nonpoliticals, and she knew the dangers of returning to the mainland: a new sentence, new torments. Even in Kolyma there was no guarantee that you wouldn't get a new sentence, but she wouldn't be hounded there the way everyone on the mainland was hounded.

I never found out anything, and I didn't want to. I saw the father's nobility, decency, and love of his child, whom he had probably seen very little of, for the child would have been in a nursery or a kindergarten.

The father's clumsy hands, undoing the child's trousers, the enormous buttons of different colors sewn on by rough, unskilled, but kind hands. The father's happiness and the boy's. This two-year-old didn't know the word "mama"; he shouted, "Papa, papa!" The child and a dark-skinned metalworker played with each other, though it was hard to find room among the drunks, the card players, and the speculators' baskets and sacks. At least these two people in our carriage were, clearly, happy.

The passenger who slept for two days and nights from Irkutsk and woke up only to drink, to down yet another bottle of vodka or brandy or liqueur, was not to sleep any more. The train was being shaken about.

The sleeping, drunken passenger thudded to the floor and groaned and groaned. When the conductor summoned medical help, it was discovered that the passenger had a fractured shoulder. He was put on a stretcher, and he vanished from my life.

Suddenly the figure of the man who had rescued me turned up in the carriage (to call him my savior would be going too far, since after all things had not got to the serious and bloody stage). My acquaintance was still sitting there but didn't recognize me and seemed not to want to. Nevertheless, we exchanged glances, and I approached him. "I want to get home at least and have a look at my family," were the last words I heard from that gangster.

All that: the sharp light of the Irkutsk station lamp, the speculator carrying other people's photographs to disguise his real purposes, the vomit that erupted onto my bunk from the young lieutenant's throat, the sad prostitute on the top bunk of the conductor's compartment, and the dirty two-year-old happily shouting "Papa, papa!"—all that has stuck in my memory as my first happiness, the constant happiness of freedom.

Moscow's Yaroslavl station. Noise, the urban tide of Moscow, a city that was dearer to me than all the cities of the world. The carriage coming to a halt. The dear face of my wife, who came to meet me, as she had done before, when I came back from my frequent journeys. This time my absence was extensive, almost seventeen years. But the main thing was that I hadn't come back from a working journey. I had come back from hell.

1964

NOTES

INTRODUCTION

1 "The Gold Medal" appears in Volume Two.
2 "Permafrost" appears in Volume Two.
3 For example, torture.
4 The date of Shalamov's request for rehabilitation.
5 See the story "The Green Prosecutor."
6 These contingents were special groups singled out for particular treatment.
7 See the story "Berries."
8 Berlin: Matthes & Seitz, 2013.

BOOK ONE: KOLYMA STORIES

1 Osip Mandelstam.
2 Pine-needle extract is still used in Russian and Chinese medicine (as a source of vitamin C) to combat scurvy.
3 Kuznetsov means "blacksmith."
4 This term (as *sherri-brendi*) hitherto only occurred in a poem by Osip Mandelstam, so the story must be read as a re-creation of the death of Mandelstam, who died on December 27, 1938, in a transit camp near Vladivostok.
5 The name given to an informal Russian association of fraudsters, operating in the early 1870s and the subject of several accounts, true and embroidered.
6 A thick cotton material, a substitute for leather.
7 A nineteenth-century poem about a railway laid over the bones of the laborers who built it.
8 A fashionable shopping street in central Moscow.
9 In 1947 Stalin personally awarded a prize for this novel, even though the prize committee had rejected it.
10 Russian ravioli, made with two sorts of meat, eaten in broth.

11   Soviet prisoners of war who agreed to fight under General Vlasov along-
      side the German army; they were mostly repatriated to the USSR in 1945
      and 1946 and shot or sent to the camps.

12   In 1922 Herriot, a French senator with Soviet sympathies, had his gold
      watch stolen on a visit to the Hermitage; underworld figures recovered it.
      The story was told by the NKVD investigator and writer Lev Sheinin.

13   Sir Williams (pseudonym of Andrea de Felipone) is the ill-fated villain in
      novels, such as *The Exploits of Rocambole*, by the nineteenth-century
      French writer Ponson du Terrail.

14   Berzin, who by then had been shot, was the founder of the Kolyma forced-
      labor mining camps.

BOOK TWO: THE LEFT BANK

1   Leonid Ramzin, a professor of engineering and a star false witness, who
      was accused at a 1930 show trial, was rewarded for his testimony by being
      allowed to continue engineering work in prison, whereafter he was
      granted amnesty.

2   An anarchist terrorist who later became an ardent Stalinist.

3   Nestor Makhno, an anarchist leader in the Civil War in Ukraine.

4   Trotsky called Stalin's concocted political trials of an unlikely assortment
      of opponents "amalgams."

5   Latin for "let us rejoice."

6   In fact, the Moscow Art Theater had existed since 1898.

7   Vitovt Putna (1893–1937) was a brilliant military commander during the
      Polish-Soviet war of 1920; he then became a military attaché and was shot
      on June 12, 1937, during Stalin's purge of senior army officers.

8   Stalin's most trusted, longest-serving general and minister.

9   A hypnotist, reputed to have worked for the NKVD after 1929.

10   An agronomist and the vice president of the United States under Franklin
      D. Roosevelt, Wallace in June 1944 spent weeks in Magadan and Kolyma
      as a guest of the NKVD. He was fooled by the guards dressed in prison
      uniforms pretending to be well-fed, happy prisoners. Not until the 1950s
      did Wallace admit his gullibility.

11   Boris Savinkov, a leading Socialist Revolutionary, killed by the Soviet se-
      cret police in 1925.

12   In February 1905, Ivan Kaliayev, a Socialist Revolutionary, killed Grand
      Duke Sergei Aleksandrovich with a bomb; he had aborted a previous at-
      tempt to avoid killing the Grand Duke's wife and nephews.

13 Right SRs, unlike left SRs, had disavowed violent revolution.

14 Maria Spiridonova, a leading left SR, was shot on Stalin's orders in 1941.

15 Prosh Proshian, a leading left SR, People's Commissariat for Post and Telegraph, died of typhus in 1918.

16 Grigori Gershuni, a Russian terrorist, died in 1908 of cancer, two years after escaping from prison by hiding in a barrel.

17 Four members of People's Will who were hung in 1881 for assassinating Tsar Alexander II.

18 Egor Sozonov committed suicide in prison in 1910 to avoid being flogged.

19 Lev Zilberberg, hanged in 1907 for assassinating the Petersburg mayor.

20 Vera Figner (1852–1942) and Nikolai Morozov (1854–1946), the two People's Will terrorists who died of natural causes.

21 Agasi Khandjian, the secretary of the Armenian Communist Party, was shot in 1936 by Beria without a trial, after a quarrel.

22 Mikhail Gots, a founder of the SR Party, died in 1906 after an operation to remove a spinal tumor.

23 No such book exists. Shalamov may be recalling Gustav Jaeckh's *History* of 1906.

24 Charles Masson, *Mémoires secrets sur la Russie* of 1802.

25 A mine winch rotated by several men pushing a wooden beam; called Egyptian because of the slave labor required.

26 Reminiscent of *Don Quixote*: "Beauty in a modest woman is like fire at a distance or a sharp sword; the one does not burn, the other does not cut, those who do not come too near."

27 In 1826 Mikhail Bestuzhev, a naval officer, before his arrest devised a system of tapping the alphabet, anticipating Morse code. It has remained in use in Russian prisons.

28 That is, informs on you.

29 Dmitri Pletniov, Russia's leading cardiologist, was sentenced to twenty-five years in prison for allegedly murdering Maxim Gorky; Pletniov was shot in 1941.

30 Georgi Dimitrov, a Bulgarian communist accused by the Nazis of burning down the Reichstag, who was acquitted after his trial.

31 Monastery islands in the White Sea used as prison camps in the 1920s.

32 A famous nineteenth-century painting of Aleksandr Menshikov, a favorite of Peter the Great, later exiled to western Siberia.

33 A real figure, his surname was Daktor, and he was generally known as Dr. Doctor.

34 Numbered camps were the harshest, reserved for political prisoners who were not expected to survive.

35 The Special Tribunal (OSO) of the secret police, a three-man committee that sentenced political prisoners without trial.

36 Leonid Zakovsky, the brutal chief of the secret police in Leningrad, was shot in 1938.

37 A German writer notorious for declaring the Soviet show trials of 1937 to be fair.

38 Professor Leonid Ramzin became a witness for the prosecution at the Industrial Party show trial of 1930 and was then reprieved.

39 Andrei Vyshinsky was Stalin's henchman, chief prosecutor in the 1930s, and eventually the minister of foreign affairs. Mikhail Ryumin, deputy head of State Security, was executed in 1954.

40 Nikolai Svishchev-Paolo (1874–1964) was a leading Soviet photographer.

41 Two lines from Nikolai Gumiliov's famous poem "Captains." He was shot in 1921 on fabricated charges of taking part in the Tagantsev conspiracy.

42 Aleksei Ignatiev, a count and major general, who as an émigré handed the Bolsheviks the tsarist government's gold reserves; he then worked for Soviet intelligence. He returned to the USSR in 1937, kept his rank, published his memoirs in 1941, and died of natural causes in 1954.

43 This popular prerevolutionary song, in fact, ends with Shalamov's preceding words "raised him to great heights / before unashamedly dropping him into the abyss."

44 Boris Savinkov was a Socialist Revolutionary politician, then an émigré agent, killed in 1925, probably on Stalin's orders. His family perished ten years later.

45 A novelist and philosopher of the 1870s whose career really did begin in the army and end in a monastery.

46 Elizaveta Drabkina, convicted of Trotskyism, spent much of her life in the camps but remained a fervent communist. Her memoirs include *Black Rusks*.

47 A river and town in northern Siberia.

48 Piotr Yakubovich's memoir about fifteen years of Siberian hard labor as a political prisoner 1884–1899.

49 The memoirs of Clément Henri Sanson were actually a mystification by Honoré de Balzac.

50 *Les Bals des gibières* started in 1794 as a protest by nobles whose relatives had been guillotined.

BOOK THREE: THE SPADE ARTIST

1   Aleksandr Chayanov and Ivan Kondratiev were highly original economists. Both were shot in the terror of 1937–38.

2   Nikolai Krylenko, famous as a chess player and mountain climber, was the People's Commissar for Justice during the 1930s. His "rubber-band" policy meant that any criminal could have his sentence reduced to one year or extended for life, depending on his behavior. "Reforging" meant reforming criminal character through productive labor. Krylenko was shot in July 1938.

3   The Serpantinnaya (the name comes from the serpentine layout of the ditches in which the dead were buried) was an NKVD camp, nominally a pretrial prison, near Magadan, used primarily for mass executions. Some thirty thousand prisoners are thought to have been killed there in the late 1930s. Only four are believed to have emerged alive.

4   Method number three was torture.

5   This railway provided a shortcut from Siberia to Vladivostok through Chinese Manchuria. In 1928 its Soviet employees were repatriated to Russia; most ended up in the camps.

6   Engineer Kiseliov resembles the engineer Kiseliov in Book Two, but Shalamov has changed his patronym from Ivanovich to Dmitriyevich.

7   A celebrated young and defiant partisan, hanged by the Germans in 1941.

8   Savva Timofeyevich Morozov was one of Russia's richest and most progressive manufacturers. He was a patron of the socialists and defended his workers' rights. In 1905 he was certified insane at his indignant family's request and was found shot later the same year. It is not known if he was murdered, or committed suicide.

9   At the Congress of 1956 Khrushchev denounced Stalin's crimes; many surviving political prisoners were then "rehabilitated."

10 This story is based on the lives of the author's parents, Father Tikhon Nikolayevich Shalamov (1868–1933) and Nadezhda Aleksandrovna (1870–1934).

11 Foreign ambassadors to Russia retreated to Vologda in spring 1918, fearing a German invasion of Saint Petersburg. Three of them (Joseph Noulens of France, Bruce Lockhart of Great Britain, and David Francis of the U.S.) were accused of fomenting an anti-Bolshevik conspiracy with tsarist officers there.

12 Lomonosov and Lavoisier were both chemists, as well as poets.

13 Friedrich (or Fiodor) Erismann was a Swiss ophthalmologist, who in 1870 as a hygienist in Saint Petersburg invented an ergonomic school desk,

usually constructed as a double, with an integrated bench and table. It became the standard school desk in Russia for the next century.

14 Potassium permanganate crystals are very caustic; only a 1:1,000 solution is used on burns.

15 Leonid Zakovsky, much-feared Leningrad NKVD chief, shot in 1938.

16 A reference to Pushkin's poem "The Hero": "Rather than ten thousand low truths I prefer / A deceit that uplifts us."

17 Lines from Heinrich Heine's "Doktrin." (Shalamov quotes them in a translation by Aleksei Pleshcheyev).

18 In fact Dr. Yakov (not "David") Umansky died in 1951.

19 Genetics, known as "Weismannism," was a banned topic in the USSR from 1937 until 1964.

20 These students, "*fonovtsy*," were officials and managers who in the late 1920s were enrolled in fast-track university courses to raise their qualifications.

21 The surname Blagorazumov means "prudent."

22 The manifesto of an anti-Stalinist left-wing group within the party in the mid-1920s, led by Timofei Sapronov, who was shot in 1937.

23 This statement, contradicting what was said about Zader's Russian a few paragraphs earlier, is in the original text.

24 Dr. Gaaz, who died in 1853, was the kindly chief prison doctor in Moscow. He saw Dostoevsky off on his journey to prison in Siberia.

25 In 1952 Stalin attacked Jewish doctors, accusing them of being "murderers in white coats." Although after Stalin's death Beria had the doctors released before trial, several died under torture.

26 Nikolai Muralov was a leader of the armed Bolshevik rebellion in Moscow; a Trotskyist, he was arrested in 1936 and shot in 1937.

27 Karl Maksimovich Behr (1792–1876), a founder of the Russian Geographical Society, was an Estonian geologist famous for his work on the asymmetry of riverbeds in the Russian Arctic and the shores of the Caspian Sea.

28 In the summer of 1907 the revolutionary Vladimir Zenzinov escaped exile to Yakutsk and, pretending to be a gold miner, walked 1,600 kilometers to the sea of Okhotsk, where he left Russia on a Japanese schooner.

29 Eugene Vidocq was a real French detective in the first half of the nineteenth century; Monsieur Lecoq was a fictional detective in the novels of Émile Gaboriau.

30 G. I. Chubarov was a Red Army officer who with twenty others committed a gang rape in 1927.

31 General Krasnov, the pro-German head of the Don Cossacks, was not taken prisoner until 1945, when he was handed to the Soviets and hanged. Possibly Shalamov confuses him with Ataman Annenkov, the White Russian leader who was betrayed to the Soviets by the Chinese and executed in 1927.

32 Article 16 made actions similar to crimes punishable, even if not covered by the Criminal Code.

33 Article 35 allowed for up to five years' deportation or exile for persons considered "dangerous."

34 Umberto Nobile's expedition by airship to the North Pole in 1928 ended in a crash. Soviet pilots rescued two of the three men who walked off in search of help, but Finn Malmgren's body was never found, and there were rumors that he was eaten by the others.

35 Joseph Stalin, in 1930.

36 One of the first Soviet show trials, the 1928 "Mines' Trial" accused engineers, especially foreigners, of sabotage. Over one hundred were convicted, and eleven were sentenced to death.

37 Vera Figner and Nikolai Morozov were prominent political prisoners in the 1880s.

38 Named in the second half of the 1900s after Prime Minister Piotr Stolypin, who was famed for restoring law and order.

39 Fiodor Raskolnikov, prominent revolutionary, later diplomat, who defected and was murdered in 1939 on Stalin's orders.

40 The Wild Division was a group of several thousand volunteers, mainly from the North Caucasus, led by the tsar's brother. They fought in World War I, taking few prisoners.

41 Lieutenant Kijé, the subject of a story by Yuri Tynianov and an opera by Prokofiev, was a bureaucratic blunder at the end of the eighteenth century. Kijé means "who is also." In this story, AKA Berdy means "also known as" (*onzhe*) Berdy. A nonexistent person was created for the records.

42 In the late 1940s Lidia Timashuk wrote a letter denouncing (perhaps justifiably) the Kremlin doctors for negligence in treating Stalin's henchman Andrei Zhdanov, who died of a heart attack.

OTHER NEW YORK REVIEW CLASSICS

For a complete list of titles, visit www.nyrb.com or write to:
Catalog Requests, NYRB, 435 Hudson Street, New York, NY 10014

J.R. ACKERLEY My Dog Tulip*
J.R. ACKERLEY My Father and Myself*
J.R. ACKERLEY We Think the World of You*
HENRY ADAMS The Jeffersonian Transformation
RENATA ADLER Pitch Dark*
RENATA ADLER Speedboat*
AESCHYLUS Prometheus Bound; translated by Joel Agee*
ROBERT AICKMAN Compulsory Games*
LEOPOLDO ALAS His Only Son *with* Doña Berta*
CÉLESTE ALBARET Monsieur Proust
DANTE ALIGHIERI The Inferno
KINGSLEY AMIS The Alteration*
KINGSLEY AMIS Ending Up*
KINGSLEY AMIS Girl, 20*
KINGSLEY AMIS The Green Man*
KINGSLEY AMIS Lucky Jim*
KINGSLEY AMIS The Old Devils*
KINGSLEY AMIS One Fat Englishman*
KINGSLEY AMIS Take a Girl Like You*
ROBERTO ARLT The Seven Madmen*
U.R. ANANTHAMURTHY Samskara: A Rite for a Dead Man*
WILLIAM ATTAWAY Blood on the Forge
W.H. AUDEN (EDITOR) The Living Thoughts of Kierkegaard
W.H. AUDEN W.H. Auden's Book of Light Verse
ERICH AUERBACH Dante: Poet of the Secular World
EVE BABITZ Slow Days, Fast Company: The World, the Flesh, and L.A.*
DOROTHY BAKER Cassandra at the Wedding*
DOROTHY BAKER Young Man with a Horn*
J.A. BAKER The Peregrine
HONORÉ DE BALZAC The Human Comedy: Selected Stories*
HONORÉ DE BALZAC The Memoirs of Two Young Wives*
VICKI BAUM Grand Hotel*
SYBILLE BEDFORD Jigsaw*
SYBILLE BEDFORD A Legacy*
SYBILLE BEDFORD A Visit to Don Otavio: A Mexican Journey*
MAX BEERBOHM The Prince of Minor Writers: The Selected Essays of Max Beerbohm*
STEPHEN BENATAR Wish Her Safe at Home*
FRANS G. BENGTSSON The Long Ships*
ALEXANDER BERKMAN Prison Memoirs of an Anarchist
GEORGES BERNANOS Mouchette
MIRON BIAŁOSZEWSKI A Memoir of the Warsaw Uprising*
ADOLFO BIOY CASARES The Invention of Morel
PAUL BLACKBURN (TRANSLATOR) Proensa*
RONALD BLYTHE Akenfield: Portrait of an English Village*
NICOLAS BOUVIER The Way of the World
EMMANUEL BOVE Henri Duchemin and His Shadows*
MALCOLM BRALY On the Yard*

* *Also available as an electronic book.*

Título original: *Tonight the Streets Are Ours*
Edición: Leonel Teti con Erika Wrede
Coordinación de diseño: Marianela Acuña
Diseño de tapa: Elizabeth H. Clark
Diseño de interior: Silvana López
Imágenes de cubierta: ©Uwe Umstaetter/Cultura/Corbis

Tonight the Streets are Ours ©2015 Leila Sales
© 2016 V&R Editoras
www.vreditoras.com

Argentina: San Martín 969 piso 10 (C1004AAS) Buenos Aires
Tel./Fax: (54-11) 5352-9444 y rotativas
e-mail: editorial@vreditoras.com

México: Dakota 274, Colonia Nápoles
CP 03810 - Del. Benito Juárez, Ciudad de México
Tel./Fax: (5255) 5220-6620/6621 • 01800–543–4995
e-mail: editoras@vergarariba.com.mx

ISBN: 978-987-747-143-4

Impreso en Argentina • Printed in Argentina

Julio de 2016

Sales, Leila
Esta noche las calles son nuestras / Leila Sales. - 1a ed .
Ciudad Autónoma de Buenos Aires: V&R, 2016.
376 p.; 21 x 14 cm.

Traducción de: Graciela Romero.
ISBN 978-987-747-143-4

1. Literatura Juvenil Estadounidense. 2. Novelas Realistas.
I. Romero, Graciela, trad. II. Título.
CDD 813.9283

Esta noche las calles son nuestras

Leila Sales

Traducción:
Graciela Romero

V&R
EDITORAS